JAMES LEE
Three Great Novels

Robicheaux: The Early Years

James Lee Burke

Three Great Novels
Robicheaux: The Early Years

The Neon Rain
Heaven's Prisoners
Black Cherry Blues

ORION

This omnibus edition first published in Great Britain in 2004 by Orion,
an imprint of the Orion Publishing Group Ltd.

ISBN 0 75286 830 6 (trade paperback)

Typeset at the Spartan Press Ltd,
Lymington, Hants

Printed in Great Britain by
Clays Ltd, St Ives plc

The Orion Publishing Group Ltd
Orion House
5 Upper St Martin's Lane
London, WC2H 9EA

www.orionbooks.co.uk

Contents

The Neon Rain

For the family of Walter J. Burke of New Iberia,
Louisiana, with great affection for their gentle spirit
and kind ways

1

The evening sky was streaked with purple, the color of torn plums, and a light rain had started to fall when I came to the end of the blacktop road that cut through twenty miles of thick, almost impenetrable scrub oak and pine and stopped at the front gate of Angola penitentiary. The anti-capital-punishment crowd – priests, nuns in lay clothes, kids from LSU with burning candles cupped in their hands – were praying outside the fence. But another group was there too – a strange combination of frat boys and rednecks – drinking beer from Styrofoam coolers filled with cracked ice; they were singing 'Glow, Little Glow Worm,' and holding signs that read THIS BUD IS FOR YOU, MASSINA AND JOHNNY, START YOUR OWN SIZZLER FRANCHISE TODAY.

'I'm Lieutenant Dave Robicheaux, New Orleans police department,' I said to one of the guards on the gate. I opened my badge for him.

'Oh, yeah, Lieutenant. I got your name on my clipboard. I'll ride with you up to the Block,' he said, and got in my car. His khaki sleeves were rolled over his sunburned arms, and he had the flat green eyes and heavy facial bones of north Louisiana hill people. He smelled faintly of dried sweat, Red Man, and talcum powder. 'I don't know which bunch bothers me worse. Those religious people act like we're frying somebody for a traffic citation, and those boys with the signs must not be getting much pussy over at the university. You staying for the whole thing?'

'Nope.'

'Did you nail this guy or something?'

'He was just a low-level button man I used to run in once in a while. I never got him on anything. In fact, I think he screwed up more jobs than he pulled off. Maybe he got into the mob through Affirmative Action.'

The guard didn't laugh. He looked out the window at the huge, flat expanse of the prison farm, his eyes narrowing whenever we passed a trusty convict walking along the dirt road. The main living area of the prison, a series of two-story, maximum-security dormitories contained within a wire fence and connected by breezeways and exercise yards and collectively called the Block, was as brilliantly lit as cobalt in the rain, and in the distance I could see the surgically perfect fields of sugar cane and sweet potatoes, the crumbling ruins of the nineteenth-century camps silhouetted against the sun's red afterglow, the willows bent in the breeze along the Mississippi levee, under which many a murdered convict lay buried.

'They still keep the chair in the Red Hat House?' I said.

'You got it. That's where they knock the fire out their ass. You know how the place come by that name?'

'Yes,' I said, but he wasn't listening.

'Back before they started putting the mean ones in lockdown in the Block, they worked them down by the river and made them wear striped jumpers and these red-painted straw hats. Then at night they stripped them down, body-searched them, then run them in the Red Hat House and threw their clothes in after them. There wasn't no screens on the windows, and them mosquitoes would make a Christian out of a man when a baseball bat couldn't.'

I parked the car and we entered the Block, passed through the first lockdown area, where both the snitches and the dangerous ones stayed, walked down the long, brilliantly lit breezeway between the recreation yards into the next dormitory, passed through another set of hydraulic locks and a dead space where two hacks sat at a table playing cards and where a sign overhead read NO GUNS BEYOND THIS POINT, into the rec and dining halls where the black trustees were running electric waxers on the gleaming floors, and finally walked up the spiral iron steps to a small maximum-security corner where Johnny Massina was spending the last three hours of his life.

The guard from the gate left me, and another one pulled the single lever that slid back the cell door. Johnny wore a white shirt, a pair of black slacks, and black Air Force shoes with white socks. His wiry gray and black hair was dripping with sweat, and his face was the color and texture of old paper. He looked up at me from where he was seated on his bunk, and his eyes were hot and bright and moisture was beaded across his upper lip. He held a Camel cigarette between his yellowed fingers, and the floor around his feet was covered with cigarette butts.

'Streak, I'm glad you come. I didn't know if you were going to make it,' he said.

'How you doing, Johnny?'

His hands clutched his thighs and he looked at the floor, then back at me. I saw him swallow.

'How scared you ever been?' he said.

'In Vietnam I had some moments.'

'That's right. You were over there, weren't you?'

'Way back in '64, before it got real hot.'

'I bet you were a good soldier.'

4

'I was just a live one, that's all.'

I felt instantly stupid, at my remark. He saw the regret in my face.

'Don't worry about it,' he said. 'I got a whole bunch of shit to tell you. Look, you remember when you took me to a couple of those AA meets, that step you guys take when you want to confess something, what'd you call it?'

'Step Five, admitting to yourself, God, and somebody else the exact nature of your faults.'

'That's it. Well, I done it. To a colored preacher, yesterday morning. I told him every bad thing I ever done.'

'That's good, Johnny.'

'No, you listen. I told him the truth and I come clean with some really heavy shit, sexual things I always been ashamed of and I never understood. You know what I mean? I didn't keep nothing back. I also told him about the two guys I whacked in my life. I dumped one guy over the rail of a passenger liner on the way to Havana, and in 1958 I took out Bugsy Siegel's cousin with a shotgun. You know what it means to ice a relative of Bugsy Siegel? After I confessed it to the preacher, I told the guard and the assistant warden about it. You know these dumb cocksuckers couldn't care less?

'Wait a minute, let me finish. I told all this stuff because somebody's got to believe I didn't snuff that broad. I wouldn't throw no young girl out a hotel window, Streak. I got no kick coming about being fried. I figure it all comes out even in the end, but I want these bastards to know I only pushed the button on guys that played by the same rules I did. Can you relate to that?'

'I think so. I'm glad you did a fifth step, too, Johnny.'

He smiled for the first time. His face glistened in the light. 'Hey, tell me something. Is it true Jimmie the Gent is your brother?'

'You hear a lot of bullshit in the street.'

'You both got that black Cajun hair with a white patch in it, like you got skunk blood in you.' He laughed. His mind was now moving away from the ride he would take in three hours, manacled in a waist chain, to the Red Hat House. 'Once he contracted us for some poker machines for his places. After we put them in we told him he gets all his machines from us – cigarettes, Pac-Man, and rubbers. So he says no rubbers, he's got class clubs and he don't put rubber machines in them. So we tell him he don't have a choice, he either buys the whole line or he don't get linen service, the Teamsters put a picket up on his sidewalk, and the parish health office finds out his dishwashers got leprosy. So what's he do? He invites Didoni Giacano – Didi Gee himself – and his whole family for lasagna at his restaurant, and they arrive on Sunday afternoon like a bunch of *cafoni* that just got off the boat from Palermo, because Didi thinks Jimmie has got respectable connections and is going to get him into the Knights of Columbus or something. Didi Gee probably weighs three hundred pounds and he's covered with hair like an animal and he scares the crap out of everybody in downtown New Orleans, but his mama is this little dried-up Sicilian lady that looks like a mummy wrapped in black rags and she still hits Didi on the hands with a spoon when he reaches across the table and don't ask.

'So in the middle of dinner Jimmie starts telling Mama Giacano what a great guy Didi Gee is, how everybody down at the Chamber of Commerce and Better Business Bureau think he's a big plus for the city, and how Didi don't let anybody push his friends around. For example, he says, some scumbags tried to put some machines in Jimmie's restaurants that Jimmie, a Catholic man, don't want. Mama Giacano might look like she's made out of dried-up pasta, but her hot little black eyes tell everybody she knows what he's talking about. Then Jimmie says Didi tore them machines out, smashed them up with hammers, and run a truck up and down on them behind the restaurant.

'Didi Gee's got a mouthful of beer and raw oysters and almost chokes to death. He's spitting glop all over his plate, his kids are beating him on the back, and he coughs up an oyster that could plug a sewer main. Mama Giacano waits till his face ain't purple anymore, then tells him she didn't raise her son to eat like a herd of pigs and says he should go wash out his mouth in the bathroom because everybody else at the table is getting sick looking at him, and when he don't get up right away she busts him across the knuckles with her spoon. Then Jimmie says he wants to take the whole family out on his sailboat and maybe Didi Gee ought to join the Yacht Club, too, because all these millionaires think he's a swell guy, and besides, Mama Giacano would really love the Italian-American celebrations they have on the Fourth of July and Columbus Day. And even if Didi don't join, which everybody knows he won't because he hates the water and pukes his guts out just crossing the Mississippi ferry, Jimmie is going to drive out and get Mama Giacano whenever she wants and sail her all around Lake Pontchartrain.'

He laughed again and ran his hand through his wet hair. He licked his lips and shook his head, and I saw the fear come back in his eyes.

'I bet he already told you that story, didn't he?' he said.

'They didn't give me too long, Johnny. Is there something else you wanted to tell me?'

'Yeah, there is. You always treated me decent and I thought maybe I could repay you a little bit.' He wiped the sweat out of his eyes with the flat of his fingers. 'I think maybe I got some heavy dues to pay on the other side, too. It don't hurt to try to square what you can now, does it?'

'You don't owe me.'

'A guy with my track record owes the whole fucking earth. Anyway, here's the deal. Yesterday this punk by the name of L. J. Potts from

Magazine Street is pushing a broom out in the corridor, clacking it against my bars and making all kinds of noise so I can't sleep. So I say I ain't working on the Good Housekeeping award and would this punk take his broom somewhere else before I get my hands on it and shove it up his hole. So the punk, who's got a brother named Wesley Potts, tries to impress me. He asks if I know a New Orleans homicide roach named Robicheaux, and he's smirking, see, because he thinks you're one of the cops that nailed me. I tell him maybe, and he keeps smirking and says, well, here's some good news because his brother Wesley has it that this particular homicide roach has stuck his nose in the wrong place and if he don't stop it he's going to get whacked.'

'He sounds like a gasbag, Johnny.'

'Yeah, he probably is, except the difference with him and his brother is I think they're connected up with the greasers.'

'The Colombians?'

'Fucking A. They're spreading around the country faster than AIDS. They'll take out anybody too – whole families, the children, the old people, it don't matter to them. You remember that bar on Basin that got torched? The greaser that did it stood in the doorway in broad daylight with a fucking flamethrower on his back and because he was in a good mood he gave everybody one minute to get out of the place before he melted it into a big pile of bubbling plastic. You watch out for those cocksuckers, Streak.'

He lit a fresh Camel from the butt in his hand. He was sweating heavily now, and he wiped his face on his sleeve and smelled himself simultaneously. Then his face got gray and still and he stared straight ahead with his palms gripped on his thighs.

'You better leave now. I think I'm going to get sick again,' he said.

'I think you're a stand-up guy, Johnny.'

'Not on this one.'

We shook hands. His hand was slick and light in mine.

They electrocuted Johnny Massina at midnight. Back in my houseboat on Lake Pontchartrain, with the rain beating on the roof and dancing on the water outside, I remembered the line I had heard sung once by a black inmate in Angola:

I ax my bossman, Bossman, tell me what's right.
He whupped my left, said, Boy, now you know what's right.
I wonder why they burn a man twelve o'clock hour at night.
The current much stronger; the peoples turn out all the light.

My partner was Cletus Purcel. Our desks faced each other in a small room in an old converted fire station on Basin Street. Before the building was a fire station it had been a cotton warehouse, and before the Civil War slaves had been kept in the basement and led up the stairs into a dirt ring that served both as an auction arena and a cockfighting pit.

Cletus's face looked like it was made from boiled pigskin, except there were stitch scars across the bridge of his nose and through one eyebrow, where he'd been bashed by a pipe when he was a kid in the Irish Channel. He was a big man, with sandy hair and intelligent green eyes, and he fought to keep his weight down, unsuccessfully, by pumping iron four nights a week in his garage.

'Do you know a character named Wesley Potts?' I asked.

'Christ, yes. I went to school with him and his brothers. What a family. It was like having bread mold as your next-door neighbor.'

'Johnny Massina said this guy's talking about pulling my plug.'

'Sounds like bullshit to me. Potts is a gutless lowlife. He runs a dirty movie house on Bourbon. I'll introduce you to him this afternoon. You'll really enjoy this guy.'

'I've got his file right here. Two narcotics, six obscenity busts, no convictions. Evidently one serious beef with the IRS.'

'He fronts points for the greasers.'

'That's what Massina said.'

'All right, we'll go talk to him after lunch. You notice I say "after lunch," because this guy is your real genuine bucket of shit. By the way, the parish coroner in Cataouatche returned your call and said they didn't do an autopsy on that colored girl.'

'What do you mean, they didn't do one?' I said.

He said they didn't do one because the sheriff's office didn't request it. It went down as a drowning. What's all this about, anyway, Dave? Don't you have enough open cases without finding work down in Cataouatche Parish? Those people down there don't follow the same rules we do, anyway. You know that.'

Two weeks before, I had been fishing in a pirogue on Bayou Lafourche, flycasting popping-bugs along the edge of the lily pads that grew out from the banks. The shore was thickly lined with cypress trees, and it was cool and quiet in the green-gold morning light that fell through the canopy of limbs overhead. The lily pads were abloom with purple flowers, and I could smell the trees, the moss, the wet green lichen on the bark, the spray of crimson and yellow four-o'clocks that were still open in the shade. An alligator that must have been five feet long lay up close to some cypress roots, his barnacled head and eyes just showing above the water line like a brown rock. I saw another black swelling in the water near another cypress, and I thought it was the first alligator's mate. Then an outboard boat passed, and the wake rolled the swelling up in the cypress roots, and I saw a bare leg, a band, a checked shirt puffed with air.

I set down my fly rod, rowed closer, and touched the body with my paddle. The body turned in the water, and I saw the face of a young black woman, the eyes wide, the mouth open with a watery prayer. She wore a man's shirt tied under her breasts, cut-off blue jeans, and for just a second I saw a dime tied on a string around her ankle, a good-luck charm that some Acadian and black people wore to keep away the *gris-gris*, an evil spell. Her young face looked like a flower unexpectedly cut from its stem.

I looped my anchor rope around her ankle, threw the anchor back into the trees on the bank, and tied my red handkerchief on an overhanging branch. Two hours later I watched the deputies from the parish sheriff's office lift the body onto a stretcher and carry it to an ambulance that was parked in the canebrake.

'Just a minute,' I said before they put her in. I lifted up the sheet to look again at something I'd seen when they had pulled her out of the water. There were tracks on the inside of her left arm, but only one needle hole that I could see inside the right.

'Maybe she gives blood to the Red Cross,' one of the deputies said, grinning.

'You're a pretty entertaining guy,' I said.

'It was just a joke, Lieutenant.'

'Tell the sheriff I'm going to call him about the autopsy,' I said.

'Yes, sir.'

But the sheriff was never in when I called, and he didn't return calls, either. So finally I telephoned the parish coroner's office, and now I discovered that the sheriff didn't believe an autopsy for a dead black girl was that important. Well, we'll see about that, I thought.

In the meantime, I was still curious as to why the Colombians, if Johnny Massina was right, were interested in Dave Robicheaux. I went through my case file and didn't see any connection. I had a whole file drawer of misery to look at, too: a prostitute icepicked by a psychotic john; a seventeen-year-old runaway whose father wouldn't bond him out of jail and who was hanged the next morning by his black cellmate; a murder witness beaten to death with a ball-peen hammer by the man she was scheduled to testify against; a Vietnamese boat refugee thrown off the roof of the welfare project; three small children shot in their beds by their unemployed father; a junkie strangled with baling wire during a satanic ritual; two homosexual men burned alive when a rejected lover drenched the stairwell of a gay nightclub with gasoline. My drawer was like a microcosm of an aberrant world populated by snipers, razor-wielding blacks, mindless nickel-and-dime boost artists who eventually panic and kill a convenience-store clerk for sixty dollars, and suicides who fill the apartment with gas and blow the whole building into a black and orange fireball.

What a bunch to dedicate your life to.

But there was no umbilical cord that led to the south-of the-border account.

Cletus was watching me.

'I swear, Dave, I think your feelings are going to be hurt unless you find out the greasers got the hots for you,' he said.

'We don't have a lot of perks in this business.'

'Well, I'll tell you what. Let's go to lunch early, you buy, and I'll introduce you to Potts. The guy's a delight. Your day is going to be filled with sunshine.'

It was hazy and bright when we drove into the Quarter. There was no breeze, and the palm fronds and banana trees in the courtyards were green and motionless in the heat. As always, the Quarter smelled to me like the small Creole town on Bayou Teche where I was born: the watermelons, cantaloupes, and strawberries stacked in crates under the scrolled colonnades; the sour wine and beer with sawdust in the bars; the poor-boy sandwiches dripping with shrimp and oysters; the cool, dank smell of old brick in the alleyways.

A few genuine bohemians, writers, and painters still lived in the Quarter, and some professional people paid exorbitant rents for refurbished apartments near Jackson Square, but the majority of Vieux Carré residents were transvestites, junkies, winos, prostitutes, hustlers of every stripe, and burnt-out acidheads and street people left over from the 1960s. Most of these people made their livings off middle-class conventioneers and Midwestern families who strolled down Bourbon Street, cameras hanging from their necks, as though they were on a visit to the zoo.

I couldn't find a place to park by Pearl's Oyster Bar, and I kept driving around the block.

'Dave, when does a guy know he's got a drinking problem?' Cletus asked.

'When it starts to hurt him.'

'It seems I've been getting half-stoned near every night of recent. I can't seem to go home unless I stop at the joint on the corner first.'

'How are you and Lois getting along?'

'I don't know. It's the second marriage for both of us. Maybe I've got too many problems, or maybe both of us have. They say if you don't make it the second time around, you ain't going to make it at all. You think that's true?'

'I don't know, Clete.'

'My first wife left me because she said she couldn't stay married to a man that brought a sewer home with him every day. That was when I was working vice. She said I smelled like whores and reefer all the time. Actually, vice did have its moments. Now Lois tell me she doesn't want me to bring my gun home at night. She's into Zen, meditates every day, sends our money to some Buddhist priest out in Colorado, and tells me she doesn't want her kids growing up around guns. Guns are bad, see, but this character out in Colorado that takes my bucks is good. Two weeks ago I came in wired, so she started crying and blowing her nose into a whole box of Kleenex. So I had a couple more hits of Jack Daniel's and told her how you and I had spent the afternoon combing pieces of a fourteen-year-old kid out of the garbage dump with a garden rake. Fifteen more minutes of tears and nose-honking. So I cruise for some booze and almost get nailed on a DUI. Not very good, huh?'

'Everybody has family trouble sometimes.'

He was frowning out the window, his thoughts collecting in his eyes. He lit a cigarette, drew in deeply, and flicked the match out into the sunlight.

'Man, I'm going to be a chainsaw by two o'clock,' he said. 'I'm going to have a couple of beers with lunch. Sedate the brain, the stomach, mellow the nerves. Does that bother you?'

'It's your day. You can do whatever you want to with it.'

'She's going to split. I know the signs.'

'Maybe y'all will work it out.'

'Come on, Dave, you didn't get off the boat yesterday. It doesn't work that way. You know how things were just before your wife took off.'

'That's right, I do. I know how things were. Nobody else does. You get my drift?' I grinned at him.

'All right, I'm sorry. But when it's going down the toilet, it's going down the toilet. You don't turn it around by leaving your piece in a locker. Pull into that truck zone. It's too damn hot out here.'

I parked in the loading zone by Pearl's and cut the engine. Cletus was sweating in the sunlight.

'Tell me honestly,' he said, 'would you have done something like that just to please your wife?'

I didn't even want to think about the things I had done to please my wife, my pale, dark-haired, beautiful wife from Martinique who left me for a Houston oilman.

'Hey, lunch is on you after all,' I said.

'What?'

'I didn't bring any money.'

'Use your MasterCard.'

'They wouldn't renew it. Something about exceeding my credit limit by four hundred dollars.'

'Great, I've got a buck thirty-five. What a class act. All right, we eat on the tab. If he doesn't like it, we tell him we're calling Immigration about the Haitians he's got working in his kitchen.'

'I didn't know he had any.'

'Me either. It'll be fun to see what he says.'

*

The pornographic theater was right on Bourbon Street. Bourbon had changed since I used to come here as a college student over twenty years ago. The old Dixieland bands like Papa Celestin's and Sharky Bonnano's had been replaced by imitation country bands made up of kids in designer jeans, vinyl vests, and puffed white silk shirts with lace brocade, like mambo dancers or transvestites would wear. The burlesque houses had always been seedy places where the girls hustled drinks between sets and hooked loose johns before closing, but the city code had required them to wear G-strings and pasties, and there hadn't been any dope around, except a little reefer among the desperate, burnt-out musicians who played in a small, dark pit at the bottom of the runway. But now the girls danced completely nude on the stage, their eyes glowing with black speed, their nostrils sometimes still twitching and wet from snorting coke through a rolled-up dollar bill.

The windows of Plato's Adult Theater had been walled up with cinder blocks so no one could see in, and the interior of the small, gold and purple lobby was decorated with erotic art that might have been painted by blind people. We went through the lobby into the office without knocking. A thin man with a pointed, shiny face looked up, startled, from his desk. He wore a powder-blue polyester suit and patent-leather shoes with silver buckles, and his receding, oiled hair glistened in the light from the desk lamp. Cans of movie reels were stacked in a wooden rack against one wall. The surprise and fear went out of the man's face, and he scratched his cheek with one hand and picked up a filter-tipped cigar from the ashtray.

'What do you want, Purcel?' he said indifferently.

'Dave, meet Wesley Potts, our resident bucket of shit,' Cletus said.

'I don't have time for your insults, Purcel. You got a warrant or something?'

'That's what they say on television, Pottsie,' Cletus said. 'You see any TV cameras, Dave?'

'I don't see any TV cameras,' I said.

'On television some guy is always saying "You got a warrant?" or "You got to read me my rights,"' Cletus said. 'But in big-people land we don't do it that way. You ought to know that, Pottsie.'

'I thought you didn't work vice anymore,' Potts said.

'That's right. I'm in homicide now. My partner here's last name is Robicheaux. Does that make your swizzle stick start to tingle?'

The man behind the desk blew cigar smoke out in front of him and looked into it with his eyes flat, but I saw his fingers crimp together on the desk blotter.

'Your little brother up at Angola says you're blabbing it around that Dave here is going to get snuffed,' Cletus said.

'If that's what my brother says, you ought to be talking to him. I don't know anything about it.'

'The people up at Angola don't like cops hitting on their convicts. Bad for their image and all that,' Cletus said. 'But you and us, well, that's a whole different caper, Wes.'

Potts's eyes were small and hot and staring straight ahead.

'Lighten up,' Cletus said. 'You're a businessman, you pay taxes, you're reasonable. You just got diarrhea of the mouth and you been spreading rumors around, and we want to know why you been doing that. It's no big deal. Just straighten us out about this strange stuff we heard, and you can get back to entertaining the perverts. Look at the material you got here. This is classy stuff.' Cletus began to bang through the film cans on the wooden rack. He picked up one in both hands, and looked at the penciled title with a critical eye. 'This one is state-of-the-art porn, Dave. In one scene a guy kills a naked broad with a nail gun. She screams and begs, but the guy chases her around the house and staples pieces of her all over the woodwork.' Cletus opened the can, held on to one end of the film, and dropped the reel bouncing on the floor. He held the film strip up to the light. 'The funny thing, Wes, is sometimes a john goes apeshit and tears a hooker up, and I get the feeling that maybe the guy just finished eating popcorn out there in your theater. What do you think?'

'I never look at that stuff. I couldn't tell you what's in it. I just manage the place. It's a movie house, with a license, with fire exits, with sanitary bathrooms just like any other movie house. You don't like the place, go talk to the people that give out the permit.'

Cletus began opening the other film cans, dropping the reels to the floor, and walking on them as he worked his way down the rack. Thick tangles of film were looped around his ankles and shoes.

'You cut it out, you bastard,' Potts said.

'How'd you get into the IRS beef?' Cletus said.

'Fuck off.'

'You're fronting points for the spicks, aren't you?' Cletus said. 'You probably don't have fifteen people out there right now, but you show profits like you have the patent on the wheel. Why is that?'

'I sell lots of popcorn.'

'All that coke and brown scag money finds a ledger to get written down on,' Cletus said. 'Except the Treasury boys are about to ream your butthole.'

'I don't see any Treasury men. All I see is a plain-clothes prick that never grew up from high school,' Potts said. 'Where the fuck you get off with this stuff? You smash up my films, you come down on me because of something my little brother said which I don't even know he said, and you give me some bullshit about Mexican scag, when if I remember right you never busted anybody more serious than a junkie with a couple of balloons in his crotch. Maybe you took a little juice while you were in vice, huh? You're a fucking joke, Purcel.'

13

'Listen to this man carry on,' Cletus said. 'We're going to have to have privacy. Does this door go into the theater? Thanks, that's what I thought.'

He opened a side door that gave onto a small theater that looked like a remodeled garage. In the flickering darkness a dozen or so men stared fixedly at the screen.

'What's happening, geeks?' Cletus said loudly, and began flicking the light switch on and off. 'I'm the New Orleans heat. I just wanted to make sure everything was working all right. Enjoy your show.'

They rose quickly from their seats and moved as a group up the aisles farthest from Cletus and went through the curtained exit.

'Big deal. The same guys'll be sitting out there tonight,' Potts said.

'Could you leave me and Wesley alone a few minutes?' I said.

'I thought you might say that,' Cletus said, and crunched again through the tangle of ruined film on the floor and closed the door behind him.

I sat on the corner of Potts's desk and folded my hands on my thigh.

'How do you think this is going to end?' I said.

'What d'you mean?'

'Just what I said. Do you think you can tell people somebody is going to blow me away and I'm just going to walk out of here?'

He sucked in his lips and looked at the wall.

'Tell me what you think is going to happen,' I said.

'I don't know. I never saw you before. Why would I go around talking about you?'

'Who wants to drop the hammer on me, Wes?'

'I don't know any such thing.'

'Do you think I'm a dumb guy?'

'I don't know what you are.'

'Oh, yes you do. I'm the guy you never thought you'd see, just a vague figure in your mind you could laugh about getting snuffed. I've sort of showed up like a bad dream, haven't I?'

'I got nothing against you,' he said. 'I run a legal business. I don't cause you guys no trouble.'

'But I'm sitting here on your desk now. It's like waking up with a vulture on your bedpost, isn't it?'

'What are you going to do? Trash the place, knock me around? Big fucking deal.'

I took out my five-inch, single-blade Puma pocket knife and opened it. The blade could fillet bass like a barber's razor. It trembled with light.

'Jesus Christ, man, what are you doing?' he said.

I picked up his cigar from the ashtray, sliced off the burning end on the desktop, and put the still-warm stub in Potts' shirt pocket.

'You can smoke the rest of that later,' I said.

'What the fuck! Are you crazy, man?' he said. His face had gone white. He swallowed and stared at me, his eyes full of fear and confusion.

'You know who Didi Gee is, don't you?'

'Sure, everybody does. Why you ask about—'

'What's he do?'

'What d'you mean?'

'What's he do? Tell me now.'

'Everything. Whores, numbers, unions, y'all know that.'

'We're going to have lunch with him and I'm going to tell him what you told me.'

'What?'

'He has lunch in Jimmie the Gent's restaurant every Tuesday at two o'clock. You and I are going to sit at the next table and have a chat with the fat boy himself. Believe me, he'll find you an entertaining guy.'

'I ain't going.'

'Yes you are. You're under arrest.'

'What for? I didn't do anything,' he said desperately.

'You said something about cash. That sounded like an attempted bribe to me.'

His eyes flicked back and forth frantically. Pinpoints of sweat broke out on his forehead.

'I said "trash." I said "trash the place."'

'I'm hard of hearing. Anyway. I'll think about it on the way over to the restaurant. Do you believe that story about Didi Gee's aquarium, the one full of piranha? I heard he held a Teamster's hand in it for a full minute. Maybe that's just another one of those bullshit Mafia stories, though. Put your hands out in front of you, I'm going to cuff you. You can carry your coat across your wrist if it embarrasses you.'

'I don't rattle. You're running a game on me.'

'You dealt the hand, Wes. Play it out. But right now you put your wrists in front of you or I'm going to break open your fucking worthless face.'

He was breathing loudly now, his hands clenched in fists on the desk blotter.

'Listen, Lieutenant, I heard the other guys say something. Lot of times they're just blowing gas. It don't necessarily mean anything. I didn't hear it from Mr Segura. It didn't come from Mr Segura. You understand that? It's just street talk, a bunch of guys' bullshit.'

'You're talking about the Colombian?'

'He's from Nicaragua.'

'Go on.'

He wiped his lips with his fingers, then pulled at the flap of skin under his chin.

'It's got something to do with a nigger girl. I think she used to be a street whore. Didn't you pull a nigger out of the bayou in Cataouatche Parish?'

'You just keep telling me what you know, Wes.'

'Jesus Christ, Lieutenant, what d'you think I am? I'm just a theater manager. Maybe once a month Mr Segura has a bunch of guys out to his place on the lake. A buffet, a lot of booze, some broads in the pool. He shakes everybody's hand, maybe has a collins with us or plays cards a few minutes under the beach umbrella, then disappears inside.'

'What's the girl have to do with Julio Segura?'

'You're not understanding me, Lieutenant. He don't tell me things like that. He don't talk to me about anything, in fact. Look, this a heavy-metal cat. I think he's wired into big people. Why mess with him? The feds deal with guys like this.'

I continued to stare silently at him. His hands flicked on the desk blotter as though wires were attached to them.

'They say you're making noise about a nigger girl you found in another parish,' he said. 'That ain't your territory, so they wonder why the interest. For some reason they think you're after them. Don't ask me why. I don't even like to be around that kind of talk. I walk away from it. That's the God's truth.'

'You really bother me, Wes. I have great concern about your sincerity. I also have the feeling you think you're omniscient.'

'Wha—'

'Tell me if I'm wrong. You think you can intuit exactly what I'll accept. You're going to jerk me around and tell me bedtime stories, then snort a line or two after I'm gone to calm your nerves, and your day will be back intact again. That indicates a serious problem with vanity and pride. What do you think?'

'Look—' he began, his mouth smiling, his eyes cast down self-deprecatingly.

'No, no, it's time for Wes to listen and me to talk. You see, when you shoot off your mouth about the murder of a police officer, you invite some dangerous complications into your life. Number one, foreknowledge can make an accomplice out of you, Wes. Then, on a more basic level, there are several men I work with who would simply cool you out. Are we communicating here?'

'Yes,' he said weakly.

'There's no confusion?'

'No.'

'All right, Wes. We'll talk again later. You understand that, don't you?'

'Yes.'

I stood up from his desk and walked toward the door. I could hear him expel his breath.

Then: 'Lieutenant?'

I turned and looked at him. His face was small and pale.

'Will this get back to Mr Segura?' he said. 'A couple of the Latin guys that work for him . . . cruel guys . . . they were cops or national guardsmen or something in Nicaragua . . . I don't like to think about the stuff they do.'

'No guarantees. You sniff something bad in the wind, come to us and we'll get you out of town.'

The sun was blazing outside. Across the street, three black kids were tap dancing for the tourists in the shade of the scrolled iron colonnade. The huge taps they wore sounded like drumsticks clicking on the metal. Cletus stood out of the sunlight's glare, watching, with his seersucker coat over one arm. 'What'd you get from old Pottsie?'

'It was the black girl I found in Bayou Lafourche. It's got the smell of dope and the Barataria pirates. Did you ever run up against Julio Segura when you were on vice?'

'You better believe it. He's your genuine, certified greaseball. The guy's got Vitalis oozing out of every pore.'

'I thought he was a Colombian.'

'He's hooked in with them, but he's from Managua. I heard he owned a hundred whorehouses down there. They say the Sandinistas shot holes all over his plane just as it cleared the field. The guy's a survivor. We tried to get him two or three times. I think he's got a lot of high-up juice going for him.'

We walked in the warm shade back toward Royal Street, where we had left the car parked in front of the oyster bar. I went into a small, dark grocery store cooled by a wooden-bladed overhead fan, and bought a *Times-Picayune*. The interior of the store smelled of bananas, coffee, blocks of cheese, and big wooden bins filled with grapes and plums. I opened the *Picayune* to the sports page as we walked along.

'Y'all want to go to the races tonight?' I said.

'Forget the races. Let's front the spick. We tell the captain about it first, then we go out to his house and flip his necktie in his face.'

'Nope. Too soon.'

'Bullshit. The only way to handle these guys is jump up and down on their nuts. In this case we want the guy to know it's personal. We deliver the Candygram right in his living room.'

'I appreciate it, Clete, but I'll let you know when it's time to toggle out there. Don't worry. You won't miss out on the party.'

'You're too laid back. I'm telling you, this guy is subhuman. He makes an animal like Didi Gee look like the archbishop by comparison.'

'Damn,' I said.

'What's wrong?'

'Next time, we take your car to lunch.'

'What for?'

'That's my car on the back of that tow truck.'

The light was soft on the lake as I dressed on the houseboat that evening. Up the shore I could see the palm and cypress trees blowing in the wind off the Gulf. The air smelled like rain again. I felt very alone and quiet inside, and I wondered if my feeling of confident solitude, my peculiar moment of serenity inside, was not a deceptive prelude to another turbulent time in my life. Maybe it was just a brief courtship with narcissism. My body was still hard and lean, my skin brown, the old scar from the dung-tipped *pungi* stick like a broken gray snake embossed on my stomach. My hair and brush mustache were still as black as ink, except for the white patch above one ear, and I convinced myself every morning that living alone was no more a mark of age and failure than it was of youth and success. The dark purple clouds piled on the Gulf's southern horizon trembled with heat lightning.

I sat alone in a box at the races that night and looked with the same quiet and tranquil fascination at the lighted track, the dampened and raked sod, the glistening clipped grass in the center field. It was the kind of vague, almost numb euphoria that I used to feel when I slid off the edge of a two-day binge into delirium tremens. I had become omniscient; my white tropical suit glowed from the arc light overhead; I cashed three place bets and two wins in a row. The peach-complexioned waitresses in the clubhouse brought me shelled shrimp on ice, and lobster and steak, and brushed their hips unnecessarily against my arm when they took away my soiled napkin and blood-streaked plate.

Someone once told me that the gambler's greatest desire, knowledge of the future, would drive us insane. On that warm summer evening as I drove back home, with the moon denting the lake and the fireflies lighting in the palm and oak trees, I felt a thin tremolo inside me, like the faint tinkling of crystal or the almost silent vibration of sympathetic guitar strings, just a hint of Cassandra's tragic gift, and I tried to ascribe it to my old alcoholic fears that writhed in the unconscious as blind snakes would. But a winner at the track usually cares little for caution or moonlit nuances.

2

Early the next morning I drove southwest of New Orleans, into the bayou country. It was the south Louisiana I had grown up in, around New Iberia. Oak, cypress, and willow trees lined the two-lane road; the mist still clung like torn cotton to the half-submerged dead tree trunks back in the marsh; the canebrakes were thick and green, shining in light, and the lily pads clustered along the bayou's banks were bursting with flowers, audibly popping, their leaves covered with drops of quicksilver. The bream and bass were still feeding in the shadows close to the cypress roots; egrets were nesting in the sand where the sun had risen above the tree line, and occasionally a heron would lift from its feeding place on the edge of the cattails and glide on gilded wings down the long ribbon of brown water through a corridor of trees.

Now these same bayous, canals, and marshlands where I had grown up were used by the Barataria pirates. But their namesakes, Jean Lafitte's collection of brigands and slavers, were romantic figures by comparison. The current group was made up of marijuana, cocaine, and heroin smugglers who would murder a whole family out on the Gulf simply for the one-time use of their boat, after which they'd open up the cocks and sink it. Occasionally the Coast Guard would find one half-filled with water and beached on a sandbar, the gunwales painted with blood.

But why should this shock or revile? The same people sometimes killed infants by injection, embalmed the bodies, and filled the stomachs with balloons of heroin so women transporters could walk through customs as though they were carrying their sleeping children.

The Cataouatche Parish sheriff was not at the courthouse. He was at his horse farm outside of town, galoshes on his feet, feeding two Arabians in a side lot. His house had a fresh coat of white paint and a wide screen porch, and was surrounded by azalea bushes and flaming hibiscus. The long white fence along the back horse pasture was entwined with climbing roses. The Sheriff was around fifty, a man in control of his property and his political life. His blue uniform fitted tightly on his compact, hard body, and his round, freshly shaved face and direct eyes gave you the impression of a self-confident rural law officer who dealt easily with outside complexities.

Unfortunately for him, I proved to be the exception.

'She drowned,' he said. 'My deputies said a bucket of water came out of her when they flipped her off the gurney.'

'She had tracks on her arms.'

'So? Addicts drown too. You need an autopsy to tell you that?'

'Do you know if she was right-handed or left-handed?'

'What the hell are you talking about?' he said.

'She'd been shooting regularly into the left arm, but she had only one needle hole on the right. What's that tell you?'

'Not a goddamn thing.'

'When a junkie flattens the vein in one arm, he starts on the other. I don't think she'd been shooting up that long. I think somebody gave her a hotshot.'

'The parish coroner signed the death certificate. It says "drowned". You take it up with him if you want to pursue it. I'm late for work.' He walked out of the horse lot, pulled off his muddy galoshes on the grass, and slipped on his polished, half-topped boots. His round face was turned away from me as he bent over, but I could hear the repressed anger in his breathing.

'Those are fine Arabians,' I said. 'I understand they can bring thirty thousand or so when they're trained.'

'That wouldn't touch them, Lieutenant. Like I say, I don't mean to be rude, but I'm late. You want me to introduce you to the coroner?'

'I don't think so. Tell me, as a matter of speculation, how do you figure a healthy young woman, wearing all her clothes, would come to drown in a narrow bayou?'

'What's going to make you happy, Lieutenant? You want somebody to write down for you that she died of a hotshot? You want to take that back to New Orleans with you? All right, you have my permission. It's no skin off our ass. But how about her family? She was raised up in the quarters on a sugar plantation about five miles south of here. Her mother is feeble-minded and her daddy is half-blind. You want to drive out there and tell them their daughter was a junkie?'

'Everything in this case stinks of homicide, Sheriff.'

'I've only got two more things to say to you, podna, and it's important you understand this. I trust what my deputies told me, and if you got a complaint, you take it to the coroner's office. And number two, this conversation is over.'

Then he looked away at his horses in a distant field, as though I were not there, slipped on his pilot's sunglasses, got into his Cadillac, and drove down his pea-gravel lane to the blacktop. I felt like a post standing in the ground.

*

The dead girl's name had been Lovelace Deshotels. Her parents lived in one of the weathered, paintless shacks along a dirt road on the back of a corporate sugar plantation. All the shacks were identical, their small front porches so evenly aligned that you could fire an arrow through the receding rectangle of posts, roofs, and bannisters for the entire length of the quarters without striking wood. The thick green fields of cane stretched away for miles, broken only by an occasional oak tree and the distant outline of the sugar mill, whose smokestacks in the winter would cover these same shacks with a sickening sweet odor that made the eyes water.

The shack was like thousands of others that I had seen all my life throughout Louisiana and Mississippi. There was no glass in the windows, only hinged board flaps that were propped open on sticks. The walls had been insulated with pages from the Sears catalog, then covered with wallpaper that was now separated and streaked brown with rainwater. The outhouse, which was set next to a small hog lot, had a rusted RC Cola sign for a roof.

But there were other things there that leaped at your eye when you walked through the door: a color television set, an imitation Bavarian clock above the woodburning stove, plastic flowers set in jelly glasses, a bright yellow Formica breakfast table next to an ancient brick fireplace filled with trash.

The parents would tell me little. The mother stared vacantly at a game show on television, her huge body stuffed in a pair of lime-green stretch pants and a man's army shirt cut off at the armpits. The father was gray and old and walked with a cane as though his back were disjointed. He smelled of the cob pipe in his shirt pocket. His eyes were scaled over and frosted with cataracts.

'She gone off to New Orleans. I tolt her a colored girl from the country dint have no business there, her,' he said, sitting on the couch, his hand curved along the top of his cane. 'She only a country girl. What she gonna do with them kind of people they got in New Orleans? I tell her that, me.'

'Who did she work for, Mr Deshotels?'

'What I know about New Orleans? I ain't got no truck there, me.' He smiled at me, and I saw his toothless blue gums.

'Do you believe she drowned?'

He paused and the smile went out of his face. His eyes seemed to focus on me for the first time.

'You think they care what some old nigger say?' he said.

'I do.'

He didn't answer. He put his dead pipe in his mouth, made a wet sound with his tongue, and stared blankly at the television screen.

'I'll be going now,' I said, standing up. 'I'm sorry about what happened to your daughter. I really am.'

His face turned back toward me.

'We had eleven, us,' he said. 'She the baby. I call her *tite cush-cush* cause she always love *cush-cush* when she a little girl. He'p me walk out front, you.'

I put my hand under his arm and we stepped out into the bright sunlight on the porch. The wind was ruffling the green fields of surgarcane on the opposite side of the road. The old man's arm was webbed with veins. He limped along with me to my automobile before he spoke.

'They kilt her, them, dint they?' he asked.

'I think they did.'

'She just a little colored jellyroll for white mens, then they throw her away,' he said. His eyes became wet. 'I tolt her "Jerryroll, jellyroll, rollin' in the cane, lookin' for a woman ain't got no man." She say "Look the television and the clock and the table I give Mama." She say that, her. Little girl that don't know how to read can buy a five-hundred-dollar television set for her mama. What you gonna do when they nineteen? Ain't no listenin', not when she got white men's money, drive a big car down here from New Orleans, tellin' me she gonna move us up North, her. Little girl that still eat *cush-cush* gonna outsmart the white mens, her, move her old nigger daddy up to New York. What she done they got to kill her for?'

I didn't have an answer for him.

I was on an empty stretch of road bordered on one side by a flat, shimmering lake and on the other by a flooded woods, when I saw a blue and white patrol car in my rearview mirror. The driver already had on his bubblegum light, and when he drew close to my bumper he gave me a short blast with his siren. I started to pull to the shoulder, but there were shards of beer-bottle glass like amber teeth shining in the weeds and gravel. I tried to drive on to a clear spot before I stopped, and the patrol car leaped abreast of me, the engine roaring, and the deputy in the passenger's seat pointed to the side of the road with an angry finger. I heard my tires crunch over the beer glass.

Both deputies got out of the car, and I knew it was going to be serious. They were big men, probably Cajuns like myself, but their powerful and sinewy bodies, their tight-fitting, powder-blue uniforms, polished gun-belts and holsters, glinting bullets and revolver butts made you think of backwoods Mississippi and north Louisiana, as though they'd had to go away to learn redneck cruelty.

Neither of them had a citation book in his hand or pocket.

'The siren means pull over. It don't mean slow down, Lieutenant,' the driver said. He smiled back at me and took off his sunglasses. He was older than the other deputy. 'Step out of the car, please.'

I opened the door and stepped out on the road. They looked at me without speaking.

'All right, I'll bite. What have you got me for?' I said.

'Sixty in a fifty-five,' the other deputy said. He chewed gum, and his eyes were humorless and intent.

'I didn't think I ever got over fifty,' I said.

''Fraid it creeped up on you,' the older man said. 'On a pretty morning like this you get to looking around, maybe looking at the water and the trees, maybe thinking about a piece of ass, and before you know it you got lead in your pecker and foot, both.'

'I don't guess we're going to have an instance of professional courtesy here, are we?' I said.

'The judge don't allow us to let too many slide,' the older man said.

'So write me a ticket and I'll talk to the judge about it.'

'Lot of people from outside the parish don't show up in court,' the older deputy said. 'Makes him madder than a hornet with shit on its nose. So we got to take them down to the court.'

'You guys didn't get completely dressed this morning,' I said.

'How's that?' the other deputy said.

'You forgot to put on your name tags. Now, why would you do that?'

'Don't worry about any goddamn name tags. You're coming back to the courthouse with us,' the younger deputy said. He had stopped chewing his gum, and his jawbone was rigid against his cheek.

'You got a flat tire, anyway, Lieutenant,' the older man said. 'I figure that's kind of our fault, so while you ride in with us I'll radio the tow to come and change it for you.'

'Facts-of-life time,' I said. 'You don't roust a City of New Orleans detective.'

'Our territory, our rules, Lieutenant.'

'Fuck you,' I said.

They were both silent. The sun was shimmering brilliantly on the flat expanse of water behind them. The light was so bright I had to force myself not to blink. I could hear both of them breathing, see their eyes flick at each other uncertainly, almost smell the thin sweat on their skin.

The younger man's shoe shifted in the gravel and his thumb fluttered toward the strap on the holster that held his chrome-plated .357 Magnum revolver. I tore my .38 out of the clip holster on my belt, squatted, and aimed with two hands into their faces.

'Big mistake, podjo! Hands on your head and down on your knees!' I shouted.

'Look—' the older deputy began.

'Don't think, do it! I win, you lose!' My breath was coming hard in my throat.

They looked at each other, laced their hands on their heads, and knelt in front of their car. I went behind them, pulled their heavy revolvers from their holsters, and pitched them sideways into the lake.

'Take out your cuffs and lock up to the bumper,' I said.

'You're in over your head,' the older deputy said. The back of his suntanned neck was beaded with sweat.

'That's not the way I read it,' I said. 'You guys thought you'd be cowboys and you got your faces shoved into the sheepdip. What was it going to be, a day or so in the tank, or maybe some serious patty-cake in the backseat on the way to the jail?'

They didn't reply. Their faces were hot and angry and pained by the rocks that cut their knees.

'Put the cuffs through the bumper and lock your wrists,' I said. 'You didn't answer me, which makes me wonder if I was going to make the jail. Are you guys into it that big?'

'Kiss my ass,' the younger deputy said.

'Tell me, are y'all that dumb? You think you can pop a New Orleans cop and walk out of it?'

'We'll see who walks out of what,' the older deputy said. He had to twist sideways on his knees and squint up into the sun to talk to me.

'The Sheriff is letting you clean up his shit for him, isn't he?' I said. 'It looks like lousy work to me. You ought to get him to spread the juice around a little more. You guys probably rip off a little change now and then, maybe get some free action in the local hot-pillow joint, but he drives a Cadillac and raises Arabians.'

'For a homicide cop you're a stupid bastard,' the older deputy said. 'What make you think you're so important you got to be popped? You're just a hair in somebody's nose.'

'I'm afraid you boys have limited careers ahead of you.'

'Start figuring how you're going to get out of here,' the younger deputy said.

'You mean my flat tire? That is a problem,' I said thoughtfully. 'What if I just drive your car down the road a little ways with you guys still cuffed to it?'

For the first time their faces showed the beginnings of genuine fear.

'Relax. We have our standards in New Orleans. We don't pick on the mentally handicapped,' I said.

In the distance I saw a maroon car approaching. The two deputies heard it and looked at each other expectantly.

'Sorry, no cavalry today,' I said, then squatted down at eye level with them. 'Now look, you pair of clowns, I don't know how far you want to take this, but if you really want to get it on, you remember this: I've got more juice than you do, more people, more brains, more everything that counts. So give it some thought. In the meantime I'm going to send somebody back for my car, and it had better be here. Also, tell that character you work for that our conversation was ongoing. He'll get my drift.'

I flagged down the maroon car with my badge and got in the passenger's seat before the driver, a blond woman in her late twenties with windblown hair and wide eyes, could speak or concentrate on the two manacled deputies. Her tape player was blaring out Tchaikovsky's First Concerto, and the backseat was an incredible litter of papers, notebooks, and government forms.

'I'm a New Orleans police officer. I need you to take me to the next town,' I shouted above the music.

Her eyes were blue and as round as a doll's with surprise and fear. She began to accelerate slowly, her eyes sliding past the handcuffed cops but then riveting on them again in the rearview mirror.

'Are those men locked to the car?' she said.

'Yes. They were bad boys,' I yelled back. 'Can I turn this down?'

'I'm sorry, but I have to do this. You can go ahead and shoot if you want to.'

And with that she slammed on the brakes, dropped the transmission into reverse, and floorboarded the car backwards in a screech of rubber and a cloud of black smoke. My head hit the windshield, then I saw my old Chevrolet coming up fast. 'Watch it!' I shouted.

But it was too late. Her bumper caught my front fender and raked both doors. Then she careened to a stop, flipped off the stereo, leaned across me, and yelled at the deputies, 'This man says he's a police officer. Is that true?'

'Call the Cataouatche Sheriff's office, lady,' the older deputy said. He was squatting on one knee, and his face was strained with discomfort.

'Who is this man in my car?'

'He a piece of shit that's going to get ground into the concrete,' the younger deputy said.

The woman yanked the car into low, pushed the accelerator to the floor, and roared past my car again. I felt her back bumper carom off my front fender. She drove like a wild person, papers blowing in the backseat, the lake and flooded woods streaking past us.

'I'm sorry about your car. I have insurance. I think I still do, anyway,' she said.

'That's all right. I've always wanted to see the country from inside a hurricane. Are you still afraid, or do you always drive like this?'

'Like what?' Her hair was blowing in the wind and her round blue eyes were intent over the wheel.

'Do you still think I'm an escaped criminal?' I said.

'I don't know what you are, but I recognized one of those deputies. He's a sadist who rubbed his penis all over one of my clients.'

'Your clients?'

'I work for the state handicapped services.'

'You can put him away.'

'She's scared to death. He told her he'd do it to her again, and then put her in jail as a prostitute.'

'God, lady, look out. Listen, there's a restaurant on stilts just across the parish line. You pull in there, then we're going to make a phone call and I'm going to buy you lunch.'

'Why?'

'Because you're wired and you don't believe who I am. By the way, what you did back there took courage.'

'No, it didn't. I just don't give rides to weird people. There's a lot of weirdness around these days. If you're a police detective, why are you driving a wreck of an automobile?'

'A few minutes ago it wasn't entirely a wreck.'

'That's what I mean by weirdness. Maybe I saved your life, and you criticize my driving.'

Don't argue with God's design on a sun-spangled morning in a corridor of oak trees, Robicheaux, I thought. Also, don't argue with somebody who's doing eighty-five miles an hour and showering rocks like birdshot against the tree trunks.

The restaurant was a ramshackle board place with screen windows, built up on posts over the lake. Metal Dixie 45 and Jax beer signs were nailed all over the outer walls. Crawfish were out of season, so I ordered fried catfish and small bowls of shrimp gumbo. While we waited for the food, I bought her a drink at the bar and used the phone to call my extension at First District headquarters in New Orleans. I put the receiver to her ear so she could hear Clete answer, then I took the receiver back.

'I'm having lunch with a lady who would like you to describe what I look like,' I told him, and gave the phone back to her. I saw her start to smile as she listened, then her eyes crinkled and she laughed out loud.

'That's outrageous,' she said.

'What'd he say?'

'That your hair is streaked like a skunk's and that sometimes you try to walk the check.'

'Clete's always had satirical ambitions.'

'Is this how you all really do things? Chaining up other cops to cars, terrifying people on the highway, playing jokes over the phone?'

'Not exactly. They have a different set of rules in Cataouatche Parish. I sort of strayed off my turf.'

'What about those deputies back there? Won't they come after you?'

'I think they'll be more worried about explaining themselves to the man they work for. After we eat, can you take me back to the city?'

'I have to make a home call at a client's house, then I can.' She sipped from her Manhattan, then ate the cherry off the toothpick. She saw me watching her, and she looked out the window at the lake, where the wind was blowing the moss in the cypress trees.

'Do you like horse racing?' I said.

'I've never been.'

'I have a clubhouse pass. Would you like to go tomorrow night, provided I have my car back?'

She paused, and her electric blue eyes wandered over my face.

'I play cello with a string quartet. We have practice tomorrow night,' she said.

'Oh.'

'But we'll probably finish by eight-thirty, if that's not too late. I live by Audubon Park,' she said.

See, don't argue with design and things will work out all right after all, I told myself.

But things did not go well back at the District the next day. They never did when I had to deal with the people in vice, or with Sergeant Motley in particular. He was black, an ex-career enlisted man, but he had little sympathy for his own people. One time a black wino in a holding cell was giving Motley a bad time, calling him 'the white man's knee-grow, with a white man's badge and a white man's gun,' and Motley covered him from head to foot with the contents of a can of mace before the turnkey slapped it out of his hand.

But there was another memory about Motley that was darker. Before he made sergeant and moved over to vice, he had worked as a bailiff at the court and was in charge of escorting prisoners from the drunk tank to morning arraignment. He had seven of them on a wrist-chain in the elevator when a basement fire blew the electric circuits and stalled the elevator between floors. Motley got out through the escape door in the elevator's roof, but the seven prisoners were asphyxiated by the smoke.

'What do you want to know about her?' he said. He was overweight and had a thick mustache, and his ashtray was full of cigar butts.

'You busted her three times in a month – twice for soliciting, once for holding. You must have had an interest in her,' I said.

'She was a ten-dollar chicken, a real loser.'

'You're not telling me a lot, Motley.'

'What's to tell? She was freebasing and jacking guys off in a massage parlor in Decatur. She was the kind a john cuts up or a pimp sets on fire. Like I say, a victim. A country girl that was going to make the big score.'

'Who went her bail?'

'Probably her pimp. I don't remember.'

'Who was he?'

'I don't remember. There's a new lowlife running that joint every two months.'

'You know anybody who'd have reason to give her a hotshot?'

'Ask me her shoe size. When'd she become your case, anyway? I heard you fished her out of the bayou in Cataouatche Parish.'

'It's a personal interest. Look, Motley, we cooperate with you guys. How about being a little reciprocal?'

'What is it you think I know? I told you she was just another brainless whore. They all come out of the same cookie cutter. I lost contact with her, anyway.'

'What do you mean?'

'We busted the massage parlor a couple of times and she wasn't working there anymore. One of the other broads said Julio Segura moved her out to his place. That don't mean anything, though. He does that all the time, when he gets tired of them, gives them a few balloons of Mexican brown, and has that dwarf chauffeur of his drive them to the bus stop or back to the crib.'

'You're unbelievable.'

'You think a guy like him is interested in snuffing whores? Write it off, Robicheaux. You're wasting your time.'

Fifteen minutes later, Captain Guidry walked into the office I shared with Clete. He was fifty and lived with his mother and belonged to the Knights of Columbus. But recently he had been dating a widow in the city water department, and we knew it was serious when the captain began to undergo a hair transplant. His gleaming bald scalp was now inlaid with tiny round divots of transplanted hair, so that his head looked like a rock with weeds starting to grow on it. But he was a good administrator, a straight arrow, and he often took the heat for us when he didn't have to.

'Triple-A called and said they towed in your car,' he said.

'That's good,' I said.

'No. They also said somebody must have broken all the windows out with a hammer or a baseball bat. What went on over there with the sheriff's department, Dave?'

I told him while he stared at me blankly. I also told him about Julio Segura. Cletus kept his face buried in our file drawer.

'You didn't make this up? You actually cuffed two sheriff's deputies to their own car?' the captain said.

'I wasn't holding a very good hand, Captain.'

'Well, you probably had them figured right, because they haven't pursued it, except for remodeling your windows. You want to turn the screws on them a little? I can call the state attorney general's office and probably shake them up a bit.'

'Clete and I want to go out to Segura's place.'

'Vice considers that their territory,' Captain Guidry said.

'They're talking about killing a cop. It's our territory now,' I said.

'All right, but no cowboy stuff,' he said. 'Right now we don't have legal cause to be out there.'

'Okay.'

'You just talk, let him know we're hearing things we don't like.'

'Okay, Captain.'

He rubbed his fingernail over one of the crusted implants in his head.

'Dave?'

'Yes, sir?'

'Forget what I said. He's threatening a New Orleans police officer and we're not going to tolerate it. Put his head in the toilet. Tell him it came from me, too.'

Oleander, azalea, and myrtle trees were planted thickly behind the scrolled iron fence that surrounded Segura's enormous blue-green lawn. Gardeners were clipping the hedges, watering the geranium and rose beds, cutting away the dead brown leaves from the stands of banana trees. Back toward the lake I could see the white stucco two-story house, its red tile roof gleaming in the sun, the royal palms waving by the swimming pool. Someone sprang loudly off a diving board.

A muscular Latin man in slacks and a golf shirt came out the front gate and leaned down to Clete's window. There were faded tattoos under the black hair on his forearms. He also wore large rings on both hands.

'Can I help you, sir?' he said.

'We're police officers. We want to talk to Segura,' Clete said.

'Do you have an appointment with him?'

'Just tell him we're here, partner,' Clete said.

'He's got guests right now.'

'You got a hearing problem?' Clete said.

'I got a clipboard with some names on it. If your name's on it, you come in. If it ain't, you stay out.'

'Listen, you fucking greaseball . . .' Without finishing his sentence, Clete got out of the car and hit the man murderously in the stomach with his fist. The man doubled over, his mouth dropped open as though he had been struck with a sledgehammer, and his eyes looked like he was drowning.

'Got indigestion troubles? Try Tums,' Clete said.

'What's the matter with you?' I said to him.

'Nothing now,' he said, and pushed back the iron gate so we could drive through. The Latin man held on the fence with one hand and labored to get his breath back. We drove up the driveway toward the stucco house. I continued to look at Clete.

'You never worked vice. You don't know what kind of scum these bastards are,' he said. 'When a greaseball like that gets in your face, you step all over him. It defines the equations for him.'

'Did you get drunk last night?'

'Yeah, but I don't need an excuse to bash one of these fuckers.'

'No more of it, Clete.'

'We're in, aren't we? We're the surprise in Julio's afternoon box of Cracker Jacks. Look at that bunch by the pool. I bet we could run them and connect them with every dope deal in Orleans and Jefferson parishes.'

About a dozen people were in or around the clover-shaped pool. They floated on rubber rafts in the turquoise water, played cards on a mosaic stone table and benches that were anchored in the shallow end, or sat in lawn chairs by the slender gray trucks of the palms while a family of dwarf servants brought them tall tropical drinks filled with fruit and ice.

Clete walked directly across the clipped grass to an umbrella-shaded table where a middle-aged man in cream-colored slacks and a yellow shirt covered with blue parrots sat with two other men who were as dark as Indians and built like fire hydrants. The man in the print shirt was one of the most peculiar-looking human beings I had ever seen. His face was triangular-shaped, with a small mouth and very small ears, and his eyes were absolutely black. Three deep creases ran across his forehead, and inside the creases you could see tiny balls of skin. On his wrist was a gold watch with a black digital dial, and he smoked a Bisonte with a cigarette holder. The two dark men started to get up protectively as we approached the table, but the man in the yellow and blue shirt gestured for them to remain seated. His eyes kept narrowing as though Clete's face were floating toward him out of a memory.

'What's happening, Julio?' Clete said. 'There's a guy out front puking his lunch all over the grass. It really looks nasty for the neighborhood. You ought to hire a higher-class gate man.'

'Purcel, right?' Segura said, the recognition clicking into his eyes.

'That's good,' Clete said. 'Now connect the dots and figure out who this guy with me is.'

One of the dark men said something to Segura in Spanish.

'Shut up, greaseball,' Clete said.

'What do you think you're doing, Purcel?' Segura asked.

'That all depends on you, Julio. We hear you're putting out a very serious shuck about my partner,' Clete said.

'Is this him?' Segura asked.

I didn't answer. I stared straight into his eyes. He puffed on his cigarette holder and looked back at me without blinking, as though he were looking at an object rather than a man.

'I heard you been knocking the furniture around,' he said finally. 'But I don't know you. I never heard of you, either.'

'I think you're a liar,' I said.

'That's your right. What else you want to tell me today?'

'Your people killed a nineteen-year-old girl named Lovelace Deshotels.'

'Let me tell you something, what's-your-name,' he said. 'I'm an American citizen. I'm a citizen because a United States senator introduced a bill to bring me here. I got a son in West Point. I don't kill people. I don't mind Purcel and his people bothering me sometimes. You got *la mordida* here just like in Nicaragua. But you don't come out here and tell me I kill somebody.' He nodded to one of the dark men, who got up and walked to the house. 'I tell you something else, too. You know why Purcel is out here? It's because he's got a guilty conscience and he blames other people for it. He took a girl out of a massage parlor in the French Quarter and seduced her in the back of his car. That's the kind of people you got telling me what morality is.'

'How'd you like your teeth kicked down your throat?' Clete asked.

'I got my attorneys coming out right now. You want to make threats, you want to hit people, you'll make them rich. They love you.'

'You're a pretty slick guy, Julio,' I said.

'Yeah? Maybe you're a cute guy, like your partner,' he answered.

'Slick as Vaseline, not a bump or a handle on you,' I said. 'But let me tell you a story of my own. My daddy was a trapper on Marsh Island. He used to tell me, "If it's not moving, don't poke it. But when it starts snapping at your kneecaps, wait till it opens up real wide, then spit in its mouth." What do you think of that story?'

'You're a mature man. Why you want to be a fool? I didn't do nothing to you. For some reason you're finding this trouble for yourself.'

'What's the worst thing you've ever seen happen to somebody, Julio?' I asked.

'What're you talking about?' he said. His brow was furrowed, and the tiny balls of skin in the creases looked like strings of purple BBs.

'I hear you have some cruel guys working for you. Probably some of Somoza's old national guardsmen, experts in garroting journalists and murdering Catholic priests.'

'You don't make no sense.'

'Sure I do,' I said. 'You probably got to visit the basement in some of Somoza's police-stations. You saw them hung up by their arms, with a cloth bag soaked in insecticide tied over their heads. They screamed and went blind and suffocated to death, and even a piece of shit like yourself had a few nightmares about it. You also knew about that volcano where the army used to drop the Sandinistas from a helicopter into the burning crater. It's pretty awful stuff to think about, Julio.'

'They really sent us a pair today. A Vice cop with *puta* in his head and another one that talks like a Marxist,' he said. Some of the people around the pool laughed.

'You're not following my drift,' I said. 'You see, to you a bad fate is what you've seen your own kind do to other people. But once you got away from the horror show down there in Managua, you figured you were safe. So did Somoza. He got out of Dodge with all his millions, then one day his chauffeur was driving him across Asuncion in his limo, with a motorcycle escort in front and back, and somebody parked a three-point-five bazooka rocket in his lap. It blew him into instant lasagna. Are you following me, Julio?'

'You going to come after me, big man?' he asked.

'You still don't get it. Look, it's almost biblical. Eventually somebody eats your lunch, and it always comes from a place you didn't expect it. Maybe a redneck cop puts a thumbbuster forty-five behind your ear and lets off a hollow-point that unfastens your whole face. Or maybe they strap you down in the Red Hat House at Angola and turn your brains into fried grits.'

'You ought to get a job writing comic books,' he said.

'Then maybe you're sitting by your pool, secure, with your prostitutes and these trained monkeys around you, and something happens out of sequence,' I said, and picked up his tropical drink full of ice and fruit and poured it into his lap.

He roared back from the table, raking ice off his cream-colored slacks, his face full of outrage and disbelief. The squat, dark man seated across from him started from his chair. Clete slammed him back down.

'Start it and we finish it, Paco,' he said.

The dark man remained seated and gripped the wrought-iron arms of his chair, staring at Clete with a face that was as flat and latently brutal as a frying pan.

'There's a good fellow,' Clete said.

'You get out of here!' Segura said.

'This is just for openers. The homicide people are a creative bunch,' I said.

'You're spit on the side walk,' he said.

'We've got a whole grab bag of door prizes for you, Julio. But in the end I'm going to send you back to the tomato patch,' I said.

'I got guys that can cut a piece out of you every day of your life,' Segura said.

'That sounds like a threat against a police officer,' Clete said.

'I don't play your game, *maricón*,' Segura said. 'You're amateurs, losers. Look behind you. You want to shove people around now?'

Two men had parked their canary-yellow Continental at the end of the drive and were walking across the grass toward us. Both of them looked like upgraded bail bondsmen.

'Whiplash Wineburger, up from the depths,' Clete said.

'I thought he'd been disbarred for fixing a juror,' I said.

'That was his brother. Whiplash is too slick for that,' Clete said. 'His specialty is insurance fraud and ripping off his own clients.'

'Who's the oilcan with him?'

'Some dago legislator that's been peddling his ass around here for years.'

'I heard you were wired into some heavy connections. These guys need lead in their shoes on a windy day,' I said to Segura.

'*Me cago en la puta de tu madre*,' he replied.

'You hotdogs got two minutes to get out of here,' the lawyer said. He was lean and tan, like an aging professional tennis player, and he wore a beige sports jacket, a yellow open-necked shirt, and brown-tinted glasses.

'We were just on our way. It looks like the neighborhood is going to hell in a hurry,' Clete said.

'By the way, Wineburger,' I said, 'bone up on your tax law. I hear the IRS is about to toss Segura's tax records.'

'Yeah? You got a line to the White House?' he said.

'It's all over the Federal Building. You haven't been doing your homework,' I said.

We walked back to our car and left Segura and his lawyer staring at each other.

We headed back down the lake toward the Pontchartrain Expressway. The palm trees were beating along the shore, and small waves were whitecapping out on the lake. Several sailboats were tacking hard in the wind.

'You think we stuck a couple of thumbtacks in his head?' Cletus asked. He drove without looking at me.

'We'll see.'

'That touch about the IRS was beautiful.'

'You want to tell me something, Clete?'

'Am I supposed to go to confession or something?'

'I don't like to see a guy like Segura trying to jerk my partner around.'

'It was three years ago. My wife and I had broke up and I'd been on the shelf for six weeks.'

'You let the girl walk?'

'She was never busted. She was a snitch. I liked her.'

'That's why you put your fist through that guy's stomach?'

'All right, so I don't feel good about it. But I swear to you, Dave, I never got any free action because of my badge, and I never went on the pad.' He looked across at me with his poached, scarred face.

'So I believe you.'

'So buy me a *beignet* and a coffee at the Café du Monde.'

An afternoon thundershower was building out over Lake Pontchartrain. The sky on the distant horizon had turned green, and waves were scudding all across the lake now. The few sailboats still out were drenched with spray and foam as they pounded into the wind and headed for their docks. It started to rain in large, flat drops when we turned onto the

Expressway, then suddenly it poured down on Clete's car in a roar of tackhammers.

The city was soaked and dripping when I went to pick up the social worker, whose name was Annie Ballard, by Audubon Park. The street-lamps lighted the misty trees along the esplanade on St Charles; the burnished streetcar tracks and the old green streetcar glistened dully in the wet light, and the smoky neon signs, the bright, rain-streaked windows of the restaurants and the drugstore on the corner were like part of a nocturnal painting out of the 1940s. This part of New Orleans never seemed to change, and somehow its confirmation of yesterday on a rainy summer night always dissipated my own fears about time and morality. And it was this reverie that made me careless, let me ignore the car that parked behind me, and let me walk up her sidewalk with the vain pre-sumption that only people like Julio Segura had things happen to them out of sequence.

3

She lived in an old brick rowhouse that was connected to several others by a common porch and a shrub-filled front yard. I heard footsteps behind me, turned and glanced at three men who were joking about something and carrying a wine bottle wrapped in a paper sack, but I paid no attention to them after they turned toward a lighted house where a party was going on.

She smiled when she opened the door. She wore a blue dress with transparent shoulders, and her blond curls stuck out from under a wide straw hat. She was very pretty with the light behind her, and I didn't care whether we made it to the track or not. Then I saw her eyes focus over my shoulder, saw her expression break apart, heard the feet on the porch behind me, this time fast and running. Just as I turned, one of the three men shoved me hard into Annie Ballard's living room and aimed a Browning automatic pistol straight into my face.

'Don't try to pull it, biscuit-eater, unless you want your brains running out your nose,' he said, and reached inside my sports coat and pulled my .38 from my waist holster.

He was tall and angular, his hair mowed into his scalp like a peeled onion, his stomach as flat as a shingle under the big metal buckle on his blue jeans. The accent was Deep South, genuine peckerwood, and on his right arm was a tattoo of a grinning skull in a green beret with crossed bayonets under the jaw and the inscription KILL THEM ALL . . . LET GOD SORT THEM OUT.

The second man was short and olive-skinned, with elongated Semitic eyes and a hawk nose. He went quickly from room to room, like a ferret. But it was the third man who was obviously in charge. His hands rested comfortably in his raincoat pockets; his face looked impassively around the room as though he were standing at a bus stop. He was in his early fifties, with a paunch, a round Irish chin, a small mouth with down-turned corners, and cheeks that were flecked with tiny blue and red veins. The vaguely dissolute edges of his face, with his tangled eyebrows and untrimmed gray hair, gave you the impression of a jaded Kiwanian.

'There's nobody else,' the olive-skinned man said. He spoke with a Middle Eastern accent.

'Do you already know I'm a police officer?' I said quietly.

'We know a lot about you, Lieutenant. You've really spread your name around recently,' the man in the raincoat said.

'I thought Segura was smarter than this,' I said.

'I don't know. I've never met the man. But you're not smart at all.' He took a revolver casually out of his raincoat pocket and nodded to the man with the tattoo, who went into the bathroom, dropped my .38 into the toilet bowl, and started the water in the bathtub. Annie's eyes were wide under her hat, and she was breathing rapidly through her mouth.

'I have friends coming over,' she said.

'That's why you got your hat on,' the man with the tattoo said, smiling from the bathroom door. His hair was cut so close to his scalp that the light made his head glow with an aura. He held a large roll of adhesive tape in his hand.

'I'm going to walk out my door,' she said. Her face was flushed and spotted as though she had a fever, and her voice was filled with strain. 'I have friends next door and out in the yard and over on the next block and they can hear everything through these walls and you're not going to do anything to us—'

'Annie,' I said quietly.

'We're going to leave now and they're not going to hurt us,' she said.

'Annie, don't talk,' I said. 'These men have business with me, then they're going to leave. You mustn't do anything now.'

'Listen to the voice of experience,' the man in the raincoat said.

'No,' she said. 'They're not going to do this. I'm walking outside now. These are weak people or they wouldn't have guns.'

'You dumb cunt,' the man with the tattoo said, and swung his fist into the back of Annie's head. Her hat pitched into the air, and she fell forward on her knees, her face white with shock. She remained bent over and started to cry. It was the kind of crying that came from genuine, deep-seated pain.

'You sonofabitch,' I said.

'Put her in back,' the man in the raincoat said. The other two men pulled Annie's arms behind her and taped her wrists, then her mouth. Her curly hair hung in her eyes, and there were tears on her cheeks. The two men started to walk her to the bedroom.

'Bobby Joe, nothing except what we have to do here,' the man in the raincoat said.

'You wanted her to walk out on the front porch?' said Bobby Joe, the man with the tattoo.

'That's not what I mean. *Nothing except what we have to do.* Do you understand?'

'There's better broads for two bucks in Guatemala City,' Bobby Joe said.

'Shut your mouth, tape her ankles, and get back out here,' the man with the raincoat said.

'Who are you?' I asked.

'You're in way over your head, Lieutenant. I'm just not sure of your own degree of awareness. That's the problem we have to resolve tonight.'

'I'll give you something else to resolve. I'm going to square everything that happens in here.'

'You're presuming a lot.'

'Yeah? We can make New Orleans an uncomfortable place for crackers that beat up on women. Or for over-the-hill spooks.'

He looked amused.

'You think you've made me?' he said.

'You have a strong federal smell.'

'Who knows, these days, employment being what it is? But at least you're professional and you recognize characteristics in people. So you know that Bobby Joe and Erik in there are hired help, not professional at all. They get carried away sometimes. Do you know what I mean? Bobby Joe, in particular. Bad army life, doesn't like authority, certainly doesn't like women. A bad combination for your situation. Tell me where Fitzpatrick is and we'll walk out of here.'

'Who?'

'I was afraid we'd hear that from you.'

The other two men, Bobby Joe and Erik, came out of the bedroom, crossed my wrists behind me, and wound the adhesive tape deep into my flesh. I could feel the blood swelling in my veins. Then the man in the raincoat nodded to Bobby Joe, who jerked my head down with both hands and brought his knee up into my face. I crashed against the coffee table, my nose ringing with pain, my eyes watering uncontrollably. Bobby Joe and Erik picked me up by each arm. Their hands were like Vise-Grips on me. Then Bobby Joe hit me twice in the stomach, and I doubled over and gagged a long string of saliva on the rug.

'Now you're a cooperative biscuit-eater,' Bobby Joe said, and they led me into the bathroom.

The tub was running over now. Erik turned off the taps, and the man in the raincoat lowered the toilet-seat cover, sat on it, and lighted a Camel cigarette.

'In 'Nam we wrapped a towel around Charlie's face and soaked it in water,' he said. 'It was kind of like a portable river to drown in. But it always worked. Even better than calling him up on the telephone crank. Let's have it, Lieutenant, so we don't have to go through this bullshit.'

They had me on my knees, bent over the tub now. My nose was

dripping blood into the water. They waited a moment in silence, then shoved my head under.

I fought to get up, but it didn't do any good. My knees felt like they were greased with Vaseline; my stomach was pressed hard over the tub's rim, and Bobby Joe was leaning all his weight on the back of my neck. My breath bubbled out my nose and mouth, I shook my head violently from side to side with my eyes open, my teeth gritted, then the closure apparatus in my throat broke and I sucked water inside my head and lungs like a series of doors slamming forever.

They pulled me up roaring with water and air, and threw me against the metal legs on the sink.

'This isn't so bad. There's no permanent damage done,' the man in the raincoat said. 'It'd be a lot worse if Segura's people handled it. It has something to do with the Latin tradition. I think they got it from the Romans. Did you know that Nero killed himself because the Senate sent word to him that he was to be executed in "the old way," which meant being whipped to death with his head locked in a wooden fork? If you don't want to say where Fitzpatrick is, you can write it on a piece of paper. It's funny how that makes a difference for people sometimes.'

My heart was thundering, my breath laboring in my throat.

'I never heard of the cocksucker,' I said.

I felt Bobby Joe begin to lift me by one arm.

'Wait a minute,' the man in the raincoat said. 'The lieutenant's not a bad fellow. He just doesn't know what's involved. If he did, he might be on our team. Fitzpatrick probably gave you a patriotic shuck and you thought you were helping out the good guys.'

'I don't know what the fuck you're talking about.'

'You're probably a good cop, but don't tell us you're shaking the bushes all over New Orleans and Cataouatche Parish because of a drowned colored girl,' he said.

'Two minutes this time. He'll tell,' Erik said.

The man in the raincoat leaned down and looked intensively in my face.

'He means it,' he said. 'Two minutes under water. Maybe you'll make it, sometimes they don't. It happens.'

'All he's got to do is nod his head up and down, then he can have all the air he wants,' Bobby Joe said.

He jerked me up half-erect by my arm and started to slide me across the wet tiles to the tub's rim again. But this time I was dripping with water and sweat and I slipped loose from him, fell on my buttocks, and shot one leather-soled shoe like a hammer into his ribcage. He wasn't ready for it, and I felt a bone go like a stick. The blood drained out of his face, his tongue lay pink on his teeth, his skin tightened on his skull as though he were silently absorbing an intolerable pain and rage.

'Oh my, you shouldn't have done that,' the man in the raincoat said.

Erik grabbed my hair and slammed my head against the side of the tub. I kicked at all of them blindly, but my feet struck at empty air. Then Bobby Joe locked his powerful arms around my neck and took me over the rim again, his body trembling rigidly with a cruel and murderous energy, and I knew that all my past fears of being shotgunned by a psychotic, of being shanked by an addict, of stepping on a Claymore mine in Vietnam, were just the foolish preoccupations of youth; that my real nemesis had always been a redneck lover who would hold me upside down against his chest while my soul slipped through a green, watery porcelain hole in earth, down through the depths of the Mekong River, where floated the bodies of other fatigue-clad men and whole families of civilians, their faces still filled with disbelief and the shock of an artillery burst, and farther still to the mossy base of an offshore oil rig in the Gulf of Mexico, where my father waited for me in his hardhat, coveralls, and steeltipped drilling boots after having drowned there twenty years ago.

Then Bobby Joe's arms let go of my neck, as though he had tired of me, and I collapsed in a gasping, embryonic heap on the floor. I lay with one eye pressed against the wet tile.

'Get out there and see what it is!' the man in the raincoat said.

Bobby Joe stood erect, stepped over me, and was gone.

'Had a mind-change about Fitzpatrick?' the man in the raincoat said.

I couldn't answer. In fact, at that point I didn't even remember the name. Then I heard Bobby Joe in the doorway.

'His bitch got her feet loose from the bedstead and kicked a lamp through the window. The whole goddamn backyard is full of people from a party,' he said.

'Travel time,' the man in the raincoat said. He stood up and combed his hair as he walked past me. 'You're a big winner tonight, Lieutenant. But let the experience work for you. Don't try to play in the major leagues. It's a shitty life, believe me. Big risks, lot of crazy people running around, few side benefits like the piece you've got in the next room. You've got *cojones*, but the next time around, Bobby Joe and Erik will cut them off.'

Then they went out the front door into the dark like three macabre harlequins who on impulse visited the quiet world of ordinary people with baseball bats.

Three patrol cars from the Second District, an ambulance and a fire truck answered the neighbor's emergency call. Revolving red and blue lights reflected off the trees and houses; the lawn and house were filled with patrolmen, paramedics, firemen in yellow slickers, neighbors drinking beer and sangria, people writing on clipboards and talking into static-filled radios, and all of it signified absolutely nothing. Any candid policeman will tell you that we seldom catch people as a result of investigation or detective work; in other words, if we don't grab them during the commission of the crime, there's a good chance we won't catch them at all. When we do nail them, it's often through informers or because they trip over their own shoestrings and turn the key on themselves (drunk driving, expired license plates, a barroom beef). We're not smart; they're just dumb.

That's why the feds were made to look so bad back in the late sixties and early seventies when they couldn't nail a bunch of middle-class college kids who ended up on the 'Ten Most Wanted' list. Instead of dealing with predictable psychopaths like Alvin Karpis and Charles Arthur Floyd, the FBI had to second-guess Brandeis and Wisconsin English majors who dynamited research labs and boosted banks and Brinks' trucks and then faded back into the quiet life of the suburbs. For a time, the amateurs ruined crime for everybody.

The last one to leave was the scene investigator whom I'd requested. He dusted the doors, the bedroom, the bath, looked at me with a shrug, and walked out the door without speaking, which was his way of telling me what he thought of the fruitless work I had just created for him.

'Did he find something?' Annie said. She sat at the dining room table with a tumbler of whiskey between her fingers. Her face was wan, her voice and blue eyes listless.

'Everything was probably smeared. Fingerprints never do us much good anyway, not unless we have a body or someone in custody. Even if an examiner has a whole handprint set in blood, he still has to compare it with tens of thousands of file prints, and it's as much fun as threading a needle with your eyes closed. That's why he looked so happy when he left here. Look, I'm sorry I brought all this stuff into your house. I got careless tonight. I should have made those guys when they stepped out of their car.'

'It wasn't your fault.' Her voice was flat, distant.

'I think you should have gone in the ambulance. A concussion can fool you sometimes.'

'It doesn't have anything to do with a concussion.'

I looked at her colorless, depleted face.

'Listen, let me go to my boat and change clothes, then I'll take you to an Italian restaurant on the lake where they serve lasagna that'll break your heart,' I said.

'I don't think I can go anywhere now.'

'All right, I'll go to that Chinese place on St Charles and bring us something back. I'll be gone only a few minutes.'

She stared quietly into space for a moment.

'Do you mind not going for a while?' she asked.

'All right, but I tell you what – no booze. Instead, I'm going to fix some hot milk for you, and an omelette.'

I took the tumbler of whiskey from her fingertips. Then her eyes looked desperately into mine, her mouth trembled, and the tears ran down her cheeks.

'He put his hands all over me,' she said. 'He put them everywhere. While the other one watched.'

She started to cry hard now, her chin on her chest, her shoulders shaking.

'Listen, Annie, you're a brave person,' I said. 'You don't know it, but you saved my life. How many people could do what you did? Most people just roll over when violence comes into their lives. A guy like that can't harm a person like you.'

She had her arms folded tightly across her stomach, and she kept her face turned down toward the table.

'You come in the living room and sit on the couch with me,' I said. I put my arm around her shoulders and walked her to the divan. I sat down next to her and picked up her hands in mine. 'What happens outside of us doesn't count. That's something we don't have control over. It's what we do with it, the way that we react to it, that's important. You don't get mad at yourself or feel ashamed because you catch a virus, do you? Listen, I'll be straight-up with you. You've got a lot more guts than I have. I've been in a situation where something very bad happened to me, but I didn't have your courage.'

She swallowed, widened her eyes, and touched at her wet cheeks with the back of her wrist. Her face jerked slightly each time she breathed, but she was listening to me now.

'I was in Vietnam in the early days of the war,' I said, 'a hotshot lieutenant with a degree in English who really thought he could handle the action. Why not? It had never been very rough while I was there. The Vietcong used to pop at us with some old Japanese and French junk that had been heated up and bent around trees. Half the time it blew up in their faces. Then one day we were going through the rubber plantation and we ran into a new cast of characters – North Vietnamese regulars armed with AK-47s. They sucked us into a mined area, then blew us apart. If a guy tried to turn around and crawl out, he'd either set off a mine right under his face or get chopped up in their crossfire. We lost ten guys in fifteen minutes, then the captain surrendered. They marched us through rubber trees down to a coulee where ARVN artillery had killed a bunch of civilians from VC village. There were dead children and women and old people in the water and all along the banks of the coulee. I figured they were going to line us up and blow us into the water with the rest of them. Instead, they stripped off our web gear and tied our hands around trees with piano wire they tore out of a smashed-up piano in the plantation house. Then they ate our rations and smoked our cigarettes and took turns urinating on us. We sat on the ground like kicked dogs while they did it to us. I blamed the captain for surrendering. I even felt pleasure when they urinated on him. But something else happened that really put some boards in my head later on.

'A gunship spotted us, and about ten minutes later a bunch of rangers and pathfinders came through that same mined area to bail us out. We were the bait in the rat trap. I could hear the AKs and the mines going off, hear our guys screaming, even see blood and parts of people explode on the tree trunks, and I was glad that I was out of it, drenched in piss and safe from all that terror out there where those guys were dying, trying to save us.

'I used to pretend to myself that I didn't have the thoughts that I did, that what went through my head didn't have anything to do with the outcome anyway, or other times I just wanted to kill every VC or North Vietnamese I could, but the real truth of that whole scene, before a couple of Hueys turned the place into a firestorm, was that I was glad somebody else was getting shredded into dog-food instead of me.

'That's what I mean about rolling over. You're not that kind of girl. You've got a special kind of courage, and it can't be compromised by some peckerwood dimwit who's going to end up as Vienna sausage if I have anything to do with it.'

'Your feelings were just human. You couldn't help it,' she said.

'That's right, but you were a better soldier tonight than I was in Vietnam, except you don't want to give yourself any credit.' Then I brushed back her blond curls from her forehead. 'You're a prettier soldier, too.'

Her eyes looked back at me without blinking.

'Pretty and brave. That's a tough combo,' I said.

The blueness of her eyes, the childlike quality in them, made something sink inside me.

'Do you think you'd like to eat now?' I said.

'Yes.'

'My daddy was a wonderful cook. He taught me and my half-brother all his recipes.'

'I think he taught you some other things, too. I think you're a very good man.'

Her eyes smiled at me. I squeezed her hand, which was still cold and formless, then went into the kitchen and heated a pan of milk and cooked an omlette with green onions and white cheese. We ate at the coffee table, and I saw the color come back into her face.

I made her talk about her family, her home, her music, and her work, everything that defined who she was before Bobby Joe had touched her with this probing hands. She told me she had grown up on a wheat and milo farm north of Wichita, Kansas, that her mother was a Mennonite peace worker and her father a descendant of John Brown's people. She described Kansas as a rolling green country traced with slow-moving rivers, dotted with clumps of oak and poplar and cottonwood, a wide, horizonless place under a hot blue sky that would fill with the drone of cicadas on a summer evening. But it was also a country peopled with religious fanatics, prohibitionists, and right-wing simpletons, and on the other side of the equation were the anti-nukers and dozens of vigilant peace groups. It sounded like an open-air mental asylum. Or at least it was to her, because she had gone to Tulane to study music and had not left New Orleans since.

But sleep was stealing into her face now.

'I think it's time for a kiddo I know to go to bed,' I said.

'I'm not tired. Not really.'

'Oh, yes?' I put my arm around her, placed her head on my shoulder, and touched her eyes closed with my fingertips. I could feel her breathing evenly on my chest.

'I'm not a kiddo. I'm twenty-seven,' she said sleepily.

I slipped my other arm under her legs and carried her into her bedroom and laid her down on the bed. I took off her shoes and pulled the sheet over her. She looked up at me from the pillow and put her hand on the back of my neck.

'Don't go,' she said.

'I'll be on the couch in the living room. Tomorrow morning we'll have breakfast at the French Market. If you hear a noise later, it's just me. I walk around a lot at night,' I said, and turned off the light.

It was true, I usually didn't sleep well. Sometimes it was latent memories of the war, but most often I was sleepless simply because I was alone. Even the monastic saints never wrote in praise of nocturnal solitude. I watched three late-hour movies on television, until I saw the light turn gray in the trees outside. When I finally fell asleep, it was with the confidence that the full radiance of day was only a short time away, and that my night's aching celibacy, my battered set of ethics, all my alcoholic dragons would soon resolve themselves in a predictable and manageable way.

The man I sometimes thought of as my father's misplaced seed called me just before noon and told me to come to lunch at his restaurant on Dauphine. Actually, my half-brother, Jimmie, who people said looked like my twin, was a gentleman in his way. He had our father's sense of humor and fairness; he treated his equals as well as his inferiors with respect, and he paid his gambling debts on time; and he had an honorable attitude toward women, one that was almost Victorian, possibly because his mother was supposedly a prostitute from Abbeville, although neither of us remembered her. But he was also locked into off-track betting and trafficking in poker and slot machines, which brought him into a casual but dangerous association with Didoni Giacano.

I often got mad at him because of that association and his cavalier attitude toward it, as well as some of the other things he had continued to do for a lifetime to prove somehow that he was both different from me and at the same time that he was not simply my half-brother and his father's illegitimate son. But I could never stay mad at him long, no more than I could when we were children and he was always devising schemes that invariably went wrong and got us both in trouble.

Even though he was fifteen months younger than I, we did everything together. We washed bottles in the hot-sauce factory on the bayou, plucked chickens for a nickel apiece at the slaughterhouse, set pins at the bowling alley when few white kids would work in those 110-degree pits that were filled with cursing, sweating Negroes, exploding pins, and careening bowling balls that could snap your shinbone in half. But he got us both fired at the hot-sauce factory, since the owner couldn't tell us apart, when he tried to wash bottles en masse by filling a dozen gunnysacks with them and weighting them down in the bayou's current. We got canned at the slaughterhouse after he decided to streamline the operation and take six dozen chickens out of the cages at one time and herd them into the yard where we were to butcher and then scald them in big cauldrons of water; instead, they panicked and many of them flew into the big window fan and were chopped to pieces in the metal blades.

One hot night at the bowling alley, a group of tough kids who lived down by Railroad Avenue came in and started rolling the second ball before the pin boy could reset the rack. These were kids who went nigger-knocking on Saturday nights with slingshots and marbles and ball bearings. The Negroes in the pits couldn't do much when they were abused by drunks or bad high-school kids, but Jimmie imposed no restraints upon himself and always practiced immediate retaliation. He was picking up four pins at a time in the pit next to me, his T-shirt streaked with dirt, sweat running out of his hair, when a ball sailed past his kneecap and thudded into the leather backstop. A minute later it happened again. He set the rack down to block the alley, went over to one of the other pits, and came back with a spit can filled with chewed Red Man. He poured it into the thumb hole of the bowling ball, packed a wad of bubblegum on top of it, then rolled the ball back down the chute.

A moment later we heard a loud curse, and we looked out from under the racks and saw a big, burr-headed boy staring at his hand with a horrified expression on his face.

'Hey, podna, smear some of it on your nose, too. It'd be an improvement,' Jimmie yelled.

Three of them caught us in the parking lot after the alley closed and knocked us down on the gravel for five minutes before the owner came out, chased them off, and told us we were both fired. Jimmie ran after their truck, throwing rocks at the cab.

'We'll get a paper route,' he said, his face hot and dusty and streaked with dried perspiration. 'Who wants to be a pinsetter all his life? There's a lot of money in paper routes these days.'

Both of us would change a lot when we went to college in Lafayette, and in many ways we would begin to leave our father's Cajun world behind us. Eventually I would go into the army and be sent to Vietnam, and Jimmie would join the national guard, borrow money on the small house and seven-acre farm our father left us, and open a café on Decatur Street in New Orleans. Later he would buy into the first of several restaurants, wear expensive jewelry and Botany 500 suits and learn the manners of the people who lived in the Garden District and belonged to the Southern Yacht Club, primarily because he thought they knew something about money and power that he didn't, and there would be any number of attractive women who floated in and out of his life. But whenever I saw him on Canal or in his restaurant with a group of jocular businessmen, his eyes crinkling good-naturedly at the banal humor, an earlier image would glint briefly in my memory like a small mirror, and I would see again the kid in overalls panicking a swirl of chickens into a window fan or flinging a rock at a pickup truck receding in the darkness.

Didi Gee and my brother were eating in a red leather booth in the back of the restaurant when I walked in. Didi's waistline and stomach had the contours of three inner tubes stacked on top of each other. His hands were as big as skillets, his neck as thick as a fire hydrant, his curly black head as round and hard as a cannon-ball. As a young man he'd been a collector for a group of shylocks across the river Algiers, hence the story about his holding people's hands down in an aquarium filled with piranha. I also knew for a fact that a cop in Gretna shot a plug out of his shoulder the size of an apple core, refused to call for an ambulance, and left him to bleed to death on the sidewalk. Only he lived and got the cop fired from the force, then fired from every job he tried to hold thereafter, until finally he had to go to work for Didi Gee as a numbers runner, a sort of pathetic human exhibit that Didi kept around like a voodoo doll with pins stuck in it.

Jimmie grinned at me with his white teeth, shook hands, and motioned for the waiter to serve me a steak-and-lobster plate from the warmer on the back counter. Didi Gee's mouth was so full of food that he had to put down his knife and fork and continue chewing for almost a half-minute, then drink a glass of red wine, before he could speak.

'How you doing, Lieutenant?' he said flatly. He always spoke as though his nose were clotted with cartilage.

'Pretty good,' I said. 'How's life, Didi?'

'Not so hot, to tell you the truth. I got cancer of the colon. They're going to cut out some of my entrail tract and sew up my hole. I got to walk around with a bag of shit hanging on my side.'

'I'm sorry to hear about that,' I said.

'My doctor says I either get it done or they nail me down in a piano crate. Be glad you're young.' He put a meatball wrapped with spaghetti and half a slice of bread in his mouth.

'We heard some rumors about you,' Jimmie said, smiling. He wore a charcoal suit and gray tie, and his gold watch and rings gleamed in the restaurant's soft light. Ever since he was a kid he had used his grin to hide guilt, to address complexity, or to deny a basic goodness in himself.

'Like they say, you hear a lot of bullshit in the street,' I said.

'Mashing on Julio Segura's nuts is not bullshit,' Jimmie said.

'You have to enrich a guy's day sometimes,' I said.

'Some guys are better left alone,' Jimmie said.

'What did you hear?' I said.

'There's talk about a heavy fall for a homicide cop.'

'It's old news, Jim. I heard it first up at Angola from Johnny Massina.'

'Don't take it lightly,' Jimmie said.

'We're talking about a very low class of people, Lieutenant,' Didi Gee said. 'They're part Indian or colored or something. I bought a nice winter home in Hallendale, Florida, then some Colombians moved in next to me and dug the whole fucking yard into a vegetable patch. Their kids pissed out the second-story window on my car. This is in a neighborhood you don't get into without three hundred thou. They put raw chicken shit on their tomato plants. The smell made your nose fall off.'

'Why are we having this lunch, Jimmie?' I said.

'Julio Segura is real garbage. He doesn't go by anybody's rules. Not yours, not Didi's. There's lots of people that would like to see this guy canceled out. But he's still around and it's because certain other people want him around. I don't want to see you get burned finding out something that's not going anywhere.'

Then Jimmie was silent. Didi Gee stopped eating, lit a cigarette, and dropped the burnt match into his empty plate.

'There's a couple of guys that used to work for me. They don't work for me now,' he said. 'But they hang around my places of business sometimes. They like to talk about what's going on around town. As Jimmie will tell you, I'm not interested in listening to gossip. Also, these are guys that follow their cocks. I don't spend no time thinking of what these kind of young guys got to say. To tell you the truth, Lieutenant, I've been changing my attitudes about people a great deal lately. I think it's my age and this awful disease in my colon. There are classes of people I don't want to have no association with anymore. Like these guys. If you was to ask me their names later, I'd have to honestly tell you I don't remember. I think it's a mental block when it comes to some trashy people that I've been forced to hire in my business.'

'I'm not big on names these days, Didi,' I said.

'Because this story, if it's true, is a horrible one and shows what kind of scum the country has been letting across its border,' he said. 'This colored girl was a parlor chippie for this spick that lives out by the lake. The spick – and I use that word only because he's a genuine lowlife – has got broads on the brain and is always moving them in and out of his mansion, primarily because he's a fucking geek that no normal woman would touch unless she was blind. So the colored girl moved in and the geek really had the hots for her. The girl thought it was going to be hump city from there on out. The spick lets his pet dwarf drive her shopping around town, gives her all the coke she wants, introduces her to a lot of import-ant greasers like she wasn't just another broad with a ten-dollar ass and a five-cent brain. But the girl didn't know this guy went through his own chippies like Jimmy Durante went through Kleenex. One morning after she got drunk and threw up in his pool he told the dwarf to drive her back to the parlor. What the spick didn't figure on was ambition in a colored girl that grew up pulling sweet potatoes out of the ground with her toes.

'Because this broad had ears and a memory like fly-paper. All the time she was poking plastic straws up her nose or balling the geek, she was also getting onto some heavy shit, and I'm talking government, military shit, Lieutenant, that the geek and the other spicks are playing around with.'

'What do you mean "government"?' I said.

'I'm repeating the gossip, I don't analyze. It don't interest me. I think Immigration ought to take these people to a factory and turn them into bars of soap. The girl tried to put his tit through a wringer. That got her out of the parlor all right. They took her fishing out on the bayou and let her shoot up until her eyes crossed. When she didn't pull it off on her own, they loaded her a hotshot that blew her heart out her mouth.'

'I appreciate the story you've told me, Didi, but I'd be offended if I thought you believed we were in the business of running your com-petition out of town.'

'You hurt my feelings,' he answered.

'Because we already knew just about everything you told me, except the mention about the government and the military. You're very vague on that. I think we're being selective here. I don't believe that's good for a man of your background who enjoys the respect of many people in the department.'

'I have been candid, Lieutenant. I do not pretend to understand the meaning of everything I hear from people that sometimes lie.'

'You're a mature man, Didi. You shouldn't treat me as less.'

He blew smoke out his nose and mashed out his cigarette in his plate. His black eyes became temporarily unmasked.

'I don't know what he's into. It's not like the regular business around the city,' he said. He paused before he spoke again. 'A guy said the girl was giggling about elephants before they dumped her in the water. You figure that one out.'

A few minutes later Didi Gee picked up his check and the two hoods who waited for him at the bar, and left. The red leather upholstery he had sat on looked like it had been crushed with a wrecking ball.

'He tips everybody in the place on his way out. Under it all he's a bit insecure,' Jimmie said.

'He's a psychopath,' I said.

'There's worse people around.'

'You think it's cute to mess around with characters like that? You better give it some serious thought if you're fronting points for him. Guys like Didi Gee don't have fall partners. Somebody else always takes the whole jolt for them.'

He grinned at me.

'You're a good brother,' he said. 'But you worry too much about me. Remember, it was always me that got us out of trouble.'

'That's because you always got us into it.'

'I'm not the one that almost got drowned in a bathtub last night. You threw a bucket of shit into a cage full of hyenas, bro.'

'How'd you hear about last night?'

'Forget about how I hear things or what I'm doing with Didi Gee. You worry about your own butt for a change, or those greasers are going to hang it out to dry.'

'What do you think this elephant stuff is?'

'How the hell should I know?'

'You ever hear of a guy named Fitzpatrick?'

'No. What about him?'

'Nothing. Thanks for the lunch. By the way, Johnny Massina told me about you smashing up Didi's rubber machines. The old man would have enjoyed that one.'

'Like they say, you hear a lot of bullshit in the street, Dave.'

I sat out on the deck of my houseboat that evening in the green-yellow twilight with a glass of iced tea and mint leaves, and disassembled my three pistols – my departmental .38 revolver, a hideaway Beretta .25, and a US Army-issue .45 automatic. As I reamed out the barrel of the .45 with a bore brush, I thought about some of the mythology that Southern boys of my generation had grown up with. And like all myth, it was a more or less accurate metaphorical reflection of what was actually going on inside us, namely our dark fascination with man's iniquity. In moments like these I suspected that John Calvin was much more the inventor of our Southern homeland than Sir Walter Scott.

Southern Myths to Contemplate While Cleaning One's Guns – Substitute Other Biographical Names or Geographical Designations to Suit the Particular State in the Old Confederacy in Which You Grew Up:

1. A town in east Texas used to have a sign on the main street that read, 'Nigger, don't let the sun go down on your head in this country.'
2. Johnny Cash did time in Folsom Prison.
3. Warren Harding was part Negro.
4. Spanish fly and Coca-Cola will turn a girl into an instant drive-in-movie nymphomaniac.
5. The crushed hull of a Nazi submarine, depth-charged off Grand Island in 1942, still drifts up and down the continental shelf. At a certain spot on a calm night, shrimpers out of Morgan City can hear the cries of drowning men in the fog.
6. A Negro rapist was lynched outside of Lafayette and his body put inside a red wooden box and nailed up in a pecan tree as a warning to others. The desiccated wood, the strips of rag, the rat's nest of bones hang there to this day.
7. The .45 automatic was designed as a result of a Filipino insurrection. The insurrectionists would bind up their genitals with leather thongs, which would send them into a maniacal agony that would allow them to charge through the American wire while the bullets from our Springfields and .30–40 Kraigs passed through their bodies with no more effect than hot needles. The .45, however, blew holes in people the size of croquet balls.

There is usually a vague element of truth in all mythology, and the basic objective truth about the .45 automatic is simply that it is an absolutely murderous weapon. I had bought mine in Saigon's Bring-Cash Alley, out by the airport. I kept it loaded with steel-jacketed ammunition that could blow up a car engine, reduce a cinder-block wall to rubble, or, at rapid fire, shred an armored vest off someone's chest.

The darkness of my own meditation disturbed me. My years of drinking had taught me not to trust my unconscious, because it planned things for me in a cunning fashion that was usually a disaster for me, or for the people around me, or for all of us. But by this time I also knew that I was involved with players who were far more intelligent, brutal, and politically connected than the kind of psychotics and losers I usually dealt with.

If I had any doubts about my last conclusion, they were dispelled when a gray, US government motor-pool car stopped on the dock and a redheaded, freckle-faced man in a seersucker suit who could have been anywhere from fifteen to thirty years old walked down the gangplank onto my houseboat.

He flipped open his identification and smiled.

'Sam Fitzpatrick, US Treasury,' he said. 'You expecting a war or something?'

4

'It doesn't look like you believe me,' he said. 'Do you think I boosted the ID and a government car too?' He wouldn't stop grinning.

'No, I believe you. It's just that you look like you might have escaped from "The Howdy Doody Show."'

'I get lots of compliments like that. You New Orleans people are full of fun. I hear you've been taking a little heat for me.'

'You tell me.'

'Are you going to offer me some iced tea?'

'You want some?'

'Not here. You're too hot, Lieutenant. In fact, almost on fire. We need to get you back on the sidelines somehow. I'm afraid it's not going to be easy. The other team is unteachable in some ways.'

'What are you talking about?'

'They have fixations. Something's wrong with their operation and they target some schmoe that's wandered into the middle of it. It usually doesn't do them any good, but they think it does.'

'I'm the schmoe?'

'No, you're a bright guy with stainless steel balls, evidently. But we don't want to see you a casualty. Let's take a ride.'

'I'm taking a lady to the track tonight.'

'Another time.'

'No, not another time. And let's stop this business of Uncle Sam talking in his omniscience to the uninformed local flatfoot. If the shit's burning on the stove, I suspect it's yours and it's because you federal boys have screwed things up again.'

He stopped grinning. He looked at me thoughtfully for a moment, then wet his lips. He suddenly seemed older.

'You have to have faith in what I tell you, Lieutenant,' he said. 'You're a good man, you've got courage, you've never been on a pad, you go to Mass on Sundays, you treat the street people decently, and you put away a lot of the bad guys. We know these things about you because we don't want you hurt. But believe me, it's dumb for the two of us to be out here in the open talking to each other.'

'Who's this "we" you're talking about?'

'Uh, actually the "we" is more or less just me, at least right now. Come on, I'll explain it. Trust me. Somebody who looks like Howdy Doody has got to be a straight shooter. Besides, I'll buy you a poor-boy sandwich on my expense account.'

So this was the state of the art down at the Federal Building, I thought. We didn't see much of the federal boys, primarily because they operated on their own as a rule, and even though they said otherwise, they looked down upon us as inept and uneducated. On the other hand, we didn't have much liking for them, either. Any number of television serials portray the feds as manicured, dapper altruists dressed in Botany 500 suits, who dispassionately hunt down the oily representatives of the Mafia and weld the cell door shut on them. The reality is otherwise. As Didi Gee would probably point out, syndicate gangsters have little fear of any police agency or court system. They own judges, cops, and prosecutors, and they can always get to a witness or a juror.

The Treasury Department is another matter. Law enforcement people everywhere, as well as criminals, consider Treasury agents incorruptible. Within the federal government they are to law enforcement what Smokey the Bear and the US Forest Service are to environmental integrity. Even Joe Valachi, the Brooklyn mob's celebrity snitch, had nothing but admiration for the T-men.

Fitzpatrick drove us across town to a Latin American restaurant on Louisiana Avenue. We sat at an outdoor table in the small courtyard under the oak and willow trees. There were electric lights in the trees and we could see the traffic on the avenue through the scrolled iron gate. The banana trees along the stone wall rattled in the wind. He ordered shrimp and oyster poor-boy sandwiches for us and poured himself a glass of Jax while I sipped my iced tea.

'You don't drink, do you?' he said.

'Not anymore.'

'Heavy sauce problem?'

'You not only look like a kid, you're as subtle as a shithouse, aren't you?' I said.

'Why do you think I brought us to this restaurant?'

'I don't know.'

'Almost everybody working here is a product of our fun in-the-sun policies south of the border. Some of them are legals, some brought their papers from coyotes.'

'That's only true of about five thousand restaurants in Orleans and Jefferson parishes.'

'You see the owner over by the cash register? If his face looks out of round, it's because Somoza's national guardsmen broke all the bones in it.'

He waited, but I didn't say anything.

'The man running the bar is an interesting guy too,' he said. 'He's from a little village in Guatemala. One day the army came to the village and without provocation killed sixteen Indians and an American priest from Oklahoma named Father Stan Rother. For kicks they put the bodies of the Indians in a US Army helicopter and threw them out at high altitudes.'

He watched my face. His eyes were a washed-out blue. I'd never seen a grown man with so many freckles.

'I'm not big on causes anymore,' I said.

'I guess that's why you went out to Julio Segura's and put a hot plate under his nuts.'

'This dinner is getting expensive.'

'I'm sorry I've been boring you,' he said, and broke up a bread stick in three pieces and stood each piece upright. 'Let's talk about your immediate concerns. Let's talk about the three guys who gave you gargling lessons in the bathtub last night. I bet that'll hold your interest.'

'You don't hide hostility well.'

'I get a little emotional on certain subjects. You'll have to excuse me. I went to Jesuit schools. They always taught us to be up front about everything. They're the Catholic equivalent of the jarheads, you know. Get in there and kick butt and take names and all that stuff. I just think you're a lousy actor, Lieutenant.'

'Look, Fitzpatrick—'

'Fuck off, man. I'm going to give you the scam and you can work out your own options. I'm surrounded by indifferent people and I don't need any more of them. I just don't want you on my conscience. Also, as a matter of principle I don't like another guy taking the heat for me, particularly when he blunders into something he doesn't know anything about. You're damn lucky they didn't blow out your light last night. The girl's too.'

He stopped talking while the waiter put down our plates of oyster and shrimp sandwiches, then he took a bite out of his sandwich as though he hadn't eaten for weeks.

'You don't like the food?' he said, his mouth still full.

'I lost my appetite.'

'Ah, you're a sensitive fellow after all.'

'Tell me, do all you guys have the same manners?'

'You want it straight, Lieutenant? We've got some firemen and pyromaniacs on the same side of the street.'

'Who was that bunch last night?' I said.

'That's the easy part. The one named Erik is an Israeli. He's somebody's little brother back in Haifa and they keep him around to clean up their mess, change toilet-paper rolls, stuff like that. The one you called Bobby Joe in your report is a real cut-up. That's Robert J. Starkweather of Shady Grove, Alabama. The state took away his kid from him and his wife for the kid's own protection. They think he fragged an NCO in Vietnam but they couldn't prove it, so they eased him out on a BCD. How do you like that tattoo about killing them all and letting God sort them out? He's sincere about it, too.'

'How about the guy in charge?'

'He's a little more complex. His name is Philip Murphy, at least we think it is. We've run this guy all kinds of ways and we come up with some blank spots – no addresses, no record of earnings, no tax returns for a couple of years here and there. Or he shows up owning a shoe store in Des Moines. With this kind of guy it usually means protected witness or CIA. He's probably one of those that bounces in and out of the Agency or freelances around. I suspect he's off their leash right now. But it's hard to tell sometimes.'

I picked up my poor-boy sandwich and started to eat. The shrimp, oysters, lettuce, onions, tomato, and *sauce piquante* tasted wonderful. The shadows of the oak and willow leaves moved in etched, shifting patterns across our table.

'I still don't understand the connections. What have these guys got to do with Segura's whores and dope?' I said.

'Nothing directly.' Then he started grinning again. 'Come on, you're a detective. Give me your opinion.'

'Are you sure these guys aren't after you because of what you fancy is a sense of humor?'

'Maybe. Come on, give me your opinion.'

'I have a hard time believing you're a Treasury agent.'

'Sometimes my supervisor does too. Come on.'

'You're with the Bureau of Alcohol, Tobacco and Firearms.'

'Good.'

'Are we talking about guns?' I said.

'Excellento.'

'Nope, not excellento. I still don't see it, and I already told you this meal had gotten expensive.'

'It's simple. I think Segura is putting his dope money back into military equipment for the Contras in Nicaragua. It explains these other guys. The Israelis supplied arms to Somoza for years and they still sell it to right-wing guys like Pinochet in Chile. From what we know about Buffalo Bob, who almost pinched your head off at the shoulders, he's cowboyed for the CIA down on the Honduran border when he wasn't mixing up his phallus with an M-16, and I'll bet Philip Murphy is the tie-in to some arms contractors and military people here in the States. There's nothing new or unusual about it. It's the same kind of unholy trinity we had working for us down in Cuba. Look, why do you think the CIA tried to use some Chicago wiseguys to whack Castro? The mob had a vested interest. They got along very well with Batista, then Castro shut down all their casinos.'

'How did you get onto this current stuff?'

'We had our eye on a paramilitary training camp in Florida and one in Mississippi, then Buffalo Bob left a submachine gun in a Biloxi bus locker. We could have picked him up, but instead we let him keep ricocheting off the walls for a while. Philip Murphy showed up and it got a lot more interesting.'

He paused for a minute, then looked me flatly in the face again with those washed-out blue eyes that seemed to be immune to both protocol and insult.

'Have you ever had to dust anyone?' he said.

'Maybe.'

'Be straight.'

'Twice.'

'How'd you feel about it?'

'They dealt the play.'

'The next time you see Murphy or Buffalo Bob and Erik, they're going to take you out. You know that, don't you?'

'You said you're an up-front guy. Let me tell you a couple of my own meditations. I don't think you're an up-front guy.'

'Oh?'

'I don't think you want me out,' I said. 'I think you want a partner. I've already got one. He's paid by the city, just like I am.'

'You're a pretty slick cop.'

'I don't like somebody trying to use me.'

'I can't blame you. There's something I didn't tell you. The American priest that was killed in Guatemala was a friend of mine. Our government is into some real bullshit down there, buddy, but everybody who works for the government isn't necessarily on the same team. Some of us still believe in the old rules.'

'Good for you. But if you're into the Boy Scout Manual, don't try to run a game on another cop.'

'Nobody's asking you to sign a loyalty oath. What are you so afraid of?'

'You're genuinely starting to piss me off,' I said.

'I didn't write this script. You got into it on your own. I'll tell you something else, too: you're not going to walk out of it easily. I guarantee it. Guys like Segura and Murphy are just functionary jackoffs for much bigger people. Here's another question for you, too, Mr Clean. What were you thinking about while you were oiling your guns out on your boat deck? Maybe blowing bone and cartilage all over Buffalo Bob's walls?'

'I think with luck I can still make the fifth race.'

'I'll drive you back.'

'Don't worry about it. The city's got a tab with Yellow Cab.'

'Take this card. My motel's number is on it.'

'I believe the phone is still out of order. See you around,' I said, and walked out of the courtyard onto Louisiana Avenue. Some black children roared past me on roller skates, and heat lightning flickered above the huge oak trees across the street.

I called Annie from the pay phone to try to save part of the evening, but no one was home. It started to rain and I waited a half hour under a leaky awning for my cab to arrive. I made a quiet resolution about accepting invitations from federal employees.

But, as Fitzpatrick had said, I'd written my own script, and the next morning I continued to write it, only with some disastrous consequences that made me wonder if my alcoholic, self-destructive incubus was not alive and well.

I started by looking for Bobby Joe Starkweather. I didn't have many threads, but he was the kind of guy who showed up at certain places. I tried a couple of indoor target ranges, outlaw motorcycle bars, sex shops, and a survivalist store that catered to people who relished the unlimited prospects of living in a post-World War II wasteland. But I struck out.

Then, at noon, while Cletus and I were eating a pizza out of a box on a bench in Jackson Square, I wondered why I was chasing after an unknown quantity like Bobby Joe Starkweather when the primary connection was already available. We sat under a mimosa tree, and St Louis Cathedral and the square itself were drenched in hot sunlight. There were drops of perspiration and flecks of red pizza sauce on Clete's face while he ate. His eyes were looking abstractedly at the sidewalk artists in Pirates Alley.

'What have you got on the burner for this afternoon?' I asked.

'Not much. Figure out what I'm going to do with my goddamn wife. Get this. She just sent a check for six hundred dollars to the Buddhist priest out in Colorado. I tried to put a stop-payment on it, but it already went through. That's thousands she's given to this guy. When I say anything about it, she says I'm drunk.'

'Maybe y'all should separate for a while.'

'I can't. She's become suicidal. Her psychiatrist says she shouldn't even be driving an automobile.'

'I'm hoping to take a girl out to dinner tonight, if I can get ahold of her. Why don't you and Lois think about coming along? It's on me.'

'Maybe so, Dave. Thanks.'

'I want to go out to Julio Segura's this afternoon.'

'What for?'

'I'm going to roust him and take him in for questioning.'
'He might file a harassment charge this time.'
'He was the last person to see a murder victim alive.'
'Sounds shaky. It's not our jurisdiction.' His eyes smiled.
'You coming or not?'
'Hell, yes.'

We drove in Clete's car along the lakefront road. There was a light chop on the slate-green surface, and pelicans were diving for fish out of the white sun. The palm trees on the esplanade clicked dryly in the wind; and on the right-hand side of the road beyond the pink stucco walls, the long iron pike fences, the impassable hedges and rows of myrtle trees, lay the terraced lawns and mansions of the rich. I knew liberals out at Tulane who would tell me these were the people whom we served. But I didn't like them any better than anybody else did. Actually, they didn't like the police, either, or at least trust us, because they hired their own security, kept attack dogs on the grounds, and maintained floodlight and burglar alarm systems that were an electronic miracle. They lived in fear of kidnappers of their children, sophisticated jewel creeps, minorities who would compromise their property values. The irony was that they were among the most secure people upon earth – secure from disease, poverty, political oppression, virtually everything except death.

'How much you think these places cost?' Cletus asked.

'I don't know, maybe a million bucks.'

'My pop was a milkman in the Garden District, and sometimes in the summer I'd go on the route with him. One morning I was messing around in front of this big house right off St Charles and this lady came out and said I was the cutest little fellow she'd ever seen and I should come back at three o'clock for some ice cream. That afternoon I took a bath and put on my nice clothes and knocked on her door right at three. At first she didn't remember who I was, then she told me to go around to the back door. I didn't know what the hell was going on. When I got into the backyard I saw the maid handing out ice cream to all these raggedy little colored kids that belonged to the yardmen around the neighborhood.

'This lady had a greenhouse back there. I came back that night with a box full of rocks and broke damn near every pane in it. She got it repaired and three weeks later I came back and broke them again. When my pop figured out I'd done it, he whipped me with a switch till blood ran down my legs.'

Clete turned onto Julio Segura's street, which was filled with trees and blooming shrubs.

'You ever get that mad when you were a kid?' he asked.

'I don't remember.'

'You told me once you and your brother had some rough times.'

'Who cares, Clete? It's yesterday's ball game.'

'So I know that. What's the big deal?' he said.

'You've got a rusty nail sideways in your head. Let it go, quit feeding it.'

'You get a little personal sometimes, Streak.'

'There he goes! Hit it!' I said.

Julio Segura's lavender Cadillac had just bounced out through his front gate onto the street. A dwarf was driving, and a blond woman sat in the front passenger's seat. Segura and another man were in the back. Cletus floored the accelerator until we were abreast of them. The dwarf's face was frightened behind the glass, and he kept driving. I held my badge out at him. He put his foot on the brake, both of his hands on the steering wheel, his chin pointed upward under his purple chauffeur's cap, and scraped the front tire in a long black line against the curb.

'How do you want to play it?' Clete asked before we got out of the car.

'We run up the black flag,' I said.

Clete had stopped our own car in front of the Cadillac, and we walked back on opposite sides of it. I tapped on the passenger's window and on Segura's back window for them to roll down the glass. Later I was to go over this scene again and again in my mind, as well as the careless remark I'd made to Clete about the black flag, and wonder at how differently that afternoon might have turned out if I had approached the driver's side of the Cadillac or if I had kept my own counsel.

Clete reached down into the ignition, pulled the keys, and threw them into a hedge. The dwarf was petrified with fear. His little hands gripped the wheel and his jug head swiveled back and forth between Clete and the back seat.

'You don't have a blowgun hidden in your shorts, do you?' Clete said to him, then sniffed the air inside the Cadillac. 'My, my, what is that aroma I smell? Colombian coffee? Or maybe we've been toking on a little *muta* on our way to the golf course?'

The air was heavy with the smell of marijuana. The blond woman's face looked sick. I saw the cigarette lighter from the dash lying on the floor, and I suspected she'd been snorting the roach off the lighter and had eaten it when we'd pulled them over. She had a nice figure and was dressed in white shorts and heels and a low blouse, but her hair was lacquered with so much hair spray that it looked like wire, and her face was layered with cosmetics to cover the deep pockmarks in her complexion.

I opened the door for her. 'Walk on back home,' I said.

'They lock the gate,' she said.

'Then do the best thing you've done in years and keep on walking,' I said.

'I don't know what to do, Julio,' she said to the back-seat.

'Do what I tell you, hon. Your Latino gumball is going to take a big fall today,' I said.

Her eyes shifted nervously and she bit her lips, then she picked up her purse, eased past me, and clicked hurriedly down the sidewalk.

I leaned down in Segura's window. He and the gatekeeper whom Clete had hit in the stomach the other day sat behind a fold-out bar with vodka drinks in their hands. Rubber bands held the napkins around the drink glasses. Segura wore yellow golf slacks, polished brown loafers, and a flowered white shirt unbuttoned to his stomach. His peculiar triangular face, with the tiny balls of purple skin in the furrows of his forehead, looked up at me in the slanting sunlight.

'What the fuck you think you're doing now, Robicheaux?' he asked.

'Teaching you what a real bad day can be,' I said.

'What do you want? Some kind of action? A piece of something downtown?'

'You're going to give me Philip Murphy, Bobby Joe Starkweather, and the little Israeli.'

'I don't know none of these people. You keep coming around my house talking about things I don't know nothing about.'

'Ole Streak's in a bad mood today, Julio,' Clete said. 'Your friends messed it up the other night and did some real bad things. They're not around now, but you are. You and Paco the barfer here.' He blew his cigarette smoke into the gatekeeper's face.

'You trying to squeeze me? Okay, I'm a realist. I got business arrangements with policemen,' Segura said.

'You don't fly this time, Julio,' I said. 'All the doors are closed. It's just me and you.'

'Call Wineburger,' he said to the gatekeeper.

The other man reached for the telephone that was in a mahogany box inset in the back of the front seat.

'You touch that telephone and I'll stuff it crossways down your throat,' Clete said.

The man sat back in the deep leather of the seat, his face tight, his hands flat on his knees.

'You don't have anything, you don't know anything, you're just a noise like a fart in somebody's pants,' Segura said.

'Try this, my friend,' I said. 'Lovelace Deshotels was a little black girl from the country who had big aspirations for herself and her family. She thought she'd made the big score, but you don't like broads that slop down your booze and throw up in your pool, so you eighty-sixed her back to the geek circuit. Except you had a badass black girl on your hands that wouldn't eighty-six. On top of it, she developed this fixation about elephants.' I watched his face. It twitched like a rubber band. 'So what does a macho guy like you do when one of his whores gets in his face? He has a couple of his lowlifes take her out on a boat and launch her into the next world with the same stuff she'd already sold her soul for.

'Right now you're wondering how I know all this, aren't you, Julio? It's because the guys that work for you have diarrhea of the mouth. It's information you can get across a lunch table. There are probably only several dozen people we can march by a grand jury right now.'

'Then do it, smart guy.'

'Let me give you the rest of it, just so you'll be fully informed when Wineburger tries to bond you out this afternoon. I'm going to have your car towed in, vacuumed, and torn apart with crowbars. Possession in Louisiana is fifteen years, and all we need is the carbon ash, either off that cigarette lighter or the upholstery.

'Any way you cut it, your ass is busted.'

Then Cletus committed what was probably the stupidest and most senseless act of his career.

'And this little piggy is busted, too,' he said, and reached in the window and caught the gatekeeper's nose between his fingers and twisted.

The gatekeeper's eyes filled with tears; his hand slapped at Clete's, then his hairy, tattooed arm dipped into the leather pouch on the side door.

'*No lo hagas! No lo hagas!*' Segura screamed.

But it was forever too late for all of us. The gatekeeper's hand came up with a nickel-plated automatic and let off one round that hit the window frame and blew glass all over Clete's shirt. It was very fast after that. Just as I pulled the .45 from the back of my trousers, I saw Clete rip his nine-millimeter from his belt holster, crouch, and begin firing. I stepped back a foot, to clear the angle away from Segura, and fired simultaneously with my left hand locked on my wrist to hold the recoil down. I fired five times, as fast as I could pull the trigger, the explosions roaring in my ears, and saw not one thing distinctly inside the car. Instead, it was as though an earthquake had struck the inside of the Cadillac. The air was filled with divots of leather, stuffing from the seats, flying shards of glass and metal, splinters of mahogany, broken liquor bottles, cordite, smoke, and a film of blood and vodka that drained down the back window.

There was no place for Julio Segura to hide. He tried to shrink into an embryonic ball away from Clete's line of fire, but his position was hopeless. Then he suddenly leaped up into the window with his hands pressed out toward me like claws. His eyes were pleading, his mouth open with a silent scream. My finger had already squeezed tight in the trigger guard, and the round caught him in the top of the mouth and blew the back of his head all over the jerking body of the gatekeeper.

I was trembling and breathless when I fell back from the Cadillac and leaned on top of Clete's car, the .45 hanging from my hand. Clete's scarred, poached face was so bloodless and tight you could have struck a kitchen match to it. His clothes were covered with flecks of glass.

'The sonofabitch missed me from two feet,' he said. 'Did you see that? That fucking window glass saved my life. Go back and look inside. We blew them apart.'

Then the dwarf chauffeur climbed down from the driver's seat and ran down the middle of the esplanade on his stubby legs amid a wail of sirens. Clete began to giggle uncontrollably.

5

The next morning Cletus and I sat across from each other at our desks in our small, glass-enclosed office with its smudged yellow walls that made you think of a dressing cubicle at YMCA. Cletus pretended to read a long memo from the superintendent's office, but his eyes were either empty or glazed with the pain of his hangover. He was chain-smoking and eating breath mints, but last night's Scotch was down deep in his lungs. Both of us had already made written reports to Captain Guidry.

'I'm not going to bail you out again, Clete,' I said.

'What do you mean, bail out? I put one through his brisket before you popped your first cap.'

'I'm not talking about that. You provoked it. It didn't have to happen.'

'You're sure about that, huh? What if Paco had come up with the automatic while you were cuffing Segura? There was a nine-round clip in there. He could have cut both of us in half.'

'You provoked it.'

'So what if I did? Scratch two lowlifes that should have been fertilizer a long time ago. Save the hearts and flowers, Dave. Nobody's going to be interested in how Julio Segura bought it. I don't think you could find three people to attend the guy's funeral.'

'Don't bet on it.'

Sergeant Motley came down the corridor and stopped in our doorway. He had just come in from outside, and his round, black head glistened with perspiration. He was eating an ice cream cone, and there were flecks of ice cream in his thick mustache.

'Somebody in the lab said they had to wash Segura's brains off the seat with a hose,' he said.

'Oh yeah? That sounds like it might make a clever Excedrin ad,' Clete said.

'Guess what else I heard?' Motley said.

'Who cares?' Clete said.

'You'll care, Purcel. The lab says the Cadillac was dirty. Reefer on the

62

cigarette lighter, coke in the rug. Who would have thought Segura would let his broads be so careless?' He smiled. 'You guys didn't salt the mine shaft, did you?'

'Why are you so obnoxious, Motley?' Clete said. 'Is it because you're fat and ugly, or is it because you're fat and dumb? It's a mystery to all of us.'

'Except I hear the broad says you told Segura he was going to take a big fall. Not smart of the Bobbsey Twins in homicide,' Motley said.

'Here's to the rapid spread of sickle cell,' Clete said, and toasted Sergeant Motley with his coffee cup.

'My dick in your ear,' Motley said.

'Lay off it,' I said.

'With this guy you've either got to use some humor or a can of insecticide,' Clete said.

A few minutes later Captain Guidry told me to come into his office. I wasn't looking forward to talking with the captain, but I was relieved to get away from Clete.

Captain Guidry scratched the hair implants in his head and looked up at me from behind his horn-rimmed glasses. My report and Clete's were side by side on his desk.

'The lab found some marijuana ash and grains of cocaine in the car,' he said. His voice was flat and reserved.

'Motley just told us.'

He picked up a pencil and began drumming it on his palm.

'They also said a round fired from inside the car bounced off the window frame and blew glass out into the street,' he said. 'A second round went up through the roof, which would indicate the shooter was hit by that time. A yardman across the street says he heard a sound like a firecracker inside the Cadillac, then he saw you two start shooting. It's all working for you, Dave.'

'What's the dwarf say?' I asked.

'Nothing. All he wants is an airplane ticket to Managua.'

'Something's not getting said here, Captain.'

'I've been over your reports. Very neat stuff. I think they'll get you by Internal Affairs.'

'That's good.'

'My own opinion is they stink. Tell me why a guy with no arrests, who Whiplash Wineburger would have had back on the street in thirty minutes, would throw down on two armed cops.'

I didn't answer.

'Do you think he had a suicidal personality?' the captain asked.

'I don't know.'

'Did Segura tell him to do it?'

'No.'

'Then why did this guy pull his own plug?' His hand closed on the pencil.

'Internal Affairs gets paid to sort that stuff out.'

'To hell with Internal Affairs. I don't like reading a report on two deaths that says "fill in the blanks." '

'I can't tell you anything else, Captain.'

'I can. I think something else happened out there. I think also you're covering Purcel's butt. That's not loyalty. It's stupidity.'

'The essential fact of my report is that somebody pulled a pistol on a police officer and fired it at him.'

'You keep telling yourself that. In the meantime, let me tell you a couple of my observations. The guys in Internal Affairs will mutter around over this stuff, ask you a few hard questions, make you feel uncomfortable a little while, maybe even really try to stick a finger in your eye. But eventually they'll cut you loose and everybody around here will ask you guys out for a beer. But you're going to take the suspicion of a wrongful death with you. It's like a cloud you drag along everywhere you go. Sometimes it even grows into a legend. How about Motley and those guys on the wrist-chain that suffocated to death in the elevator?'

I had to look away from his face.

'It's between Purcel and other people, Captain. I didn't deal the play out there,' I said.

'I'm sorry to see you take that position, Dave.' He opened his palm and dropped his pencil on the top of his desk blotter. 'I'll make one other suggestion before you go. Take Purcel with you to some meetings. Also, if you're going to cover for a partner who's going out of control, you'd damn well better be able to take the consequences.'

It wasn't the best of all possible mornings.

A half hour later the phone in our office rang.

'Guess who,' the voice said.

'The Howdy Doody Show.'

'Guess what I'm doing.'

'I'm not interested.'

'I'm looking at the photographic art on the front page of the *Picayune*,' Fitzpatrick said. 'I underestimated your flair for the dramatic. These are the kinds of pictures we used to see in *The Police Gazette* – grainy black and white stuff, car doors thrown open, bodies hanging out on the street, pools of black blood on the seats. Congratulations, you greased the one solid connection we had.'

'If you want to get on my case this morning, you'll have to stand in line. As far as I'm concerned, your meter is already on overtime. In fact—'

'Shut up, Lieutenant.'

'What did you say?'

'You heard me. I'm mad as hell right now. You've done a lot of damage.'

'You weren't out there, bud.'

'I didn't have to be. I had a real strong tingle down in the genitals that it might go like this, and you didn't disappoint me.'

'You want to explain that?'

'I'm not sure you can handle it. I thought you were a bright guy. Instead, it doesn't look like you can put one foot after another without somebody painting Arthur Murray dance steps on the floor for you.'

I didn't answer. My hand was clenched on the telephone receiver and starting to perspire. Clete was looking curiously at my face.

'Are you where you can talk?' Fitzpatrick said.

'I'm in my office.'

'Who's there with you?'

'My partner, Purcel.'

'Yeah, sure you can talk,' he said irritably. 'I'll pick you up in front of the Acme Oyster Bar on Iberville in ten minutes. I'll be driving a blue Plymouth rental.'

'I don't think so.'

'You either be there or I'll come up to your houseboat tonight and knock out your goddamn teeth. That's a personal promise.'

I waited ten minutes for him in front of the Acme, then went inside and bought a Dr Pepper in a cup of crushed ice with a sliced lime and drank it outside in the sunlight. I could see the spires of St Louis Cathedral, where I sometimes went to mass, shining in the clear morning air. By the time Fitzpatrick drew up to the curb, my anger had subsided to the point that I was no longer going to pull him out of his automobile by his necktie. But when I sat down in the passenger's seat I did reach across and turn off his ignition.

'Before we go anywhere, let's sort out a couple of things,' I said. 'I don't think you've paid enough dues to be telling people to shut up or making threats to them over the phone. But if you think you're a serious rock-and-roller, we can go over to the Y and slip on the gloves and see what develops.'

He nodded and clicked his fingernails indifferently on the steering wheel.

'Don't worry, they've got a first-aid man there in case you're a bleeder,' I said.

'Okay, you've made your point.'

'You're not too big on hanging tough, are you?'

'I wanted you out of your office. If you'll notice your present geography, you're sitting in my automobile and not at the First District. Is it all right if I start the car now?'

'I think you federal guys just have to do everything with three-cushion shots. Wouldn't it be easier for you and me to go into Captain Guidry's office and talk about this stuff in a reasonable way? We don't want guys like Philip Murphy and his trained psychopaths running around New Orleans any more than you do. The captain's a good man. He'll help you if he can.'

He started the engine and pulled into the traffic. The sunlight fell across his freckled face and candy-striped Arrow shirt.

'Is Purcel a good man?' he asked.

'He's got some problems, but he's working on them.'

'You think he's clean?'

'As far as I know.'

'Six weeks ago we had reason to be in a trick pad. His name was in the girl's book. He was a weekly banger. There was no entry about charge, either.'

I took a deep breath.

'He's had marital trouble,' I said.

'Come off it. We're talking about a compromised cop who started popping caps yesterday on a possible government witness. Which of you nailed Segura?'

'I did. He was trying to get out the door, and he raised up right in front of me.'

'I'll bet one of Purcel's rounds was already in him. What did the autopsy say?'

'I don't know.'

'Great.'

'You're telling me Clete wanted to kill Segura?'

'It's a possibility.'

'I don't buy it.'

'You don't buy lots of things, Lieutenant. But there's people just like you in my bureau. That's why they're sending me back to Boston next week.'

'You're off it?'

'I will be. I haven't made my case and there's other work waiting.'

He looked across at me, and for the first time I felt a liking for him. Under all the invective he was a full nine-inning pitcher. We bought a bucket of fried shrimp and two cartons of dirty rice and ate it in a small, shady part off Napoleon Avenue. A bunch of black and white and Chicano kids were playing a workup game in front of an old chicken-wire backstop. They were rough, working-class boys and they played the game with a fierce physical courage and recklessness. The pitcher threw spitters and beanballs; the base runners broke up double plays with elbows and knees, and sanded their faces off in headlong slides; the catcher stole the ball out from under the batter's swing with his bare hand; and the third baseman played so far in on the grass that a line drive would tear his head off. I thought it no wonder that foreigners were awed by the innocent naïve nature of American aggressiveness.

'Does anything about elephants figure in all this?' I asked.

'Elephants? No, that's a new one. Where'd you get it?'

'I heard Lovelace Deshotels was giggling about elephants when Segura's people shot her up. I dropped it on Segura, and his face twitched like a plumber's helper.'

'Well, we've got a second chance. I found her roommate, a Mexican girl from the same massage parlor, and she wants to stick it to all these bastards.'

'Why is she talking to you instead of me?'

'She seems to think you guys are cretins. Is there a vice sergeant down there named Motley?'

'Yep.'

'She says his zipper's open.'

'Sounds accurate.'

'She's a dancer in a nude bar out by the airport now. For three hundred dollars she says she can turn a couple of interesting people for us, then she wants to take her little girl back to San Antonio and study to be a hairdresser.'

'It sounds like a shuck to me.'

'I think she's straight. Her boyfriend was a Nicaraguan ex-national guardsman who worked for Segura. Then he beat her up and stole her money. They're a class bunch, those guys. Now she wants to blow Dodge. It seems reasonable to me.'

'I think she's selling the same information Didi Gee already gave me.'

'She's hip about Bobby Joe Starkweather. She says he's a latent bone-smoker and can't make it with women. He threw a waitress out of a hotel window, and some local hood got fired for it up at Angola.'

I looked away at the boys playing workup.

'What's the matter?' Fitzpatrick asked.

'I knew him. His name was Johnny Massina.'

'Were you tight with him or something?'

'I tried to help him get off the hooch once. Does she know where Starkweather might be?'

'She's vague on that.'

'I thought so,' I said. 'Write her name and address down for me, would you, but I'm going to pass on her right now. They've got me on a short leash, anyway.'

'Lieutenant, can I broach something personal?'

I started to say 'Why not?' since he had never shown any restraint about anything before, but he kept right on talking before I could speak.

'It's obvious you're a good cop and a private kind of man, but you're a Catholic and you must have feelings about what's going on down there,' he said.

'Where?' I already knew the answer but I wasn't ready to pursue the discussion.

'Central America. They're doing some bad shit to our people. They're killing priests and Maryknoll nuns and they're doing it with the M-16s and M-60 machine guns we give them.'

'I don't think you ought to take all that responsibility on yourself.'

'It's our church. They're our people. There's no way to get around the fact, Lieutenant.'

'Who's asking you to? You've just got to know your limits, that's all. The Greeks understood that. Guys like you and me need to learn from them.'

'You think that's good advice, huh?' he said.

'It beats walking around with a headful of centipedes.'

'Since you're fond of classical metaphors, try this one: Why do we admire Prometheus and have contempt for Prolonius? Don't try to tilt with a Jesuit product, Lieutenant. We've been verbally demolishing you guys for centuries.'

He grinned at me the way a high school pitcher would after throwing you a Carl Hubbel screwball that left you twisted in your swing.

That night I drove to the Tulane campus to hear Annie Ballard's string quartet play. She was pretty on the lighted stage in her dark skirt and jacket and frilly white blouse. Her face was both eager and concentrated while she read the music sheet on the metal stand in front of her and drew her bow back and forth on her cello. In fact, her face had a lovely childlike quality in it while she played her music, the kind you see in people who seem to go through a photogenic transformation when they do that private thing that they hold separate for themselves. Afterwards, we were invited to a lawn party in the Garden District. The trees were strung with Japanese lanterns; the swimming-pool lights glowed smokily below the emerald surface; the air smelled of jasmine and roses and the freshly turned, watered dirt in the flower beds; and Negro waiters carrying trays of champagne glasses and cool tropical drinks moved deferentially among the groups of laughing people in evening dresses and summer tuxedoes.

She was having a good time. I saw that her eyes were empty now of the fear and self-loathing that Bobby Joe Starkweather had put in them, and she was doing her best, also, to make me forget what had happened in the back of Julio Segura's Cadillac yesterday. But I was selfish.

I couldn't let go of those ten seconds between the time the gatekeeper pulled the automatic out of the door pouch and the moment when the .45 roared upward in my hand and Segura's head exploded all over the inside of the car. I'm convinced that, unlike most of the hapless and pathetic people whom we usually dealt with, he was truly an evil man, but anyone who has ever fired a weapon at another human being knows the terrible adrenaline-fed sense of omnipotence and arrogance that you feel at that moment and the secret pleasure you take in the opportunity being provided you. I had done it in Vietnam; I had done it twice before as a police officer, and I knew that simian creature we descend from was alive and well in my breast.

I was also bothered by Sam Fitzpatrick and his admonition to me about my religion and my humanity. I wanted to dismiss him. He was a kid, an idealist, a federal hotdog who probably broke a lot of bureau rules and would eventually blow out his doors. If he hadn't become a Treasury agent, he would probably be pouring chicken blood on draft files. A half-dozen like him could have a whole city in flames.

But I couldn't get rid of him. I liked him and he had gotten to my pride.

I genuinely tried to enjoy myself that night. The people at the lawn party came from another world than mine, but they were pleasant and friendly and went out of their way to be courteous to me. Annie was a fine girl, too. When she saw my expression wandering away from the conversation, she would touch the back of my hand with hers and smile at me with her eyes. But it wasn't any good. I gave it up, made an excuse about having to go to work in the morning, and drove her home. On her porch I saw the faint look of hurt in her face when I said I couldn't come in.

'Do you like to be alone, Dave?' she asked.

'No. It's not a good life.'

'Another time, huh?'

'Yes. I'm sorry about tonight. I'll call tomorrow.'

She smiled and then she was gone, and I drove home more depressed than I had been in years.

Why? Because the truth was that I wanted to drink. And I don't mean I wanted to ease back into it, either, with casual Manhattans sipped at a mahogany and brass-rail bar with red leather booths and rows of gleaming glasses stacked in front of a long wall mirror. I wanted busthead boilermakers of Jack Daniel's and draft beer, vodka on the rocks, Beam straight up with water on the side, raw tequila that left you breathless and boiling in your own juices. And I wanted it all in a rundown Decatur or Magazine Street saloon where I didn't have to hold myself accountable for anything and where my gargoyle image in the mirror would be simply another drunken curiosity like the neon-lit rain striking against the window.

After four years of sobriety I once again wanted to fill my mind with spiders and crawling slugs and snakes that grew corpulent off the pieces of my life that I would slay daily. I blamed it on the killing of Julio Segura. I decided my temptation for alcohol and self-destruction was maybe even an indication that my humanity was still intact. I said the rosary that night and did not fall asleep until the sky went gray with the false dawn.

That afternoon I still had Sam Fitzpatrick on my mind. I called the Bureau of Alcohol, Tobacco and Firearms, and was told by the assistant Special Agent in Charge that Fitzpatrick was not in.

'Who is this please?' he asked.

I told him my name and who I was.

'Are you calling from your office?'

I said I was.

'I'll call you there in two minutes,' he said, and hung up.

Sure enough, the phone rang a minute and a half later. They were a very careful bunch down at the Federal Building.

'We're worried about him. He hasn't checked in and he's not at his motel,' he said. 'Are you the guy who smoked Segura?'

'Yes.'

'Bad day at Black Rock, huh?' he said, and laughed.

'Do all you guys have the same sense of humor?'

'We've got an agent out of the nest, Lieutenant. Do you have something we ought to know?'

'He was going to see a Mexican girl, a nude dancer out by the airport. She told him she could turn a couple of Segura's people.'

'We already know about her. What else?'

'That's it.'

'Stay in touch. Drop by and have coffee sometime. We need a better liaison with you people. By the way, Lieutenant, Agent Fitzpatrick has a way of wandering beyond some of our parameters. That doesn't mean that some local authorities should reciprocate by wandering themselves into a federal jurisdiction. You get the picture, don't you.'

There was a pause, then the receiver went dead.

Late that afternoon I went to the Mexican girl's apartment building out in Metairie. No one was home, and the apartment manager said she had not seen the girl, whose name was Gail Lopez, or her daughter in a couple of days. I stuck a small piece of Scotch tape between the bottom of the door and the doorjamb, and drove out to the strip bar by the airport in the fading twilight.

Jet airliners lifted off the runway across the road and roared over the top of the bar into the lavender sky. The building was constructed of cinder blocks that had been painted purple; the door was fingernail-polish red; and the interior smelled of cigarette smoke, refrigerated air, and bathroom antiseptic. Behind the bar was a burlesque runway where a stand-up comic with a face like crinkled parchment went through a lifeless and boring routine that no one at the tables or bar listened to. In the middle of his routine, some bikers in the corner plugged in the jukebox and turned it on full tilt.

The bartender was a big man, about thirty, with a huge granite head that was bald and shining on top with oiled ducktails combed back on the sides. He wore black trousers, a white shirt, and a black velvet vest like a professional bartender, but his thick arms and neck and massive chest and the wooden mallet on a shelf behind him indicated something about his other potential. I asked him about Gail Lopez.

'You don't recognize me, Lieutenant?' he asked, and smiled.

I squinted at him in the smoke and against the glare of lights on the burlesque stage.

'Five or six years ago, right?' I said. 'Something about driving a *Picayune* delivery truck over a Teamster steward.'

'Actually, it's been eight years and I never really got to tell my side of that story, Lieutenant. But it don't matter now. I'm always walking toward something rather than away from something. You know what I mean? Let me ask a little favor of you, though. My PO don't need to know about this situation, does he? He's a good guy and kind of protective and he don't want me working in no shitholes, but some of the guys down at the union hall hold a grudge and don't want to give me my card back and there ain't many places I can make six bucks an hour and tips. Hell, it's degrading to work in a dump like this. I got to pick up cigarette butts from the urinals with my hands and scrub out toilets and mop up the vomit every time one of these fuckers pukes. What do you want to drink? It's on me.'

'Uh, nothing right now. What about Gail Lopez?'

'Well, all these broads get a lot of traffic, you know what I mean? It's a lowlife clientele here, Lieutenant. Greasers, hitters, bull dykes, jerks that like to get in my face till they're way out on the edge, you know what I mean? There's a guy comes in here every night and melts Demerol down in a glass of Wild Turkey, then when I say "Nice weather we're having" or "Hard rain we had this afternoon," he says "no, duh." I ask him if he wants another drink and he says "No duh." "You want some more peanuts?" "No duh." "You want some more peanuts." "No duh." "You're in the wrong place to be a wise-ass." "No duh."'

'No, Charlie, I'm talking about a guy who looks like a human freckle.'

'I haven't seen him. Look around you, Lieutenant. A guy like that in here would stand out like shit in an ice cream factory. Anyway, ask her. She'll be here in an hour.'

I sat through two floor shows that consisted of a half-dozen naked girls dancing to a three-piece band whose instruments could have been tuned to a snare drum. The girls wore thin gold chains around their ankles and stomachs, and their faces seemed lit with some inner narcissistic pleasure that had nothing to do with the world outside them. They undulated and raised their arms above their heads as though they were moving in water, and occasionally their eyes would meet and light with some secret recognition.

During all this the bartender washed glasses indifferently in a tin sink while his cigarette ashes fell into the dishwater. Someone in the back caught his attention and he left the bar for a few minutes, then returned with an uncomfortable look on his face.

'Lieutenant, I got an embarrassing situation here,' he said. 'The manager, Mr Rizzo, is very happy you're here and he don't want you to pay for anything. But a guy that sits at the bar drinking 7-Up with a piece showing under his coat is kind of like—'

'Anthrax?' I said.

'Well, if you notice, there's nobody else at the bar, Lieutenant, which is not meant as a reflection on you, but on the degenerate pus-bags that drink in here. Even the guy that gets off saying "No duh" to me is sitting way in the back tonight. You got to understand the degenerate mind. See, they all got hard-guy fantasies, but when they take it out too far and step on the nuts of some heavy-metal badass, like some cat that just got out of Angola and has already got a Coke bottle kicked up his ass, I got to bail them out.'

I paid for the 7-Ups I'd drunk and waited another half hour at a small table in a dark part of the room. Gail Lopez didn't show up. I gave the bartender my office card with my telephone number and asked him to call me if she came in. He put down his bar rag and leaned forward and spoke a few inches from my face.

'One of her boyfriends is a tall Nicaraguan dude with a mustache,' he said. 'Don't let him blind-side you, Lieutenant. One night out in the parking lot he cut a guy from his armpit down to his liver. He's the kind of cat if you got to dust him you take him off at the neck.'

I drove back out to the Mexican girl's apartment in Metairie and found the tape still in place between the door and the jamb. I told the building manager that I couldn't ask him to open the apartment, but I suspected that if he did, all he would find would be empty clothes hangers. It took him less than two minutes to get the passkey.

I was wrong, however. She hadn't simply left behind empty clothes hangers. In the wastebasket were several crumpled travel brochures that advertised scenic tours of the Caribbean, not San Antonio and hairdressing school. Fitzpatrick, you poor fish, I thought.

I was tired when I drove home along Lake Shore Drive, past the amusement park with its Ferris wheel lighted against the sky, past the University of New Orleans and its quiet, dark lawns and black trees, and I entered into a self-serving dialogue with myself that almost extricated me from my problems. Let Fitzpatrick's own people take care of him, I thought. Illegal guns and explosives are their jurisdiction, not yours. You took on an obligation about the murdered black girl in the bayou and you fulfilled it, whether you wanted to or not, when you translated Julio Segura's brains into marmalade. If you're interested in revenge against Philip Murphy, Starkweather, and the little Israeli, you're in the wrong line of work. Somewhere down the road they'll step in their own flop and somebody'll be there to put them away. So disengage, Robicheaux, I told myself. You don't have to be a long-ball hitter every time. A well-placed bunt has its merits.

I had almost achieved some tranquility by the time I parked my car on the short, darkened street that dead-ended into a sand dune and three coconut palms and the dilapidated dock where I kept my houseboat moored. A smooth, hard path with salt grass growing on the edges cut through the dune, and the waving palm fronds made shadows on the sand and the roof of my houseboat. I could hear the water slapping against the hull, and the moonlight fell across the lake itself in a long silver band. I walked across the gangplank with the wind cool in my face, the bend of the wood easy and familiar and comforting under my foot, the froth of the incoming tide sliding up on the sand under me. The mahogany and yellowish brown teak and glass panes and brass fittings of my boat were as rectangularly beautiful as metal and wood could be. I opened the hatch, stepped down into the main cabin, and turned on the light switch.

Bobby Joe Starkweather rose up quickly from the floor and swung a short length of pipe at my face. It was crowned on one end with pipe bonnet and wrapped with friction tape on the other. I ducked and put my hands in front of me and took part of the blow on my forearm, but the cast-iron bonnet raked down the side of my face and my ear felt torn loose from my head. I tried to get my .38 out of my belt holster, but someone pinned my arms to my sides from behind and the three of us fell into my rack of musical records on the far wall. My collection of historical jazz, old seventy-eight records that were as stiff and delicate as baked ceramic, shattered in black shards all over the floor. Then a third man was on top of me, a tall man with a pencil mustache and pomade-scented, reddish Negroid hair, and I was covered by their hands, arms, thighs, scrotums, buttocks, knees, their collective weight and strength and visceral odor so powerful and smothering now that I couldn't move or breathe under them. I felt a needle sink into my neck, an unspoken wish clicked dryly in my throat, and my mouth locked open as though the joints of my jaw had been broken. Then my trio of friends squeezed the remaining air out of my chest, the blood out of my heart, the light from my eyes.

6

I awoke in an auto garage of some kind. The roof was made of tin and it was raining outside. I was stretched out on a wooden table, my arms handcuffed around a post behind me, my feet tied to another post at the opposite end. The only light came from a mechanic's portable lamp that was hung on one wall among rows of tools, fan belts, grease guns, and clusters of sparkplug wires. The air was close and hot and smelled of oil and rust. When I turned my head, my neck felt as though it would crack like a dry flower stem.

Then I saw Fitzpatrick in a wooden chair four feet from me. His forearms were tied flush to the arms of the chair, wrapped with clothes-line from the elbow to the wrist so that his hands stuck out like broken claws; his clothes were torn, streaked with grease and blood, and his battered and bleeding head hung down in the shadow, obscuring his face. By his feet was a telephone crank, the kind that was used on army field phones.

'Sam,' I said.

He made a sound and moved his head.

'Sam, it's Dave Robicheaux,' I said. 'Where are they?'

He raised his head up into the light and I saw his face. His eyes were swollen shut like a beaten prize-fighter's, his nose broken, his saliva red in his teeth.

'Where are they, Sam?' I said again.

Then he started breathing hard, rattling down in his throat, as though he were trying to generate enough power to speak a solitary line.

'Elephant walk,' he said.

I heard a tin door scrape open on the concrete floor, and the cool smell of the rain blew into the room. Philip Murphy, the little Israeli, and the tall man with the pencil mustache and the kinky reddish hair walked into the light from the mechanic's lamp. They carried paper bags of ham-burgers and french fries in their hands.

'You must have a strong constitution,' Murphy said. 'They shot you up with enough Thorazine to knock out a dinosaur.' His wet gray hair was still uncut; he hadn't shaved that day, and stubble grew through the tiny blue and red veins in his cheeks. He took a bite of his hamburger and looked at me while he chewed. His hazel eyes were devoid of either feeling or meaning.

'You're a miserable excuse for a man,' I said.

'Why's that, Lieutenant? You don't like the way things have gone? You didn't have warning about the rules? People have been unfair to you, have they?'

'It takes a special kind of degenerate to torture a defenseless man.'

'People get hurt in wars. Your friend is one of them. You probably don't like that definition, but your sort never does.'

'You're a punk, Murphy. You never fought a war in your life. Guys like you take them off the cattle cars and run the ovens.'

For a moment I saw a flash in his eyes.

'Would you like to live in a communist country, Lieutenant?' he said. 'Would you like Louisiana run by the Sandinistas the way they run things in Nicaragua? You know the Marxists are puritans, don't you? No casinos or horse tracks, no booze or poontang when you want it, no chance for the big fat score that keeps everybody's genitals aglow. Instead, you wait in a sweaty line with a lot of other mediocre people for whatever the government dole is that day. If you lived down there, you'd put a gun in your mouth from boredom.'

'So somehow it's acceptable to tie down a kid and take him apart? What nails me about your kind is that you're always willing to sacrifice half the earth to save the other half. But you're never standing in the half that gets blitzed.'

'You're a disingenuous man, Lieutenant. You remember what Patton said? You don't win wars by giving your life for your country. You make the other sonofabitch give his. I think you're just a poor loser. Look at Andres here. You see the little gray scars around his mouth? He has a right to be bitter but he's not, at least not excessively. Say something for us, Andres. *Que hora es?*'

'*Doce menos veinte,*' the tall man with the mustache replied. His voice was a wheeze, a rasp, as though his lungs were perforated with small holes.

'Andres used to have a regular *puta* in one of Somoza's whorehouses. Then one day he talked a little too casually in front of her about the work his firing squad did. They'd shot a Sandinista girl named Isabella whom they'd captured in the hills. He thought it was a good story, because she'd confessed before she died and turned a couple of dozen other Sandinistas. What he didn't say was that his whole firing squad had raped her before they shot her, and what he didn't know was that Isabella was his *puta*'s sister. So the next time he dropped in for a little dirty boogie between the sheets, it was hotter than the devil's skillet and she fixed him a tall, cool

Cuba libre with ice and lime slices and he swallowed it straightaway like the lusty fellow he is. Except she loaded it with muriatic acid, and poor old Andres has been spitting up his insides like burnt cork ever since.'

'You're a piece of shit, Murphy.'

'No, you've got it all wrong, Lieutenant. Some of us serve, others like Fitzpatrick here get in the way, and the majority, such as yourself, go about your games and your self-delusion while we take care of things for you. I don't like to pick on you in your situation, but it's not fair of you to start calling people names, either. Now you're an educated man of some experience, and I want you to answer me something truthfully. You've seen the people who are on the other side of the fence in this country – the peace marchers, the nuke freezers, the out-of-Central-America gang. Who are they?' The down-turned corners of his mouth tugged backwards in a slight smile and his eyes wandered over my face with a sense of merriment. 'Some of them are lesbians, aren't they? Not all of them, but at least some, you've got to admit that. Then there are others that just don't like men. They didn't like their fathers, their brothers, or their husbands, and finally they zero their sights in on any male authority – the President, congressmen, generals, anything with a cock.

'Now we come to the general malcontents,' he continued. 'These are your professional losers who couldn't tell a history book from a Sears, Roebuck catalog, but they do love a parade. I'm sure you got to see a lot of them on television while you were in Vietnam. My favorite bunch, though, is the pussy-whipped contingent. Their wives drag them around to endless meetings that are going nowhere, and if they're good little fellows, Mommy will give them a piece every week or so.

'I don't think that's your kind of group, Lieutenant, but maybe I'm wrong about you. I guess the bottom line is you wanted to be a player. Too bad, because now we've got to take a couple of players off the board.'

'I'll suggest some reading for you,' I said. 'Go down to the *Picayune* morgue and read the clippings on what's happened to people who snuffed New Orleans cops. It's not our finest hour, but the lesson's unmistakable.'

He smiled in a self-amused way, and began eating his hamburger again while his eyes glanced expectantly at the back door. Five minutes later, Bobby Joe Starkweather burst in out of the rain with a paper sack under his arm. His T-shirt and blue jeans were soaked through, and his muscles stood out against the wet cloth like intertwined serpents.

'I got it. Let's put the biscuit-eater under and get it on the road,' he said. 'Did you bring me a hamburger?'

'I didn't think you wanted it cold,' Murphy said.

'You're a great guy to work with, Murphy,' Starkweather said.

'Would you like mine?' Murphy asked quietly.

'I haven't had my rabies shots.'

'Suit yourself, then, and spare us your complaining wit.'

'Look, Murphy, I went after the booze, which you owe me twelve dollars for, and I got rainwater running out my crotch while you guys are in the dry, licking your greasy fingers. Don't provoke me.'

Murphy chewed on his food and looked at nothing. Starkweather wiped his face and arms slick, lighted a Lucky Strike from his Zippo, snapped the lighter shut and stuck it in his watch pocket with a thick thumb, and inhaled the smoke without removing the cigarette from his mouth while he took a fifth of Seagram's whiskey, six-pack of Jax, a capped vial of pills, and a brown medicine bottle from the sack and put them on the table. Then he rummaged around on the workbench until he found a rubber funnel and a glass jar filled with rusty nails. He dumped the nails out on the workbench and walked back to the table with the jar and the funnel. His shaved head was shaped like a question mark.

'You should have been here earlier,' he said. 'We got some real high notes out of your friend. You remember what they used to say in 'Nam. Call up Charlie on the telephone and he always answers.'

He filled the glass jar with beer and whiskey and the liquid from the brown bottle, then poured in the pills and screwed on the cap and shook it all together as though he were making a martini. His saliva was wet on the tip of his cigarette, and he breathed with a mean energy.

'It must be terrible to know you're a lush that can't hold his liquor,' he said.

'I've spilled more in a week than you've drunk in your lifetime, asshole,' I said.

'I'll bet. My first wife was a juicer,' he said. 'She'd do anything for it. She screwed a cabdriver once for a quart of beer. I found out about it, cut me a switch as thick as my finger, and whipped the dress off her back. I took her money and clothes away and locked her in the bedroom and she'd drink hair tonic. Finally they come and took her off to a crazyhouse in Montgomery.'

'No matter what happens here tonight, I've got some friends who are going to cool out your action, Starkweather,' I said.

'Maybe so, maybe so. But in the meantime I've got a drunkard's dream for you. When those 'ludes hit you, I can pull your teeth with pliers and you won't twitch. The castor oil is just to round out your evening, bring back those old three-day benders when you used to shit your pants. If you're a good boy, we'll let you sit up and drink it by yourself.'

'Get on with it,' Murphy said.

'Stop giving orders for a while, Murphy,' Starkweather said. 'A lot of this mess is yours. We should have taken these guys out the first time they got in our face. Instead, you had to make an intelligence operation out of it to impress Abshire.'

'Why is it in any given situation you never disappoint us?' Murphy
said.

'You got a way of letting other people clean the pot after you get off it.
Maybe you ought to do some grunt work yourself. You ought to be there
when them Indians close off a village and start pulling them out of the
huts. The amusement park really lights up. I don't think you'd have the
guts for it.'

'It's not a matter of guts, my friend,' Murphy said. There were small
breadcrumbs in the whiskers on his chin. 'Some people are adverbs,
others are nouns.'

'It'd be fun watching you hump it.'

'You might not believe this, but I had a role of some minor historical
importance at the Bay of Pigs and Dien Bien Phu. The latter was about the
time you were trying to figure out the difference between your mother's
ovaries and a bowl of grits.'

'You got a great record, Murph. If you'd been at Omaha Beach, we'd
be speaking German today.'

Erik, the little Israeli, snickered, and the Nicaraguan looked back and
forth hot-eyed at the joke he didn't understand.

'You idiots, he's burning his wrists with the handcuffs,' Murphy said.

'Always the intelligence man,' Starkweather said.

'You do your job and shut your mouth, Starkweather. The lieutenant
could operate on one brain cell and outwit you. If you screw something
up here tonight, or open your face one more time—'

He stopped and breathed hard through his nose.

'I'm going to bring his car in now. You wrap this package up,' he said.
'We're going to talk later.'

'You heard the bossman,' Starkweather said to me. 'Time to go to
work, earn our pay, fetch that barge and tote that bale. Goodbye, fart-
breath.'

They forced the spout of the rubber funnel past my teeth and into the
back of my mouth. I gagged and coughed, my eyes filled with water, and I
felt my chest convulse under their hands. Then they held my nose and
poured the mixture of beer, castor oil, whiskey, and Quaaludes down my
throat. The sudden raw taste of alcohol after four years of abstinence was
like a black peal of thunder in my system. My stomach was empty and
it licked through me like canned heat, settled heavily into my testicles and
phallus, roared darkly into my brain, filled my heart with the rancid,
primordial juices of a Viking reveling in his own mortal wound.

The light went out of my mind, and in a few moments' time I was
caught again in my drunken world of all-night bars, taxi drivers, guiding
me through my own front door in the false dawn, the delirium tremens
that covered me with sweat and filled the inside of my houseboat with
spiders and dead Vietnamese. I heard beer-bottle glass break in my head,

saw myself pushed out the back door of a wino bar, saw the contempt in a bouncer's face when he stuffed me in my automobile and threw my hat in after me, felt myself heaving my insides into a public toilet, felt the hands of a pimp and a whore turning my trouser pockets inside out.

Then a strange thing happened. Most of my dreams about Vietnam were nightmares that at one time made me fear sleep. Even before I became a full-blown drunk, I used to drink three beers before bed so I would sleep through to the morning. But now somebody was carrying me in the warm rain and I knew that I was once again in the loving care of the soldiers from my platoon. I had heard the *klitch* under my foot in the dark on the jungle trail; then, as though I were a spectator rather than a participant, I saw myself covered with cobalt light, my body crawl with electricity, my soul light the trees like an enormous candle.

When I awoke, the smoke was still rising from the rent holes in my fatigues and they were carrying me between them on a poncho while the rain ticked on the trees and the shells from an offshore battery ripped through the sky overhead. In the humid darkness I could hear the labored breathing of the four men carrying me. They were running in a half-trot, the tree branches and vines slapping against their faces and steel pots, their expressions stonelike and heedless of the other Claymores that must have been set on the trail. One of the four was a hillbilly boy from northern Georgia. He had a large American flag tattooed on his flexed, sun-browned arm, and he was so strong and he pulled so hard on his corner of the poncho that he almost tipped me out on the trail. But when a couple of AK-47s went off and they had to set me down suddenly, he crouched close to my face and whispered in his mountain accent, 'Don't you worry none, Lieutenant. If they ain't at the LZ, we'll tote you plumb to Saigon if we have to.'

They carried me the rest of the night. Their faces were exhausted and beaded with pinpoints of sweat and dirt, their fatigues stiff with their own salt. I should have been afraid but I was not. They never faltered, even though their arms and backs ached miserably and their hands were rubbed raw and blistered. The moon broke through the clouds overhead, the mist hung like strips of wet cotton along the jungle trail, and I fell into a deep morphine dream, a prenatal quietness in which the only sound was my own breathing and the labored breath of the four men carrying me, which finally became a collective hum like blood coursing through an umbilical cord. I heard them stop once and set me down gingerly while they changed my serum albumin bottle, but I didn't wake until morning, when I heard the blades of the medevac roaring over the LZ and I looked up out of my black cocoon and saw the boy from northern Georgia lean down out of the light and touch my face with hands that were as tender as a woman's.

But the hands that lifted me out of the trunk of my own automobile on the third level of a parking garage above the river didn't belong to the men of my platoon. In the darkness and the swirling rain I saw the faces of the little Israeli, the Nicaraguan, Philip Murphy, and Bobby Joe Starkweather staring down at me as though I were a loathsome object whose smell made their nostrils dilate and whiten with shock. They lifted me to my feet, then wedged me behind the steering wheel of my car and slammed the door closed. My head felt as though it had been stunned with Novocain, my mouth hung open uncontrollably, my chin and neck were slick with vomit, the sickening sweet stench of excrement rose from my trousers. Through the windshield I could see the green and red running lights of barges out on the Mississippi and clouds of vapor rising from the rain-dented water like a scene out of purgatory.

They propped Sam Fitzpatrick next to me and splashed whiskey and beer on his clothes. I tried to hold my head up straight, to reach out and touch him, but my chin kept falling on my chest and my words became thick bubbles on my lips. His eyes were rolled upward, and when he breathed, fresh blood drained from his nose onto his shirt-front. My face was numb, dead to the touch, stretched tight across the skull the way skin is over a death's head, and I felt my lips splitting apart in a wicked grin, as though I wanted to share an obscene joke with the world about our execution. Then an awful taste rose out of my stomach, my head pitched forward, and I felt something like wet newspaper rip loose inside my chest and then I heard a splattering through the steering wheel onto the floorboards.

Someone had started the car engine now, and a bare arm ridged with muscle like rolls of nickels reached across me and dropped the transmission into gear. The rain was blowing hard on the river.

The car rolled toward the guardrail, gaining speed, as I slapped limply at the door handle and tried to pull the lock free with fingers that felt sewed together with needle thread. At first I could see the river levee, a lighted street down below with cars on it, the black tops of one-story warehouses; then as my car neared the guardrail and the end of the concrete shelf I could see only the sky and the rain twisting out of it and a distant airplane with its wing lights flashing against the blackness.

I heard the rail fold under my bumper, then snap loose altogether from its fastenings just as the front wheels dropped over the edge of the concrete and my car tilted forward and slid out into space like it was beginning the first downward rush of a rollercoaster ride. The back end started to roll over, and I was pressed flat against the steering wheel, watching the street below roar up at me through the windshield, my mouth open wide with a sound that would be caught forever in my throat.

The car hit the corner of another building or concrete abutment of some kind, because I heard metal shear, as though the underside of the car had been surgically gutted, smelled a drench of gasoline briefly, then we crashed upside down in the middle of a sidewalk in a thunderous roar of glass, crumpling metal, and doors exploding off the hinges.

I was outside on the pavement, my clothes covered with oil and glass shards. We had beat it, I thought. The bad guys had done their worst and hadn't been able to pull it off. We were painted with magic, Fitzpatrick and I, and after we had recuperated it would be our turn to kick butt and take names.

But only drunkards and fools believe in that kind of poetic simplicity. The fuel tank was gashed open and the car was soaking in gasoline. I saw wisps of smoke rise from the crushed hood like pieces of dirty string, then there was a *poof* and a burst of light from the engine, and a strip of flame raced along the pavement to the gas tank and the whole car went up in an orange and black ball that snapped against the sky.

I hope he didn't suffer. The inside of the car was a firestorm. I couldn't see anything except flames swirling inside the gutted windows. But in my mind's eye I saw a papier-mâché figure, with freckles painted on its face, lying quietly between the roaring yellow walls of a furnace, ridging and popping apart in the heat.

The next morning the sun was bright through the windows of my hospital room, and I could see the green tops of the oak trees against the red brick of the nineteenth-century homes across the street. I was only half a block off St Charles, and when the nurse cranked up my bed I could see the big dull-green streetcar passing along the esplanade.

I had concussion and the doctor took seventeen stitches in my scalp, and small pieces of oily glass were embedded in my shoulder and all down one arm, so that the skin felt like alligator hide. But my real problem was the whiskey and Quaaludes that were still in my system, and the series of people who came through my door.

The first one was Sam Fitzpatrick's supervisor from the Treasury Department. He wasn't a bad guy, I guess, but he didn't like me and I believe he felt it was Fitzpatrick's involvement with me, rather than with Philip Murphy and Central American guns, that had led to his death.

'You keep talking about an elephant walk. There's nothing like that in Fitzpatrick's notes and he never talked about it, either,' he said. He was forty, wore a business suit and a deep tan, and his gray hair was cut short like an athlete's. His brown, green-flecked eyes were steady and intent.

'He didn't have a chance to,' I said.

'You tell a strange story, Lieutenant.'

'Psychopaths and government fuckheads out of control do strange things.'

'Philip Murphy isn't government.'

'I'm not sure about that.'

'Take my word,' he said.

'Then why don't you take mine?'

'Because you have a peculiar history. Because you keep meddling in things that aren't your business. Because you killed a potential major government witness and because one of our best agents burned to death in your automobile.'

My eyes broke and I had to look away from his face. The trees were green in the sunlight outside and I thought I heard the streetcar clatter on the esplanade.

'Have you heard of a guy named Abshire?' I asked.

'What about him?' he replied.

'I think these guys work for somebody named Abshire.' His eyes looked into space, then back at me. But I had seen the recognition in them.

'Who is this guy?' I asked.

'How would I know?'

'You circling up the wagons?'

'We can't afford to have you around,' he said.

'Too bad.'

'What does it take for you to get the message, Lieutenant?'

'I liked that kid, too.'

'Then make a tribute to his memory by staying out of federal business.'

He left without saying good-bye and I felt foolish and alone in the sunlit whiteness of my room. I was also starting to shake inside, like a tuning fork that starts to tremble at a discordant sound. There was a bottle of Listerine on my nightstand. I walked stiffly to the bath, rinsed my mouth, and spat into the sink. Then I sucked the juice out of my cheeks and tongue and swallowed it. Then I rinsed again, but this time I didn't spit it out. I could feel the alcohol in my stomach like an old friend.

A half hour later, two detectives from Internal Affairs stood over my bed. It was the same two who had investigated the shooting at Julio Segura's. They wore sports clothes and mustaches, and had their hair cut by a stylist.

'You guys are making me nervous. You look like vultures sitting on my bedposts. How about sitting down?' I said.

'You're a fun guy, Robicheaux, a laugh a minute,' the first detective said. His name was Nate Baxter and he had worked for CID in the army before he joined the department. I had always believed that his apparent military attitudes were a disguise for a true fascist mentality. He was a bully, and one night a suspended patrolman punched him headlong into a urinal at Joe Burton's old place on Canal.

'We don't need too much from you, Dave,' his partner said. 'We're just vague on a couple of points.'

'Like what you were doing in that snatch-patch out by the airport,' Baxter said.

'I heard about a girl that wanted to turn a couple of Segura's people.'

'You didn't find her.'

'No.'

'Then why did you have to spend all that time out there watching the gash?' Baxter said.

'I waited to see if she'd come in.'

'What'd you have to drink?'

'7-Up.'

'I didn't know 7-Up caused people to shit their pants,' Baxter said.

'You've read the report. If you don't believe me, that's your problem.'

'No, it's your problem. So run through it again.'

'Stick it up your butt, Baxter.'

'What did you say?'

'You hear me. You get out of my face.'

'Slow down, Dave,' his partner said. 'It's a wild story. People are going to ask questions about it. You got to expect that.'

'It's supposed to be a wild story. That's why they did it,' I said.

'I don't think there's any mystery here. I think you fell off the wagon, got a snootful, and crashed right on your head,' Baxter said. 'The paramedics say you smelled like an unflushed toilet with whiskey poured in it.'

'I keep defending you. No matter what everybody says. I tell them that under that Mortimer Snerd polyester there's a real cop who can sharpen pencils with the best administrators in the department. But you make it hard for me to keep on being your apologist, Baxter.'

'I think your mother must have been knocked up by a crab,' he said.

His partner's face went gray.

'I'm going to be out of here by tomorrow,' I said. 'Maybe I ought to call you up off-duty, meet you someplace, talk over some things. What do you think?'

'You call me up off-duty, you better be asking for the bus fare to an AA meeting.'

'I've got a feeling it won't make much difference if I go out of control here today.'

'I wish you would, wise-ass. I'd love to stomp the shit out of you.'

'Get out of here, Baxter, before somebody pours you out with the rest of the bedpans.'

'Keep popping those Quaaludes, hotshot, because you're going to need them. It's not me that's dropping the hammer on you, either. You blew out your own doors this time. I hope you enjoy the fall, too, because it's a big one.' Then he turned to his partner. 'Let's get out in the fresh air. This guy's more depressing every time I see him.'

They went out the door, brushing past a young Irish nun in a white habit who was bringing in my lunch on a tray.

'My, what an intense pair,' she said.

'That's probably the nicest thing anyone has ever said about them. Sister.'

'Are they after the men who did this to you?'

'I'm afraid they get paid for catching other cops.'

'I don't understand.' Her face was round and pretty inside her nun's wimple.

'It's nothing. Sister, I don't think I can eat lunch. I'm sorry.'

'Don't worry about it. Your stomach will be better by tonight.'

'You know what I'd really like, that I'd give anything to have?'

'What?'

The words wouldn't come. My eyes swept around the brightly lit room and went outside the window to the green tops of the oak trees moving in the breeze.

'Could you get me a big glass of Coca-Cola? With a lot of ice in it, maybe with cherry juice and slices of lime in it?'

'Of course.'

'Thanks very much, Sister.'

'Do you want anything else?'

'No. Just the Coca-Cola. I'm sure that's all I need.'

That afternoon Captain Guidry sat on the foot of my bed, snuffed down in his nose, and wiped his glasses on my bedsheet.

'One time after every newspaper in the country condemned George Wallace as a racist, he told a reporter, "Well, that's one man's opinion,"' Captain Guidry said. 'I was never his admirer, but I always liked that statement.'

'How bad is it going to be?'

'They stiffed you. Indefinite suspension without pay.'

'That's what they give cops who get caught dealing dope.'

'For what it's worth, I argued against it. They dumped on you, Dave, but you've got to see their side of it, too. In a week's time your name has gotten into a lot of paperwork. We're also talking about two people shot to death in one of the richest neighborhoods in New Orleans, and a Treasury agent killed in your automobile that falls three stories in the middle of a city street. That's a tough act to follow.'

'Do you believe my report?'

'You've always been a good cop. There's none better.'

'Do you believe me?'

'How the hell do I know what happened out there? To tell you the truth, I'm not sure you do, either, Dave. The paramedics said you were half crazy when they brought you in here. I saw what was left of your car.

I don't know how you survived it. The doctor said you had enough dope and booze in your blood to embalm the Russian army.'

'You want me to resign?'

'Don't let them call the plays for you. You let parasites like Baxter see that you're wounded and they'll try to file a manslaughter charge against you.'

'That special agent, Fitzpatrick's supervisor, knows who this guy Abshire is. I saw it in his eyes.'

'You shake a federal tree, and all you get in your face is birdshit. Secondly, you're suspended. You're out of it. That's absolute.'

'What am I supposed to do, Captain?'

'It's your turn in the barrel. I just hope it passes quick. Tell them all go fuck themselves and take up needle-point if you have to.'

I watched the sunset through the open window that evening. The sky was crimson above the trees and the rooftops, then it turned lavender and finally a deep purple as the sun burned itself out in a crack of brilliant fire on the horizon. I sat alone in the dark awhile, then used the remote television control to switch on the twenty-four-hour cable news. I watched pictures of Salvadoran guerrillas threading their way through a jungle trail at the base of a dead volcano. Their faces were very young, with wispy beards like Orientals, and their bodies were hung with bandoliers and cloth belts of shotgun shells. Each of them had laced his straw hat with long blades of pampas grass.

A moment later the screen showed an unrelated scene of government troops in GI issue moving through a forest of banana trees and enormous clumps of green elephant grass. A Cobra gunship streaked across the glassy sky, hovered at an angle over a deep, rocky ravine, then unloaded a succession of rockets that blew water, powdered coral, and bits of trees and scrub brush out of the bottom of the ravine. The footage closed with a shot of government troops retreating out of the banana trees with their wounded on stretchers. The heat in those trees must have been terrible, because the wounded were covered with sweat and the medics were washing their faces with water from canteens. It all looked very familiar.

Having been raised in Louisiana, I had always thought that politics was the province of moral invalids. But as a gambler I had certain instincts about which side I would wager my money on in certain situations. On one side of the equation were people who had been conscripted into the army and were either forced or paid to fight, and who sometimes sold their weapons to the enemy if given the chance. On the other side was a group that lived off the jungle, scavenged guns and ammunition wherever they could buy or steal them, had absolutely nothing of economic value to lose, and who, because they had no illusions about their fate if they were captured, would go down to the last man in a firefight. I doubted there was a bookie in New Orleans who would take a bet on that one.

But my war was over, and maybe my career as well. I turned off the set and looked out the window at the reflection of the lights against the sky. The room was quiet, the sheets were cool and clean, and my stomach didn't feel sick anymore; but the tuning fork was still vibrating inside me. I brushed my teeth, I showered, I rinsed my mouth with Listerine again; then I got back in bed and pulled my knees up in front of me and started to shake all over.

Fifteen minutes later I checked myself out of the hospital and took a cab to my houseboat. It was a dark, hot night and the heat had built up all day in the cabin. My collection of historical jazz records – irreplaceable seventy-eights of Blind Lemon, Bunk Johnson, Kid Ory, Bix Beiderbecke – lay scattered and broken and tattooed with footprints on the floor. I opened the windows wide, turned on my floor fan, picked up the few records that were still hard and stiff in their jackets, cleaned them with a soft cloth, and set them in the wall rack. Then I swept the rest into a paper bag and lay down to sleep on the couch with my clothes on.

Small waves chucked against the hull, and the boat rocked rhythmically under me. But it was no good; I couldn't sleep. I was sweating and trembling and when I took my shirt off I shivered as though I'd been struck with a blast of arctic air. Each time I closed my eyes I felt the earth's surface drop away under me, felt myself spinning end over end inside my automobile toward the distant bottom of a rock-strewn canyon, saw words form like a bubble on the dead lips of Sam Fitzpatrick sitting next to me.

Later, Annie Ballard tapped softly on the cabin door. I unlocked it and went back to the couch in the dark. A sailing yacht out on the lake had a floodlamp lighted on its deck, and it made gold lights in Annie's hair. I saw her feel for the switch on the wall.

'Don't turn it on,' I said.

'Why not?'

'People just out of the hospital don't look good.'

'I don't care.'

'I do.'

'You knew I was coming up there. Didn't you want to leave me a message?'

'I thought I did. Maybe I didn't. There were cops in there all day.'

She walked closer to the couch. She wore a pair of white jeans with a blue denim shirt tucked inside.

'What's wrong?' she said.

'I guess it's malaria. I picked it up in the Philippines.'

'I'm going to turn on the light.'

'No.'

'You don't have to hide anything, Dave.'

'I'm suspended without pay. I don't feel well right now. To tell you the truth, I feel like killing somebody.'

'I don't understand.'

'When they suspend you indefinitely without pay, it means you're probably not coming back. It's the kind of stuff they drop on cops that are about to be indicted.'

She sat down on the edge of the couch and put her hand on my bare shoulder. Her face was a dark silhouette against the glass behind her. She touched my forehead with her fingers.

'I can't believe they would do that to you.'

'It's my past history. You don't know about it. I was a full-blown drunk for years. They figure I'm back into it.'

'They can't hold the past against you.'

'Why the hell not? It makes it easier. Most cops couldn't think their way out of a wet paper bag. They think categorically about virtually every situation. That's why we don't put a lot of people away. Look, four pieces of human slime that wouldn't even make good bars of soap are out there right now drinking beer, celebrating burning a kid to charcoal, while some of our own people are wondering if they should hang a DUI on me, or a DUI and a manslaughter charge.'

'You're not talking like yourself.'

'Annie, in the real world we fry paupers in the electric chair and send priests to prison for splashing chicken blood on draft files. It's the nature of ritual. We deal with the problem symbolically, but somebody has to take the fall. In this case, a guy that looked like he escaped from a Popsicle wrapper launched a one-man crusade against an entire government policy in Central America. If you were an administrative pencil-pusher, don't you think it would be easier to deal with a drunk-driving fatality than a story about a lot of right-wing crazies who are killing peasant villagers in Nicaragua?'

'Why do you think you're the only person who sees the truth?'

'I didn't say that.'

'But it's the way you feel, Dave. That's too big a burden for a person.' Her face was soft and composed and she looked out the windows across the water for a moment, then stood up and began undressing in the dark.

'Annie, I'm not a charity case. I'm just not doing too good today.'

'If you want me to go away, tell me. But look me directly in the face and tell me honestly, with no weirdness or bullshit this time.'

'I like you a great deal.'

She sat back on the couch and leaned her face close to mine.

'Loving somebody is being there when nobody else is. When it's not even a choice. You should understand that, Dave,' she said. She bent and kissed me lightly on the mouth.

She was beautiful to look at, and her skin was smooth and warm and I could smell the sun and a perfume like the scent of four-o'clocks in her hair. She kissed me again and blew her breath on the side of my face and slipped her arms around my neck and pressed her breasts tight against me. I sat up in the side of the couch and took off my trousers; then she pressed me back into the cushions, raised herself up on her knees, and with her hand guided me inside her. Her eyes closed, she moaned and her mouth opened wide, and she leaned down over me on her arms with her breasts close to my face. She had ignored all my anger – no, my self-pity – and I felt humbled and dizzy and physically weak when I looked up into the electric blueness of her eyes.

There was a strawberry birthmark on her right breast, and it seemed to grow darker and fill with blood as her breathing became more rapid. I felt her warmth drawing me into her, felt her wet palms slip under me, felt her thighs flex and tighten around me, then her hands held my face and my heart twisted in my chest and I felt an aching hardness crest inside of me and burst apart like a heavy stone ripping loose in a rushing streambed.

'Oh, you fine man,' she said, and brushed the drops of sweat out of my eyes with her fingers, her body still shaking.

She fell asleep next to me, and I covered her with a sheet from the bedroom. The moon was out now, and the light through the glass made her curly blond hair look like it was touched with silver. Just the edge of her strawberry birthmark showed above the sheet.

I knew I was very fortunate to have a girl like this. But the great nemesis of the gambler is that he's never satisfied with just winning the daily double; he'll reinvest his winnings in every race remaining that afternoon, and if he's still ahead when the window closes on the last race, he'll be at the dog track that night and stay with it until he loses everything.

I didn't have a parimutuel window handy, so I left Annie asleep and started walking down the lakefront toward Pontchartrain Beach Amusement Park. The wind had picked up and the waves were cresting against the hard-packed sand of the beach and the palm fronds were rattling dryly against the darkening sky. By the time I reached the amusement park the air was cool and filled with flying grains of sand and smelled of the gale blowing out of the south. Most of the rides were closed, with tarpaulins stretched over them to protect them from the coming rain, and the red neon signs over the empty funhouse looked like electrified blood in the sky.

But I found what I had been looking for all day.

'A double Jack Daniel's with a Pearl draft on the side,' I told the bartender.

'You look like you already lost a fight to a chainsaw, buddy,' he said.

'You ought to see the chainsaw,' I said.

But it was a dark, cheerless place, not given to either humor or protocol, and the bartender poured silently into my shot glass.

7

At five o'clock the next morning the eastern sky was gray and pink beyond the tree line on the far side of the Mississippi. I was in an all-night bar set back from old Highway 90 under the long, black, looming expanse of the Huey Long Bridge. Mist hung in clouds on the river's surface and around the brush-choked pilings of the bridge; the air itself seemed to drip with moisture, and the shale rock in the parking lot glistened with a dull shine as the pinkness of the sun spread along the earth's rim.

A bus loaded with carnival and circus people from Sarasota, Florida, had broken down on the highway, and the bar and the café counter were crowded with a strange collection of roustabouts, acrobats, and sideshow performers. I sat at a table with the Crocodile Boy, the Pencil Man, and a dwarf named Little Mack. The Pencil Man had arms and legs that were so thin and soft that they looked as though all the bone had been surgically removed from them, like rubbery snakes attached to his torso, which in itself could not have been much greater in circumference than a telephone pole. His kinky red hair was waxed and brushed into a conk so that it resembled a pencil eraser. The skin of the Crocodile Boy was covered with hard black bumps like barnacles, and his teeth looked as if they had been filed to points. In rotating order he sipped from his muscatel wine, chased it with beer, smoked a cigar, and ate out of a bowl of pickled hogs' feet. Little Mack sat next to me, his tiny feet not able to touch the floor, his elongated jug face filled with concern at my situation.

I looked at the long-distance number I had written on a damp napkin. My head was filled with a steady buzzing sound, like a neon short circuit.

'You shouldn't call those CIA people again, Lieutenant,' Little Mack said in his high-pitched mechanical voice. 'They're the ones tied in with those UFOs. We saw one once in the desert outside of Needles, California. It was glowing green and orange and it streaked over the top of the bus at maybe a thousand miles an hour. The next day the paper said a bunch of cows on a ranch were all mangled up. Maybe those UFO guys were trying to take some food on board.'

'That could be,' I said, and I motioned to the bartender to bring us two more shots of Jack Daniel's.

'The government will mess you up,' the Pencil Man said. 'Each time you have contact with a government agency, it creates a piece of paper on you. There's people that's got whole rooms of paper on their lives. I don't have any, not even a birth certificate. My mother squatted down just long enough to squirt me out in the back of a boxcar. I been moving ever since. I never had a social security card, a driver's license, a draft card. I never filed an income tax return. You let them get papers on you and they'll jerk you around.'

'You guys are my kind of situational philosophers,' I said.

'What's that?' the Crocodile Boy asked. He had stopped eating a hog's knuckle, and his narrow green eyes were curious and perplexed.

'You deal with the action on your own terms, whether it's a UFO or a bunch of government buttholes. Right?' I said.

'Have you seen a UFO?' Little Mack asked.

'I've heard reports on them,' I said.

I poured a jigger of whiskey into my beer glass, drank it down, then looked at the telephone number on the napkin again. I raked my change off the table into my palm and started toward the pay phone on the wall.

'Lieutenant, don't use dirty words to anyone this time,' Little Mack said. 'I read a story once they even put poison inside a guy's condom.'

I called the number in McLean, Virginia, and asked for a duty officer. My ear felt thick and wooden against the phone receiver. I tried to focus my eyes through the front window on the clouds of steam rising off the river in the soft light. The neon buzz in my head wouldn't stop. Finally the voice of an annoyed man came on the line.

'Who's this?' I asked.

'The same guy you were talking to a half hour ago.'

'Then put somebody else on.'

'I'm all you get, pal.'

'Tell me your name so I can look you up sometime.'

'Let me give you the facts of life, Lieutenant. We traced your call, we know what bar you're in, we ran your sheet, we know everything about you. If you weren't such a pathetic asshole, I'd have your own people pick you up.'

'All right, try this with your morning coffee, motherfucker. I'm the loose cannon on your deck and I'm going to leave blood and shit all over the gunwales.'

'If you didn't have the alcoholic titty in your mouth, I might even take you seriously. Call here one more time and you're going to be sitting in your own drunk tank.'

The line went dead. When I lowered the receiver from my ear, the side of my face felt numb, as though I had been slapped with a thick hand.

'What's the matter? Your face don't look good,' Little Mack said.

'We need some more drinks,' I said.

'They threaten to assassinate you or something? The cocksuckers. You ever read *The Black Star*? There was a story about how the CIA used these Nazi scientists to make clones from Elvis and Marilyn Monroe, then they killed the clones when they couldn't use them to spy anymore. I think they got the idea from this show about these seed-pod people taking over the earth. They put a seed pod under your bed, and when you go to sleep the pod sucks out all your ectoplasm and turns you into a dry shell that just blows away in the wind . . . Where you going?'

'I don't know.'

'Better sit down, get something to eat,' the Pencil Man said. 'You can ride with us when the bus is fixed.'

'Thanks, I need to walk. This last round is on me.'

But when I opened my wallet I had no money.

'You all right, Lieutenant?' Little Mack said.

'Sure.'

'I mean, you're listing pretty bad,' he said.

'I'm okay.'

'You got to be careful out there in the fog and all,' he said. 'There's crazy people on the highway, drunks and such. You going to be safe?'

'Sure,' I said. 'Believe me.'

I started walking in the gray dawn toward the shining black outline of the Huey Long Bridge. I could hear car tires whir on the steel grid of the bridge. The air was cool and damp and smelled of the wet earth along the riverbanks. I began the long walk up toward the apex of the bridge, my breath coming hard in my throat, my heart swelling with exertion. Far down below in the dark waters, a Standard Oil barge was headed north to the refineries in Baton Rouge. The spires, cables, and girders of the bridge seemed to sing and whip and groan in the wind. Then the sun broke through the clouds in a yellow ball, flooding the bridge with light, and for some reason I saw deep down in my mind a black cluster of jungle birds rise clattering into a hot tropical sky.

Late that afternoon I sat under an umbrella on the deck of my houseboat and tried to mend my day and mind back together with a bottle of Jax. I wasn't having much luck. The sun reflected off the water and struck my eyes like broken shards from a mirror. I wanted to call Annie and apologize, but how do you explain that your craving for alcohol can be stronger than your need for someone's love? And in truth, at that moment I didn't have either the courage or the energy to face my own irresponsibility and weakness. Instead, I brooded on the relativity of time, the stark realization that no amount of years could successfully separate me from my nightmarish alcoholic past, that Philip Murphy's cocktail had launched me totally back into a surreal world where the dragons and monsters frolicked.

I also brooded on my drowned father and wondered what he would have done in my situation. He was a big, powerful man, a dark laughing Cajun with white teeth and turquoise eyes who had been raised on *boudin, cush-cush,* and garfish balls. He had been a fur trapper on Marsh Island and a derrick man on oil rigs, working high up on the monkey board, and he had done his best to take care of Jimmie and me after my mother ran away with a *bourée* dealer from Morgan City. But when he was out of work he drank hard and sometimes brawled in bars and got thrown in the parish jail; the white streak in Jimmie's and my hair was caused by a vitamin deficiency associated with malnutrition. However, during those bad times he could be imaginative and kind in ways that we would never forget. On a Halloween evening, when the pecan trees stood full and black against the orange sky, he would come home with carved pumpkins, chopped lengths of sugar cane, and blocks of hot gingerbread, or at our birthday breakfasts we would find by our plates of *cush-cush* and *boudin* a dozen Civil War minié balls or rose quartz Indian arrowheads, and one time a rusty Confederate revolver he had dug out of the bank on Bayou Teche.

He usually spoke to us in French, and he entertained us for years with an endless number of admonitions, observations, and folk stories that he said he'd learned from his father but that I think he made up as the situation demanded. An English paraphrase of a few:

- Never do anything you don't want to, you.
- If everybody agrees upon it, it's got to be wrong.
- Rather than the eagle, the crawfish should be the symbol of the United States. If you put an eagle on a rail road track and a train comes along, what's the eagle going to do? He's going to fly, him. But you put a crawfish on that railroad track and what's he going to do? He's going to put up his claws to stop that train, him.

But there was a piece of serious advice that he used to give us, and I could almost hear him whispering it to me now from below the green depths far out in the Gulf: When you've hunted through the whole marsh for the bull 'gator that ate your hog and you come up empty, go back where you started and commence again. You walked right over him.

A cop had never been given a better suggestion.

I slept through the rest of the afternoon and woke in the cooling dusk when the cicadas were loud in the purple haze and the fireflies were lighting in the trees. I showered and felt some of the misery begin to go out of my mind and body, then I took a taxi to the Hertz agency and rented a small Ford.

Because most of the Quarter was closed to automobile traffic at night, I parked the car near the French Market, by the river, and walked back to Bourbon. The street was loud with music from the bars and strip houses, and the sidewalks were filled with tourists, drunks, and street people who were trying to hold on to their last little piece of American geography. My favorite bunch of hustlers and scam artists, the black sidewalk tap dancers, were out in force. They wore enormous iron taps that clipped onto their shoes, and when they danced to the music from the bars, their feet rang on the concrete like horseshoes. A tap dancer would stop a tourist, rivet him in the eyes, and say, 'I bet you a half-dollar I can tell you where you got yo' shoes.' If the tourist accepted the wager, the dancer would then say, 'You got yo' shoes on yo' feet, and yo' feet is on Bourbon Street. You ain't the kind, now, to back out on yo' bet, is you?'

I went inside Plato's Adult Theater, stopped in the men's room, and removed the clip from my .45 automatic. I dropped the empty pistol in one coat pocket, the clip in the other, and opened Wesley Pott's office door without knocking.

'What's happening Wes? Community Outreach here,' I said.

He sat behind the desk in his powder-blue polyester slacks, with his feet up in a chair, watching the baseball game on television and eating fried chicken out of a box propped on his stomach. His pate shone with hair oil, and his eyes looked at me like uncertain blue marbles. He resumed chewing, and swallowed the chicken in his mouth.

'I'm looking for a fellow named Bobby Joe Starkweather,' I said. 'I suspect he's a fan of the Tijuana visual arts.'

His eyes clicked back and forth.

'I hear they pulled your ticket, Lieutenant,' he said.

'You hear a lot of rumors in troubled times.'

'This is more like the *Times-Picayune*.'

'Those are bureaucratic matters that guys like you and me don't need to pay much attention to.'

'I think I already went on the line once for you, Lieutenant. I didn't get nothing for it, either, except my films smashed up by Purcel. I could've got into some real ugly shit because of that.'

'I'm temporarily disconnected from the snitch fund, so we're operating on good faith here.'

'I went through a lot of anxiety because of that day. I think you ought to understand that. No matter what you think about me, I'm not some kind of geek for the mob that hops around in the pan like a piece of popcorn. I got a family, my kids go to Sunday school, I pay a lot of taxes. Maybe my IRS records are a little creative, but how about Nixon's? A guy wants a little respect, a little recognition that he's got his own space, his own problems.'

'I know all that, Wes. That's why it makes me feel bad when I do this to you.'

I took the .45 from my coat pocket, slid back the loading receiver, let it clack back loudly into place, and aimed it at a downward angle between his eyes so he could see the cocked hammer.

He gasped, his face jumped, pinpoints of sweat broke out on his coarse skin, and his eyes almost crossed as they went out of focus on the pointed pistol. He fluttered his fingers at the barrel.

'Don't point it at me, Lieutenant,' he pleaded. 'I was in the war. I can't take guns.'

'Your sheet says you got a peacetime BCD.'

'I don't care. I hate guns. I hate all violence. God, I'm gonna wet my pants!'

He was trembling badly. The box of fried chicken had spilled to the floor, and he was swallowing dryly, the pulse jumping in his throat, and kneading and rubbing his hands in front of him as though something obscene were on them. Then he began to weep uncontrollably.

'I can't do this to you. I'm sorry, Wesley,' I said, and lowered the .45.

'What?' he said weakly.

'I apologize. I shouldn't have done that. If you don't want to drop the dime on somebody, that's your business.'

He couldn't stop hiccuping and shaking.

'Lighten up. It was empty. Here, look.' I pointed the barrel at my palm and snapped the trigger. His head jerked at the sound.

'I'm gonna have a heart attack. I had rheumatic fever when I was a kid. I can't take high-level stress like this,' he said.

'I'll get you a whiskey from next door. What do you drink?'

'A double Black Jack on ice, with a Tuborg chaser.' He paused and blinked. 'Make sure the beer's cold, too. The Jew that runs that joint is always trying to cut down on his refrigeration bill.'

I went to the bar next door and had to pay eight dollars for the imported beer and the double shot of Jack Daniel's in a cup of ice. When I got back to Wesley's office the air reeked of marijuana, and his face had the blank, stiff look of somebody who had just eaten the roach.

'My doctor gives it to me for glaucoma,' he said. 'It's a condition I got in the army. A hand grenade blew up in one of the pits. That's how come I'm nervous all the time and can't take stress.'

'I see.'

'The beer cold?'

'You bet. Are you all right now?'

'Sure.' He drank down the whiskey and crunched the ice between his teeth, his close-set eyes narrowing and focusing like BBs. 'Lieutenant, I can give you that fucker.'

'Why is that?'

'He's a creep. Besides, he was muling Mexican brown for Segura. I still live down in the Irish Channel. They hook up neighborhood kids with that stuff.'

'Yeah, the Rotary and the Knights of Columbus have been talking a lot about that lately. Have you been attending some of their breakfasts on that, Wes?'

'I sell dirty fantasies in a dark theater. I don't steal people's souls. You haven't found that tattooed ass-wipe because he don't live in New Orleans. He's got a fish camp over by Bayou des Allemands in St Charles Parish. He spends his time busting bottles in the backyard with a shotgun. The guy's a walking advertisement for massive federal aid to mental health.'

'Dropping the dime's not always enough.'

'I'm turning him for you. What else you want?'

'You know the rules, Wes. We don't let the customers write the script. Give me the rest of it. Like Didi Gee told me, treat people with respect.'

He drank his beer and looked intently at the wall, his face coloring with remembered anger. I could hear his breath in his nose.

'Segura invited a bunch of guys out to his pool to play cards, have drinks, and fool around with the gash. Starkweather is shooting off his mouth about how he was a Green Beret in 'Nam and how he cut some gooks' throats in their sleep and painted their faces yellow so the other gooks would wake up in the morning and find them like that. Except people are eating their shrimp salad and trying not to puke on the grass, and so I say, "Hey, give it a break or hand out barf bags with all these sickening war stories." He stared at me like I was some kind of bedbug. Then, right in front of all them people, with all them broads watching, he jabbed me in both eyeballs with his fingers, the way Moe Stooge was always doing to Shemp and Larry. A broad started laughing real loud, and then he pushed me in the pool.'

'Wes, somehow I believe you,' I said.

I waited until dawn to hit Starkweather's fish camp. Clouds of fog swirled off the bayou through the flooded woods as I banged over an old board that had been cut through the swamp by an oil company. The dead cypresses were wet and black in the gray light, and green lichen grew where the waterline touched the swollen bases of the trunks. The fog was so thick and white in the trees that I could barely see thirty feet ahead of the car. A rotted plank snapped under my wheel and whanged off the oil pan. In the early morning stillness the sound made the herons and egrets rise in a sudden flapping of wings toward the pink light above the treetops. Then to one side of the road, in a scoured-out clearing in the trees, I saw a shack built of Montgomery Ward brick and clapboard, elevated from the muddy ground by cinder blocks and cypress stumps, with a Toyota jeep parked in front. A knobby beagle that looked like it had been hit with birdshot was tied to the front porch.

I cut the car's ignition in the center of the road, opened the door quietly, and walked through the wet trees on one side of the clearing until I was abreast of the porch. The oaks that ringed the clearing were covered with shredded rifle targets; perforated tin cans and shattered bottles dangled from bits of baling wire; the bark on the trunks was ripped and gouged white by bullets.

The screen door to the shack was ajar, but I couldn't see or hear any movement inside. Out back, hogs were snuffing and grunting inside a wood pen.

I pulled back the receiver on my .45 and eased a round from the clip into the chamber. I took a deep breath, then raced across the dirt yard, cleared the porch steps in one jump, almost caused the beagle to break its neck on its rope, and crashed through the screen door.

I crouched and swung the .45 around the room, my heart hammering against my ribcage, my eyes wide in the gloom. The wooden floor was littered with beer cans, bread wrappers, Red Man pouches, chicken bones, bottle caps, and the chewed stuffing from a rotted mattress that was piled in the corner. But there was nobody in the room. Then someone slid back the curtain on the doorway to the single bedroom in the back. I aimed the .45 right at her face, both of my hands sweating on the grip.

'Wow, who the fuck are you?' she said drowsily. She was maybe twenty and wore cut-off blue jeans and only a bra for a top. Her face looked numb, dead, and she had to keep widening her eyes to focus on me. Her hair was the color of weathered wood.

'Where's Starkweather?' I said.

'I think he went out back with that other dude. Are you the heat or something?'

I pushed open the back screen and dropped into the yard. In the mist I could see an outhouse, an upside-down pirogue beaded with dew, a wooden hog pen, a wheelless and rusted-out car body pocked with silvery bullet holes. The sun was lighting the trees now, and I could see the dead green water in the swamp, the levee covered with buttercups, the Spanish moss that was lifting in the breeze off the Gulf. But there was no one back here. Then I heard the hogs grunting and snuffing again, and I realized they were eating something inside the pen.

They were in a circle, their heads dipped down as though they were eating from a trough; then one of them would rattle its head, grunt, crunch something loudly in its jaws, and dip its snout down again. Their faces and mouths were shiny with gore; then I saw one of them tear a long string of blue entrails out of Bobby Joe Starkweather's stomach and run heavily across the pen with it. Starkweather's face was bloodless, the eyes and mouth open, his shaved scalp flecked with mud. Right above one eyebrow was a black hole the size of a dime.

A bucket of kitchen slops was spilled on the ground. His arms were spread out beside him, and he looked as if he'd been shot from the front side of the pen. I looked carefully over the wet ground, which was dented with boot and dog and chicken prints, until I saw the smooth impression of a street shoe in a ridge of mud, and right in the center of it the stenciled outline of a pistol shell that the shooter must have stepped on and then prized up with his finger.

I went back in the shack. The girl was fumbling in a food cabinet.

'Are you heat?' she said.

'It depends on who you talk to.'

'You got any whites?'

'You look like you already did a drugstore.'

'If you had to ball him, you'd be doing Thorazines like M & M's.'

'I hope you got paid up front.'

Her eyes closed and opened and refocused on mine.

'Where is he?' she said.

'Feeding the pigs.'

She looked at me uncertainly, then started out the back door.

'Let it go. You don't want to look back there,' I said.

But she didn't listen. A minute later I heard her make a sound like she had suddenly stepped into an envelope of fouled air. Her face was gray when she came back through the door.

'That's gross,' she said. 'Shouldn't you take him to a funeral home or something? Yuk.'

'Sit down. I'll fix you a cup of coffee.'

'I can't hang around here. I've got an aerobics and meditation class at ten o'clock. The guy I work for enrolls us in the class so we won't build up a lot of tensions. He gets mad if I miss. God, how do I get around all these crazy people? You know what *he* did? He got naked in his army boots and started lifting weights on the front porch. The dog got off the leash and chased a chicken into the privy and he shot the dog with a shotgun. Then he tied it up and gave it a bowl of milk like nothing had happened.'

'Who was the dude he went out back with?'

'He looked like he had a pink bicycle patch on his face.'

'What?'

'I don't know what he looked like. He was big. I was kind of indisposed, you know what I mean?'

'Say it again about his face.'

'His nose and part of his eyebrow were messed up. Like with a scar.'

'What did he say?'

Her eyes seemed to reach out into space. Her mouth was slightly parted, her facial muscles collapsed with thought.

'He said, "They want you to find some new geography. Work on your golf game." Then what's-his-name said, "Money talks and bullshit walks, biscuit-eater. I got to feed my pigs." '

She chewed on a hangnail and her eyes went flat again.

'Look, I got a problem,' she said. 'He didn't pay me. I got to give the guy I work for twenty bucks when I get back to the bar. Will you get his wallet for me?'

'Sorry. I think the hogs got it, anyway.'

'You want some action?'

'I'll drop you where you want to go, kiddo. Then I'm going to call the sheriff's office about Starkweather. But I'll deal you out of it. If you want to tell them something later, that's up to you.'

'You are heat, aren't you?'

'Why not?'

'Why you cutting me loose? You got something in mind for later?'

'They might lock you up as a material witness. That guy out there in the hog lot has killed dozens, maybe hundreds of people. But he was a novice and a bumbler compared to the people he worked for.'

She sat against the far door of my car, her face thick with a drug hangover, and didn't speak during the long ride through the marsh to the parish road. Her yellowed fingers were wrapped tightly in her lap.

Like many others, I learned a great lesson in Vietnam: Never trust authority. But because I had come to feel that authority should always be treated as suspect and self-serving, I had also learned that it was predictable and vulnerable. So that afternoon I sat under my beach umbrella on my houseboat deck, dressed only in swimming trunks and an open tropical shirt, with a shot of Jim Beam and a beer chaser on the table in front of me, and called Sam Fitzpatrick's supervisor at the Federal Building.

'I ran down Abshire,' I said. 'I don't know why you held out on me at the hospital. He's not exactly well concealed.'

There was a moment's silence on the line.

'Have you got wax in your ears or something?' he said. 'How do I get through to you? You stay off federal turf.'

'I'm going to kick a board up his ass.'

'You're not going to do a goddamn thing, except get a warrant filed on you for obstruction.'

'You want in on it or not?' I asked.

'I have a strong feeling you're drunk.'

'So what? I'm going to cool him out. You want to be there for the party, or do you want us local boys to write the story for you in the *Picayune*? It's going to be socko stuff, partner.'

'What the hell is the matter with you? You don't seem to have any bottom. One of my best men is burned to death in your car. Your own people dump you like a sack of dog turds. You're evidently working on becoming a full-time drunk again, and now you're talking about taking out a retired two-star general. You think it's possible you're losing your mind?'

'You're a good man, but don't take up poker.'

'What?'

'It's a terrible vice. It'll lead you to ruin.'

'You bastard, you're not going to get away with this,' he said.

I hung up the phone, knocked back the jigger of Jim Beam, and sipped from the glass of beer. The sun looked like a yellow balloon trapped under the lake's surface. The wind was warm, and sweat ran down my bare chest in the hot shade of the umbrella. My eyes burned with the humidity of the afternoon. I dialed Clete down at the First District.

'Where are you?' he asked.

'At home.'

'There's a bunch of people asking about you. You sure spit in the soup, Dave.'

'I'm not hard to find. Who's curious about me?'

'Who else? Feds. Did you really call up the CIA? Man, that's unbelievable.'

'I have a lot of time on my hands. A guy has to do something for kicks.'

'I don't know as I'd want to fire up these babies. A nasty bunch. They're not our crowd.'

'You think I ought to get lost for a while?'

'Who knows? I just wouldn't pull on their tally-wackers anymore.'

'Actually, I called you for a point of information, Clete. In all the shootings you've investigated, how many times have you known the shooter to recover his brass?'

'I don't understand.'

'Sure you do.'

'I don't guess I ever gave it much thought.'

'I've never seen it once,' I said. 'Except when a cop was the shooter.'

'What's the point?'

'It's funny how that can be trained into a guy, isn't it?'

'Yeah. Imagine that.'

'If I was the shooter, I'd rather leave the shell casing than my signature.'

'Maybe some things aren't worth speculating about, Dave.'

'Like I said, I'm idle now. It fills the time. I spent two hours this morning over at the St Charles sheriff's department answering questions about Bobby Joe Starkweather. Did they contact you all yet?'

'We heard about it.' His voice was becoming irritated.

'A truly big mess out there. Another hour or so and I don't think there would have been anything left of Bobby Joe except his belt buckle and his boot nails.'

'He's better off as sausage links. A guy finds his proper level after a while. I got to split, partner.'

'Do me a favor. How about punching on the computer and seeing if you can turn up a retired two-star general named Abshire?'

'Stay idle, Dave. Adjust. We'll get out of this bullshit eventually. You'll see. *Adios.*'

The phone went dead in my head, and I looked at the smoky green surface of the water in the summer haze and poured another jigger of Jim Beam. What did they have on him? I wondered. Whores? Juice from narcotics? It seemed sometimes that the best of us became most like the people whom we loathed. And whenever a good cop took a big fall, he could never look back and find that exact moment when he made a hard left turn down a one-way street. I remembered sitting in a courtroom when an ex-major-league baseball pitcher from New Orleans was sentenced to ten years in Angola for extortion and trafficking in cocaine. Seventeen years earlier he had won twenty-five games, had thrown fastballs that could destroy barn doors, and now he weighed three hundred pounds and walked as though a bowling ball were slung between his thighs. When asked if he had anything to say before sentencing, he stared up at the judge, the rings of fat on his neck trembling, and replied, 'Your Honor, I have no idea how I got from *there to here.*'

I believed him, too. But as I sat in the warm breeze with the drowsy heat of the whiskey working in my head, my concern was not for Clete or an ex-baseball pitcher. I knew that my own fuse was lit, and it was only a matter of time before my banked fires would roar out of control in my life. I had never felt more alone, and I uttered a prayer that seemed a contradiction of everything I had learned back at the Catholic School: *Dear God, my higher power, even though I've abandoned You, don't abandon me.*

8

Late that afternoon I fixed a poor-boy sandwich of oysters, shrimp, lettuce and a *sauce piquante*, then drove through the cooling, tree-shaded street toward the *Times-Picayune*, where a night editor sometimes let me use their morgue.

But first I wanted to make amends to Annie for deserting her at the houseboat the other night. Afternoon Jim Beam always endowed me with that kind of magical power.

I bought a bottle of Cold Duck and a box of pralines wrapped in orange cellophane and yellow ribbon, kept my freshly pressed seersucker coat on, and strolled up her sidewalk in the dusky light. The air smelled of lilac and spaded flower beds and clipped lawns and water sprinklers clicking across hedges and the trunks of trees.

When she didn't answer the bell, I walked around the back and found her barbecuing steaks on a portable grill on a brick patio under a china-berry tree. She wore white shorts and Mexican straw shoes and a yellow shirt tied under her breasts. Her eyes were watering in the smoke, and she stepped away from the fire and picked up a gin gimlet from a glass tabletop that was set with plates and silverware. The gimlet glass was wrapped in a paper napkin with a rubber band around it. Her eyes lighted briefly when she saw me, then she looked away.

'Oh, hello, Dave,' she said.

'I should have called. I caught you at a bad time.'

'A little bit.'

'I brought these pralines and some Cold Duck,' I said.

'That was nice of you.'

'I'm sorry I left you the other night. It's something you won't under-stand very well, I'm afraid.'

The light came back in her blue eyes. I could see the red birthmark on the top of her breast.

'The best way to end a conversation is to tell somebody she can't understand something,' she said.

'I meant there was no excuse for it.'

'There was a reason. Maybe you just don't want to look at it.'

'I went after liquor. I was drunk all night. I ended up in a bar on Old 90 with a bunch of sideshow performers. I called up the CIA and cussed out the duty officer.'

'I guess that prevented you from finding a telephone for two days.'

'I tried to find Bobby Joe Starkweather. Somebody canceled him out in a hog lot.'

'I'm not interested, Dave. Did you come by to screw me?'

'You think I'm giving you a shuck?'

'No, I think you're singleminded and you're bent on revenge. I made the overture the other night and complicated things for you. Now you're feeling a gentleman's obligation. Sorry, I'm not in the absolution business. I don't have any regrets. If you do, that's your problem.'

She began to poke the meat on the grill with a fork. The fire flared up and her eyes winced in the smoke. She poked at the meat all the harder.

'I'm truly sorry,' I said. 'But you're right about my being singleminded. There's only one girl I'm interested in.'

I wanted to put my arms around her waist and take her out of the smoke, hold her against me and feel her curly hair under my hands.

'You just can't leave a woman alone in the night, Dave.'

I looked away from her face.

'I woke up and you were gone and I thought maybe those defective people had come back. I drove up and down the beach looking for you until dawn,' she said.

'I didn't know that.'

'How could you, if you were with some sideshow people?'

'Annie, I'd like another chance with you. I can't make you many promises, except I won't deliberately hurt you again. That's probably not very adequate, but it's all I have.'

She turned her face away from me, and I saw her brush her eye with the back of her wrist.

'Another night. There's someone coming over now,' she said.

'All right.'

'Are those people out there worth all this?'

'They'll find me if I don't find them. You can bet on it.'

'My great-grandparents were part of the Underground Railway. Quantrill's Raiders tore down their sod houses and burned their cornfields. Long after Quantrill and Bloody Bill Anderson and Jesse James were dead, they were raising children and Russian wheat in a free state.

'But somebody canceled Quantrill and Company's action first, namely, federal cavalry.'

I smiled at her, but her face suddenly looked wan in the electric light that was hung in the chinaberry tree. I didn't care about propriety or restraint or the fact that her friend would arrive any minute now; I set the Cold Duck and the pralines on the glass tabletop and put my arms around her and kissed her curly hair. But she didn't respond. Her shoulders were stiff, her eyes turned down, her arms angular and dead.

'Call me tomorrow,' she whispered.

'Sure.'

'I want you to.'

'I will. I promise.'

'Things just aren't right with me tonight. I'll be all right tomorrow.'

'I'll leave the pralines. I'll call early. Maybe we'll have breakfast at the Café du Monde.'

'That sounds nice,' she said. But her eyes were veiled, and I couldn't read them. Under all her fascination with weirdness, she had the sensitive heart of a small-town Midwestern girl.

On my way down the front walk I passed a young man who looked like a graduate student at Tulane. He wore cream-colored slacks, a pale blue shirt, and a striped tie, and his smile was good-natured and his face very handsome. I asked him if he was having dinner with Annie Ballard.

'Why, yes,' he said, and smiled again.

'Here, take this,' I said, and handed him the bottle of Cold Duck. 'It's on the fuzz tonight.'

It was an *old* thing to do, and a moment later I felt foolish and rude. Then I remembered an axiom taught me in Vietnam by a line officer who used to cut through Gordian knots with a sentence: Fuck it. Who wants to be a good loser?

That night as I sat in the morgue of the *Times-Picayune* and turned the yellowed pages of old newspapers or flipped the strips of microfilm up on the viewing screen, I reflected upon the ambiguous importance of the past in our lives. In order to free ourselves from it, I thought, we treat it as a decaying memory. At the same time, it's the only measure of identity we have. There is no mystery to the self; we are what we do and where we have been. So we have to resurrect the past constantly, erect monuments to it, and keep it alive in order to remember who we are.

For some, even our darkest past moments are preferable somehow to those few interludes of peace and sunshine in the world. Why? God only knows. I thought about the followers of Pancho Villa who found his assassination and the end of his violent era so unacceptable that they dug up his corpse, sawed the head from the trunk, sank it in a huge glass jar of white rum, and brought it in a Model T Ford to the Van Horn Mountains outside of El Paso, where they entombed it under a pile of orange rocks. At night for years thereafter, they would remove the rocks and drink mescal and smoke marijuana in the hot wind and talk to his bloated, leering face floating against the glass.

But I was looking at another kind of dark history now. The retired two-star general had not been hard to find. His full name was Jerome Gaylan

Abshire, and he lived right here in New Orleans, in the Garden District off St Charles Avenue. He was a West Point graduate, and he'd had a distinguished combat record in World War II and Korea. A 1966 color photograph showed him eating out of a GI mess kit with his men in an LZ cut out of the elephant grass in the central highlands of Vietnam. He wore an automatic pistol in a shoulder holster over his bare, leathery chest; his face was deeply tanned, his eyebrows and hair very white, his eyes the intense blue of a butane flame. A creative journalist had called him 'The Happy Warrior' in the cutline.

But I ran across another Jerome Gaylan Abshire in the newspaper files, this one a junior, a US Army lieutenant, obviously his son. His name first appeared in a 1967 story when he was listed as missing in action; then I found a second clipping dated November 1, 1969, that described how two American prisoners held by the Vietcong in an area called Pinkville had been tied to posts with their heads inserted in wooden cages filled with rats. The article said one of these soldiers may have been Lieutenant Jerome Abshire of New Orleans.

The word 'Pinkville' leaped off the page like a sin not confessed and deliberately forgotten. It was the name that GIs called the area around My Lai.

Then, as though the newspaper librarian had made the same associations as I, he or she had attached a crossreferenced Xerox copy of an article about some testimony at the court-martial of Lieutenant William Calley, when he was tried for ordering the My Lai massacre. One of the grunts who had taken the stand said in a parenthetical aside that some captured Vietcong had told him that two American prisoners had helped them string mines through a rice field, the same field in which his company had been blown apart.

I was tired. My system was beginning to crave alcohol again, and the place names, the dates, a photograph of villagers executed on a trail, filled me with a sadness and despair that made me close the file, flick off the viewing screen, walk to the window, and stare out into the darkness for a full minute, hoping that no one in the room saw my eyes.

I never saw an American atrocity, at least not a deliberate one, so I did not have those kinds of memories from the war. Instead, if there was one experience that encapsulated my year in Vietnam, it was a strange incident involving two men in my platoon and a drowning water buffalo.

They were almost all Southerners, from textile and cannery and cotton-gin towns where young people seldom expected more than Saturday nights at the drive-in movie with others like themselves who would wear their high school jackets years after their graduation. We had walked twenty miles out of Indian country into a secured area by a tree-lined, milky brown river, and the men had dropped their packs and rifles and undressed, and were splashing around in the shallows like boys. The late-afternoon sun was warm through the trees and dappled the ground with shadow. I hadn't slept in a day and a half, and I lay down in the cool, short grass under a banyan tree, put my arm across my eyes, and in seconds I was asleep.

I awoke a half hour later to giggling and laughter and the drowsy smell of marijuana. Somebody had scored some Cambodian red, and the whole platoon was getting loaded. I got up stiffly from under the tree, walked down the bank, and realized they were all being entertained by a scene taking place in the middle of the river. A water buffalo had wandered out into the hard current, had become stuck in the silt on the bottom, and was now floundering and barely able to keep its nostrils above the surface. Its eyes were wide with terror, its horns webbed with debris from the river. The owner of the buffalo, who wore a French legionnaire's flop hat on his pointed head and who was so thin and bony that he looked like he was made of coat hangers, ran up and down the bank, waving his arms and shouting at us in Vietnamese and scraps of French.

Two cousins from Conroe, Texas, had waded in after the buffalo with a lariat they had fashioned from a rope they had taken out of the back of a Marine Corps six-by. Their brown backs were wet and ridged with muscle and vertebrae, and they were grinning and laughing and flinging out their lariat with all the stoned confidence of nineteen-year-old cowboys.

'There's dropoffs out there,' I said.

'Watch this, Lieutenant,' one of them called back. 'We'll slide this honker out slicker than a hog's pecker.'

Then suddenly out of the brown current I saw the gnarled, black roots of a floating tree break through the surface and reach into the air like an enormous claw.

It hit them broadside with such force that their faces went white. Their mouths gasped open, then spat water. They tried to push away from the roiling, yellow foam around the tree and the roots that spiked their eyes and twisted their faces into contortions. The tree spun around in the current, shining with mud, caught new momentum, and pressed them under. We waited for them to surface on the other side, to pop up in a calm place, rattling water and light from their hair, but we never saw them again.

We probed the river with poles and dragged it with a grappling hook for three hours. Instead of our own people, we dredged up belts of French machine-gun ammunition, a box of unexploded Japanese potato mashers that leaked rust and green slime on the bank, American soda-pop cans, and a cargo net filled with Vietcong dead that must have been dropped by one of our helicopters. When the hook pulled the net tautly from the water's surface, we saw arms and heads draped through the webbing like those of prisoners long since tired of their eternal sentence.

I wrote letters to the families of the two boys in Conroe, Texas. I said they had given their lives in trying to help others. Their lives had not been *taken*; they were *given*. I did not say I regretted there were no medals for innocence and the trusting courage it took to keep being a Texas country boy in a land that seemed created for jaded and transient colonials.

An hour later I was in a wonderful old bar on Magazine Street, which separated the Garden District from a huge black residential area of paintless, wooden nineteenth-century houses whose sagging galleries and dirt yards reminded me of the Negro quarters on the plantations in Iberia Parish. The bar, like many buildings along Magazine, had a wooden colonnade in front, big windows and screen doors, and inside was a long mahogany counter with a brass rail, overhead fans, walls filled with Hadacol and Dixie 45 and Dr Nut signs, and Earl K. Long political posters, and a blackboard with the name of major-league teams and ball scores chalked all over it. The owner used to be a submarine pitcher for the Lafayette Bulls in the defunct class-C Evangeline League, and he had never been quite able to extricate himself from yesterday. He sold loose-string Virginia Extra tobacco and cigarettes out of cartons on the shelf, covered the pool table with oilcoth on Thursday nights and served free chicken gumbo as bar owners often did back in the bayou country, never called the cops to settle a beef, kept hard-boiled eggs in big pickle jars on the bar, and made hot *boudin* that would break your heart. It was always cool and softly lighted inside, and the jukebox was full of *zydeco* and Cajun records, and workingmen shot pool in the back under a red Jax sign and a tin-shaded swinging light.

Archie, the owner, picked up my empty *boudin* plate and wiped under it with a rag. He was a dark Cajun with a big round face and a small mouth. His arms were covered with black hair. I motioned with my shot glass for a refill.

'You know why they call them boilermakers, Dave?' he asked. 'Because they put pieces of foundry plate in your head, like broken metal teeth.'

'Sounds like bad stuff.'

'Then one day it chews its way through your brain.'

'Can I have another shot of Beam?'

'I don't like to argue against my own profits, but I hate to see you sit on the porch and listen to your liver rot.'

'Would it make you feel better if I told you I'm not enjoying it?'

'Ease up tonight. You can have a shithouse of misery any day you want.'

I looked away from his face. He was a friend and an honest man, and because I had no defense, I knew I was capable of insulting people, even an old friend, to save my situation.

'I got another problem, too. Your slip's showing,' he said.

'What?'

'Wearing a pistol as big as a cornbread pan on your hip gives anxiety to some people.'

'Here,' I said, unsnapping the holster from my belt. 'Stick it under the bar till I leave.'

'What the hell is wrong with you, Dave? Are you trying to take a big fall? Why invite more trouble in your life?'

'It came free of charge.'

'I'm talking about tonight. They took your badge. That means you can't walk around like Wyatt Earp.'

'Do you know anything about a retired general named Jerome Abshire over on Prytania?'

'A little bit. His kid used to come in here.'

'Is he a right-wing crazy?'

'No, I don't think so. I always heard he was a kind of classy guy. His kid was a hell of a fine boy, though. He used to come in here with his baseball team when he went to Tulane. He was a big, blond boy with a pitching arm like a whip. He was always arm-wrestling and tussling and having fun. It was a shame he disappeared over there in Vietnam.'

'Does anybody know what happened to him?'

'Just a lot of stories. He was captured, he was missing, the Vietcong executed him or something. My boy was over there, but he came back home all right. I tell you the truth, Dave, if I'd lost him, I'd be afraid what I'd do.'

'I've got to cruise. We'll see you around, Archie.'

'I hope so. Don't crowd the plate when you don't have to, podna.'

I drove into the Garden District. The neighborhood was filled with homes that had been built during the 1850s. They were pillared and scrolled, marked with widow's walks and latticework, wide porches and second-story verandas, with brick courtyards and gazebos on the lawns. The streets were lined with oaks and the yards themselves seemed to explode with every type of Southern flower and tree: blooming myrtle, azalea, bamboo, umbrella and banana tree, elephant ears, hibiscus, tangles of red and yellow roses. I could smell barbecue fires and hear people diving in swimming pools. It was a neighborhood of historical security and endless summer parties that flowed from one thick, clipped lawn onto the next.

Jerome Gaylan Abshire's home was no exception. The brick walk was lighted by burning candles placed inside paper bags in the flower beds, and through the tall windows beyond the front porch I could see the guests crowded in a large living room lighted by chandeliers. The loud conversation reached all the way to the street. A band was playing on the lawn somewhere in the back.

Why not? I thought. I had on a coat and tie. Archie was right. Why crowd the plate when it was just as easy to throw the bat at the pitcher's head?

I parked the car up the street and walked back to the party. The sidewalk was buckled and peaked by the enormous roots that grew under the concrete. I buttoned my coat so my .45 wasn't apparent, combed my hair, flattened my tie with the palm of my hand, and walked up the brick entrance with my eyes fixed steadily on the face of the man checking invitations at the door.

He probably worked for a security service and was not accustomed to handling anybody more serious than college party-crashers.

'I don't have an invitation. I'm the New Orleans heat,' I said.

'May I see your identification?'

'Here's a quarter. Call the First District and tell them Lieutenant Dave Robicheaux is here.'

'I think you're drunk, sir.'

I brushed past him, went to the bar, and picked up a glass of champagne off a tray. The rooms were furnished with French antiques, gold and silver grandfather clocks, deep purple divans with scrolled walnut frames, oil portraits of a Southern military family that went back to the War of 1812. The blond hardwood floors were waxed to a shine that looked like clear plastic. Every tabletop, brass candelabra, ashtray, glass light chimney, and polished strip of seamed woodwork gleamed as though it had been rubbed incessantly with soft rags.

The people in the room were an older crowd, undoubtedly wealthy, confident in themselves and their friends and the world of manners and success in which they lived. The women had bluing in their hair and wore glittering evening dresses, and their throats and wrists dripped with jewelry. In their white tuxedo coats, the men gave you the impression that age was no more a physical problem in their lives than the remote struggles of the poor. It was obvious that I didn't belong there, but they were too polite to look directly at me.

But the security man at the door was talking with two others who looked like rent-a-cops, and all three of them were staring at me. I put down my empty champagne glass, picked up another, and walked out the French doors onto the back patio, where a half-dozen black cooks in white jackets were making mint juleps and barbecuing a pig impaled on a roasting spit. The wind rustled through the oaks, the banana trees, the bamboo border of the lawn, and ruffled the unlit water in the swimming pool that was as dark as burgundy wine. One of the elderly black cooks fanned the barbecue smoke away from his face with his hand.

'Where's the general gone to?' I asked.

'He having his julep in the library with the other gentlemens,' he said.

'I don't want to go back through that big crowd. Is there another way I can get to the library?'

'Yes suh. Go back through the kitchen. The girl tell you where it's at.' I walked across the clipped lawn, went through a huge Colonial-style kitchen with brick in the walls, where three black maids were making hors d'oeuvres, and came out in a hallway. I could see the library door partly open and two men with highball glasses in their hands talking to somebody who sat in a chair with his legs crossed. I recognized one of the standing men immediately. I pushed the door, sipped out of my champagne glass, and smiled at the three of them.

The general had gained weight since the newspaper photograph was taken, but his skin was still deeply tanned and glowing with health, the white hair was cut GI, and his acetylene-blue eyes looked at you with the unflinching clarity of a man who was never inhibited by complexity or moral doubt.

'How are you doing, General?' I said. 'It's amazing who might drop in on a cocktail party these days. I'm speaking about myself, of course. But what are you doing with a character like Whiplash Wineburger? Most people call the Orkin Company if they see this guy anywhere near their neighborhoods.'

'I'll take care of it,' Wineburger said, and moved his hand to the table phone.

'It's all right,' the general said.

'I don't know about that,' I said. 'I think some of your cadre are starting to unravel. I've got a couple of Polaroids of Bobby Joe Stark-weather lying out behind his fish camp. You can have them for post-cards.'

'You'll be treated as a guest in my home, even though you came here uninvited. You can go back to the bar, or you can leave.'

'I'm comfortable here.'

'You've had too much to drink, or perhaps you're simply obsessive,' he said. 'But there's no point in your being here.'

'You should have stuck with regular army, General. These guys work-ing for you wouldn't even measure up to Mafia standards. Wineburger here is a jewel. One time a naïve cop down at the First District asked him to defend some indigent Haitians, and he said, "I'm full up on food stamps." It's the amateurs that kill the IPs.'

'What do you know about IPs?'

'I was in Vietnam, too, except my outfit went out of its way to protect innocent people. I don't think you can say the same.'

'How dare you!' he said.

'Cut the gentlemanly rancor. You've got Sam Fitzpatrick's blood painted all over you, and I'm going to nail you for it.'

'Ignore him. He's a lush,' Wineburger said.

'I'll give you something else to work on, too,' I said. 'I visited the father of that nineteen-year-old girl that Segura's people murdered. I wonder if you'd like to confront him and explain why she had to lose her life over some elephant game you and your cretins are playing.'

'Get out.'

'You lost a son in Vietnam. I think if he were alive he'd consider you a disgrace.'

'You leave my home. Don't you ever enter it again.'

'You'll get no rest from me, General. I'm going to be the worst thing in your life.'

'No, you won't, Robicheaux,' Wineburger said. 'You're a motormouth and you smell bad. You're just a jitterbird that everybody is bored with.'

'Whiplash, how do you think you got in here? Because you're a brilliant attorney? Most of these people don't like Jews. They're paying for your ass right now, but when they don't need you anymore, you might end up like Bobby Joe or Julio. Think about it. If you were the general, would you keep a lowlife like yourself around?'

'Turn around. Some of your colleagues want to talk with you,' Wineburger said.

Two uniformed street cops stood behind me. They were young, and they had their hats off and were uncomfortable at their situation. One of them tried to smile at me.

'Bad night, huh, Lieutenant?' he said.

'Don't worry about it,' I said. 'I'm wearing my rock-'n'-roll cassette, though. Just unbutton my coat and pull it out.'

His hand brushed across my stomach, almost like a caress, and eased the .45 out of my belt holster.

'Walk this way with us. We'll go out the side door,' he said. 'But we'll have to cuff you in the car.'

'It's all right,' I said.

'Hey, Robicheaux, call that colored bondsman on Rampart. He gives credit,' Wineburger said.

I glanced back at the general, whose tanned brow was webbed with wrinkles as he stared intensely into space.

They booked me into the drunk tank downtown. I woke up with the first gray light on an iron bunk whose gray paint was covered with scratched and rusted names and obscenities. I sat up slowly, holding the bunk on each side of me, and smelled the rancid odor of stale sweat, cigarette smoke, alcohol, urine, vomit, and the seatless and caked toilet in the corner. The floor and all the bunks, which were suspended from wall chains, were filled with snoring drunks, demented street people, barroom brawlers still flecked with blood, a few genuine badasses, and anxiety-ridden, middle-class DUIs who later would expect to be treated with the courtesy due good Kiwanians.

I walked in my socks to the toilet and leaned over it. Names had been burned into the yellow paint of the ceiling with cigarette lighters. My eyes watered from the reek of the toilet, and my hangover had already started to tighten the veins in my head like a hatband. Ten minutes later a guard and a trusty in white fatigues opened the barred door and wheeled in a stainless-steel food cart loaded with powdered scrambled eggs, grits, and black coffee that tasted like iodine.

'Hors d'oeuvres time, gentlemen,' the guard said. 'Our accommodations are humble, but our hearts are warm. If you're planning to stay for lunch today, we're having spaghetti and meatballs. Please do not ask for doggy bags. Also, even though it's a temptation, don't try to take the food home in your pockets.'

'Who the fuck is this guy?' asked a soldier sitting on the floor. His tie hung loose around his neck, and the buttons were torn off his shirt.

'He's a pretty good guy,' I said.

'Some place for a fucking comedian,' he said, and flipped his cigarette butt off the wall above the toilet.

I waited until the trusty had passed out the paper plates of eggs and grits and he and the guard had gone back out the door, then I went to the bars and clicked my ring against the metal to get the guard's attention. He looked at me without expression, blinking his eyes to hide either recognition or his embarrassment.

'Is arraignment at eight?' I asked.

'They'll put you on the wrist-chain then. I don't know what time they'll get to you.' He almost said 'Lieutenant,' but he clamped his lips tightly.

'Who's on the bench this morning?'

'Judge Flowers.'

'Oh boy.'

'You want a lawyer with you?'

'No, not just yet. Thanks, anyway, Phil.'

'You bet. Hang tough. It's going to be all right. Everybody's got a right to a hard night sometimes.'

An old man with a wild, tobacco-stained beard sat down beside me on the iron bunk. He wore plastic cowboy boots, jeans that fit him like balloons, and a denim shirt cut off at the armpits.

'You ain't gonna eat your food?' he said.

'No. Go ahead.'

'Thanks,' he said, and began putting the dry eggs in his mouth with a plastic spoon. 'The spiders starting to crawl around in your head?'

'Yep.'

'Look down in my boot,' he said. 'The hack missed it when they shook me down. Take a snort. It'll swat them spiders right back into their nest.'

I looked down at the pint bottle of whiskey inside his boot. I breathed deeply and ran my tongue over my cracked lips. My own breath was stronger than the smell of the drunk tank. It wouldn't be long before I would start sweating and shaking, maybe even going into the dry heaves. I wondered what I would look like in front of Judge Flowers, a notorious morning-court jurist who could put the fear of God into a drunk with his gavel.

'I'll pass right now, but I appreciate it, partner,' I said.

'Suit yourself. Don't let them shake you up, though, son. I been up in front of this court so many times they don't even mess with me. The judge gives me thirty days and tells me to get out. That ain't nothing. We got them by the short hairs.'

A half hour later, Sergeant Motley stood at the tank door with the guard. He smoked a cigar and looked on quietly while the guard turned the key in the lock. He wore his shirt lapels pressed back so the hair on his black barrel of a chest stuck out like wire.

'Come with us, Robicheaux,' he said.

'Zoo visitors aren't allowed in until this afternoon,' I said.

'Just come along,' he said.

I walked between him and the guard to the far end of the jail corridor. A trusty was damp-mopping the floor, and our shoes left wet imprints where he had cleaned. Sunlight came through the windows high up on the corridor wall, and I could hear traffic out on the street. The guard turned the lock on an individual cell. Motley's weight made him breathe as though he had emphysema.

'I got you transferred to a holding cell,' he said.

'What for?'

'You want somebody in that tank to make you?'

I stepped inside the cell, and the guard locked me in. Motley remained at the door, his cannonball head beaded with perspiration from the heat outside.

'What are you up to?' I asked.

'I've been in your shoes. I think they're putting a RotoRooter up your hole, and all you've got going for you is your own balls. That's okay, but after a while they get ground down to the size of marbles.'

'I have a hard time buying this.'

'Who asked you to? We never got along. But I'll tell you a story, Robicheaux. Everybody thinks I let those seven guys die in that elevator to save my own buns. I was responsible, all right, but not because I was afraid. I didn't have the key to the chain. I didn't have the fucking key. I climbed up out of the shaft to find somebody with a master. When we pried the doors open, they looked like smoked oysters in there. Whether you believe me or not, that's some hard shit to live with.'

'Why don't you tell that to somebody?'

'You know why I didn't have the key? I got a freebie that morning from one of Julio Segura's broads and she rolled me. The key was in my billfold.'

'You tried to get them out, Motley.'

'Tell that to everybody in the courthouse and the First District. Tell it to Purcel. He's always got clever things to say to a black man.'

'What's he been doing?'

'I don't like those guys in Internal Affairs any more than you do. In my opinion, Purcel is operating in their area. I don't drop the dime on other cops, not even racists, so I don't comment on Purcel.'

'He's not a racist.'

'Wake up, Robicheaux. You got to get hit in the face with it? The guy's got a hard-on all the time. Quit the Little Orphan Annie routine.'

'You're determined to make people love you, aren't you?'

'Read it like you want. I hope you get out of this crap. I don't think you will.'

'You're a breath of fresh air, buddy.'

'They stiffed you on the charge. I'd get out of town if I were you. I think they're going to put you away.'

I touched the side of my face to the bar and looked at him silently. I could feel the pulse working fearfully in my throat.

'They charged you with carrying a concealed fire-arm,' he said, and looked back at me with his knowing, hard brown eyes. It was a lowball morning. I went to court on a chain with four other drunks, a street dealer, a psychotic exhibitionist, and a black kid who had murdered a filling-station attendant for sixty-five dollars. Judge Flowers was what we called at AA a white-knuckler. He had gotten off the booze on his own, but he'd stayed dry only by redirecting his intense inner misery into the lives of others, particularly those who stood before him blowing alcohol in his face. He set my bond on the concealed firearm charge at ten thousand dollars.

I didn't even have the thousand I would need to pay the bondsman's ten-percent fee. I sat on the bunk of the holding cell and stared at the scato-logical words scratched all over the opposite wall. It was the lowest morning of my life, except perhaps for the day my wife left me for the Houston oilman. We had gone to an evening lawn party out by the lake, and he had been there and did not even make a pretense about the affair they were having. He touched shoulders with her at the drink table, brushed his palm across the down on top of her arm, smiled good-naturedly at me with his rugged good looks, as though we enjoyed an intelligent understanding of our situation. Then a lesion snapped open somewhere behind my eyes; I felt color rise into my vision, the way a glass might fill with red water, then a woman screamed and I felt men's arms lifting me up from the lawn, pulling me away from his stunned, terrified face.

In the morning I found her note on the table under the big umbrella where we ate breakfast while the sun rose across Lake Pontchartrain.

Dear Dave,

I don't know what it is you're looking for, but three years of marriage to you have convinced me I don't want to be there when you find it. Sorry about that. As your pitcher-bartender friend says, Keep it high and hard, podjo.

Nicole.

'What are you doing with your clothes off?' the guard asked through the bars of the holding cell.

'It's hot.'

'There's people that walk through here.'

'Don't let them.'

'Jesus Christ, Dave, get your act together.'

'I got it solidly together. I'm very copacetic at the moment.' I opened and closed my palms. I watched the way the veins in my forearms filled with blood.

'Unless you bond out, I got to move you. You got to go into the main population unless you want lockdown.'

'Do what you need to do, Phil.'

'I can't put you in lockdown if you don't request it. Dave, there's some real badasses upstairs.'

I fingered the *pungi*-stick scar on my stomach. Somebody was shouting hysterically in a cell down the corridor, then a cop's baton rang on the bars.

'I'm going to get the doctor. You're going into lockdown whether you like it or not,' he said.

I heard him walk away. My head felt as if piano wire were twisted around it. I closed my eyes and saw balloons of orange flame erupt out of a rain forest, GIs locked up to their knees in a muddy shimmering rice field while the shards of Claymores sang through the air with the edges of boiler plate, the souls of children rising like gunsmoke from the ditch where they lay, Sam Fitzpatrick's boyish face lighted in the purgatorial fire of a holy card. The sweat leaked out from under my palms and ran down my naked thighs.

At three o'clock that afternoon, another guard walked down the corridor of the isolation unit, called 'Queen's Row,' where I was in lockdown with the snitches, pyschotics, and roaring homosexuals. The door of my small cell was made of metal grillwork, with a slit and an iron apron for the trusty to pass in the food tray. The guard was having trouble with the key in the lock, and the light behind him made his body seem to jerk and disconnect itself through the squares in the door.

'Pack it up. You're going all the way,' he said.

'What happened?'

'Somebody went bail for you. Strip your sheets and throw them into the corridor. Pick up that plastic spoon off the floor and drop your soap in the toilet.'

'What?'

'You still drunk or something? Clean out your cell if you want to leave here today.'

We walked down the corridor to the hydraulically operated double-barred doors that gave onto the booking room, where two black women were being fingerprinted. I signed at the possessions desk for the large brown envelope tied with string that contained my wallet, car keys, pocket knife, and belt.

'Happy motoring,' the trusty clerk said.

Out in the visitors' area I saw Annie sitting on a wooden bench with her hands pinched together in her lap. She wore blue tennis shoes, Clorox-faded jeans, and a print shirt covered with purple flowers. The tables in the rooms were filled with inmates and their families who had come to visit them, and each group tried to isolate themselves in their intimate moment by bending their heads forward, never focusing their eyes beyond their own table, holding one another's forearms tightly in their hands. Annie tried to smile at me, but I saw the nervousness in her face.

'Are you all right?' she asked.

'Sure.'

'My car's right at the curb. We can go now.'

'Sure, let's get out of here.'

'Dave, what's wrong?'

'The bastards took my piece. I ought to get a receipt for it.'

'Are you crazy?' she whispered.

'Forget it. Let's go.'

We went through the glass doors onto the street, and the afternoon heat hit me like somebody opening a furnace door next to my skin. We got into her car and she started the engine, then looked across at me with a cloud in her face. My arm jerked when it touched the burning metal on the window.

'Dave, are you okay? Your face is white,' she said.

'I'm running on some weird fluids. Just consider the source and don't take everything I say to heart today. How did you know I was in jail?'

'Your partner, what's his name, Clete, called. He said something strange, but he told me to tell it to you just like he said it – "You still own yourself, Streak. That's a big victory. Disconnect from this dogshit while there's time." What's he talking about?'

'It means part of him is still intact. I'm not sure if the same is true of me. I think I felt all the stitches pop today.'

She steered into the traffic. The yellow haze, the heat off the concrete, the hot leather against my back, the acrid gasoline fumes around me, filled my head with a sensation that was like breathing over a tar-roofer's pot on a summer day.

'I don't know much about alcohol and drinking problems, Dave. Do you want to stop for a beer? I don't mind. Isn't it better to taper off sometimes?'

She had made it very easy, and at that moment I think I would have cut my fingers off one at a time with tin snips for a frosted quart of Jax beer.

'I'd just appreciate it right now if you'd drive me to my houseboat. Did you have to put up a thousand for the bondsman?' I said.

'Yes.'

'I'll make it good tomorrow. I'm suspended from the credit union, but I'm going to take a loan out on the boat.'

'I'm not thinking about that. Last night you tried to make amends, and I sent you away.'

'You had someone coming for dinner.'

'He was just a friend from the music school. He would have understood.'

'Let me explain something. My getting thrown in jail doesn't have anything to do with you. I had four years of sobriety, and I blew it in.'

'You can stop again.'

I didn't answer. We were on Elysian Fields Avenue, headed out toward the lake. My seersucker suit was rumpled and stained with tobacco juice from the jail, and the skin of my face felt grimy and unshaven under my hand.

'Pull in by that eating place, will you?' I said.

She parked next to a café that had an open-air counter and tables under shade trees where people ate poor-boy sandwiches and bleeding slices of watermelon. I ordered two Dr Peppers in paper cups packed with crushed ice and asked the waiter to add a handful of candied cherries and cut limes. I sat in the car and drank out of the cup with both hands, and the slide of ice and bruised cherries and syrupy soda ached wonderfully all the way down my throat and into my stomach.

'When I was a kid in New Iberia, we had a drink called Dr Nut. It tasted just like this,' I said. 'My father always bought my brother and me a Dr Nut when we went to town. That was a big treat back then.'

'How do you think of the past, Dave?' she asked. Her curly hair blew in the wind through the window while she drove.

'What do you mean?'

'What feelings do you have when you remember your father?'

'I think of him with fondness.'

'That's right, you do, even though your family was poor and sometimes your father wasn't there when you needed him. You didn't take any
anger toward him into your adult life. You forgave him and you remember what was best about him. Why not do the same for yourself.'

'It's not that simple with some people's metabolisms.'

'Today is Saturday, and it's Saturday all day long, and I don't care
about what happened yesterday, at least not about the bad things. I like
being with you and remembering good things and knowing it's going to
get better all the time. Don't they teach something like that at AA?'

'That's pretty close.'

'Will you take me to the horse races tonight?'

I touched the damp, curly hair at the nape of her neck and brushed the
smoothness of her cheek with my fingers. She smiled at me with her eyes
and patted me on the thigh, and I felt a weakness drain through my body
like water and then settle and swell in my loins.

When we got to Lake Pontchartrain it was like walking out from under
a layer of steam into a slap of cool, salt-smelling air. Pelicans dove for
fish out of the blue sky, plummeting downward with their wings cocked
behind their heads as though they had been dropped from a bomb rack,
exploding in the smoky green water and rising suddenly with silvery fish
flipping helplessly in their beaks. Far out in the horizon the water was
capping in the sunlight, and a long, gleaming white yacht with red sails
was dipping into the troughs and sending geysers of foam bursting into
the air.

I showered and shaved in my tin stall and felt the smell of the jail, its
physical touch was like an obscene hand, go out of my body. I washed
carefully around the stitches in my scalp, then I pulled off the old dressing
on my shoulder and arm, where the chips of glass had been embedded,
and let the water run warmly on the crusted skin. Annie was cooking bass
fillets and spinach with hard-boiled eggs on my small stove, and for the
first time that day I felt hunger. I dried off, sat on the side of the bed with
the towel wrapped around my waist, and opened the plastic first-aid box
in which I kept the bandages and ointment to dress my shoulder and arm.
I could have done it myself. Pride and a larger measure of self-respect
actually required it. I looked at the closed curtain and heard Annie turn
the pots down on the stove.

'Annie, I need you to help me,' I said.

She slid back the curtain on the door.

'I have a little trouble getting these bandages into place,' I said.

She sat beside me, wiped ointment on my cuts with a piece of cotton,
snipped adhesive tape into strips with the scissors, and taped down two
big, folded squares of gauze on top of the ointment. Then she rubbed
her hands over my skin, down my shoulders and back, across my chest,
her eyes looking over my body without embarrassment, as though she

were discovering me for the first time. I leaned her back on the bed and kissed her mouth, her neck, unbuttoned her flowerprint blouse and placed my head against the red birthmark on her breast. I felt her body stretch out against mine, felt the confidence, the surrender that a woman gives in that moment when she no longer hides her hunger and instead blesses you with a caress that is always unexpected and heart-rushing and humbling in its generosity.

This time I wanted to give her more than she gave me, but I wasn't able. In seconds I was lost inside her, her hands tight against my back, her legs in mine in almost a maternal way, and when I tried to tense and stop because it was too soon, she held my face close to hers, kissed my cheek, ran her fingers through the back of my hair, saying, 'It's all right, Dave. Go ahead. It's all right.' Then I felt all the anger, the fear, and the heat of the last two days rise inside me like a dark bubble from a well, pause in its own gathered energy and momentum, and burst away into light, into the joy of her thighs, the squeeze of her arms, the blue tenderness of her eyes.

That night at the track, while heat lightning danced in the western sky, we strolled among the flower gardens by the paddock, watched the hot-walkers cool out the thoroughbreds that had already run, smelled the wonderful odors of freshly raked and dampened sod and horse sweat and manure and oats in the stables, and looked with genuine wonder and admiration at the rippling sheen of the roans and black three-year-olds walking onto the tract under a halo of electric arc lights.

We cashed the daily double, a perfecta, two win, and three place tickets. The palm trees were purple against the flickering sky; the lake in the center-ground caught the stars and the moon, and when the surface shuddered in a gust of wind off the Gulf, the water streaked with quick-silver; I could smell oak trees and moss and night-blooming flowers. Gamblers and lovers pay big dues and enjoy limited consolations. But sometimes they are enough.

9

The sky was pink over the lake at dawn the next day, and I put on my running shoes and tennis shorts and ran five miles along the lakefront with the wind cool in my face and the sun warm on my bare back. I could feel the sweat glaze and dry on my skin in the wind, and the muscles in my chest and legs seemed to have a resiliency and tension and life in them that I hadn't felt in weeks. Seagulls drifted on the air currents above the water's edge, their wings glided in the sunlight, when they would dip quickly down toward the sand and peck small shellfish from the receding foam. I waved at families in their cars on the way to church, drank orange juice at a child's street stand under a palm tree, and pounded down the asphalt with a fresh energy, my chest and head charged with blood, my heart strong, the summer morning part of an eternal song.

I could have run five more miles when I got back to the houseboat, but my phone was ringing. I sat on the edge of a chair and wiped my sweating face with a towel while I answered it.

'Why don't you trust your own family a little bit?' my brother Jimmie asked.

'What are you talking about?'

'I understand you bopped into an interesting scene the other night. Very stylish. There's nothing like crashing a Garden District party with a .45 on your hip.'

'It had been a dull night.'

'Why didn't you call me? I could have bonded you out in fifteen minutes. I might even have had a little influence on that concealed-weapons charge.'

'This is one you can't oil.'

'The point is, I don't like my brother being taken apart by some pencil-pushers.'

'You'll be the first to know the next time I'm in the bag.'

'Can you get somebody over there that speaks Spanish in the next half hour?'

'What for?'

'I told Didi Gee I'd get him in the Knights of Columbus. He likes me. Who else would eat lunch with a character like that except at gunpoint?'

'What are you doing, Jimmie?'

'It's already done. Presents come in strange packages. Don't question the fates.'

'Anything Didi Gee does has ooze and slime all over it.'

'He never said he was perfect. Stay cool, bro,' he said, and hung up.

I called a Cuban horse trainer I knew at the Fairgrounds and asked him to come to the houseboat. He arrived there ten minutes before a Cadillac limousine with tinted windows pulled up on the dead-end street by the sand dune and palm trees where my boat was moored, and two of Didi Gee's hoods, dressed in slacks, loafers, and shades, with flowered shirts hanging over their belts, got out and opened the back door with the electric motions of chauffeurs who might have been delivering a presidential envoy. Instead, an obviously terrified man sat in the gloom of the backseat with a third hoodlum next to him. He stepped out into the sunlight, swallowing, his face white, his pomade-slicked, kinky red hair and grease-pencil mustache like a parody of a 1930s leading man's. He held one palm around the fingers of his other hand.

'This guy asked us for a ride. Begged us to bring him here,' the driver said. 'We can't shut him up, though. All he wants to do is talk.'

'But give him something for his breath. It smells like sewer gas. The guy must eat dog turds for breakfast,' the other hood said.

'Hey, serious, he's got an interesting story,' the driver said. 'If somehow he don't remember it, tie a shirt on your TV antenna. I got to pick up a loaf of bread at the corner store a little later. We can help him fill in the empty spaces. We're just out for the morning air, anyway.'

I couldn't see either one of them well behind their shades, and Didi Gee's hired help tended to run of a kind – slender young Sicilians and Neapolitans who would blow out your lights as easily as they would flip away a cigarette – but I thought I'd seen the driver in a lineup two years ago after we'd prized parts of a bookie out of his own kitchen garbage compactor.

They drove off in their Cadillac, the white sun bouncing off the black-tinted glass in the rear.

'Andres, I wouldn't hang round with that bunch if I were you,' I said.

But you still can't accept gratuities when they're given to you on other people's terms, particularly when they came from somebody like Didi Gee. Besides, the fingers of the Nicaraguan's left hand were wrapped in tape, and I had an idea where they had been earlier. He sat at my kitchen table, rigid, his brown eyes riveted fearfully on me as though the lids were stitched to his forehead. I put a tape recorder, a Polaroid camera, and a pint of white rum on the table.

'I don't have a tank full of piranha here, and I'll take you to the hospital if you want to go,' I said to him through my Cuban friend, whose name was Jaime.

He did not need a hospital; the injuries were not serious; but he would very much appreciate a glass of Bacardi, no ice, please.

I opened the morning newspaper, pulled my chair around next to him, held up the front section between us so the headline and date were visible, and told Jimmie to take our picture with the Polaroid. The Nicaraguan's breath was awful, as though there were something dead in his lungs. He drank the rum and wiped his lips, and the wispy gray scars around his mouth shone like pieces of waxed string.

'I want you to understand something,' I said. 'You're going to be a cooperative person, but not because of Didi Gee's hoods and the business with your fingers. Those guys will not get to you again, at least not because of me. If you want, you can file assault and kidnapping charges against them. I'll drive you to either the police station or the FBI.'

He watched me carefully as Jaime translated. The thought of reporting Didi Gee's people to the authorities was evidently so absurd to him that his eyes didn't even register the proposal.

'But our photograph here is another matter,' I said. 'I'll make copies, many of them, and circulate them around town for those who might be interested. Maybe you have the trust of your friends, and this will be of little consequence to you. Maybe you are in command of your situation and this is childishness to you.'

His face clouded, and his eyes flicked meanly at me for a moment, the way an egg-sucking dog might if you pushed it inside a cage with a stick.

'*Qué quiere?*' his voice rasped.

It was a strange tale. It was self-serving, circumventive, filled in all probability with lies; but as with all brutal and cruel people, his most innocent admission and most defensive explanations were often more damning and loathsome in their connotations than the crimes others might accuse him of.

He had been a sergeant in Somoza's national guard for seven years, a door gunner on a helicopter, and he had flown in many battles against the communists in the jungles and the hills. It was a war of many civilian problems, because the communists hid among the villages and posed as workers in the rice fields and coffee plantations, and when the government helicopters flew too low they often took hostile fire from the ground, where the peasants denied there were any Sandinistas or weapons. What was one to do? Surely Americans who had been in Vietnam could understand. Those who fought wars could not always be selective.

The soldiers went forth in uniform, as men, in plain sight, while the communists threaded their way among the poor and fought with the methods of cowards and homosexuals. If I did not believe him, witness his eye, and he pulled down the skin on one side of his face and showed me the dead, puttylike muscle under the retina. Their gun-ship had come in low over a secured area, and down below he could see Indians stacking green hay in the field, then a rocket exploded through the armored floor of the helicopter, blew one man out the door, and left a steel needle quivering in Andres's eyeball. The American journalist who visited the army hospital in Managua did not seem interested in his story, nor did he take pictures of Andres as the journalists did of the communist dead and wounded. That was because the American press's greatest fear was to be called rightist by their own membership. Like the Maryknoll missionaries, they kept their own political vision intact by compromising the world in which others had to live.

If I was offended by his statement, I must remember that he did not choose exile in this country any more than he chose the ruination of his vocal cords and lungs.

'I heard his regular punch gave him some special gargle water,' I said.

'What?' Jaime said.

'He and some other guys gang-raped a girl before they executed her. Her sister poured muriatic acid in our friend's drink.'

'This is true?' Jaime asked. He was a small and delicate man with a sensitive face. He always wore a New York Yankees baseball cap and rolled his own cigarettes from illegal Cuban tobacco. His toylike face looked from me to the Nicaraguan.

'Our man from Managua is a big bullshitter, Jaime.'

The Nicaraguan must have understood me.

The story about the execution and the acid was a lie, he said, a fabrication of Philip Murphy and the *maricón* Starkweather. They took pleasure in the denigration of others because they were not real soldiers. Murphy was a morphine addict who made love to his own body with syringes. He pretended courage but was flaccid like a woman and could not bear pain. Did I really want to know how he, Andres, had his throat and lungs burnt out, how this terrible odor came to live in his chest like a dead serpent?

'I was blind in one eye, but I could not stop in the fight for my country,' Jaime translated for him. 'Just as they posed as priests and labor organizers, I went among them as a radical who hated the Somoza family. But a diseased *puta*, a worthless army slut, betrayed me because she thought I had given her the foulness of her organs. The Sandinistas cocked a pistol at my head and made me drink kerosene, then they lighted matches to my mouth. I suffered greatly at their hands, but my country has suffered more.'

'Where are Philip Murphy and the Israeli?' I asked.

'Who knows? Murphy lives in airports and pharmacies and finds people when he needs them. Jews stay with their own kind. Maybe Erik is with the rich Jew who owns the warehouse. They're a close and suspicious people.'

'What Jew? What warehouse?'

'The warehouse where the weapons to free Nicaragua are kept. But I don't know where it is, and I don't know their Jew. I'm only a soldier.'

His face was empty. His eyes had the muddy, stupid glaze of someone who believed that the honest expression of his ignorance was an acceptable explanation to those who had the power to make judgments.

'I'll give you an easier question, then,' I said. 'What did you all do to Sam Fitzpatrick before he died?'

Jaime translated, and the Nicaraguan's face became as flat as a shingle.

'Did you wire up his genitals?' I asked.

He looked out at the lake, his mouth pinched tight. He touched the rum glass with his fingers, then withdrew them.

'Murphy gave the orders, but I suspect you and Bobby Joe carried them out with spirit. Your experience stood you well.'

'I think this one has a big evil inside him,' Jaime said. 'I believe you should give him back to the people who brought him here.'

'I'm afraid they're not interested in him, Jaime. The man they work for just wanted to knock his competition around a little bit.'

His small face was perplexed under the brim of his baseball cap.

'We use them. They use us. It keeps everybody in business,' I said.

'If you don't need more of me, I'll go. Sunday is a bad day with this type of man. I've smelled that odor before. It comes out of a great cruelty.'

'Thank you for your help. I'll see you at the track.'

'Send him away, Dave. Even a policeman should not look into the darkness of this man's soul.'

I reflected upon Jaime's statement after he had gone. Yes, it was about time that the Nicaraguan became somebody else's charge, I thought.

I locked a handcuff on one of his wrists, walked him out to my rental car, and hooked the other end through the safetybelt anchorage on the back floor. I went back inside the houseboat, dropped the tape cassette in my pocket, and looked up the number of Nate Baxter, from Internal Affairs, in the phone book.

'I've got one of the guys that killed Fitzpatrick,' I said. 'I want you to meet me down at the office.'

'You've got who?'

'I've got the Nicaraguan in cuffs. I'm going to bring him in.'

'You're suspended, Robicheaux. You can't bring anybody in.'

'I can't book him, but I can sign a complaint.'

'Are you drinking?'

'Maybe I ought to drop by your house with him.'

'Listen, I can deal with you personally on any level you want. But you better not drag your bullshit into my life. If you haven't figured it out by this time, there's a lot of people that think you should be locked up in a detox unit. These are your friends I'm talking about. Other people think you're a candidate for a frontal lobotomy.'

'The last time you talked to me like this, I was in a hospital bed. Don't take too much for granted, Baxter.'

'You want to clarify that, make it a little more formal?'

I looked out at the sun beating on the water.

'I've got the man that helped kill a federal agent,' I said. 'He can clear me, and I'm bringing him in. If you want to ignore this phone call, that's your choice. I'm going to call Captain Guidry now, then I'm going down to the First District. Are you going to be there?'

He was silent.

'Baxter?'

'All right,' he said, and hung up.

Then I called Captain Guidry. His mother said he had gone to a band concert in the park. I poured out the rum remaining in the Nicaraguan's glass and started to wash the glass in the sink. Instead, I threw it as far as I could into the lake.

I could see the Nicaraguan's hot eyes looking at me in the rearview mirror. He had to bend forward because of the way his wrist was hand-cuffed to the floor, and his face was flushed and deaded with sweat in the seat.

'*Adónde vamos?*' he said.

I didn't answer him.

'*Adónde vamos?*'

I wondered which he feared most: Didi Gee's people, the city police, or Immigration. But, regardless, I wasn't going to help him about our destination.

'*Hijo de puta! Concha de tu madre!*' he said.

'Wherever it is, I don't think it's Kansas, Toto,' I said.

I parked in front of the First District headquarters on Basin, cuffed both of the Nicaraguan's wrists behind him, and led him by the arm into the building.

'Is Nate Baxter back there?' I asked the sergeant at the information desk.

'Yeah, he's sitting in your office. What are you doing, Dave?'

'Give Purcel a call for me. Tell him I have some freight he ought to check out.'

'Dave, you're not supposed to be down here.'

'Just make the call. It's not a big deal.'

'Maybe you should make it yourself.'

I set the Nicaraguan down on a wooden bench and used the phone on the sergeant's desk to call Clete at home. I don't know what I had in mind, really. Maybe I was still pulling for him. Or maybe like a jilted lover I wanted to deliver a little more pain in a situation that was beyond bearing it.

'I can't come down there now. Maybe later. Lois is going apeshit on me,' he said. 'She took all the beer bottles out of the icebox and busted them all over the fucking driveway. On Sunday morning. The neighbors are watering their lawns and going to church while beer foam and glass are sliding down my drive into the street.'

'Sounds bad.'

'It's our ongoing soap opera. Drop around sometime and bring your own popcorn.'

'Clete?'

'What is it?'

'Get down here.'

I led the Nicaraguan through the traffic squad room, which was filled with uniformed cops doing paperwork, into my office, where Nate Baxter sat on the corner of my desk. His sports clothes and two-toned shoes and styled hair gave you the impression of a Nevada real-estate salesman who would sell you a house lot located on an abandoned atomic test site.

I threw the tape cassette into his lap.

'What's this?' he asked.

'His confession. Also some information about gun smuggling.'

'What am I supposed to do with it?'

'Listen to it. I've got an interpreter on the tape, but you can get your own.'

'You taking coerced statements from suspects?'

'He had his options.'

'What the hell are you doing, Robicheaux? You know this isn't acceptable as evidence.'

'Not in a courtroom. But you have to consider it in an IA investigation. Right?'

'I can tell you now it's got about as much value as toilet paper.'

'Look, you're supposed to be an impartial investigator. There's a murder confession on that tape. What's the matter with you?'

'All right, I'll listen to it during working hours tomorrow. Then I'll tell you the same thing I told you today. But let's look at your real problem a minute. An unverifiable tape-recorder statement brought in by a suspended cop is worthless in any kind of investigation. You've been here fourteen years and you know that. Secondly, while you were on suspension you got yourself busted with a concealed weapon. I didn't do that to you. Nobody else around here did, either. So why not quit pretending I'm the bad actor that kicked all this trouble up your butt?

You got to deal with your own fall, Robicheaux. That's real. Your rap sheet is real, and so is your drinking history.'

'How about Andres here? Does he look like something I made up?'

My office enclosure was half glass, and the door was open and our voices carried out into the squad room.

'Is he going to make a statement?' Baxter asked.

'Is he go—'

'That's right. You got a tape. You got a guy. Now the tape's no good, so is the guy going to talk to us?'

I didn't answer. The backs of my legs were trembling.

'Come on, tell me,' Baxter said.

'He did it. He tortured a Treasury agent with a telephone crank, then burned him to death in my automobile.'

'And he's going to waive his rights and tell us all that? Then he's going to put his signature on it?'

'I'm still signing the complaint.'

'Glad to hear it.'

'Baxter, you're a sonofabitch.'

'You want to call names, be my guest.'

'Ease off, Lieutenant,' the desk sergeant said quietly in the doorway behind me.

I took my handcuff key from my pocket and unlocked one of the Nicaraguan's wrists, then hooked the loose end to the radiator pipe on the wall.

'Your trouble is you been making love to your fist so long you think you're the only guy around here with any integrity,' Baxter said.

I swung from my side, hard, with my feet set solidly, and caught him square on the mouth. His head snapped back, his tie flew in the air, and I saw blood in his teeth. His eyes were wild. Uniformed cops were standing up all over the squad room. I wanted to hit him again.

'You want to pull your piece?' I said.

'You've finished yourself this time,' he said, holding his hand to his mouth.

'Maybe so. But that doesn't get you off the hook. You want to do something?'

He lowered his hands to his sides. There was a deep purple cut, the shape of a tooth, in his lower lip and it was starting to swell. His eyes watched me carefully. My fist was still clenched at my side.

'Don't you hear well?' I said.

His eyes broke, and he looked at the uniformed cops watching him from the squad room.

'Use some judgment,' he said almost in a whisper, the threat and insult gone from his tone.

'Go on home, Lieutenant. It's no good for you here,' the sergeant said behind me. He was a big man, built like a hogshead, with a florid face and a clipped, blond mustache.

I opened my hand and wiped the perspiration off my palm on my slacks.

'Put my cuffs in my desk drawer for me,' I said.

'Sure,' the sergeant said.

'Look, tell Purcel—'

'Go home, Lieutenant,' he said gently. 'It's a nice day out. We can handle it.'

'I'm signing the complaint against this guy,' I said. 'Get ahold of Captain Guidry. Don't let anybody kick this guy loose.'

'It's no problem, Lieutenant,' the sergeant said.

I walked woodenly through the squad room, the skin of my face tight and dead against the collective stare of the uniformed officers. My hand was still shaking when I filled out the formal complaint of assault with a deadly weapon, kidnapping, and homicide against the Nicaraguan.

Outside, the glare of the sun was like a slap across the eyes. I stepped into the shade to let my eyes adjust to the light and saw Clete walking toward me in yellow and purple LSU T-shirt cut off at the armpits and a pair of red and white Budweiser shorts. The shadow of the building fell across his face and made him look like he was composed of disjointed parts.

'What's happening, Dave?' His eyes squinted at me out of the glare, but they didn't actually meet mine. He looked as though he were focusing on a thought just beyond my right ear.

'I brought in the Nicaraguan. Didi Gee's people dumped him on my dock.'

'The fat boy is rat-fucking the competition, huh?'

'I thought you might want to check him out.'

'What for?'

'Maybe you've seen him before.'

He lit a cigarette and blew the smoke out into the sunlight.

'You know you got blood on your right hand?' he said.

I took out my handkerchief and wiped my knuckles with it.

'What went on?' he said.

'Nate Baxter had an accident.'

'You punched out Nate Baxter? Jesus Christ, Dave, what are you doing?'

'Why'd you do it, Clete?'

'A lowlife is off the board. What do you care?'

'A bad cop would have used a throwaway. He would have just said Starkweather came up in his face with it and he had to smoke him. At least you didn't hide behind your badge.'

'You once told me yesterday is a decaying memory. So I got no memory of yesterday. I don't care about it, either.'

'Confront it or you'll never get rid of it, Clete.'

'You think all this bullshit is political and involves principles and national integrity or something. What you're talking about is a bunch of perverts and heroin mules. How you take them out is irrelevant. Bust 'em or smoke 'em, all anybody cares about is they're not around anymore. My uncle used to walk patrol in the Irish Channel back in the forties. When they caught some guys creeping the place, they broke their arms and legs with baseball bats and left one guy to drive the rest of them out of town. Nobody complained then. Nobody would complain if we did it now.'

'These guys don't hire part-time help.'

'Yeah? Well, I'll worry about that when I have the chance. Right now my home life is like living inside an Excedrin ad. I got a little heat rash and Lois thinks it's the gon.'

'Don't you think you've been working that domestic scam a long time?'

'Sorry to tire you with it, Streak.'

'I'm going to take those guys down. I hope you're not there when I do.'

He flipped his cigarette off the back of the passing truck. A sign showing a woman in a bathing suit was on the side.

'Why would I be?' he said. 'I'm just the guy that carried you two flights down a fire escape while a kid tried to notch our ears with a .22 rifle.'

'You can't win on the game you pitched last Saturday.'

'Yeah? Sounds like an AA meet. I'll see you around. Stay off the booze. I'll drink it for both of us. It's a lousy life.'

He walked back toward his automobile, his sandals flopping on the pavement, a big, lumbering man whose boiled, stitched face reminded me of a bleached melon about to explode in the sun.

I pretended to be a pragmatist, a cynic, a jaded war veteran, a vitriolic drunk, the last of the Louisiana badasses; but like most people I believed that justice would be done, things would work out, somebody would show up with the Constitution in his hand. That afternoon I kept the phone on the deck table while I washed down the boathouse, polished the brass and windows, and sanded and revarnished the hatch. I put on flippers and goggles and cooled off in the lake, diving down into the yellow-green light, feeling the power in my lungs and chest that were now free of alcohol, bursting to the surface with a ringing in my ears that was never the telephone.

Finally, at six-thirty Captain Guidry called and said that the Nicaraguan remained in custody and that he would question him himself in the morning and also contact Fitzpatrick's supervisor at the Federal Building.

I invited Annie over for a late supper, and we cooked steaks outside on my hibachi and ate under the umbrella in the cooling evening. The western horizon was aflame with the sun's afterglow, then the clouds became pink and purple and then finally you could see the city light the night sky.

The next morning I did one hundred sit-ups, worked out with light barbells for an hour while I listened over and over to the old original recording of Iry Lejeune's 'La Jolie Blonde,' made out a grocery list, then asked a college kid who lived down the beach to listen for my phone while I went to a loan company and borrowed three thousand dollars on my houseboat.

The sun was straight up and white in the sky when I got back. Captain Guidry had called a half hour earlier. I dialed his extension at the First District and was told he was in a meeting and would not be out for two hours. Then I called Fitzpatrick's supervisor at Alcohol, Tobacco and Firearms.

'What did you expect me to tell you this morning?' he asked. I could almost see his hand clenched on the receiver.

'I thought by this time maybe you'd questioned the Nicaraguan.'

'You must get up in the morning and brush your teeth in the toilet.'

'What's that supposed to mean?'

'You finally nail one of them and you turn him over to the same people who're letting you twist in the wind. They put him upstairs in the tank. Last night a couple of strungout blacks didn't like the way his breath smelled and they stuffed his head down the flooded floor drain and broke his neck.'

10

That afternoon I repaid Annie the one-thousand-dollar bail fee she had put up for me, then I searched in the Jefferson, Orleans, and St Bernard parish courthouses for commercial property deeds with Whiplash Larry Wineburger's name on them. I discovered that he was a slumlord of large proportions; but if he owned a warehouse in one of those three parishes, it was deeded under another name.

I went to an AA meeting that evening and later took Annie to dinner at the track. It was hot that night, and I slept on the deck of my houseboat, possibly a careless thing to do, but I felt so discredited by this time that I doubted if my now often-repeated story was a threat to anyone. The wind blew across the lake all night, and I slept so soundly in my hammock that I didn't wake until the sun was hard in my eyes.

I went to an early-morning AA meeting in the Quarter, then bought *beignets* and coffee from the Café du Monde and sat on a bench in Jackson Square and watched the sidewalk artists paint and sketch the tourists. It was still cool in the shade, and the breeze blew off the river. It smelled of coffee and pastry, shrimp in bins of ice, the trees and flowers in the Square, damp stone, the water sprinklers knocking through the banana leaves that grew over the top of the iron piked fence enclosing the park. I went inside St Louis Cathedral and bought a small book that narrated the history of the building and read it on the bench while a Negro street musician played a bottleneck guitar a few feet away from me.

I was ready to give up my pursuit. I knew I wasn't a coward or a quitter, but at some point reason had to reestablish itself in my life. I couldn't afford any more attrition. I had already had one slip, had progressed within minutes from one drink to a full-blown bender (as they say at the meetings, you pick it up where you left it off), and if I slipped again I wasn't sure I'd ever get back from it.

After I'd struck out at the courthouse, I'd even thought about creeping Wineburger's house or his law office. I knew people who would help me pull it off, too – thieves who worked in car washes, where they made impressions of the house keys on the automobile key ring; a very slick second-story man who ran a wrecking service and would pull the distributor cap off a car owner he wanted to burglarize, then tow the car around the block, cut duplicate keys on a machine he kept in the truck, return the car with a fraudulent bill for repairs, and clean out the house a week later.

But it wasn't worth it. Wineburger, the little Israeli, Philip Murphy, and the general were out there malfunctioning in society because others much more important and powerful than I allowed them to. When these guys ceased to fill a need for somebody else, they would be taken off the board. That sounds like a cynical conclusion for a man to arrive at while sitting on a shady stone bench on a cool morning under banana trees, but most honest, experienced cops will tell you the same thing. It's facile to blame the Supreme Court for the pornographic bookstores and the live sex shows. They usually exist because somebody on the zoning board is getting greased. Kids don't do dope because their parents and teachers are permissive. They do it because adults sell it to them. No psychological complexities, no sociological mysteries.

When people become tired of something, it will end. In the meantime, Dave Robicheaux isn't going to make much difference in the scheme of things. My brother Jimmie knew that. He didn't contend with the world; he dealt in electric poker machines and off-track betting, and I suspected that he sold whiskey and rum that came in from the Islands without tax stamps. But he was always a gentleman and everybody liked him. Cops ate breakfast free in his restaurant; state legislators got pig-eyed drunk at his bar; judges introduced him to their wives with expansive courtesy. His transgressions had to do with licences, not ethics, he used to tell me.

'The day those people don't want to gamble and drink, we'll both be out of jobs. In the meantime, go with the flow, bro.'

'Sorry,' I'd answered. ' "Flow" somehow suggests "effluent" to me. I guess I'm just imaginative.'

'No, you just believe in the world that should be, rather than the one that exists. That's why you'll always be the driven guy you are, Dave.'

'Is there any change for that?'

'What do I know? I'm just a restaurateur. You're that guy that fought the wars.'

As irony would have its way, my reverie was broken by a maroon Cadillac convertible with an immaculate white top that pulled to the curb twenty feet from my bench. Two of Didi Gee's hoods got out on each side. They were young, lithe, dressed in summer slacks and open-necked shirts with gold medallions around their necks. Their mirror sunglasses and tasseled Nettleton shoes were almost part of a uniform. What always struck me most about lower-level Mafia hoods were the insipid expressions, as though their faces had been glazed with tallow, and the lifeless speechpatterns that they believed passed for sophistication. The only political regime that ever dealt with them effectively was Mussolini's. The fascists tore out their hair and fingernails with pliers, shot them, or sent them to fight against the Greeks. The Mafia welcomed the Allied liberation in 1943 with great joy.

'Good morning, Lieutenant. Mr Giacano would like to invite you out to his house for brunch,' the driver said. 'You can drive out with us if you want. The road's tore up by Chalmette.'

'I'm not sure I place you with the sunglasses on. Is it Joe Milazzo?' I said.

'That's right. I used to run my uncle's pizza place right across from your office.'

But that wasn't why I remembered his name. He had been a runner for his uncle's book, and he used to lay off bets at the parimutuel when his uncle took on an overload. But I'd also heard a rumor a year ago that he and his uncle had doped a thoroughbred with a speedball that literally exploded the animal's heart on the far turn at the Fairgrounds.

'What's on Didi Gee's mind?' I said.

'He just said ask you out, Lieutenant.'

'I'm kind of tied up today.'

'He said if it's too far for you to drive, he'd like to have you as his guest for lunch at Mama Lido's.'

'Thank him for me just the same.'

'I think it's about these people that's been giving you all this trouble. If you want, you can use the phone in the car to talk with him.'

'I appreciate the help he tried to give me Sunday. But as he probably knows, it didn't do much good. In other words, take the Nicaraguans to the First District.'

He looked away toward the Pontalba Apartments on the corner, his face quietly exasperated.

'I'm kind of in a hard spot, Lieutenant,' he said. 'Mr Giacano is a nice guy to work for. He paid off my old man's hospital bills, he give my little boy a bicycle for Christmas, he don't let nobody pay for anything when we go to the club. A lot of guys would pay a lot to buy my job. But he don't like to hear words like "maybe" or "no" from a guy that waxes his cars and drives people around. If you ain't coming, I'd really appreciate you calling him up and telling him that.'

'I'm afraid you'll have to live with it, podna.'

'All right, I don't know from shit about Mr Giacano's business dealings. I'm not an ambitious person. I don't care about what don't concern me. But I got ears. I'm human. I can't turn into a potted plant just because people are talking around me. It's about some guy named Murphy. You're interested, Lieutenant, that's okay. But I done my job.'

I closed my book and took a bite of my *beignet*. I watched a woman sweeping out her storefront under the colonnade on the corner. Rolls of sausage and cheese were hung in the window, and a little black boy was spraying the boxes of grapes and plums along the front wall with a hose.

'Tell Didi Gee I'll meet him at Mama Lido's at noon,' I said.

Joe Milazzo smiled behind his sunglasses and put an unlit cigarette in his mouth.

'Don't get the wrong idea, Joe. I'm just an impulsive guy. Next time save the shuck for a Fuller Brush route,' I said.

His face went dead.

Didi Gee had reserved a private dining room at the back of the restaurant. It was hung with pink and lavender curtains that were tied back to give the illusion of windows on the walls, which were painted with wispy Venetian canal scenes, gondolas, boatmen in striped T-shirts with flat hats and mandolins. The baseboards and woodwork around the doors were painted with grapevines that wound their way up the corners to the ceiling, which was hung with clusters of green plastic grapes.

There must have been fifteen people at the long white table that was filled with bottles of red wine in wicker casks, bowls of spaghetti and meatballs, lasagna, shrimp cooked in some kind of tomato sauce that made your eyes wince, loaves of Italian bread that people broke apart with their hands and ate loudly with a shower of crumbs on the table-cloth.

What a crew to be seen with, I thought. Some of them were aging soldiers who had survived any number of gang wars and jolts in Angola and Lewisburg since 1950s, now thick-bodied and flatulent, with cigarette-and-whiskey throats and hair growing out of their ears and nostrils. Then there were the young ones like Joe Milazzo, who might have been raised in a vacant lot. There was always a hidden thought in their eyes that they couldn't quite conceal. They would hit anybody, even their own kind, just to earn a chair closer at the table to Didi Gee. They all ate like troglodytes, made the waitresses take the food back if it wasn't warm, complained about the chipped glass or a fork with dishwasher spots on it. The hostess who wandered in every ten minutes to ask if everything was all right looked as though she had swallowed a mouthful of bumblebees.

Didi Gee had saved the seat next to him for me. He wore a white suit and an orange-flowered shirt with the shirt lapels on the outside of his coat. A gold St Christopher's medal rested on the black hair that grew up to his throat. His chest and stomach were so huge that he had to keep his chair pressed back almost to the wall.

'You want wine?' he asked.

'No, thanks.'

'I heard you were drinking again. I say that only because it don't matter to me. Everybody's got a vice. It's what makes us human.'

'I'm not drinking today. Put it that way.'

'That's the one-day-at-a-time stuff, huh? I wish I could do that. I worry about stuff all the time I don't have control over.'

It was amazing, I thought, how the true indicators of a sudden change in your social status worked. Didi Gee no longer used the deferential 'Lieutenant' when he spoke to me, and his hoods were eating as though I were not there.

'I worry all the time about this operation I got to have,' he said. 'The longer I wait, the more they got to cut out of my hole. I just can't bring myself to face it. Maybe there're some things you're not supposed to accept. It ain't natural for a person to be leaking shit into a bag strapped to his side. Look what I got to sit on now. That's bad enough.'

He rose a little from his chair and exposed an inflated rubber cushion that was shaped like a toilet seat in a public restroom.

'I'm going over to Baylor Hospital in Houston and see what they say. All the best surgeons in New Orleans are Jews. A guy my size walks through the door and they start looking at my parts like they got meat prices stamped on them.'

'Maybe they'll find another way to help you, Didi.'

'That's right. Maybe I get the right doctors over there at Baylor and I'll just retire there. My brother died and left me an office building in San Antonio three blocks from this Alamo place. They got an amusement park there or something?'

'It's a historical—'

'Because even though I was born and grew up in New Orleans, I'm tired of people dumping on me, and nickel-and-dime legal farts trying to make a name by cutting off my cock.'

His voice had intensified suddenly, like heat building down in a furnace system, and the others at the table stopped talking and moved their knives and forks softly in their plates.

'I'm not sure what we're talking about,' I said.

'I got subpoenaed by the grand jury. Me and some people I'm associated with.'

'I didn't know that.'

'Businesses I run for thirty years somehow start bothering some people. Their little noses start twitching like there's a bad smell in the air. I'm talking about people that were at my children's baptisms, that always come around at election time for donations. Suddenly I'm like some kind of disease.'

'You're a professional, Didi. It comes with the geography.'

'They're serious this time. I got it straight from the prosecutors' office. They want me in Angola.'

'Like you said, maybe it's time to retire.'

'They're not cutting no deals on this one. That means I'm gonna have to break my own rules. I'm gonna have to do some stuff I don't like.' His dark eyes were flecked with black electricity.

'I guess I'm not following you.'

And I didn't want to follow him, either. The conversation had already grown old. I didn't care about his troubles with the grand jury, and his vague references to violating his own ethical system seemed at the time like another manifestation of the self-inflated grandiosity that was characteristic of his kind.

'You're right. It's personal,' he said. His glare went from me to the men around the table. They started eating and talking again. 'You want this guy Philip Murphy?'

I tapped my fingers on my water glass and looked away from his face.

'No games, partner,' I said.

'You think I play games? A guy that run Orleans and half of St Bernard Parish when you were a schoolboy? You think I brought you out here for games?'

'How is it you have a string on this guy?'

'He's an addict. An addict's one day away anytime you want him. This guy used to be a joy-popper. Now he's a two-ballon-a-day regular. You want him, try this restaurant.' He dropped a matchbox on the tablecloth. On the cover was a palm tree and the words GULF SHORES. FINE FOOD. BILOXI, MISSISSIPPI. 'His connection's the guy that runs the valet parking.'

'What do you care about Philip Murphy, Didi?'

'I got my reasons, a bunch of them maybe.'

'He plays in a different ballpark. He's not a competitor.'

'He's screwing up some things over in Fort Lauderdale. There's some people there want him out of the way.'

'I know this guy. He's not your crowd.'

'That's right, he ain't. But he messes with it. What you don't under-stand is south Florida's not New Orleans. Miami and Fort Lauderdale are open cities. Nobody's got a lock on the action, nobody gets cowboyed down there. Everybody always respected that. Now there's coloreds, Cubans, and Colombians in everything. They're fucking animals. They'll cowboy you for fifty bucks, they kill each other's children. Then guys like Murphy come around and make political deals with them – plots against Castro or some bullshit down in Central America. People that's cannibals, that was born in a chicken yard, end up working for the government. In the meantime, guys like me are in front of a grand jury.'

I picked up the matchbox and put it in my shirt pocket.

'Thank's for the information, Didi. I hope things turn out better for you over at Baylor,' I said.

'You ain't eat your lunch. You don't like Italian food?'

'You know how us old-time boozers are, scarred stomach and all that.'

'Maybe you don't like eating as my guest, huh?'

'I've appreciated your hospitality. You're always a generous man. We'll see you, Didi.'

'Yeah, sure. You're welcome. Keep one thing in mind, though. I never did time. Not in thirty years. You can tell that to any of those farts you know in the prosecutor's office.'

It was boiling when I got back to the houseboat. Heat waves bounced off the roof, and every inch of metal and wood on the deck was hot to the touch. I put on my trunks and snorkel mask and swam out into the lake. The surface was warm, but I could feel the layers of coldness below me grow more intense the farther I swam from the shoreline. I watched three pelicans floating in the groundswell in front of me, their pouched beaks swollen with fish, and tried to figure out what Didi Gee was up to. I hadn't accepted his explanation about Murphy creating complication for the mob in southern Florida, and his anger at the government's support of Cuban political gangsters seemed manufactured for the moment. But who was to say? In terms of law enforcement, south Florida was the La Brea Tar Pits East.

The real problem was that nobody knew what went on in the mind of Didi Gee except Didi Gee. Most cops categorize criminals as dimwits and degenerates, or we assume that the intelligent ones think more or less in the same logical patterns as we do. The truth is that absolutely no one knows what goes on in the mind of a psychopath. Didi Gee was a vicious, sentimental fat man who could just as easily tip a waitress fifty dollars as put an icepick in her husband's stomach. When he was a collector for the shylocks across the river in Algiers, his logo had been a bloodstained baseball bat that he kept propped up in the back seat of his convertible.

But somehow he and his kind always had their apologists. Journalists would treat them as honorable men who lived by an arcane private code; television documentaries dwelt on their families, the attendance at Mass, their patriotism – and made only fleeting reference to their connections with semiacceptable forms of organized crime, such as numbers and union takeovers. They were simply businessmen who were no more unethical than large corporations.

Maybe so. But I'd seen their victims: some grocers and dry cleaners who borrowed money from them and who became employees in their own stores; nightclub entertainers, beer and meat distributors, horse jockeys who couldn't move out of town without permission; addicts who were always looking for more mules to pull their wagons; and those who became object lessons, their faces blown all over a car windshield with double-ought buck-shot.

Maybe the deeper problem was that the Didi Gees of the world understood us, but we did not understand them. Were they genetically defective, or evil by choice? I took a breath through the snorkel and dove down to the bottom of the lake and glided above the gray, rippling sand while small fish scurried away in the green-yellow light. The salt water I swam in contained the remains of people who symbolized to me the greatest possible extremes in human behavior. They were created by the same Maker. The similarity ended there.

Three years ago a small plane with a family on board from Tampa hit a bad headwind over the Gulf, used up all its gas, and pancaked into the lake ten miles out. They got out with only one life preserver. Both the father and mother were strong swimmers and could have struck out for the shore or the causeway, but they stayed with their three children and kept them afloat for two days. One by one the parents and the two oldest children slipped under the waves. The smallest child survived because their father had strapped him in the life preserver and tied his shirt around the child's head to protect it from the sun.

Some miles to the west and just south of Morgan City was the crushed and barnacle-encrusted hull of a German U-boat that an American destroyer had nailed in 1942, when Nazi submarines used to lie in wait for the oil tankers that sailed from the refineries in Baton Rouge and New Orleans. Shrimpers in New Iberia told stories of the orange fires that burned on the southern horizon late at night, and of the charred bodies they pulled up in their nets. I didn't understand then who the Nazis were, but I imagined them as dark-uniformed, slit-eyed creatures who lived beneath the water and who could burn and murder people of goodwill whenever they wished.

Years later, when I was in college, I dove down to that wreck with an air tank and a weight belt. It was in sixty feet of water, lying on its side, the deck railing and forward gun shaggy with moss, the painted identification numbers still visible on the conning tower. The stern was tilted downward into deeper water, and I thought I could see the frenetic turning movements of sand sharks near the screws. My heart was clicking in my chest, I was breathing oxygen rapidly from my tank, and actually sweating inside my mask. I determined that I wasn't going to be overcome by my childhood fears, and I swam down to the dark, massive outline of the conning tower and knocked against the steel plate with the butt of my bowie knife.

Then the strangest occurrence of my life took place as I hovered above the wreck. I felt a cold current blow across me, a surge from the darkness beyond the submarine's screws, and air bubbles rose from under the hull.

I heard the metal plates start to grate against the bottom, then there was a crunching, sliding sound, a dirty cloud of moss and floating sand, and suddenly the sub trembled almost erect and began sliding backwards off the continental shelf. I watched it, horrified, until it disappeared in the blackness. The sand sharks turned like brown minnows in its invisible wake.

I learned that this particular wreck moved several miles up and down the Louisiana coastline, and it was only coincidence that its weight had shifted in a strong current while I was on top of it. But I could not get out of my mind the image of those drowned Nazis still sailing the earth after all those years, their eye sockets and skeletal mouths streaming seaweed, their diabolical plan still at work under the Gulf's tranquil, emerald surface.

A navy destroyer broke the spine of their ship with depth charges in 1942. But I believed that the evil they represented was held in check by the family who sacrificed their lives so their youngest member could live.

The phone was ringing when I climbed the ladder onto my deck. I sat in the hot shade of the umbrella and wiped my face with a towel while I held the receiver to my ear. It was Captain Guidry.

'Dave, is that you?' he said.

'Yes.'

'Where've you been? I've been calling you for two hours.'

'What is it?'

'I hate to have to call with bad news. It's your brother, Jimmie. Somebody shot him twice in a public rest room by the French Market.'

I squeezed my hand on my forehead and looked out at the heat waves hammering on the lake's surface.

'How bad is it?' I asked.

'I won't kid you. It's touch-and-go. It looks like the guy put two .22 rounds in the side of his head. Look, Jimmie's a tough guy. If anybody can make it, he will. You want me to send a car for you?'

'No, I have a rental. Where is he?'

'I'm here with him at Hotel Dieu Sisters. You drive careful, hear?'

The traffic was bad all the way across town. It was a half hour before I got to the hospital and found a place to park. I walked hurriedly up the tree-shaded walkway into the building, my sandals clacking on the tiles, my sweaty, unbuttoned print shirt hanging outside my slacks. I had to swallow and breathe quietly for a moment before I could ask the receptionist where Jimmie's room was. Then I turned and saw Captain Guidry standing behind me.

'He's in recovery on the fifth floor, Dave. They got the bullets out,' he said.

'What's it look like for him?'

'Better than it did when I talked with you. Let's walk down to the elevator.'

'What happened?'

'I'm going to tell you everything we know. But slow down now. There's some real good docs taking care of him. We're going to ride this one out all right.'

'Tell me what happened.'

The elevator door opened, and a nurse pushed out a wheelchair in which sat a pretty woman in a pink nightgown. She was smiling and she held a spray of flowers in her lap. We stepped inside and the doors closed behind us.

'He walked down to the Café du Monde for *beignets*, then stopped at the public restroom next door. The one that's under the levee. A black kid that was taking a piss in the wall urinal said Jimmie went into one of the stalls and closed the door. A minute later a guy came in, kicked open the door, and fired twice, point-blank. The kid says the gun had something on the barrel and it made a spitting sound. It sounds like a professional hit.'

'What'd the guy look like?'

'The kid was scared shitless. He still is. We got him looking in mug books, but don't expect anything.'

I clenched and unclenched my fists. The elevator was a slow one, and it kept stopping at floors where no one was waiting.

'Maybe this is the wrong time to tell you this, but some people are starting to think twice about your story,' the captain said.

'How's that?'

'Maybe they were after you instead. Jimmie looks like your twin. There might be other explanations, but the local talent tends toward shotguns and car bombs.'

'It's damn poor consolation to be believed because your brother was shot.'

'People are human. Give an inch.'

'I don't have that kind of charity. That's my whole family up there.'

'I can't blame you. But for what it's worth, we've got uniforms all over the floor. Nobody'll get to him here.'

'If he doesn't make it, you might be arresting me, Captain.'

'I hate to hear you talk like that, Dave. It brings me great worry,' he said.

Jimmie remained three more hours in the recovery room before they brought him into intensive care on a gurney. I wanted to go inside, but the surgeon wouldn't let me. He said both rounds had hit Jimmie at an angle, which was the only factor that saved his life. One had caromed off the skull and exited the scalp at the back of the head, but the second round had fractured the skull and put lead and bone splinters into the brain tissues. The surgeon's concern was about paralysis and loss of sight in one eye.

Captain Guidry had already gone back to the office, and I spent the rest of the afternoon alone in the waiting room. I read magazines, drank endless cups of bad coffee from a machine, and watched the light fade outside the window and the shadows of the oak trees fall on the brick-paved street down below. At eight o'clock I went downstairs and ate a sandwich in the cafeteria. I wanted to call Annie, but I thought I had already caused her enough traumatic moments and should spare her this one. Upstairs again, I talked with nurses, made friends with an elderly Cajun lady from Thibodaux who spoke English poorly and was afraid for her husband who was in surgery, and finally I watched the late news on television and went to sleep in a fetal position on a short couch.

In the morning a Catholic sister woke me up and gave me a glass of orange juice and told me it was all right to see my brother for a few minutes. Jimmie's jaws and head were wrapped thickly with bandages, almost like a plaster cast. His face was white and sunken, both eyes were hollow and blackened as though he had been beaten with fists. An IV needle was taped down to the blue vein inside his right arm; an oxygen tube was attached to his nose; his bare chest was crisscrossed with curlicues of electronic monitoring wires. He looked as though all the life had been sucked out of him through a straw and the lighted machines around him had more future and viability than he.

I wondered what my father would think of this. My father brawled in bars, but he always fought for fun and he never bore a grudge. He wouldn't carry a gun for any reason, even when he played *bourée* with gamblers who were known as dangerous and violent men. But this was a different world from the New Iberia of the 1940s. Here people with the moral instincts of piranha would pump two bullets into the brain of a man they didn't know and spend the contract money on cocaine and whores.

There were small lights in Jimmie's dark eyes when he looked at me. His eyelids looked like they were made of paper, stained with purple dye.

'How you doing, boy?' I said. I rubbed the back of his arm and squeezed his palm. It was lifeless and felt like Johnny Massina's had when I shook hands with him the night of his execution.

'Did you see who it was?'

His throat swallowed and his tongue made small saliva bubbles on his lower lip.

'Was it this guy Philip Murphy?' I asked. 'A late-middle-aged, frumpy-looking guy with glasses? Like somebody who'd be selling dirty postcards around a schoolyard?'

His eyes looked away from me, the lids fluttering.

'How about a dark little guy?'

Jimmie started to whisper, then choked on the fluids in his throat.

'All right, don't worry about it now,' I said. 'You're safe here. There's three uniformed cops with you, and I'll be in and out of here all the time. But while you get well, I'm going to find out who did this to us. You remember what the old man used to say – "You pull on dat 'gator's tail, he gonna clean your kneecaps, him."'

I smiled at him, then I saw his eyes flicker with an urgent light. His mouth opened and clicked dryly.

'Not now, Jim. There'll be time later,' I said.

He worked his hand off the bed onto my chest. Then his fingers began to trace lines against my skin, but he was so weak that the frail pattern he made was like a cobweb spread across my breastbone. I nodded as though I understood, and placed his hand back on the bed. The energy and effort in his eyes were now used up, and he looked at the ceiling with the expression of those who are suddenly forced to deal in a very different and dark dimension.

'I've bent your ear too long. You sack out now. I'll be back a little later,' I said.

But he was already disconnected from our conversation. I left the room quietly, with the sense of both guilt and relief that we feel when we're allowed to walk away from the bedside of someone who reminds us of our mortality.

The two uniformed cops on the door nodded to me. At the end of the corridor I saw Captain Guidry walking toward me with a potted geranium wrapped in green and silver foil. The implants in his scalp had grown, and his head looked as though a badly made wig had been grafted to it.

'I'm going to leave this at the nurse's station. How's he doing?' he asked.

'He's a tough little brother.'

'You look like hell. Go home and get some sleep.'

'I slept all right on the couch last night. I just need a shower and a change of clothes.'

Captain Guidry's eyes stared into mine. 'What did he tell you in there?'

'Nothing.'

'Don't jerk me around, Dave.'

'He didn't say anything.'

'I've worked with you a long time. You don't hide things well.'

'Ask the nurse. He can't talk. I'm not sure he even knows how he got here.'

'Listen, I think you're about to get out of all this trouble you've been in. Don't blow it now with an obstruction charge.'

'Do I get my badge back?'

His lips pinched together, and he looked down the corridor.

'You shouldn't have hit Baxter,' he said.

'So nothing is changed.'

'We do it one step at a time. Have some patience, will you? Trust people a little bit.'

'I'm out on ten thousand dollars' bond. I'm going to have to go to trial unless I can negotiate a misdemeanor plea.'

'You're a reader. You know about Saint John of the Cross and the long night of the soul. So this is your long night. Why make it longer?'

At the houseboat I took my Remington twelve-gauge pump out of its sheepskin-lined case. The blueing shone with the thin layer of oil that I kept on it. My father had given me the twelve-gauge when I went away to college in Lafayette, and I had knocked down mallards and geese with it from Cypremont Point to Whiskey Bay almost every year since. I rubbed my fingers along the polished, inlaid stock, then wrapped the barrel with a rag and locked it in the machinist's vise that I kept anchored to one end of the drainboard. I made a pencil mark three inches in front of the pump, then sawed through the barrel with a hacksaw. The end of the barrel clanged to the floor. I picked it up and started to drop it in the garbage but, instead, ran a piece of Christmas ribbon through it and hung it on the wall over what was left of my historical jazz collection.

I sat at the kitchen table and rubbed the sawed edges of the gun's muzzle smooth with emery paper and removed the sportsman's plug from the magazine so that it would now hold five shells instead of three. I went to the closet and took out my duffel bag of decoys, my army-surplus bandolier I used when the hunting weather was too warm for a coat. I emptied everything out on the table and stood all my shells up in an erect row like toy soldiers. Then I selected out the street cop's buffet – deer slugs and double-ought buckshot – slipped them one at a time into the magazine with my thumb until the spring came tight, slid the breech shut, and clicked on the safety.

In my mind were images that I didn't want to recognize. I looked out the window and saw a man turning a raw steak on a barbecue fire, saw the two kids trying to burn each other out in a pitch-and-catch game, their faces sweaty and narrow, saw a waxed red car parked next to a sand dune under the murderous white sun.

Annie ate lunch every day in a delicatessen by Canal and Exchange, not far from where she worked at the social welfare agency. I sat in a wooden chair across the street and read the *Times-Picayune* and waited for her. Just after noon I saw her coming down the sidewalk in the lunchtime crowd, wearing sunglasses, her wide straw hat, and a pale yellow dress.

She could live in New Orleans the rest of her life, I thought, but she would always be from Kansas. She had the tan of a farm girl, the kind that never seemed to change tone, and even though her legs were beautiful and her hips a genuine pleasure to look at, she walked in high heels as though she were on board a rocking ship.

I watched her sit by herself at a table, her back to me, remove her sunglasses, and give her order to the waiter while she moved both her hands in the air. He looked perplexed, and I could almost hear her ordering something that wasn't on the menu, which was her habit, or telling him about some 'weirdness' that she had seen on the street.

Then I heard the metal-rimmed wheels of a huge handcart on the pavement and an elderly black man's voice crying out, 'I got melons, I got 'loupes, I got plums, I got sweet red strawberries.' His cart was loaded with tiers of fruit and also with boxes of pralines, roses wrapped in green tissue paper, and small bottles of grape juice shoved down in an ice bucket.

'How you doing, Cappie?' I said.

'Good afternoon, Lieutenant,' he said, and grinned. His head was bald and brown, and he wore a gray apron. He had grown up in Laplace next door to Louis Armstrong's family, but he had sold produce in the Quarter for years and was so old that neither he nor anyone else knew his age.

'Is your wife still in the hospital?' I asked.

'No suh, she fit and fine and out do'-popping again.'

'I beg your pardon.'

'She do'-popping. She pop in dis do', she pop out dat do'. You want your grape drink today?'

'No, I tell you what instead. You see that pretty lady in the yellow dress eating across the street?'

'Yes suh, I think so.'

'Give her some of these roses and a box of pralines. Here, you keep the change, Cappie.'

'What you want me to tell her?'

'Just tell her it's from a good-looking Cajun fellow,' I said, and winked at him.

I looked once more in Annie's direction. Then I turned and walked back to where I had left my rented car parked on Decatur Street.

The beach outside of Biloxi was white and hot-looking in the afternoon sun. The palm trees along the boulevard beat in the wind, and the green surface of the Gulf was streaked with light and filled with dark patches of blue, like floating ink. A squall was blowing up in the south, and waves were already breaking against the ends of the jetties, the foam leaping high into the air before you heard the sound of the wave, and in the groundswell I could see the flicker of bait fish and the dark, triangular outlines of stingrays, almost like oil slicks, that had been pushed in toward shore by the approaching storm.

I found the Gulf shores restaurant, but the man who ran the valet parking service wasn't there. I walked a short way down the beach, bought a paper plate of fried catfish and hush puppies from a food stand, and sat on a wooden bench under a palm tree and ate it. Then I read a paperback copy of *A Passage to India*, watched some South American teenagers play soccer in the sand, and finally walked out along the jetty and skipped oyster shells across the water's surface. The wind was stiffer now, with a sandy bite in it, and as the sun seemed to descend into an enormous flame across the western sky, I could see thin white streaks of lightning in the row of black clouds that hovered low on the watery horizon in the south. When the sun's afterglow began to shrink from the sky, and the neon lights of the amusement rides and beer joints along the beach began to come on, I walked back to my car and drove to the restaurant.

Two black kids and a white man in his thirties were taking cars from under the porch at the entrance and parking them in back. The white man had crewcut brown hair and small moles all over his face, as though they had been touched there with a paintbrush. I drove up to the entrance, and one of the black kids took my car. I went inside and ate a five-dollar club sandwich that I didn't want. When I came back out, the white man walked up to me for my parking ticket.

'I can get it. Just show me where it is,' I said.

He stepped out of the light from the porch and pointed toward the lot.

'The second-to-last-row,' he said.

'Where?'

He walked farther into the dark and pointed again.

'Almost to the end of the row,' he said.

'My girlfriend said you can sell me some sneeze,' I said.

'Sell you what?' He looked me up and down for the first time. The neon light from a liquor store next door made his lips look purple.

'A little nose candy for the sinuses.'

'You got the wrong guy, buddy.'

'Do I look like a cop or something?'

'You want me to get your car, sir?'

'I've got a hundred bucks for you. Meet me someplace else.'

'Maybe you should talk to the manager. I run the valet service here. You're looking for somebody else.'

'She must have told me about the wrong place. No offence,' I said, and I walked to the back of the lot and drove out onto the boulevard. The palm trees on the esplanade were crashing in the wind.

I drove through a residential neighborhood away from the beach, then circled back and parked on a dark street a block inland from the restaurant. I took my World War II Japanese field glasses from the glove compartment and focused them on the lighted porch where the man with the moles was parking cars.

In the next three hours I watched him go twice to the trunk of his own automobile before he delivered a car to a customer out front. At midnight the restaurant closed, and I followed him across town to an unpaved neighborhood of clapboard houses, open drainage ditches, and dirt yards littered with rusted engine parts and washing machines.

Most of the houses on the street were dark, and I left my car a block away and walked to a sandy driveway that led up to the lighted side door of a boxlike wooden house surrounded by unwatered and dying hedges. Through the screen I could see him in his undershirt, with a beer in his hand, changing the channels on his television set. His shoulders were as white as a frog's belly and speckled with the same brown moles that covered his face. He sat back in a stuffed chair, a window fan blowing in his face, salted his beer can, and sipped at it while he watched television. The first raindrops clicked flatly on the roof.

I slipped my hand through the screen-door handle, then jerked it backward and tore the latch loose from the jamb. He sat erect, his eyes wide, the beer can rolling across the floor in a trail of foam.

'Some customers are persistent as hell,' I said, stepping inside.

But I should have come in holding the .25 Beretta that was in my pocket. He reached behind him on a workbench, grabbed a ball-peen hammer, and flung it into my chest. The steel head hit me just to the right of my breastbone, and I felt a pain, a breathlessness, shoot through my heart cavity as though I had been stunned with a high-voltage wire. Then he charged me, his arms flailing like a kid fighting on a school ground, and he caught me once on the eye and again on the ear before I could get my guard up. But I had been a good boxer at New Iberia High, and I had learned long ago that either in the ring or in a street fight there was nothing to equal setting your feet square, tucking your chin into your shoulder, raising your left to guard your face, and coming across with a right hook aimed somewhere between the mouth and the eyes. I got him right across the bridge of the nose. His eyes snapped straight with shock, the light glazed in them, and I hit him again, this time on the jaw, and knocked him over his chair into the television set. He looked up at me, his face white, his nose bleeding on his upper lip.

'You want to do it some more?' I said.

'Who are you, man?'

'What did you care, as long as you come out of this all right?'

'Come out of what? What you want with me? I never saw you before tonight.'

He started to get up. I pushed him down on the floor.

'You come here to rip me off, you're going to deal later with a couple of bad dudes. That's no joke, buddy,' he said.

'You see this in my hand? I'm not going to point it at you, because I don't think you're up to it. But we're upping the stakes now.'

'You come in my goddamn house and attack me and wave a gun around, and *I'm* in trouble? You're unbelieveable, man.'

'Get up,' I said, and pulled him erect by his arm. I walked him into the bedroom.

'Turn on the light,' I said.

He flicked the light switch. The bed was unmade, and dirty clothes were piled on the wood floor. A jigsaw puzzle of Elvis Presley's face was half completed on a card table. I pushed him through the hallway into the tiny kitchen at the back of the house.

'You forget where the light switch is?' I said.

'Look, man, I just work for some people. You got a problem with the action around here, you take it up with them, I'm just a small guy.'

I felt the wall with my hand and clicked on the overhead light. The kitchen was the only clean room in the house. The drainboards were washed down, the dishes put away in a drying rack, the linoleum floor waxed and polished. A solitary chair was placed at the large Formica-topped table in the center of the room, and on the table were three black plastic bags closed with masking tape, an ether bottle, and boxes of powdered milk and powdered sugar.

He wiped his nose on his hand. The moles on his face looked like dead bugs. Beyond the drawn window shades I could hear the rain falling in the trees.

'It looks like you've been watering down the stock,' I said.

'What do you want? You're looking at everything I got.'

'Where's Philip Murphy?'

He looked at me curiously, his brow furrowed.

'I don't know the guy,' he said.

'Yes, you do. He's a two-poke-a-day regular.'

'That's lots of people. Look, if I could give you the dude and get you out of my life, you'd have him.'

'He's in his fifties, wears glasses, tangled gray hair and eyebrows, talks a little bit like an Englishman sometimes.'

'Oh, that fucker. He told me his name was Eddy. You out to pop him or something?'

'Where is he?'

'Look, this dude has a lot of money. Around here we piece off the source. Everybody gets along that way.'

'Last chance,' I said, and moved towards him. His back bumped against the sink and he raised his hands up in front of his chest.

'All right,' he said. 'The last stucco duplex on Azalea Drive. It's straight north of Jefferson Davis's house. Now get the fuck out of here, man.'

'Do you rent or own this place?'

'I own it. Why?'

'Bad answer,' I said, and I unscrewed the cap from the ether bottle and poured it over the black plastic bags on the kitchen table.

'What are you doing?' he said.

'Better get moving, partner,' I said, and folded back the cover on a book of matches.

'Are you crazy? That stuff's like napalm. Don't do it, man.'

He stared at me wild-eyed, frozen, waiting until the last second to see if I was serious. I lighted the whole book, and he broke for the window, put one foot through the shade, balanced for a moment on the sill like a clothespin while he stared back at me incredulously a last time, and then crashed to the ground outside with the torn shade dangling behind him.

I backed out the door and threw the flaming match-book at the table. The air seemed to snap apart with a yellow-blue flash like lightning arching back on itself. Then the Formica tabletop erupted into a cone of flame that was absolutely white at the center. Within seconds the paint on the ceiling burned outward in a spreading black blister that touched all four walls.

When I walked away from the house, the fire had already cracked through the shingles of the kitchen roof and I could see the rain turning in the red light.

I drove along the beach boulevard next to the sea wall in the dark. The surf was loud, the waves crashing hard on the sand, and the shrimp boats that were moored in their slips were knocking against the pilings. I passed Beauvoir, the rambling, one-story home of Jefferson Davis, set back on a dark lawn under spreading oak trees. The wide veranda was lighted, and in the darkness and the sweep of rain through the trees, the building seemed like an inverted telescopic vision into that spring of 1865 when Davis watched his failed medieval romance collapse around him. If the grass in that same lawn was a darker green than it should have been, perhaps it was because of the two hundred Confederate soldiers who were anonymously buried there. The road to Roncevaux lures the poet and the visionary like a drug, but the soldier pays for the real estate.

I turned north and followed the road to a pink stucco duplex at the end of an unfinished subdivision. There was no moon, the sky was totally black now, and I parked my car down the street under a dripping oak tree. Murphy wasn't going to be easy, and I had to make some decisions. My father used to say that an old armadillo is old because he's smart, and he doesn't leave his hole unless you give him an acceptable reason. I had packed a change of clothes and a raincoat and a rain hat in a small suitcase before I had left New Orleans. I put on the hat and coat, slipped the shotgun out of its sheep-lined cover, and hung it through the trigger guard from under my armpit with a coat hanger. I buttoned the coat over the shotgun and walked to the duplex, which was set apart from the other houses by a vacant lot filled with construction rubble.

Both sides of the duplex were dark, but the driveway on the far side was empty and newspapers moldered on the lawn. I went behind the apartment closest to me, cut the telephone wire at the box with my Puma knife, and unscrewed the lightbulb on the porch. The rain beat against my hat and coat, and the shotgun knocked against my side and knee like a two-by-four. I pulled my hat low on my eyes, put a pencil between my teeth, then hammered on the door with my fist and stepped back out into the rain.

A light went on in back, and a moment later I saw the curtain move behind the door glass.

'Who is it?' a voice called.

'Gulf Coast Gas and Electric. We got a busted main. Turn off your pilot.'

'What?' the voice asked from behind the door.

'The main's busted. We can't get it shut down at the pump station. If you smell gas, go to the National Guard armory. Don't light no matches, either,' I said, and walked into the darkness as though I were headed toward another house.

But instead I cut behind a pile of bulldozed fiber-board in the vacant lot next door, circled through a stand of pines along a coulee, and came out in back of the duplex. I suspected that Murphy had stayed at the window until he gave up trying to locate me in the darkness and rain, then had gone to the telephone. I was right. As I eased under the window I heard him dialing, a pause, then the receiver rattling in the cradle. I stopped and walked quickly along the side wall toward the front porch, trying to keep the barrel of the shotgun out of the mud. At the corner I stopped and listened. He unlocked the deadbolt and opened the door on the chain.

Come on, you've got to prove you have *cojones*, I thought. Big boys wear them on the outside of their pants. You kicked gook ass with the Legionnaires, crouched in the bottom of an LST at the Bay of Pigs, hung parts of Sandinista farmers in trees like Christmas-tree ornaments. What good is life if you're not willing to risk it?

Then I heard him slide the chain and let it swing back against the door. I raised the shotgun in front of me, my body pressed tightly against the stucco wall. He stepped out into the slanting rain, his pajama top unbuttoned over his white pot belly, a flashlight in one hand and a blue two-inch .38 in the other.

I clicked off the safety and came around the corner and aimed the twelve-gauge's barrel at the side of his head in one motion.

'Throw it away! Don't think about it! Do it!' I said.

He was frozen, the flashlight's glow illuminating his face like a piece of dead wax. But I could see thought working in his eyes.

'I'll cut you in half, Murphy.'

'I suspect you would, Lieutenant,' he said, and he bent his knees, almost as though he were going to genuflect, and set the revolver on the porch slab.

I pushed him inside, turned on the light switch, and kicked the door closed behind me.

'Facedown on the floor, arms straight out,' I said.

'We don't need all this street theater, do we?' He looked again at my face in the light. 'All right, I don't argue. But there's nobody else here. It looks like you've won the day.'

The inside of the duplex looked like a motel room. An air-conditioning suit hummed in one window and dripped water on the shag carpet; the wallpaper had been roller-painted a pale green; the furniture was either plastic or made of composite wood; the air smelled of chemical deodorizer. I looked quickly in the bedroom, the bath, the small kitchen and dinette.

'It's a simple place,' he said. He had to turn his head sideways on the rug to talk. The pink fat around his hips was striped with gray hair. 'No women, no guns, no mysteries. This might be a disappointing bust for you, Lieutenant.'

'Take off your shirt and sit in that chair.'

'All right,' he said, and a smile flickered around the corner of his lips.

'Do I amuse you for some reason?'

'Not you. Just your attitude. I told you once before you had puritan sympathies. At some point in your career, you need to realize that nobody cares about these things. Oh, they say they do. But they really don't, and I think you know it.'

He dropped his pajama top on the arm of a stuffed chair and sat down. His chest was small and gray, and his stomach pushed up high on his breastbone.

'Turn them up,' I said.

He shrugged his shoulders and turned up his forearms so I could see the flat, gray scar tissue along the veins. The scars were so thick they could have been traced there with a barber's razor.

'I heard you were just a two-pop-a-day man. I think you've worked up to the full-tilt boogie,' I said.

'Does that somehow make you feel better?' The smile was gone, and I could see the contempt, the cynicism, the glint of evil in his eyes.

'If I allowed myself to have feelings about you, I would have blown you up on the porch.'

'And we thought you were a professional.'

'I hope you shot up a lot of dope tonight. You're going on a long dry. Figure what it's going to be like after two days in lockdown.'

'I'm trembling already. See the cold sweat on my face. Oh Lawsie, what's I going to do?'

At that moment I felt a genuine rush of hatred in my chest.

'If my brother dies and you somehow get back on the street, God help you,' I said.

'Your brother?'

I watched his face carefully.

'He's still alive, and he saw the guy you sent to do it,' I said.

'You think we tried to kill your brother?'

I watched the head of light in his eyes, the curve of his palms on the arm of the chair.

'That's what all this bullshit is about? Somebody hit your brother and you think we were behind it?' he said.

He widened his eyes, pursed his lips with his own question. He started to smile but glanced at my face and thought better of it.

'I'm sorry to tell you this, old boy. It wasn't us,' he said. 'Why would we want to hurt your brother?'

'He looks like my twin.'

'Ah yes, I heard something like that. Give us our innings, though. We don't make those kinds of mistakes, at least not as a rule. Actually, we'd marked you off, thought you'd be working on some of your own problems for a while.'

'Get back on the floor.'

'What are we doing now, Lieutenant?'

'You go well with the rug.'

I cut the light cord, tied his wrists behind him, pulled his bare feet up in the air, and wrapped the cord tightly around his ankles. Then I emptied all the drawers on the floor, went through all the clothes in his closets, dumped his suitcases on the bed, looked in his mailbox, went through everything in his wallet, and poured his garbage can out on the kitchen table. There was nothing in the duplex that would indicate that he had any life at all outside of Biloxi, Mississippi. There wasn't a matchbook cover, a canceled check, a credit-card receipt, an unpaid bill that would indicate he had even been out of the duplex. Almost everything in the apartment could have been purchased yesterday at K-Mart. The exception was a box of Trojan rubbers in the drawer of his nightstand, and his works – a very clean syringe, two shining hypodermic needles, a spoon with a bent and tape-wrapped handle and three packets of high-grade scag, all kept lovingly in a velvet-line, zippered leather case.

'My, my, we do like to probe after a man's vices, don't we?' he said. He was on his side in the middle of the living room rug. 'Give you a little rush, doesn't it, like watching a dirty movie? Your secret sins aren't so bad after all.'

I closed the leather case and tapped my fingers on it a moment.

'What to do, what to do, he thinks,' Murphy said. 'He can drop the dime with the locals and have the depraved old junkie locked up in a county slam. But then there's the problem of breaking into a man's house with a shotgun, isn't there?

'Or maybe a trip back to New Orleans. But, zounds, that's kidnapping. The worries of our chivalric detective seem endless. It's a great burden, being one of the good guys, isn't it? There are so many lofty standards to uphold. Your little piece of tail from Kansas isn't so discriminating.'

'What?'

'We checked her out. She has a file.'

'You are a CIA, then.'

'Are you so dumb you think the government is one group of people? Like the US Forest Service in their Smoke Bear suits? Even your regular punch knows better than that. Ask her. She's had some interesting experiences as a peace groupie back in the land of Oz. Except she was so committed she balled everything in sight and got herself knocked up. So she took a little horseback ride across the prairie and bounced the little fellow right out of there. Almost as messy as a coat hanger. But fortunately for you they have good doctors in Wichita, and they took out the baby carriage and left the playpen intact.'

I flipped the leather case through the kitchen door onto the pile of garbage I had poured over the table, then I went into the bedroom and picked up a shirt and a pair of slacks and shoes from the closet floor. Lightning splintered the sky outside, and thunder reverberated through the house. The rain was hitting hard against the windowpanes. I dropped the clothes next to him, untied his hands, and picked up the shotgun again.

'Put them on,' I said.

'Travel time?' he said, and smiled.

'Get dressed, Murphy.'

'I don't think this is going to be a pleasant trip.'

'Think of your alternatives. This is Mississippi.'

'I suspect I'll be riding in the trunk.' He sat on the floor and put on his shirt. 'Do you mind if I use the bathroom? I was headed there when you knocked.'

'Leave the door open,' I said.

He walked flatfooted to the toilet, like an old man, in his pajama bottoms and unbuttoned shirt. He looked back at me while he took out his penis and urinated loudly in the water. His face was composed, pink in the fluorescent light, as though he had surrendered both to the situation and the release in his kidneys. Out of decency or revulsion, I suppose, I looked away from him. The trees were thrashing against the windows, and through the edge of the shades I could see the lawn flicker whitely as lightning leaped across the sky. I was tired, my hands thick with fatigue so that they didn't want to curve around the stock and pump of the shotgun.

He might have pulled it off if he hadn't scraped the ceramic top of the toilet tank when he lifted it up to get the Walther 7.65 millimeter that was taped inside. But he had gotten his hand securely around the handle just as I snapped off the safety on the trigger guard, lifted the sawed-off barrel from the hip, and fired at his chest. The angle was bad, and the explosion of buckshot blew the side of the doorjamb away in a shower of white splinters and tore the shirt off his shoulder and streaked a long pattern of blood on the wallpaper, as though it had been slung there by a paintbrush. Later, I would never be able to decide whether the second shot was necessary. But the Walther was in his hand, the black electrician's tape hanging loose from the barrel, the broken ceramic top lying in the toilet bowl. I ejected the spent shell from the magazine, pumped the next round into the chamber, smelled the smoke and cordite in the air, and almost simultaneously pulled the trigger. It was a deer slug, and it caught him just below the heart and blew him backwards, his arms outspread, his face filled with disbelief, through the glass shower doors into the bathtub.

I picked up the warm shells off the rug and put them into my pocket. I looked down at Murphy in the tub. The deer slug had flattened inside him and had made an exit hole in his back the size of a half-dollar. His eyes were open and staring, and his face was absolutely white, as though the wound had drained every drop of his blood out of him. One hand still twitched convulsively on his pot belly.

But I took no joy in it.

I hung the shotgun on the hanger under my arm, buttoned my raincoat, and walked back out in the storm. The air was cool and smelled of wet trees and torn leaves blowing in the wind and the sulfurous odor of lightning that licked across the black sky over the Gulf. The rain sluiced off my hatbrim and blew in my face, and I walked through the dark puddles of water on the sidewalk as though they were not there. In a few more hours it would be dawn, the eastern sky would be pink with the new day, the palm trees and the beach and the fingers of surf sliding up on the sand would light slowly as the sun climbed in the sky, and I would be back in New Orleans with this night in my life somehow arranged in the proper compartment.

But my thought processes of convenience and my attempts at

magic were seldom successful. The storm blew all night and well into the next day, and back on my houseboat I didn't feel better about anything.

11

That afternoon I visited Jimmie in the hospital. He was still in intensive care, his condition unchanged, his voice still locked inside his chest. His hands and face looked as though they had been painted with wet ash.

At five-thirty I drove over to Annie's place. The sky had cleared and the air was suddenly blue and gold when the sun broke through the clouds, but the wind was still loud in the oak trees along the lane, and torn leaves were scattered across the lawns. She fixed both of us iced coffee, tuna sandwiches, and deviled eggs, and we took them out on the back porch and ate on the glass table under the chinaberry tree. She wore white Levi's, a pink pullover blouse, and gold hoop earrings that made her look like a flower child of the sixties. I hadn't told her about Jimmie, or anything about Biloxi, but she had caught my mood when I came through the door, and now as I sat with my food half eaten, her anxiety and incomprehension in having to deal with a representative of a violent and unfathomable world stole back into her face.

'What is it, Dave? Can't you trust me a little? Are we always going to stake out our private areas that we don't let the other one into?'

So I told her about Jimmie.

'I thought it was probably in the newspaper,' I said. 'He's a well-known guy in the Quarter.'

'I don't—' she began.

'You don't read those kinds of stories.'

She looked away, her eyes hurt.

'I'm sorry. Jimmie might not make it, and I might not be around to help him, either. I'm in some very big trouble right now.'

Her blue eyes looked intently into mine.

'The roses and the pralines in the delicatessen,' she said. 'That's why you didn't want to see me. You were going somewhere, and you thought I'd try to stop you.'

'There's no reason I should bring all my problems into your life. Loving a girl shouldn't include making her miserable.'

'Dave, why do you think you're the only person who can bear

hardship? A relationship is more than just sleeping with somebody, at least it is with me. I don't want to be your part-time lover. If you really want to do some damage, keep treating me like somebody who can't take it, who has to be protected.'

'I'm going to hurt you tonight, and I don't have any way around it.'

'I don't understand.'

'I had to kill Philip Murphy last night in Biloxi.'

Her face jumped, and I saw her throat swallow.

'He didn't give me a choice,' I said. 'I guess I wanted to do it when I went over there but wanting to do something and deliberately choosing to do it are two different things. I was going to take him back to New Orleans. I got careless, and he thought he could drop me.'

'Was he the one who shot your brother?' Her voice was quiet, the knowledge I had given her an enormous pain behind her eyes.

'I don't think so.'

'What are you going to do?'

'I'm not quite sure yet. Somebody'll find the body soon. In this weather, even with the air conditioning on—'

I saw her mouth form a tight line and her nostrils dilate slightly.

'The point is, sooner or later I'll be arrested,' I said.

'You did it in self-defense.'

'I broke into somebody's house with a shotgun, with no legal authority. Then I left the scene of a homicide. It'll take them a while, but they'll run my prints and eventually get a warrant out.'

'We have to talk with somebody. It isn't fair,' she said. 'Everything you do turns back on you. You're an innocent man. It's these other people who should be in jail. Doesn't anybody in that police department see that?'

'I've told you all this for another reason, Annie.' I let out my breath. 'Murphy said some things I have to ask you about. He was an evil man who tried to make others think the world was as evil as he was. But if any part of what he said is true, he had connections with a government agency or somebody in one.'

'What—'

'He said you were a peace groupie back in Kansas. He said you got pregnant and lost the child riding a horse.'

I waited. Her face flushed and her eyes filmed with tears.

'They reach far into your life, don't they?' she said.

'Annie—'

'What else did he have to say?'

'Nothing. Don't let a man like that wound you.'

'I don't care about him. It's you. Do you think I aborted my own child on a horse?'

'I don't think anything.'

'You do. It's in your face. Is she the person I thought she was? Was she an easy piece for those weird people back in Kansas?'

'I don't have a doubt in the world about who or what you are. Annie, you're everything to me.'

She put her fork down on her plate and looked into the evening shadows on the yard.

'I don't think I can handle this,' she said.

'There nothing to handle. It's over. I just had to find out if he was wired into the government. The Treasury people told me he wasn't.'

But she wasn't hearing me.

She looked down at her plate, then back at me again. Her eyes were wet and her chin was dented with tiny dimples.

'Dave, I feel just like I did the night that man put his hands on me.'

'Your family is involved with the peace movement, and the FBI probably collected some gossip on you all. It doesn't mean anything. They have files on all kinds of people, most of it for no explainable reason. They followed Ernest Hemingway around for twenty-five years, even when he was receiving electroshock treatments right before his death. Joe Namath's and John Wayne's names were on a White House enemies list.' I touched her on the arm and smiled at her. 'Come on, who was more American than the Duke?'

'I was seventeen. He was a Mennonite student from Nebraska, working in the home-repair program in Wichita for the summer.'

'You don't need to tell me this.'

'No, goddamn it, I'm not to have the lies of those people in our lives. I didn't tell him about the baby. He was too young to be a husband. He went back to school in Nebraska and never knew about it. When I was seven months pregnant we had a terrible electric storm at the farm. My parents had gone to town, and my grandfather was harrowing on the edge of an irrigation ditch. He was an old-order Mennonite and he harrowed with a team instead of a tractor. But he'd never quit work because of weather, unless it washed him right out of the field. I was watching him from the front porch, and I could see the wind blowing dust around him and lightning jumping all over the horizon. The sky was blue-gray, the way it gets in Kansas when you see tornadoes start spinning out of the earth, way off in the distance. Then a bolt of lightning hit a cotton wood tree next to the irrigation ditch, and I saw him and the team and the harrow topple over the side.

'I ran across the field in the rain. He was under the harrow, with his face pressed down in the mud. I couldn't get him out, and I thought he was going to suffocate. I cleaned the dirt out of his mouth and nose and put my shirt under his head. Then I got one of the mules untangled from the harness. The phone in the house was dead, and I had to ride four miles down the road to a neighbor's house to get help. I miscarried in their front yard. They put me in the back of a pickup with a roof on it and drove me to the hospital in Wichita. I almost bled to death on the way.'

'You're one hell of a girl, Annie.'

'Why did that man tell you those things?'

'He wanted to rattle me, get my mind on something else. He figured he had one play left, and he was going to take it.'

'I feel afraid for you.'

'You shouldn't. Four of them are dead, and I'm still walking around. When I was in Vietnam I used to try and think everything through. Then one day a friend told me, "Forget the complexities. The only thing that counts is that you're still on top of the ground, sucking air."'

'Except you don't believe that.'

'A person has to act and think in the way that works for him. I can't control all this bullshit in my life. I didn't deal any of it. In fact, I tried to deal myself out. It didn't work out that way.'

I saw the sadness in her eyes, and I took her hands in mine.

'The only thing I'm sorry about is having brought problems into your life,' I said. 'It's the cop's malaise.'

'And problems I have with you are problems I want.'

'You don't understand, Annie. When I told you about Biloxi I made you an accessory after the fact. So when I came over here this evening, I guess I did know what I have to do. I'd better go now. I'll call later.'

'Where are you going?'

'I've got to set things straight. Don't worry. Things always work out before the ninth race.'

'Stay.'

She stood up from the table and looked down at me. I got up and put my arms around her, felt her body come against me, felt it become small and close under my hands, felt her hands under my chin and her sandaled foot curve around my ankle. I kissed her hair and her eyes, and when she opened them again, all I could see was the electric blueness in them.

'Let's go inside,' she said. Her voice was a low, thick whisper in my ear, her fingers like the brush of a bird's wing on my thigh.

Later, in the darkness of her bedroom, the sunset an orange and purple glow beyond the half-closed blinds, she lay against my chest and rubbed her hand over my skin.

'One day you'll have a quiet heart,' she said.

'It's quiet now.'

'No, it isn't. You're already thinking about the rest of the night. But one day you'll feel all the heat go out of you.'

'Some people aren't made like that.'

'Why do you think that?' she asked quietly.

'Because of the years I invested in dismantling myself, I was forced to learn about some things that went on in my head. I don't like the world the way it is, and I miss the past. It's a foolish way to be.'

I left Annie's and drove over toward St Mary's Dominican College, where Captain Guidry lived with his mother in a Victorian house, not far from the Mississippi levee. It was a yellow house, in need of paint, and the lawn hadn't been cut and the lower gallery was overgrown with trees and untrimmed shrubs. The windows were all dark, except for the light of a television screen in the living room. I unlatched the picket gate and walked up the cracked walkway to the front porch. The porch swing hung at an angle on rusted chains, and the door bell was the kind you twisted with a handle. I thought it was about time the captain seriously considered marrying the widow in the water department.

'Dave, what are you doing out here?' he said when he opened the door. He wore a rumpled sports shirt, slippers, and old slacks with paint stains on them. He held a cup with a tea bag in it.

'I'm sorry to bother you at home. I need to talk with you.'

'Sure, come in. My mother just went to bed. I was watching the ball game.'

The living room was dark, smelled of dust and Mentholatum, and was filled with nineteenth-century furniture. The furniture wasn't antique; it was simply old, like the clutter of clocks, vases, religious pictures, coverless books, tasseled pillows, and stacked magazines that took up every inch of available space in the room. I sat down in a deep, stuffed chair that was threadbare on the arms.

'You want tea or a Dr Pepper?' he said.

'No, thanks.'

'You want anything else?' He looked at me carefully.

'Nope.'

'Thataboy. Jimmie's still holding his own, isn't he?'

'He's the same.'

'Yeah, I checked on him at noon. He's going to make it, Dave. If they get through the first day, they usually make it all the way. It's like something down inside of them catches a second breath.'

'I'm in some serious trouble. I thought about just riding it out, then I thought about getting out of town.'

He reached over from where he sat on the couch and clicked off the ball game.

'Instead, I figured I better face it now before it gets worse, if that's possible,' I said.

'What is it?'

'I had to kill Philip Murphy last night in Biloxi.' I saw his jaw set and his eyes light angrily.

'I was going to bring him in,' I said. 'That's the truth, Captain. I let him go into the bathroom to take a leak, and he had a Walther taped inside the toilet tank. He called the play.'

'No, you called the play when you started acting on your own authority, when you refused to accept the terms of your suspension, when you went as a vigilante into another state. I asked you at the hospital to have a little patience, a little trust. I guess those were wasted words.'

'I respect you, Captain, but how much trust have people had in me?'

'Listen to what you're saying. Can you imagine making a statement like that in a courtroom?'

I felt my face flush, and I had to look away from his eyes.

'You still haven't told me everything, though, have you?' he said.

'No.'

'You left the scene and you didn't report it?'

'Yes.'

'What else?'

'I think Purcel killed Bobby Joe Starkweather.'

'What for?'

'I don't know.'

'Maybe he was just riding in St Charles Parish one morning and decided he wanted to blow away a redneck,' the captain said.

'There was a witness. I have her name and where she works.'

'But you didn't bother telling this to anyone before?'

'She's a doper and a hooker, Captain. Her brains are as soft as yesterday's ice cream. I didn't know what would happen to her if they kept her as a material witness, either.'

'I'm having a hard time assimilating all this, Dave. I hate to tell you this, but this Purcel business sounds like it came out of a bottle. Maybe his personal problems are about to screw up his career with the department, but he's not an assassin, for God's sake.'

I felt tired, empty, my options all spent, and all of it for no purpose whatsoever. The captain was a good man. I didn't know what I had expected of him, actually. In going to his house with my strange stories, I had given him even fewer alternatives than I had myself.

'Give me the address,' he said. 'I'm going to call the Biloxi police department. Then we need to go down to the station, and I think you should call an attorney.'

He made the long-distance call, and I listened glumly while he talked with someone in their homicide division. I felt like a child whose errant behavior would now have to be taken over by a group of bemused authority figures. The captain finished and hung up the phone.

'They're sending a car out there and they'll call me back,' he said.

I sat in the silence. 'Did that black kid ever find anything in the mug books?'

'No, he was too scared, poor kid. We found out he's a little bit retarded too. You don't think Murphy pulled the trigger?'

'No.'

The captain blew air out of his nose. His fingers made a design on the arm of the couch as we sat in the gloom.

'Captain, did you hear anything about Didi Gee being indicted?'

'No, but you know how they are in the prosecutor's office. They dummy up on us sometimes, particularly when they're thinking about a roll of drums on the six-o'clock news. What did you hear?'

'He thinks he's going to he indicted.'

'He told you this? You've been talking with Didi Gee?'

'He asked me out to Mama Lido's. He gave me the line on Murphy.'

'Dave, I'm advising you at this point that you should be careful of what you tell me.'

'I believe he thinks he might actually go to Angola.'

'If the prosecutor's office is taking Didi Gee before the grand jury, it doesn't have anything to do with homicide. We had two cases I thought we could tie to his tail, and the prosecutor sat on his hands until one witness blew town and another time a clerk threw away a signed confession. You remember two years ago when somebody cut up a bookie named Joe Roth and stuffed him into the trash compactor in his own house? The next-door neighbor heard a Skilsaw whining in the middle of the night, and saw two guys leave the house at dawn, carrying a bloody paper sack. We found out later it contained the overalls they wore while they sawed up Roth's body. The neighbor picked out one of Didi Gee's hoods from a lineup, the guy had no alibi, his car had blood on the seat, he was a two-time loser and psychotic who would have sold Didi Gee's ass at a garage sale to stay out of the electric chair. But the prosecutor's office messed around for five months, and our witness sold his house at a loss and moved to Canada. So I can't take their current efforts too seriously. If they want to put the fat boy away, they should be talking to us, and they're not.

'I'm not sure what you're getting at, Dave, but it doesn't make any difference. It's our territory now, not yours, even though we're talking about your brother. What's the word they use when they're talking about characters in Shakespeare's plays?'

'Hubris?'

'Yeah, that's the word. Pride, a guy not knowing when he should sit one out. I think maybe that's the origin of our problem here.'

Captain Guidry turned the ball game on and pretended to watch it while we waited for the call. He was clearly uncomfortable. I suppose I was thinking he might actually have to arrest me. Finally, he got up, went into the kitchen, and brought us back two bottles of Dr Pepper.

'You remember a drink called Dr Nut when we were kids?' he said.

'Sure.'

'Boy, those were good, weren't they? The closest thing to it is a Dr Pepper. I guess that's why Southerners drink Dr Pepper all the time.' He paused in the silence and brushed the tops of his fingers with his palms. 'Look, I know you think the bottom's dropped out of everything, but try to look at what you got. You've put the cork in the jug, you've still got good friends, and you have a hell of a fine record as a police officer behind you.'

'I appreciate it, Captain.'

The phone rang, and he answered it with obvious relief. He listened for almost a full minute, his eyes blinking occasionally, then he said, 'That's what he said – on Azalea Drive, the last pink stucco duplex. Next to a vacant lot.' He looked at me. 'That's right, isn't it Dave? It's the last place on the street, and the apartment next door has newspapers on the lawn?'

I nodded.

'You got the right house,' he said into the phone. 'Did you find the landlord? . . . I see . . . No, sir, I don't understand it, either. I'd appreciate it, though, if you'd keep us informed, and we'll do the same . . . Yes, sir, thank you for your time and courtesy.'

He hung up the phone and touched the hair implants in his scalp.

'The place is empty,' he said.

'What?'

'There's no Philip Murphy, no body in the shower, no clothes in the closets, nothing in the cabinets or drawers. The next-door neighbor says a couple of guys were there this morning with a U-Haul trailer. The only thing that checks out is that the glass is gone from the shower doors, and it looks like somebody sawed a piece out of the bathroom doorjamb. Did it have some lead in it?'

'Yeah, I caught the edge of it with the first round.'

'I don't know what to tell you, Dave.'

'What about the landlord?'

'He lives in Mobile. They haven't talked with him yet.'

'What about blood?'

'The place is clean. You're off the hook, at least for now.'

'This means there's more of them out there. They're like army ants that trundle off their dead.'

'I have thirty-two years in the department. Only once before have I run into something like this, and to tell you the truth it unnerved me for a long time. About twenty-two or twenty-three years ago, a car with three soldiers in it got hit by a train on Tchoupitoulas. They were all killed, and I mean really ground up under the engine. What bothered me was that all three of them were wearing seat belts. What are the odds of three fatalities all wearing their seat belts? Also, guys that are that careful don't put themselves in front of trains. Anyway, it was winter and they were supposed to be on leave from Fort Dix, New Jersey, but they had suntans like they'd been lying on the beach for six months. I think they were dead before the train ever hit them. Somebody belted them in their car and put them on the track at three in the morning.

'But I'll never know for sure, because the army claimed their bodies, bagged them up, and that's the last I heard of it. We'd better talk to the Treasury people tomorrow morning.'

'They have a way of becoming comatose when they hear my voice on the phone.'

'I'll call them. You did the right thing, coming here tonight. Things look a little better than they did a while ago, don't they?'

'Yes, sir, they do.'

'There's something else I want to tell you. It looks like the prosecutor's office is going to drop the concealed-weapon charge against you.'

'Why?'

'Elections are coming around again. It's law-and-order time. They're going to make a lot of newsprint about gambling and narcotics, and they don't want people accusing them of wasting taxpayers' money while they try a cop on a chickenshit weapons charge.'

'Are you sure?'

'That's what I heard. Don't take it to the bank yet. But those guys over there are on their way up to higher things, and they don't care about our little problems in the department. Anyway, coast awhile, will you, Dave?'

But scared money never wins. You don't ease up on the batter in the ninth, you don't give up the rail on the far turn.

The next day it rained just before dawn, and when the sun came up, the trees along Carondelet were green and dripping, and the air was so thick with moisture it was almost foglike, suffused with a pink light the color of cotton candy. I parked down the street from Clete's house in a working-class neighborhood that would eventually be all black. His lawn had been recently mowed, but it had been cut in uneven strips, with ragged tufts of grass sticking up between the mower's tracks, and the cracks in the sidewalk and driveway were thick with weeds. His garbage cans had been emptied yesterday, but they still lay out front, their battered sides glistening with dew. At seven-thirty he came out the front door, dressed in a white short-sleeved shirt, a striped tie, and seersucker pants, his coat over his arm. His belt was hitched under his navel, the way a retired football player might wear it, and his big shoulders made him look as if he had put on a boy's shirt by mistake.

I followed him across town in the traffic. Up ahead at a red light, as the heat and humidity of the day began to gather and intensify among the tall buildings and jammed automobiles, I saw him yawn widely, rub his face as though he were trying to put life back in dead tissue, and rest his head against the door. There was a man with a real dose of the yellow-dog blues, I thought. By midmorning he would be sweating heavily, emptying the water cooler, debating whether he should eat more aspirin, hiding with his misery in the darkness of a toilet stall; at noon he would emerge into the sun's glare and the roar of traffic, drive across Canal to a café where nobody knew him so he could drink beer with his meal until one o'clock and glue his day back together. He was serving hard time, but it was about to get worse.

He double-parked in front of the Greyhound bus depot and went inside, putting on his coat. Five minutes later he was back in his car, working his way into the traffic, looking around as though the whole world were coming at him in the rearview mirror.

I went back to my houseboat, called the hospital about Jimmie, pumped iron, ran four miles along the lakefront, cleaned and oiled my twelve-gauge, and cooked some redfish and dirty rice for lunch while I listened to a recording of Blind Lemon Jefferson:

Dig my grave with a silver spade
And see that my grave is kept clean
Oh dear Lord, lower me down on a golden chain.

I wondered why it was that only black people seemed to treat death realistically in their art. White people wrote about it as an abstraction, used it as a poetic device, concerned themselves with it only when it was remote. Most of Shakespeare's and Frost's poems about death were written when both men were young. When Billie Holiday, Blind Lemon Jefferson, or Leadbelly sang about it, you heard the cock of the prison guard's rifle, saw the black silhouette suspended from a tree against a dying red sun, smelled the hot pine box being lowered into the same Mississippi soil a sharecropper had labored against all his life.

That afternoon I went up to the hospital and spent two hours with Jimmie. He slept with the remoteness of someone who had moved off into another dimension. Occasionally his mouth twitched, as though a fly had settled on it, and I wondered what painful shard of memory was at work under the almost featureless, ashlike mask that had become his face. I hoped he was not remembering the gun flashes fired point blank at his head through the door of the toilet stall. Few people appreciate the level of terror that a person experiences at that moment. Soldiers learn not to talk about it. Civilian victims try to explain it to friends and therapists, and are often treated with the sympathy we extend to babbling psychotics. But the best description I ever heard of it was not from a soldier or victim. We had a serial killer in an isolation cell at the First District, and he gave an interview to a woman reporter from the *Times-Picayune*. I'll never forget his words:

'There's no rush in the world like it. They drown when you point it at them. They beg and piss their pants. They cry, they tell you to do it to somebody else, they try to hide behind their own hands. It's like watching somebody melt into pudding.'

But I had no way of knowing what battle Jimmie was fighting inside himself. Maybe nothing went on inside Jimmie. Tomorrow they were going into his skull with the brace and bit to pick out the fragments of lead and bone that were stuck in his brain. But maybe they wouldn't simply find brain cells that were prized and broken as though they had been teased with an icepick; it was possible that the injuries were larger, the doctor said, like the dead and pulpy edges of bruised fruit. If so, his mind could deteriorate to the point that his thoughts would be little more than sand pattern drifting back and forth under the currents of a dull sea.

At five o'clock I was parked a block down Basin from First District headquarters when Clete walked out the front door. I followed him again to the Greyhound bus depot and watched him double-park, go inside, then return a few minutes later to his automobile. Even though I was now sure what he was up to, I had trouble believing it. We were required by department policy to carry our weapons both on and off duty, but his wife's fears and objections about guns were evidently enough to make him put himself in a position that was incredibly vulnerable.

I watched his car head off into the traffic, then I drove to an open-air café on Decatur across from the French Market, sat at the raw bar and ate a bowl of shrimp gumbo and two dozen oysters on the half-shell, and read the afternoon newspaper. A young crowd was in the café, and they were playing Island music on the jukebox, drinking Jax on tap, and eating oysters as fast as the Negro barman could rake them out of the ice bins and shuck them open on a tray. After the traffic had thinned and the streets had cooled in the lengthening shadows, I drove back to Clete's house off Carondelet.

When he opened the door he had a can of beer in his hand, and he wore a pair of baggy swimming trunks and a T-shirt that said DON'T MESS WITH MY TOOT-TOOT on the front. His eyes were bleary, and I suspected that he had skipped supper and had already committed himself to a serious evening of mentally sawing himself apart.

'Hey, Dave what's happening? he said. 'Come on out on the back porch. I'm tying some flies. I think I'm going out to Colorado and do some trout fishing.'

'Where's Lois?'

'She took the girls to a show. I think they go to about ten shows a week. I don't care, though. She gets discount tickets from the bank, and it's better for them than watching that MTV stuff. They're her kids, anyway, right? Say, tell me something. Did I see you down on Canal this morning?'

'Maybe.'

'Going down to see Jimmie?'

'I saw him this afternoon.'

'Oh. How is he?'

'He goes into surgery again tomorrow. We'll know a lot more then.'

'I'm real sorry about Jimmie. He's a fine guy.'

'I appreciate it, Clete.'

'Excuse the mess out here. Just throw those magazines on the floor and sit down. You want a Coke or coffee or something?'

'No, thanks.'

He had built the sun porch himself three years ago. It looked like a cracker hammered onto the back of the house. Vases of unwatered brown ferns and wilted spider plants hung in the windows, and the throw rugs he used to cover the concrete pad looked like discarded colored towels. He had set up a card table in the center of the room, and on it was a fly-tying vise, spools of thread, different types of bird feathers, and a tangle of tiny hooks. An unfinished, ragged fly was clamped in the vise.

He sat down in a canvas chair and took another beer from an ice-filled cooler.

'I'm going to take two weeks' vacation time, and we're going to head out to Colorado,' he said, 'Lois is going to visit her Buddhist priest, maybe get him out of her system, then we're going to camp on the Gunnison River, fish, backpack, live in a tent, do all that health stuff. I can get off cigarettes, lose some weight, maybe cut down on the booze. It's a chance for us to get a fresh start. I'm really looking forward to it.'

'I've got your nine-millimeter.'

'What?'

'I followed you to the bus depot.'

The stiff skin around his mouth tried to wrinkle into a smile.

'What are we talking about?' he said.

'I followed you there this morning and again this afternoon. Then I got Bobo Getz to open your locker for me. You remember him. He used to buy room keys off the hookers at the Ramada.'

His face became wooden. He lowered his eyes and slid a cigarette in and out of the pack.

'What are you trying to do to me, Dave?' he asked.

'Nobody has done anything to you. You jumped into the pig flop by yourself.'

'So I'm ashamed of leaving my weapon in a bus locker. But this isn't a home. It's a goddamn lunatic asylum. Who the hell set you up as my judge?'

'Run that game on somebody else. Ballistics will match your weapon to the bullet that come out of Bobby Joe Starkweather. You should have lost it somewhere.'

'Yeah? Maybe I didn't expect my partner to boost it from me.' He took the cigarette out of the pack, lighted it with a Zippo, dropped the lighter loudly on the tabletop, and rubbed his hand over his face while he blew out the smoke. 'So you gonna put me in the wringer?'

'Why'd you do it?'

'Ten thousand bucks.'

I didn't say anything. I looked at his big hands, the way a cigarette looked so small in them, his scarred, poached face, and wondered what had happened to the good-humored and intelligent man I used to work with.

'Come on, he was garbage and you know it,' he said. 'The credit union wouldn't give me another loan, I'm still paying alimony to my first wife, I owe the finance company, and I was paying fifty a week to a shylock. I could have handled it, but I had some complications with a girl. She said she was a month late, and she stiffed me for a grand to get lost without having a talk with Lois, That's about all it would have taken to put her in hospital.'

'Who paid you, Clete?'

'Murphy.'

'Why did he want him killed? Why did he want a cop to do it?'

'What difference does it make?'

'You're going to have to explain it sometime.'

'He said the guy was an asshole, he was out of control or something.'

'Murphy didn't need to pay cops to hit somebody.'

His brow wrinkled. He wiped a piece of tobacco off the corner of his mouth.

'You said "didn't".'

'He's not a player anymore.'

It took a second for the recognition to work into his eyes.

'Man, you don't fuck around, do you?' he said.

'Come on, Clete, why a cop?'

He waited a moment, and I saw the heat come back in his face.

'He said he worked for a guy. I suppose that general, what's his name, the guy whose house you got busted at, he said the guy didn't believe in whacking his own people. It's probably bullshit. All of them are slime, anyway.'

'So you knew Murphy before?'

'No. He knew me. At least he knew I was paying a shylock.' He drank from his beer can, inhaled from his cigarette, studied his hands, then raised his eyes again.

'Where do we go from here, partner?' he asked.

'I don't know.'

'Is a piece of shit like Starkweather this important?'

'You not only killed a man for money, you could have brought him and Murphy in. You could have gotten me off the hook.'

'I don't read it that way. But I don't guess that's important now. Are you going to give them my piece?'

'I don't have it.'

'What?'

'I just guessed you were dropping it and picking it up at the bus locker.'

He shook his head and blew out his breath as though I'd kicked him in the stomach.

'Damn, if you aren't slick, Streak.' He began to flick the fly clamped in the vise with his fingernail. 'What do you think I ought to do now?'

'I don't care what you do,' I said. 'Get out of town. Go to Colorado. Take up Zen with Lois. I just know one thing for sure – don't ever call me "partner" again.'

12

Jimmie went into surgery at eight the next morning, and they didn't wheel him into the recovery room until almost noon. The doctor found me in the waiting room and sat down in his greens on the leather couch next to me. He was prematurely bald and talked with a west Texas accent. His fingers looked as though they could cover a basketball.

'I call this kind a dusting-and-cleaning situation,' he said. 'There was a messy spot or two, but most everything was on the surface. All things considered, it cleaned up beautifully. I'm still concerned about that eye, but at least I don't think we're talking about paralysis anymore. I hope that's good news for you this morning.'

'It is, Doctor.'

'Now, about the other stuff – general recovery, post-effects, psychological trauma, we can't really tell you. There's a lot about the brain we don't understand. I've had to cut 'em open and go in with an ice-cream scoop, and somehow the other parts of the brain compensate and the person can live a fairly normal life. Then I've seen a simple fracture cause a guy headaches that almost drove him to suicide. It's like the jack-in-the box. Sometimes you just don't know what's going to jump up at you. But we've got a great eye man here and fine therapists, and every day it's going to get better for your brother. You follow me? In other words, we've got it turned around, and that's what counts.'

We shook hands, then I stopped by the gift shop downstairs and had fresh flowers sent up to Jim's room. I saw a big plastic crawfish in the gift case, and I had the salesgirl tie it with a bow to the flower vase.

I went back to the files and the *Picayune*'s morgue. Once again, the photographs and news stories sent me back across the sea, back into the era that would always be mine, whether I had wanted it or not. As I stared at the pictures of grunts loading their wounded into a dustoff, the elephant grass flattening around them, their dust-filmed faces streaked with dried sweat, their heads twisted back at the gunfire they still heard behind them, I felt like a leper who could not stop picking at his own crusted lesions. And like that leper, I knew I was about to sink my finger into a dark recess of pain and grief that did not cauterize with time. I flipped the frames of microfilm up on the viewing screen until I saw again the series of photographs taken during and after the My Lai massacre. I had never been able to rid myself of one of those photographs since I had first seen it in *Newsweek* magazine fifteen years ago. The villagers had been herded together, a GI with an M-16 was facing them, and a woman was begging with clasped hands while her little boy, not more than five, held her skirt and looked out from behind her with uncomprehending terror on his face. His mouth was open, the skin of his face was stretched tight with fear, and his eyes were wide with the knowledge that his mother's words could not protect him from what was about to happen.

The next frame on the microfilm showed the ditch where they were executed. On the floor of the ditch, amid the tangle of dead adults, was the body of a little boy who wore the same short pants and T-shirt as the child in the first picture. This was the war that an American called a holy cause.

I knew that I would always be caught in that lens, too, locked inside a frame of film that people would never be able to deal with, because to deal with it would require an admission of responsibility that would numb an entire nation.

That is why the word *obsession* is a convenient one in the analytical vocabulary. We apply it to those who were trapped inside the camera, who can never extricate themselves from those darker periods in history that were written for them by somebody else. But I had a feeling that the general would understand what I meant, that he too had heard the click of the shutter in an unexpected moment, had realized with a quickening of the heart that some of us are meant to be only sojourners in the present.

Then a strange thing happened that afternoon. I drove back to my houseboat, ate a sandwich and drank a glass of iced tea, and suddenly felt very tired. I took a nap, with the fan blowing across me in the hot cabin, and awoke an hour later with the thick heat of the afternoon in my head. I pumped water into the kitchen sink, splashed my face and dried it with a paper towel, and stared abstractedly out the window into the gleaming sunlight. Then my eyes focused on a man who stood under a palm tree farther down the beach. His hair was absolutely white, his skin deeply tanned, his posture erect as he smoked a cigarette in a holder and looked out at the shimmering lake from behind pilot's sunglasses. I rubbed the moisture out of my eyes with my fingers and looked again. I suspected that possibly I was obsessed after all. I went out on my deck and saw him turn and look at me. Cigarette smoke drifted away from his mouth in the wind. I walked quickly across the gangplank onto the dock and headed down the beach toward him. He looked at me a moment longer, removed the cigarette from his holder and dropped it into the sand, then casually walked to a gunmetal gray Chrysler and drove away. The heat was like steam rising from a stove.

I put on my running shoes and shorts, did four miles along the beach, showered in my tin stall, and called Annie and told her I would pick her up for supper after I visited Jimmie at the hospital. But just as I was locking up, Captain Guidry parked his car under the palm trees by my dock and walked down the path through the sand dune toward me. He carried his coat over his shoulder, and he wore his badge on one side of his belt and his clip-on .38 holster on the other. He wore long-sleeved white shirts and a tie even in the summer, and there were huge loops of sweat under his arms.

'Give me a few minutes of your time,' he said.

I unlocked the door, fixed him a rum and Coke, made myself a glass of instant iced coffee, and sat down with him at my deck table under the canvas umbrella. The heat and humidity of the afternoon had started to lift and break apart in the evening breeze, and there were patches of dark blue floating in the green of the lake.

'I shouldn't drink this,' he said. 'I had a couple of belts right after work, and I probably don't need any more. But . . . so what? Cheers, Dave.'

'You're not a man we can accuse of many vices, Captain.'

'Yeah, but my life is pretty boring as a consequence. At least it is until I get hung up on a case. I want to get you back into the department. You're too valuable to be marking time out here on your boat. I'll tell you something straight out. You're probably the best investigative officer I ever had under me. You have honest-to-God talent and ability. There's nobody else I can depend on like I've depended on you.'

'That's kind of you, Captain.'

'Forget the kindness. I want people in custody for Jimmie's shooting. I'm ashamed of the number of homicides and attempted homicides we're not prosecuting. I'm convinced that almost every guy we don't nail keeps killing people until he finally falls. I've never bought this number that a murder is usually a one-time excursion. You remember that hit man from New Jersey we busted about five or six years ago? He's been a suspect in something like eighteen contract murders. That's hard to believe, isn't it? He'd still be out there if one of his kind hadn't stuck an icepick in his ear. Anyway, they're not going to walk on this one. I'm going to tie the ribbon on the package and carry it over to the prosecutor's office myself, but I might need a little help. Now don't you bullshit me, Dave. You knew something when you came out of Jimmie's room the day he was shot. I want to know what it is.'

'I didn't hold out on you. I just wasn't sure it meant very much. I'm still not sure it does.'

'What?'

'Jimmie put his fingers on my chest, like he was trying to trace the letters of somebody's name.'

'Okay.'

'I think he knew he couldn't spell out an entire name. But what about initials? Whose name sounds like initials?'

'No, you tell me.'

'Didi Gee. He used me. He had me out to lunch with him and his collection of assholes while Jimmie was being hit. I not only gave him an alibi, I allowed him to shoot off his mouth about his ethics and how people were forcing him to break his own rules.'

'Why would he want to hit Jimmie?'

'He's going up in front of the grand jury, and I'll bet you Jimmie's going to be subpoenaed, too. He knew Jimmie wouldn't perjure himself. He'd take his own fall, and Didi would end up falling with him.'

Captain Guidry drank from his rum and Coke and took his pipe and pouch out of his coat pocket.

'I'm going to tell you a few things, but I need to extract your word of honor about something first,' he said.

'I've stopped dealing in those terms, Captain. That's not meant to be cynical. Considering the kind of mileage I have on my odometer, I just have a hard time thinking about personal honor.'

'That's because you've convinced yourself you're one of the world's great sinners. Let me tell you something. Real honor means you're still intact and functioning after your soul's been shot out of a cannon.'

'What do you want?'

'A promise you won't try to take down Didi Gee.'

'I didn't plan to.'

'You didn't plan that situation over in Biloxi, but it happened anyway, didn't it?'

'As a police officer I've shot four people, and I won't tell you about my record in Vietnam, except that I'm sick of all of it. There's always somebody there to convince you we got to blow 'em away, just this one more time, and the world will be a safer place. If Didi Gee deals the play, that's another matter. But I'm off rock-'n'-roll, Captain.'

He fiddled with his pipe for a while, then stuck it inside the tobacco pouch and put the pouch on the table.

'I got a call from the Fort Lauderdale police department,' he said. 'They try to monitor their local talent, but one of them slipped off the leash and left town for a couple of days. They think he might have been over here.'

'Who is he?'

'A hit man that works for the mob in New Jersey and south Florida. They sent me a picture on the wire, and I showed it to the black kid with five others. He said that's our man.'

'Where's this guy now?'

'Eating lobster on the beach, but we're going to jerk him up short. We'll cut the warrant on the kid's make, they'll pick him up for us, and we'll extradite back to New Orleans. By that time maybe Jimmie can identify him, too. The important thing is we don't let this guy fly.'

'You'd better get a damn high bond, then.'

'It will be. Also, the word's going to be on the street that this guy is a traveling man, a very bad risk. There's one thing you got to remember, though, Dave. We'll need Jimmie for a solid case. I don't think the kid will hold up too well by himself.'

'What about Didi Gee?'

'We'll take it a step at a time. We won't have any trouble showing motive – the prosecutor was going to indict Jimmie and use him as a witness against Didi Gee. I think it comes down to how much time our contact man wants to spend chopping sugar cane in Angola. Fort Lauderdale says he's never had to do any hard time. The possibility of a thirty-year jolt in the Louisiana prison system might really increase his instinct for negotiation.'

'Don't send Purcel after him.'

'Purcel's *my* problem. Don't worry about him.'

'He got ten thousand for Starkweather. He'll take money again. It's never a one-time thing. If you don't believe me, run his nine-millimeter through ballistics. But I bet his house will be robbed by then. Maybe you can get a match off the slugs from the Segura shooting, if they're not too beat up.'

'I hope you have my job one day, Dave. Then you can be responsible for everything that's wrong in the First District. It's something to look forward to.'

'I'm just squaring with you.'

'Yeah, but give me some credit. I'm the one that warned you about protecting Purcel's butt in the first place. Right?'

I didn't answer. The wind was cool now, and it flapped the canvas umbrella over our heads. Twenty yards out, a half-dozen pelicans sailed low over the water, their shadows racing ahead of them on the green surface.

'Right or wrong?' he said, and grinned at me.

'You're right.'

Then his face became serious again.

'But no Didi Gee, no cowboy stuff, no bullshit of any kind,' he said. 'The fat boy's going away, you can count on it, but it's going to be by the numbers. Right?'

'Right,' I said.

But even as I spoke, I thought, *if we break promises to God, shouldn't we be allowed an occasional violation of our word to our friends and superiors?*

*

Monday morning I had to go through another interview with Internal Affairs, this time concerning my last encounter with Internal Affairs. The three of us sat in a closed, immaculate white room that was furnished with a wooden table and three chairs. My interviewers were takers of notes. The yellow legal pads they wrote on were covered with swirls of calligraphy from their black felt pens. I didn't know either of them.

'Why did you strike Lieutenant Baxter?'

'He provoked me.'

'How's that?'

'What do you care?'

'I beg your pardon?'

'I said why are you asking me these questions? You work with the man every day. You know him better than I do.'

'Should we just indicate that you do not choose to answer the question?'

'I punched Nate Baxter because he's a bad cop. He tries to bully and degrade people. In my case, he tried to ignore evidence in the torture and murder of a federal law officer. Those things aren't demonstrable, but they're true, and both of you guys know it.'

Both of them looked at me blankly across the table. I could hear the air-conditioning humming through a duct in the white silence.

On the way out I got a clerk to pull the computer sheet they had gotten on the hit man from the National Crime Information Center in Washington. It was brief, almost hazy, in its description, in the way that a facial image burned into rock with acid would be hazy and brutal at the same time.

B. 1957, CAMDEN, NJ, GRADUATED HS 1975, ATTENDED MIAMI-DADE CC 2 YRS. VOC: DRY CLEANER, APT. MANAGER, SALESMAN. SUSPECTED INVOLVEMENT IN 6 HOMICIDES ORDERED BY ORGANIZED CRIME FIGURES. 1 CONTEMPT CITATION RESULTING IN 3 MONTHS' CONFINEMENT BROWARD COUNTY STOCKADE. CURRENT ADDRESS: CASA DEL MAR, GALT MILE, FT. LAUDERDALE, FL.

I tried to envision the man. The face remained an empty, dark oval, like the pitted center of a rotten piece of fruit, but I could see the simian hands. They were strong, ridged with knuckles, thick across the palm, but they were not made for work or for touching a woman's breast or even for tossing a ball back and forth with boys. Instead, they curved readily around certain tools that in themselves were only discardable means to an end: the .22 Magnum revolver, the .410 pistol, the barber's razor, the cork-tipped icepick, the Uzi. He loosed the souls from their bodies, the grief and terror from their eyes; he unstuck them from their mortal fastenings, sawed the sky loose from the earth's rim, eased them as a lover might into the wheeling of the stars. Sometimes at night he watched his deeds on the ten-o'clock news, ate ice cream out of a carton with a spoon, and felt a strange sexual arousal at the simplicity of it all, the purity, the strobelike glow where their bodies had been outlined with chalk, the remembered smell of death that was also like the smell of the sea, like copulation, like birth.

He had been busted at nine-thirty that morning and was now being held in the deadlock of the Fort Lauderdale jail, with no bond, while he awaited extradition to Louisiana. With good luck Jimmie would identify him, and with the right turn of the screw he would be willing to feed Didi Gee into an airplane propeller.

It should have been enough. But it wasn't.

I went back to the houseboat and found an old canvas money bag that I used to collect pennies in. The canvas had been cut out of a sail and sewn with a thick double stitch, and it closed and tied at the top with a leather drawstring. Then I sorted through my toolbox and found a half-dozen tire lugs, three ball bearings, and a huge iron nut that I used as a weight on my crab traps.

Rain clouds drifted by overhead, and my houseboat and the lake were suddenly covered with shadow, and the waves were capping on the slate-green surface. The air was cool and smelled of trees and salt and wet sand that was alive with shellfish. I could feel caution lights start to flash in my head, the way you do when you watch the amber light shimmer in a whiskey glass; you raise the glass to your lip and you're almost eyeball to eyeball with that protean and dancing balloon of yellow light, then its heated energy hits your stomach, surges through your chest, and rips open sealed places in your brain that you did not know existed. But the marriage is made, the hyena will have its way, the caution light is locked on red, you can't even have the pleasure of loathing yourself because the metamorphosis to which you've committed yourself is now the only self you have.

No, I wasn't out of control. It wasn't whiskey or an adrenaline surge like it that was loose in my system. I simply had to set some things right. And sometimes you don't set things right by being reasonable. *Reason* is a word I always associated with bureaucrats, paper shufflers, and people who formed committees that were never intended to solve anything. I don't mean to be hard. Maybe I'm just saying that what works for other people never worked very well for me, and that's probably because I shorted out a lot of my wiring a long time ago. I was never good at complexities, usually made a mess of them when I tried to cope with them, and for that reason I was always fond of a remark that Robert Frost made when he was talking about his lifetime commitment to his art. He said the fear of God asks the question, Is my sacrifice acceptable, is it worthy, in His sight? When it's all over and done with, does the good outweigh the bad, did I pitch the best game I could, even though it was a flawed one, right through the bottom of the ninth?

No, maybe I'm simply talking about honor. I could not define it in myself, but I recognized it when I saw it in others, and I was convinced that as a virtue it had little to do with being reasonable. And I knew absolutely that it was as dishonorable for a man to allow himself to be used as it was for him to use others. I also knew as a cop that the use of people, which is probably our worst sin, was considered the stuff of moralistic rhetoric by the legal fraternity.

So it wasn't an afternoon for caution lights, even though they reminded me of that amber-yellow heat that could almost soak through glass into my palm and crawl up my arm. It was a day of wind, of whitecaps turning into froth on the lake, of salt spray blowing through my windows, of palm leaves straightening against the gray sky, of swimmers chopping for the shore as thunder rolled overhead and I pointed my car toward the Eastern Expressway and the first raindrops clicked flatly against my windshield.

His office was in a huge liquor store he owned on Huey P. Long Avenue in Gretna, out of which he operated two beer distributorships, a catering and valet parking service, and a half-dozen delicatessens. The liquor store took up almost an entire block. It had wide, well-lighted aisles and buffed floors; music played from hidden speakers; spider plants and philodendron grew in the windows; glass collection jars for crippled children and stand-up posters advertising LSU, Tulane, and the Saints' fall football schedules stood on the front counter. Shoppers used arm baskets while they browsed through the aisles. The enclosed and refrigerated delicatessen counter was filled with shelled shrimp, squid, deviled eggs, lox, sliced cheeses, and meats from all over the world.

It was a place that probably compensated in some way for the deprivation he had known in childhood. There was an endless supply of food and drink; the interior was made entirely of glass, plastic, chrome, stainless steel, the stuff of technology, of *now*; and the people who bought his booze and gourmet trays belonged to the Timber Lane Country Club and treated him with the respect due a successful businessman. It wasn't that far to the waterfront neighborhood of Algiers where he grew up, but it must have seemed light-years away from the time when the sight of his convertible, with the bloodstained baseball bat propped up in the rear seat, made Italian merchants walk sweatily to the curb with the taped brown envelope already in their hands.

I felt a lick of fear in the back of my throat, like a pocket of needles in the voicebox, as I walked through the electronic sliding doors. The leather drawstring of the money bag was wrapped around my hand, and I could feel the collection of ball bearings, tire lugs, and the one big iron nut striking against my thigh as I walked. The shoppers in the aisles were the type you see in liquor stores only in the afternoons: by and large they're amateurs, they examine the labels on bottles because they don't know what they want, and they move about with the leisurely detachment of people who will not drink what they buy until hours or even days later. At the back of the store was an office area with a mahogany rail around it, much like the office area in a small bank. Didi Gee sat behind an executive's glass-topped desk, talking to a clerk in a gray apron and two middle-aged men who had the kind of heavy-shouldered, thick-chested breadth and slightly stooped stance that comes from a lifetime of walloping freights or lifting weights and drinking and eating whatever you want, with disregard for what you look like. Didi Gee saw me first and stopped talking, then all their heads were turned toward me and their faces were as flat and expressionless as people looking up the street at a bus about to arrive. I saw Didi Gee's lips move, then the two middle-aged men walked toward me with the clerk behind them. He was much younger than the other two, and his eyes would not focus on mine.

We stood in the center of the wide aisle, and I could feel the shoppers moving away from us, their eyes a bit askance, their brows slightly furrowed, as though a violent presence could come into their midst only if they looked directly at it. Both of the big men wore slacks and short-sleeved shirts and rested easily on the soles of their feet, the way boxers and oldtime career soldiers do.

'What do you want?' the larger of the two asked. He wore big rings on his thick fingers, and a gold watch with a black face that matched the black hair on his arms.

'So far you guys aren't in it,' I said.

'We're in everything. What do you want, Robicheaux?' the second man asked. He had a puckered scar in the center of his throat. He had been chewing gum, but now he had stopped.

'It's *Lieutenant* Robicheaux.'

'You want to buy some liquor? Go get him a fifth of Jack Daniel's,' the first man said to the clerk. 'It's on the house. Now what else you want before you leave?'

'It's not worth it for you,' I said.

'We'll walk you to your car. Charlie, put his bottle in a sack.'

Then the first man touched me slightly on the arm, just a brush with the callused inside of his palm. I swung the canvas bag from the side and caught him across the eye and the bridge of the nose, felt the lugs and ball bearings flatten against the bone, saw the pain and shock grab the rest of his face like a fist. He stumbled backward through a conically stacked display of green bottles, and the stack folded into a rain of wine and glass all over the aisle. I saw the second man's fist leap out at the side of my head; I bobbed, bent my knees, felt a ring rake across my scalp, and came around with the bag full circle and laid it right across his chin and mouth. His lips went crooked, his teeth were streaked red, and his eyes stared straight into mine with a fearful knowledge. I swung at him again, but he had his shoulders bent and his arms over his head now. A woman was screaming somewhere behind me, and I saw a man drop a red arm basket on the floor and walk quickly toward the electronic sliding doors. Others had formed into a crowd at the far end of the aisle.

Then the first man crunched through the glass and spilled wine and came at me holding a broken bottle of vermouth by the neck. The side of his face where I had hit him was red and swollen. His head was low, his shoulders rounded, his weight flat-footed, his eyes close-set and glaring. He poked at me with a bottle, as though it were a pike. I swung at his wrist, missed, heard the canvas clink on the bottle's tip, and he came forward again and lunged at my face. He must have been a knife fighter at one time, and even though he was heavy and breathed with the controlled rasp of the cigarette smoker, his reflexes were fast, his thighs and big buttocks were cocked like springs, and there was no fear in his eyes, but only a steady heated light that would accept any attrition to get to a murderous end.

But impatience was his undoing. He jabbed the bottle at my eyes again, and when he thought I was going to jerk backward, he raised it to slash at my head. But I didn't give ground, and I swung the heavy knot of metal from behind me, the canvas actually whipping in the air, and caught him solidly on the temple. His face went gray, his eyes rolled, the lids fluttered like bruised flower petals, and he crashed into the shelves and lay still.

Somebody was calling the police on the telephone. The second middle-aged man and the clerk in the apron retreated in front of me as I walked through the broken glass and the pools of wine, whiskey, and vermouth. Didi Gee rose from his desk like a leviathan surfacing from the depths. He had knocked over the ashtray when he stood up, and his perfumed cigarette was burning on the desk blotter. His face was still filled with disbelief, but there was something else at work in his eyes, too – a flicker, a twitch, the rippling edge of a fear he had hidden inside himself all his life.

'You're fucked,' he said.

Don't talk. Do it. Now, I thought.

'You hear me? Fucked. Your brother, your girl, you're all a package deal.'

'He thought you were his friend. You bastard,' I said.

I saw his eyes sweep the store, look impotently at his employees, who were having no part of it now, then his hand went inside the desk drawer and flattened on top of a blue automatic. I came straight overhead with the canvas bag, struck him across the forearm, and snapped the side panel out of the drawer. His fingers straightened and trembled with the shock, and he wrapped his hand around the swelling on top of his forearm, held it against his chest, and backed away from me. His lower buttocks and the backs of his thighs hit against the mahogany rail that surrounded the office area, bolts popped loose from their fastenings, and the rail suddenly snapped flat against the floor. Then he turned and ran with his head twisted back at me.

I followed him behind the delicatessen counter, onto the duckboards, into the midst of his countermen and butchers, whose faces at that moment dared show no partisan expression. Didi's breath was wheezing, his huge chest laboring, his black curly hair hanging in his face like snakes, his dark eyes hot and desperate. His breath sounded as though he was strangling on air bubbles in his throat. The fat across his heart quivered under his shirt. He tried to speak, to gain control of the situation a last time, to click over the tumblers that he had always used to make terrified suppliants of his enemies. Instead, he fell against the wooden butcher's block and held on to the sides for support. The block was streaked brown and covered with bits of chopped chicken. His stomach hung down like a huge, water-filled balloon. His face was sweating heavily, and his mouth worked again on the words that wouldn't come.

'You got a free pass, Didi,' I said, and dropped the canvas money sack on the butcher's block. 'Give your help a raise.'

I heard the sirens outside.

'Tell them cops to get an ambulance,' one of the clerks said. 'He's got blood coming out of his seat.'

They opened up Didi Gee that night. The surgeons said he had malignant polyps the size of duck's eggs inside his bowels. They cut and snipped, sewed and stapled until almost dawn. They closed his colon, implanted a drip tube in his side, and fed him through his veins. Later he would wear a plastic bag on an emaciated frame that would lose a hundred and fifty pounds in a month. He would listen to pyschologists talk to him in a vocabulary he couldn't fathom, learn to stand on a walker, sit in group-therapy sessions with people who talked about life when it was clearly evident they were dying, look dumbly at brochures describing vacations in the Islands, watch his children's discomfort at the smell that came from under his sheets.

He would sign over his power of attorney to others, draw his signatures across bits of paper that seemed now to have no more value than confetti, and try to think about the coming fall, about red leaves flying in the wind, about Christmas trees and brandy cakes and eggnog, and about the following spring that would surely come a-borning if only he could hold its shape clearly in his mind.

Somewhere down inside him, he knew that his fear of death by water had always been a foolish one. Death was a rodent that ate its way inch by inch through your entrails, chewed at your liver and stomach, severed tendon from organ, until finally, when you were alone in the dark, it sat gorged and sleek next to your head, its eyes resting, its wet muzzle like a kiss, a promise whispered in the air.

The next night I couldn't sleep. At first I thought it was the heat, then I decided that it was the insomnia that plagued me two or three nights a month and left me listless and disordered in mind the next morning. Then finally I knew that it was simply the price of ambition – the Fort Lauderdale hit man was in jail, Didi Gee was dealing with a punishment far worse than any court could impose on him, and I wanted to get Wineburger and the general. But I knew they had won the day, and accepting the fact was as easy as swallowing a razor blade.

Then about 3:00 AM I fell asleep and I dreamed. Shakespeare said that all power lies in the world of dreams, and I believe him. Somehow sleep allows us to see clearly those very things that are obscured by the light of day. I heard my father talking to me again, saw his huge muscles working under his flannel shirt as he pulled a ten-foot dead alligator upon a hook over the barn door. He pushed the point of the skinning knife into the thick yellow hide under the neck and then pulled it with both hands in a red line that ran from the mouth to the white tip under the tail.

I didn't see him, no, he said. *That's 'cause I was thinking like me, not like him. That 'gator don't get out on them log when he hungry. He hide under them dead leafs floating next to the levee and wait for them big far coon come down to drink.*

I woke up at dawn, dripped a pot of chicory coffee, heated a small pan of milk, cooked a half-dozen pieces of toast in the skillet, and ate breakfast out on the deck while the pink light spread across the sky and the gulls began to wheel and squeech overhead. I had always thought I was a good cop, but I was still amazed at how I sometimes overlooked what should have been obvious. My father didn't read or write, but in many ways he had learned more from hunting and fishing in the marsh than I had from my years of college education and experience as a policeman. I wondered if he wouldn't have made a better cop than I, except that he didn't like the rules, authority, and people who took themselves seriously. But maybe that was his gift, I thought; he laughed at seriousness in people and consequently was never distracted by their subterfuge.

I left the houseboat at seven-thirty and was at the Jefferson Parish courthouse when it opened at eight o'clock. I found what I was looking for in a half hour. I was actually shaking when I went into the phone booth in the marble corridor and called Fitzpatrick's supervisor at the Federal Building.

'I found Larry Wineburger's warehouse,' I said.

'Oh yeah?' he said.

'Yeah, that's right.'

He didn't respond.

'The one the Nicaraguan mentioned on the tape,' I said. 'I assume you've listened to the tape.'

'We did.'

'It's way down in Jefferson Parish, off Barataria Road. I was looking for it under "deeds" in the parish clerk's office. Then it hit me: Why would a slumlord like Wineburger want to buy warehouse property? He makes his real-estate money off welfare clients. A guy like Whiplash doesn't own anything that doesn't bring in a high, immediate return. So I checked leases in the Registrar of Deeds office. The law doesn't require anyone to record a lease, but a lawyer would do it automatically to protect himself.'

'Can you tell me why it is you have to share this omniscience with us?'

'What?'

'Who gave you this divine calling? Why is it incumbent upon you to direct our investigation?'

'You want the information or not?'

'We sealed that place yesterday afternoon and cut the warrant on Wineburger last night. This morning he's developed an enormous interest in the protected-witness program.'

I felt the skin of my face pinch tight in the half-light of the phone booth. The line was quiet a moment.

'What was inside?' I said.

'It's not really your business, Lieutenant.'

'It is. You know it is.'

'A lot of modified AR-15s, ammunition, medical supplies, and, believe it or not, a Beech King-Air B-200, outfitted with racks for electronic surveillance gear.'

'A big day for the cavalry,' I said.

'We're high achievers.'

'What about Abshire?'

'Plays second base for the Dodgers, right? Take it easy Robicheaux.'

'You'll never win their hearts and minds.'

'Before I hang up, let me add one thing. You didn't do half bad for a guy locked out in the cold. You were a good friend to Sam Fitzpatrick, too. We're not unappreciative of that. And finally, I hope this is the last conversation I ever have with you.'

So I didn't know what plans, if any, they had for the general, but I knew I had to see him. I didn't like him, certainly, but I felt a peculiar kind of kinship with him. I felt I had learned something about him in the morgue at the *Times-Picayune* that most other people would not understand. Like those Confederate soldiers buried under the lawn of Jefferson Davis's home, some people share historical real estate that will always be their private country. And I also knew that to be free of the tiger you sometimes had to look right into the beaded orange light of his eye.

After lunch, I visited Jimmie in the hospital. He was out of intensive care now, and the blinds were open in his room and the sunlight struck across the vases of roses, carnations, and dahlias on the windowsill and dresser. The nurses had him propped up on pillows, and although one of his eyes was taped and his face was still gray, he was able to smile at me.

'In a few more weeks we're going to be stringing some green trout,' I said.

He started to whisper something, and I had to sit on the edge of the bed and lean over him to hear his words.

'*Je t'aime, frère,*' he said.

I didn't answer him right away. I didn't need to. He knew I loved him as much as he loved me, in the way that only two men can love each other. I picked up his water and glass straw and helped him drink.

'It's always today, Jim, and it's just going to get better and better,' I said.

His mouth was like a bird's on the glass straw.

I left the hospital and drove my rental car back to the Hertz office downtown. I couldn't afford to keep it anymore. I figured if I was reinstated with the department, and hence with the credit union, I would buy a new automobile; and if I wasn't reinstated, it would probably be time to liquidate and look for new horizons, anyway. There were always options. I remembered the worst afternoon in my gambler's career. My wife and I had gone on a vacation to Miami, and by the end of the ninth race on our first day at Hialeah I had dropped six hundred dollars. I sat in the emptying grandstand, dozens of torn parimutuel tickets at my feet, a cold wind blowing paper across the track, and tried not to look at the disappointment and anger in my wife's face. Then I heard a small plane's straining roar overhead, and I looked up into the gray sky and saw a biplane towing a long canvas sign that read, GET EVEN AT BISCAYNE DOG TRACK TONIGHT. Even the loser had a future.

I took the streetcar down St Charles Avenue to the Garden District. It was wonderful riding down the esplanade with the window open under the trees, the iron wheels clicking on the tracks, the sunlight and shadow flicking across my arm. At each stop, black and working-class white people and college students waited in the shade of the oaks and palm trees, and black teenagers sold icecream bars and snow cones out of bicycle carts, and the sidewalk cafés in front of the hotels had already started to fill with the early supper crowd. For some reason every day in

New Orleans seems like a holiday, even when you have to work, and there is no better way to enjoy it than rattling down the esplanade in the breezy streetcar that has been running on those same tracks since the turn of the century. I watched the pillared and scrolled antebellum homes roll by, the spreading oaks hung with Spanish moss, the small courtyards with their iron gates and whitewashed brick walls, the palm fronds and banana trees that shaded the old, root-cracked sidewalks. Then we crossed Jackson Avenue and I got off at my stop, drank a lime coke in Katz and Besthoff, and walked down the short, brickpaved street to the general's home on Prytania.

I paused at the front gate. Through the umbrella trees along the fence I saw him sitting at a white iron table in the side yard, peeling oranges and avocados into a bowl. He wore sandals and khaki shorts with no shirt, and his sun-browned skin and white hair were dappled with the light shining through the oak tree overhead. Under his arms were the wrinkled webs of tissue that old people have, but his physique was still robust, the movement of his hands strong and confident as he pared the fruit into the bowl. By his elbow were an ashtray with a cigarette holder in it and a corked bottle of wine. He unstoppered the bottle, poured into a small glass, and then his acetylene-blue eyes fastened on mine.

I unlatched the iron gate and walked across the lawn toward him. His face was empty, but his eyes watched me as they would a creature who had suddenly been released from a cage.

'Are there others with you?' he asked.

'Nope. I'm still operating on my own.'

'I see.' He looked up and down my body, watched my hands. He slipped the paring knife into an orange and peeled back the rind. 'Do you want revenge?'

'They'll come for you. It's just a matter of time.'

'Maybe. Maybe not.'

'There's no maybe about it, General. If the feds don't, my supervisor will. He's a better cop than I am. He does it by rules, and he doesn't mess things up.'

'I don't understand why you're here.'

'What were you doing out by my houseboat?'

'Sit down. Do you drink wine or do you want some fruit?'

'No, thank you.'

He put a cigarette in his holder, but he didn't light it. His eyes looked across the yard where some gray squirrels were running up an oak tree.

'I want to apologize,' he said.

'Oh?'

'For all the things that have happened to you. You shouldn't have been involved in it.'

'Cops automatically become involved when you break the law.'

'I've brought you serious grief, Lieutenant. Some of it was done without my knowledge, but ultimately I'm responsible. I offer you my apology now. I don't expect you to accept it.'

'I came here for a personal reason, too. I won't be the one who comes up your walk with a warrant. Somebody else will do that. But I think I'm the only one who knows why you got into this Elephant Walk project, or whatever you call it.'

'What makes you privy to my soul, Lieutenant?'

'You were a soldier's soldier. You're not a right-wing crazy. You have the reputation of an honorable man. I suspect that people like Wineburger, Julio Segura, and Philip Murphy make your skin crawl. But you went on the other side of the street with the lowlifes and the paranoids and started shipping arms down to Central America. A couple of innocent people are dead in this country, and God only knows what damage those guns have done in Guatemala and Nicaragua. So a man who probably doesn't respect politicians in the first place has become part of a political conspiracy. It doesn't fit, does it? I think it has to do with your son.'

'Maybe you're well-intentioned, but you're being intrusive.'

'I was over there, General. Your knowledge and mine won't go away. But you've got to look at it for what it is. You can't bury something awful inside yourself, then pretend it's not there while you fight another war that makes you break all your own rules.'

'What do you mean?'

'The massacre at My Lai. You're blaming it on your son. Or you're blaming it on the VC that made him set those mines.'

'No.'

'Yes. Tear it out of yourself and look at it in the light. They captured him around Pinkville and made him string mines through those rice paddies. Then Calley's people got blown up by those same mines before they went into My Lai.'

He set the orange and the paring knife down on the table. His hands were flat on the table's surface. His eyes blinked rapidly and I could see the pulse in his neck. His deeply tanned, smooth skin was spotted with the sunlight shifting through the oak leaves overhead.

'I've apologized to you, I'm deeply sorry for what's happened to you. But you haven't the right to do this.'

'It wasn't your son's fault. He was forced to set those mines, and you have to forgive him for it. Maybe you even have to forgive the people that made him do it.'

'Do you know what they did to him?' One blue eye trembled at the edge.

'Yes.'

'They put his head in a cage full of rats.'

'I know.'

'He didn't like the army. He was going to medical school. But he was never afraid of anything.'

'I bet he was a fine young man, General. A friend of mine over on Magazine knew him. He said your kid was first rate.'

'I don't want to talk any more about this, if you don't mind.'

'All right.'

'Your supervisor . . . you say he's a good man?' He picked up the orange and pulled a piece of rind off it absently.

'Yes.'

'Will he see that you're given back your position?'

'Probably.'

'I'm sure that he's a man who keeps his word. How long before they'll be out here?'

'Today, tomorrow. Who knows? It probably depends on who takes jurisdiction. Why not walk in on them?'

'I don't think so.'

'You must know by now they've got Wineburger. He'll turn you for the pennies on your eyes.'

He lit his cigarette. The smoke curled around his holder. His eyes looked into the shade of the trees.

'Well, I guess it's not your style,' I said, and got up from the table. 'I'll go now. Read Saint John of the Cross. It's a long night, General. Don't try to get through it with apologies. They're all right between gentlemen, but they don't have much value for the dead.'

I walked back to the streetcar stop on St Charles. The esplanade was shady under the spreading oaks, and the wind blew pieces of newspaper through the intersection. The streetcar tracks were burnished the color of copper, and they trembled slightly from the rumbling weight of the car that was still far down the esplanade. The wind was dry, full of dust, the burnt-out end of a long, hot afternoon, and I could smell the acrid scorch in the air that the streetcars made when they popped across an electric circuit. Overhead, clouds that had the dull sheen of steam floated in from the Gulf, where the sun was already sinking into a purple thunderhead. An elderly black woman who waited at the stop with me carried a flowered umbrella hooked on her arm. She wore a pillbox hat clamped down on her small head.

'It gonna rain frogs by tonight,' she said. 'First it get hot and windy, then it smell like fish, then lightning gonna jump all over my little house.'

She smiled at me with her joke. I helped her on the streetcar, which was crowded with black people who worked as servants in the Garden District. She and I shared a wooden seat in the back of the car as it rumbled along the esplanade under the trees, past the scrolled iron balconies, the sidewalk cafés in front of the hotels, the green-blue lawns that were now streaked with shadow, the marble-columned porches where Confederate officers once tethered their horses and drank bourbon with their ladies. Out over the Gulf I heard a long peal of thunder, like a row of ancient cannon firing in a diminishing sequence. The black lady shook her head gravely and made a wet, humming sound in the back of her throat.

Epilogue

I was reinstated in the department with no disciplinary action other than a letter of reprimand for punching out Nate Baxter. In two days a half-dozen cops called up to congratulate me. I had heard from none of them while I was on suspension. I discovered that I was not ready to return to work, that my file drawer of gargoyles and grief would have to remain in abeyance in that old Basin Street building that had once housed slave auctions and cock-fights. I took two weeks of my vacation time, and Annie and I went to Key West, walked along the ficus-shaded streets by the bay where Ernest Hemingway and James Audubon had once lived, scuba-dived on Seven Mile Reef, where the water was so clear and green at thirty feet that you could count the grains of sand like fragments of diamond in your palm, fished for cobia, grouper, and wahoo, and ate trays of boiled shrimp and conch fritters down on the dock while the shrimp boats rose and knocked inside their mooring slips.

When it was time to return to work, I put in for my remaining week's vacation. Finally I had no days left. The summer had burnt itself out; the heat had lifted one day in a breeze off the Gulf, the sky turned a darker blue, the trees a deeper green. Stubborn boys still tried to hold on to baseball games in sand lots, but each morning was cooler now, the sunlight gold and warm at noon, and you could hear high-school marching bands thundering on afternoon practice fields. I walked into the First District at eight o'clock on the day I was to resume work, filled out a request for return of my retirement funds, and resigned.

It was time for somebody else to fight the wars. Captain Guidry argued with me and said that I had been vindicated. But vindication is of value only if you're interested in keeping score. I think by that time I had learned that the score takes care of itself. You just keep bearing down on the batter, then one day you look over your shoulder and you're pleasantly surprised at the numbers that are up on the board.

Clete blew Dodge like the town was burning down. He packed two suitcases, forged his wife's signature on a check against their joint account, and left his car double-parked in front of the airport with both front doors open. A month later I received a postcard from him that had been mailed in Honduras. The card showed a Mayan pyramid in Guatemala.

Dear Streak,

Greetings from Bongo-Bongo Land. I'd like to tell you I'm off the sauce and working for the Maryknolls. I'm not. Guess what skill is in big demand down here? A guy that can run through the manual of arms is an automatic captain. They're all kids. Somebody with a case of Clearasil could take the whole country.

See you in the next incarnation,
C.

PS If you run into Lois, tell her I'm sorry for ripping her off. I left my toothbrush in the bathroom. I want her to have it.

I used my retirement money to buy a boat-rental and bait business in New Iberia, and had my houseboat towed from New Orleans through Morgan City and up the Bayou Teche. Annie and I rode on the boat the last few miles into New Iberia, and we ate crawfish *étouffée* on the deck and watched our wake slip up into the cypress and oak trees along the bank, watched yesterday steal upon us – the black people in straw hats, cane-fishing for goggle-eye perch, the smoke drifting out through the trees from barbecue fires, the crowds of college-age kids at fish-fries and crab-boils in the city park, the red leaves that tumbled out of the sky and settled like a whisper on the bayou's surface. It was the Louisiana I had grown up in, a place that never seemed to change, where it was never a treason to go with the cycle of things and let the season have its way. The fall sky was such a hard blue you could have struck a match against it, the yellow light so soft it might have been aged inside oak.

Heaven's Prisoners

For my agent, Philip Spitzer, a prizefighter who hung in there for the full fifteen, and those wonderful friends down in Louisiana to whom I owe an enormous debt of gratitude: John Easterly, Martha Lacy Hall, and Michael Pinkston

1

I was just off Southwest Pass, between Pecan and Marsh islands, with the green, whitecapping water of the Gulf Stream to the south and the long, flat expanse of the Louisiana coastline behind me – which is really not a coastline at all but instead a huge wetlands area of sawgrass, dead cypress strung with wisps of moss, and a maze of canals and bayous that are choked with Japanese water lilies whose purple flowers audibly pop in the morning and whose root systems can wind around your propeller shaft like cable wire. It was May and the breeze was warm and smelled of salt spray and schools of feeding white trout, and high above me pelicans floated on the warm air currents, their extended wings gilded in the sunlight, until suddenly one would drop from the sky like a bomb from its rack, its wings cocked back against its sides, and explode against the water's surface and then rise dripping with a menhaden or a mullet flapping from its pouched beak.

But the sky had been streaked with red at dawn, and I knew that by afternoon thunderheads would roll out of the south, the temperature would suddenly drop twenty degrees, as though all the air had suddenly been sucked out from under an enormous dark bowl, and the blackened sky would tremble with trees of lightning.

I had always loved the Gulf, no matter if it was torn with storms or if the surf was actually frozen with green ridges of ice. Even when I was a police officer in New Orleans, I had lived in a houseboat on Lake Pontchartrain and spent my off-days fishing down in Lafourche Parish and Barataria Bay, and even though I was in homicide I sometimes worked deals through the boys in vice so I could go alone on the Coast Guard cutter when they went after the dope runners out on the salt.

Now I owned a bait and boat-rental business on the bayou south of New Iberia, and twice a week my wife, Annie, and I headed out Southwest Pass in my converted jug boat and trawled for shrimp. It was called a 'jug boat' because years ago it had been designed by an oil company for retrieving the long, thick, rubber-coated cables and seismic instruments used in marine oil exploration; it was long, narrow, and flat, with a big

Chrysler engine, two screws, and the pilot's cab flush against the stern. Annie and I had outfitted it with ice bins, a bait well, winches for the nets, a small galley, fishing and scuba gear boxes welded to the gunnels, and even a big, canvas Cinzano umbrella that I could open up over a bridge table and folding chairs.

On mornings like this we'd trawl in a big circle through the Pass, the bow almost out of the water with the bursting weight of the net, then we'd load the ice bins full with pink-blue shrimp, set out the rods for gafftop catfish, and fix lunch in the galley while the boat drifted against the anchor rope in the warm wind. On this morning Annie had boiled a pot of shrimp and bluepoint crabs and was cleaning the shrimp in a bowl to mix with a pan of dirty rice we had brought from home. I had to smile as I watched her; she was my Mennonite-Kansas girl, with curly gold hair that lifted on the nape of her neck in the breeze, and eyes that were the most electric blue I had ever seen. She wore a man's faded denim shirt with the tails hanging over her white ducks, and canvas shoes with no socks; she had learned to clean fish and shrimp and handle a boat in a gale as well as if she had been born in the bayou country, but she would always remain my Kansas girl, sewn together from bluebonnets and sun-flowers, tilting awkwardly on high heels, always awed by cultural differ-ence and what she called 'weirdness' in other people, although she came from a background of wheat-farmer pacifists that was so pervasively eccentric that she couldn't recognise normality when she saw it.

She had a tan even in winter, and the smoothest skin I had ever touched. Small lights played in her eyes when you looked into them. She saw me smiling at her, set down the bowl of shrimp, and walked past me as though she were going to check the rods, then I felt her behind me, felt her breasts touch the back of my head, then her hands collapsed my hair like a tangle of black snakes in my eyes, and her fingers traced my face, my brush mustache, my shoulders, the *pungi*-stick scar on my stomach that looked like a flattened, gray worm, until her innocent love made me feel that all my years, my love handles, my damaged liver were not important after all. Maybe I had grown foolish, or perhaps fond is a better word, in the way that an aging animal doesn't question its seduction by youth. But her love wasn't a seduction; it was unrelenting and always there, even after a year of marriage, and she gave it eagerly and without condition. She had a strawberry birthmark high up on her right breast, and when she made love her heart filled it with blood until it became a dark red. She moved around the chair, sat on my lap, rubbed her hand across the thin film of sweat on my chest, and touched her curly hair against my cheek. She shifted her weight in my lap, felt me under her, looked knowingly into my eyes, and whispered as though we could be heard, 'Let's get the air mattress out of the locker.'

'What are you going to do if the Coast Guard plane goes over?'

'Wave.'

'What if one of the reels goes out?'

'I'll try to keep your mind on something else.'

I looked away from her toward the southern horizon.

'Dave?'

'It's a plane.'

'How often do you get propositioned by your own wife? Don't let opportunity pass, skipper.' Her blue eyes were merry and full of light.

'No, look. He's in trouble.'

It was a bright yellow, two-engine job, and a long trail of thick black smoke blew from behind the cabin all the way across the sky to the horizon. The pilot was trying hard to gain altitude, gunning both engines, but the wingtips wobbled from side to side and wouldn't stabilise and the water was coming up fast. He went past us and I could see faces in the glass windows. The smoke twisted out of a ragged hole just in front of the tail.

'Oh, Dave, I thought I saw a child,' Annie said.

The pilot must have been trying to make Pecan Island so he could pancake into the salt grass, but suddenly pieces of the rudder shredded away like strips of wet cardboard and the plane dipped violently to port and turned in a half-circle, both engines stalling now, the smoke curling as thick and black as smoke from an oil fire, and went down hard on one wing against the water's surface, flipped over in the air like a stick toy, and landed upside-down in a huge spray of green and white water and floating seaweed.

The water boiled and danced on the overheated engine housings, and the hole in the back actually seemed to create and suck a river deep inside the plane. In seconds the bright yellow underside of the plane was dimming in the low waves that slid across it. I couldn't see the doors, but I kept waiting for somebody in a life preserver to break through the surface. Instead, big balloons of air rose from the cabin, and a dirty slick of oil and gasoline was already obscuring the sun's winking refraction off the wings.

Annie was on the shortwave to the Coast Guard. I pulled the anchor free of the mud, threw it rattling into the bow, turned the big Chrysler engine over, heard the exhausts cough below the waterline, and hit it full throttle for the wreck. The wind and spray were like a cool slap in my face. But all I could see of the plane now were small gold lights in the floating blue-green stain of oil and gas leaking from broken fuel lines.

'Take the wheel,' I said.

I saw her thoughts gathering in her face.

'We didn't refill the air tanks last time,' she said.

'There's still some in there. It's not more than twenty-five feet here, anyway. If they haven't settled into the silt, I can get the doors open.'

'Dave, it's deeper than twenty-five feet. You know it is. There's a trench right through the Pass.'

I got the two air tanks out of the gear box and looked at the gauges. They both showed almost empty. I stripped down to my skivvies, hooked on a weight belt, put on one air tank and a mask, and slipped the canvas straps of the other tank over my arm. I picked up a crowbar out of the gear box.

'Anchor outside so one of them doesn't come up under the boat,' I said.

'Leave the other tank. I'm going down, too.' She had cut back the throttle, and the boat was pitching in its own wake. The side of her tanned face was wet with spray, and her hair was stuck to it.

'We need you up here, babe,' I said, and went over the side.

'Damn you, Dave,' I heard her say just as I plummeted with a clank of metal tanks through the water's surface.

The bottom of the Gulf was a museum of nautical history. Snorkel and scuba diving over the years, I had found clusters of Spanish cannon-balls welded together with coral, US Navy practice torpedoes, and the flattened hull of a Nazi submarine that had been depth-charged in 1942, a cigarette boat that dope runners had opened the cocks on before the Coast Guard had nailed them, and even the collapsed and twisted wreckage of the offshore oil rig on which my father drowned over twenty years ago. It lay on its side in the murk in eighty feet of water, and the day I swam down to it the steel cables whipped and sang against the stanchions like hammers ringing against an enormous saw blade.

The plane had settled upside down on the edge of the trench, its propellers dug deep in the gray sand. Strings of bubbles rose from the wings and windows. I felt the water grow colder as I went deeper, and now I could see crabs and jewfish moving quickly across the bottom and puffs of sand from the wings of stingray that undulated and glided like shadows down the sides of the trench.

I got down to the pilot's door, slipped the spare tank off my arm, and looked through the window. He stared back at me upside down, his blond hair waving in the current, his sightless green eyes like hard, watery marbles. A short, thick-bodied woman with long black hair was strapped into the seat next to him, and her arms floated back and forth in front of her face as though she were still trying to push away that terrible recognition that her life was about to end. I had seen drowning victims before, and their faces had had the same startled, poached expression as the faces of people I had seen killed by shell bursts in Vietnam. I just hoped that these two had not suffered long.

I was kicking up clouds of sand from the bottom, and in the murky green-yellow light I could barely see through the window of the back door. I held myself out flat, holding on to the door handle for balance, and pressed my mask to the window again. I could make out a big, dark man in a pink shirt with pockets and cloth loops all over it, and a woman next to him who had floated free from her seatbelt. She was squat, with a square, leathery face, like the woman in front, and her flowered dress floated up around her head. Then, just as my air went, I realised with a terrible quickening of my heart that somebody was alive in the cabin.

I could see her small, bare legs kicking like scissors, her head and mouth turned upward like a guppy's into an air pocket at the rear of the cabin. I dumped the empty tank off my back and jerked on the door handle, but the door's edge was wedged into the silt. I pulled again, enough to separate the door a half-inch from the jamb, got the crowbar inside, and pried the metal back until I felt a hinge go and the door scrape back over the sand. But my lungs were bursting now, my teeth gritted against my own exhalation of breath, my ribs like knives inside my chest.

I dropped the crowbar, picked up the other tank, slapped the valve open, and got the hose in my mouth. The air went down inside me with the coolness of wind blowing across the melting snow. Then I took a half-dozen deep hits, shut the valve again, blew my mask clear, and went in after her.

But the dead man in the pink shirt was in my way. I popped loose his seatbelt buckle and tried to pull him free from the seat by his shirt. His neck must have been broken because his head revolved on his shoulders as though it were attached to a flower stem. Then his shirt tore loose in my hands, and I saw a green and red snake tattooed above his right nipple and something in my mind, like the flick of a camera shutter, went back to Vietnam. I grabbed his belt, pushed under his arm, and shoved him forward toward the cockpit. He rolled in a slow arc and settled between the pilot and the front passenger seat, with his mouth open and his head resting on the pilot's knee, like a supplicant jester.

I had to get her out and up fast. I could see the wobbling balloon of air she was breathing out of, and there wasn't room for me to come up inside of it and explain what we were going to do. Also, she could not have been more than five years old, and I doubted that she spoke English. I held her small waist lightly between my hands and paused, praying that she would sense what I had to do, then dragged her kicking down through the water and out the door.

For just an instant I saw her face. She was drowning. Her mouth was open and swallowing water; her eyes were hysterical with terror. Her close-cropped black hair floated from her head like duck down, and there were pale, bloodless spots in her tan cheeks. I thought about trying to get the air hose in her mouth, but I knew I wouldn't be able to clear the blockage in her throat and she would strangle before I could get her to the top. I unhooked my weight belt, felt it sink into the swirling cloud of sand under me, locked my arms under her chest, and shoved us both hard toward the surface.

I could see the black, shimmering outline of the jug boat overhead. Annie had cut the engine, and the boat was swinging in the current against the anchor rope. I had gone without air for almost two minutes, and my lungs felt as though they had been filled with acid. I kept my feet out straight, kicking hard, the bubbles leaking through my teeth, the closure in my throat about to break and suck in a torrent of water that would fill my chest like concrete. Then I could see the sunlight become brighter on the surface, like a yellow flame dancing on the chop and glazing the flat slicks, feel the layers of current suddenly become tepid, touch the red-brown wreaths of seaweed that turned under the waves, then we burst into the air, into the hot wind, into a dome of blue skies and white clouds and brown pelicans sailing over us like welcoming sentinels.

I grabbed the bottom of the deck rail with one hand and held the little girl up to Annie's arms. She felt as though she had the hollow bones of a bird. Annie pulled her up on deck and stroked her head and face while the little girl sobbed and vomited into Annie's lap. I was too weak to climb out of the water right away. Instead, I simply stared at the red hand-prints on the child's trembling thighs where the mother had held her up into the pocket of air while she herself lost her life, and I wished that those who handed out medals for heroism in war had a more encompassing vision about the nature of valor.

I knew that people who took water into their lungs sometimes developed pneumonia later, so Annie and I drove the little girl to the Catholic hospital in New Iberia, the small sugar town on Bayou Teche where I had grown up. The hospital was a gray stone building set in Spanish oaks on the bayou, and purple wisteria grew on the trellises above the walkways and the lawn was filled with yellow and red hibiscus and flaming azalea. We went inside, and Annie carried the little girl back to the emergency room while I sat across the reception desk from a heavyset nun in a white habit who filled out the girl's admission form.

The nun's face was as big and round as a pie plate, and her wimple was crimped as tightly across her forehead as a medieval knight's visor.

'What is her name?' she said.

I looked back at her.

'Do you know her name?' she said.

'Alafair.'

'What is her last name?'

'Robicheaux.'

'Is she your daughter?'

'Sure.'

'She's your daughter?'

'Of course.'

'Hmmm,' she said, and continued to write on the form. Then, 'I'll look in on her for you. In the meantime, why don't you look over this information and make sure I wrote it down accurately.'

'I trust you, Sister.'

'Oh, I wouldn't say that too quickly.'

She walked heavily down the hall with her black beads swinging from her waist. She had the physique of an over-the-hill prizefighter. A few minutes later she was back and I was growing more uncomfortable.

'My, what an interesting family you have,' she said. 'Did you know that your daughter speaks nothing but Spanish?'

'We're heavy into Berlitz.'

'And you're so clever, too,' she said.

'How is she, Sister?'

'She's fine. A little scared, but it looks like she's with the right family.' She smiled at me with her lumpy, round face.

Afternoon rain clouds had started to build in the south when we crossed the drawbridge over the bayou and drove out East Main toward the edge of town. Huge oak trees grew on each side of the street; their thick roots cracked through the side-walks, their spreading branches arched in a sun-spangled canopy overhead. The homes along East Main were antebellum and Victorian in design, with widow's walks, second-story verandas, marble porches, Greek columns, scrolled iron fences, and sometimes gleaming white gazebos covered with Confederate jasmine and purple bugle vine. The little girl, whom I had offhandedly named Alafair, my mother's name, sat between us in the pickup. The nuns had kept her damp clothes and had dressed her in a pair of faded child's jeans and an oversized softball shirt that read *New Iberia Pelicans*. Her face was exhausted, her eyes dull and unseeing. We rumbled over another draw-bridge and stopped at a fruit stand run by a black man under a cypress tree on the edge of the bayou. I bought us three big links of hot boudin wrapped in wax paper, snowcones, and a lug of strawberries to fix later with ice cream. Annie put the ice in Alafair's mouth with the small wooden spoon.

'Little bites for little people,' she said.

Alafair opened her mouth like a bird, her eyelashes blinking sleepily.

'Why did you lie back there?' Annie said.

'I'm not sure.'

'Dave . . .'

'She's probably an illegal. Why make problems for the nuns?'

'So what if she's an illegal?'

'Because I don't trust government pencil pushers and paper shufflers, that's why.'

'I think I hear the voice of the New Orleans police department.'

'Annie, Immigration sends them back.'

'They wouldn't do that to a child, would they?'

I didn't have an answer for her. But my father, who had been a fisherman, trapper, and derrickman all his life, and who couldn't read or write and spoke Cajun French and a form of English that was hardly a language, had an axiom for almost every situation. One of these would translate as 'When in doubt, do nothing.' In actuality he would say something like (in this case to a wealthy sugar planter who owned property next to us), 'You didn't told me about your hog in my cane, no, so I didn't mean to hurt it when I pass the tractor on its head and had to eat it, me.'

I drove along the dirt road that led to my boat-and-bait business on the bayou. The rain began to fall lightly through the oak trees, dimpling the bayou, clicking on the lily pads that grew out from the bank. I could see the bream starting to feed along the edge of the lilies and the flooded cane-brake. Up ahead, fishermen were bringing their boats back into my dock, and the two black men who worked for me were pulling the canvas awning out over the side porch of the bait house and clearing the beer bottles and paper barbecue plates off the wooden telephone spools that I used as tables.

My house was a hundred yards from the bayou, in a grove of pecan trees. It was built of unpainted oak and cypress, with a tin-roofed gallery in front, a dirt yard, rabbit hutches, and a dilapidated barn in back, and a watermelon garden just beyond the edge of the pecan trees. Sometimes in a strong wind the pecans would ring like grapeshot on the gallery's tin roof.

Alafair had fallen asleep across Annie's lap. When I carried her into the house she looked up at me once as though she were waking briefly from a dream, then she closed her eyes again. I put her to bed in the side room, turned on the window fan, and closed the door softly. I sat on the gallery and watched the rain fall on the bayou. The air smelled of trees, wet moss, flowers, and damp earth.

'You want something to eat?' Annie said behind me.

'Not now, thanks.'

'What are you doing out here?'

'Nothing.'

'I guess that's why you keep looking down the road,' she said.

'The people in that plane don't fit.'

I felt her fingers on my shoulders.

'I've got this problem, officer,' she said. 'My husband can't stop being a homicide detective. When I try to hit on him, his attention is always somewhere else. What's a girl to do?'

'Take up with a guy like myself. I'm always willing to help out.'

'I don't know. You look so busy watching the rain.'

'It's one of the few things I do well.'

'You sure you have time, officer?' she said, and slipped her arms down my chest and pressed her breasts and stomach against me.

I never had much luck at resisting her. She was truly beautiful to look at. We went into our bedroom, where the window fan hummed with a wet light, and she smiled at me while she undressed, then began singing, 'Baby love, my baby love, oh how I need you, my baby love . . .'

She sat on top of me, with her heavy breasts close to my face, put her fingers in my hair, and looked into my eyes with her gentle and loving face. Each time I pressed the back of her shoulders with my palms she kissed my mouth and tightened her thighs, and I saw the strawberry birthmark on her breast darken to a deep scarlet and I felt my heart begin to twist, my loins harden and ache, saw her face soften and grow small above me, then suddenly I felt something tear loose and melt inside me, like a large boulder breaking loose in a stream-bed and rolling away in the current.

Then she lay close to me and closed my eyes with her fingers, and I felt the fan pulling the cool air across the sheets like the wind out on the Gulf in the smoky light of sunrise.

It was late afternoon and still raining when I woke to the sound of the child's crying. It was as though my sleep were disturbed by the tip of an angel's wing. I walked barefoot into the bedroom, where Annie sat on the edge of the bed and held Alafair against her breast.

'She's all right now,' Annie said. 'It was just a bad dream, wasn't it? And dreams can't hurt you. We just brush them away and wash our face and then eat some ice cream and strawberries with Dave and Annie.'

The little girl held Annie's chest tightly and looked at me with her round, frightened eyes. Annie squeezed her and kissed the top of her head.

'Dave, we just have to keep her,' she said.

Again I didn't answer her. I sat out on the gallery through the evening and watched the light turn purple on the bayou and listened to the cicadas and the rain dripping in the trees. At one time in my life, rain had always been the color of wet neon or Jim Beam whiskey. Now it just looked like rain. It smelled of sugarcane, of the cypress trees along the bayou, of the gold and scarlet four-o'clocks that opened in the cooling shadows. But as I watched the fireflies lighting in the pecan orchard, I could not deny that a thin tremolo was starting to vibrate inside me, the kind that used to leave me in after-hours bars with the rain streaking down the neon-lit window.

I kept watching the dirt road, but it was empty. Around nine o'clock I saw some kids in a pirogue out on the bayou, gigging frogs. The headlamps of the children danced through the reeds and cattails, and I could hear their paddles chunking loudly in the water. An hour later I latched the screen, turned out the lights, and got in bed next to Annie. The little girl slept on the other side of her. In the moon's glow through the window I saw Annie smile without opening her eyes, then she laid her arm across my chest.

He came early the next morning, when the sun was still misty and soft in the trees, even before the pools of rain had dried on the road, so that his government car splashed mud on a family of Negroes walking with cane poles toward my fishing dock. I walked into the kitchen where Annie and Alafair were just finishing their breakfast.

'Why don't you take her down to the pond to feed the ducks?' I said.

'I thought we'd go into town and buy her some clothes.'

'We can do that later. Here's some old bread. Go out the back door and walk through the trees.'

'What is it, Dave?'

'Nothing, just some minor bullshit. I'll tell you about it later. Come on, off you go.'

'I'd like to know when you first thought you could start talking to me like this.'

'Annie, I'm serious,' I said.

Her eyes flicked past me to the sound of the car driving across the pecan leaves in front. She picked up the cellophane bag of stale bread, took Alafair by the hand, and went out the back screen door through the trees toward the pond at the end of our property. She looked back once, and I could see the alarm in her face.

The man got out of his gray US government motor-pool car, with his seersucker coat over his shoulder. He was middle-aged, thick across the waist, and wore a bow tie. His black hair was combed across his partially bald head.

I met him on the gallery. He said his name was Monroe, from the Immigration and Naturalization Service in New Orleans. While he talked, his eyes went past me into the gloom of the house.

'I'd ask you in, but I'm on my way down to the dock,' I said.

'That's all right. I just need to ask you one or two things,' he said. 'Why didn't you all wait for the Coast Guard after you called in on the emergency channel?'

'What for?'

'Most people would want to hang around. For curiosity, if nothing else. How often do you see a plane go down?'

'My wife gave them the position. They could see the oil and gas on the water. They didn't need us.'

'Huh,' he said, and took a cigarette out of his shirt pocket. He rolled it back and forth between his fingers without lighting it and looked away at the pecan trees. The tobacco grains crackled dryly inside the paper. 'I got a problem, though. A diver found a suitcase in there with a bunch of child's clothes in it. A little girl's, in fact. But there wasn't a kid in that plane. What's that suggest to you?'

'I'm late for work, Mr Monroe. Would you like to walk down to the dock with me?'

'You don't like federal people too much, do you?'

'I haven't known that many. Some of them are good guys, some of them aren't. I guess you tapped into my file.'

He shrugged.

'Why do you think illegals would carry a child's clothing with them when they had no child? I'm talking about people that left the banana farm one step ahead of the National Guard shredding them into dog food. Or at least that's what they tell the press.'

'I don't know.'

'Your wife told the Coast Guard you were going to dive that wreck. Are you going to tell me you only saw three people down there?'

I looked back at him.

'What do you mean, three?' I said.

'The pilot was a priest named Melancon, from Lafayette. We've been watching him for a while. We think the two women were from El Salvador. At least that's where the priest had been flying them out from before.'

'What about the guy in the pink shirt?'

His face became perplexed, his eyes muddy with confusion.

'What are you talking about?' he said.

'I damn near tore the shirt off him. He was in the back. His neck was broken and he had a tattoo over one nipple.'

He was shaking his head. He lit his cigarette and blew smoke out into the dappled sunlight.

'You're either a good storyteller or you see things nobody else knows about,' he said.

'Are you calling me a liar?' I asked quietly.

'I won't play word games with you, Mr Robicheaux.'

'It seems to me that's just what you're doing.'

'You're right, I did get feedback on your file before I came down here. You have an amazing record.'

'How's that?'

'You blew away three or four people, one of whom was a government witness. That's real hardball, all right. You want me to come back out with a warrant?'

'I don't think I'm going to see you for a while. You dumped the wheelbarrow on its side, podna. Your people are into something they haven't let you in on yet.'

I saw his eyes darken.

'I'd tend to my own business if I was you,' he said.

'There's something I didn't tell you. The UPI in New Orleans called me last night. I told them there were four dead people in that plane. I hope you guys aren't going to tell people I can't count.'

'You don't need to worry about what we do. Just keep your own act clean, and we'll get along fine.'

'I think you've been talking to wetbacks for too long. I think you should give some thought to your words before you say things to people.'

He dropped his cigarette on the ground, pressed it out with his shoe, and smiled to himself as he got in his car. He started his engine. A shaft of sunlight cut across his face.

'Well, you've made my day,' he said. 'I always like to be reassured that I'm on the right side of the fence.'

'One other thing. When you drove in here, you splashed mud on some people. Try to be more careful when you leave.'

'Anything you say,' he said, and smiled up at me, then accelerated slowly down my lane.

Very cool, Robicheaux, I thought. There's nothing like rattling the screens on the baboon cage. But what should you do in a situation like that? Most government employees aren't bad guys; they're just unimaginative, they feel comfortable in a world of predictable rules, and they rarely question authority. But if you run up against the nasty ones and they sense fear in you, they'll try to dismantle you one piece at a time.

I went down to the dock, put fresh ice in the beer and pop coolers, seined out the dead shiners from the bait tanks, started the fire in the split oil drum that I used for a barbecue pit on the side porch, oiled and seasoned the twenty-five pounds of chickens and pork chops that I would grill and sell at lunchtime, and then fixed myself a big glass of Dr Pepper filled with shaved ice, mint leaves, and cherries, and sat at a table under the porch awning and watched some Negroes fishing under a cypress on the opposite bank of the bayou. They wore straw hats and sat on wood stools close together with their cane poles motionless over the lily pads. I had never understood why black people always fished together in close groups, or why they refused to move from one spot to another, even when the fish weren't biting; but I also knew that if they didn't catch anything, no one else would, either. One of the cork bobbers started to tremble on the surface, then slide along the edge of the lily pads, then draw away toward the bottom; a little boy jerked his cane up, and a big sunfish exploded through the water, its gills and stomach painted with fire. The boy held it with one hand, worked the hook out of its mouth, then dipped his other hand into the water and lifted out a shaved willow branch dripping with bluegill and goggle-eye perch. I watched him thread the sharpened tip of the branch through the sunfish's gill and out its mouth, then replace it in the water.

But watching that scene out of my own youth, living that moment with yesterday's people, wouldn't take my mind off that ugly scar of smoke across the sky at Southwest Pass or a woman who would hold a child up into a pocket of air while her own lungs filled with water and gasoline.

That afternoon I drove into New Iberia and bought a copy of the *Times-Picayune*. The wire service story said that the bodies of three people, including that of a Catholic priest, had been removed from the plane. The source of the story was St Mary Parish sheriff's office. Which meant the sheriff's office had been told that three bodies were recovered, or that only three had been brought into the parish coroner's office.

It was hot and bright the next morning when I cut the engine off Southwest Pass and splashed the anchor overboard. The waves slapped under the bow as I put on my flippers and air tank, which I had refilled earlier in the morning. I hitched on a weight belt, went over the side, and swam down in a stream of bubbles to the wreck, which still lay upside down on the sloping edge of the trench. The water was a cloudy green from the rains, but I could see detail within a foot of my face mask. I came down on the tail section and worked my way forward toward the cabin. The hole that had gushed black smoke across the sky was jagged and sharp under my hands. The metal was twisted outward, in the same way that an artillery round would exit from iron plate.

All the doors were open forward, and the cabin was picked clean. At least almost. The torn pink shirt of the tattooed man undulated gently against the floor in the groundswell. One of the cloth loops was caught in the floor fastening for the safety strap harness. I jerked the shirt loose, wadded it into a tight ball, and swam back up to the yellow-green light on the surface.

I had long ago learned to be thankful for small favors. I had also learned not to be impetuous or careless with their use. I laid the shirt out on the deck and weighted the sleeves and collar and tails with fishing sinkers. It didn't take long for the shirt to dry in the wind and against the hot boards of the deck; the cloth was stiff and salty to the touch.

I found a plastic minnow bag in my tackle box, took the shirt back to the pilothouse out of the wind, and began cutting away the pockets with my single-blade Puma knife, which had the edge of a barber's razor. I picked out a pencil stub, tobacco grains, sodden kitchen matches, a small comb, strings of lint, and finally a swizzle stick.

A wooden swizzle stick in a tiny sanitary wrapper. A swizzle stick that I knew had letters printed on it because the purple ink had run into the paper wrapper like a smeared kiss.

2

It was midafternoon the next day when I parked my pickup truck on Decatur Street by Jackson Square in New Orleans. I had coffee and beignets in the Café du Monde, then walked on into the square and sat on an iron bench under the banana trees not far from St Louis Cathedral. It was still a little early to find the girl who I hoped would be in Smiling Jack's, so I sat in the warm shade and watched the Negro street musicians playing their bottleneck guitars in the lee of the church, and the sidewalk artists sketching portraits of tourists in Pirates Alley. I had always loved the French Quarter. Many people in New Orleans complained that it was filled with winos, burnt-out dopers, hookers, black street hustlers, and sexual degenerates. What they said was true, but I didn't care. The Quarter had always been like that. Jean Lafitte and his gang of cutthroats had operated out of old New Orleans and so had James Bowie, who was an illegal slave trader when he wasn't slicing people apart with his murderous knife. Actually, I thought the hookers and drunks, the thieves and pimps probably had more precedent and claim to the Quarter than the rest of us did.

The old Creole buildings and narrow streets never changed. Palm fronds and banana trees hung over the stone walls and iron gates of the courtyards; it was always shady under the scrolled colonnades that extended over the sidewalks, and the small grocery stores with their wood-bladed fans always smelled of cheese, sausage, ground coffee, and crates of peaches and plums. The brick of the buildings was worn and cool and smooth to the touch, the flagstones in the alleys troughed and etched from the rainwater that sluiced off the roofs and balconies overhead. Sometimes you looked through the scrolled iron door of a brick walkway and saw a courtyard in the interior of a building ablaze with sunlight and purple wisteria and climbing yellow roses, and when the wind was right you could smell the river, the damp brick walls, a fountain dripping into a stagnant well, the sour odor of spilled wine, the ivy that rooted in the mortar like the claws of a lizard, the four-o'clocks blooming in the shade, and a green garden of spearmint erupting against a sunlit stucco wall.

The shadows were growing longer in Jackson Square. I looked again at the swizzle stick I had found in the dead man's shirt pocket. The smears of purple dye on it did not look like much now, but that morning a friend of mine at the university in Lafayette had put it under an infrared microscope that was a technological miracle. It could lighten and darken both the wood and the dye, and as my friend shifted the grain in and out of focus we could identify eight of twelve letters printed on the stick: SM LI G J KS.

Why would people who went to the trouble of removing a body from a submerged plane and lying about it to the press (successfully, too) be so careless as to leave behind the dead man's shirt for a bait salesman to find? Easy answer. People who lie, run games, manipulate, and steal usually do so because they don't have the brains and forethought to pull it off otherwise. The Watergate burglars were not nickel-and-dime second-story creeps. These were guys who had worked for the CIA and FBI. They got nailed because they taped back the spring lock on an office door by wrapping the tape horizontally around the lock rather than vertically. A minimum-wage security guard saw the tape and removed it but didn't report it. One of the burglars came back and taped the door open a second time. The security guard made his rounds again and saw the fresh tape and called the DC police. The burglars were still in the building when the police arrived.

I walked through the cooling streets to Bourbon, which was now starting to fill with tourists. Families from Grand Rapids looked through the half-opened doors of the strip joints and the bars that advertised female wrestling and French orgies, their faces scrubbed and smiling and iridescent in the late-afternoon light. They were as innocent in their oblique fascination with the lascivious as the crowds of college boys with their paper beer cups who laughed at the burlesque spielers and street crazies and knew that they themselves would never be subject to time and death; or maybe they were even as innocent as the businessman from Meridian, who walked with grinning detachment and ease past the flashes of thighs and breasts through those opened doors, but who would wake trembling and sick tomorrow in a motel off the old Airline Highway, his empty wallet floating in the toilet, his nocturnal memories a tangle of vipers that made sweat pop out on his forehead.

Smiling Jack's was on the corner of Bourbon and Toulouse. If Robin Gaddis was still stripping there, and still feeding all the dragons that had lived inside her since she was a little girl, she'd be at the bar for her first vodka collins by six o'clock, do some whites on the half-shell at six-thirty, and an hour later get serious with some black speed and shift up to the full-tilt boogie. I had taken her to a couple of AA meetings with me, but she'd said it wasn't for her. I guessed she was one of those who had no bottom. In the years I had known her she had been jailed dozens of times by vice, stabbed through the thigh by a john, and had her jaw broken with an ice mallet by one of her husbands. One time when I was over at the social welfare agency I pulled her family file, a three-generation case history that was a study in institutional failure and human inadequacy. She had grown up in the public housing project by St Louis Cemetery, the daughter of a half-wit mother and an alcoholic father who used to wrap the urine soaked sheets around her head when she wet the bed. Now, in her adulthood, she had managed to move a half-mile away from the place of her birth.

But she wasn't at the bar. In fact, Smiling Jack's was almost empty. The mirrored runway behind the bar was darkened; the musical instruments of the three-piece band sat unattended in the small pit at the end of the runway; and in the empty gloom a turning strobe light overhead made a revolving shotgun pattern of darkness and light that could be equaled only by seasickness. I asked the bartender if she would be in. He was perhaps thirty and wore hillbilly sideburns, a black fedora, and a black T-shirt with the faces of the Three Stooges embossed whitely on the front.

'You bet,' he said, and smiled. 'The first show is at eight. She'll be in by six-thirty for the glug-glug hour. You a friend of hers?'

'Yes.'

'What are you drinking?'

'Do you have a Dr Pepper?'

'Are you kidding me?'

'Give me a 7-Up.'

'It's two bucks. You sure you want to drink soda pop?'

I put the two dollars on the bar.

'I know you, right?' he said, and smiled again.

'Maybe.'

'You're a cop, right?'

'Nope.'

'Hey, come on, man, I got two big talents – one as a mixologist and the other for faces. But you're not vice, right?'

'I'm not a cop.'

'Wait a minute, I got it. Homicide. You used to work out of the First District on Basin.'

'Not anymore.'

'You get moved or something?'

'I'm out of the business.'

'Early change of life, huh?' he said. His eyes were green and they stayed sufficiently narrowed so you couldn't read them. 'You remember me?'

'It's Jerry something-or-other. Five years ago you went up the road for bashing an old man with a pipe. How'd you like it up there at Angola?'

His green eyes widened a moment, looked boldly at me from under the

brim of the black fedora, then narrowed and crinkled again. He began
drying glasses with a towel, his face turned at an oblique angle.

'It wasn't bad. I was outdoors a lot, lots of fresh air, gave me a chance
to get in shape. I like farm work. I grew up on one,' he said. 'Hey, have
another 7-Up. You're impressive, man. A sharp guy like you should have
a 7-Up on the house.'

'You drink it for me,' I said, and picked up my glass and walked to the
back of the bar. I watched him light a cigarette, smoke only a few puffs
off it, then flip it angrily through the front door onto the tourist-filled
sidewalk.

She came in a half hour later, dressed in sandals, blue jeans low on her
hips, and a tank top that exposed her flat, tanned stomach. Unlike most
of the strippers, she wore her black hair cut short, like a 1940 schoolgirl's.
And in spite of all the booze, coke, and speed that went into her body, she
was still good to look at.

'Wow, they put the first team back on the street,' she said, and smiled.
'How you doing, Streak? I'd heard you were remarried and back on the
bayou, selling worms and all that jazz.'

'That's right. I'm just a tourist now.'

'You really hung it up for good, huh? That must take guts, I mean just
to boogie on out of it one day and do something weird like sell worms to
people. What'd you say, "*Sayonara*, crime-stoppers, keep your guns in
your pants"?'

'Something like that.'

'Hey, Jerry, does it look like we got AIDS down here? It's glug-glug
time for mommy.'

'I'm trying to find out something about a guy,' I said.

'I'm not exactly an information center, Streak. Didn't you ever want to
touch up that white spot in your hair? You've got the blackest hair I've
ever seen in a man, except for that white patch.' She touched the side of
my head with her fingers.

'This guy had a green and red snake tattooed on his chest. I think he
probably came in here.'

'They pay to see me take off my clothes. It's not the other way around.
Unless you mean something else.'

'I'm talking about a big, dark guy with a head the size of a watermelon.
The tattoo was just above the nipple. If you saw it, you wouldn't forget it.'

'Why's that?' She lit a cigarette and kept her eyes on the vodka collins
that Jerry was mixing for her down the bar.

'There was a tattoo artist in Bring-Cash Alley in Saigon who used the
same dark green and red ink. His work was famous in the Orient. He was
in Hong Kong for years. British sailors all over the world have his work
on them.'

'Why would I get to see it?'

'Listen, Robin, I was always your friend. I never judged what you did. Cut the bullshit.'

'Oh, that's what it is, huh?' She took the collins glass from Jerry's hand and drank from it. Her mouth looked wet and red and cold when she set the glass down. 'I don't do the other stuff anymore. I don't have to. I work this place six months, then I have two gigs in Fort Lauderdale for the winter. Ask your pals in vice.'

'They're not my pals. They hung me out to dry. When I was suspended I found out what real solitude was all about.'

'I wish you had come around. I could have really gone for you, Dave.'

'Maybe I wish I had.'

'Come on, I can't see you hooked up with a broad that whips out her jugs every night for a roomful of middle-aged titty-babies. Hey, Jerry, can you take it out of slow motion?'

He took away her glass and refilled it with vodka and mix, but didn't bother to put fresh ice or an orange slice in it.

'You're always a class guy,' she said to him.

'What can I say, it's a gift,' he said, and went back down the bar and began loading beer bottles in the cooler. He turned his face from side to side each time he placed a bottle in the cooler in case one of them should explode.

'I gotta get out of this place. It gets crazier all the time,' she said. 'If you think his burner's turned off, you ought to meet his mom. She owns this dump and the souvenir shop next door. She's got hair like a Roto-Rooter brush, you know, the kind they run through sewer pipes. Except she thinks she's an opera star. She wears muumuu dresses and glass jewelry hanging all over her, and in the morning she puts a boom-box on the bar and she and him scrub out the toilets and sing opera together like somebody stuck them in the butt with a hayfork.'

'Robin, I know this tattooed man was in here. I really need you to help me.'

She flicked her cigarette ashes into the ashtray and didn't answer.

'Look, you're not dropping the dime on him. He's dead,' I said. 'He was in a plane crash with a priest and some illegals.'

She exhaled smoke into the spinning circles of light and brushed a strand of hair out of her eye.

'You mean like with wetbacks or something?' she said.

'You could call them that.'

'I don't know what Johnny Dartez would be doing with a priest and wetbacks.'

'Who is he?'

'He's been around here for years, except when he was in the marines. He used to be a stall for a couple of street dips.'

'He was a pickpocket?'

'He tried to be one. He was so clumsy he'd usually knock the mark down before they could boost his wallet. He's a loser. I don't think this is your guy.'

'What's he been doing lately?'

She hesitated.

'I think maybe he was buying room keys and credit cards,' she said.

'I thought you were out of that, kiddo.'

'It was a while back.'

'I'm talking about now. What's the guy doing now, Robin?'

'I heard he was a mule for Bubba Rocque,' she said, and her voice fell to almost a whisper.

'Bubba Rocque?' I said.

'Yeah. Take it easy, will you?'

'I gotta go in back. You want another collins?' Jerry said.

'Yeah. Wash your hands when to go to the bathroom, too.'

'You know, Robin, when you come in here I hear this funny sound,' he said. 'I got to listen real close, but I hear it. It sounds like mice eating on something. I think it's your brain rotting.'

'Who's your PO, podna?' I said.

'I don't have one. I went out free and clear, max time, all sins forgiven. Does that mess up your day?' He grinned at me from under his black fedora.

'No, I was just wondering about some of those rum bottles behind the bar,' I said. 'I can't see an ATF Bureau seal on them. You were probably shopping in the duty-free store over in the Islands, and then you got your own bottles mixed up with your bar stock.'

He put his hands on his hips and looked at the bottles on the shelf and shook his head profoundly.

'Boy, I think you called it,' he said. 'Am I glad you brought that to my attention. Robin, you ought to hold on to this guy.'

'You better lay off it, Jerry,' she said.

'He knows I don't mean any harm. Right, chief? I don't get in people's face, I don't mess in their space. I ain't no swinging dick. You know what that is, don't you, chief?'

'Show time's over,' I said.

'You telling me? I get minimum wage and tips in this place, and I don't need the hassle. Believe me, I don't need the hassle.'

I watched him walk into the storage room at the back of the bar. He walked like a mainline con and full-time wiseguy, from the hips down, with no motion in the chest or arms, a guy who would break into jails or be in a case file of some kind the rest of his life. What produced them? Defective genes, growing up in a shithole, bad toilet training? Even after fourteen years with the New Orleans police department, I never had an adequate answer.

'About that Bubba Rocque stuff, that's just what I heard. I mean, it didn't come from me, okay?' she said. 'Bubba's crazy, Dave. I know a girl, she tried to go independent. His guys soaked her in gasoline and set her on fire.'

'You didn't tell me anything I didn't already know about Bubba. You understand that? You're not a source.'

But I could still see the bright sheen of fear in her eyes.

'Listen, I've known him all my life,' I said. 'He still owns a home outside of Lafayette. There's nothing you could tell me about him that's new.'

She let out her breath and took a drink from her glass.

'I know you were a good cop and all that bullshit,' she said, 'but there's a lot of stuff you guys never see. You can't. You don't live in it, Streak. You're a visitor.'

'I've got to run, kiddo,' I said. 'We live just south of New Iberia. If you ever want to work in the boat-and-bait business, give me a call.'

'Dave . . .'

'Yeah?'

'Come see me again, okay?'

I walked out into the dusky, neon-lit street. The music from the Dixieland and rockabilly bars was thunderous. I looked back at Robin, but her bar-stool was empty.

That night I rolled along the 1–10 causeway over the Atchafalaya flood basin. The willows and the half-submerged dead trunks of the cypress trees were gray and silver in the moonlight. There was no breeze, and the water was still and black and dented with the moon's reflection. A half-dozen oil derricks stood out blackly against the moon, then a wind blew up from the Gulf, ruffling the willows along the far shore, and wrinkled the water's surface like skin all the way out to the causeway.

I turned off at Breaux Bridge and followed the old backroad through St Martinville toward New Iberia. An electric floodlight shone on the white face of the eighteenth-century Catholic church where Evangeline and her lover were buried under a spreading oak. The trees that arched over the road were thick with Spanish moss, and the wind smelled of plowed earth and the young sugarcane out in the fields. But I could not get Bubba Rocque's name out of my mind.

He was among the few white kids in New Iberia who were tough and desperate enough to set pins at the bowling alley, in the years before air conditioning when the pits were 120 degrees and filled with exploding pins, crashing metal racks, cursing Negroes, and careening bowling balls that could snap a pinsetter's shinbone in half. He was the kid who wore no coat in winter, had scabs in his hair, and cracked his knuckles until they were the size of quarters. He was dirty and he smelled bad and he'd spit down a girl's collar for a nickel. He was also the subject of legends: he got laid by his aunt when he was ten; he hunted the neighborhood cats with a Benjamin pump; he tried to rape a Negro woman who worked in the high school lunch room; his father whipped him with a dog chain; he set fire to his clapboard house, which was located between the scrap yard and the SP tracks.

But what I remember most about him were his wide-set gray-blue eyes. They never seemed to blink, as though the lids had been surgically removed. I fought him to a draw in district Golden Gloves. You could break your hands on his face and he'd keep coming at you, the pupils of those unrelenting eyes like burnt cinders.

I needed to disengage. I wasn't a cop anymore, and my obligations were elsewhere. If Bubba Rocque's people were involved with the plane crash, a bad moon was on the rise and I didn't want anything more to do with it. Let the feds and the lowlifes jerk each other around. I was out of it.

When I got home the house was dark under the pecan trees, except for the glow of the television set in the front room. I opened the screen door and saw Annie asleep on a pallet in front of the television, the wood-bladed fan overhead blowing the curls on the back of her neck. Two empty ice cream bowls streaked with strawberry juice were beside her. Then in the corner I saw Alafair, wearing my blue-denim shirt like pajamas, her frightened face fixed on the television screen. A documentary about World War II showed a column of GIs marching along a dirt road outside of a bombed-out Italian town. They wore their pots at an angle, cigarettes dangled from their grinning mouths, a BAR man had a puppy buttoned up in his field jacket. But to Alafair these were not the liberators of Western Europe. Her thin body trembled under my hands when I picked her up.

'*Vienen los soldados aqui?*' she said, her face a terrible question mark.

She had other questions for us, too, ones not easily resolved by Annie's and my poor Spanish, or more importantly our adult unwillingness to force the stark realisation of mortality upon a bewildered child. Perhaps in her sleep she still felt her mother's hands on her thighs, raising her up into the wobbling bubble of air inside the plane's cabin; maybe she thought I was more than human, that I could resurrect the dead from water, anoint them with my hand, and make them walk from the dark world of sleep into the waking day. Alafair's eyes searched mine as though she would see in them the reflected image of her mother. But try as we might, neither Annie nor I could use the word *muerto*.

'*Adónde ha ido mi mamá?*' she said again the next morning.

And maybe her question implied the best answer we could give her. She didn't ask what had happened to her mother; she asked instead where she had gone. So we drove her to St Peter's Church in New Iberia. I suppose one might say that my attempt at resolution was facile. But I believe that ritual and metaphor exist for a reason. Words have no governance over either birth or death, and they never make the latter more acceptable, no matter how many times its inevitability is explained to us. We each held her hand and walked her up the aisle of the empty church to the scrolled metal stand of burning candles that stood before statues of Mary, Joseph, and the infant Jesus.

'*Ta maman est avec Jésus,*' I said to her in French. '*Au ciel.*'

Her face was round, and her eyes blinked at me.

'*Cielo?*' she asked.

'Yes, in the sky. *Au ciel,*' I said.

'*En el cielo,*' Annie said. 'In heaven.'

Alafair's face was perplexed as she at first looked back and forth between us, then I saw her lips purse and her eyes start to water.

'Hey, hey, little guy,' I said, and picked her up on my hip. 'Come on, I want you to light a candle. *Pour ta maman.*'

I lit the punk on a burning candle, put it in her hand, and helped her touch it to a dead wick inside a red glass candle container. She watched the teardrop of fire rise off the wax, then I moved her hand and the lighted punk to another wick and then another.

Her moist eyes were bright with the red and blue glow from inside the rows of glass containers on the stand. Her legs were spread on my hip like a frog's, her arms tight around my neck. The top of her head felt hot under my cheek. Annie reached out and stroked her back with the flat of her hand.

The light was pink in the trees along the bayou when I opened the dock for business early the next morning. It was very still, and the water was dark and quiet in the overhang of the cypress trees, and the bream were feeding and making circles like raindrops on the edge of the lily pads. I watched the light climb higher in the blue sky, touching the green of the tree line, burning away the mist that still hung around the cypress roots. It was going to be a balmy, clear day, good for bluegill and bass and sunfish, until the water became warm by mid-morning and the pools of shadow under the trees turned into mirrors of brown-yellow light. But just before three o'clock that afternoon the barometric pressure would drop, the sky would suddenly fill with gray clouds that had the metallic sheen of steam, and just as the first raindrops clicked against the water the bluegill would begin feeding again, all at once, their mouths popping against the surface louder than the rain.

I cleaned out the barbecue pit on the side porch next to the bait shop, put the ashes in a paper bag, dropped the bag in a trash barrel, spread new charcoal and green hickory in the bottom of the pit and started my lunch fire, then left Batist, one of the black men who worked for me, in charge of the shop, and went back up to the house and fixed an omelette and *cush-cush* for our breakfast. We ate on the redwood picnic table under the mimosa tree in the backyard while blue jays and mockingbirds flicked in and out of the sunlight.

Then I took Alafair with me in the truck to the grocery store on the highway to buy ice for the dock and shelled crawfish to make *étouffée* for our supper. I also bought her a big paper kite, and when we got back home she and I walked back to the duck pond at the end of my property, which adjoined a sugarcane field, and let the kite lift up suddenly into the breeze and rise higher and higher into the cloud-flecked blue sky. Her face was a round circle of incredible surprise and delight as the string tugged in her fingers and the kite flapped and danced against the wind.

Then I saw Annie walking toward us out of the dappled shade of the backyard into the sunlight. She wore a pair of Clorox-faded jeans and a dark blue shirt, and the sun made gold lights in her hair. I looked again at her face. She was trying to look unconcerned, but I could see the little wrinkle, like a sculptor's careless nick, between her eyes.

'What's wrong?' I said.

'Nothing, I guess.'

'Come on, Annie. Your face doesn't hide things too well.' I brushed her suntanned forehead with my fingers.

'There's a car parked off the side of the road in the trees with two men in it,' she said. 'I saw them a half hour or so ago, but I didn't pay any attention to them.'

'What kind of car?'

'I don't know. A white sports car of some kind. I went out on the porch and the driver raised up a newspaper like he was reading it.'

'They're probably just some oil guys goofing around on the job. But let's go take a look.'

I knotted the kite twine to a willow stick and pushed the stick deep into the soft dirt by the edge of the pond, and the three of us walked back to the house while the kite popped behind us in the wind.

I left them in the kitchen and looked through the front screen without opening it. A short distance down the dirt road from the dock, a white Corvette was parked at an angle in the trees. The man on the passenger side had his seat tilted back and was sleeping with a straw hat over his face. The man behind the wheel smoked a cigarette and blew the smoke out the window. I took my pair of World War II Japanese field glasses from the wall where they hung on their strap, braced them against the doorjamb, and focused the lens through the screen. The front windshield was tinted and there was too much shadow on it to see either of the men well, and the license plate was in back, so I couldn't get the number, but I could clearly make out the tiny metal letters *ELK* just below the driver's window.

I went into the bedroom, took my army field jacket that I used for duck hunting out of the closet, then opened the dresser drawer and from the bottom of my stack of shirts lifted out the folded towel in which I kept the US Army-issue .45 automatic that I had bought in Saigon. I picked up the heavy clip loaded with hollow-points, inserted it into the handle, pulled back the receiver and slid a round into the chamber, set the safety, and dropped the pistol into the pocket of my field jacket. I turned round and saw Annie watching me from the bedroom doorway, her face taut and her eyes bright.

'Dave, what are you doing?' she said.

'I'm going to stroll down there and check these guys out. They won't see the gun.'

'Let it go. Call the sheriff's office if you have to.'

'They're on our property, kiddo. They just need to tell us what they're doing here. It's no big deal.'

'No, Dave. Maybe they're from Immigration. Don't provoke them.'

'Government guys use economy rentals when they can't use the motor pool. They're probably land men from the Oil Center in Lafayette.'

'Yes, that's why you have to take the pistol with you.'

'So I have some bad habits. Leave it alone, Annie.'

I saw the hurt in her face. Her eyes flicked away from mine, then came back again.

'Yes, I wouldn't want to tell you anything,' she said. 'A good Cajun girl stays barefoot and pregnant in the kitchen while her macho man goes out and kicks ass and takes names.'

'I had a partner eight years ago who walked up on a guy trying to change a tire two blocks from the French Market. My partner had just gotten off work and he still had his badge clipped to his belt. He was a nice guy. He was always going out of his way to help people. He was going to ask this guy if he needed a bigger jack. The guy shot him right through the mouth with a nine-millimeter.'

Her face twitched as though I had slapped her.

'I'll be back in a minute,' I said, and went out the screen door with the field jacket over my arm.

The pecan leaves in the yard were loud under my feet. I looked back over my shoulder and saw her watching me through the screen, with Alafair pressed against her thigh. Lord, why did I have to talk to her like that, I thought. She was the best thing that had ever happened to me. She was kind and loving and every morning she made me feel that somehow I was a gift in her life rather than the other way around. And if she ever had any fears, they were for my welfare, never for her own. I wondered if I would ever exorcise the alcoholic succubus that seemed to live within me, its claws hooked into my soul.

I walked on into the trees toward the dirt road and the parked white car. Then I saw the driver flip his cigarette out into the leaves and start the engine. But he didn't drive past me so I could look clearly into the car or see the license plate in the rear. Instead, he backed down the dirt road, the spangled sunlight bouncing off the windshield, then straightened the car abruptly in a wide spot and accelerated around a bend that was thick with scrub oak. I heard the tires thump over the wooden bridge south of my property and the sound of the engine become thin through the trees.

I went back to the house, slipped the clip out of the .45, ejected the shell from the chamber, snicked the shell into the top of the clip again, and folded the towel over the .45 and the clip and replaced them in the dresser drawer. Annie was washing dishes in the kitchen. I stood beside her but didn't touch her.

'I'll say it only once and I'll understand if you don't want to accept it right now,' I said. 'But you mean a lot to me and I'm sorry I talked to you the way I did. I didn't know who those guys were, but I wasn't going to find out on their terms. Annie, when you love somebody dearly, you don't put limits on your protection of them. That's the way it is.'

Her hands were motionless on the sink, and she gazed out the window into the backyard.

'Who were they?' she said.

'I don't know,' I said, and went into the front room and tried to concentrate on the newspaper.

A few minutes later she stood behind my chair, her hands on my shoulders. Then I felt her bend down and kiss me in the hair.

After lunch I got a telephone call at the dock from the Drug Enforcement Administration in Lafayette. He said his name was Minos P. Dautrieve. He said he was the resident agent in charge, or 'RAC,' as he called it. He also said he wanted to talk with me.

'Go ahead,' I said.

'No. In my office. Can you come in?'

'I have to work, Mr Dautrieve.'

'Well, we can do it two or three ways,' he said. 'I can drive over there, which I don't have time for. Also, we don't usually interview people in bait shops. Or you can drive over here at your convenience, since it's a beautiful day for that sort of thing. Or we can have you picked up.'

I paused a moment and looked across the bayou at the Negroes fishing in the shallows.

'I'll be there in about an hour,' I said.

'Hey, that's great. I'm looking forward to it.'

'Were your people out at my place this morning?'

'Nope. Did you see somebody who looked like us?'

'Not unless you guys are driving Corvettes.'

'Come in and let's talk about it. Hell, you're quite a guy.'

'What is this bullshit, Mr Dautrieve?'

The receiver went dead in my hand.

I went out on the dock where Batist was cleaning a string of mudcat in a pan of water. Each morning he ran a trotline in his pirogue, then brought his fish back to the dock, gutted them with a double-edged knife he had made from a file, ripped the skin and spiked fins from their flesh with a pair of pliers, and washed the fillets clean in the pan of red water. He was fifty, as hairless as a cannonball, coal black, and looked as though he'd been hammered together out of angle iron. When I looked at him with his shirt off and the sweat streaming off his bald head and enormous black shoulders, the flecks of blood and membrane on his arms, his knife slicing through vertebrae and lopping the heads off catfish into the water like wood blocks, I wondered how southern whites had ever been able to keep his kind in bondage. Our only problem with Batist was that Annie often could not understand what he was saying. Once when she had gone with him to feed the livestock in a pasture I rented, he had told her, '*Mais t'row them t'ree cow over the fence some hay, you.*'

'I have to go to Lafayette for a couple of hours,' I said. 'I want you to watch for a couple of men in a Corvette. If they come around here, call the sheriff's department. Then go up to the house and stay with Annie.'

'*Qui c'est une Corvette*, Dave?' he said, his eyes squinting at me in the sun.

'It's a sports car, a white one.'

'What they do, them?'

'I don't know. Maybe nothing.'

'What you want I do to them, me?'

'You do nothing to them. You understand that? You call the sheriff and then you stay with Annie.'

'*Qui c'est ti vas faire si le sheriff pas vient pour un neg, Dave. Dites Batist fait plus rien?*' He laughed loudly at his own joke: 'What are you going to do if the sheriff doesn't come for a Negro, Dave? Tell Batist to do more nothing?'

'I'm serious. Don't mess with them.'

He grinned at me again and went back to cleaning his fish.

I told Annie where I was going, and a half-hour later I parked in front of the federal building in downtown Lafayette where the DEA kept its office. It was a big, modern building, constructed during the Kennedy-Johnson era, filled with big glass doors and tinted windows and marble floors; but right down the street was the old Lafayette police station and jail, a squat, gray cement building with barred windows on the second floor, an ugly sentinel out of the past, a reminder that yesterday was only a flick of the eye away from the seeming tranquillity of the present. My point is that I remember an execution that took place in the jail in the early 1950s. The electric chair was brought in from Angola; two big generators on a flatbed truck hummed on a side street behind the building; thick, black cables ran from the generators through a barred window on the second story. At nine o'clock on a balmy summer night, people in the restaurant across the street heard a man scream once just before an arc light seemed to jump off the bars of the window. Later, townspeople did not like to talk about it. Eventually that part of the jail was closed off and was used to house a civil defense siren. Finally, few people even remembered that an execution had taken place there.

But on this hazy May afternoon that smelled of flowers and rain, I was looking up at an open window on the second story of the federal building, through which flew a paper airplane. It slid in a long glide across the street and bounced off the windshield of a moving car. I had a strong feeling about where it had come from.

Sure enough, when I walked through the open door of Minos P. Dautrieve's office I saw a tall, crewcut man tilted back in his chair, his knit tie pulled loose, his collar unbuttoned, one foot on the desk, the other in the wastebasket, one huge hand poised in the air, about to sail another paper plane out the window. His blond hair was cut so short that light reflected off his scalp; in fact, lights seemed to reflect all over his lean, close-shaved, scrubbed, smiling face. On his desk blotter was an open manila folder with several telex sheets clipped inside. He dropped the airplane on the desk, clanged his foot out of the wastebasket, and shook hands with such energy that he almost pulled me off balance. I thought I had seen him somewhere before.

'I'm sorry to drag you in here,' he said, 'but that's the breaks, right? Hey, I've been reading your history. It's fascinating stuff. Sit down. Did you really do all this bullshit?'

'I'm not sure what you mean.'

'Come on, anybody with a sheet like this is genuinely into rock'n'roll. Wounded twice in Vietnam, the second time on a mine. Then fourteen years with the New Orleans police department, where you did some very serious things to a few people. Why's a guy with a teacher's certificate in English go into police work?"

'Is this a shake?'

'Be serious. We don't get to have that kind of fun. Most of the time we just run around and prepare cases for the US attorney. You know that. But your file's intriguing, you've got to admit. It says here you blew away three people, one of whom was the *numero uno* greaseball, drug pusher, and pimp in New Orleans. But he was also on tap as a federal witness, at least until you scrambled his eggs for him.' He laughed out loud. 'How'd you manage to snuff a government witness? That's hard to pull off. We usually keep them on the game reserve.'

'You really want to know?'

'Hell, yes. This is socko stuff.'

'His bodyguard pulled a gun on my partner and took a shot at him. It was a routine possession bust, and the pair of them would have been out on bond in an hour. So it was a dumb thing for the bodyguard to do. It was dumb because it was unnecessary and it provoked a bad situation. A professional doesn't do dumb things like that and provoke people unnecessarily. You get my drift?'

'Oh, I get it. We federal agents shouldn't act like dumb guys and provoke you, huh? Let me try this one on you, Mr Robicheaux. What are the odds of anybody being out on the Gulf of Mexico and witnessing a plane crash? Come on, your file says you've spent lots of time at racetracks. Figure the odds for me.'

'What are you saying, podna?'

'We know a guy named Johnny Dartez was on that plane. Johnny Dartez's name means one thing – narcotics. He was a transporter for Bubba Rocque. His specialty was throwing it out in big rubber balloons over water.'

'And you figure maybe I was the pickup man.'

'You tell me.'

'I think you spend too much time folding paper airplanes.'

'Oh, I should be out developing some better leads? Is that it? Some of us are hotdog ball handlers, some of us are meant for the bench. I got it.'

'I remember now. Forward for LSU, fifteen years or so ago. Dr Dunkenstein. You were All-American.'

'Honorable Mention. Answer my question, Mr Robicheaux. What are the odds of a guy like you being out on the salt when a plane goes down right by his boat? A guy who happened to have a scuba tank so he could be the first one down on the wreck?'

'Listen, the pilot was a priest. Use your head a minute.'

'Yeah, a priest who did time in Danbury,' he said.

'Danbury?'

'Yeah, that's right.'

'What for?'

'Breaking and entering.'

'I think I'm getting the abridged version here.'

'He and some nuns and other priests broke into a General Electric plant and vandalised some missile components.'

'And you think he was involved with drug smugglers?'

He wadded up the paper airplane on his desk and dropped it into the wastebasket.

'No, I don't,' he said, his eyes focused on the clouds outside the window.

'What does Immigration tell you?'

He shrugged his shoulders and clicked his nails on the desk blotter. His fingers were so long and thin and his nails so pink and clean that his hands looked like those of a surgeon rather than of an ex-basketball player.

'According to them, there was no Johnny Dartez on that plane,' I said.

'They have their areas of concern, we have ours.'

'They're stonewalling you, aren't they?'

'Look, I'm not interested in Immigration's business. I want Bubba Rocque off the board. Johnny Dartez was a guy we spent a lot of money and time on, him and another dimwit from New Orleans named Victor Romero. Does that name mean anything to you?'

'No.'

'They both disappeared from their usual haunts about two months ago, just before we were going to pick them up. Since Johnny has done the big gargle out at Southwest Pass, Victor's value has appreciated immensely.'

'You won't get Bubba by squeezing his people.'

He pushed his large shoe against the wall so that his chair spun around in a complete circle, like a child playing in the barber's chair.

'How is it that you have this omniscient knowledge?' he said.

'In high school he'd put on different kinds of shows for us. Sometimes he'd eat a lightbulb. Or he might open a bottle of RC Cola on his teeth or push thumbtacks into his kneecaps. It was always a memorable exhibition.'

'Yeah, we see a lot of that kind of psychotic charisma these days. I think it's in fashion with the wiseguys. That's why we have a special lockdown section in Atlanta where they can yodel to each other.'

'Good luck.'

'You don't think we can put him away?'

'Who cares what I think? What's the National Transportation Safety Board say about the crash?'

'A fire in the hold. They're not sure. It was murky when their divers went down. The plane slipped down a trench of some kind and it's half covered in mud now.'

'You believe it was just a fire?'

'It happens.'

'You better send them down again. I dove that wreck twice. I think an explosion blew out the side.'

He looked at me carefully.

'I think maybe I ought to caution you about involving yourself in a federal investigation,' he said.

'I'm not one of your problems, Mr Dautrieve. You've got another federal agency trespassing on your turf, maybe tainting your witnesses, maybe stealing bodies. Anyway, they're jerking you around and for some reason you're not doing anything about it. I'd appreciate it if you didn't try to lay off your situation on me.'

I saw the bone flex against the clean line of his jaw. Then he began to play with a rubber band on his long fingers.

'You'll have to make allowances for us government employees who have to labor with bureaucratic manacles on,' he said. 'We've never been able to use the simple, direct methods you people have been so good at. You remember a few years back when a New Orleans cop got killed and some of his friends squared it on their own? I think they went into the guy's house, it was a black guy, of course, and blew him and his wife away in the bathtub. Then there were those black revolutionaries that stuck up an armored car in Boston and killed a guard and hid out in Louisiana and Mississippi. We worked two years preparing that case, then your people grabbed one of them and tortured a statement out of him and flushed everything we'd done right down the shithole. You guys sure knew how to let everybody know you were in town.'

'I guess I'll go now. You want to ask me anything else?'

'Not a thing,' he said, and fired a paper clip at a file cabinet across the room.

I stood up to leave. His attention was concentrated on finding another target for his rubber band and paper clip.

'Does a white Corvette with the letters ELK on the door bring any of your clientele to mind?' I said.

'Were these the guys out at your place?' His eyes still avoided me.

'Yes.'

'How should I know? We're lucky to keep tabs on two or three of these assholes.' He was looking straight at me now, his eyes flat, the skin of his face tight. 'Maybe it's somebody you sold some bad fish to.'

I walked outside in the sunshine and the wind blowing through the mimosa trees on the lawn. A Negro gardener was sprinkling the flower beds and the freshly cut grass with a hose, and I could smell the damp earth and the green clippings that were raked in piles under the trees. I looked back up at the office window of Minos P. Dautrieve. I opened and closed my hands and took a breath and felt the anger go out of my chest.

Well, you asked for it, I told myself. Why poke a stick at a man who's already in a cage? He probably gets one conviction out of ten arrests, spends half his time with his butt in a bureaucratic paper shredder, and on a good day negotiates a one-to-three possessions plea on a dealer who's probably robbed hundreds of people of their souls.

Just as I was pulling out into the traffic, I saw him come out of the building waving his arm at me. He was almost hit by a car crossing the street.

'Park it a minute. You want a snowcone? It's on me,' he said.

'I have to get back to work.'

'Park it,' he said, and bought two snowcones from a Negro boy who operated a stand under an umbrella on the corner. He got in the passenger side of my truck, almost losing the door on a passing car whose horn reverberated down the street, and handed me one of the snowcones.

'Maybe the Corvette is Eddie Keats's,' he said. 'He used to run a nickel-and-dime book in Brooklyn. Now he's a Sunbelter, he likes our climate so much. He lives here part of the time, part of the time in New Orleans. He's got a couple of bars, a few whores working for him, and he thinks he's a big button man. Is there any reason for a guy like that to be hanging around your place?'

'You got me. I never heard of him.'

'Try this – Eddie Keats likes to do favors for important people. He jobs out for Bubba Rocque sometimes, for free or whatever Bubba wants to give him. He's that kind of swell guy. We heard he set fire to one of Bubba's hookers in New Orleans.'

He stopped and looked at me curiously.

'What's the matter? You never got a case like that in homicide?' he said. 'You know how their pimps keep them down on the farm.'

'I talked to a stripper in New Orleans about Johnny Dartez. She told me he worked for Bubba Rocque. I've got a bad feeling about her.'

'This disturbs me.'

'What?'

'I'm serious when I warn you about fooling around in a federal investigation.'

'Listen, I reported four dead people in that plane. The wire service was told there were only three. That suggests that maybe I was drunk or that I'm a dumb shit or maybe both.'

'All right, for right now forget all that. We can pick her up and give her protective custody, if that's what you want.'

'That's not her style.'

'Getting the shit kicked out of her is?'

'She's an alcoholic and an addict. She'd rather eat a bowl of spiders than disconnect from her source.'

'Okay, if you see that car around your place again, you call us. We handle it. You're not a player, you understand?'

'I don't intend to be one.'

'Watch your ass, Robicheaux,' he said. 'If I see your name in the paper again, it had better be in the fishing news.'

*

I crossed the Vermilion River and took the old two-lane road through Broussard to New Iberia. At almost exactly three o'clock it started to rain. I watched it move in a gray, lighted sheet out of the south, the shadows racing ahead of the clouds as the first drops clicked across the new sugar-cane and then clattered on the abandoned tin sugar factory outside of Broussard. In the middle of the shower, shafts of sunlight cut through the clouds like the depictions of spiritual grace on a child's holy card. When the sun shone through the rain my father used to say, 'That how God tell you it ain't for long, Him.'

When I got back home the rain was still dancing on the bayou, and Annie had walked Alafair down to the dock to help Batist take care of the fishermen who were drinking beer and eating *boudin* under the canvas awning. I went up to the house and called New Orleans information for Robin's number, but she had no listing. Then I called Smiling Jack's. The man who answered didn't identify himself, but the voice and the manner were unmistakable.

'She isn't here. She don't come in till six,' he said.

'Do you have her home number?'

'Are you kidding? Who is this?'

'What's her number, Jerry?'

'Oh yeah, I should have known. It's Fearless Fosdick, isn't it?' he said. 'Guess what? She don't have a phone. Guess what again? This isn't an answering service.'

'When'd you see her last?'

'Throwing up in the toilet at three o'clock this morning. I just got finished cleaning it up. Look, fun guy, you want to talk to that broad, come down and talk to her. Right now I got to wash out my mops. You two make a great couple.'

He hung up the phone, and I looked out into the rain on the bayou. Maybe she would be all right, I thought. She had survived all her life in a world in which male use of her body and male violence against it had been as natural to her as the vodka collins and speed on the half-shell that started each of her days. Maybe it was just a vanity that I felt a conversation with me could bring additional harm into her life. Also, I didn't know for sure that the driver of the Corvette was some Brooklyn character named Eddie Keats.

Saints don't heed warnings because they consider them irrelevant. Fools don't heed them because they think the lightning dancing across the sky, the thunder rolling through the woods, are only there to en-hance their lives in some mysterious way. I had been warned by both Robin and Minos P. Dautrieve. I saw a solitary streak of lightning tremble like a piece of heated wire on the southern horizon. But I didn't want to think anymore that day about dope runners and local wiseguys, federal agents and plane crashes. I listened to the rain dripping through the pecan trees, then walked down to the dock in the flicker of distant lightning to help Annie and Batist get ready for the late-afternoon fishermen.

3

If, as a child, I had been asked to describe the world I lived in, I'm sure my response would have been in terms of images that in general left me with a sense of well-being about myself and my family. Because even though my mother died when I was young and we were poor and my father sometimes brawled in bars and got locked in the parish jail, he and my little brother and I had a home – actually a world – on the bayou that was always safe, warm in the winter from the woodstove, cool in the summer under the shade of the pecan trees, a place that was ours and had belonged to our people and a way of life since the Acadians came to Louisiana in 1755. In describing that world I would have told my questioner about my pet three-legged coon, my pirogue tied to a cypress into which was driven a rusty spike with a chain supposedly used by Jean Lafitte, the big, black iron pot in the backyard where my father fried us *sac-a-lait* and bream almost every night in the summer, the orange and purple sunsets in the fall when the ducks would cover the sky from horizon to horizon, the red leaves spinning out of the trees onto the water in that peculiar gold October light that was both warm and cold at the same time, and the dark, wet layers of leaves deep in the woods where we dug for nightcrawlers, the smokehouse in back that glistened in the morning frost and always smelled of pork dripping into smoldering ash, and most of all my father – a big, dark, laughing Cajun who could break boards into kindling with his bare hands, throw a washtub full of bricks over a fence, or pull a six-foot 'gator out of the water by his tail.

But what images would you find if you unlocked the mind of a six-year-old child who had been flown out of a virtual Stone Age, a Central American village, where the twentieth century intruded itself in the form of the most sophisticated and destructive infantry weapons in the world?

The only Spanish-speaking person I knew in New Iberia was a pari-mutuel window seller named Felix who worked at Evangeline Downs in Lafayette and the Fairgrounds in New Orleans. He had been a casino card dealer in Havana during the Batista era, and his lavender shirts and white

French cuffs, crinkling seersucker suits and pomade-scented hair gave him the appearance of a man who still aspired to a jaded opulence in his life. But like most people I knew around the track, his chief defect was that he didn't like regular work or the world of ordinary people.

The skies had cleared almost completely of rain clouds an hour after I had returned from Lafayette and my visit to the DEA, and now the western horizon was aflame with the sunset, cicadas droned in the trees, and fireflies were starting to light in the dusk. We sat in the living room while Felix spoke quietly to Alafair in Spanish about her parents, her village, the small geographic, tropical postage stamp that constituted the only world she had ever known but that sent my own mind back across the seas, back across two decades, to other villages that smelled of fish heads, animal dung, chicken yards, sour mud, stagnant water, human feces, ulcerated children with no pants on who urinated in the road; and then there was that other smell, the reek of soldiers who hadn't bathed for days, who lived enclosed in their own fetid envelope, whose fantasies vacillated from rut to dissolving their enemies and the source of their discomfort into a bloody mist.

But I digress into my own historical myopia. Her story is more important than mine because I chose to be a participant and she did not. I chose to help bring the technology of napalm and the M-16 and AK-47 meat-cutters to people who harvested rice with their hands. Others elected Alafair and her family to be the recipients of our industrial gifts to the Third World.

She spoke as though she were describing the contents of a bad picture show of which she understood only parts, and Annie and I had trouble looking at each other's eyes lest we see reflected there the recognition of the simian creature that was still alive and thriving in the human race. Felix translated:

– The soldiers carry knives and pliers to steal the faces of the people in the village. My uncle ran away into the cane, and the next day we found him where they had left him. My mother tried to hide my eyes but I saw anyway. His thumbs were tied together with wire, and they had taken away his face. It was hot in the cane and we could hear the flies buzzing. Some of the people got sick because of the smell and vomited on themselves.

– That was when my father ran away, too. My mother said he went into the hills with the other men from the village. The helicopters chased them sometimes, I think, because we saw the shadows go across our house and then across the road and the fields, then they would stop in the air and begin shooting. They had tubes on their sides that made puffs of smoke, and the rocks and trees on the hillside would fly in the air. The grass and bushes were dry and caught fire, and at night we could see them burning high up in the darkness and smell the smoke in the wind –

'Ask her what happened to her father,' I said to Felix.

'*Dónde está tu padre ahora?*'

– Maybe he went away with the trucks. The trucks went into the hills, then came back with many men from the village. They took them to a place where the soldiers live, and we did not see them again. My cousin said the soldiers have a prison far away and they keep many people there. Maybe my father is with them. The American priest said he would try to find out but that we had to leave the village. He said they would hurt my mother the way they hurt the other lady because of the clinic –

She went silent on the couch and stared out the screen door at the fireflies' lightning in the dusk. Her tan face was now discolored with the same pale, bloodless spots it had had when I pulled her out of the water. Annie stroked her close-cropped hair with her palm and squeezed her around the shoulders.

'Dave, maybe that's enough,' she said.

'No, she's got to tell it all. She's too little a kid to carry that kind of stuff around by herself,' I said. Then, to Felix, 'What other lady?'

'*Quién es la otra señora?*' he asked.

– She worked at the clinic with my mother. Her stomach was big and it made her walk like a duck. One day the soldiers came and pulled her out in the road by her arms. She was calling the names of her friends to help her, but the people were afraid and tried to hide. Then the soldiers made us go outside and watch the thing they did to her in the road –

Her eyes were wide and had the empty, dry, glazed expression of someone who might be staring into a furnace.

'*Qué hicieron los soldados?*' Felix said softly.

– They went to the woodcutter's house and came back with his machete. They were chopping and the machete was wet and red in the sunlight. A soldier put his hands in her stomach and took out her baby. The people were crying now and covering their faces. The priest ran to us from the church, but they knocked him down and beat him in the road. The fat lady and her baby stayed out there by themselves in the sun. The smell was like the smell in the cane when we found my uncle. It was in all the houses, and when we woke up in the morning it was still there but worse –

The cicadas were loud in the trees. There was nothing we could say. How do you explain evil to a child, particularly when the child's experience with it is perhaps greater than your own? I had seen children in a Saigon burn ward whose eyes rendered you mute before you could even attempt to apologize for the calamity that adults had imposed upon them. My condolence became a box of Hershey bars.

We drove to Mulate's in Breaux Bridge for pecan pie and listened to the Acadian string band, then took a ride down Bayou Teche on the paddle-wheel pleasure boat that operated up and down the bayou for

tourists. It was dark now, and the trees on some of the lawns were hung
with Japanese lanterns, and you could smell barbecue fires and crabs
boiling in the lighted and screened summerhouses beyond the cane that
grew along the bayou's banks. The baseball diamond in the park looked
as if it were lit by an enormous white flare, and people were cheering
on an American Legion game that had all the innocent and provincial
intensity of a scene clipped from the summer of 1941. Alafair sat on a
wooden bench between Annie and me and watched the cypress trees and
shadowy lawns and the scrolled nineteenth-century homes slip past us.
Maybe it wasn't much to offer in recompense, but it was all we had.

The air was cool and the eastern sky plum-colored and striped with low-
hanging red clouds when I opened up the bait shop the next morning. I
worked until about nine o'clock, then left it with Batist and walked back
up to the house for breakfast. I was just having my last cup of coffee when
he called me on the phone.

'Dave, you 'member that colored man that rent from us this morning?'
he said.

'No.'

'He talked funny. He not from around here, no.'

'I don't remember him, Batist. What is it?'

'He said he run the boat up on the bar and bust off the propeller. He ax
if you want to come get it.'

'Where is he?'

'Sout' of the four-corners. You want me go after him?'

'That's all right. I'll go in a few minutes. Did you give him an extra
shearing pin?'

'*Mais* sure. He say that ain't it.'

'Okay, Batist. Don't worry about it.'

'Ax him where he's from he don't know how to keep the boat in the
bayou, no.'

A few minutes later I headed down the bayou in an outboard to pick
up the damaged rental. It wasn't unusual for me to go after one of our
boats. With some regularity, drunks ran them over sandbars and floating
logs, bashed them against cypress stumps, or flipped them over while
turning across their own wakes. The sun was bright on the water, and
dragonflies hung in the still air over the lily pads along the banks. The V-
shaped wake from the Evinrude slapped against the cypress roots and
made the lily pads suddenly swell and undulate as though a cushion of
air were rippling by underneath them. I passed the old clapboard general
store at the four-corners where the black man must have used the phone
to call Batist. A rusted Hadacol sign was still nailed to one wall, and a
spreading oak shaded the front gallery where some Negro men in overalls
were drinking soda pop and eating sandwiches. Then the cypress trees

and cane along the banks became thicker, and farther down I could see my rental boat tied to a pine sapling, swinging empty in the brown current.

I cut my engine and drifted into the bank on top of my wake and tied up next to the rental. The small waves slapped against the sides of both aluminium hulls. Back in a clearing a tall black man sat on a sawed oak stump, drinking from a fifth of apricot brandy. By his foot were an opened loaf of bread and a can of Vienna sausages. He wore Adidas running shoes, soiled white cotton trousers, and an orange undershirt, and his chest and shoulders were covered with tiny coils of wiry black hair. He was much blacker than most south Louisiana people of color, and he must have had a half-dozen gold rings on his long fingers. He put two fingers of snuff under his lip and looked at me without speaking. His eyes were red in the sun-spotted shade of the oak trees. I stepped up onto the bank and walked into the clearing.

'What's the trouble, podna?' I said.

He took another sip of the brandy and didn't reply.

'Batist said you ran over the sandbar.'

He still didn't answer.

'Do you hear me okay, podna?' I said, and smiled at him. But he wasn't going to talk to me.

'Well, let's have a look,' I said. 'If it's just the shearing pin, I'll fix it and you can be on your way. But if you bent the propeller, I'll have to tow you back and I'm afraid I won't be able to give you another boat.'

I looked once more at him, then turned around and started back toward the water's edge. I heard him stand up and brush crumbs off his clothes, then I heard the brandy gurgle in the bottle as though it were being held upside down, and just as I turned with that terrible and futile recognition that something was wrong, out of time and place, I saw his narrowed red eyes again and the bottle ripping down murderously in his long, black hand.

He caught me on the edge of the skull cap, I felt the bottle rake down off my shoulder, and I went down on all fours as though my legs had suddenly been kicked out from under me. My mouth hung open, my eyes wouldn't focus, and my ears were roaring with sound. I could feel blood running down the side of my face.

Then, with a casual, almost contemptuous movement of his body, he straddled me from behind, held my chin up with one hand so I could see the open, pearl-handled barber's razor he held before my eyes, then inserted the razor's edge between the back of my ear and my scalp. He smelled of alcohol and snuff. I saw the legs of another man walk out of the trees.

'Don't look up, my friend,' the other man said, in what was either a Brooklyn or Irish Channel accent. 'That'd change everything for us. Make it real bad for you. Toot's serious about his razor. He'll sculpt your ears off. Make your head look like a mannequin.'

He lit a cigarette with a lighter and clicked it shut. The smoke smelled like a Picayune. Out of the corner of my eye I could see his purple suede cowboy boots, gray slacks, and one gold-braceleted white hand.

'Eyes forward, asshole. I won't say it again,' he said. 'You can get out of this easy or Toot can cut you right across the nipples. He'd love to do it for you. He was a *tonton macoute* down in Haiti. He sleeps in a grave one night a month to stay in touch with the spirits. Tell him what you did to the broad, Toot.'

'You talk too much. Get finished. I want to eat,' the black man said.

'Toot had a whole bunch of surprises for her,' the white man said. 'He's an imaginative guy. He's got a bunch of Polaroids from Haiti. You ought to see them. Guess what he did to her.'

I watched a drop of my blood run off my eyelash and fall and break like a small red star in the dirt.

'Guess!' he said again, and kicked me hard in the right buttock.

I clenched my teeth and felt the clods of dirt bite into my palms.

'You got dirty ears, huh?' he said, and kicked me in the thigh with the toe of his boot.

'Fuck you, buddy.'

'What?'

'You heard me. Whatever you do to me today I'm going to square. If I can't do it, I've got friends who will.'

'I've got news for you. You're still talking now because I'm in a good mood. Second, you brought this down on yourself, asshole. When you start talking to somebody else's whores, when you poke your nose into other people's shit, you got to pay the man. That's the rules. An old-time homicide roach ought to know that. Here's the last news flash. The chippy got off easy. Toot wanted to turn her face into one of his Polaroids. But that broad is money on the hoof, got people depending on her, so sometimes you got to let it slide, you know what I mean? So he put her finger in the door and broke it for her.

'Hey,' he said in an almost happy fashion, 'don't look sad. I'm telling you, she didn't mind. She was glad. She's a smart girl, she knows the rules. It's too bad, though, you don't have a pussy between your legs, 'cause you ain't money on the hoof.'

'Get finished,' the black man said.

'You ain't in a hurry, are you, Robicheaux? Huh?' he said, and nudged me in the genitals with his boot.

The blood dripped off my eyelash and speckled the dirt.

'Okay, I'll make it quick, since you're starting to remind me of a dog down there,' he said. 'You got a house, you got a boat business, you got a wife, you got a lot to be thankful for. So don't get in nobody else's shit.

Stay home and play with mama and your worms. If you don't know what I'm talking about, think about screwing a wife that don't have a nose.

'Now let the man pay his tab, Toot.'

I felt the weight of the razor lift from behind my ear, then the white man's pointed boot ripped between my thighs and exploded in my scrotum. A furnace door opened in my bowels, a piece of angle iron twisted inside me, and a sound unlike my own voice roared from my throat. Then, for good measure, as I shuddered on my knees and elbows, heaving like a gutted animal, the black man stepped back and drop-kicked me across the mouth with the long-legged grace of a ballet dancer.

I lay in an embryonic ball on my side, blood stringing from my mouth, and saw them walk off through the trees like two friends whose sunny day had been only temporarily interrupted by an insignificant task.

I look out of the door of the dustoff into the hot, bright morning as we lift clear of the banyan trees, and the elephant grass dents and flattens under us as though it were being bruised by a giant thumb. Then the air suddenly becomes cooler, no longer like steam off an oven, and we're racing over the countryside, our shadow streaking ahead of us across rice paddies and earthen dikes and yellow dirt roads with bicyclists and carts on them. The medic, an Italian kid from New York, hits me with a syrette of morphine and washes my face from his canteen. He's barechested and sweaty, and his pot is strung with rubber spiders. Say goodbye to Shitsville, Lieutenant, he says. You're going back alive in '65. I smell the foulness of my wounds, the dried urine in my pants, as I watch the geographic history of my last ten months sweep by under us: the burnt-out ville where the ash rises and powders in the hot wind; a ditch that gapes like a ragged incision in the earth, where we pinned them down and then broiled them alive with Zippo-tracks; the ruptured dike and dried-out and baked rice paddy still pocked with mortar rounds where they locked down on us from both flanks and marched it right through us like a firestorm. Hey, Lieutenant, don't touch yourself there, the medic is saying. I mean it, it's a mess down there. You can't lose no more blood. You want I should tie your hands? They got refrigeration at the aid station. Plasma. Hey, hold his goddamn wrists. He's torn it open.

'That's an ice bag you feel down there,' the doctor was saying. He was a gray, thick-bodied man who wore rimless glasses, greens, and a T-shirt. 'It'll take the swelling down quite a bit. It looks like you slept well. That shot I gave you is pretty strong stuff. Did you have dreams?'

I could tell from the sunlight on the oak trees outside that it was late afternoon. The wisteria and blooming myrtle on the hospital lawn moved in the breeze. The drawbridge was up over Bayou Teche, and the two-deck pleasure boat was going through, its paddle wheel streaming water and light.

My mouth was dry, and the inside of my lip felt as though it were filled with wire.

'I had to put stitches in your scalp and six in your mouth. Don't eat any peanut brittle for a while,' he said, and smiled.

'Where's Annie?' I asked thickly.

'I sent her for a cup of coffee. She'll be back in a minute. The colored man's outside, too. He's a big fellow, isn't he? How far did he carry you?'

I had to wet the row of stitches inside my lip before I could talk again.

'About five hundred yards, up to the four-corners. How bad am I down below, Doc?'

'You're not ruptured, if that's what you mean. Keep it in your pajamas a couple of nights and you'll be all right. Where'd you get those scars around your thighs?'

'In the service.'

'I thought I recognized the handiwork. It looks like some of it is still in there.'

'I set off metal detectors at the airport sometimes.'

'Well, we're going to keep you with us tonight, but you can go home in the morning. You want to talk with the sheriff now, or later?'

I hadn't seen the other man, who was sitting in a leather chair in the corner. He wore a brown departmental uniform, held his lacquered campaign hat on his knee, and leaned forward deferentially. He used to own a dry-cleaning business in town before someone talked him into running for sheriff. The rural cops had changed a lot in the last twenty years. When I was a boy the sheriff wore a blue suit with a vest and a big railroad watch and chain and carried a heavy revolver in his coat pocket. He was not bothered by the bordellos on Railroad Avenue and the slot machines' all over Iberia Parish, nor was he greatly troubled when white kids went nigger-knocking on Saturday nights. He'd tip his John B. Stetson hat to a white lady on Main, and talk to an elderly Negro woman as though she were a post. This one was president of the Downtown Merchants Association.

'You know who they were, Dave?' he said. He had the soft, downturned lines in his face of most Acadian men in their late middle age. His cheeks were flecked with tiny blue and red veins.

'A white guy named Eddie Keats. He owns some bars in Lafayette and New Orleans. The other guy is black. His name's Toot.' I swallowed from the water glass on the table. 'Maybe he's a Haitian. You know anybody like that around here?'

'No.'

'You know Eddie Keats?'

'No. But we can cut a warrant for him.'

'It won't do any good. I never saw his face. I couldn't make him in a lineup.'

'I don't understand. How do you know it was this guy Keats?'

'He was messing around my house yesterday. Call the DEA agent in Lafayette. He's got a sheet on him. The guy works for Bubba Rocque sometimes.'

'Oh boy.'

'Look, you can pick up Keats on suspicion. He's supposed to be a low-level hit man. Roust him in his automobile, and maybe you'll turn something. Some weed, a concealed weapon, hot credit cards. These fuckers always have spaghetti hanging off the place somewhere.' I drank from the water again and laid my head back on the pillow. My scrotum, with the ice bag under it, felt as big as a bowling ball.

'I don't know about that. That's Lafayette Parish. It's a little like going on a fishing trip in somebody else's pond.' He looked at me quietly, as though I should understand.

'You want him back here again?' I said. 'Because unless you send him a hard telegram, he will be.'

He was silent a moment, then he wrote in a pad and put the pad and pencil back in his shirt pocket and buttoned it.

'Well, I'll give the DEA and the Lafayette sheriff's office a call,' he said. 'We'll see what happens.'

Then he asked some more questions, most of which were the formless and irrelevant after-thoughts of a well-meaning amateur who did not want to seem unsympathetic. I didn't reply when he said good-bye.

But what did I expect? I couldn't be sure myself that the white man was Eddie Keats. New Orleans was full of people with the same Italian-Irish background that produced the accent you would normally associate with Brooklyn. I had admitted I couldn't make him in a lineup and I didn't know anything about the black man except that his name was Toot and he slept in a grave. What is an ex-dry cleaner who dresses like a Fritos delivery man supposed to do with that one? I asked myself.

But maybe there was a darker strain at work inside me that I didn't want to recognize. I knew how local cops would have dealt with Eddie Keats and his kind twenty years ago. A couple of truly vicious coonass plainclothes (they usually wore J. C. Higgins suits that looked like clothes on a duck) would have gone to his bar, thrown his framed liquor license in the toilet, broken out all his car windows with a baton, then pointed a revolver between his eyes and snapped the hammer on an empty chamber.

No, I didn't like them then; I didn't like them now. But it was a temptation.

Batist came in smelling of wine and fish, with some flowers I suspected he had taken from a hall vase and put in a CocaCola bottle. When I told him that the black man named Toot was possibly a *tonton macoute* from Haiti who practiced black magic, Batist got him confused with the *loup-*

garou, the bayou equivalent of the lamia or werewolf, and was convinced that we should see a *traiteur* in order to find this *loup-garou* and fill his mouth and nostrils with dirt from a witch's grave. He saw my eyes light on the pint wine bottle, with the paper bag twisted around its neck, that protruded from the back pocket of his overalls, and he shifted sideways in the chair to block my vision, but the bottle clanked loudly against the chair's arm. His face was transfused with guilt.

'Hey, podna, since when did you have to hide things from me?' I said.

'I shouldn't drink, me, when I got to look after Miss Annie and that little girl.'

'I trust you, Batist.'

His eyes averted mine and his big hands were awkward in his lap. Even though I had known him since I was a child, he was still uncomfortable when I, a white man, spoke to him in a personal way.

'Where's Alafair now?' I said.

'Wit' my wife and girl. She all right, you ain't got to worry, no. You know she talk French, her? We fixing po'-boys, I say *pain,* she know that mean "bread," yeah. I say *sauce piquante,* she know that mean "hot sauce." How come she know that, Dave?'

'The Spanish language has a lot of words like ours.'

'Oh,' he said, and was thoughtful a moment. Then, 'How come that?'

Annie came through the door and saved me from an impossible discussion. Batist was absolutely obsessive about understanding any information that was foreign to his world, but as a rule he would have to hack and hew it into pieces until it would assimilate into that strange Afro-Creole-Acadian frame of reference that was as natural to him as wearing a dime on a string around his ankle to ward off the gris-gris, an evil spell cast by a *traiteur,* or conjuror.

Annie stayed with me through the evening while the light softened on the trees outside and the shadows deepened on the lawn, the western sky turned russet and orange like a chemical flame, and high school kids strolled down the sidewalks to the American Legion baseball game in the park. Through the open window I could smell barbecue fires and water sprinklers, magnolia blossoms and night-blooming jasmine. Then the sky darkened, and the rain clouds in the south pulsated with white streaks of lightning like networks of veins.

Annie lay next to me and rubbed my chest and touched my face with her fingers and kissed me on the eyes.

'Take away the ice bag and push the chair in front of the door,' I said.

'No, Dave.'

'Yes, it's all right. The doctor said there was no problem.'

She kissed me on the ear, then whispered, 'Not tonight, baby love.'

I felt myself swallow.

'Annie, please,' I said.

She raised up on one elbow and looked curiously into my face.

'What is it?' she said.

'I need you. You're my wife.'

She frowned and her eyes went back and forth into mine.

'Tell me what it is,' she said.

'You want to know?'

'Dave, you're my whole life. How could I not want to know?'

'Those sonsofbitches put me on my hands and knees and worked me over like they would a dog.'

I could see the pain in her eyes. Her hand went to my cheek, then to my throat.

'Somebody will catch them. You know that,' she said.

'No, they're hunting on the game reserve. They're mainline badasses, and they don't have anybody more serious to deal with than a dry cleaner in a sheriff's suit.'

'You gave it up. We have a good life now. This is the place you've always wanted to come back to. Everybody in town likes you and respects you, and the people up and down the bayou are the best friends anyone could have. Now we have Alafair, too. How can you let a couple of criminals hurt all that?'

'It doesn't work that way.'

'Yes, it does, if you look at what's right with your life instead of what's wrong with it.'

'Are you going to push the chair in front of the door?'

She paused. Her face was quiet and purposeful. She turned off the light on the bedstand and pushed the heavy leather chair until it caught under the doorknob. In the moonlight through the window her curly gold hair looked as if it were flecked with silver. She pulled back the sheet and took away the ice bag, then touched me with her hand. The pain made both my knees jump.

I heard her sigh as she sat back down on the side of the bed.

'Are we going to fight with each other when we have a problem?' she said.

'I'm not fighting with you, kiddo.'

'Yes, you are. You can't turn loose of the past, Dave. You get hurt, or you see something that's wrong in the world, and all the old ways come back to you.'

'I can't help that.'

'Maybe not. But you don't live alone anymore.' She took my hand and lay down beside me again. 'There's me, and now there's Alafair, too.'

'I'll tell you what it feels like, and I won't say any more. You remember when I told you about how those North Vietnamese regulars overran us and the captain surrendered to them? They tied our hands around trees with piano wire, then took turns urinating on us. That's what it feels like.'

She was quiet a long time. I could hear breathing in the dark. Then she took a deep breath and let it out and put her arm across my chest.

'I have a very bad feeling inside me, Dave,' she said.

There was nothing more to say. How could there be? Even the most sympathetic friends and relatives of a battery or assault victim could not understand what that individual experiences. Over the years I had questioned people who had been molested by degenerates, mugged by street punks, shanked and shot by psychopaths, gang-banged and sodomized by outlaw bikers. They all had the same numb expression, the same drowning eyes, the same knowledge that they somehow deserved their fate and that they were absolutely alone in the world. And often we made their grief and humiliation even greater by ascribing the responsibility for their suffering to their own incaution, so that we could remain psychologically invulnerable ourselves.

I wasn't being fair to Annie. She had paid her share of dues, but there are times when you are very alone in the world and your own thoughts flay your skin an inch at a time. This was one of them.

I didn't sleep that night. But then insomnia and I were old companions.

Two days later the swelling between my legs had gone down and I could walk without looking like I was straddling a fence. The sheriff came out to see me at the boat dock and told me he had talked to the Lafayette city police and Minos P. Dautrieve at the DEA. Lafayette had sent a couple of detectives to question Eddie Keats at his bar, but he claimed that he had taken two of his dancers sailing on the day I was beaten up, and the two dancers corroborated his story.

'Are they going to accept that?' I said.

'What are they supposed to do?'

'Do some work and find out where those girls were two days ago.'

'Do you know how many cases those guys probably have?'

'I'm not sympathetic, Sheriff. People like Keats come into our area because they think they have a free pass. What did Minos P. Dautrieve have to say?'

The sheriff's face colored and the skin at the corner of his mouth tugged slightly in a smile.

'I think he said you'd better get your ass into his office,' the sheriff replied.

'Those were his words?'

'I believe so.'

'Why's he mad at me?'

'I get the impression he thinks you're messing around in federal business.'

'Does he know anything about a Haitian named Toot?'

'No. I went through Baton Rouge and the National Crime Information Center in Washington and couldn't find out anything, either.'

'He's probably an illegal. There's no paper on him,' I said.

'That's what Dautrieve said.'

'He's a smart cop.'

I saw a look of faint embarrassment in the sheriff's eyes, and I felt instantly sorry for my remark.

'Well, I promise you I'll give it my best, Dave,' he said.

'I appreciate what you've done.'

'I'm afraid I haven't done very much.'

'Look, these guys are hard to put away,' I said. 'I worked two years on the case of a syndicate hit man who pushed his wife off a fourth-floor balcony into a dry swimming pool. He even told me he did it. He walked right out of it because we took her diary out of the condo without a warrant. How about that for first-rate detective work? Every time I'd see him in a bar, he'd send a drink over to my table. It really felt good.'

He smiled and shook hands.

'One more thing before I go,' he said. 'A man named Monroe from Immigration was in my office yesterday. He was asking questions about you.'

The sunlight was bright on the bayou. The oaks and cypress on the far side made deep shadows on the bank.

'He was out here the day after that plane went down at Southwest Pass,' I said.

'He asked if you had a little girl staying with you.'

'What'd you tell him?'

'I told him I didn't know. I also told him it wasn't my business. But I got the feeling he wasn't really interested in some little girl. You bother him for some reason.'

'I gave him a bad time.'

'I don't know those federal people that well, but I don't think they drive up from New Orleans just because a man with a fish dock gives them a bad time. What's that fellow after, Dave?'

'I don't know.'

'Look, I don't want to tell you what to do, but if you and Annie are helping out a little girl that doesn't have any parents, why don't you let other folks help you, too? People around here aren't going to let anybody take her away.'

'My father used to say that a catfish had whiskers so he'd never go into a hollow log he couldn't turn around in. I don't trust those people at Immigration, Sheriff. Play on their terms and you'll lose.'

'I think maybe you got a dark view sometimes, Dave.'

'You better believe it,' I said.

I watched him drive away on the dirt road under the canopy of oak trees. I clicked my fingers on the warm board rail that edged my dock, then walked up to the house and had lunch with Annie and Alafair.

An hour later I took the .45 automatic and the full clip of hollow-points from the dresser drawer and walked with them inside the folded towel to the pickup truck and put them in the glove box. Annie watched me from the front porch, her arm leaned against a paintless wood post. I could see her breasts rise and fall under her denim shirt.

'I'm going to New Orleans. I'll be back tonight,' I said.

She didn't answer.

'It's not going to take care of itself,' I said. 'The sheriff is a nice guy who should be cleaning stains out of somebody's sports coat. The feds don't have jurisdiction in an assault case. The Lafayette cops don't have time to solve crimes in Iberia Parish. That means we fall through the cracks. Screw that.'

'I'm sure that somehow that makes sense. You know, rah, rah for the penis and all that. But I wonder if Dave is giving Dave a shuck so we can march off to the wars again.'

Her face was cheerless and empty.

I watched the wind flatten the leaves in the pecan trees, then I opened the door of the pickup.

'I need to take some money out of savings to help somebody,' I said. 'I'll put it back next month.'

'What can I say? Like your first wife told you, "Keep it high and hard, podjo,"' she said, and went back inside the house.

The sweep of wind in the pecan trees seemed deafening.

I gassed up the truck at the dock, then as an afterthought I went inside the bait shop, sat at the wooden counter with a Dr Pepper, and called Minos P. Dautrieve at the DEA in Lafayette. While the phone rang I gazed out the window at the green leaves floating on the bayou.

'I understand you want my ass in your office,' I said.

'Yeah, what the fuck's going on over there?'

'Why don't you drive over and find out?'

'You sound funny.'

'I have stitches in my mouth.'

'They bounced you around pretty good, huh?'

'What's this about you wanting my ass in your office?'

'I'm curious. Why are a bunch of farts who deal dope and whores so interested in you? I think maybe you're on to something we don't know about.'

'I'm not.'

'I think also you may have the delusion you're still a police officer.'

'You've got things turned around a little bit. When a guy gets his *cojones* and his face kicked in, he becomes the victim. The guys who kick in his *cojones* and face are the criminals. These are the guys you get mad at. The object is to put them in jail.'

'The sheriff said you can't identify Keats.'

'I didn't see his face.'

'And you never saw the Zulu before?'

'Keats, or whoever the white guy was, said he was one of Baby Doc's *tontons macoute*.'

'What do you want us to do, then?'

'If I remember our earlier conversation right, y'all were going to handle it.'

'It's after the fact now. And I don't have authority in this kind of assault case. You know that.'

I looked out the window at the leaves floating on the brown current.

'Do you all ever salt the mine shaft?' I said.

'You mean plant dope on a suspect? Are you serious?'

'Save the Boy Scout stuff. I've got a wife and another person in my home who are in jeopardy. You said you were going to handle things. You're not handling anything. Instead I get this ongoing lecture that somehow I'm the problem in this situation.'

'I never said that.'

'You don't have to. A collection of moral retards runs millions in drugs through the bayous, and you probably don't nail one of them in fifty. It's frustrating. It looks bad on the monthly report. You wonder if you're going to be transferred to Fargo soon. So you make noise about civilians meddling in your business.'

'I don't like the way you're talking to me, Robicheaux.'

'Too bad. I'm the guy with the stitches. If you want to do something for me, figure out a way to pick up Keats.'

'I'm sorry you got beat up. I'm sorry we can't do more. I understand your anger. But you were a cop and you know our limits. So how about easing off the Purple Heart routine?'

'You told me Keats's bars have hookers in them. Get the local heat to park patrol cars in front of his bars a few nights. You'll bring his own people down on him.'

'We don't operate that way.'

'I had a feeling you'd say that. See you around, partner. Don't hang on the rim too long. Everybody will forget you're in the game.'

'You think that's clever?'

I hung up on him, finished my Dr Pepper, and drove down the dirt road in the warm wind that thrashed the tree limbs overhead. The bayou was covered with leaves now, and back in the shadows on the far bank I could see cottonmouths sleeping on the lower branches of the willow trees, just above the water's languid surface. I rumbled across the drawbridge into town, withdrew three hundred dollars from the bank, then took the back road through the sugarcane fields to St Martinville and caught the interstate to New Orleans.

The wind was still blowing hard as I drove down the long concrete causeway over the Atchafalaya swamp. The sky was still a soft blue and filled with tumbling white clouds, but a good storm was building out on the Gulf and I knew that by evening the southern horizon would be black and streaked with rain and lightning. I watched the flooded willow trees bend in the wind, and the moss on the dead cypress in the bays straighten and fall, and the way the sunlight danced and shattered on the water when the surface suddenly wrinkled from one shore to the next. The Atchafalaya basin encompasses hundreds of square miles of bayous, willow islands, sand bogs, green leaves covered with buttercups, wide bays dotted with dead cypress and oil-well platforms, and flooded woods filled with cotton-mouths, alligators, and black clouds of mosquitoes. My father and I had fished and hunted all over the. Atchafalaya when I was a boy, and even on a breezy spring day like this we knew how to catch bull bream and goggle-eye perch when nobody else would catch them. In the late afternoon we'd anchor the pirogue on the lee side of a willow island, when the mosquitoes would start to swarm out of the trees, and cast our bobbers back into the quiet water, right against the line of lilly pads, and wait for the bream and goggle-eye to start feeding on the insects. In an hour we'd fill our ice chest with fish.

But my reverie about boyhood moments with my father could not get rid of the words Annie had said to me. She had wanted to raise a red welt across the heart, and she had done a good job of it. But maybe what bothered me worse was the fact that I knew she had hurt me only because she had an unrelieved hurt inside herself. Her reference to a statement made by my first wife was an admission that maybe there was a fundamental difference in me, a deeply ingrained character flaw, that neither Annie nor my ex-wife nor perhaps any sane woman would ever be able to accept. I was not simply a drunk; I was drawn to a violent and aberrant world the way a vampire bat seeks a black recess within the earth.

My first wife's name was Niccole, and she was a darkhaired, beautiful girl from Martinique who loved horse racing almost as much as I. But unfortunately she loved money and clubhouse society even more. I could have almost forgiven her infidelities in our marriage, until we both discovered that her love affairs were not motivated by lust for other men but rather contempt for me and loathing for the dark, alcoholic energies that governed my life.

We had been at a lawn party out by Lake Pontchartrain, and I had been drinking all afternoon at Jefferson Downs and now I had reached the point where I didn't even bother to leave the small bar under the mimosa trees at the lawn party and make a pretense of interest at the conversation around me. The wind was balmy and it rattled the dry palm fronds on the lakeshore, and I watched the red sun set on the horizon and reflect on the green, capping surface of the water. In the distance, white sailboats lurched in fountains of spray toward the Southern Yacht Club. I could feel the whiskey in my face, the omniscient sense of control that alcohol always brought me, the bright flame of metaphysical insight burning behind my eyes.

But my seersucker sleeve was damp from the bar, and my words were thick and apart from me when I asked for another Black Jack and water.

Then Niccole was standing next to me with her current lover, a geologist from Houston. He was a summer mountain climber, and he had a rugged, handsome profile like a Roman's and a chest that looked as hard as a barrel. Like all the other men there, he wore the soft tropical colors of the season – a pastel shirt, a white linen suit, a purple knit tie casually loose at the throat. He ordered Manhattans for both of them, then while he waited for the Negro bartender to fix their drinks he stroked the down on top of Niccole's arm as though I were not there.

Later, I would not be able to describe accurately any series of feelings or events after that moment. I felt something rip like wet newspaper in the back of my head; I saw his startled face look suddenly into mine; I saw it twist and convulse as my fist came across his mouth; I felt his hands try to grab my coat as he went down; I saw the genuine fear in his eyes as I rained my fists down on him and then caught his throat between my hands.

When they pulled me off him, his tongue was stuck in his throat, his skin was the color of ash, and his cheeks were covered with strings of pink spittle. My wife was sobbing uncontrollably on the host's shoulder.

When I awoke on our houseboat the next morning, my eyes shuddering in the hard light refracting off the lake, I found the note she had left me:

Dear Dave,
I don't know what it is you're looking for, but three years of marriage to you have convinced me I don't want to be there when you find it. Sorry about that. As your pitcher-bartender friend says, Keep it high and hard, podjo.

Niccole

I followed the highway through the eastern end of the Atchafalaya basin. White cranes rose above the dead cypress in the sunlight just as the first drops of rain began to dimple the water below the causeway. I could smell the wet sand, the moss, the four-o'clock flowers, the toadstools, the odor of dead fish and sour mud blowing on the wind out of the marsh. A big willow tree by the water's edge looked like a woman's hair in the wind.

4

The rain was falling out of a blue-black sky when I parked the pickup truck in front of the travel agency in New Orleans. I knew the owner, and he let me use his WATS line to call a friend in Key West. Then I bought a one-way ticket there for seventy-nine dollars.

Robin lived in a decrepit Creole-style apartment building off South Rampart. The cracked brick and mortar had been painted purple; the red tiles in the roof were broken; the scrolled iron grillwork on the balconies had burst loose from its fastenings and was tilted at odd angles. The banana and palm trees in the courtyard looked as though they had never been pruned, and the dead leaves and fronds clicked loudly in the rain and wind. Dark-skinned children rode tricycles up and down the second-floor balcony, and all the apartment doors were open and even in the rain you could hear an incredible mixed din of daytime television, Latin music, and people shouting at each other.

I walked up to Robin's apartment, but as I approached her door a middle-aged, overweight man in a rain–spotted gray business suit with an American-flag pin in his lapel came toward me, squinting at a small piece of damp paper in his hand. I wanted to think he was a bill collector, a social worker, a process server, but his eyes were too furtive, his face too nervous, his need too obvious. He realized that the apartment number he was looking for was the one I was standing in front of. His face went blank, the way a man's does when he suddenly knows that he's made a commitment for which he has no preparation. I didn't want to be unkind to him.

'She's out of the business, partner,' I said.

'Sir?'

'Robin's not available anymore.'

'I don't know what you're talking about.' His face had grown rounder and more frightened.

'That's her apartment number on that piece of paper, isn't it? You're not a regular, so I suspect somebody sent you here. Who was it?'

He started to walk past me. I put my hand gently on his arm.

'I'm not a policeman. I'm not her husband. I'm just a friend. Who was it, partner?' I said.

'A bartender.'

'At Smiling Jack's, on Bourbon?'

'Yes, I think that was it.'

'Did you give him money?'

'Yes.'

'Don't go back there for it. He won't give it back to you, anyway. Do you understand that?'

'Yes.'

I took my hand away from his arm, and he walked quickly down the stairs and out into the rain-swept courtyard.

I looked through the screen door into the gloom of Robin's apartment. A toilet flushed in back, and she walked into the living room in a pair of white shorts and a green Tulane T-shirt and saw me framed against the wet light. The index finger of her left hand was wrapped in a splint. She smiled sleepily at me and I stepped inside. The thick, drowsy odor of marijuana struck at my face. Smoke curled from a roach clip in an ashtray on the coffee table.

'What's happening, Streak?' she said lazily.

'I just ran off a client, I'm afraid.'

'What d'you mean?'

'Jerry sent a john over. I told him you were out of the business. Permanently, Robin. We're moving you to Key West, kiddo.'

'This is all too weird. Look, Dave, I'm down to seeds and stems, if you know what I mean. I'm going out to buy some beer. Mommy has to get a little mellow before she bounces her stuff for the cantaloupe lovers. You want to come along?'

'No beer, no more hooking, no Smiling Jack's tonight. I've got you a ticket on a nine o'clock flight to Key West.'

'Stop talking crazy, will you? What am I going to do in Key West? It's full of faggots.'

'You're going to work in a restaurant owned by a friend of mine. It's a nice place, out on the pier at the end of Duval Street. Famous people eat in there. Tennessee Williams used to come there.'

'You mean that country singer? Wow, what a gig.'

'I'm going to square what those guys did to you and me,' I said. 'When I do, you won't be able to stay in New Orleans.'

'That's what's wrong with your mouth?'

'They told me what they did to your finger. I'm sorry. It's my fault.'

'Forget it. It comes with my stage career.' She sat down on the stuffed couch and picked up the roach clip, which now held only smoldering ash. She toyed with it, studied it, then dropped it on top of the glass ashtray. 'Don't make them come back. The white guy, the one with the cowboy boots, he had some Polaroid pictures. God, I don't want to remember them.'

'Do you know who these guys are?'

'No.'

'Did you ever see them before?'

'No.'

'Are you sure?'

'Yes.' She squeezed one hand around the fingers of the other. 'In the pictures, some colored people were tied up in a basement or something. They had blood all over them. Dave, some of them were still alive. I can't forget what their faces looked like.'

I sat down beside her and picked up her hands. Her eyes were wet, and I could smell the marijuana on her breath.

'If you catch that plane tonight, you can start a new life. I'll check on you and my friend will help you, and you'll put all this stuff behind you. How much money do you have?'

'A couple of hundred dollars maybe.'

'I'll give you two hundred more. That'll get you to your first pay-check. But no snorting, no dropping, no shooting. You understand that?'

'Hey, is this guy out there one of your AA pals? Because I told you I don't dig that scene.'

'Who's asking you to?'

'I got enough troubles without getting my head shrunk by a bunch of ex-drunks.'

'Make your own choice. It's your life, kiddo.'

'Yeah, but you're always up to something on the side. You should have been a priest. You still go to Mass?'

'Sure.'

'You remember the time you took me to midnight Mass at St Louis Cathedral? Then we walked across the square and had beignets at the Café du Monde. You know, I thought maybe you were serious about me that night.'

'I have to ask you a couple of questions before I go.'

'Sure, why not? Most men are interested in my jugs. You come around like a census taker.'

'I'm serious, Robin. Do you remember a guy named Victor Romero?'

'Yeah, I guess so. He used to hang around with Johnny Dartez.'

'Where's he from?'

'Here.'

'What do you know about him?'

'He's a little dark-skinned guy with black curls hanging off his head, and he wears a French beret like he's an artist or something. Except he's bad news. He sold some tainted skag down on Magazine, and I heard a couple of kids were dead before they got the spike out of their arms.'

'Was he muling for Bubba Rocque, too?'

'I don't know. I don't care. I haven't seen the guy in months. Why do you care about those dipshits? I thought you were the family man now. Maybe things aren't too good at home.'

'Maybe.'

'And you're the guy that's going to clean up mommy's act so she can wipe off tables for the tourists. Wow.'

'Here's the airline ticket and the two hundred dollars. My friend's name is written on the envelope. Do whatever you want.'

I started to get up, but she pressed her hands down on my arms. Her breasts were large and heavy against her T-shirt, and I knew secretly that I had the same weakness as the men who watched her every night at Smiling Jack's.

'Dave?'

'What?'

'Do you think about me a little bit sometimes?'

'Yes.'

'Do you like me?'

'You know I do.'

'I mean the way you'd like an ordinary woman, somebody who didn't have a pharmacy floating around in her bloodstream.'

'I like you a lot, Robin.'

'Stay just a minute, then. I'll take the plane tonight. I promise.'

Then she put her arm across my chest, tucked her head under my chin like a small girl, and pressed herself against me. Her short-cropped, dark hair was soft and smelled of shampoo, and I could feel her breasts swell against me as she breathed. Outside it was raining hard on the courtyard. I brushed her cheek with my fingers and held her hand, then a moment later I felt her shudder as though some terrible tension and fear had left her body with sleep. In the silence I looked out at the rain dancing on the iron grillwork.

The neon lights on Bourbon looked like green and purple smoke in the rain. The Negro street dancers, with their heavy metal clip-on taps that clattered like horseshoes on the sidewalk, were not out tonight, and the few tourists were mostly family people who walked close against the buildings, from one souvenir shop to the next, and did not stop at the open doors of the strip joints where spielers in straw boaters and candy-striped vests were having a hard time bringing in the trade.

I stood against a building on the opposite corner from Smiling Jack's and watched Jerry through the door for a half hour. He wore his fedora and an apron over an open-necked sports shirt that was covered with small whiskey bottles. Against the glow of stage lights on the burlesque stage behind him, the angular profile of his face looked as though it were snipped out of tin.

The weight of the .45 was heavy in my raincoat pocket. I had a permit to carry it, but I never had occasion to, and actually I had fired it only once since leaving the department, and that was at an alligator who attacked a child on the bayou. But I had used it as a police officer when the bodyguard of New Orleans's number-one pimp and drug dealer threw down on my partner and me. It had kicked in my hand like a jackhammer, as though it had a life of its own; when I had stopped shooting into the back of the Cadillac, my ears were roaring with a sound like the sea, my face was stiff with the smell of the cordite, and later my dreams would be peopled by two men whose bodies danced disjointedly in a red haze.

This district had been my turf for fourteen years, first as a patrolman, then as a sergeant in robbery investigation, and finally as a lieutenant in homicide. In that time I got to see them all: male and female prostitutes, Murphy artists, psychotic snipers, check writers, pete men, car boosters, street dealers, and child molesters. I was punched out, shot at, cut with an ice pick, stuffed unconscious behind the wheel of a car and shoved off the third level of a parking garage. I witnessed an electrocution in Angola penitentiary, helped take the remains of a bookie out of a garbage compactor, drew chalk outlines on an alley floor where a woman had jumped with her child from the roof of a welfare hotel.

I turned the key on hundreds of people. A lot of them did hard time in Angola; four of them went to the electric chair. But I don't think my participation in what politicians call 'the war on crime' ever made much difference. New Orleans is no safer a town now than it was then. Why? Narcotics is one answer. Maybe another is the fact that in fourteen years I never turned the key on a slumlord or on a zoning board member who owned interests in pornographic theaters and massage parlors.

I saw Jerry take off his apron and walk toward the back of the bar. I crossed the street in the slanting rain and entered the bar just as Jerry disappeared through a curtained doorway in back. On the lighted stage in front of a full-wall mirror, two topless girls in sequined G-strings with gold chains around their ankles danced barefoot to a 1950s rock 'n' roll record. I had to wait for my eyes to adjust to the turning strobe light that danced across the walls and floor and the bodies of the men staring up at the girls from the bar, then I headed toward the curtained doorway in back.

'Can I help you, sir?' the other bartender said. He was blond and wore a black string tie on a white sports shirt.

'I have an appointment with Jerry.'

'Jerry Falgout?'

'The other bartender.'

'Yeah. Have a seat. I'll tell him you're here.'

'Don't bother.'

'Hey, you can't go back there.'

'It's a private conversation, podna. Don't mess in it.'

I went through the curtain into a storage area that was filled with cases of beer and liquor bottles. The room was lit by a solitary bulb in a tin shade, and a huge ventilator fan set in the far window sucked the air out into a brick alley. The door to a small office was partly ajar, and inside the office Jerry was bent on one knee in front of a desk, almost as if he were genuflecting, while he snorted a line of white powder off a mirror with a rolled five-dollar bill. Then he rose to his feet, closed each nostril with a finger, and sniffed, blinked, and widened his eyes, then licked his finger and wiped the residue off on a small square of white paper and rubbed it on his gums.

He didn't see me until he was out the door. I caught both of his arms behind him, put one hand behind his head and ran him straight into the window fan. His fedora clattered in the tin blades, and then I heard them thunk and whang against his scalp and I pulled his head up the way you would a drowning man's and shoved him back inside the small office and shut the door behind us. His face was white with shock, and blood ran out of his hairline like pieces of string. His eyes were wild with fright. I pushed him down in a chair.

'Goddamn, goddamn, man, you're out of your fucking mind,' he said, his voice almost hiccupping.

'How much did you get for dropping the dime on Robin?'

'What? I didn't get nothing. What are you talking about?'

'You listen to me, Jerry. It's just you and me. No Miranda, no lawyer, no bondsman, no safe cell to be a tough guy in. It all gets taken care of right here. Do you understand that?'

He pressed his palm against the blood in his hair and then looked at his palm stupidly.

'Say you understand.'

'What?'

'Last chance, Jerry.'

'I don't understand nothing. What the fuck's with you? You come on like a crazy person.'

I took the .45 out of my coat pocket, pulled back the receiver so he could see the loaded magazine, and slid a round into the chamber. I sighted between his eyes.

His face twitched with fear, his mouth trembled, his hair glistened with sweat. His hands were gripped on both his thighs as though there were a terrible pain in his bowels.

'Come on, man, put it away,' he said. 'I told you I ain't no swinging dick. I'm just a guy getting by. I tend bar, I live off tips, I mop up bathrooms. I'm no heavy dude you got to come down on like King Kong. No shit, man. Put away the piece.'

'What did they pay you?'

'A hunnerd bucks. I didn't know they were going to hurt her. That's the truth. I thought they'd just tell her not to be talking to no ex-cops. They don't beat up whores. It costs them money. I don't know why they broke her finger. They didn't have to do it. She don't know anything anyway. Come on, man, put it away.'

'Did you call Eddie Keats?'

'Are you kidding? He's a fucking hit man. Is that who they sent?'

'Who did you call?'

His eyes went away from the gun and looked down in his lap. He held his hands between his legs.

'Does my voice sound funny to you?' I said.

'Yeah, I guess so.'

'It's because I have stitches in my mouth. I also have some in my head. A black guy named Toot put them there. Do you know who he is?'

'No.'

'He broke Robin's finger, then he came to New Iberia.'

'I didn't know that, man. Honest to God.'

'You're starting to genuinely piss me off, Jerry. Who did you call?'

'Look, everybody does it. You hear something about Bubba Rocque or somebody talking about him or maybe his people getting out of line, you call up his club about it and you get a hunnerd bucks. It don't even have to be important. They say he just likes to know everything that's going on.'

'Hey, you all right in there, Jerry?' the voice of the other bartender said outside the door.

'He's fine,' I said.

The doorknob started to turn.

'Don't open that door, podna,' I said. 'If you want to call the Man, do it, but don't come in here. While you're at it, tell the heat Jerry's been poking things up his nose again.'

I looked steadily into Jerry's eyes. His eyelashes were beaded with sweat. He swallowed and wiped the dryness of his lips with his fingers.

'It's all right, Morris,' he said. 'I'm coming out in a minute.'

I heard the bartender's feet walk away from the door. Jerry took a deep breath and looked at the gun again.

'I told you what you want. So cut me some slack, okay?' he said.

'Where's Victor Romero?'

'What the fuck I know about him?'

'You knew Johnny Dartez, didn't you?'

'Sure. He was in all these skin joints. He's dead now, right?'

'So you must have known Victor Romero, too.'

'You don't get it. I'm a bartender. I don't know anything that anybody on the street don't know. The guy's a fucking geek. He was peddling some bad Mexican brown around town, it had insecticide in it or something. So he had to get out of town. Then I heard him and Johnny Dartez got busted by Immigration for trying to bring in a couple of big-time greasers from Colombia. But that must be bullshit because Johnny was still flying around when he went down in the drink, right?'

'They were busted by Immigration?'

'I don't know that, man. You stand behind that bar and you'll hear a hunnerd fucking stories a night. It's a soap opera. How about it, man? Do I get some slack?'

I eased the hammer down carefully and let the .45 hang from my arm. He expelled a long breath from his chest, his shoulders sagged, and he wiped his damp palms on his pants.

'There's one other thing,' I said. 'You're out of Robin's life. You don't even have thoughts about her.'

'What am I supposed to do? Pretend I don't see her? She works here, man.'

'Not anymore. In fact, if I were you, I'd think about finding a job outside the country.'

His face looked confused, then I could see a fearful comprehension start to work in his eyes.

'You got it, Jerry. I'm going to have a talk with Bubba Rocque. When I do, I'll tell him who sent me. You might think about Iran.'

I dropped the .45 in the pocket of my raincoat and walked back out of the bar into the rain that had now thinned and was blowing in rivulets off the iron-scrolled balconies along the street. The air was clean and cool and sweet-smelling with the rain, and I walked in the lee of the buildings toward Jackson Square and Decatur, where my truck was parked, and I could see the lighted peaks of St Louis Cathedral against the black sky. The river was covered with mist as thick as clouds. The waiters had stacked the chairs in the Café du Monde, and the wind blew the mist over the tabletops in a wet sheen. In the distance I could hear a ship's horn blowing across the water.

It was eleven o'clock when I got back home, and the storm had stopped and the house was dark. The pecan trees were wet and black in the yard, and the slight breeze off the bayou rustled their leaves and shook water onto the tin roof of the gallery. I checked on Alafair, then went into our bedroom, where Annie was sleeping on her stomach in her panties and a pajama top. The attic fan was on, and it drew the cool air from outside and moved the curly hair on the back of her neck. I put the .45 back in the drawer, undressed, and lay down beside her. I could feel the fatigue of the day rush through me like a drug. She stirred slightly, then turned her head away from me on the pillow. I placed my hand on her back. She rolled over with her face pointing at the ceiling and her arm over her eyes.

'You got back all right?' she said.

'Sure.'

She was quiet a moment, and I could hear the dryness of her mouth when she spoke again: 'Who was she, Dave?'

'A dancer in a joint on Bourbon.'

'Did you take care of everything?'

'Yes.'

'You owed her, I guess.'

'Not really. I just had to get her off the hook.'

'I don't understand why she's your obligation.'

'Because she's a drunk and an addict and she can't do anything for herself. They broke her finger, Annie. If they catch her again, it'll be much worse.'

I heard her take a breath, then she put her hands on her stomach and looked up into the dark.

'It's not over, though, is it?' she said.

'It is for her. And the guy who was partly responsible for me getting my face kicked in is going to be blowing New Orleans in a hurry. I admit that makes me feel good.'

'I wish I could share your feeling.'

It was quiet in the room, and the moon came out and made shadows in the trees. I felt I was about to lose something, maybe forever. I put my foot over hers and took one of her hands in mine. Her hand was pliant and dry.

'I didn't seek it out,' I said. 'The trouble came to us. You have to confront problems, Annie. When you don't, they follow you around like pariah dogs.'

'You always tell me that one of the main axioms in AA is "Easy does it." '

'It doesn't mean you should avoid your responsibilities. It doesn't mean you should accept the role of victim.'

'Maybe we should talk about the price we should all be willing to pay for your pride.'

'I don't know what to say anymore. You don't understand, and I don't think you're going to.'

'What should I feel, Dave? You lie down next to me and tell me you've been with a stripper, that you've run somebody out of New Orleans, that it makes you feel good. I don't know anything about a world like that. I don't think anybody should have to.'

'It exists because people pretend it's not there.'

'Let other people live in it, then.'

She sat up on the side of the bed with her back to me.

'Don't go away from me,' I said.

'I'm not going anywhere.'

'Lie down and talk.'

'It's no good to talk about it anymore.'

'We can talk about other things. This is just a temporary thing. I've had a lot worse trouble in my life than this,' I said.

She remained seated on the side of the bed, her panties low on her bottom. I put my hand on her shoulder and eased her back down on the pillow.

'Come on, kiddo. Don't lock your old man out,' I said.

I kissed her cheeks and her eyes and stroked her hair. I could feel myself grow against her side. But her eyes looked straight ahead, and her hands rested loosely on my shoulders, as though that were the place that obligation required them to be.

I could see the water dripping out of the pecan trees in the moonlight. I didn't care about pride or the feelings that I would have later. I needed her, and I slipped off her panties and pulled off my underwear and held her against me. Her arms rested on my back and she kissed me once lightly on the jaw, but she was dry when I entered her, and her eyes stayed open and unseeing as though she were focused on a thought inside herself.

Out on the bayou I heard the peculiar cry of a bull 'gator calling to its mate. I was sweating now, even in the cool wind drawn by the attic fan through the window, and in the mire of thoughts that can occur in such a heart-rushing and selfdefeating moment, I tried to justify both my lustful dependency and my willingness to force her to be my accomplice.

I stopped and raised myself off her, my body trembling with its own denial, and worked my underwear back over my thighs. She turned her head on the pillow and looked at me as a patient might from a hospital bed.

'It's been a long day,' she said quietly.

'Not for me. I think I'd like to go out and blow the shit out of some tin cans and bottles right now.'

I stood up from the bed and put on my shirt and pants.

'Where are you going?' she said.

'I don't know.'

'Come back to bed, Dave.'

'I'll lock the front door on the way out. I'll try not to wake you when I come back.'

I slipped on my loafers and went outside to my truck. The few black clouds in the sky were rimmed with moonlight, and shadows fell through the oaks on the dirt road that led back into New Iberia. The bayou was high from the rain, and I could see the solitary V-shaped ripple of a nutria swimming from the cattails to the opposite shore. I banged and splashed through the muddy pools in the road, and gripped the steering wheel so tightly that my fists were ridged with bone. When I went across the drawbridge, the spare tire in the bed of the pickup bounced three feet in the air.

Main Street in New Iberia was quiet and empty when I parked in front of the poolroom. The oaks along the street stirred in the breeze, and out on the bayou the green and red running lights of a tug moved silently through the opened drawbridge. I could see the bridge tender in his little lighted office. Down the block a man in shirt sleeves, smoking a pipe, was walking his dog past the old brick Episcopalian church that had been used as a hospital by federal soldiers during the War Between the States.

The inside of the poolroom was like a partial return into the New Iberia of my youth, when people spoke French more often than English, when there were slot and race-horse machines in every bar, and the cribs on Railroad Avenue stayed open twenty-four hours a day and the rest of the world was as foreign to us as the Texans who arrived after World War II with their oil rigs and pipeline companies. A mahogany bar with a brass rail and spittoons ran the length of the room; there were four green-felt pool tables in back that the owner sometimes covered with oilcloth and served free gumbo on, and old men played *bourée* and dominoes under the wood-bladed fans that hung from the ceiling. The American and National League scores were written on a big chalkboard against one wall, and the television above the bar always seemed to have a baseball game on it. The room smelled of draft beer and gumbo and talcum, of whiskey and boiled crawfish and Virginia Extra tobacco, of pickled pig's feet and wine and Red Man.

The owner was named Tee Neg. He was an old-time pipeliner and oil-field roughneck who looked like a mulatto and who had had three fingers pinched off by a drilling chain. I watched him draw a beer in a frosted schooner, rake the foam off with a ladle, and serve it with a jigger of neat whiskey to a man in denim clothes and a straw hat who stood at the bar and smoked a cigar.

'I hope you're here to play pool, Dave,' Tee Neg said.

'Give me a bowl of gumbo.'

'The kitchen's closed. You know that.'

'Give me some *boudin*.'

'They didn't bring me none today. You want a Dr Pepper?'

'I don't want anything.'

'Suit yourself.'

'Give me a cup of coffee.'

'You look tired, you. Go home and sleep.'

'Just bring me a cup of coffee, Tee Neg. Bring me a cigar, too.'

'You don't smoke, Dave. What you mad at, you?'

'Nothing. I didn't eat tonight. I thought your kitchen was open. You got today's paper?'

'Sure.'

'I'm just going to read the paper.'

'Anyt'ing you want.'

He reached under the bar and handed me a folded copy of the *Daily Iberian*. There were beer rings on the front page.

'Give those old gentlemen in back a round on me,' I said.

'You don't have to do that.'

'I want to.'

'You don't have to do that, Dave.' He looked me steadily in the face.

'So I'm flush tonight.'

'Okay, podna. But they buy you one, you go behind the bar and get it yourself. You don't use Tee Neg, no.'

I shook open the paper and tried to read the sports page, but my eyes wouldn't focus on the words. My skin itched, my face burned, my loins felt as though they were filled with concrete. I folded the paper, dropped it on the bar, and walked back outside into the late-spring night.

I drove down to the bay at Cypremort Point and sat on a jetty that extended out into the salt water and watched the tide go out. When the sun came up in the morning the sky was empty and looked as white as bone. Seagulls flew low over the wet, gray sand flats and pecked at the exposed shellfish, and I could smell the odor of dead fish on the wind. My clothes felt stiff and gritty with salt as I walked back to my truck. All the way back to town my visit to the poolroom remained as real and as unrelenting in its detail as a daylong hangover.

Later, Batist and I opened up the bait shop and dock, then I went up to the house and slept until early afternoon. When I woke, it was bright and warm, and the mockingbirds and blue jays were loud in the trees. Annie had left me two waxpaper-wrapped ham and onion sandwiches and a note on the kitchen table.

Didn't want to wake you but when I get back from town can you help me find a horny middle-aged guy with a white streak in his head who knows how to put a Kansas girl on rock 'n' roll?

Love,
A.

PS Let's picnic in the park this evening and take Alafair to the baseball game. I'm sorry about last night. You'll always be my special guy, Dave.

It was a generous and kind note. I should have been content with it. But it disturbed me as much as it reassured me, because I wondered if Annie, like most people who live with alcoholics, was not partly motivated by fear that my unpredictable mood might lead all of us back into the nightmarish world that AA had saved me from.

Regardless, I knew that the problems that had been caused us by the plane crash at Southwest Pass would not go away. And having grown up in a rural Cajun world that was virtually devoid of books, I had learned most of my lessons for dealing with problems from hunting and fishing and competitive sports. No book could have taught me what I had learned from my father in the marsh, and as a boxer in high school I had discovered that it was as important to swallow your blood and hide your injury as it was to hurt your opponent.

But maybe the most important lesson I had learned about addressing complexity was from an elderly Negro janitor who had once pitched for the Kansas City Monarchs in the old Negro leagues. He used to watch our games in the afternoon, and one day when I'd been shotgunned off the mound and was walking off the field toward the shower, he walked along beside me and said, 'Sliders and screwballs is cute, and spitters shows 'em you can be nasty. But if you want to make that batter's pecker shrivel up, you throw a forkball at his head.'

Maybe it was time to float one by the batter's head, I thought.

Bubba Rocque had bought a ruined antebellum home on the Vermilion River outside of Lafayette and had spent a quarter-million dollars rebuilding it. It was a massive plantation house, white and gleaming in the sun, the three-story Doric columns so thick that two men could not place their arms around them and touch hands. The front gallery was made of Italian marble; the second-story veranda ran completely around the building and was railed with ironwork from Seville and hung with boxes of petunias and geraniums. The brick carriage house had been expanded to a three-car garage; the stone wells were decorated with ornamental brass pulleys and buckets and planted with trumpet and passion vine; the desiccated wood outbuildings had been replaced with a clay tennis court.

The lawn was blue-green and glistening in the water sprinklers, dotted with oak, mimosa, and lime and orange trees, and the long gravel lane that led to the front door was bordered by a white fence entwined with yellow roses. A Cadillac convertible and a new cream-colored Oldsmobile were parked in front, and a fire-engine red collector's MG stuck out of the carriage house. Through the willows on the riverbank I could see a cigarette boat moored bow and stern to the dock, a tarp pulled down snugly on the cockpit.

It was hard to believe that this scene clipped out of *Southern Living* belonged to Bubba Rocque, the kid who used to train for a fight by soaking his hands in diluted muriatic acid and running five miles each morning with army boots on. An elderly Negro servant opened the door but didn't invite me in. Instead, he closed the door partly in my face and walked into the back of the house. Almost five minutes later I heard Bubba lean over the veranda and call down to me, 'Go on in, Dave. I'll be right down. Sorry for our crummy manners. I was in the shower.'

I let myself in and stood in the middle of the front hall under a huge chandelier and waited for him to come down the winding staircase that curled back into the second floor. The interior of the house was strange. The floors were blond oak, the mantelpiece carved mahogany, the furnishings French antiques. Obviously an expensive interior decorator had tried to recreate the Creole antebellum period. But somebody else had been at work, too. The cedar baseboards and ceiling boards had been painted with ivy vines; garish oil paintings of swampy sunsets, the kind you buy from sidewalk artists in New Orleans's Pirates Alley, hung over the couch and mantel; an aquarium filled with paddle wheels and plastic castles, even a rubber octopus stoppered to one side, sat in one window, green air bubbles popping from a clown's mouth.

Bubba came down the stairs on the balls of his feet. He wore white slacks and a canary-yellow golf shirt, sandals without socks and a gold neck chain, a gold wristwatch with a diamond-and-ruby face, and his spiked butch hair was bleached on the tips by the sun and his skin was tanned almost olive. He was still built like a fighter – his hips narrow, his stomach as flat as a boiler plate, the shoulders an axhandle wide, the arms longer than they should be, the knuckles as pronounced as ball bearings. But it was the wideset, gray-blue eyes above the gap-toothed mouth that leaped at you more than anything else. They didn't focus, adjust, stray, or blink; they locked on your face and they stayed there. He smiled readily, in fact constantly, but you could only guess at whatever emotion the eyes contained.

'What's happening, Dave?' he said. 'I'm glad you caught me when you did. I got to go down to New Orleans this afternoon. Come on out on the patio and have a drink. What do you think of my place?'

'It's impressive.'

'It's more place than I need. I got a small house on Lake Pontchartrain and a winter house in Bimini. That's more my style. But the wife likes it here, and you're right, it impresses the hell out of people. You remember when you and me and your brother used to set pins in the bowling alley and the colored kids tried to run us off because we were taking their jobs?'

'My brother and I got fired. But I don't think they could have run you off with a shotgun, Bubba.'

'Hey, those were hard times, podna. Come out here, I got to show you something.'

He led me through some French doors onto a flagstone patio by a screen-enclosed pool. Overhead the sun shone through the spreading branches of an oak and glinted on the turquoise water. On the far side of the pool was a screened breezeway, with a peaked, shingled roof, that contained a universal gym, dumbbells, and a body and timing bag.

He grinned, went into a prizefighter's crouch, and feinted at me.

'You want to slip on the sixteen-ounce pillows and waltz around a little bit?' he said.

'You almost put out my lights the last time I went up against you.'

'The hell I did. I got you in the corner and was knocking the sweat out of your hair all over the timekeeper and I still couldn't put you down. You want a highball? Clarence, bring us some shrimp and *boudin*. Sit down.'

'I've got a problem you might be able to help me with.'

'Sure. What are you drinking?' He took a pitcher of martinis out of a small icebox behind the wet bar.

'Nothing.'

'That's right, I heard you were fighting the hooch for a while. Here, I got some tea. Clarence, bring those goddamn shrimp.' He shook his head and poured himself a drink in a chilled martini glass. 'He's half senile. Believe it or not, he used to work on the oyster boat with my old man. You remember my old man? He got killed two years ago on the SP tracks. I ain't kidding you. They say he took a nap right on the tracks with a wine bottle on his chest. Well, he always told me he wanted to be a travelling man, poor old bastard.'

'A Haitian named Toot and maybe a guy by the name of Eddie Keats came to see me. They left a few stitches in my mouth and head. A bartender in Smiling Jack's on Bourbon told me he sicked them on me by calling one of your clubs.'

Bubba sat down across the glass-topped table from me with his drink in his hand. His eyes were looking directly into mine.

'You better explain to me what you're saying.'

'I think these guys job out for you. They also hurt a friend of mine,' I said. 'I'm going to square it, Bubba.'

'Is that why you think you're sitting in my house?'

'You tell me.'

'No, I'll tell you something else instead. I know Eddie Keats. He's from some toilet up North. He doesn't work for me. From what I hear, he doesn't put stitches in people's heads, he smokes them. The Haitian I never heard of. I'm telling you this because we went to school together. Now we eat some shrimps and *boudin* and we don't talk about this kind of stuff.'

He ate a cold shrimp off a toothpick from the tray the Negro had placed on the table, then sipped from his martini and looked directly into my face while he chewed.

'A federal cop told me Eddie Keats jobs out for you,' I said.

'Then he ought to do something about it.'

'The feds are funny guys. I never figured them out. One day they're bored to death with a guy, the next day run him through a sausage grinder.'

'You're talking about Minos Dautrieve at the DEA, right? You know what his problem is? He's a coonass just like you and me, except he went to college and learned to talk like he didn't grown up down here. I don't like that. I don't like these things you're saying to me, either, Dave.'

'You dealt the play, Bubba, when those two guys came out to my house.'

He looked away at a sound in the front of the house, then tapped his fingertips on the glass tabletop. His nails were chewed back to the quick, and the fingertips were flat and grained.

'I'm going to explain it to you once because we're friends,' he said. 'I own a lot of business. I got a dozen oyster boats, I got a fish-packing house in New Iberia and one in Morgan City. I own seafood restaurants in Lafayette and Lake Charles, I own three clubs and an escort agency in New Orleans. I don't need guys like Eddie Keats. But I got to deal with all kinds of people in my business – Jews, dagos, broads with their brains between their legs, you name it. There's a labor lawyer in New Orleans I wouldn't spit on, but I pay him a five-thousand-dollar-a-year retainer so I don't get a picket in front of my clubs. So maybe I don't like everybody on my payroll, and maybe I don't always know what they do. That's business. But if you want me to, I'll make some calls and find out if somebody sent Keats and this colored guy after you. What's the name of this motormouth at Smiling Jack's?'

'Forget him. I already had a serious talk with him.'

'Yeah?' He looked at me curiously. 'Sounds mean.'

'He thought so.'

'Who's the friend that got hurt?'

'The friend is out of it.'

'I think we got a problem with trust here.'

'I don't read it that way. We're just establishing an understanding.'

'No. I don't have to establish anything. You're my guest. I look at you and it's like yesterday I was watching you leaning over the spit bucket, your back trembling, blood all over your mouth, and all the time I was hoping you wouldn't come out for the third round. You didn't know it, but in the second you hit me so hard in the kidney I thought I was going to wet my jock.'

'Did you know I found Johnny Dartez's body in that plane crash out at Southwest Pass, except his body disappeared?'

He laughed, cut a piece of *boudin*, and handed it to me on a cracker.

'I just ate,' I said.

'Take it.'

'I'm not hungry.'

'Take it or you'll offend me. Christ, have you got a one-track mind. Listen, forget all these clowns you seem to be dragging around the countryside. I told you I have a lot of businesses and I hire people to run them I don't even like. You're educated, you're smart, you know how to make money. Manage one of my clubs in New Orleans, and I'll give you sixty thou a year, plus a percentage that can kick it up to seventy-five. You get a car, you cater trips to the Islands, you got your pick of broads.'

'Did Immigration ever talk to you?'

'What?'

'After they busted Dartez and Victor Romero. They tried to smuggle in some high-roller Colombians. You must know that. I heard it in the street.'

'You're talking about wetbacks or something now?'

'Oh, come on, Bubba.'

'You want to talk about the spicks, find somebody else. I can't take them. New Orleans is crawling with them now. The government ought to send massive shipments of rubbers down to wherever they come from.'

'The weird thing about this bust is that both these guys were mules. But they didn't go up the road, and they didn't have to finger anybody in front of a grand jury. What's that lead you to believe?'

'Nothing, because I don't care about these guys.'

'I believe they went to work for the feds. If they'd been muling for me, I'd be nervous.'

'You think I give a fuck about some greasers say they got something on me? You think I got this house, all these businesses because I run scared, because the DEA or Immigration or Minos Dautrieve with his thumb up his pink ass say a lot of bullshit they never prove, that they make up, that they tell to the newspapers or people that's dumb enough to listen to it?'

His eyes were bright, and the skin around his mouth was tight and gray.

'I don't know. I don't know what goes on inside you, Bubba,' I said.

'Maybe if a person wants to find out, he's just got to keep fucking in the same direction.'

'That's a two-way street, podna.'

'Is that right?'

'Put it in the bank. I'll see you around. Thanks for the *boudin*.'

I stood up to leave, and he rose from the table with me. His face was flat, heated, as unknowable as a shark's. Then suddenly he grinned, ducked into a boxer's crouch again, bobbed, and feinted a left at my face.

'Hey, got you!' he said. 'No shit, you flinched. Don't deny it.'

I stared at him.

'What are you looking at?' he said. 'All right, so I was hot. You come on pretty strong. I'm not used to that.'

'I've got to go, Bubba.'

'Hell, no. Let's slip on the pillows. We'll take it easy on each other. Hey, get this. I went to this full-contact karate club in Lafayette, you know, where they box with their feet like kangaroos or something. I'm in the ring with this guy, and he's grunting and swinging his dirty foot around in the air, and all these guys are yelling because they know he's going to cut my head off, and I stepped inside him real fast and busted him three times before he hit the deck. They had to lead him back to the dressing room like somebody took his brains out with an ice cream scoop.'

'I'm over the hill for it, and I still have to work this afternoon, anyway.'

'Bullshit. I can see it in your eyes. You'd still like to take me. It's that long reach. It's always a big temptation, isn't it?'

'Maybe.'

I was almost disengaged from Bubba and his mercurial personality when his wife walked through the French doors onto the patio. She was at least ten years younger than he. Her black hair was tied with ribbon behind her head; her skin was dark, and she wore a two-piece red and yellow flower-print bathing suit with a matching sarong fastened on one hip. In her hand she carried an open shoe box filled with bottles and emery boards for her nails. She was pretty in the soft, undefined way that Cajun girls often are before they gain weight in the middle years. She smiled at me, sat at the patio table, crossed her legs, arching one sandal off her foot, and put a piece of *boudin* in her mouth.

'Dave, you remember Claudette, from New Iberia?' Bubba said.

'I'm sorry, I'm a little vague on people from home sometimes,' I said. 'I lived in New Orleans for fourteen years or so.'

'I bet you remember her mother, Hattie Fontenot.'

'Oh yes, I think I do,' I said, my eyes flat.

'I bet you lost your cherry in one of her cribs on Railroad Avenue,' Bubba said.

'I'm not always big on boyhood memories,' I said.

'You and your brother had a paper route on Railroad Avenue. Are you going to tell me y'all never got paid in trade?'

'I guess I just don't remember.'

'She had two colored joints on the corner,' he said. 'We used to go nigger-knocking down there, then get laid for two dollars.'

'Bubba just likes to talk rough sometimes. It doesn't bother me. You don't have to be embarrassed,' she said.

'I'm not.'

'I'm not ashamed of my mother. She had a lot of good qualities. She didn't use profane language in polite company, unlike some people I know.' She had a heavy Cajun accent, and her brown eyes had a strange red cast in them. They were as round as a doll's.

'Bubba, will you make me a gin rickey?' she said.

'Your thermos is in the icebox.'

'So? I'd like one in a glass, please.'

'She can drink gin rickeys all day and not get loaded,' Bubba said. 'I think she's got hollow buns.'

'I don't think Dave is used to our kind of talk,' she said.

'He's married too, isn't he?'

'Bubba . . .'

'What?'

'Would you please get me a drink?'

'All right,' he said, taking the thermos and a chilled glass out of the icebox. 'I wonder what I pay Clarence for. I damn near have to show him a diagram just to get him to dust.'

He poured from the thermos into his wife's glass, then put it in front of her. He continued to look at her with an exasperated expression on his face.

'Look, I don't want to get on your case all the time, but how about not filing your nails at the table?' he said. 'I can do without nail filings in my food.'

She wiped the powdered filings off the glass top with a Kleenex, then continued filing her nails over the shoe box.

'Well, I have to go. It was nice meeting you,' I said.

'Yeah, I got to pack and get on the road, too. Walk him out to his truck, Claudette. I'm going to make some calls when I get to New Orleans. I find out somebody's been causing you problems, I'll cancel their act. That's a promise. By the way, that bartender better be out of town.'

He looked at me a moment, balancing on the balls of his feet, then cocked his fists and jerked his shoulders at an angle as quickly as a rubber band snapping.

'Hey!' he said, grinned and winked, then walked back out the patio toward the circular staircase. His back was triangular, his butt flat, his thighs as thick as telephone posts.

His wife walked with me out to my pickup truck. The wind blew across the lawn and flattened the spray from the sprinklers into a rainbow mist among the trees. Gray clouds were building in the south, and the air was close and hot. Upstairs, Bubba had turned on a 1950s Little Richard record full blast.

'You really don't remember me?' she said.

'No, I'm sorry.'

'I dated your brother, Jimmie, in New Orleans about ten years ago. One night we went out to visit you at your fish camp. You were really plastered and you kept saying that the freight train wouldn't let you sleep. So when it went by, you ran outside and shot it with a flare pistol.'

I suddenly realized that Bubba's wife wasn't so uncomplicated after all.

'I'm afraid I was ninety-proof a lot of the time back then,' I said.

'I thought it was funny.'

I tried to be polite, but like most dry alcoholics I didn't want to talk about my drinking days with people who saw humor in them.

'Well, so long. I hope to see you again,' I said.

'Do you think Bubba's crazy?'

'I don't know.'

'His second wife left him two years ago. He burned all her clothes in the incinerator out back. He's not crazy, though. He just wants people to think he is because it scares them.'

'That could be.'

'He's not a bad man. I know all the stuff they say about him, but not many people know the hard time he had growing up.'

'A lot of us had a hard time, Mrs Rocque.'

'You don't like him, do you?'

'I guess I just don't know your husband well, and I'd better go.'

'You get embarrassed too easy.'

'Mrs Rocque, I wish you good luck because I think you're going to need it.'

'I heard him offer you a job. You should take it. The people that work for him make a lot of money.'

'Yes, they do, and there's a big cost to lots of other people.'

'He doesn't make them do anything they don't already want to.'

'Your mother ran brothels, but she wasn't a white-slaver and she didn't sell dope. The most polite thing I can say about Bubba is that he's a genuine sonofabitch. I don't even think he'd mind.'

'I like you. Come have dinner with us sometime,' she said. 'I'm home a lot.'

I drove back down the pea-gravel lane and headed toward New Iberia and the picnic in the park with Annie and Alafair. The sun was bright on the tin roofs of the barns set back in the sugarcane fields. The few moss-hung oaks along the road made deep pools of shadow on the road's surface. I had to feel sorry for Bubba's wife. In AA we called it denial. We take the asp to our breast and smile at the alarm we see in the eyes of others.

I had gotten to him when I mentioned Immigration busting two of his mules. Which made me wonder even more what role Immigration played in all of this. They had obviously stone-walled Minos Dautrieve at the DEA, and I believed they were behind the disappearance of Johnny Dartez's body after it was recovered from the plane crash by the Coast Guard. So if I was any kind of cop at all, why hadn't I dealt with Immigration head-on? They probably would have thrown me out of their office, but I also knew how to annoy bureaucrats, call their supervisors in Washington collect, and file freedom of information forms on them until their paint started to crack. So why hadn't I done it, I asked myself. And in answering my own question, I began to have a realization about presumption and denial in myself.

5

Annie and Alafair were wrapping fried chicken in wax paper and fixing lemonade in a thermos when I got back home. I sat at the kitchen table with a glass of iced tea and mint leaves and looked out the window at the blue jays swooping over the mimosa tree in the backyard. The ducks in my pond were shaking water off their backs and waddling onto the bank in the shade created by the cattails.

'I feel foolish about something,' I said.

'We'll take care of that tonight,' she said, and smiled.

'Something else.'

'Oh.'

'Years ago when I was a patrolman there was a notorious street character in the Quarter named Dock Stratton. The welfare officer would give him a meal-and-lodging ticket at one of their contract hotels, and he'd check into the place, then throw all the furniture out the window – tables, chairs, dresser drawers, lamps, mattresses, everything he could squeeze through the window, it would all come crashing down on the sidewalk. Then he'd run downstairs before anybody could call the heat and haul everything to the secondhand store. But no matter what this guy did, we never busted him. I was new and didn't understand. The other guys told me it was because Dock was a barfer. If he got a finger loose in the back of the car, he'd stick it down his throat and puke all over the seats. He'd do it in a lineup, in a holding cell, in a courtroom. He was always cocked and ready to fire. This guy was so bad a guard at the jail threatened to quit rather than take him on the chain to morning court. So Dock was allowed to drive welfare workers and skid-row hotel managers crazy for years, and when rookies like me asked why, we got treated to a good story.

'Except I discovered there was another reason why Dock stayed on the street. He not only knew every hustler and thief in downtown New Orleans, but he'd been a locksmith before he melted his head with Thunderbird, and he could get into a place faster than a professional house creep. So there were a couple of detectives in robbery and homicide who would use him when things weren't working right in a case. One time they knew a hit man from Miami was in town to take out a labor union agent. They told Dock they were making him a special agent with the New Orleans police department and got him to open up the guy's motel room, steal his gun, his suitcase, all his clothes and traveler's checks, then they picked up the guy on suspicion – it was a Friday, so they could hold him until Monday morning – and kept him in a small cell for two days with three drag queens.'

'What's the point?' Annie said. Her voice was flat, and her eyes looked at the sunlight in the trees when she spoke.

'Cops leave certain things and people in place for a reason.'

'I know these people you talk about are funny and unusual and interesting and all that, Dave, but why not leave them in the past?'

'You remember that guy from Immigration that came around here? He's never been back to the house, has he? He could make a lot of trouble for us if he wanted to, but he hasn't. I told myself that was because I'd given him reason to avoid us.'

'Maybe he has other things to do. I just don't think the government is going to be interested in one little girl.' She wore a pair of wash-faded Levi's and a white sun halter, and I could see the brown spray of sun freckles on her back. Her hips creased softly above her belt line while she filled the picnic hamper at the drainboard.

'The government is interested in what they choose to be interested in,' I said. 'Right now I think they've got us on hold. They sent me a signal, but I didn't see it.'

'To tell you honestly, this sounds like something of your own creation.'

'That guy from Immigration, Monroe, was asking questions about us at the sheriff's office. He didn't need to do that. He could have cut a warrant, come out here, and done anything he wanted. Instead, he or somebody above him wanted me to know their potential in case I thought I could make problems for them about Johnny Dartez.'

'Who cares what they do?' Annie said.

'I don't think you appreciate the nature of bureaucratic machinery once it's set in motion.'

'I'm sorry. I'm just not going to invest my life in speculating about what people can do to me.'

Alafair was looking back and forth between the two of us, her face clouded with the tone of our voices. Annie had dressed her in pink shorts, a Mickey Mouse T-shirt, and pink tennis shoes with the words LEFT and RIGHT stamped boldly on the rubber tip of each shoe. Annie rubbed her hand over Alafair's head and gave her the plastic draw bag in which we kept the old bread.

'Go feed the ducks,' she said. 'We'll leave in a minute.'

'Feed ducks?'

'Yes.'

266

'Feed ducks now?'

'That's right.'

'Dave viene al parque?'

'Sure, he's coming,' Annie said.

Alafair grinned at me and went out the back screen to the pond. The sunlight through the trees made patterns on her brown legs.

'I'll tell you one thing, Dave. No matter what those people from Immigration do, they're not going to take her away. She's ours, just as if we had conceived her.'

'I didn't tell you the rest of the story about Dock Stratton. After he finished blowing out his wiring with synthetic wine and wasn't any good to anybody, they shipped him off to the asylum at Mandeville.'

'So what does this mean? Are you going to become the knight-errant, tilting with the US government?'

'No.'

'Do you still want to go to the park?'

'That's the reason I came home, kiddo.'

'I wonder. I really do,' she said.

'I'd appreciate it if you'd explain that.'

'Don't you see it, Dave? It's like you want to taint every moment in our lives with this conspiratorial vision of yours. It's become an obsession. We don't talk about anything else. Either that or you stare into space. How do you think I feel?'

'I'll try to be different.'

'I know.'

'I really will.'

Her eyes were wet. She sat down across the table from me.

'We haven't been able to have our own child. Now one's been given to us,' she said. 'That should make us the happiest people in the world. Instead, we fight and worry about what hasn't happened yet. Our conversation at home is filled with the names of people who shouldn't have anything to do with our lives. It's like deliberately inviting an obscene presence into your home. Dave, you say at AA they teach you to give it all up to your Higher Power. Can't you try that? just give it up, cut it out of your life? There's not a problem in the world that time can't help in some way.'

'That's like saying a black tumor on your brain will get better if you don't think about it.'

The kitchen was silent. I could hear the blue jays in the mimosa tree and the wings of the ducks beating across the pond as Alafair showered bread crumbs down on their heads. Annie turned away, finished wrapping the fried chicken, closed the picnic hamper, and walked out to the pond. The screen door banged on the jamb after her.

*

267

That evening there was a big crowd in the park for the baseball game, and the firemen were having a crawfish boil in the open-air pavilion. The twilight sky was streaked with lilac and pink, and the wind was cool out of the south with the promise of rain. We ate our picnic supper on a wooden table under the oak trees and watched the American Legion game and the groups of high school and college kids who drifted back and forth between the bleachers and the tailgates of pickup trucks where they kept beer in washtubs of ice. Out on the bayou the paddle-wheel pleasure boat with its lighted decks slid by against the dark outline of cypress and the antebellum homes on the far bank. The trees were full of barbecue smoke, and you could smell the crawfish from the pavilion and the hot *boudin* that a Negro sold from a handcart. Then I heard a French string band play 'Jolie Blonde' in the pavilion, and I felt as though once again I were looking through a hole in the dimension at the south Louisiana in which I had grown up.

> *Jolie blonde, gardez donc c'est t'as fait.*
> *Ta m'as quit-té pour t'en aller,*
> *Pour t'en aller avec un autre que moi.*
> *Jolie blonde, pretty girl,*
> *Flower of my heart,*
> *I'll love you forever*
> *My Jolie blonde.*

But seldom did Annie and I speak directly to each other. Instead we talked brightly to Alafair, walked her to the swing sets and seesaws, bought snow-cones, and avoided one another's eyes. That night in the almost anonymous darkness of our bedroom we made love. We did it in need, with our eyes closed, without words, with a kiss only at the end. As I lay on my back, arms across my eyes, I felt her fingers leave the top of my hand, felt her turn on her side toward the opposite wall, and I wondered if her heart was as heavy as mine.

I woke up a half hour later. The room was cool from the wind sucked through the window by the attic fan, but my skin was hot as though I had a sunburn, the stitches in my scalp itched, my palms were damp on my thighs when I sat on the side of the bed.

Without waking Annie, I washed my face, put on a pair of khakis and an old Hawaiian shirt, and went down to the bait shop. The moon was up, and the willows along the bank of the bayou looked silver in the light. I sat in the darkness at the counter and stared out the window at the water and the outboard boats and pirogues knocking gently against the posts on my dock. Then I got up, opened the beer cooler, and took out a handful of partly melted ice and rubbed it on my face and neck. The amber necks of the beer bottles glinted in the moon's glow. The smooth aluminum caps, the wet and shining labels, the brassy beads inside the bottles were like an illuminated nocturnal still life. I closed the box, turned on the lightbulb over the counter, and called Lafayette information for Minos P. Dautrieve's home number.

A moment later I had him on the phone. I looked at the clock. It was midnight.

'What's happening, Dunkenstein?' I said.

'Oh boy,' he said.

'Sorry about the hour.'

'What do you want, Robicheaux?'

'Where are these clubs that Eddie Keats owns?'

'You called me up to ask me that?'

I didn't answer, and I heard him take a breath.

'The last time we talked, you hung up the phone in my ear,' he said. 'I didn't appreciate that. I think you have a problem with manners.'

'All right, I apologize. Will you tell me where these clubs are?'

'I'll be frank about something else, too. Are you drinking?'

'No. How about the clubs?'

'I guess things never work fast enough for you, do they? So you're going to cowboy our Brooklyn friend?'

'Give me some credit.'

'I try to. Believe me,' he said.

'There are a dozen people I can call in Lafayette who'll give me the same information.'

'Yeah, which makes me wonder why you had to wake me up.'

'You ought to know the answer to that.'

'I don't. I'm really at a loss. You're truly a mystery to us. You don't hear what you're told, you make up your own rules, you think your past experience as a police officer allows you to mess around in federal business.'

'I'm talking to you because you're the only guy around here with the brains and juice to put these people away,' I said.

'I'm not flattered.'

'So it's no dice, huh?'

He paused.

'Look, Robicheaux, I think you have a cinder block for a head, but basically you're a decent guy,' he said. 'That means we don't want you hurt anymore. Stay out of it. Have some faith in us. I don't know why you went out to Bubba Rocque's house this afternoon, but I don't think it was smart. You don't—'

'How'd you know I was out there?'

'We have somebody who writes down licence tags for us. You don't flush these guys by flipping lighted matches at them. If you do, they pick the time and the place and you lose. Anyway, go to bed and forget Eddie Keats, at least for tonight.'

'Does he have a family?'

'No, he's a gash-hound.'

'Thanks, Minos. I'm sorry I woke you up.'

'It's all right. By the way, how'd you like Bubba Rocque's wife?'

'I suspect she's ambitious more than anything else.'

'What a romantic. She's a switch-hitter, podna. Five years ago she did a three-spot for shanking another dyke. That Bubba can really pick them, can't he?'

I called an old bartender friend in Lafayette. Minos had given me more information than he thought. The bartender told me Keats owned two bars, one in a hotel off Canal in New Orleans, the other on the Breaux Bridge highway outside of Lafayette. If he was at either bar, and if what Minos had said about him was correct, I knew which one he would probably be in.

When I was in college, the Breaux Bridge highway contained a string of all-night lowlife bars, oilfield supply yards, roadhouses, a quarter horse track, gambling joints, and one Negro brothel. You could find the pimps, hoods, whores, ex-cons, and white-knuckle crazies of your choice there every Saturday night. Emergency flares burned next to the wrecked automobiles and shattered glass on the two-lane blacktop, the dance floors roared with electronic noise and fistfights. You could get laid, beat up, shanked, and dosed with clap, all in one night and for less than five dollars.

I parked across the road from the jungle Room. Eddie Keats had kept up the tradition. His bar was a flat, wide building constructed of cinder blocks that were painted purple and then overprinted with green coconut palms that were illuminated by the floodlights that were hung in the oak trees in front. But I could see two house trailers in the back parking lot, which was kept dark, that were obviously being used by Keat's hot-pillow action. I waited a half hour and did not see the white Corvette.

I had no plan, really, and I knew that I should have listened to Minos's advice. But I still had the same hot flush to my skin, my breath was quicker than it should have been, my back teeth ground together without my being aware of it. At 1:30 AM I stuck the .45 down in the front of my khakis, pulled my Hawaiian shirt over the butt, and walked across the road.

The front door, which was painted fingernail-polish red, was partly open to let out the smoke from inside. Only the bar area and a pool table in a side room were lighted, and the dance floor in back that was enclosed by a wooden rail, where a redheaded girl who had powdered her body heavily to cover her freckles was grinning and taking off her clothes while the rockabilly band in the corner pounded it out. The men at the bar were mostly pipeliners and oilfield roughnecks and roustabouts. The white-collar johns stayed in the darkness at the tables and booths. The waitresses wore black cutoff blouses that exposed the midriff, black high heels, and pink shorts so tight that every anatomical line was etched through the cloth.

A couple of full-time hookers were at the bar, and with a sideways flick of their eyes, in the middle of their conversation with the oilfield workers, they took my inventory as I walked past them to one of the booths. Above the bar a monkey in a small cage sat listlessly on a toy trapeze among a litter of peanut shells and his own droppings.

I knew I was going to have to order a drink. This wasn't a place where I could order a 7-Up without either telling them I was a cop or some other kind of bad news. I just wasn't going to drink it. I wasn't going to drink it. The waitress brought me a Jax that cost three dollars. She was pretty, and she smiled at me and poured from the bottle into my glass.

'There's a two-drink minimum for the floor show,' she said. 'I'll come back when you're ready for your second.'

'Has Toot been in?' I said.

'Who?'

'Eddie's friend, the black guy.'

'I'm new. I don't guess I know him,' she said, and went away.

A few minutes later three of the oilfield workers went out and left one of the hookers alone at the bar. She finished her drink, picked up her cigarette from the ashtray, and walked toward my booth. She wore white shorts with a dark blue blouse, and her black hair was tied off her neck with a blue bandanna. Her face was round and she was slightly overweight, and when she sat next to me I could smell her hair spray, her perfume, and a nicotine odor that went deep into the lungs. In the glow of the light from the bar, her facial hair was stiff with makeup. Her eyes, which never quite focused on my face, were glazed with alcohol, and her lips seemed to constantly suppress a smile that had nothing to do with either of us.

The waitress arrived right behind her. She ordered a champagne cocktail. Her accent was northern. I watched her light a cigarette and blow smoke up into the air as though it were a stylized art.

'Has Toot been around lately?' I said.

'You mean the space-o boon?' she said. Her eyes had a smile in them while she looked abstractly at the bar.

'That sounds like him.'

'What are you interested in him for?'

'I just haven't seen him or Eddie for a while.'

'You interested in girls?'

'Sometimes.'

'I bet you'd like a little piece in your life, wouldn't you?'

'Maybe.'

'It you don't get a little piece, it really messes you up inside, doesn't it? It makes everything real hard for you.' She put her hand on my thigh and worked her fingers on my knee.

'What time is Eddie going to be in?'

'You're trying to pump me, hon. That's going to give me bad thoughts about you.'

'It's just a question.'

Her lips made an exaggerated pout, and she raised her hand, touched my cheek, and slid it down my chest.

'I'm going to think maybe you're not interested in girls, that maybe you're here for the wrong reasons,' she said.

Then her hand went lower and hit the butt of the .45. Her eyes looked straight into mine. She started to get up, and I put my hand on top of her arm.

'You're a cop,' she said.

'It doesn't matter what I am. Not to you, anyway. You're not in trouble. Do you understand that?'

The alcohol shine had gone from her eyes, and her face had the look of someone caught between fear and an old anger.

'Where's Eddie?' I said.

'He goes to dogfights sometimes in Breaux Bridge, then comes in here and counts the receipts. You want some real trouble, get in his face and see what happens.'

'But that doesn't concern you, does it? You've got nothing to gain by concerning yourself with other people's problems, do you? Do you have a car?'

'What?'

'A car.' I pressed her arm slightly.

'Yeah, what d'you think?'

'When I take my hand off your arm you're going on your break. You're going out the door for some fresh air, and you're not going to talk to anybody, and you're going to drive your car down the road and have a late supper somewhere, and that phone on the bar is not going to ring, either.'

'You're full of shit.'

'Make your choice, hon. I think this place is going to be full of cops tonight. You want to be part of it, that's cool.' I took my hand away from her arm.

'You sonofabitch.'

I looked at the front door. Her eyes went angrily over my face again, then she slid off the vinyl seat and walked to the bar, the backs of her legs creased from sitting in the booth, and asked the bartender for her purse. He handed it to her, then went back to washing glasses, and she went out a side door into the parking lot.

Ten minutes later the phone did ring, but the bartender never looked in my direction while he talked, and after he hung up he fixed himself a scotch and milk and then started emptying ashtrays along the bar. I knew, however, that I didn't have long before her nerves broke. She was afraid of me or of cops in general, but she was also afraid of Eddie Keats, and eventually she would call to see if a bust or a shooting had gone down and try to make the best of her situation.

I had another problem, too. The next floor show was about to start, and the waitress was circling through the tables, making sure everyone had had his two-drink minimum. I turned in the booth and let my elbow knock the beer bottle off the table.

'I'm sorry,' I said when she came over. 'Let me have another one, will you?'

She picked up the bottle from the floor and started to wipe down the table. The glow from the bar made highlights in her blond hair. Her body had the firm lines of somebody who had done a lot of physical work in her life.

'You didn't want company?' she said.

'Not now.'

'Expensive booze for a dry run.'

'It's not so bad.' I looked at the side of her face as she wiped the rag in front of me.

'It's the wrong place for trouble, sugar,' she said quietly.

'Do I look like bad news?'

'A lot of people do. But the guy that owns this place really is. For kicks, he heats up the wires in that monkey's cage with a cigarette lighter.'

'Why do you work here?'

'I couldn't get into the convent,' she said, and walked away with her drink tray as though a door were closing behind her.

Later a muscular, powerful man came in, sat at the bar, had the bartender bring him a collins, and began shelling peanuts from a bowl and eating them while he talked to one of the hookers. He wore purple suede cowboy boots, expensive cream-colored slacks, a maroon V-necked terrycloth shirt, and gold chains and medallions around his neck. His long hair was dyed blond and combed straight back like a professional wrestler's. He took his package of Picayune cigarettes from his pants pocket and set it on the bar while he shelled peanuts from the bowl. He couldn't see me because I was sitting far back in the gloom and he had no reason to look in my direction, but I could see his face clearly, and even though I had never seen it before, its details had the familiarity of a forgotten dream.

His head was big, the neck as thick as a stump, the eyes green and full of energy; a piece of cartilage flexed behind the jawbone while he ground peanuts between his back teeth. The tanned skin around his mouth was so taut that it looked as if you could strike a kitchen match on it. His hands were big too – the fingers like sausages, the wrists corded with veins. The hooker smoked a cigarette and tried to look cool while he talked to her, watching the red tracings of her cigarette in the bar mirror, but whenever she replied to him her voice seemed to come out in a whisper.

However, I had no trouble hearing his voice. It sounded like there was a blockage in the nasal passages; it was a voice that didn't say but told things to people. In this case he was telling the hooker that she had to square her tab, that she was juicing too much, that the Jungle Room wasn't a trough where a broad got free soda straws.

I said earlier I didn't have a plan. That wasn't true. Every drunk always has a plan. The script is written in the unconscious. We recognize it when the moment is convenient.

I slipped sideways out of the vinyl booth. I almost drank from the filled beer glass before I did. In my years as a practicing alcoholic I never left an unemptied glass or bottle on a table, and I always got down that last shot before I made a hard left turn down a one-way street. Old habits die hard.

I took down one of the cues from the wall rack by the entrance to the poolroom. It was tapered and made of smooth-sanded ash and weighted heavily at the butt end. He didn't pay attention to me as I walked toward him. He was talking to the bartender now, snapping peanut shells apart with his thick thumb and popping the nuts into his mouth. Then his green eyes turned on me, focused in the dim light, his glance con-centrating as though there were a stitch across the bridge of his nose, then he brushed his hands clean and swivelled the stool casually so that he was facing me directly.

'You're on my turf, butthole,' he said. 'Start it and you'll lose. Walk on out the door and you're home free.'

I kept walking toward him and didn't answer. I saw the expression in his eyes change, the way green water can suddenly cloud with a ground-swell. He reached over the bar for a collins bottle, the change rattling in his slacks, one boot twisted inside the brass foot rail. But he knew it was too late, and his left arm was already rising to shield his head.

Most people think of violence as an abstraction. It never is. It's always ugly, it always demeans and dehumanizes, it always shocks and repels and leaves the witnesses to it sick and shaken. It's meant to do all these things.

I held the pool cue by the tapered end with both hands and whipped it sideways through the air as I would a baseball bat, with the same force and energy and snap of the wrists, and broke the weighted end across his left eye and the bridge of his nose. I felt the wood knock into bone, saw the skin split, saw the green eye almost come out of its socket, heard him clatter against the bar and go down on the brass rail with his hands cupped to his nose and the blood roaring between his fingers.

He pulled his knees up to his chin in the litter of cigarette butts and peanut hulls. He couldn't talk and instead trembled all over. The bar was absolutely silent. The bartender, the hookers, the oilfield workers in their hardhats, the waitresses in their pink shorts and cut-off black blouses, the rockabilly musicians, the half-undressed mulatto stripper on the dance floor, all stood like statues in the floating layers of cigarette smoke.

I heard someone dial a telephone as I walked out into the night air.

The next morning I drove into New Iberia and picked up a supply of red worms, nightcrawlers, and shiners. It was a clear, warm day with little wind, and I rented out almost all my boats. While I worked behind the counter in the bait shop and, later, started the fire in the barbecue pit for the lunch customers, I kept looking down the dirt road for a sheriff's car. But none came. At noon I called Minos Dautrieve at the DEA in Lafayette.

'I need to come in and talk to you,' I said.

'No, I'll come over there. Stay out of Lafayette.'

'Why's that?'

'I don't think the town's ready for Wyatt Earp this morning.'

An hour later he came down the dirt road under the oak trees in a government car, parked by the dock, and walked into the shop. He stooped automatically as he came through the door. He wore a pair of seersucker slacks, shined loafers, a light blue sports shirt, and a red and gray striped tie pulled loose at the collar. His scalp and crewcut blond hair shone in the light. He looked around the shop and nodded with a smile on his face.

'You've got a nice business here,' he said.

'Thanks.'

'It's too bad you're not content to just run it and stop over-extending yourself.'

'You want a soft drink or a cup of coffee?'

'Don't be defensive. You're a legend this morning. I came into the office late, because somebody woke me up last night, and everybody was having a big laugh about the floor show at the Jungle Room. I told you we don't get to have that kind of fun. We just fill out forms, advise the slime-o's of their rights, and make sure they have adequate counsel to stay on the street. I heard they had to use a mop to soak up all the blood.'

'Are they cutting a warrant?'

'He wouldn't sign the complaint. A sheriff's detective took it to the hospital on a clipboard.'

'But he identified me?'

'He didn't have to. One of his hookers got your license number. Eddie Keats doesn't like courtrooms. But don't mess with the Lafayette cops anymore. They get provoked when somebody comes into their parish and thinks he can start strumming heads with a pool cue.'

'Too bad. They should have rousted him when I got my face kicked in.'

'I'm worried about you. You don't hear well.'

'I haven't been sleeping a lot lately. Save it for another time, all right?'

'I'm perplexed, too. I know you've been into some heavy-metal shit before, but I didn't figure you for a cowboy. You know, you could have put out that guy's light.'

Two fishermen came in and bought a carton of worms and a dozen bottles of beer for their ice chest. I rang up their money on my old brass cash register and watched them walk out into the bright sunlight.

'Let's take a ride,' I said.

I left Batist in charge of the shop, and Minos and I rode down the dirt lane in my pickup. The sunlight seemed to click through the thick green leaves overhead.

'I called you up for a specific reason this morning,' I said. 'If you don't like the way I do things, I'm sorry. You're not in the hotbox, partner. I didn't invite any of this bullshit into my life, but I got it just the same. So I don't think it's too cool when you start making your observations in the middle of my shop, in front of my help and my customers.'

'Okay. You've got your point.'

'I never busted up a guy like that before. I don't feel good about it.'

'It's always dumb to play on the wiseguys' terms. But if you needed to scramble somebody's eggs, Keats was a fine selection. But believe it or not, we have a couple of things in his file that are even worse. The kid of a federal witness disappeared a year ago. We found him in a—'

'Then why don't you put the fucker away?'

He didn't answer. He turned the wind vane in his face and looked out at the Negro families fishing in the shade of the cypress trees.

'Is he feeding you guys?' I said.

'We don't use hit men as informants.'

'Don't jerk me around, Minos. You use whatever works.'

'Not hit men. Never. Not in my office.' He turned and looked me directly in the face. There was color in his cheeks.

'Then give him a priority and weld the door shut on him.'

'You think you're twisting in the wind while we play pocket pool. But maybe we're doing things you don't know about. Look, we never go for just one guy. You know that. We throw a net over a whole bunch of these shitheads at once. That's the only way we get them to testify against each other. Try learning some patience.'

'You want Bubba Rocque. You've got a file on everybody around him. In the meantime his clowns are running loose with baseball bats.'

'I think you're unteachable. Why did you call me up, anyway?'

'About Immigration.'

'I didn't eat breakfast this morning. Stop up here somewhere.'

'You know this guy Monroe that was sniffing around New Iberia?'

'Yeah, I know him. Are you worried about the little girl you have in your house?'

I looked at him.

'You have a way of constantly earning our attention,' he said. 'Stop there. I'm really hungry. You can pay for it, too. I left my wallet on the dresser this morning.'

I stopped at a small wooden lunch stand run by a Negro, set back in a grove of oak trees. We sat at one of the tables in the shade and ordered pork chop sandwiches and dirty rice. The smoke from the stove hung in the sunlit branches of the trees.

'What's this about Immigration?' Minos said.

'I heard they busted both Johnny Dartez and Victor Romero.'

'Where'd you get that?' He watched some black children playing pitch-and-catch next to the lunch stand. But I could see that his eyes were troubled.

'From a bartender in New Orleans.'

'Sounds like a crummy source.'

'No games. You knew that a government agency of some kind had a connection with Dartez or his body wouldn't have disappeared. You just weren't sure about Victor Romero.'

'So?'

'I think Immigration was using these guys to infiltrate the sanctuary movement.'

He put his hand on his chin and watched the children throwing the baseball.

'What does your bartender friend know about Romero now?' he said.

'Nothing.'

'What's this guy's name? We'd like to chat with him.'

'So would Bubba Rocque. That means that Jerry – that's his name, and he works at Smiling Jack's on Bourbon – is probably looking for a summer home in Afghanistan.'

'You never disappoint me. So you've managed to help scare an informant out of town just out of curiosity, how is it that people tell you these things they don't care to share with us?'

'I stuck a cocked .45 up his nose.'

'That's right, I forgot. You learned a lot of constitutional procedure from the New Orleans police department.'

'I'm correct, though, aren't I? Somehow Immigration got these two characters into the underground railway, or whatever the sanctuary people call it.'

'That's what they call it. And no matter what you might have figured out, it's still not your business. Of course, that doesn't make any difference to you. So I'll put it another way. We're nice guys at the DEA. We try to lodge as many lowlifes as we can in our gray-bar hotel chain. And we respect guys like you who are well intended but who have their brains encased in cement. But my advice to you is not to fuck with Immigration, particularly when you have an illegal in your home.'

'You don't like them.'

'I don't think about them. But you should. I once met a regional INS commissioner, an important man wired right into the White House. He said, "If you catch 'em, you ought to clean 'em yourself." I wouldn't want somebody like that on my case.'

'It sounds like folksy bullshit to me,' I said.

'You're a delight, Robicheaux.'

'I don't want to mess up your lunch, but aren't you bothered by the fact that maybe a bomb sent that plane down at Southwest Pass, that somebody murdered a Catholic priest and two women who were fleeing a butcher shop we helped create in El Salvador?'

'Are you an expert on Central American politics?'

'No.'

'Have you been down there?'

'No.'

'But you give me that impression just the same. Like you've got the franchise on empathy.'

'I think you need a whiff of a ville that's been worked over with Zippo-tracks.'

'Don't give me that righteous dogshit. I was there, too, podna.' The bread in the side of his mouth made an angry lump along his jaw.

'Then don't let those farts at Immigration jerk you around.'

He put his sandwich in his plate, drank from his iced tea, and looked away reflectively at the children playing under the trees.

'Have you ever thought that maybe you'd be better off drunk than sober?' he said. 'I'm sorry. I really didn't mean that. What I meant to say is I just remembered that I have a check in my shirt pocket. I'll pay for my own lunch today. No, don't argue. It's just been a real pleasure being out with you.'

The inside of the church was cool and dark and smelled of stone, burning candles, water, and incense. Through the side door I could see the enclosed garden where, as a child, I used to line up with the other children before we made the Stations of the Cross on Good Friday. It was sunny in the garden, and the St Augustine grass was green and clipped, and the flower beds were full of yellow and purple roses. At the head of the garden, shaded by a rain tree with bloodred blooms on it, was a rock grotto with a waterfall at the bottom and a stone statue of the crucified Christ set back in the recess.

I walked into the confessional and waited for the priest to slide back the small wooden door in the partition. I had known him for twenty-five years, and I trusted his working-class instincts and forgave him his excess of charity and lack of admonition, just as he forgave me my sins. He slid back the door, and I looked through the wire screen at the round head, the bull neck, the big shoulders in silhouette. He had a small, rubber-bladed fan in the box with him, and his crewcut gray hair moved slightly in the breeze.

I told him about Eddie Keats. Everything. The beating I took, the humiliation, the pool cue shattered across his face, the blood stringing from the fingers cupped over his nose.

The priest was quiet a moment.

'Did you want to kill this man?' he said.

'No.'

'Are you sure of that?'

'Yes.'

'Do you plan to hurt him again?'

'Not if he leaves me alone.'

'Then put it behind you.'

I didn't reply. We were both quiet in the gloom of the box. 'Are you still bothered?' he said.

'Yes.'

'Dave, you've made your confession. Don't try to judge the right and wrong of what you did. Let it go. Perhaps what you did was wrong, but you acted with provocation. This man threatened your wife. Don't you think the Lord can understand your feelings in a situation like that?'

'That's not why I did it.'

'I'm sorry, I don't understand.'

'I did it because I want to drink. I burn inside to drink. I want to drink all the time.'

'I don't know what to say.'

I walked out the side door of the church into the garden. I could hear the waterfall in the grotto, and the odor of the yellow and purple roses and the red flowers on the rain tree was heavy and sweet in the warm, enclosed air. I sat on the stone bench by the grotto and stared at the tops of my shoes.

Later I found Annie weeding the vegetable garden behind our old smokehouse. She was barefoot and wore blue jeans and a denim shirt with no sleeves. She was on her hands and knees in the row, and she pulled the weeds from between the tomato plants and dropped them into a bucket. Her face was hot with her work. I had told her that morning in bed about Eddie Keats. She had said nothing in reply, but had merely gone into the kitchen and started breakfast.

'I think maybe you should go visit your family in Kansas and take Alafair along,' I said. I had a glass of iced tea in my hand.

'Why?' She didn't look up.

'That guy Keats.'

'You think he's going to come around?'

'I don't know. Sometimes when you bash his kind hard enough, they stay away from you. But then sometimes you can't tell. There's no point in taking chances.'

She dropped a handful of weeds into the bucket and stood up from her work. There was a smear of dirt and perspiration on her forehead. I could smell the hot, dusky odor of the tomato plants in the sunlight.

'Why didn't you think of that earlier?' she said. She looked straight ahead.

'Maybe I made a mistake. I still want you and Alafair to go to Kansas.'

'I don't want to sound melodramatic, Dave. But I don't make decisions in my life or my family's because of people like this.'

'Annie, this is serious.'

'Of course it is. You're trying to be a rogue cop of some kind, and at the same time you have a family. So you'd like to get one part of the problem out of Louisiana.'

'At least give it some thought.'

'I already did. This morning, for about five seconds. Forget it,' she said, and walked to the coulee with the weed-filled bucket and shook the weeds down the bank.

When she came back she continued to look at me seriously, then suddenly she laughed.

'Dave, you're just too much,' she said. 'At least you could offer us Biloxi or Galveston. You remember what you said about Kansas when you visited there? "This is probably the only place in the United States that would be improved by nuclear war." And now you'd like to ship me back there?'

'All right, Biloxi.'

'No deal, baby love.' She walked toward the shade of the backyard, the bucket brushing back and forth against her pants' leg.

That evening we went to a *fais dodo* in St Martinville. The main street was blocked off for the dancers, and an Acadian string band and a rock 'n' roll group took turns playing on a wooden platform set back against Bayou Teche. The tops of the trees were green against the lavender and pink light in the sky, and the evening breeze blew through the oaks in the churchyard where Evangeline and her lover were buried. For some reason the rock 'n' roll music in southern Louisiana has never changed since the 1950s. It still sounds like Jimmie Reed, Fats Domino, Clifton Chenier, and Albert Ammons. I sat at a wooden table not far from the bandstand, with a paper plate of rice and red beans and fried *sac-a-lait,* and watched the dancers and listened to the music while Annie took Alafair down the street to find a rest room.

Then rain clouds blackened the western sun temporarily and the wind came up strong and blew leaves, newspapers, beer cups, and paper plates through the streets. But the band kept playing, as though the threat of rain or even an electric storm were no more important a consideration than time and mortality, and for some reason I began to muse on why any of us are what we are, either for good or bad. I didn't choose to be an alcoholic, to have the oral weakness of a child for a bottle, but nevertheless that self-destructive passion, that genetic or environmental wound festered every day at the center of my life. Then I thought about a sergeant in my platoon who was perhaps the finest man I ever knew. If environment was the shaping and determining factor in our lives, his made no sense.

He grew up in a soot-covered foundry town in Illinois, one of those places where the sky is forever scared with smoke and cluttered with the blackened tops of factories and the river so polluted with chemicals and sludge that once it actually caught fire. He lived with his mother in a block of row houses, a world that was bordered on one end by a Saturday night beer joint and pool hall and on the other by his job as a switchman in the train yard. By all odds he should have been one of those people who live out their lives in a gray and undistinguished way with never a bolder ambition than a joyless marriage and a cost-of-living raise. Instead, he was both brave and compassionate, caring about his men and uncompromising in his loyalties; his intelligence and courage carried both of us through when mine sometimes failed. But even though we served together for seven months, I'll always retain one essential image of him that seemed to define both him and what is best in our country's people.

We had just gotten back to a hot, windblown firebase after two days out in Indian country and a firefight in which the Viet Cong were sometimes five feet from us. We had lost four men and we were drained and sick and exhausted the way you are when even in sleep you feel that you're curled inside a wooden box of your own pain and your soul twitches like a rubber band. I had taken my platoon down a trail at night, a stupid and reckless act, had walked into their ambush, lost our point man immediately, and had gotten flanked, and there was only one person to blame for it – me. Although it was now noon and the sun was as hot and bright as a welder's arc overhead, in my mind's eye I still saw the flash of the AK-47s against the black-green of the jungle.

Then I looked at Dale, my sergeant, wringing out his shirt in a metal water drum. His back was brown, ridged with vertebrae, his ribs like sticks against his skin, the points of his black hair shiny with sweat. Then his lean Czechoslovakian face smiled at me, with more tenderness and affection in his eyes than I had yet seen in a woman's.

He was killed eight days later when a Huey tipped the treetops by an LZ and suddenly dipped sideways into the clearing.

But my point about the origins of the personality and the mysteries of the soul concerns someone else and not my dead friend. A half-dozen stripped-down Harleys, mounted by women in pairs, pulled to the edge of the street barricade, and Claudette Rocque and her friends strolled into the crowd. They wore greasy jeans and black Harley T-shirts without bras, wide studded belts, bandannas around their foreheads like Indians, chains, tattoos, half-topped boots with metal taps. They had six-packs of beer hooked in their fingers, folders of Zig-Zag cigarette papers protruding from their Tshirt pockets. They wore their strange form of sexuality like Visigoth warriors in leather and mail.

But not Bubba's wife. Her breasts hung heavy in a black sun halter that was covered with red hearts, and her jeans were pulled low on her soft, tanned stomach to expose an orange and purple butterfly tattooed by her navel. She saw me through the dancers and walked toward my table, a smile at the edge of her mouth, her hips creasing and undulating with her movement, the top of her blue jeans damp with perspiration against her skin.

She leaned down on the table and smiled into my eyes. There were sun freckles on the tops of her breasts. I could smell beer on her breath and the faint odor of marijuana in her hair. Her eyes were indolent and merry at the same time, and she bit down on her lip as though she had come to a sensuous conclusion for both of us.

'Where's the wifey?' she said.

'Down the street.'

'Will she let you dance with me?'

'I'm not a good dancer, Mrs Rocque.'

'I bet you're good at other things, then. Everybody has their special talent.' She bit down on her lip again.

'I think maybe I'm one of those people who was born without any. Some of us don't have to seek humility.'

She smiled sleepily.

'The sun went behind the clouds,' she said. 'I wanted to get some more tan. Do you think I'm dark enough?'

I ate from my paper plate and tried to grin good-naturedly.

'Some people say my family has colored and Indian blood in it,' she said. 'I don't care, though. Like my mother's colored girls used to say, "The black berry got the sweet juice."'

Then she touched away a drop of sweat on my forehead with her finger and put it in her mouth. I felt my face redden in the stares from the people on each side of me.

'Last chance to dance,' she said, then put her hands behind her head and started to sway her hips to a Jimmy Clanton song the rock 'n' roll band was playing on the stage. She flexed her breasts and rolled her stomach and her eyes looked directly into mine. Her tongue moved around the edges of her mouth as though she were eating an ice cream cone. A family seated next to me got up and moved. She bent her knees so her rear came tight against her jeans, and held her elbows close against the sides of her breasts with her fingers pointed outward, her wet mouth pouting, and went lower and lower toward the ground with the pale tops of her breasts exposed to everyone at the table. I looked away at the bandstand, then saw Annie walk through the crowd with Alafair's hand in hers.

Claudette Rocque and Annie looked at each other with that private knowledge and recognition of intention that women seem to have between one another. But there was no embarrassment in Claudette's face, only that indolent, merry light in her reddish brown eyes. Then she smiled at both of us, put her hand idly on a man's shoulder, and in a moment had moved off with him into the center of the street.

'What was that?' Annie said.

'Bubba Rocque's wife.'

'She seems to have enjoyed entertaining you.'

'I think she's been hitting on the *muta* this afternoon.'

'The what?'

'The reefer.'

'I loved the dancing butterfly. She wiggles it around so well.'

'She learned it at Juilliard. Come on, Annie, no screws today.'

'Butterfly? Butterfly dance?' Alafair said. She wore a Donald Duck cap with a yellow bill that quacked when you squeezed it. I picked her up on my knee and quacked the cap's bill, happy to be distracted from Annie's inquiring eye. Out of the corner of my vision, I saw Claudette Rocque dancing with the man she had found in the crowd, her stomach pressed tightly against his loins.

The next day the doctor snipped the stitches out of my scalp and mouth. When I ran my tongue along the inside of my lip, the skin felt like a rubber bicycle patch with welts in it. Later that afternoon I went to an AA meeting. The air conditioner was broken, and the room was hot and smoky. My mind wandered constantly.

It was almost summer now, and the afternoon seemed to grow hotter as the day wore on. We ate supper on the redwood table in the backyard amid the drone of the cicadas and the dry rumble of distant thunder. I tried to read the newspaper on the porch, but I couldn't concentrate on the words for more than a paragraph. I went down to the dock to see how many boats were still out, then went back up to the house and closed myself in the back room where I kept my weight set and historical jazz collection. I put on an old Bunk Johnson 78, and as the clear, bell-like quality of his horn lifted out of the static and mire of sound around him, I started a series of curls with ninety pounds on the bar, my biceps and chest swelling with blood and tension and power each time I brought the bar from my thighs up to my chin.

In fifteen minutes I was dripping sweat on the wooden floor. I took off my shirt, put on my gym trunks and running shoes, and did three miles on the dirt road along the bayou. The soreness was almost completely gone from my genitals, where I had been kicked by Eddie Keats, and my wind was good and my heartbeat steady all the way down the road. I could have done another two miles. Normally, I would have felt good about all the energy and resilience in my middleaged body, but I well knew the machinery that was working inside me, and it had nothing to do with health or the breathless twilit evening or the fireflies sparkling in the black-green trees or the bream popping the water's surface along the lily pads. Summer in south Louisiana has always been, to me, part of an eternal song. Tonight I simply saw the fading red spark of sun on the horizon as the end of spring.

It was a strange night. The stars looked hot in the black sky. There was absolutely no wind, and each leaf on the pecan trees looked as though it were etched out of metal. The surface of the bayou was flat and still, the willows and cattails along the banks motionless. When the moon rose, the clouds looked like silver horsetails against the sky.

I showered with cold water and lay in my underwear on top of the sheets in the dark. Annie traced her fingers on my shoulder. Her head lay facing me on the pillow, and I could feel her breath on my skin.

'We can work through it, Dave. Every marriage has a few bad moments,' she said. 'We don't have to let them dominate us.'

'All right.'

'Maybe I've been selfish. Maybe I've wanted too much on my terms.'

'What do you mean?'

'I've wanted you to be something you're not. I've tried to pretend for both of us that you're finished with police work and all that world back in New Orleans.'

'I left it on my own. You didn't have anything to do with it.'

'You turned in a resignation, but you didn't leave it, Dave. You never will.'

I looked up into the darkness and waited. The moonlight made patterns on our bodies through the turning window fan.

'If you want to go back to it, maybe that's what we should do,' she said.

'Nope.'

'Because you don't think I can handle it?'

'Because it's a toilet.'

'You say that, but I don't think that's the way you feel.'

'My first partner was a man I admired a great deal. He had honest-to-God guts and integrity. One time on Canal a little girl was thrown through a windshield and had her arm cut off. He ran into a bar, filled his coat with ice, and wrapped the arm in it, and they sewed it back on. But before that same guy retired he took juice, he—'

'What?'

'He took bribes. He shook down whores for freebies. He blew away a fourteen-year-old black kid on the roof of the welfare project.'

'Listen to the anger in your voice. It's like a fire inside you.'

'It's not anger. It's a statement of fact. You stay in it and you start to talk and think like a lowlife, and one day you find yourself doing something that you didn't think yourself capable of, and that's when you know you're really home. It's not a good moment.'

'You were never like that, and you never will be.' She put her arm across my chest and her knee across my thigh.

'Because I got out of it.'

'You thought you did, but you didn't.' She rubbed her knee and the inside of her thigh up and down my leg and moved the flat of her hand down my chest and stomach. 'I know an officer whose physical condition needs some attention.'

'Tomorrow I want to talk with the nuns about enrolling Alafair in kindergarten.'

'That's a good idea, skipper.'

'Then we'll go to the swimming pool and have lunch in St Martinville.'

'Whatever you say.' She pressed tightly against me, blew her breath in my hair, and hooked her leg across both my thighs. 'What other plans do you have?'

'There's an American Legion game tomorrow night, too. Maybe we'll just take the whole day off.'

'Can I touch you here? Oh my, and I thought you were so stoic, couldn't be swayed by a girl's charms. My babylove is a big actor, isn't he?'

She kissed my cheek, then my mouth, then got on top of me in her maternal way, as she always did, and stroked my face and smiled into my eyes. The moonlight fell on her tan skin and heavy white breasts, and she raised herself slightly on her knees, took me in her hand, and pressed me inside her, her mouth forming a sudden O, her eyes suddenly looking inward upon herself. I kissed her hair, her ear, the tops of her breasts, I ran my hands along her back and her shaking, hard thighs, and finally I felt all the day's anger and heat, which seemed to live in me like hot sunlight trapped in a bottle of whiskey, disappear in her rhythmic breathing against my cheek and her hands and arms that pressed and caressed me all over as though I could escape from under her love that was as warm, unrelenting, and encompassing as the sea.

My dreams took me many places. Sometimes I would be in a pirogue with my father, deep in the Atchafalaya swamp, the fog thick in the black trees, and just as the sun broke on the earth's rim, I'd troll my Mepps spinner next to the cypress stumps and a largemouth bass would sock into it and burst from the quiet water, rattling with green-gold light. But tonight I dreamed of Hueys flying low over jungle canopy and milky-brown rivers. In the dream they made no sound. They looked like insects against the lavender sky, and as they drew closer I could see the door-gunners firing into the trees. The downdrafts from the helicopter blades churned the treetops into a frenzy, and the machine-gun bullets blew water out of the rivers, raked through empty fishing villages, danced in geometrical lines across dikes and rice paddies. But there was no sound and there were no people down below. I saw a door-gunner's face, and it was stretched tight with fear, whipped with wind, throbbing with the action of the gun. I could see only one of his eyes – squinted, cordite-bitten, liquid with the reflected images of dead water buffalo in the heat, smoking villages, and glassy countryside, where the people had scurried into the earth like mice. His hands were swollen and red, his finger wrapped in a knot around the trigger, the flying brass cartridge casings kaleidoscopic in the light. There were no people to shoot at anymore, but no matter – his charter was clear. He was forever wedded and addicted to this piece of earth that he'd helped make desolate, this land that was his drug and nemesis. The silence in the dream was like a scream.

I woke to the sounds of dry lightning, a car passing on the dirt road by the bayou, the bullfrogs croaking down by the duck pond. I had no analytical interest in the interpretation of dreams. The strange feelings and mechanisms they represented always went away at dawn, and that was all that mattered. I hoped that one day they would go away alto-gether. I once read that Audie Murphy, the most decorated US soldier of World War II, slept with a .45. I believe he was a brave and good man, but for some the nocturnal landscape is haunted by creatures forged in a devil's furnace. The Greeks called upon Morpheus to abate the Furies. I simply waited on the false dawn, and sometimes with luck I fell asleep again before it arrived.

But this night was alive with too many sounds, too many shards of memory that worked on the edge of the mind like rat's teeth, for me to regain sleep easily. I put on my clack sandals, poured a glass of milk in the kitchen, and walked down to the duck pond in my skivvies. The ducks were bunched in the shadows of the cattails, and the moon and lighted clouds were reflected as perfectly in the still water as though they had been trapped under dark glass. I sat on a bench by the collapsed barn that marked the end of my property, and looked out over my neighbor's pasture and sugarcane field in the moonlight. On the barn wall behind me, whose red paint had long since flaked away, was a tin Hadacol sign from thirty-five years ago. Hadacol had been manufactured by a state senator from Abbeville, and it not only contained enough vitamins and alcohol to make you get up from your deathbed, but the boxtop would allow you admission to the traveling Hadacol show, which one year had featured Jack Dempsey, Rudy Vallee, and an eight-foot Canadian giant. I marveled at the innocence of the era in which I had grown up.

Then I saw the heat lightning flash brightly in the south, and a breeze came up suddenly and broke the moonlight apart in the water and dented the leaves of the pecan trees in my front yard. The cows in the pasture were already bunched, and I could smell rain and sulfur in the air and feel the barometric pressure dropping. I finished the milk in my glass, leaned back against the barn wall with my eyes closed, breathed the wet coolness on the wind, and realized that without even trying I was going to overcome my insomnia that night and go back to bed and sleep by my wife while the rain *tinked* on the window fan.

But when I opened my eyes I saw two dark silhouettes move as quickly and silently as deer out of the pecan trees in the front yard, past my line of vision, onto my front porch. Even as I rose to my feet, widening my eyes in the futile wish that I had seen only shadows, my heart sank with a terrible knowledge that I had experienced only once before, and that was when I had heard the *klatch* of the mine under my foot in Vietnam. Even as I started to run toward the darkened house, even before I heard the crowbar bite into the doorjamb, before the words burst out of my throat, I knew that my nocturnal fears would have their realization tonight and not be dispelled by a false dawn that only fools waited upon. I tripped on my sandals, kicked them from my feet, and ran barefoot over the hard ground, the litter of broken boards and rusty nails from the barn roof, the cattails that grew up the bank from the pond, shouting. 'I'm out here! I'm out here!' like a hysterical man lost on a piece of moonscape.

But my words were lost in the thunder, the wind, the splatter of raindrops on the tin roof, the crowbar that splintered the doorjamb, sprung the hinges, snapped the deadbolt, ripped the door open into the living room. Then I heard my own voice again, a sound like an animal's cry breaking out of a wet bubble, and I heard the shotguns roar and saw the flashes leap in the bedroom like heat lightning in the sky. They fired and fired, the pump-actions clacking loudly back into place with each fresh shell, the explosions of flame dissecting the darkness where my wife lay alone under a sheet. Their buckshot blew window glass and curtain material out into the yard, tore divots of wood from the outside wall, rang off the window fan blades. A bolt of lightning struck somewhere behind me, and my own skin looked white and dead in the illumination.

They had stopped shooting. I stood breathless and barefoot in my underwear in the rain and looked through the broken window and ragged curtains at the outline of a man who stared back at me, motionless, his shotgun held at an angle across his chest. Then I heard the pump clack back to feed another shell into the chamber.

I ran to the side of the house, pressed myself against the cypress boards, moved under the windows toward the front, and crouched in the darkness. I heard one of them knock into a wall or door in the dark, trip over the telephone extension, rip the phone from its jack, and throw it down the hall. There was blood on the tops of my feet, a ragged tear in my ankle, but my body had no feeling. My head reeled as though it had been slapped hard with a rolled newspaper, and I could taste the bile rising uncontrollably from my stomach. I had no weapon; my neighbors were away; there was nothing I could do to help Annie. Sweat and rainwater ran out of my hair like insects.

There was nothing else to do but run for the phone in the bait shop. Then I heard the front screen fly back against the wall and both of them come out on the gallery. Their feet were loud on the wood, their steps going in one direction, then another. I pressed against the side of the house and waited. All one of them had to do was jump over the side railing of the gallery, and he would have me at point-blank range. Then their feet stopped, and I realized that their attention was focused on something else. A pickup truck was banging down the dirt road toward the dock, the rain slanting in the beam of a single headlight that bounced off the trees. I knew it must be Batist. He lived a quarter-mile down the road, slept on his screened gallery in the summer, and would have heard and recognized the gunfire, even in the thunder.

'Shit on it. Let's get out of here,' one man said.

The other man spoke, but his voice was lost in the rain on the tin roof and a peal of thunder.

'So you come back and do him. It's a lousy hit, anyway. You didn't say nothing about a broad,' the first man said. 'Sonofabitch, the truck's turning in here. I'm gone. Clean up your own mess next time.'

I heard one man jump off the steps and start running. The second man paused, his feet scraped hesitantly on the wood planks, then I heard the step bend under his weight, and a moment later I could see the two of them running at an angle through the trees toward a car parked down by the bayou. With their shotguns at port-arms, they looked like infantry fleeing through a forest at night.

I raced through the front door into the bedroom and hit the light switch, my heart thundering in my chest. Red shotgun shells littered the doorway area; the mahogany foot and headboards of the bed were gouged and splintered with buckshot and deer slugs; the flowered wallpaper above the bed was covered with holes like black dimes. The sheet, which still lay over her, was drenched with her blood, the torn cloth embedded in wounds that wolves might have chewed. Her curly blond head was turned away from me on the pillow. One immaculate white hand hung over the side of the mattress.

I touched her foot. I touched her blood-flecked ankle. I put my hands around her fingers. I brushed my palm across her curly hair. I knelt like a child by the bed and kissed her eyes. I picked her hand up and put her fingers in my mouth. Then the shaking started, like sinew and bone separating inside me, and I pressed my face tightly into the pillow with my wet hair against her forehead.

I don't know how long I knelt there. I don't remember getting up from my knees. I know that my skin burned as though someone had painted it with acid, that I couldn't draw enough air into my lungs, that the room's yellow light was like a flame to my eyes, that all my joints seemed atrophied with age, that my hands were blocks of wood when I fumbled in the dresser drawer, found the .45, and pushed the heavy clip into the magazine. In my mind's eye I was already running through the yard, across my neighbor's pasture, through the sloping woods of oak and pine on the far side where the dirt road passed before it reached the drawbridge over the bayou. I heard a black kid from my platoon yell, *Charlie don't want to boogie no more. He running for the tunnel. Blow up their shit, Lieutenant.* I saw parts of men dissolve in my fire, and when the breech locked open and I had to reload, my hands shook with anticipation.

But the voice was not a black kid's from my platoon, and I was not the young lieutenant who could make small yellow men in black pajamas hide in their earthen holes. Batist had his big hands on each of my arms, his bare chest like a piece of boilerplate, his brown eyes level and unblinking and staring into mine.

'They gone, Dave. You can't do no good with that gun, you,' he said.

'The drawbridge. We can cut across.'

'*C'est pas bon. Ils sont pa'tis.*'

'We'll take the truck.'

He shook his head to say no, then slipped his huge hand down my arm and took the automatic from my palm. Then he put his arm around my shoulders and walked me into the living room.

'You sit here. You don't got to do nothing, you,' he said. The .45 stuck up out of the back pocket of his blue jeans. 'Where Alafair at?'

I looked at him dumbly. He breathed through his mouth and wet his lips.

'You stay here. Don't you move, no. *T'comprends*, Dave?'

'Yes.'

He walked into Alafair's room. The pecan trees in the yard flickered whitely when lightning jumped across the sky, and the wind swept the rain across the gallery and through my shattered front door. When I closed my eyes I saw light dancing inside a dark window frame like electricity trapped inside a black box.

I rose woodenly from the couch and walked to the doorway of Alafair's room. I paused with one hand on the doorjamb, almost as though I had become a stranger in my preoccupation with my own grief. Batist sat on the side of the bed with Alafair in his lap, his powerful arms wrapped around her. Her face was white and jerking with sobs against his black chest.

'She all right. You gonna be all right, too, Dave. Batist gonna take care of y'all. You'll see,' he said. 'Lord, Lord, what the world done to this little child.'

He shook his head from side to side, an unmasked sadness in his eyes.

6

It rained the day of Annie's funeral. In fact, it rained all that week. The water dripped from the trees, ran in rivulets off the eaves, formed brown pools filled with floating leaves in the yard, covered the fields and cane-brakes with a dull, gray-green light. Her parents flew down from Kansas, and I picked them up at the airport in Lafayette and drove them in the rain to a motel in New Iberia. Her father was a big, sandy-haired wheat farmer with square, callused hands and thick wrists, and he looked out the car window silently at the sopping countryside and smoked a cigar and spoke only enough to be polite. Her mother was a thick-bodied Mennonite country woman with sun-bright blond hair, blue eyes, and red cheeks. She tried to compensate for her husband's distance by talking about the flight from Wichita, her first experience in an airplane, but she couldn't concentrate on her words and she swallowed often and her eyes constantly flicked away from my face.

They had had reservations about me when I married Annie. I was a divorced older man with an alcoholic history, and as a homicide detective I had lived in a violent world that was even more foreign to rural Kansas than my Cajun accent and French name. I felt they blamed me for Annie's death. At least her father did, I was sure of that. And I didn't have the strength to argue against that unspoken accusation even with myself.

'The funeral is at four o'clock,' I said. 'I'll let you all rest up at the motel, then I'll be back for you at three-thirty.'

'Where's she at now?' her father said.

'The funeral home.'

'I want to go there.'

I paused a moment and looked at his big, intent face and his wide-set gray eyes.

'The casket's closed, Mr Ballard,' I said.

'You take us there now,' he said.

We buried Annie in my family's plot in the old cemetery by St Peter's Church in New Iberia. The crypts were made of brick and covered with white plaster, and the oldest ones had cracked and sunk into the earth and had become enwrapped with green vines that rooted into the mortar. The rain fell out of the gray sky and danced on the brick street by the cemetery and drummed on the canvas canopy over our heads. Before the attendants from the funeral home slid Annie's coffin into the crypt and sealed it with an inscribed marble slab, one of them unscrewed the metal crucifix from the top and put it in my hands.

I don't remember walking back to the limousine. I remember the people under the canopy – her parents, Batist and his wife, the sheriff, my friends from town – but I don't remember leaving the cemetery. I saw the rain swirling out of the sky, saw it glisten on the red bricks of the street and the black spiked fence that surrounded the cemetery, felt it run out of my hair and into my eyes, heard a train whistle blow somewhere and freight cars clicking on the tracks that ran through town, and then I was standing in the middle of the manicured lawn of the funeral home, with its hollow wooden columns and false antebellum façade looking the color of cardboard in the dull light, and cars were driving away from me in the rain.

'The truck over here, Dave,' Batist was saying. 'Come on, we got supper already fixed. You ain't eat all day.'

'We've got to take her folks back to the motel.'

'They done already gone. Hey, put this coat over your head. You wanta stand out here and be a duck, you?'

He smiled at me, his cannonball head beaded with raindrops, his big teeth like pieces of carved whalebone. I felt his hand go around my arm, squeeze into the muscle, and lead me to the pickup truck, where his wife stood by the open door in a cotton print dress with an umbrella over her head. I sat quietly between them on the way back to the house. They stopped trying to speak to me, and I stared out the windshield at the muddy pools on the dirt road, the wet sheen on the trunks of the oak trees, the water that rattled down from the limbs overhead, the clouds of mist that hung on the bayou and broke across the truck's hood like the offering of sleep. In the gray light, the row of trees along the road looked like a tunnel that I could safely fall through until I reached a cold, enclosed room beneath the earth where wounds healed themselves, where the flesh did not yield to the worm, where a sealed casket could be opened to reveal a radiant face.

I went back to work at the dock. I rented boats, filled people's minnow cans with shiners, fixed barbecue lunches, opened bottles of pop and beer with the mechanical smile and motions of a man in a dream. As always, when one unexpectedly loses someone close, I discovered how kind people could be. But after a while I almost wanted to hide from their well-meaning words of condolence, their handshakes and pats on the back. I learned that grief was a private and consuming emotion, and once it chose you as its vessel it didn't share itself easily with others.

And maybe I didn't want to share it, either. After the scene investigators from the sheriff's department had bagged the bloody sheets from the bed and dug the buckshot out of the bedstead and walls, I closed and locked the door as though I were sealing up a mausoleum filled with pain, which I could resurrect simply by the turn of a key. When I saw Batist's wife heading for the house with scrub brushes and buckets to clean the bloodstains out of the splintered wood, I ran from the bait shop, yelled at her in French with the sharpness of a white man speaking to a Negro woman, and watched her turn back toward her pickup truck, her face hurt and confused.

That night I was awakened by the sound of bare feet on the wooden floor and a door handle turning. I sat up from the couch where I had fallen asleep with the television on, and saw Alafair sitting by the locked bedroom door. She wore her pajama bottoms without a top, and in her hands was the plastic draw bag in which we kept the stale bread. Her eyes were open, but her face was opaque with sleep. I walked toward her in the moonlight that fell through the front windows. Her brown eyes looked at me emptily.

'Feed ducks with Annie,' she said.

'You're having a dream, little guy,' I said.

I started to pull the plastic bag gently from her hands. But her eyes and hands were locked inside the dream. I touched her hair and cheek.

'Let's take you back to bed,' I said.

'Feed ducks with Annie?'

'We'll feed them in the morning. *En la mañana.*' I tried to smile into her face, then I raised her to her feet. She put one hand on the doorknob and twisted it from side to side.

'*Dónde está?*'

'She's gone away, little guy.'

There was nothing for it. I lifted her up on my hip and carried her back into her room. I lay her down on her bed, put the sheet over her feet, sat down beside her, and brushed her soft, downlike hair with my hand. Her bare chest looked small in the moonlight through the window. Then I saw her mouth begin to tremble, as it had in the church, her eyes look into mine with the realization that I could not help, that no one could, that the world into which she had been born was a far more terrible one than any of her nightmares.

'*Los soldados llegaron en la lluvia y le hicieron daño a Annie?*'

The only Spanish words that I understood in her question were 'soldiers' and 'rain.' But even if I had understood it all, I could not have answered her anyway. I was more lost than she, caught forever in the knowledge that when my wife had needed me most, I had left the house to sit by a duck pond in the dark and dwell on the past and my alcoholic neurosis.

I lay down beside Alafair and pulled her against me. I felt the wetness of her eyelash against my face.

Then, one hot, bright afternoon, exactly a week after I had buried Annie, with no dramatic cause at work, with fleecy clouds blowing across the blue sky, I snapped the cap off a bottle of Jax, watched the foam slide over the amber bottle and drip flatly on the wooden floor of the bait shop, and drank it empty in less than a minute.

Two fisherman friends of mine at a table looked briefly at me with dead expressions on their faces, and in the silence of the room I heard Batist drag a kitchen match on wood and light a cigar. When I looked at his face, he flicked the match out the open window and I heard it hiss in the water. He turned away from me and stared out into the sunlight, a curl of smoke rising from his wide-spaced teeth.

I popped open a double-paper bag, put two cartons of Jax inside, poured a small bucked of crushed ice on top of the bottles, and hefted the bag under my arm.

'I'm going to take an outboard down the bayou,' I said. 'Close it up in a couple of hours and keep Alafair with you till I get back.'

He didn't answer and continued to look out at the sunlight on the lily pads and the cane growing along the bank.

'Did you hear me?' I asked.

'Do what you gotta do, you. You ain't got to tell me how to take care of that little girl.' He walked up toward the house, where Alafair was coloring a book on the porch, and didn't look back at me.

I opened the throttle on the outboard and watched my yellow-white wake slap against the cypress roots on the bank. Each time I tilted a bottle of Jax to my mouth the sunlight danced like brown fire inside the glass. I had no destination, no place of completion for all the energy that throbbed through my palm, no plan for the day, my life, or even the next five minutes. What was the great value in plans, anyway? I thought. A forest fire didn't have one, or a flood that buried a Kentucky town in mud, or lightning that splintered down into a sodden field and blew a farmer out of his shoes. Those things happened and the world went on. Why did Dave Robicheaux have to impose all this order and form on his life? So you lose control and total out for a while, I thought. The US Army certainly understood that. You declare a difficult geographical and political area a free-fire zone, then you stand up later in the drifting ash and the smell of napalm and define with much more clarity the past nature of the problem.

The gas tank went empty toward evening, and at the bottom of my feet was a melted pile of ice, soggy brown paper, and empty Jax bottles. I rowed the boat to shore, threw the iron anchor weight up on the bank, and walked in the dusk down a dirt road to a Negro juke joint and bought another six-pack of beer and a half-pint of Jim Beam. Then I pushed the boat back out into the center of the bayou and drifted in the current among the trailings of fireflies and the dark tracings of alligator gar just below the water's surface. I sipped from the lip of the whiskey bottle, chased it with the beer, and waited. Sometimes whiskey kicked open a furnace door that could consume me like a piece of cellophane. Other times I could operate for days with a quiet euphoria and kind of control that would pass for sobriety. Then sometimes I looked into memory and saw forgotten moments that I wished I could burn away like film negatives dissolving on a hot coal.

I remembered a duck-hunting trip with my father when I was thirteen years old. We were in a blind on a cold, gray, windswept day, just off Sabine Pass where it dumped into the Gulf, and the mallards and *poules d'eau* had been coming in low all morning since dawn, and we had busted them like dirty smudges all over the sky. Then my father had gotten careless, maybe because he had been drunk the night before, had gotten mud in the barrel of the automatic twelve-gauge, and when three Canadian honkers went over, really too high for a good shot, he stood up quickly, turned with the shotgun at an angle over my head, and blew the barrel into a spray of wadding, cordite, birdshot, and steel needles all over the water's surface. My ears rang with the explosion, and bits of hot powder covered my face like grains of black pepper. I saw the shame in his eyes and smelled the stale beer on his breath as he washed my skin with his wet handkerchief. He tried to make light of it, said that's what he got for not going to Mass yesterday, but there was a troubled realization in his eyes as well as shame, and it was the same look he had whenever he'd been locked up in the parish jail for brawling in a bar.

It was only a quarter-mile back to the camp; it was right across the bay, up a canal that cut back through the sawgrass and cane, a shack built on stilts that looked out on the Gulf. He would be gone only a short time and bring back the sixteen-gauge. I could start shucking out the ducks, which lay in a soft green and blue pile on the flattened yellow grass at the bottom of the blind. Besides, them honker coming back, yeah, he said.

But back in the canal he ran the outboard across a submerged log and snapped off the propeller shaft like a stick.

I waited for him for two hours, my knife bloody from the warm entrails of the ducks. The wind picked up from the south, small waves chucked against the blind, the sky was the color of incinerator smoke. On the Texas side of the shore I heard the dull popping of another hunter's shotgun.

A pirogue was tied to the back of the blind. I broke open my dogleg twenty-gauge, picked up the string of decoys we had set out in a

J-formation, filled the canvas game bag with the stiffening, gutted bodies of the ducks, loaded it all in the pirogue's bow, and shoved off toward the canal and the long expanse of sawgrass.

But the wind had shifted and was now blowing hard out of the northeast, and no matter how strongly I rowed on both sides of the pirogue, I drifted toward the mouth of the Pass and the slate-green water of the Gulf of Mexico. I paddled until blisters formed on my hands and broke against the grain of the wood, then I threw the anchor weight overboard, realized when the rope hung straight down that the bottom was too deep to catch, and looked desperately at the Louisiana wetlands sliding farther away from me.

Foam blew off the waves in my face, and I could taste salt water in my mouth. The pirogue dipped with such force into the troughs that I had to hold on to the gunwales, and my buttocks constricted with fear each time the wooden bottom slammed up into my tailbone. I tried to bail with a tin can, lost the paddle, and watched it float away from me like a yellow stick between the waves. The string of decoys, my shotgun, and the canvas bag of ducks were awash in the bow; uprooted cypress trees and an upside-down wooden shack revolved in the dark current just under the surface beside me. The shack had a small porch, and it broke through the waves into the winter light like a gigantic mouth streaming water.

The state fish-and-game boat with my father on board picked me up that afternoon. They dried me off and gave me warm clothes, and fixed me fried Spam sandwiches and hot Ovaltine in the galley. But I wouldn't talk to my father until the next day, and I talked with him only then because sleep gave me back the familiar relationship that his explanation about the sheared propeller shaft would not.

'It's because you was alone out there,' he said. 'When somebody make you alone, it don't matter why. You suppose to be mad at them. When your mama run off with a *bourée* man, I didn't care I made her do it, no. I knocked him down on the barroom floor in front of her. When he got up, I knocked him down again. Later I found out he had a pistol in his coat. He could have killed me right there, him. But she didn't let him do it, 'cause she knew I gonna get over it. That's why, me, I ain't mad at you, 'cause I know you suppose to be disappoint with me.

'The bad thing is when you make yourself alone. Don't never do that, Dave, 'cause it's like that coon chewing off its own foot when he stick it in the trap.'

As I sat in the outboard on the bayou and looked at the red sky and the purple clouds in the west, the breathless air as warm as the whiskey that I raised to my lips, I knew what my father had meant.

A coon can chew through sinew and bone in a few minutes. I had a whole night to work on dismantling myself. I found a good place to do it, too – a Negro bar made of Montgomery Ward brick, set back from a dusty yellow road in a grove of oak trees, a place where they carried barber's razors, mixed bourbon in Thunderbird, and played zydeco music so loud it shook the cracked and taped glass windows in front.

Two days later a big-breasted Negro woman in a purple dress picked up my head from a puddle of beer. The sun was low in the east and shining through the window like a white flame.

'Your face ain't no mop, honey,' she said, looking down at me with her hand on her hip, a lighted cigarette between her fingers.

Then her other hand went into my back pocket and took out my wallet. I reached for it impotently while she splayed it open.

'I ain't got to steal white men's money,' she said. 'I just waits for y'all to give it to me. But it's trick, trade, or travel, honey, and it looks like you got to travel.'

She put my wallet in my shirt pocket, mashed out her cigarette in the ashtray in front of me, and dialed the phone on the bar while I remained slumped in the chair, the side of my face wet with beer, red balls of light dancing in my brain. Ten minutes later a St Martin Parish sheriff's car drove me back to the bayou where I had tied my boat and left me standing sick and alone, like a solitary statue, in the wet weeds on the bank.

After I finally got back to the boat dock that afternoon, I asked Batist to keep Alafair until that evening and I slept for three hours on the couch under an electric fan, then got up and shaved and showered and thought I could return a degree of normalcy to my day. Instead, I went into the shakes and the dry heaves and ended up on my knees in front of the wash basin.

I got back into the shower again, sat under the cold water for fifteen minutes, brushed my teeth, dressed in a pair of clean khakis and a denim shirt, and forced myself to eat a bowl of Grape-Nuts. Even in the breeze from the electric fan, my denim shirt was spotted with sweat.

I picked up Alafair at Batist's house and took her to the home of my cousin, a retired schoolteacher, in New Iberia. I had already deserted Alafair for two days while I was on a drunk, and I felt bad about moving her again to another home, but both Batist and his wife worked and could not watch her full-time, and at that moment I wasn't in sufficient physical or emotional condition to be responsible even for myself, much less anyone else, and also the possibility existed that the killers would come back to my house again.

I asked my cousin to keep Alafair for the next two days, then I drove to the courthouse to find the sheriff. But when I parked my truck I was sweating heavily, my hands left wet prints on the steering wheel, the veins in my brain felt like twisted pieces of cord. I drove to the poolroom on Main Street, sat in the coolness of the bar under the wood-bladed fans, and drank three vodka collinses until I felt the rawness of yesterday's whiskey go out of my chest and the tuning fork stop trembling inside me.

But I was mortgaging today for tomorrow, and tomorrow I would probably postpone the debt again, and the next day and the next, until I would be very far in arrears with a debt that would eventually present itself like an unfed snake given its choice of a wounded rabbit's parts. But at that point I guess I didn't care. Annie was dead because I couldn't leave things alone. I had quit the New Orleans police department, the bourbon-scented knight-errant who said he couldn't abide any longer the political hypocrisy and the addictive, brutal ugliness of metropolitan law enforcement, but the truth was that I enjoyed it, that I got high on my knowledge of man's iniquity, that I disdained the boredom and predictability of the normal world as much as my strange alcoholic metabolism loved the adrenaline rush of danger and my feeling of power over an evil world that in many ways was mirrored in microcosm in my own soul.

I bought a bottle of vodka to take home and didn't touch it again until the next morning.

The four inches I drank for breakfast sat in my stomach like canned heat. I had to keep wiping my face with a towel for a half hour, until I stopped sweating, then I brushed my teeth, showered, put on my cream-colored slacks, charcoal sports shirt, and gray and red striped tie, and an hour later I was sitting in the sheriff's office while he listened indecisively to what I had to say and looked peculiarly at my face.

'Are you hot? You look flushed,' he said.

'Go outside. It must be ninety-five already.'

He nodded absently. He scratched the blue and red lines in his soft cheek with a fingernail and pushed a paper clip around on his desk blotter. Through the glass window of the closed office door I could see his deputies doing paperwork at their desks. The building was new and had the cool, neutral, refrigerated smell of a modern office, which was the image it was intended to convey, but the deputies still looked like the raw-boned rednecks and coonasses of an earlier time and they still kept cuspidors by their desks.

'How'd you know the department had an opening?' the sheriff said.

'It was in the paper.'

'It's detective rank, Dave, but eighteen thousand isn't near what you made in New Orleans. It seems to me you'd be going back to the minor leagues.'

'I don't need a lot of money. I've got the boat-and-bait business, and I own my house free and clear.'

'There's a couple of deputies out there who want that job. They'd resent you.'

'That's their problem.'

He opened his desk drawer, dropped the paper clip in it, and looked at me. The soft edges of his face flexed with the thought that had been troubling him since I had told him I wanted the job.

'I'm not going to give a man a badge so he can be an executioner,' he said.

'I wouldn't need a badge for that.'

'The hell you wouldn't.'

'I was a good cop. I never popped a cap unless they dealt the play.'

'You don't have to convince me about your past record. We're talking about now. Are you going to tell me you can investigate your own wife's murder with any objectivity?'

I licked my tongue across my lips. I could feel the vodka humming in my blood. Ease up, ease up, ease up, you're almost home, I thought.

'I was never objective in any homicide investigation,' I said. 'You see the handiwork and you hunt the bastards down. Then, as my old partner used to say, "You bust 'em or grease 'em." But I didn't cool them out, Sheriff. I brought them in when I could have left them on the sidewalk and sailed right through Internal Affairs. Look, you've got some deputies out there who probably give you the cold sweats sometimes. It's because they're amateurs. One day they'll own bars or drive trucks or just go on beating up their wives. But they're not really cops.'

His eyes blinked.

'They tell you a guy resisted arrest or fell down when they put him in the car,' I said. 'They're supposed to bring in a hooker, but they can't ever seem to find her. You send them into a Negro neighborhood and you wonder if the town is going to be burning by midnight.'

'There's another problem, too. It comes in bottles.'

'If I go out of control, fire me.'

'Everybody around here likes and respects you, Dave. I don't like to see a man go back to his old ways because he's trying to fly with an overload.'

'I'm doing all right, Sheriff.' I looked him steadily in the eyes. I didn't like to run a con on a decent man, but most of the cards in my hands were blanks.

'You look like you've been out in the sun too long,' he said.

'I'm dealing with it. Sometimes I win, sometimes I lose. If I come in here blowing fumes in your face, pull my plug. That's all I can tell you. Where do you think those killers are now?'

'I don't know.'

'They're doing a few lines, getting laid, maybe sipping juleps at the track. They feel power right now that you and I can't even guess at. I've heard them describe it as being like a heroin rush.'

'Why are you telling me this?'

'Because I know how they think. I don't believe you do. Those other guys out there don't, either. You know what they did after they murdered Annie? They drove to a bar. Not the first or the second one they saw, but one way down the road where they felt safe, where they could drink Jack Daniel's and smoke cigarettes without speaking to one another, until that moment when their blood slowed and they looked in each other's eyes and started laughing.

'Look at it another way. What evidence do you have in hand?'

'The lead we dug out of the walls, the shotgun shells off the floor, the pry bar they dropped on the porch,' he said.

'But not a print.'

'No.'

'Which means you have almost nothing. Except me. They were out to kill me, not Annie. Every aspect of the investigation will eventually center around that fact. You'll end up interviewing me every other day.'

He lit a cigarette and smoked it with his elbow on the desk blotter. He looked through the door glass at the deputies in the outer office. One of them leaned to the side of his desk and spit tobacco juice into a cuspidor.

'I'll have to run it by a couple of other people, but I don't think there'll be any trouble,' he said. 'But you don't work on just this one case, Dave. You carry a regular load just like the other detectives and you go by the same rules.'

'All right.'

He puffed on his cigarette and widened his eyes in the smoke, as though dismissing some private concerns from his mind, then he watched my expression closely and said, 'Who do you think did it?'

'I don't know.'

'You told me that the day after it happened, and I accepted that. But you've had a lot of time to think in the last ten days. I can't believe you haven't come to some conclusion. I wouldn't want to feel you're being less than honest here, and that maybe you're going to try to operate on your own after all.'

'Sheriff, I gave motive to any number or combination of people. The bartender at Smiling Jack's is the kind of vicious punk who could blow out your light and drink a beer while he was doing it. I not only ran his head into a window fan and cocked a .45 between his eyes, I turned Bubba Rocque loose on him and made him get out of New Orleans. I messed up Eddie Keats with a pool cue in front of his whores, and I went into Bubba Rocque's house and told him I was going to put my finger in his eye if I found out he sent Keats and the Haitian after me.

'Maybe it was Toot and a guy I don't know. Maybe it was two contract men Bubba or Keats brought in from out of state. Maybe it's somebody out of the past. Once in a while they get out of Angola and keep their promises.'

'New Orleans thinks the bartender went to the Islands.'

'Maybe, but I doubt it. He's a rat, and a rat goes into a hole. He's more afraid of Bubba than he is of cops. I don't believe he'll be walking around on a beach anywhere. Besides, he's a mama's boy. He probably won't run far from home.'

'I'll be truthful with you, Dave. I don't know where to start on this one. We just don't have this kind of crime around here. I sent two deputies to question Keats, and he picked his nose in front of them and told them to bust him or beat feet. His bartender and one of his hookers said he was in the club when Annie was killed.'

'Did they question the bartender and the hooker separately?'

He looked away from me. 'I don't know,' he said.

'That's all right. We can talk to them again.'

'I went out to Bubba Rocque's myself. I don't know what to think about a guy like that. You could scratch a match on those eyes and I don't think they'd blink. I remember thirty years ago when he was a kid and he dropped a fly ball in the city park and lost the game for his side. After the game he was eating a snowcone and his daddy slapped it out of his hand and hit him across the ear. His eyes didn't show any more feeling than a couple of zinc pennies.'

'What did he tell you?'

'He was home asleep.'

'What'd his wife say?'

'She said she was in New Orleans that night. So Bubba doesn't have an alibi.'

'He knows he doesn't need one yet. Bubba's a lot smarter than Eddie Keats.'

'He said he was sorry about Annie. I think maybe he meant it, Dave.'

'Maybe.'

'You think he's bad through and through, don't you?'

'Yep.'

'I guess I just don't have your mileage.'

I started to tell him that any cop who gave the likes of Bubba Rocque an even break would probably not earn much mileage, but fortunately I kept my own counsel and simply asked when I could get a badge.

'Two or three days,' he answered. 'In the meantime, take it easy. We'll get these guys sooner or later.'

As I said, he was a decent man, but the Rotary Club had a larger claim on his soul than the sheriff's department. The fact is that most criminals are not punished for their crimes. In New York City only around two percent of the crimes are punished, and in Miami the figure is about four percent. If you want to meet a group of people who have a profound distrust of, and hostility toward, our legal system, don't waste your time on political radicals; interview a random selection of crime victims, and you'll probably find that they make the former group look like utopian idealists by comparison.

I shook hands with him and walked out into the hazy noon-day heat and humidity. In the meadows along the road, cattle were bunched in the hot shade of the oak trees, and white egrets were pecking in the dried cow flop out in the grass. I pulled my tie loose, wiped my forehead on my shirt sleeve, and looked at the long wet streaks on the cloth.

Fifteen minutes later I was in a dark, cool bar south of town, a cold, napkin-wrapped collins glass in my hand. But I couldn't stop perspiring.

Vodka is an old friend to most clandestine drunks. It has neither odor nor color, and it can be mixed with virtually anything without the drinker being detected. But its disadvantage for a whiskey drinker like me was that it went down so smoothly, so innocuously, in glasses filled with crushed ice and fruit slices and syrup and candied cherries, that I could drink almost a fifth of it before I realized that I had gone numb from my hairline to the soles of my feet.

'Didn't you say you had to leave here at four?' the bartender asked.

'Sure.'

He glanced up at the illuminated clock on the wall above the bar. I tried to focus my eyes on the hands and numbers. I pressed my palm absently to my shirt pocket.

'I guess I left my glasses in my truck,' I said.

'It's five after.'

'Call me a cab, will you? You mind if I leave my truck in your lot awhile?'

'How long?' He was washing glasses, and he didn't look at me when he spoke and his voice had the neutral tone that bartenders use to suppress the disdain they feel for some of the people whom they serve.

'I'll probably get it tomorrow.'

He didn't bother to answer. He called a cab and went back to washing glasses in the aluminum sink.

Ten minutes later my cab arrived. I finished my drink and set it on the bar.

'I'll send somebody for my truck, podna,' I said to the bartender.

I rode back to my house in the cab, packed two changes of clothes in my suitcase, got Batist to drive me to the airport in Lafayette, and by six-thirty I was aboard a commercial flight to Key West, by way of Miami, the late red sun reflecting like pools of fire among the clouds.

I sipped from my second double Beam and soda and looked down at the dark blue and turquoise expanse of water off the western tip of the island, where the Gulf and the Atlantic met, and at the waves sliding across the coral reefs below the surface and breaking against the beaches that were as white as ground diamond. The four-engine plane dipped, made a wide turn out over the water, then flattened out for its approach to the airport, and I could see the narrow strip of highway that ran from Key West to Miami, the coconut palms along the beaches, the lagoons full of sailboats and yachts, the kelp rising in the groundswell, the waves bursting in geysers of foam at the ends of the jetties, and then suddenly the tree-lined and neon-lit streets of Key West in the last red wash of sunset.

It was a town of ficus, sea grape, mahogany and umbrella trees, coconut and royal palms, hanging geraniums, Confederate jasmine, and bougainvillea that bloomed as brightly as blood. The town was built on sand and coral, surrounded by water, the wooden buildings eventually made paintless and gray by salt air. At one time or another it has been home to Indians, Jean Lafitte's pirates, salvagers who deliberately lured commercial ships onto the reefs so they could gut the wrecks, James Audubon, rum runners, Cuban political exiles, painters, homosexuals, dope smugglers, and burnt-out street people who had been pushed so far down in the continent now that they had absolutely no place else to go.

It was a town of clapboard and screened-in beer joints, raw-oyster bars, restaurants that smelled of conch fritters and boiled shrimp and deep-fried red snapper, clearings in the pine trees where fishermen stacked their lobster traps, nineteenth-century brick warehouses and government armories, and shady streets lined with paintless shotgun houses with wooden shutters and sagging galleries. The tourists were gone now because of the summer heat, and the streets were almost empty in the twilight; the town had gone back into itself. The cabdriver had to buy gas on the way to the motel, and I looked out the window at some elderly Negro men sitting on crates in front of a tiny grocery store, at the ficus roots that cracked the sidewalks into concrete peaks, at the dusky purple light on the brick streets and the darkening trees overhead, and for just a moment it was as though I had not left New Iberia, had not taken another step deeper into my problems.

But I had.

I checked into a motel on the southern tip of the island and had a fifth of Beam and a small bucket of ice sent to the room. I had a couple of hits with water, then showered and dressed. Through my window I could see the palm trees thrashing on the deserted beach and the light dying on the horizon. The water had turned as dark as burgundy, and waves were pitching upward against a coral reef that formed a small harbor for a half-dozen sailboats. I opened the glass jalousies wide to let the cool breeze into the room, then I walked downtown to Duval Street and my friend's restaurant where Robin worked as a waitress.

But my metabolism was on empty before I made it to the foot of Duval. I stopped in at Sloppy Joe's and had a drink at the bar and tried to examine all the vague thoughts and strange movements of my day. True, not everything I had done had been impetuous. Robin was still the best connection I had to the collection of brain-fried New Orleans people who served Bubba Rocque, and I had called my friend long-distance to make sure she was working at the restaurant, but I could have questioned her on the phone, or at least tried, before deciding I would have to fly to Key West.

Which made me confront, at least temporarily, the real reason I was there: it's lousy to be alone, particularly when you're not handling anything properly. Particularly when you're drunk and starting to fuck up your life again on an enormous scale. And because somebody was playing 'Baby Love' on the jukebox.

'Why don't you put some records on that jukebox that aren't twenty years old?' I said to the bartender.

'What?'

'Put some new music on there. It's 1987.'

'The jukebox is broken, pal. You better slip your transmission into neutral.'

I walked back out onto the street, my face warm with bourbon in the wind blowing off the backside of the island. On the dock by the restaurant I watched the waves slide through pilings, small incandescent fish moving about like smoky green lights below the surface. The restaurant was crowded with customers, and the bar was a well-lighted and orderly place where people had two drinks before dinner. When I walked inside I felt like a diver stepping out of a bathysphere into a hostile and glaring brilliance.

The maitre d' looked at me carefully. I had fixed my tie and tried to smooth the wrinkles in my seersucker coat, but I should have put on sunglasses.

'Do you have a reservation, sir?' he said.

'Tell Robin Dave Robicheaux's here. I'll wait in the bar.'

'I beg your pardon?'

'Tell her Dave from New Orleans. The last name's hard to pronounce sometimes.'

'Sir, I think you'd better see her outside of working hours.'

'Say, you're probably a good judge of people. Do I look like I'm going away?'

I ordered a drink at the bar, and five minutes later I saw her come through the door. She wore a short black dress with a white lace apron over it, and her figure and the way she walked, as though she were still on a burlesque runway, made every man at the bar glance sideways at her. She was smiling at me, but there was a perplexed light in her eyes, too.

'Wow, you come a long way to check up on a girl,' she said.

'How you doing, kiddo?'

'Not bad. It's turned out to be a pretty good gig. Hey, don't get up.'

'How long till you're off?'

'Three hours. Come on and sit in the booth with me. You're listing pretty heavy to port.'

'A drunk front came through New Iberia this morning.'

'Well, walk over here with mommy and let's order something to eat.'

'I ate on the plane.'

'Yeah, I can tell,' she said.

We sat in a tan leather booth against the back wall of the bar. She blew out little puffs of air with her lips.

'Dave, what are you doing?' she said.

'What?'

'Like, *this*.' She flicked her fingernail against my highball glass.

'Sometimes I clean out my head.'

'You bust up with your old lady or something?'

'I'm going to get another Beam. You want a cup of coffee or a Coke?'

'Do *I* want coffee? God, that's great, Dave. Look, after the dinner rush I can get off early. Take the key to my apartment and I'll meet you there in about an hour. It's right around the corner.'

'You got any hooch?'

'Some beer is all. I've been doing good, Dave. No little white pills, no glug-glug before I go to work. I can't believe how good I feel in the mornings.'

'Pick me up at Sloppy Joe's.'

'What do you want to go there for? It's full of college dopes who think Ernest Hemingway wrote on the bathroom walls or something.'

'See you in an hour, kiddo. You're a sweet girl.'

'Yeah, the guys at Smiling Jack's used to tell me that all the time. While they were trying to cop a feel under the table. I think you got hit in the head by lightning this morning.'

When she came for me later at Sloppy Joe's, I was by myself at a table in the back, the breeze from a floor fan rising up my trouser leg, fluttering the wet sleeve of my seersucker coat that hung over the side of the table. The big sliding doors on two sides of the building were rolled wide open, and the neon light shone purple on the sidewalk. On the corner, two cops were rousting a drunk. They weren't cutting him any slack, either. He was going to the bag.

'Let's go, Lieutenant,' Robin said.

'Wait till the man leaves. My horizon keeps tilting. Key West is a bad town to have trouble in.'

'All I do is flex my boobs and they tip their hats. Such gentlemen. No more booze, honey pie.'

'I need to tell you some things. About my wife. Then you have to tell me some more about those people in New Orleans.'

'Tomorrow morning. Mommy's going to fix you a steak tonight.'

'They killed her.'

'What?'

'They blew her to pieces with shotguns. That's what they did, all right.'

She stared at me with her mouth parted. I could see the edges of her nostrils discolor.

'You mean Bubba Rocque killed your wife?' she said.

'Maybe it was him. Maybe not. Ole Bubba's a hard guy to second-guess.'

'Dave, I'm sorry. Jesus Christ. Did it have something to do with me? God, I don't believe it.'

'No.'

'It does, though, because you're here.'

'I just want to see if you can remember some things. Maybe I just wanted to see you, too.'

'I guess that's why you had the hots for me when you were single. Tell me about it when your head's not ninetyproof.' She looked around the bar. The floor fan ruffled her short black hair. 'This place's a drag. The whole town's a drag. It's full of low-rent dykes and man-eaters that drift down from New York. Why'd you send me over here?'

'You told me you were doing well here.'

'Who's doing well when people are out there killing a guy's wife? You messed with them, didn't you, Dave? You wouldn't listen to me.'

I didn't answer, but instead picked up my highball glass.

'Forget it. Your milk cow has gone dry for tonight,' she said, then took the glass out of my hand and poured it in a pool of whiskey and ice on the table.

She lived on the first floor of an old two-story stucco building with a red tile roof just off Duval Street. A huge banyan tree had cracked one wall, and the tiny yard was overgrown with weeds and untrimmed banana trees. Her apartment had a small kitchen, a bedroom separated by a sliding curtain, and a couch, breakfast table, and chairs that looked like they had come from a Goodwill store.

Robin had a good heart, and she wanted to be kind, but her cooking was truly a challenge, particularly to someone on a bender. She turned the steak black on one side, fried the potatoes in a half-inch of grease, and filled the apartment with smoke and the smell of burned onions. I tried to eat but couldn't. I'd reached the bottom of my drunk. The cogs on my wheels were sheared smooth, all my wiring was blown, and the skin of my face was thick and dead to the touch. I suddenly felt that I had aged a century, that someone had slipped a knife along my breastbone and scooped out all my vital organs.

'Are you going to be sick?' she said.

'No, I just need to go to bed.'

She looked at me a moment in the light of the unshaded bulb that hung from the ceiling. Her eyes were green, and unlike most of the strippers on Bourbon, she had never needed to wear false eyelashes. She brought two sheets from her dresser in the bedroom and spread them on the couch. I sat down heavily, took off my shoes, and rubbed my hand in my face. I was already starting to dehydrate, and I could smell the alcohol against my palm like an odor climbing out of a dark well. She carried a pillow back to the couch.

'Robin?' I said.

'What are you up to, Lieutenant?' She looked down at me with the light behind her head.

I put my hand on her wrist. She sat down beside me and looked straight ahead. Her hands were folded, and her knees were close together under her black waitress uniform.

'Are you sure this is what you want?' she said.

'Yes.'

'Did you come all the way over here just to get laid? There must be somebody available closer to home.'

'You know that's not the way I feel about you.'

'No, I don't. I don't know anything of the sort, Dave. But you're a friend, and I wouldn't turn away from you. I just don't want you to lie about it.'

She turned off the light and undressed. Her breasts were round and soft against me, her skin tan and smooth in the dark. She hooked one leg in mine, ran her hands over my back, kissed my cheek and breathed in my ear and made love to me as she might to an emotional child. But I didn't care. I was used up, finished, as dead inside as I was the day they slid Annie's casket inside the crypt. The street light made shadows on the banyan and banana trees outside the window. Inside my head was a sound like the roar of the ocean in a conch shell.

The next morning the early light was gray in the streets, then the sun came up red on the eastern horizon, and the banana leaves clicking against the screen window were beaded with humidity. I filled a quart jar with tap water, drank it down, then threw up in the toilet. My hands shook, the backs of my legs quivered, flashes of color popped like lesions behind my eyes. I stood in my underwear in front of the washbasin, cupped water into my face, brushed my teeth with toothpaste and my finger, then threw up again and went into a series of stomach spasms so severe that finally my saliva was pink with blood in the bottom of the basin. My eyes were watering uncontrollably, my face cold and twitching; there was a pressure band across one side of my head as though I had been slapped with a thick book, and my breath was sour and trembled in my throat each time I tried to breathe.

307

I wiped the sweat and water off my face with a towel and headed for the icebox.

'No help there, hon,' Robin said from the stove, where she was soft-boiling eggs. 'I poured the beer out at four this morning.'

'Have you got any ups?'

'I told you mommy's clean.' She was barefoot and wearing a pair of black shorts and a denim shirt that was unbuttoned over her bra.

'Some of those PMS pills. Come on, Robin. I'm not a junkie. I've just got a hangover.'

'You shouldn't try to run a shuck on another juicer. I took your wallet, too. You got rolled, Lieutenant.'

It was going to be a long morning. And she was right about trying to con a pro. Normally an alcoholic can jerk just about anybody around except another drunk. And Robin knew every ploy that I might use to get another drink.

'Get in the shower, Dave,' she said. 'I'll have breakfast ready when you come out. You like bacon with soft-boiled eggs?'

I turned on the water as hot as I could stand it, pointed my face with my mouth open into the shower head, washed the cigarette smoke from the bar out of my hair, scrubbed my skin until it was red. Then I turned on the cold water full blast, propped my arms against the tin walls of the stall, and held on while I counted slowly to sixty.

'The bacon's kind of crisp, I guess,' she said after I had dressed and we were sitting at the table.

The bacon looked like strips torn out of a rubber tire. And she had hard-boiled the eggs and mashed them up with a spoon.

'You don't have to eat it,' she said.

'No, it's really good, Robin.'

'Do you feel a lot of remorse this morning? That's what your AA buddies call it, don't they?'

'No, I don't feel remorse.' But my eyes went away from her face.

'I was turning tricks when I was seventeen. So you got a free one. Deal me out of your guilt, Dave.'

'Don't talk about yourself like that.'

'I don't like morning-after bullshit.'

'You listen to me, Robin. I came to you last night because I felt more alone than I've ever felt in my life.'

She drank from her coffee and set the cup in her saucer.

'You're a sweet guy, but I've got too much experience at it. It's all right.'

'Why don't you give yourself some credit? I don't know another person in the world who would have taken me in the way you did last night.'

She put the dishes in the sink, then walked up behind me and kissed my hair.

'Just get through your hangover, Streak. Mommy's been fighting her own dragons for a long time,' she said.

It wasn't simply a hangover, however. This slip had blown a year of sobriety for me, and in that year of health and sunshine and lifting weights and jogging for miles in the late evening, my system had lost all its tolerance for alcohol. It was similar to pouring a five-pound bag of sugar in an automobile gas tank and opening up the engine full-bore. In a short time your rings and valves are reduced to slag.

'Can I have my wallet?' I said.

'It's under the cushion on the couch.'

I found it and put it in my back pocket, then slipped on my loafers.

'You headed for a beer joint?' she said.

'It's a thought.'

'You're on your own, then. I'm not going to help you mess yourself up anymore.'

'That's because you're the best, Robin.'

'Save the baby oil for yourself. I don't need it.'

'You've got it wrong, kiddo. I'm going to buy a bathing suit and we're going down to the beach. Then I'm going to take you out to lunch.'

'It sounds like a good way to ease yourself back into the bar and keep mommy along.'

'No bars. I promise.'

Her eyes searched mine, and I saw her face brighten.

'I can fix food for us here. You don't have to spend your money,' she said.

I smiled at her.

'I would really like to take you to lunch,' I said.

It was a morning of abstinence in which I tried to think in terms of five minutes at a time. I felt like a piece of cracked ceramic. In the clothing store my hands were still trembling, and I saw the salesman step back from my breath. In an open-air food stand on the beach, I drank a glass of iced coffee and ate four aspirins. I squinted upward at the sunlight shining through the branches of the palm tree overhead. I would have swallowed a razor blade for a shuddering rush of Jim Beam through my system.

The snakes were out of their baskets, but I hoped they would have only a light meal and be on their way. I paid a Cuban kid a dollar to borrow his mask and snorkel, then I waded through the warm waves of the lagoon and swam out to open deep water over a coral reef. The water was as clear as green Jell-O, and thirty feet down I could see the fire coral in the reef, schools of clown fish, bluepoint crabs drifting across the sand, a nurse shark as motionless as a log in the reef's shadow, gossamer plants that bent with the current, black sea urchins whose spikes could go all the way through your foot. I held my breath and dove as deep as I could, dropping into a layer of cold water where a barracuda looked directly into my mask with his bony, hooked snout, then zipped past my ear like a silver arrow fired from an archer's bow.

I felt better when I swam back in and walked up on the sand where Robin was lying on a towel among a stand of coconut palms. Also, I had already invested too much of the day in my own misery. It was time to go to work again, although I knew she wasn't going to like it.

'The New Orleans cops think Jerry's in the Islands,' I said.

She unsnapped her purse, took out a cigarette and lit it. She pulled her leg up in front of her and brushed sand off her knee.

'Come on, Robin,' I said.

'I closed the door on all those dipshits.'

'No, I'm going to close the door on them. And like we used to say in the First District, "weld it shut and burn their birth certificates."'

'You're a barrel of laughs, Dave.'

'Where is he?' I smiled at her and ticked some grains of sand off her knee with my fingernail.

'I don't know. Forget the Islands, though. He used to have a mulatto chick in Bimini. That was the only reason he went over there. Then he got stoned on ganja and dropped her baby on its head. On concrete. He said they've got a coralrock jail over there that's so black it'd turn a nigger into a white man.'

'Where's his mother go when she's not in New Orleans?'

'She's got some relatives in north Louisiana. They used to come in the bar and ask for Styrofoam spit cups.'

'Where in north Louisiana?'

'How should I know?'

'I want you to tell me everything Eddie Keats and the Haitian said when they were in your apartment.'

Her face darkened, and she looked out toward the surf where some high school kids were sailing a frisbee back and forth over the waves. Out beyond the opening of the lagoon, pelicans were diving into a patch of blue water that was as dark as ink.

'You think my head's a tape deck?' she asked. 'Like I should be collecting what these people say while they break my finger in a door? You know what it feels like for a woman to have their hands on her?'

Her face was still turned away from me, but I could see the shiny film on her eyes.

'What do you care what they say, anyway?' she said. 'It never makes any sense. They're morons that went to the ninth grade, and they try to act like wiseguys they see on TV. Like Jerry always saying, "I ain't no swinging dick. I ain't no swinging dick." Wow, what an understatement. I bet he was in the bridal suite every night at Angola.'

I waited for her to continue. She drew on the cigarette and held the smoke down as though she were taking a hit on a reefer.

'The spade wanted to cut my face up,' she said. 'What's-his-name, Keats, says to him, "The man don't want us throwing out his pork chops. You just give her a souvenir on her hand or her foot, and I'll bet she'll wear it to church. Under it all, Robin's a righteous girl." Then the boogie says, "You always talk with a mouth full of shit, man." '

'What's-his-name thought that was funny. So he laughs and lights a Picayune and says, "At least I don't live in a fucking slum so I can be next to a dead witch." '

'How about that for clever conversation? Listening to those guys talk to each other is like drinking out of a spittoon.'

'Say that again about the witch.'

'The guy lives in a slum around a witch. Or a dead witch or something. Don't try to make sense out of it. These guys buy their brains at a junkyard. Why else would anybody work for Bubba Rocque? They all end up doing time for him. I hear when they get out of Angola he won't give them a job cleaning toilets. What a class guy.'

I picked up her hand and squeezed it. It was small and brown in mine. She looked at me in the warm shade, and her mouth parted slightly so I could see her white teeth.

'I have to go back this afternoon.'

'Big news flash.'

'No cuteness, kiddo. Do you want to go to New Iberia with me?'

'If your conscience bothers you, go to church.'

'I have a bait business I could use some help with. I have a little girl living with me, too.'

'Life down on the bayou isn't my style, Streak. Come on back here when you're serious.'

'You always think I'm running a shuck on you.'

'No, you're just a guy that makes impossible rules for himself. That's why you're a mess. Buy a girl lunch, will you?'

Sometimes you leave a person alone. This was one of them.

Out on the ocean a pelican lifted from a green trough and flew by overhead, a bloody fish dripping from its beak.

7

The next morning when I awoke, back in New Iberia, I heard blue jays and mockingbirds in my pecan trees. I put on my gym shorts and tennis shoes and jogged all the way to the drawbridge in the early blue light, drank coffee with the bridge tender, then hit it hard all the way home. I showered and dressed, ate a breakfast of strawberries and GrapeNuts on the picnic table in the backyard, and watched the breeze ruffle the delicate leaves of the mimosa tree. It had been over thirty hours since I had had a drink. I was still weak, my nerve endings still felt as though they had been touched with lighted matches, but I could feel the tiger starting to let go.

I drove to Lafayette and talked with two priests who had worked with the pilot of the plane that had gone down at Southwest Pass. What they told me was predictable: Father Melancon, the drowned priest, had been a special piece of work. He had been an organizer of migrant farm workers in Texas and Florida, had been busted up with ax handles by company goons outside Florida City, and had served three months' county time in Brownsville for slashing the tires of a sheriff's van that was loaded with arrested strikers. Then he got serious and broke into a General Electric plant and vandalized the nose cone of a nuclear missile. Next stop; the federal pen in Danbury for three years.

I was always fascinated by the government's attempt to control political protest by the clergy in the country. Usually the prosecutor's office would try to portray them as naive idealists, bumblers who had strayed from their pulpits and convents, and when that didn't work, they were sent up the road with the perverts, geeks, and meltdown cases, which are about the only types that do hard time anymore. However, once they were in the slam, they had a way of spreading their message throughout the convict population.

But the priest in Lafayette didn't recognize the names of Johnny Dartez and Victor Romero. They simply said that Father Melancon had been a trusting man with unusual friends, and that sometimes his unusual friends went with him when he ferried refugees out of villages in El Salvador and Guatemala.

312

'Romero is a little, dark guy with black curls hanging in his face. He wears a beret,' I said.

One of the priests tapped his finger on his cheek.

'You remember him?' I said.

'He didn't wear a beard, but the rest of it was like you say. He was here a month ago with Father Melancon. He said he was from New Orleans but he had relatives in Guatemala.'

'Do you know where he is now?'

'No, I'm sorry.'

'If he comes round again, call Minos Dautrieve at the Drug Enforcement Administration or call me at this number.' I wrote Minos's name and my home number on a piece of paper and gave it to him.

'Is this man in trouble?' the priest said.

'I'm not sure what he is, Father. He used to be a drug courier and street dealer. Now he may be an informer for Immigration and Naturalization. I'm not sure if he's moving up or down in his moral status.'

I drove back to New Iberia through Breaux Bridge so I could stop for lunch at Mulate's. I had deep-fried soft-shell crabs with a shrimp salad and a small bowl of étouffée with French bread and iced tea. Mulate's was a family place now, with only the long mahogany bar and the polished dance floor to remind me of the nightclub and gambling spot it had been when I was in college. The last twenty-five years had changed southern Louisiana a great deal, much of it for the better. The laws of segregation were gone; kids didn't go nigger-knocking on Saturday nights; the Ku Klux Klan didn't burn crosses all over Plaquemines Parish; the dema-gogues like judge Leader Perez had slipped into history. But something else was gone, too: the soft pagan ambience that existed right in the middle of a French Catholic culture. Oh, there was still plenty of sleaze around – and narcotics, where there had been none before – but the horse race and slot machines, with their winking lights and rows of cherries and plums and gold bells, had been taken out of the restaurants and replaced with video games; the poolrooms and working-class bars with open *bourée* games were fewer; the mulatto juke joints, where Negroes and dark-skinned Cajuns had lost their racial identity at the door, were now frequented by white tourists who brought cassette recorders to tape zydeco music. The old hot-pillow joints – Margaret's in Opelousas, the Column Hotel in Lafayette, the cribs on Railroad Avenue in New Iberia – were shut down.

I'd like to blame it on the boys at the Rotary and the Kiwanis. But that's not fair. We had just become a middle-class people, that's all.

But one local anachronism had held on to the past successfully and burgeoned in the present, and that was Bubba Rocque. The kid who would eat a lightbulb for a dollar, set you up with a high-yellow washer-woman for two dollars, throw a cat into the grille of an oncoming car for free, had gone modern. I suspect that he had to piece off a lot of his action to the mob in New Orleans and they probably pulled strings on him sometimes and perhaps eventually they would cannibalize his whole operation, but in the meantime he had taken to drug dealing and big time pimping like a junkyard dog to lamb chops.

But had he sent the two killers to my house with shotguns? I had a feeling that the net would have to go over a lot of people before I found out. Bubba didn't leave umbilical cords lying around.

That afternoon my detective's appointment with the sheriff's department was approved. I was given a photo identification card and a gold badge, which were contained inside a soft leather wallet; a packet of printed information on departmental policies and employee benefits, which I threw away later without reading; and a Smith & Wesson .38 revolver with worn blueing and two notches filed in the grip. I was to report to work at the sheriff's office at eight the next morning.

I picked up Alafair at my cousin's house in New Iberia, bought ice cream cones for both of us, and played with her on the swing sets in the park. She was a beautiful little girl when the cloud of violent memories and unanswered questions went out of her eyes. Her face was hot and bright with excitement as I swung her on the chains, high up to the edge of the oak limbs, and she was so dark with tan she seemed almost to disappear in the tree's shadows; then she would swish past me in the sunlight, in a roar of squeals, her dusty bare feet just tickling the earth.

We went home and fixed catfish poor-boy sandwiches for supper, then I drove down the road and hired an elderly mulatto woman, whom I had known since I was a child, as a live-in baby-sitter. That night I packed my suitcase.

I woke early the next morning to the rain falling on the pecan trees and drumming on the gallery. Alafair and the baby-sitter were still asleep. I screwed a hasp and a staple into the door and jamb of Annie's and my bedroom, closed the windows, drew the curtains, and padlocked the door.

Why?

I can't answer. Maybe because it's unholy to wash away the blood of those we love. Maybe because the placement of a tombstone on a grave is a self-serving and atavistic act. (Just as primitive people did, we weight the dead and their memory safely down in the earth.) Maybe because the only fitting monument to those who die violently is the memory of pain they've left behind.

I loaded the .38 revolver with five shells in the cylinder, set the hammer on the empty chamber, and put it in my suitcase. I drank a cup of coffee and hot milk at the kitchen table, took apart my .45 automatic, oiled it, reamed out the barrel with a bore brush, reassembled it, and stuck a full clip back up into the magazine. Then I opened a fresh box of hollow-points and inserted them one at a time with my thumb into a second clip. They were heavy and round in my hand, and they snapped cleanly against the tension of the loading spring. When they flattened out they could blow holes the size of croquet balls in an oak door, destroy the inside of an automobile, leave a keyhole wound in a human being that no physician could heal.

A dark meditation? Yes. Guns kill. That's their function. I had never deliberately kicked a situation into the full-tilt boogie. The other side had always taken care of that readily enough. I was sure they would again.

I called the sheriff at his office. He wasn't in. I left a message that I was on my way to New Orleans, that I would see him in one or two days. I looked in on Alafair, who was sleeping with her thumb in her mouth in front of the window fan, then picked up my suitcase, draped my raincoat over my head, and ran through the mud puddles and dripping trees to my truck.

The sun was out but it was still raining when I reached New Orleans at eleven o'clock. I parked my truck on Basin and walked into the old St Louis Cemetery No. 1, the warm rain hitting on the brim of my hat. There were rows and rows of white-painted brick crypts, the bottom level of tombs often pressed deep into the earth so that you could not read the French on the cracked and worn marble tablets that covered the coffins. Glass jars and rusted tin cans filled with withered flowers littered the ground. Many of the dead had died during one of the city's nineteenth-century epidemics of yellow fever, when the corpses were collected in wagons and stacked like firewood, sprinkled with lime and interred by convicts in chains who were allowed to get drunk before they began their work. Some of the crypts had been gutted by looters, the pieces of bone and moldy cloth and rotted wood raked out onto the ground. On rainy or cold nights, winos crawled inside and slept in fetal positions with bottles of synthetic wine pulled against their chests.

New Orleans's wealthiest and most famous were here: French and Spanish governors, aristocrats killed in duels or in the battle against the British of Chalmette, slave dealers and skippers of clipper ships who ran the Yankee blockade of the city. I even found the grave of Dominique You, the Napoleonic soldier of fortune who became Jean Lafitte's chief gunnery officer. But I was interested in only one grave that day, and even when I found it I couldn't be sure that Marie Laveau was inside it (some people said she was buried in an old oven a couple of blocks away, in St Louis Cemetery No. 2).

She was known as the voodoo queen of New Orleans during the mid-nineteenth century. She was called a witch, a practitioner of black magic from the Islands, a mulatto opportunist. But regardless, her following had been large, and I suspected that there was still at least one man in this neighborhood who would scoop dirt from her grave and carry it in a red flannel pouch, divine the future by shaking out pigs' bones on the top of her crypt, or one night a month climb into the guttered ruin next to it.

I had no real plan, and it would probably be a matter of luck if I grabbed Toot in that rundown neighborhood around the cemetery. In fact, I was out of my jurisdiction and didn't even have authority to be there. But if I went through official procedure, I would still be in New Iberia and a couple of New Orleans street cops would ask a couple of questions around the neighborhood, provided they had time, and when that didn't work, a night-shift plainclothes with sheaves of outstanding warrants wrapped in rubber bands on his car seat would add Toot's name to the list of wanted suspects in that area and the upshot would be absolutely nothing.

Most criminals are stupid. They creep $500,000 homes in the Garden District, load up two dozen bottles of gin, whiskey, vermouth, and collins mix in a $2,000 Irish linen tablecloth and later drink the booze and throw the tablecloth away.

But I guess my greatest fear was that the locals would scare Toot out of the area, or maybe even nail him and then kick him loose before we could bring him back to New Iberia. It happens. The criminals aren't the only dumb guys in town.

When I was a homicide detective in the First Division on Basin we busted a serial killer from Georgia who had murdered people all the way across the South. He was a thirty-five-year-old carnival worker, a blond, rugged-looking man of fearsome physical proportions who wore earrings made out of gold crucifixes. He had a third-grade education, drew his signature as a child might, and plugged up his toilet with a blanket and flooded the deadlock section of the jail because he couldn't watch television with the other men in the main holding area; but nevertheless he was able to convince two homicide detectives that he could show them where a young girl was buried in the levee down in Plaquemines Parish. They put him in handcuffs rather than leg and waist chains, and drove him down a board road deep into a swamp.

But he had hidden a paper clip in his mouth. He picked the lock on his handcuffs, ripped the .357 Magnum out of the driver's shoulder holster, and blew both detectives all over the front windshield.

He was never caught again. The bucket of a Ferris wheel fell on him in Pocatello, Idaho.

I spent the day driving and walking the streets of the neighborhood, from Canal all the way over the Esplanade Avenue. I talked with blacks, Chicanos, and blue-collar white people in shoe-shine stands, seven AM bars, and corner grocery stores that smelled of chitlins and smoked carp. Yesterday I had been a small-town businessman. Today I was a cop, and I got the reception that cops usually get in a poor neighborhood. They made me for either a bill collector, a bondsman, a burial insurance man, a process server for a landlord, or Mr Charlie with his badge (it's strange how we as white people wonder at minority attitudes towards us, when we send our worst emissaries among them).

Once I thought I might be close. An ex-boxer who owned a bar that had a Confederate flag auto tag nailed in the middle of the front door took the wet end of his cigar out of his mouth, looked at me with a face that was shapeless with scar tissue, and said, 'Haitian? You're talking about a boon from the Islands, right?'

'Right.'

'There's a bunch of those cannibals over on North Villere. They eat all the dogs in the neighborhood. They even seine the goldfish out of the pond in the park. Don't stay for supper. You might end up in the pot.'

The yard of the one-story, wood-frame yellow house he directed me to was overgrown with wet weeds and littered with automobile and washing-machine parts. I drove down the alley and tried to see through the back windows, but the shades were pulled against the late-afternoon sun. I could hear a baby crying. Sacks of garbage that smelled of rotting fish were stacked on the back steps, and the diapers that hung on the clothesline were gray and frayed from handwashing. I went around front and knocked on the door.

A small, frightened black man with a face like a cooked apple came to within three feet of the screen and looked at me out of the gloom.

'Where's Toot?' I said.

He shook his head as though he didn't understand.

'Toot,' I said.

He held his palms outward and shook them back and forth. His eyes were red in the gloom. Two children were coloring in a book on the floor. A wide-hipped woman with an infant on her shoulder watched me from the kitchen door.

'*Vous connaissez un homme qui s'appelle Toot?*' I said.

He answered me in a polyglot of French and English and perhaps African that was incomprehensible. He was also terrified.

'I'm not from Immigration,' I said. '*Comprenez? Pas Immigration.*'

But he wasn't buying it. I couldn't reach past his fear nor make him understand my words, and then I made matters worse when I asked again about Toot and used the term *tonton macoute*. The man's eyes widened, and he swallowed as though he had a pebble in his throat.

But it was hopeless. Good work, Robicheaux, I thought. Now these poor people will probably stay frightened for days, shuddering every time an automobile slows out front. They would never figure out who I was and would simply assume that I was only a prelude of worse things to come. Then I had another thought. Police officers and Immigration officials didn't give money to illegal immigrants.

I took a five-dollar bill out of my wallet, creased it lengthwise, and slipped it through the jamb of the latched screen.

'This is for your baby,' I said *'Pour vot' enfant.'*

He stared at me dumbfounded. When I looked back at the screen from my truck, he and his wife were both staring at me.

I bought a block of cheese, a half-pound of sliced ham, an onion, a loaf of French bread, and a quart of milk in a Negro grocery store, parked by the cemetery, and ate supper while the rain began failing out of the purple twilight. Over on Basin I saw a neon Jax signal light over a barroom.

When you don't nail a guy like Toot in his lair, you look for him in the places that take care of his desires. Most violent men like women. The perverts bust them up; contract hit men use them as both reward for their accomplishment and testimony of their power. I knew almost every black and high-yellow pick-up bar and hot-pillow joint in New Orleans. It was going to be a long night.

I was exhausted when the sun came up in the morning. It had stopped raining at about three AM, and the pools of water in the street were drying in the hot sunlight, and you could feel the moisture and heat radiate up from the concrete like steam.

I brushed my teeth and shaved in a filling station rest room. My eyes were red around the rims, my face lined with fatigue. I had gone into a dozen lowlife Negro bars during the night, had been propositioned, threatened, and even ignored, but no one knew a Haitian by the name of Toot.

I had coffee and beignets in the Café du Monde, then gave the neighborhood around the cemetery one more try. By now my face had. become so familiar up and down Iberville and St Louis that grocery and drugstore owners and bartenders looked the other way when they saw me coming. The sun was white in the sky; the elephant ears, philodendron, and banana trees that grew along the back alleys were beaded with moisture; the air had the wet, fecund taste of a hothouse. At noon I was ready to give it up.

Then I saw two police cars, with their bubble-gum lights on, parked in front of a stucco house one block up North Villere from the yellow house where the frightened man lived. An ambulance was backed up the driveway to the stairway of the garage apartment. I parked my truck by the curb and opened my badge in my hand and walked up to two patrolmen in the drive. One was writing on a clipboard and trying to ignore the sweat that leaked out of his hatband.

'What have you got?' I said.

'A guy dead in the bathtub,' he said.

'What from?'

'Hell if I know. He's been in there two or three days. No air-conditioning either.'

'What's his race?'

'I don't know. I haven't been up there. Check it out if you want to. Take your handkerchief with you.'

Halfway up the stairs the odor hit me. It was rotten and acrid and sweet at the same time, reeking of salt and decay, fetid and gray as a rat's breath, penetrating and enveloping as the stench of excrement. I gagged and had to press my fist against my mouth.

Two paramedics with rubber gloves on were waiting patiently with a stretcher in the tiny living room while the scene investigator took flash pictures in the bath. Their faces were pinched and they kept clearing their throats. An overweight plainclothes detective with a florid, dilated face stood in the doorway so that I couldn't see the bathtub clearly. His white shirt was so drenched with sweat that you could see his skin through the cloth. He turned and looked at me, puzzled. I thought I might know him from my years in the First District, but I didn't. I turned up my badge in my palm.

'I'm Dave Robicheaux, Iberia Parish sheriff's office,' I said. 'Who is he?'

'We don't know yet. The landlord's on vacation, there's nothing in the apartment with a name on it,' he said. 'A meter reader came up the stairs this morning and tossed his cookies over the railing. It's all over the rosebush. It really rounds out the smell. What are you looking for?'

'We've got a warrant on a Haitian.'

'Be my guest,' he said, and stepped aside.

I walked into the bathroom with my handkerchief pressed over my mouth and nose. The tub was an old iron, rust-streaked one on short metal legs that looked like animal claws. A man's naked black calves and feet stuck up out of the far end of the tub.

'He was either a dumb shit that liked to keep his radio on the washbasin, or somebody threw it in there with him,' the detective said. 'Any way you cut it, it cooked him.'

The water had evaporated out of the tub, and dirty lines of grit were dried around the drain hole. I looked at the powerful hands that were now frozen into talons, the muscles in the big chest that had become flaccid with decomposition, the half-closed eyes that seemed focused on a final private thought, the pink mouth that was still locked wide with a silent scream.

'It must have been a sonofabitch. He actually clawed paint off the sides,' the detective said. 'There, look at the white stuff under his nails. You know him?'

'His name's Toot. He worked with Eddie Keats. Maybe he worked for Bubba Rocque, too.'

'Huh,' he said. 'Well, it couldn't have happened to a nicer guy, then. What a way to get it. Once over in Algiers I had a case like this. A woman was listening to this faith healer while she was washing dishes. So the faith healer told everybody to put their hands on the radio and get healed, and it blew her right out of her panty hose. What'd y'all have on this guy?'

'Assault and battery, suspicion of murder.'

The scene investigator walked past us with his camera. The detective crooked his finger at the two paramedics.

'All right, bag him and get him out of here,' he said, and turned to me again. 'They'll have to burn the stink out of this place with a flame-thrower. You got everything you want?'

'You mind if I look around a minute?'

'Go ahead. I'll wait for you outside.'

Propped against the back corner of the closet, behind the racked tropical shirts, the white slacks, the flowered silk vests, I found a twelve-gauge pump shotgun. I opened the breech. It had been cleaned and oiled and the cordite wiped out of the chamber with a rag. Then I unscrewed the mechanism to the pump action itself and saw the sportsman's plug had been taken out so the magazine could hold five rather than three rounds. On the floor was a half-empty box of red double nought shotgun shells of the same manufacture as the ones that had littered the floor of Annie's and my bedroom. I rolled one of the shells back and forth in my palm and then put it back in the box.

The detective lit a cigarette as he walked down the stairs into the yard. Afternoon rain clouds had moved across the sun, and he wiped the sweat out of his eyebrows with the flat of his hand and widened his eyes in the breeze that had sprung up from the south.

'I'd like for you to come down to the District and file a report on your man,' he said.

'All right.'

'Who's this guy supposed to have killed?'

'My wife.'

He stopped in the middle of the yard, a dead palm tree rattling over his head, and looked at me with his mouth open. The wind blew his cigarette ashes on his tie.

I decided I had one more stop to make before I headed back to New Iberia. Because of my concern for Alafair, I had given the Immigration and Naturalization Service a wide berth. But as that Negro janitor had told me in high school, you never let the batter know you're afraid of him. When he spreads his feet in the box and gives you that mean squint from under his cap, as though he's sighting on your throat, you spit on the ball and wipe his letters off with it. He'll probably have a change in attitude toward your relationship.

But Mr Monroe was to surprise me.

I parked the truck in the shade of a spreading oak off Loyola and walked back in the hot sunlight to the INS office. His desk was out on the floor, among several others, and when he looked up from a file, folder in his hands and saw me, the skin around his ears actually stretched across the bone. His black hair, which was combed like wires across his pate, gleamed dully in the fluorescent light. I saw his throat swallow under his bow tie.

'I'm here officially,' I said, easing my badge out of my side pants pocket. 'I'm a detective with the Iberia sheriff's office now. Do you mind if I sit down?'

He didn't answer. He took a cigarette out of a pack on his desk and lit it. His eyes were straight ahead. I sat down in the straight-backed chair next to his desk and looked at the side of his face. By his desk blotter in a silver frame was a picture of him and his wife and three children. A clear vase with two yellow roses in it sat next to the picture.

'What do you want?' he said.

'I'm on a murder investigation.'

He held his cigarette to his mouth between two fingers and smoked it without ever really detaching it from his lips. His eyes were focused painfully into space.

'I think you guys have a string on somebody I want,' I said.

Finally he looked at me. His face was as tight as paper.

'Mr Robicheaux, I'm sorry,' he said.

'Sorry for what?'

'For . . . about your wife. I'm truly sorry.'

'How did you know about my wife?'

'It was in the area section of the *Picayune*.'

'Where's Victor Romero?'

'I don't know this man.'

'Listen, this is a murder investigation. I'm a police officer. Don't you jerk me around.'

He lowered his cigarette toward the desk blotter and let out his breath. People at the other desks were obviously listening now.

'You have to understand something. I do field work with illegal immigrants in the workplace. I check green cards. I make sure people have work permits. I've done that for seven years.'

'I don't care what you do. You answer me about Victor Romero.'

'I can't tell you anything.'

'You think carefully about your words, Mr Monroe. You're on the edge of obstruction.'

His fingers went to his temple. I saw his bottom lip flutter.

'You have to believe this,' he said. 'I'm very sorry about what's happened to you. There's no way I can express how I feel.'

321

I paused before I spoke again.

'When somebody's dead, apologies have as much value as beating off in a paper bag,' I said. 'I think you need to learn that, maybe go down to the courthouse and listen to one of the guys on his way up to Angola. Are you following me? Because this is what I believe you guys did: you planted Johnny Dartez and Victor Romero inside the sanctuary movement, and four people ended up dead at Southwest Pass. I think a bomb brought that plane down. I think Romero had something to do with it, too. He's also hooked up with Bubba Rocque, and maybe Bubba had my wife killed. You shield this guy and I'm going to turn the key on you.'

I could hear him breathing now. His pate was slick with oil and perspiration under the light. His eyes clicked back and forth.

'I don't care who hears this, and you can make of it what you want,' he said. 'I'm a career civil servant. I don't make policy or decisions. I try to keep illegals from taking American jobs. That's all I do here.'

'They made you a player. You take their money, you take their orders, you take their fall.'

'I'm not an articulate man. I've tried to tell you my feelings, but you won't accept that. I don't blame you. I'm just sorry. I don't have anything else to say, Mr Robicheaux.'

'Where's your supervisor?'

'He's gone to Washington.'

I looked at the picture of his family on the desk.

'My wife's casket had to be kept closed at the funeral,' I said. 'You think about that a minute. Also, you tell your supervisor I'm going to run that heroin mule to ground. When I do, I'm going to squeeze him. You better hope none of y'all's names come out of his mouth.'

When I walked out the door the only sound in the room was the telex machine clacking.

It was evening when I got home, and Alafair and the babysitter had already had their supper. I was hungry and too wired to sleep, so I heated up some dirty rice, shelled crawfish, and cornbread, wrapped it in foil, and packed it in my canvas rucksack with my army mess kit and walked down the road in the flaming sunset to a spot of the bayou where my father and little brother and I used to dig for minié balls when I was a boy.

A sugar planter's home had been built there in the 1830s, but the second story had been torched by General Banks's soldiers in 1863 and the roof and the blackened cypress timbers had collapsed inside the brick shell. Over the years the access road had filled with pine seedlings and undergrowth, vandals had prized up the flagstones in the fireplaces, looking for gold coins, and the grave markers had been knocked down in the family burial ground and the graves themselves were recognizable only because of their dark green color and the blanket of mushrooms that grew across them.

Four-o'clocks and wild rosebushes grew along the rim of a small coulee that flowed through the edge of the clearing, past a rotted-out cistern by the side of the house and a blacksmith's forge that was now only a rusty smear in the wet soil. The breeze off the bayou was still strong enough to push the mosquitoes back into the trees, and I sat on a dead cypress stump in the last wash of red sunlight and ate supper from my mess kit. The water was clear, copper-colored, flowering over the rocks in the bottom of the coulee, and I could see small bream hiding under the moss that swung in the current. Along these same banks my father, my brother, and I had dug out a bucket full of minié balls as well as cannister and grapeshot, bits of chain, and chopped-up horseshoes fired by union cannon into the Confederate rearguard. We used rakes to clear the vines and damp layers of dead leaves from the coulee walls, and the minié balls would drop from the loam like white teeth. They were conical-shaped on one end, with a hollow indentation and three grooved rings on the other, and they always felt heavy and smooth and round in your palm.

In our innocence we didn't think about them as objects that blew muscle away from bone, ripped through linkage and webs of vein, tore the jaw and tongue from a face. I had to become a new colonial and journey across the seas to learn that simple fact. I had to feel a shotgun shell touched by the long black fingers of a man whose mission was to create and capture human misery on Polaroid film.

I put aside my mess kit and tore the petals from a pink rose and watched them drift down onto the water, float along the riffle through the ferns and out into the sunlight. I had more to think about than I wanted to. True, I was sober; the physical pain of my last bender was gone, and the tiger seemed to be in his cage; but I had a lot of tomorrows to face, and in the past the long-distance view of my life had a way of getting me drunk again. Tomorrow at noon I would go to an AA meeting and confess my slip in front of the group, which was not an easy thing to do. I had once again failed not, only myself and my Higher Power, but I had betrayed the trust of my friends as well.

I knocked out my mess kit on the cypress stump, and put it away in my rucksack. I thought I heard a car door open and close on the road, but I paid it little attention. The shadows had fallen across the clearing now, and the mosquitoes were lifting in clouds from the trees and undergrowth. I flipped one of the rucksack straps over my shoulder and walked through the pine seedlings toward the sun's last red glare above the main road.

Through the tree trunks I saw the dark outline of a man standing by a maroon Toyota parked on the road. He stood on the far side of the hood, looking at me, his face covered with shadow, motionless, as though he were taking a leak by his tire. For a moment I couldn't see him at all because of a big spreading oak, then the trees thinned and I saw him suddenly swing a bolt-action rifle to his shoulder, the leather sling already wrapped tight around his left forearm, saw the lens of the telescopic sight glint as dark as firelight in a whisky glass, saw his chest and elbows lean across the low roof of the car with the quick grace of an infantry marksman who never cants his sights and delivers the mail somewhere between your breastbone and throat.

I jumped sideways and rolled through the underbrush just as the rifle roared and a bullet popped leaves off a half-dozen limbs and splintered the side of a pine trunk as though it had been touched lightly with a chainsaw. I heard him work the bolt, even heard the empty shell casing clink off the car metal, but I was running now, zigzagging through the woods, pine branches whipping back across my face and chest, the carpet of dead leaves an explosion of sound under my feet I had the canvas straps of the rucksack bunched in my left hand, and when his second round went off and tore through the undergrowth and pinged away off the brick of the plantation ruin, I dove on my chest, ripped the sack flap loose from its leather thong, and got my hand around the butt of my .45 automatic.

I think he knew it had turned around on him. I heard him work the bolt, but I also heard the barrel knock against the car roof or windshield and I could hear him shaking the bolt as though he had tried to jam a shell too fast into the chamber. I was up and running again, this time at an angle toward the road so I would exit the woods behind his car. The trees were thickly spaced here, and he fired at my sound rather than shape, and the bullet thropped through a briar patch fifteen feet behind me.

I crashed through the undergrowth and came out onto the lighted edge of the woods just as he threw his rifle across the car. He was a dark, small man, in jeans and running shoes and a purple T-shirt, with black hair that hung in curls. But I was running so fast and breathlessly that I slipped to my knees on the side of the drainage ditch and almost filled the .45's barrel with dirt. He floored his car, popped the clutch, and spun water out of a muddy pool. I fell forward on my elbows, my arms extended, my left palm cupped under the .45's butt, and began firing.

The roar was deafening. I whanged the first round off his bumper, punched two holes in the trunk, went high once, then blew out the back window with such force that it looked as if it had been gutted by a baseball bat. I rose to my knees and kept firing, the recoil knocking my arm higher with each explosion. His car slid sideways at the bend of the road, smashed against an oak trunk before he righted the front wheels, and I saw my last round blow his taillight into a tangle of wires and broken red plastic. But I didn't hit his gas tank or a tire, or punch through his firewall into the engine block, and I heard him winding up his gearbox until it almost screamed as he disappeared beyond a flooded canebreak on the side of the road.

8

After I had called in a description of the shooter and his Toyota at the boat dock, I went back out on the road with a flashlight and hunted for the shells he had ejected from his rifle. Two fully loaded gravel trucks had passed on the road and crushed one of the .30–06 shells flat in the dirt and half buried the other in a muddy depression, but I prised each of them out with the awl of my Swiss army knife and dropped them in a plastic bag. They were wet and muddy and scoured from being ground under the truck's tires, but a spent cartridge thrown from a bolt-action rifle is always a good one to recover a print from, because usually the shooter presses each load down with his thumb and leaves a nice spread across the brass surface.

The next morning I listened quietly while the sheriff shared his feelings about my going to New Orleans for two days without authorization. His face was flushed, his tie pulled loose and he talked with his hands folded on his desk in order to conceal his anger. I couldn't blame him for the way he felt, and the fact that I didn't answer him only made him more frustrated. Finally he stopped, shifted his weight in the chair, and looked at me as though he had just abandoned everything he had said.

'Forget that bullshit about procedure. What bothers me is the feeling I've been used,' he said.

'I called before I left. You weren't in,' I said.

'That's not enough.'

Again I didn't answer him. The bagged rifle shells were on his desk.

'Tell the truth. What would you have done if you'd found the Haitian alive?' he asked.

'Busted him.'

'I want to believe that.'

I looked out of the window at a bright green magnolia tree in the morning haze.

'I'm sorry about what I did. It won't happen again,' I said.

'If it does, you won't have to resign. I'll take your badge myself.'

I looked at the magnolia tree a moment and watched a hummingbird hang over one of the white flowers.

'If we get a print off those shells, I want to send it to New Orleans,' I said.

'Why?'

'The scene investigator dusted the radio that was in the bathtub with the Haitian. Maybe there's a connection with our shooter.'

'How?'

'Who knows? I want New Orleans to give us a copy of Victor Romero's sheet and prints, too.'

'You think he was the shooter?'

'Maybe.'

'What's the motive?'

'Hell if I know.'

'Dave, do you think maybe you're trying to tie too many things together here? I mean, you want your wife's killers. But you've only got one set of suspects that you can reach out and touch, so maybe you've decided to see some threads that aren't there. Like you said, you put a lot of people in Angola.'

'The ex-con who snuffs you wants you to see his face and enjoy a couple of memories with him. The guy who shot at me last night did it for money. I don't know him.'

'Well, maybe the guy's car will show up. I don't know how he got it out of the parish with all those holes in it.'

'He boosted it, and it's in the bayou or a garage somewhere. We won't find it. At least not for a while.'

'You're really an optimist, aren't you?'

I spent the day doing the routine investigative work of a sheriff's detective in a rural parish, I didn't enjoy it. For some reason, probably because he was afraid I'd run off again, the sheriff assigned me a uniformed deputy named Cecil Aguillard, an enormous, slow-witted redbone. He was a mixture of Cajun, Negro and Chitimacha Indian; his skin was the color of burnt brick, and he had tiny, turquoise-green eyes and a pie-plate face you could break a barrel slat across without his changing expression. He drove seventy miles an hour with one hand, spit Red Man out of the window, and pressed on the pedals with such weight and force that he had worn the rubber off the metal.

We investigated a stabbing in a Negro bar, the molestation of a retarded girl by her uncle, an arson case in which a man set fire to his own fish camp because his drunken guests wouldn't leave his party by the next morning, and finally, late that afternoon, the armed robbery of a grocery store out on the Abbeville road. The owner was a black man, a cousin of Cecil Aguillard, and the robber had taken ninety-five dollars from him, walked him back to the freezer, hit him across the eye with his pistol barrel, and locked him inside. When we questioned him he was still shaking from the cold, and his eye was swollen into a purple knot. He could only tell us that the robber was white, that he had driven up in a small brown car with an out-of-state license plate, had walked inside with a hat on, then suddenly rolled down a nylon stocking over his face, mashing his features into a blur of skin and hair.

'Somet'ing else. He took a bottle of apricot brandy and a bunch of them Tootsie Roll,' the Negro said. 'I tell him "Big man with a gun, sucking on Tootsie Roll." So he bust me in the face, him. I need that money for my daughter's col'ech in Lafeyette. It ain't cheap, no. You gonna get it back?'

I wrote on my clipboard and didn't reply.

'You gonna get it back, you?'

'It's hard to tell sometimes.'

I knew better, of course. In fact, I figured our man was in Lake Charles or Baton Rouge by now. But time and chance happeneth to us all, even to the lowlifes.

On our radio we heard a deputy in a patrol car run a check on a 1981 tan Chevette with a Florida tag. He had stopped the Chevette out on the Jeanerette road because the driver had thrown a liquor bottle at a road sign. I called the dispatcher and asked her to tell the deputy to hold the driver until we got there.

Cecil drove the ten mile distance in less than eight minutes. The Chevette was pulled over on the oyster-shell parking lot of a ramshackle clapboard dance hall built back from the road. It was five PM, the sun was orange over the rain clouds piled in the west, and Haliburton and cement and pickup trucks were parked around the entrance to the bar. A deeply tanned man in blue jeans, with no shirt on, leaned with one arm hooked over the open door of his Chevette, spitting disgustedly between his legs. His back was tattooed with a blue spider caught in a web. The web extended over both of his shoulder blades.

'What have you got him on?' I said to the deputy who had held him for us.

'Nothing. Littering. He says he works seven-and-seven offshore.'

'Where's he break the bottle?'

'Back there. Against the railroad sign.'

'We'll take it from here. Thanks for you help,' I said.

The deputy nodded and drove off in his car.

'Shake this guy down. Cecil. I'll be back in a minute,' I said.

I walked back to the railroad crossing, where an old LOUISIANA LAW – STOP sign was postholed by the side of the gravel bedding. The wooden boards were stained with a dark, wet smear. I picked up pieces of glass out of the gravel and soot-blackened weeds until I found two amber-colored pieces that were hinged together by an apricot brandy label.

I started back toward the parking lot with the two pieces of wet glass in my shirt pocket. Cecil had the tattooed man spread on the front of the fender of the Chevette and was ripping his pockets inside out. The tattooed man turned his head backwards, said something, and started to stand erect, when Cecil simultaneously picked him up in the air by his belt and slammed his head down on the hood. The man's face went white with concussion. Some oil-field roughnecks in tin hats, their denims spattered with drilling mud, stopped in the bar entrance and walked towards us.

'We're not supposed to bruise the freight, Cecil,' I said.

'You want to know what he said to me?'

'Ease up. Our man here isn't going to give us any more trouble. He's already standing in the pig slop up to his kneecaps.'

I turned to the oilfield workers, who obviously didn't like the idea of a redbone knocking around a white man.

'Private party, gentlemen,' I said. 'Read about it in the paper to-morrow, just don't try to get your name in the story today. You got my drift?'

They made a pretense of staring me sullenly in the face, but a cold beer was much more interesting to them than a night in the parish jail.

The tattooed man was leaning on his arms against the front fender again. There were grains of dirt on the side of his face where it had hit the hood, and a pinched, angry light in his eyes. His blond hair was uncut and as thick and dry as old straw. Two Tootsie Roll wrappers lay on the floor of his car.

I looked under the seats. Nothing was there.

'You want to open the hatchback for us?' I said.

'Open it yourself,' he said.

'I asked you if you wanted to do that. You don't have to. It beats going to jail, though. Of course, that doesn't mean you're necessarily going to jail. I just thought you might want to be a regular guy and help us out.'

'Because you got no cause.'

'That's right. It's called "probable cause." Were you in Raiford? I like the artwork on your back,' I said.

'You want to look in my fucking car? I don't give a shit. Help yourself,' he said, pulled the keys from the ignition, popped up the hatchback, and pulled open the tire well. There was nothing inside it except the spare and a jack.

'Cuff him and put him behind the screen,' I told Cecil.

Cecil pulled the man's hands behind his back, snapped the handcuffs tightly onto his wrists, and walked him back to our car as though he were a wounded bird. He locked him behind the wire mesh that separated the back and front seats, and waited for me to get into the passenger's seat. When I didn't, he walked back to where I stood by the Chevette.

'What's the deal? He's the one, ain't he?' he said.

'Yep.'

'Let's take him in.'

'We've got a problem, Cecil. There's no gun, no hat, no nylon stocking. Your cousin's not going to be able to identify him in a lineup, either.'

'I seen you pick up them brandy glass. I seen you look at them Tootsie Roll paper.'

'That's right. But the prosecutor's office will tell us to kick him loose. We don't have enough evidence, podna.'

'My fucking ass. You get a beer, you. Come see in ten minutes. He give you that stocking, you better believe, yeah.'

'How much money was in his wallet?'

'A hunnerd maybe.'

'I think there's another way to do it, Cecil. Stay here a minute.'

I walked back to our car. It was hot inside and the handcuffed man was sweating heavily. He was trying to blow a mosquito away from his face with his breath.

'My partner wants to bust you,' I said.

'So?'

'There's a catch. I don't like you. That means I don't like protecting you.'

'What are you talking about, man?'

'I went off duty at five o'clock. I'm going to get me a shrimp sandwich and a Dr Pepper and let him take you in. Are you starting to see the picture now?'

He shook back his damp hair from his eyes and tried to look indifferent, but he didn't hide fear well.

'I have a feeling that somewhere between here and the jail you're going to remember where you left that gun and stocking,' I said. 'But anyway it's between you and him now. And I don't take stock in rumors.'

'What? What the fuck you talking about rumors, man?'

'That he took a suspect into the woods and put out his eye with a bicycle spoke. I don't believe it.'

I saw him swallow. The sweat ran out of his hair.

'Hey, did you see *The Treasure of the Sierra Madre?*' I asked. 'There's a great scene in there when this Mexican bandit says to Humphrey Bogart, "I like your watch. I think you give me your watch." Maybe you saw it on the late show at Raiford.'

'I ain't playing this bullshit, man.'

'Come on you, you can do it. You pretend you're Humphrey Bogart. You drive your car back to that convenience store and you give the owner your hundred dollars and that Gucci watch you're wearing. It's going to brighten up your day. I guarantee it.'

The mosquito sat on the end of his nose.

'Here comes Cecil now. Let him know what you've decided,' I said.

The light was soft through the trees as I drove along the bayou road toward my house that evening. Sometimes during the summer the sky in southern Louisiana actually turns lavender, with strips of pink cloud in the west like flamingo wings painted above the horizon, and this evening the air was sweet with the smell of watermelons and strawberries in somebody's truck patch and the hydrangeas and nightblooming jasmine that completely covered my neighbor's wooden fence. Out on the bayou the bream were dimpling the water like raindrops.

Before I turned into my lane I passed a fire-engine-red MG convertible with a flat tire by the side of the road, then I saw Bubba Rocque's wife sitting on my front step with a silver thermos next to her thigh and a plastic cup in her fingers. She wore straw Mexican sandals, beige shorts, and a low-cut white blouse with blue and brown tropical birds on it, and she had pinned a yellow hibiscus in her dark hair. She smiled at me as I walked toward her with my coat over my shoulder. Once again I noticed that strange red cast in her brown eyes.

'I had a flat tire. Can you give me a ride back to my aunt's on West Main?' she asked.

'Sure. Or I can change it for you.'

'There's no air in the spare, either.' She drank from the cup. Her mouth was red and wet, and she smiled at me again.

'What are you doing down this way, Mrs Rocque?'

'It's Claudette, Dave. My cousin lives down at the end of the road. I come over to New Iberia about once a month to see all my relatives.'

'I see.'

'Am I putting you out?'

'No. I'll be just a minute.'

I didn't ask her in. I went inside to check on Alafair and told the baby-sitter to go ahead and serve supper, that I would be back shortly.

'Help a lady up. I'm a little twisted this evening,' Claudette Rocque said, and reached her hand out to mine. She felt heavy when I pulled her erect. I could smell gin and cigarettes on her breath.

'I'm sorry about your wife,' she said.

'Thank you.'

'It's a terrible thing.'

I held the truck door open for her and didn't answer.

She sat with her back at an angle to the far door, her legs slightly apart, and moved her eyes over my face.

Oh boy, I thought. I drove out of the shadows of the pecan trees, back onto the bayou road.

'You look uncomfortable,' she said.

'Long day.'

'Are you afraid of Bubba?'

'I don't think about him,' I lied.

'I don't think you're afraid of very much.'

'I respect your husband's potential. I apologize for not asking you in. The house is a mess.'

'You don't get backed into a corner easily, do you?'

'Like I said, it's been a long day, Mrs Rocque.'

She made an exaggerated pout with her mouth.

'And you're not going to call a married lady by her first name. What a proper law officer you are. Do you want a gin rickey?'

'No, thanks.'

'You're going to hurt my feelings. Has someone told you bad things about me?'

I watched a sparrow hawk glide on extended wings down the length of the bayou.

'Did someone tell you I was in St Gabriel?' she said. Then she smiled and reached out and ticked the skin above my collar with her nail. 'Or maybe they told you I wasn't all girl.'

I could feel her eyes moving on the side of my face.

'I've made the officer uncomfortable. I think I even made him blush,' she said.

'How about a little slack, Mrs Rocque?'

'Will you have a drink with me, then?'

'What do you think the odds are of your having a flat tire by my front lane?'

Her round doll's eyes were bright as she looked at me over her raised drinking cup.

'He's such a detective,' she said. 'He's thinking so hard now, wondering what the bad lady is up to.' She rubbed her back against the door and flattened her thighs against the truck seat. 'Maybe the lady is interested in you. Are you interested in me?'

'I wouldn't go jerking Bubba around, Mrs Rocque.'

'Oh my, how direct.'

'You live with him. You know the kind of man he is. If I was in your situation, I'd give some thought to what I was doing.'

'You're being rude, Mr Robicheaux.'

'Read it like you want. Your husband has black lightning in his brain. Mess around with his pride, embarrass him socially, and I think you'll get to see that same kid who wheeled his crippled cousin into the coulee.'

'I have some news for you, sir,' she said. Her voice wasn't coy anymore, and the red tint in her brown eyes seemed to take on a brighter cast. 'I did three years in a place where the bull dykes tell you not to come into the shower at night unless you want to lose your cherry. Bubba never did time. I don't think he could. I think he'd last about three days until they had to lock him in a box and put handles on it and carry it out in the middle of an empty field.'

I drove onto the drawbridge. The tires thumped on the metal grid. I saw the bridge tender look at Claudette Rocque and me with a quizzical expression on his face.

'Another thought for you, sir,' she said. 'Bubba has a couple of sluts he keeps on tap in New Orleans. I'm not supposed to mention them. I'm just his cutie-pie Cajun girl that's supposed to clean his house and wash his sweat suits. I've got a big flash for you boys. Your jockstrap stinks.'

In the cooling dusk I passed a row of weathered Negro shacks with sagging galleries, a bar and a barbecue joint under a spreading oak, an old brick grocery store with a lighted Dixie beer sign in the window.

'I'm going to drop you at the cab stand,' I said. 'Do you have money for cabfare?'

'Bubba and I own cabs. I don't ride in them.'

'Then it's a good night for a walk.'

'You're a shit,' she said.

'You dealt it.'

'Yeah, you got a point. I thought I could do something for you. Big mistake. You're one of those full-time good losers. You know what it takes to be a good loser? Practice.' On East Main she pointed ahead in the dusk. 'Drop me at that bar.'

Then she finished the last of her thermos and casually dropped it out the truck window into the street. It sprang end over end on the concrete. A group of men smoking cigars and drinking canned beer in front of the bar turned and stared in our direction.

'I was going to offer you a hundred-thousand-dollar-a-year deal to run Bubba's fish-packing house in Morgan City,' she said. 'Think about that on your way back to your worm sales.'

I slowed the truck in front of the bar. The neon beer signs made the inside of the cab red. The men outside the bar entrance had stopped talking and were looking at us.

'Also, I don't want you to drive out of here thinking you've been in control of things tonight,' she said, and got up on her knees, put her arms around my neck, and kissed me wetly on the cheek. 'You just missed the best lay you'll ever have, pumpkin. Why don't you try some pocket pool at your AA meetings? It really goes with your personality.'

But I was too tired to care whether she had won the day or not. It was a night of black clouds rolling over the Gulf, of white electricity jumping across the vast, dark dome of sky above me, of the tiger starting to walk around in his cage. I could almost hear his thick, leathery paws scudding against the wire mesh, see his hot orange eyes in the darkness, smell his dung and the fetid odor of rotted meat on his breath.

I never had an explanation for these moments that would come upon me. A psychologist would probably call it depression. A nihilist might call it philosophical insight. But regardless, it seemed there was nothing for it except the acceptance of another sleepless night. Batist, Alafair, and I took the pickup truck to the drive-in movie in Lafayette, set out deck chairs on the oyster shells, and ate hot dogs and drank lemonade and watched a Walt Disney double feature, but I couldn't rid myself of the dark well I felt my soul descending into.

In the glow of the movie screen I looked at Alafair's upraised and innocent face and wondered about the victims of greed and violence and political insanity all over the world. I have never believed that their suffering is accidental or a necessary part of the human condition. I believe it is the direct consequence of corporate avarice, the self-serving manipulations of politicians who wage wars but never serve in them themselves, and, perhaps worse, the indifference of those of us who know better.

I've seen many of those victims myself, seen them carried out of the village we mortared, washed down with canteens after they were burned with napalm, exhumed from graves on a riverbank where they were buried alive.

But as bad as my Indochinese memories were, one image from a photograph I had seen as a child seemed to encapsulate the dark reverie I had fallen into. It had been taken by a Nazi photographer at Bergen-Belsen, and it showed a Jewish mother carrying her baby down a concrete ramp toward the gas chamber, while she led a little boy with her other hand and a girl of about nine walked behind her. The girl wore a short cloth coat like the ones children wore at my elementary school. The lighting in the picture was bad, the faces of the family shadowy and indistinct, but for some reason the little girl's white sock, which had worked down over her heel, stood out in the gloom as though it had been struck with a shaft of gray light. The image of her sock pushed down over her heel in that cold corridor had always stayed with me. I can't tell you why. But I feel the same way when I relive Annie's death, or remember Alafair's story about her Indian village, or review that tired old film strip from Vietnam. I commit myself once again to that black box that I cannot think myself out of.

Instead, I sometimes recall a passage from the Book of Psalms. I have no theological insight, my religious ethos is a battered one; but those lines seem to suggest an answer that my reason cannot, namely, that the innocent who suffer for the rest of us become anointed and loved by God in a special way; the votive candle of their lives has made them heaven's prisoners.

It rained during the night, and in the morning the sun came up soft and pink in the mist that rose from the trees across the bayou. I walked out to the road and got the newspaper from the mailbox and read it on the front porch with a cup of coffee. The phone rang. I went inside and answered it. 'What are you doing driving around with the dyke?' 'Dunkenstein?' I said.

'That's right. What are you doing with the dyke?'

'None of your business.'

'Everything she and Bubba do is our business.'

'How'd you know I was with Claudette Rocque?'

'We have our ways.'

'There wasn't a tail.'

'Maybe you didn't see him.'

'There wasn't a tail.'

'So?'

'Have you got their phone tapped?'

He was silent.

'What are you trying to tell me, Dunkenstein?' I asked.

'That I think you're crazy.'

'She used the phone to tell somebody I gave her a ride into New Iberia?'

'She told her husband. She called him from a bar. Some people might think you're a dumb shit, Robicheaux.'

I looked at the mist hanging in the pecan trees. The leaves were dark and wet with dew.

'A few minutes ago I was enjoying a cup of coffee and the morning paper,' I said. 'I think I'm going to finish the paper now and forget this conversation.'

'I'm calling from the little grocery store by the drawbridge. I'll be down to your place in about ten minutes.'

'I think I'll make a point of being on my way to work by then.'

'No, you won't. I already called your office and told them you'd be late. Hang loose.'

A few minutes later I watched him drive his US government motor pool car up my front lane. He closed his car door and stepped around the mud puddles in the yard. His loafers were shined, his seersucker slacks ironed with knifeedge creases, his handsome blond face gleaming with the closeness of his shave. He wore his polished brown belt high up on his waist, which made him look even taller than he was.

'Have you got another cup of coffee?' he said.

'What is it you want, Minos?' I held the screen open for him, but I imagine my face and tone were not hospitable.

He stepped inside and looked at Alafair's coloring book on the floor.

'Maybe I don't want anything. Maybe I want to help you,' he said.

335

'Why don't you try not to be so sensitive all the time? Every time I talk with you, you're bent out of joint about something.'

'You're in my house. You're running on my meter. You haven't given me any help, either. Cut the bullshit.'

'All right, you've got a legitimate beef. I told you we'd handle the action. We didn't. That's the way it goes sometimes. You know that. You want me to catch air?'

'Come on in the kitchen. I'm going to fix some GrapeNuts and strawberries. You want some?'

'That sounds nice.'

I poured him a cup of coffee and hot milk at the kitchen table. The light was blue in the backyard.

'I didn't talk to you at the funeral. I'm not good at condolences. But I wanted to tell you I was sorry,' he said.

'I didn't see you there.'

'I didn't go to the cemetery. I figure that's for family. I think you're a stand-up guy.'

I filled two bowls with Grape-Nuts, strawberries, and sliced bananas, and set them on the table. He put a big spoonful in his mouth, the milk dripping from his lips. The overhead light reflected off his crewcut scalp.

'That's righteous, brother,' he said.

'Why am I late to work this morning?' I sat down at the table with him.

'One of those shells you picked up had a beautiful thumbprint on it. Guess who New Orleans PD matched it with?'

'You tell me, Minos.'

'Victor Romero is shooting at you, podna. I'm surprised he didn't get you, too. He was a sniper in Vietnam. I hear you shot the shit out of his car.'

'How do you know New Orleans matched his print? I haven't even heard that.'

'We had a claim on him a long time before you did. The city co-ordinates with us anytime his name pops up.'

'I want you to tell me something, with no bullshit. Do you think the government can be involved in this?'

'Be serious.'

'You want me to say it again?'

'You're a good cop. Don't fall for those conspiracy fantasies. They're out of style,' he said.

'I went down to Immigration in New Orleans. That fellow Monroe is having some problems with personal guilt.'

'What did he tell you?' His eyes were looking at me with new interest.

'He's one of those guys who wants to feel better. I didn't let him.'

'You mean you actually think somebody in the government, the INS, wants you hit?'

'I don't know. But no matter how you cut it, right now they've got shit on their noses.'

'Look, the government doesn't knock off its own citizens. You're sidetracking into a lot of claptrap that's not going to lead you anywhere.'

'Yeah? Try this. What kind of Americans do you think the government uses down in Central America? Boy Scouts? Guys like yourself?'

'That's not here.'

'Victor Romero sure is.'

He let out his breath.

'All right, maybe we can stick it to them,' he said.

'When's the last time you heard of the feds dropping the dime on each other? You're a laugh a minute, Minos. Finish your cereal.'

'Always the PR man,' he said.

That afternoon the street was filled with hot sunshine when Cecil Aguillard and I parked our car in front of the poolroom on Main in New Iberia. Some college boys from Lafayette had pried the rubber machine off the wall of the men's room and had taken it out the back door.

'They ain't got rubbers in Lafayette? Why they got to steal mine?' said Tee Neg, the owner. He stood behind the bar, pointing his hand with the three missing fingers at me. The wood-bladed fans turned overhead, and I could smell *boudin* and gumbo in the kitchen. Several elderly men were drinking draft beer and playing *bourée* at the felt tables in back. 'They teach them that in col'ech? What I'm gonna do a man come in here for his rubber?'

'Tell them to take up celibacy,' I said.

Tee Neg's mouth was round with surprise and insult.

'*Mais* I don't talk that, me. What's the matter you say something like that to Tee Neg? I think you gone crazy, Dave.'

I walked out of the coolness of the poolroom into the hot sunlight to find Cecil, who had gone next door to get a description of the college boys' car. Just then a cream-colored Oldsmobile with tinted windows pulled out of the traffic. The driver didn't try to park; he simply stopped the car at an angle to the curb, dropped the transmission into neutral, flung open the door, and stepped onto the street with the engine still running. His hair was brushed with butch wax, his skin tanned as dark as a quadroon's. He wore expensive gray slacks, loafers with tassels, a pink polo shirt; but his narrow hips, wide shoulders, and boilerplate stomach made his clothes look like an unnecessary accident on his body. The wide-set, gray-blue eyes were round and staring and showed no expression, but the skin of his face was stretched so tight there were nests of fine white lines below his temples.

'What's happening, Bubba?' I said.

His fist shot out from his side, caught me squarely on the chin, and knocked me back through the open door of the poolroom. My clipboard clattered to the floor, I tried to catch myself against the wall, and then I saw him come flailing toward me out of the bright square of sunlight. I took two off the side of the head, ducked into a crouch, and smelled his cologne and sweat and heard his breath go out between his teeth as he missed with a roundhouse. I had forgotten how hard Bubba could hit. He rose on the balls of his feet with each punch, his muscular thighs and buttocks flexing like iron against his slacks. He never defended; he always attacked, swinging at the eyes and nose with such a vicious energy that you knew that once you were hurt he wouldn't stop until he had chopped your face into raw pork.

But I still had the reach on him, and I jabbed him in the eye with my left, saw his head come erect with the shock of the blow, and then I caught him flat on the jaw with a right cross. He reeled backwards and knocked over a brass cuspidor that rolled wetly across the floor. There was a red circle around his right eye, and I could see my knuckle marks on his cheek. He spit on the floor and hitched his slacks up on his navel with his thumb.

'If that's your best shot, your ass is glue,' he said.

Suddenly Cecil burst through the doorway, his jaw filled with Red Man, his baton and handcuffs clattering on his pistol belt, and picked up Bubba from behind, pinning his arms to his sides, and threw him headlong onto a *bourée* table and circle of chairs.

Bubba got to his feet, his slacks stained with tobacco juice, and I saw Cecil slip his baton out of its plastic ring and grip it tightly around the handle.

'You turning candy-ass on me, Dave?' Bubba said.

'How you like I break your face?' Cecil said.

'You were messing with Claudette. Don't lie about it, either, you sonofabitch. Keep Bruno on his chain, and I'll put out your lamp.'

'You're a dumb guy, Bubba.'

'So I didn't get to go to college like you. You want to finish it or not?'

'You're busted. Turn around and put your hands on the table.'

'Fuck you. I'll put that deputy's badge up your butt.'

Cecil started toward him, but I motioned him back. I grabbed Bubba's arm, which was as hard as a cedar post in my hand, and spun him toward the table.

Vanity, vanity.

His torso turned back toward me as though it were powered by an overstressed spring, his fist lifting into my face like a balloon. His eyes were almost crossed with the force he put into his blow. But he was off balance, and I bobbed sideways, felt his knuckles rake across the top of my ear, then drove my right fist as hard as I could into his mouth. Spittle

flew from his lips, his eyes snapped open wide, his nostrils flared white
with pain and shock. I caught him again with my left, above the eye, then
swung under his guard into his ribcage, right below the heart. He doubled
over and fell back against the bar and had to hold on to the mahogany
trim to keep from going down.

I was breathless, and my face felt numb and thick where he had hit me.
I pulled my handcuffs loose from the back of my belt. I snapped one cuff
over Bubba's wrist, then pulled his other arm behind him and locked on
the second cuff. I sat him down in a chair while he hung his head forward
and spit a string of bloody saliva between his knees.

'You want to go to the hospital?' I asked.

He was grinning, with a crazy light in his eyes. There was a red smear,
like lipstick, on his teeth.

'*Brasse ma chu*, Dave,' he said.

'You going to cuss me because you lost a fight?' I said. 'You've got
more class than that, Bubba. Do you want to go to the hospital or not?'

'Hey, Tee Neg,' he said to the owner. 'Give everybody a round. Put it
on my tab.'

'You ain't got a tab,' Tee Neg said. 'You ain't getting one, either.'

Cecil walked Bubba out to the car and locked him in behind the wire
screen. Green flecks of sawdust from the poolroom floor were stuck to
the butch wax in his hair. Through the car window he looked like a caged
animal. Cecil started the engine.

'Drive over into the park for a minute,' I said.

'What for?' Cecil asked.

'We're in no hurry. It's a nice day. Let's have a spearmint snowcone.'

We crossed the drawbridge over Bayou Teche. The water was brown
and high, and dragonflies flicked over the lily pads in the sunlight. Close
along the banks I could see the armored backs of cars turning in the shade
of the cypress trees. We drove through the oak-lined streets into the park,
passed the swimming pool, and stopped behind the baseball bleachers. I
gave Cecil two one-dollar bills.

'How about getting us three cones?' I said.

'Dave, that man belong in jail, not eating snowcones in the park, no,'
he said.

'It's something personal between me and Bubba, Cecil. I'm going to
ask you to respect that.'

'He's a pimp. He don't deserve no slack.'

'Maybe not, partner. But it's my collar.' I winked at him and grinned.

He didn't like it, but he walked away through the trees toward the
concession stand by the swimming pool. I could see kids springing off the
diving board into the sunlit blue water.

'Do you really think I was messing around with your wife?' I asked
Bubba through the wire-mesh screen.

'What the fuck do *you* call it?'

'Clean the shit out of your mouth and answer me straight.'

'She knows how to get a guy on the bone.'

'You're talking about your wife.'

'So? She's human.'

'Don't you know when you're being jerked around? You're supposed to be a smart man.'

'You thought about it when she was in your truck, though, didn't you?' he said, and smiled. His teeth were still pink with his blood. His arms were pulled behind him by the handcuffs, and his chest looked as round and hard as a small barrel. 'She just likes to flash her bread around sometimes. They all do. That doesn't mean you get to unzip your pants.

'Hey, tell me the truth, I really shook your peaches with that first shot, didn't I?'

'I'm going to tell you something, Bubba. I don't want you to take it the wrong way, either. Go to a psychiatrist. You're a rich man, you can afford it. You'll understand people better, you'll learn about yourself.'

'I bet I pay my gardener more than you make. Does that say something?'

'You're not a good listener. You never were. That's why one day you're going to take a big fall.'

I got out of the car and opened his door.

'What are you doing?' he said.

'Step out.'

I put one hand under his arm and helped him off the seat.

'Turn around,' I said.

'What's the game?'

'No game. I'm cutting you loose.'

I unlocked the cuffs. He rubbed his wrists with his hands. In the shade, the pupils of his gray-blue eyes stared at me like burnt cinders.

'I figure what happened at Tee Neg's was personal. So this time you walk. If you come at me again, you're going up the road.'

'Sounds like a Dick Tracy routine to me.'

'I don't know why, but I have a strong feeling you're a man without a future.'

'Yeah?'

'They're going to eat your lunch.'

'Who's this "they" you're talking about?'

'The feds, us, your own kind. It'll happen one day when you never expect it. Just like when Eddie Keats set one of your hookers on fire. She was probably thinking about a vacation in the Islands when he knocked on her door with a smile on his face.'

'I've had cops give me that shuck before. It always comes from the same kind of guys. They got no case, no evidence, no witness, so they make a lot of noise that's supposed to scare everybody. But you know what their real problem is? They wear J. C. Higgins suits, they drive shit machines, they live in little boxes out by an airport. Then they see a guy that's got all the things they want and can't have because most of them are so dumb they'd fuck up a wet dream, so they get a big hard-on for this guy and talk a lot of trash about somebody cooling out his action. So I'll tell you what I tell these other guys. I'll be around to drink a beer and piss it on your grave.'

He took a stick of gum out of his pocket, peeled off the foil, dropped it on the ground, and fed the gum into his mouth while he looked me in the eyes.

'You through with me?' he asked.

'Yep.'

'By the way, I got drunk last night, so don't buy yourself any boxing trophies yet.'

'I gave up keeping score a long time ago. It comes with maturity.'

'Yeah? Tell yourself that the next time you look at your bank account. I owe you one for cutting me loose. Buy yourself something nice and send me the bill. I'll see you around.'

'Don't misunderstand the gesture. If I find out you're connected to my wife's death, God help you, Bubba.'

He chewed his gum, looked off at the swimming pool as though he were preparing to answer, but instead walked away through the oak trees, the soles of his loafers loud on the crisp, dead leaves. Then he stopped and turned around.

'Hey, Dave, when I straighten out a problem, the person gets to see this face. You give that some thought.'

He walked on farther, then turned again, his spiked hair and tan face mottled with sun and shadow.

'Hey, you remember when we used to play ball here and yell at each other, "I got your Dreamsicle hanging"?' he said, grinning, and grabbed his phallus through his slacks. 'Those were the days, podna.'

I bought a small bag of crushed ice, took it back to the office with me, and let it melt in a clean plastic bucket. Every fifteen minutes I soaked a towel in the cold water and kept it pressed to my face while I counted to sixty. It wasn't the most pleasant way to spend the afternoon, but it beat waking up the next day with a face that looked like a lopsided plum.

Then, just before quitting time, I sat at my desk in my small office, while the late sun beat down on the sugarcane fields across the road, and looked once again at the file the New Orleans police department had sent us on Victor Romero. In his front and side mug shots his black curls hung down on his forehead and ears. As in all police station photography, the black-and-white contrast was severe. His hair glistened as though it were oiled; his skin was the color of bone; his unshaved cheeks and chin looked touched with soot.

His criminal career wasn't a distinguished one. He had four misdemeanor arrests, including one for contributing to prostitution; he had done one hundred eighty days in the parish jail for possession of burglar tools; he had an outstanding bench warrant for failing to appear on a DWI charge. But contrary to popular belief, a rap sheet often tells little about a suspect. It records only the crimes he was charged with, not the hundreds he may have committed. It also offers no explanation of what goes on in the mind of a man like Victor Romero.

His eyes had no expression in the photographs. He could have been waiting for a bus when the camera lens clicked. Was this the man who had murdered Annie with a shotgun, who had fired point-blank at her with buckshot while she screamed and tried to hide her face behind her arms? Was he made up of the same corpuscle, sinew, and marrow as I? Or was his brain taken hot from a furnace, his parts hammered together in a shower of sparks on a devil's anvil?

Next morning the call came in from the St Martin Parish sheriff's office. A black man, fishing in his pirogue by the Henderson levee, had looked down into the water and seen a submerged automobile. A police diver had just gone down on it. The automobile was a maroon Toyota and the driver was still in it. The parish coroner and a tow truck were on their way from St Martinville.

I called Minos at the DEA in Lafayette and told him to meet me there.

'This impresses me,' he said. 'It's professional, it's cooperative. Who said you guys were rural bumblers?'

'Put the cork in it, Minos.'

Twenty minutes later, Cecil and I were at the levee on the edge of the Atchafalaya swamp. It was already hot, the sun shimmered on the vast expanse of water, and the islands of willow trees looked still and green in the heat. Late-morning fishermen were trying for bluegill and goggle-eye in the pilings of the oil platforms that dotted the bays or in the shade of the long concrete causeway that spanned the entire marsh. Turkey buzzards floated high on the updrafts against the white sky. I could smell dead fish in the lily pads and cattails that grew along the shore. Farther out from the bank, the black heads of water moccasins stuck out of the water like motionless twigs.

The ground had been wet when the car went off the crown of the levee. The tire tracks ran down at an angle through the grass and buttercups, cut deeply through a slough, and disappeared in the slit beyond a deep-water dropoff. The tow-truck driver, a sweating, barrel-chested man in Levi's with no shirt, fed the hook and cable off the truck to the police diver, who stood in the shallows in a bright yellow bikini with a mask and snorkel strapped to his face. Under the rippling sunlight on the water, I could see the dim outline of the Toyota.

Minos parked his car and walked down the levee just as the tow-truck driver engaged his winch and the cable clanged taut against the Toyota's frame.

'What do you figure happened?' Minos said.

'You got me.'

'You think you parked one in him, after all?'

'Who knows? Even if I did, why would he drive out here?'

'Maybe he went away to die. Even a piece of shit like this guy probably knows that's one thing you got to do by yourself.'

He saw me look at the side of his face. He bit off a hangnail, spit it off the end of his tongue, and looked at the wrecker cable quivering against the surface of the water.

'Sorry,' he said.

A cloud of yellow sand mushroomed under the water, and suddenly the rear end of the Toyota burst through a tangle of lily pads and up-rooted cattails into the sunlight. The tow-truck driver dragged the car clear of the water's edge and bounced it on the bank, the broken back window gaping like a ragged mouth. Two St Martin Parish sheriff's deputies opened the side doors, and a flood of water, silt, moss, yellowed vegetation, and fish-eels cascaded out on the ground. The eels were long and fat, with bright silver scales and red gills, and they writhed and snapped among the buttercups like tangles of snakes. The man in the front seat had fallen sideways so that his head hung out the passenger's door. His head was strung with dead vines and covered with mud and leeches. Minos tried to see over my shoulder as I looked down at the dead man.

'Jesus Christ, half his face is eaten off,' he said.

'Yep.'

'Well, maybe Victor wanted to be part of the bayou country.'

'It's not Victor Romero,' I said. 'It's Eddie Keats.'

9

A deputy started to pull him by his wrists onto the grass, then wiped his palms on his pants and found a piece of newspaper in the weeds. He wrapped it around Keats's arm and jerked him out on the ground. The water sloshed out of Keats's suede cowboy boots, and his shirt was unbuttoned and pulled up on his chest. There was a black, puffed hole the size of my thumb in his right ribcage, with a seared area around the skin flap, and an exit wound under the left arm pit. The deputy nudged Keats's arm with his shoe to expose the wound better.

'It looks like somebody scooped it out with a tablespoon, don't it?' he said.

The coroner motioned to two paramedics who stood by the back of an ambulance parked at the top of the levee. They pulled the gurney out of the ambulance and started down the slope with it. A black body bag was folded under one of the canvas straps.

'How long has he been in the water?' I asked the coroner.

'Two or three days,' he said. He was a big, fat, bald man, with a shirt pocket full of cigars. His buttocks looked like watermelons. He squinted in the brightness of the sun's reflection off the water. 'They turn white and ripen pretty fast in this weather. He hasn't gotten mushy yet, but he was working on it. Y'all know him?'

'He was a low-level button man,' I said.

'A what?'

'A contract killer. The bargain-basement variety,' Minos said.

'Well, somebody sure stirred his hash for him,' the coroner said.

'What kind of gun are we talking about?' Minos said.

'It's going to be guesswork because there's no bullet. Maybe some fragments, but they won't help much. Offhand, I'd rule out a rifle. The muzzle flash burned his skin, so it was pressed right up against him. But the angle was upward, which would mean the shooter would have to hold the rifle low and depress the stock he fired, which wouldn't make much sense. So I'd say he was killed with a pistol, a big one, maybe a .44 Magnum or a .45 loaded with soft-nosed shells or hollowpoints. He must

344

have thought somebody stuffed a hand grenade down his throat. Y'all look perplexed.'

'You might say that,' Minos said.

'What's the problem?' the coroner said.

'The wrong guy's in the car,' I said.

'He sounds like the right guy to me. Count your blessings,' the coroner said. 'You want to look through his pockets before we bag him up?'

'I'll be over to St Martinville later,' I said. 'I'd like a copy of the autopsy report, too.'

'Hell, come on over and watch. I'll have him apart in ten minutes.' His eyes were bright and a smile worked around the corners of his mouth. 'Relax. I just like to have a little fun with you guys sometimes. I'll have a copy ready for you by tonight.'

The paramedics unzipped the body bag and lifted Eddie Keats into it. A fish-eel fell out of his pants leg and flipped in the weeds as though its back were broken.

A few minutes later, Minos and I watched the ambulance, the coroner's car, and the two St Martin parish sheriff's cars disappear down the levee. The tow-truck driver was having trouble with his winch, and he and Cecil were trying to fix it. A hot wind blew across the marsh and ruffled the water and flattened the buttercups around our feet. I could smell the schools of bluegill that were feeding on the mosquitoes in the shade of the willow islands.

Minos walked down to the Toyota and rubbed his thumb over one of my .45 holes in the trunk. The hole was smooth and silver around the edges, as though it had been cut by a machinist's punch.

'Are you sure Keats wasn't in the car when Romero shot at you?' he said.

'Not unless he was hiding on the floor.'

'Then how did he get into the Toyota, and what did somebody have to gain by blowing up his shit and then dumping him with a car we were bound to find?'

'I don't know.'

'Give me your speculations.'

'I told you, I don't know.'

'Come on, how many people had reason to snuff him?'

'About half the earth.'

'Around here, how many people?'

'What are you getting at?'

'I'm not sure. I just know I want Bubba Rocque, and the people who could help me put him away keep showing up dead. That pisses me off.'

'It probably pissed Keats off a lot worse.'

'I don't think that's clever.'

'I've got a revelation for you, Minos. Homicide isn't like narcotics.

Your clientele breaks the law for one reason – money. But people kill each other for all kinds of reasons, and sometimes the reasons aren't logical ones. Particularly when you're talking about Keats and his crowd.'

'You know, you always give me the feeling you tell other people only what you think they should know. Why is it that I always have that feeling about you?'

'Search me.'

'I also have the feeling that you don't care how these guys get scratched, as long as they're off the board.'

I walked down to the Toyota's open passenger door, rested my arm on top, and looked inside again. There wasn't much of significance to see: shards of glass on the floorboards, two exit holes in the cloth of the passenger's seat, pieces of splintered lead embedded in the dashboard, a long furrow in the headliner. A warm, wet odor rose from the upholstery.

'I think Romero drove the Toyota out here to dump it,' I said. 'I think Keats was supposed to meet him with another car. Then for some reason Romero blew him away. Maybe it was just an argument between the two of them. Maybe Keats was supposed to whack him and it didn't go right.'

'Why would Keats want to whack Romero?'

'How the hell should I know? Look, we shouldn't even be talking about Romero. He should have been sent up the road when he first got busted. Why don't you turn the screws on your colleagues?'

'Maybe I have. Maybe they're not happy with the situation, either. Sometimes these assholes get off their leashes. One time we put a street dealer in the protected-witness program and he paid us back by shooting a liquor store clerk. It works out like that sometimes.'

'I'm not sympathetic. Come on, Cecil. See you around, Minos.'

Cecil and I headed down the levee past boat rentals, the bait shops and beer joints, the fish camps set up on stilts. Out in the water, the strips of moss on the dead cypress trees lifted and fell in the wind. I bought Cecil a catfish plate in a Negro café in Breaux Bridge, then we drove back to New Iberia while the heat danced on the road in front of us.

I spent the next two hours doing paperwork at the office, but I couldn't concentrate on the forms and folders that were spread around my desk-top. I was never good at administration or clerical tasks, primarily because I always felt they had little to do with the job at hand and were created for people who made careers of running in place. And like most middle-aged people who hear the clock ticking in their lives, I had come to resent a waste or theft of my time that was far greater than any theft of my goods or money.

I fixed a cup of coffee and stared out the window at the trees in the sunlight. I called home to check on Alafair, then called Batist at the dock. I went to the rest room when I really didn't have to go. Then once again I looked at my uncompleted mileage report, my time and activity report, my arrest reports on local characters who had already bonded out and would probably be cut loose altogether before court appearance. I opened the largest drawer in my desk and dropped all my paperwork into it, eased the drawer shut with my shoe, signed out of the office, and went home just in time to see a taxicab leave Robin Gaddis with her suitcase on my front porch.

She wore patent leather spiked heels with Levi's, and a loose blouse that looked as if it was touched with pink and gray shades from a water-color brush. I turned off the truck's engine and walked toward her across the dead pecan leaves in the yard. She smiled and lighted a cigarette, blowing the smoke up into the air, and tried to look relaxed and pleasant, but her eyes were bright and her face tight with anxiety.

'Wow, this is really out among the pelicans and the alligators,' she said. 'You got snakes and nutrias and all that stuff crawling around under your house?'

'How you doing, Robin?'

'Ask me after I'm sure I'm back on earth. I flew on one of those greaseball airlines where the pilot's got a three-day beard and blows garlic and Boone's Farm all over the place. We were dropping through the air pockets so fast you couldn't hear the engines, and all the time they're playing mambo music on the loudspeakers and I'm smelling reefer out of the front of the plane.'

I took her hand, then felt as awkward as she. I put my arms lightly around her shoulders and kissed her cheek. Her hair was warm and there were fine drops of perspiration behind her neck. Her stomach brushed against me, and I felt my loins quiver and the muscles in my back stiffen.

'I guess it's not your day for Cro-Magnon bear hugs,' she said. 'That's cool, Streak. Don't worry about it. I'm copacetic. Don't worry about what you might have to tell me, either. Mommy's been taking care of herself a long time. I just got this urge to get on a thirty-nine-dollar flight with Kamikaze Airlines and couldn't resist.'

'What happened in Key West?'

'I made a change that didn't work out.'

'Like what?'

Her eyes went away from me and looked out into the hot shade of the pecan trees.

'I couldn't take serving corn fritters to the Howdy Doody crowd from Des Moines any longer. I met this guy who owns a disco on the other side of the island. It's supposed to be a high-class joint, full of big tippers. Except guess what? I find out it's full of queers, and the guy and his head bartender are running a clever late-hour scam on these guys. A tourist comes in, some guy who's not out of the closet yet, who's probably got a wife and kiddies in Meridian, and when he's good and shitfaced and trying to cop some kid's bread, they use his MasterCard to run off a half-dozen charges for thirty-dollar magnum bottles of champagne and trace his signature on them later. When he gets the bill a month later in Meridian, he's not going to holler about it because he either doesn't remember what he did or he doesn't want anybody to know he was hanging around with Maneaters Incorporated.

'So one night just after closing I told the owner and his bartender I thought they were a couple of pricks. The owner sits on the stool next to me, with a kindly smile on his face like I just walked off the cattle truck, and slides his hand up my leg. All the time he's looking me in the eyes because he knows that mommy doesn't have any money, that mommy doesn't have another job, that mommy doesn't have any friends. Except I'm drinking a cup of coffee that's hot enough to take the paint off a battleship, and I pour it right on his oysters.

'I heard the next day he was walking around like he had a mousetrap hanging off his equipment. But' – she clicked her tongue and tossed back her hair – 'I've got a hundred and twelve bucks, Streak, and no compo because the guy and his bartender told the state employment office I was fired for not ringing up drinks and pocketing the money.'

I rubbed the back of her neck with my hand and picked up her suitcase.

'We have a big house here. It gets hot during the day sometimes, but it's cool at night. I think you'll like it,' I said, and opened the screen for her. 'I need somebody to help me at the dock, too.'

And I thought, *Oh Lord.*

'You mean sell worms and that stuff?' she said.

'Sure.'

'Wow, Worms. Out of sight, Streak.'

'I have a little girl and a baby-sitter who live with me, too. But we have a room in back we don't use. I'll put a fold-out bed in it and a fan in the window.'

'Oh.'

'I sleep out here on the couch, Robin.'

'Yeah, I see.'

'Insomnia and all that bullshit. I watch the late show every night until I fall asleep.'

I saw her eyes stray to the lock and hasp on my bedroom door.

'It looks like a great place. Did you grow up here?' she said.

'Yes.'

She sat down on the couch and I saw the fatigue come into her face. She put out her cigarette in the empty candy dish on my coffee table.

'You don't smoke, do you? I'm probably polluting your house,' she said.

'Don't worry about it.'

'Dave, I know I'm making complications for you. I don't mean to.

A girl just gets up against the wall sometimes. You know, it was either hit on you or go back to the T-and-A circuit. I just can't cut that anymore.'

I sat down next to her and put my arm around her shoulder. I felt her resist at first, then she lay her head under my chin. I touched her cheek and her mouth with my fingers and kissed her forehead. I tried to tell myself that I would be only a friend to her and not her ex-lover whose heart could be so easily activated by a woman's quiet and regular breathing against his chest.

But my life's history was one of failed promises and resolutions. Alafair, the baby-sitter, Robin, and I ate red beans, rice, and sausage on the kitchen table while it thundered outside and the wind shook the trees against the house and the rain clattered on the roof in sheets and poured off the eaves. Then the skies cleared, and the moon came up over the wet fields and the breeze smelled of earth and flowers and sugar-cane. She came into the living room after midnight. The moonlight fell in ivory squares on the floor, and the outline of her long legs and bare shoulders and arms seemed to glow with a cool light. She sat on the couch, leaned over me, and kissed me on the mouth. I could smell her perfume and the baby powder on her neck. She put her fingers on my face, slipped them through my hair, brushed the white patch above my ear as though she were discovering a curiosity in me for the first time. She wore a short negligée, and her breasts were stiff against the nylon, and when I moved my hands up her sides and along her back, her skin was as hot to the touch as if she had been in the sun all day. I pulled her lengthwise against me, felt her thighs open, felt her hand take me inside her. Then I was lost inside her woman's heat, the sound her mouth made against my ear, the pressure of her calves inside mine, and finally my own confession of need and dependency and my inability to impose order on my life. Once I thought I heard a car on the road, I felt myself jerk inside, as though I were being pulled violently from sleep, but she propped herself up on her elbows over me, looked quietly into my face with her dark eyes, and kissed me on the mouth while her hand pressed me inside her again, as though her love were enough to dispel shadows from the corners of my nocturnal heart.

The telephone woke me at four AM. I answered it in the kitchen and closed the door to the hall so as not to wake the rest of the house. The moon was still up, and a soft ivory light fell on the mimosa tree and redwood picnic table in the backyard.

'I found a bar with an honest-to-God *zydeco* band,' Minos said. 'You remember Clifton Chenier? These guys play just like Clifton Chenier used to.'

I could hear a jukebox, then the record stopped and I could hear bottles clinking.

'Where are you?'

'I told you. In a bar in Opelousas.'

'It's pretty late for *zydeco*, Minos.'

'I've got a story for you. Hell, I've got a bunch of them. Did you know I was in army intelligence in Vietnam?'

'No.'

'Well, it's no big deal. But sometimes we had problems that fell outside the rulebook. There was this French civilian who gave us a lot of trouble.'

'Do you have your car?'

'Sure.'

'Leave it in the parking lot. Take a cab to a motel. Don't drive back to Lafayette. You understand?'

'Listen, this French civilian was hooked in with the VC in Saigon. He had whores and some people on our bases reporting to him, and maybe he helped torture one of our agents to death. But we couldn't prove it, and because he had a frog passport, he was a touchy item to deal with.'

'I'm not interested in talking with you about Vietnam.'

'In the meantime the major is looking like a dumb shit that can't handle the action. So we call in a sergeant who did little jobs for us from time to time, like crawl into a ville at night and slit somebody's throat from ear to ear with a barber's razor. He was going to get the frog with a night scope, nail him from fifty yards out and be back at the NCO club for beers before they could blot the guy's brains off the wallpaper. But guess what? He got the wrong fucking house. A Dutch businessman was eating snails with his chopsticks, and our good sergeant blew his face all over his wife's blouse.'

'I've got some advice for you, Minos. Fuck Vietnam. Get it the hell out of your life.'

'I'm not talking about Vietnam. I'm talking about you and me, podna. It's like something F. Scott Fitzgerald wrote. We serve a vast, vulgar, meretricious enterprise.'

'Look, get something to eat and I'll come up there.'

'There's some government people who want to cut a deal with Romero.'

'What?'

'He's got a lot of shit on a lot of people. He's valuable to us. Or at least to somebody.'

I felt my hand clench on the telephone receiver. The wooden chair I sat on felt hard against my bare thighs and back.

'Is this straight?' I said. 'Your people are talking with Romero? They know where he is?'

'Don't say "my people." He got word to some other federal agents in New Orleans. They don't know where he is, but he says he'll come in for the right deal. You know what I told them?'

I could hear my breath against the holes in the telephone.

'I told them, "Cut all the fucking deals you want. Robicheaux ain't going to play," ' he said. 'I have to say that made me feel kind of good.'

'Which bar are you in?'

'Forget about me. I was right, though, wasn't I? You're not going to bargain?'

'I want to talk with you tomorrow.'

'Hell, no. What you hear now is all you get. Now I want you to tell me something fair and square. You don't have to admit anything. Just tell me I'm wrong. You found the Toyota, you rounded up Keats, you took him out to the levee and put that .45 of yours between his ribs and blew his lungs out his mouth, Right?'

'Wrong.'

'Come on, Robicheaux. You showed up at the Haitian's in New Orleans right after the cops did. What are the odds of you just blundering into a situation like that? Then another guy you truly hate, somebody whose nose you crushed into marmalade with a pool cue, shows up dead by the Henderson levee. Keats was from Brooklyn. He didn't know anything about that area. Neither does Romero. But you've been fishing that swamp all your life. If anybody else but a bunch of coonass cops were handling this case, you'd be in jail.'

'Take two vitamin B and four aspirins before you go to bed,' I said. 'You won't run the four-minute mile tomorrow, but at least the snakes won't be crawling.'

'I'm all wet, huh?'

'You've got it. I'm going to sign off now. I hope they don't put you through the wringer. For a government man, you're a pretty good guy, Dunkenstein.'

He was still talking when I eased the phone receiver back into the cradle. Outside, I could hear night birds calling to each other in the fields.

After work that day, I took Robin and Alafair down to Cypremort Point for dinner. We ate boiled shrimp and bluepoint crabs in a ramshackle, screened-in restaurant by the bay, and in the mauve twilight the water looked flat and gray, rippled in places by a slight breeze, like wrinkles in a skim of paint, and in the west the distant islands of sawgrass were edged with the sun's last red glow on the horizon. Behind us I could see the long, two-lane road that led down through the Point, the dead cypress trees that were covered with shadows now, the fishing shacks built up on stilts above the flooded woods, the pirogues tied to the cabin pilings, the carpet of blooming lily pads on the canals, the herons that lifted on extended wings into the lavender sky like a whispered poem.

The big electric fans in the restaurant vibrated with their own energy; the wood tables were littered with crab shells; bugs beat against the screen as the light went out of the sky; and somebody played 'La Jolie Blonde' on the jukebox. Robin's dark hair moved in the breeze, and her eyes were bright and happy, and there was a smear of *sauce piquante* on the corner of her mouth. With all her hard mileage, she was a good girl inside and she took hold of my affections in a funny way. You fall in love with women for different reasons, I guess. Sometimes they are simply beautiful and you have no more control over your desire for them than you do in choosing your nocturnal dreams. Then there are others who earn their way into your soul, who are kind and loyal and loving in the way that your mother was or should have been. Then there's that strange girl who walks unexpectedly off a side street into the middle of your life, the one who is nothing like the indistinct and warm presence who has lived with you for so long on the soft edge of sleep. Instead, her clothes are all wrong, her lipstick mismatched, her handbag clutched like a shield, her eyes wide and bright, as though the Greek Furies were calling to her from the stage wings.

Robin and I made an agreement. I would discharge the baby-sitter, and she would help me take care of Alafair and work at the bait shop. She promised me she was off the booze and the dope, and I believed her, although I didn't know how long her resolution would last. I don't understand alcoholism, and I cannot tell you for sure what an alcoholic is. I've known some people who quit on their own, then became white-knucklers who boiled with a metabolic and psychological misery that finally caused them to blow out their doors and come into AA on their kneecaps. I've known others who simply stopped drinking one day and lived out their lives in a gray, neutral area like people who had clipped all the sharp edges off their souls until they seemed to be operating on the spiritual energies of a moth. The only absolute conclusion I ever made about alcoholics was that I was one of them. What others did with booze had no application to my life, as long as they didn't press it on Dave Robicheaux, who was altogether too willing a victim.

We drove back through the long corridor of dead cypress trees, the fireflies lighting in the dark, and rented a VCR and a Walt Disney movie at the video store in New Iberia. Later, Batist came by the house with some fresh *boudin,* and we heated it in the oven and made lemonade with cracked ice and mint leaves in the glasses and watched the movie in the living room under the wood-bladed fan. When I got up to fill the lemonade pitcher again, I looked at the flicker of the screen on Robin's and Alafair's and Batist's faces and felt a strange sense of family belonging that I hadn't felt since Annie's death.

I went home for lunch the next day and was eating a ham and onion sandwich at the kitchen table when the phone rang. It was a beautiful, sunny day, the sky a clear blue above the trees, and through the back window I could see Alafair playing with one of my calico cats in the backyard. She wore her LEFT and RIGHT pink tennis shoes, a pair of denim pedal pushers, and the yellow Donald Duck T-shirt that Annie had bought for her, and she swung a piece of kite twine back and forth in front of the cat's churning paws. I chewed on the ham and bread in my mouth and placed the telephone receiver idly against my ear. I could hear the dull whirring of a long-distance connection, like wind blowing in a conch shell.

'Is this Robicheaux?'

'Yes. Who's this?'

'The cop, right?' His voice sounded as if it were strained through wet sand.

'That's right. You want to tell me who this is?'

'It's Victor Romero. I got a lot of people on my case, and I'm hearing a lot of stuff I don't like to hear. Most of it's got your name in it.'

The piece of sandwich felt stiff and dead in my jaw. I pushed my plate away and felt myself sit up straight in my chair.

'You still there?' he said. I heard a peculiar thump, then a hissing sound in the background.

'Yes.'

'Everybody wants to cut a slice out of my ass, like I'm responsible for every crime in Louisiana. They got the word on the street that maybe I'm going away for thirty years. They're talking that maybe I killed some people in a plane, that maybe they'll turn me over to the locals and get me fried in Angola. So everybody in New Orleans hears the feds got a big hard-on for me, that don't nobody touch me because I'm like the stink on shit and they better not get it on their hands, either. You listening to me?'

'Yes.'

'So I told them I'd deal. They want these big fuckers, and I get some slack. I tell them I'll come in for three. No more than three, that's it. Except what do I hear? This cat Robicheaux is a hardtail and he don't play. So you're fucking me, man.'

I could feel my heart beating, feel the blood in the back of my neck and in my temples.

'Do you want to meet somewhere and talk?' I said.

'You must be out of your goddamn mind.'

Then I heard the thump again, followed by the hissing sound.

'I want you to talk to those cocksuckers at the DEA,' he said. 'I want you to tell them no charges because you thought somebody shot at you. You get the fuck off my back. I get that message from the right guy, and maybe I deliver something you want.'

'I don't think you've got anything to bargain with, Romero. I think you're a nickel-and-dime mule that everybody's tired of. Why don't you write all this bullshit on a postcard and I'll read it when I don't have anything else to do.'

'Yeah?'

I didn't answer. He was quiet a moment, then he spoke again.

'You want to know who set up the whack on your wife?'

I was breathing deeply now, and wires were trembling inside my chest. I swallowed and kept my voice as flat as possible.

'All I hear from you is noise. You got something to trade, get it out of your mouth or stop bothering me,' I said.

'You think I'm talking noise, huh? Try this, motherfucker. You had a fan in your bedroom window. You had a telephone in your hall, except somebody tore it out of the wall for you. And while they did your old lady, you were hiding outside in the dark.'

I felt my hand slide up and down my flexed thigh. I had to wet my lips before I could speak again. I should have been silent, said nothing, but the control was now gone.

'I'll find you,' I said hoarsely.

'Find me and you find nothing. I got all this from the boon. You want the rest of the story, you come up with a deal that don't leave me in the barrel. You got a guilty conscience, man, and I ain't taking your fall.'

'Listen—'

'No, I talk, you listen. You get together with that bunch of farts at the Federal Building and decide what you want to do. You come up with the right numbers – and I'm talking three years max, in a minimum-security joint – then you run an ad in the *Times-Picayune* that says, "Victor, your situation is approved." I see that ad, maybe a lawyer's gonna call up the DEA and see about a meet.'

'Eddie Keats tried to dust you. They're going to take you out just like they did the Haitian. You're running out of ratholes.'

'Kiss my ass. I ate bugs and lizards for thirty-eight days and came back with eleven gook ears on a stick. I'm buying the paper Sunday morning. After that, forget it. Clean up your own shit.'

Before he hung up I thought I heard a streetcar bell clang.

The rest of the afternoon I tried to recreate his voice in my mind. Had I heard it once before, in a rumble of thunder, on my front porch? I couldn't be sure. But the thought that I had held a conversation about plea-bargaining with one of Annie's murderers worked and twisted in my brain like an obscene finger.

Sometime after midnight, I woke with a thick, numb feeling in my head, the kind you have after you've been out in a cold wind a long time by yourself. I sat quietly on the edge of the couch, my bare feet resting in a square of moonlight on the floor, and opened and closed my hands as though I were seeing them for the first time. Then I unlocked Annie's and my bedroom and sat on the edge of the mattress in the dark.

The bloody sheets and bedspread had been carried off in a vinyl evidence bag, but the mattress and the wooden bedstead were filled with holes that I could fit my fingers into as though I were probing the wounds in Our Lord's hands. The brown patterns all over the bedstead and the flowered wallpaper could have been slung there by a paintbrush. I rubbed my hand across the wall and felt the stiff, torn edges of the paper where the buckshot and deer slugs had torn through the wood. The moon shone through the pecan tree outside and made an oval of light in my lap. I felt as solitary as if I had been sitting in the bottom of a dry, cool well, with strips of silver cloud floating by against a dark sky.

I thought about my father and wished he were there with me. He couldn't read or write and never once traveled outside the state of Louisiana, but his heart possessed an intuitive understanding about our lives, our Cajun vision of the world, that no philosophy book could convey. He drank too much and he'd fistfight two or three men in a bar at the same time, with the enthusiasm of a boy hitting baseballs, but inside he had a gentle heart, a strong sense of right and wrong, and a tragic sense about the cruelty and violence that the world sometimes imposes upon the innocent.

He told me a story once about a killing that he'd seen as a young man. In my father's mind, the victim's death was emblematic of all the unjust and brutal behavior that people are capable of in groups, although in reality the victim was not an innocent man. It was the winter of 1935, and a criminal who had robbed banks with John Dillinger and Homer Van Meter had been flushed out of Margaret's whorehouse in Opelousas, a brothel that had been operating since the War Between the States. Cops chased him all the way to Iberia Parish, and when his car slid into a ditch, he struck out across a frozen field of sugarcane stubble. My father and a Negro were pulling stumps with a mule and trace chains and burning them in big heaps when the robber ran past them toward the old barn by our windmill. My father said he wore a white shirt with cufflinks and a bow tie, with no coat, and he gripped a straw boater in his hand as though it were his last possession on earth.

A cop fired a rifle from the road, and one of the robber's legs collapsed and he went down in the middle of the stubble. The cops all wore suits and fedoras, and they walked in a line across the field as though they were flushing quail. They formed a half-circle around the wounded man, while he sat with his legs straight out before him and begged for his life. My father said that when they started shooting with their revolvers and automatic pistols, the man's shirt exploded with crimson flowers.

With crimson flowers, that turned brown, that can be bruised into the grain of wood, that flake and shale away under the touch of my fingers. Because they impaled her upon this bedstead and this wall, drove her screams and her fear and her agony deep into this wood, translated these cypress boards, hewn by my father, into her crucifix.

I felt a hand on my shoulder. I stared up at Robin, whose face and body looked strangely pale in the moonlight that fell through the pecan tree into the room. She slipped her hand under my arm and pulled me up gently from the edge of the bed.

'It's no good for you in here, Streak,' she said quietly. 'I'll fix us warm milk in the kitchen.'

'Sure. Is the phone still ringing?'

'What?'

'The phone. I heard it ringing.'

'No. It didn't ri– Dave, come on out of here.'

'It didn't ring, huh? When I used to have the DTs, dead people would call me up on the phone. It was a crazy way to be back then.'

That morning I drove back to New Orleans to look for Victor Romero. As I said before, his sheet wasn't much help, and I knew that undoubtedly he was a more intelligent and far more dangerous man that it indicated. However, it was also obvious from his record that he had the same vices and sordid preoccupations and worm's-eye view of the world as did most of his kind. I talked with street people in the Quarter, bartenders, some strippers who hooked on the side, late-hour cabdrivers who pimped for the strippers, a couple of black Murphy artists, door spielers on Bourbon, a fence in Algiers, a terminal junkie who was down to shooting into his wasted thighs with an eye-dropper insulated with the white edge of a one-dollar bill. If they admitted having known Romero, they said they thought he was dead, out of the country, or in federal custody. In each instance, I might as well have held a conversation with a vacant lot.

But sometimes what you don't hear is a statement in itself. I was convinced he was still in New Orleans – I had heard the streetcar bell in the background when he called – and if he was in town, somebody was probably hiding or supporting him, because he wasn't pimping or deal-ing. I went down to First District headquarters on the edge of the Quarter and talked to two detectives in vice. They said they had already tried to find Romero through his relatives, and there weren't any. His father had been a fruit picker who disappeared in Florida in the 1960s, and the mother had died in the state mental hospital at Mandeville. There were no brothers or sisters.

'How about girlfriends?' I said.

'Outside of whores, you're talking about his fist,' one of the detectives said.

I drove back to New Iberia in a late-afternoon shower. The sun was shining while it rained, and the yellow surface of the Atchafalaya marsh danced with light.

I turned off at Breaux Bridge and parked my truck on the Henderson levee and stood among the buttercups and blue-bonnets and watched the light rain fall on the bays and the flooded cypress trees. The levee was thick with enormous black and yellow grasshoppers that sprang out of the grass, their lacquered backs shining in the wet light. When I was a boy, my brother and I would trap them with our straw hats, bait our trotline with them at sunset and string it between two abandoned oil platforms, and in the morning the line would be so taut and heavy with mudcat that it would take both of us to lift it clear of the water.

I was becoming tired of being a policeman again. Hold your soul against an emery wheel long enough, and one day you'll have only air between your hands. And with that thought in mind, I left Alafair with Batist that night and took Robin to the races at Evangeline Downs in Lafayette. We ate shrimp and steak in the clubhouse, then went back out to the open-air seats and sat in a box by the finish line. It was a balmy night, and heat lightning flickered all over the southern horizon; the sod, still damp from the afternoon shower, had been freshly raked, and halos of moisture glowed in the arc lamps over head. Robin wore a white cotton sundress with purple and green tiger lilies printed on it, and her tanned neck and shoulders looked smooth and cool in the shadowy light. She had never been to a horse race before, and I let her pick the horses in the first three races. She chose one horse because of the white stockings on its feet, a second because of the jockey's purple silks, a third because she said the jockey's face was shaped like a toy heart. All three placed or showed, and she was hooked. Each time the horses thundered around the last turn and then spread out from the rail as they went into the home stretch, the jockeys whipping the quirts into their flanks, the torn sod flying in the air, she would be on her feet, her arms locked in mine, her breast pressed hard against me, her whole body jiggling and bouncing in excitement. We cashed $178 worth of tickets at the pay window that night, and on the way home we stopped at a late-hour market and bought Batist and his wife a fruit-and-cheese basket with a bottle of Cold Duck in it. When I turned the truck off on the dirt road that led along the bayou south of New Iberia, she was asleep with her head on my shoulder, her hand limp inside my shirt, her lips parted in the moonlight as though she were going to whisper a little girl's secret to me.

I hadn't been able to find the living, so I thought I might have better luck investigating the dead. The next afternoon Cecil and I drove to the Jungle Room on the Breaux Bridge road to see what we could learn, if anything, about Eddie Keats's connection to Victor Romero. In the blazing sunlight, the white shale parking lot and the purple cinder-block front wall with its painted coconut trees and fingernail-polish-red front door were like a slap across the eyes. But the inside was as dark as a cave, except for the soft lights behind the bar, and it smelled of the insecticide that an Orkin man was spraying with a tank in the corners of the building. Two weary and hungover-looking women were smoking cigarettes and drinking Bloody Marys at the bar. The bartender was putting long-necked beer bottles in the cooler, his wide back ridging with muscle each time he bent over. He had platinum hair and bronze arms and he wore no shirt and a flowered silver vest that shone like dull tin. High up on the wall was the wire cage where the monkey sat among his peanut hulls and soiled newspapers.

I showed my badge to the two women and asked them when was the last time they had seen Eddie. Their eyes looked at nothing; they blew smoke up in the air, flipped their ashes into ashtrays, and were as unknowledgeable and lifeless as cardboard cutouts.

Had they seen Victor Romero lately?

Their eyes were vague and empty, and their cigarettes moved back into their mouths in slow motion and then back out into the exhaled smoke.

'I understand the funeral was this morning. Did Eddie get a nice service?' I said.

'They cremated him and put him in a vase or something. I got up too late to go,' one of the women said. Her hair was dyed red and tied back tight against her head like wire. Her skin was white and shiny, tight as a lampshade over the bone, and there was a knot of blue veins in her temple.

'I bet he was a great guy to work for,' I said.

She turned on the barstool and looked me full in the face. Her brown eyes were liquid and malevolent.

'I'm supposed to talk to people that buy me a drink,' she said. 'Then I'll put my hand in your lap and we'll talk about your rising expectations. You want somebody to help you with your rising expectations, officer?'

I put my office card in front of her.

'If you ever get tired of comic-book routines, call this number,' I said.

The bartender put the last beer bottle in the cooler and walked toward me on the dockboards behind the bar, pressing a stick of Num-Zit against his tooth and gum.

'I'm Eddie's brother. You want something?' he said. His tan was almost gold, the kind that comes from applying chemicals to the skin in the sun, and the exposed hair sticking out from under his arms was bleached on the tips. He had the same thick, veined neck, powerful shoulders and adenoidal Brooklyn accent that his brother had had. I asked him when he had seen Eddie Keats last.

'Two years ago, when he come up to visit in Canarsie,' he said.

'You know Victor Romero?'

'No.'

'How about Bubba Rocque?'

'I don't think I know the name.'

'Did you know a Haitian named Toot?'

'I don't know none of these people. I just come down to take care of Eddie's business affairs. It's a big tragedy.'

'I think you're violating the law, Mr Keats.'

'What?'

'I think you're contributing to prostitution.'

His green eyes looked at me carefully. He took a Lucky Strike from a pack on the liquor counter behind him and lit it. He removed a piece of tobacco from his tongue with his fingernails. He blew the smoke out the side of his mouth.

'What's the game?' he said.

'No game. I'm just going to see if I can get you closed up.'

'You had some kind of deal with Eddie?'

'No, I didn't like Eddie. I'm the guy who busted a pool cue across his face. What do you think of that?'

He looked away and took another puff off his cigarette. Then he focused again on my face, a wrinkled wedge of concern between his eyes.

'Look, you didn't like my brother, that's your problem. But I ain't Eddie. You got no reason to be down on me, man. I'm a cooperative guy. If I got to piece off a little action, that's cool. I ran a nigger bar in Bedford-Stuyvesant. I got along with everybody. That ain't easy to do in Bed-Stuy. I want to get along here, too.'

'No. I don't have the problem. You do. You're a pimp and you're cruel to animals. Cecil, come over here,' I said.

Cecil was leaning against the wall by the cue rack, with his arms folded in front of him, a dark light in his face. Like many people of color, he didn't like the class of white people that Keats's brother and the two prostitutes represented to him. He walked toward us with his massive weight, his mouth a tight line, a lump of Red Man as taut as a golf ball inside his jaw. He opened and closed his hands at his sides.

The bartender stepped backwards.

'Now wait a minute,' he said.

'Mr Keats wants us to take down that monkey cage,' I said.

'I was t'inking that same t'ing myself,' Cecil said, and used the barstool to climb up on the bar. Then he stepped with one foot over onto the liquor counter and shook the monkey cage loose from a hook screwed into the ceiling. His huge shoe knocked over a half-dozen bottles of whiskey that rolled off the counter and crashed on the duck-boards. The monkey's eyes were wide with fright, his leathery paws enmeshed in the wire screen. Cecil held the cage out stiffly with one arm and dropped to the floor again.

'The lady has my office card. You can file a complaint if you don't like it. Welcome to south Louisiana, podjo,' I said.

Cecil and I went outside into the white glare of sunlight on the shale parking lot. Then we walked into the shady grove of live oaks behind the bar and set the cage down in the grass. I unfastened the wire on the door and pulled it open. The monkey sat in his wet tangle of newspaper, too frightened to move, his tail pressed up one side of the cage. Then I tilted the cage forward and he toppled out on the grass, chattered and squeaked once, and climbed high into the fork of an oak, where he looked back at us with his wide eyes. The wind blew the moss in the trees.

'I like working wit' you, Dave,' Cecil said.

But sometimes when an investigation seems to go nowhere, when the street people stonewall you and lowlife like Victor Romero seems to have Vaseline all over him, a door quietly drifts open on the edge of your vision. It was Saturday, the day after Cecil and I had gone to Keats's bar, and I was reading the *Times-Picayune* under the canvas umbrella on the dock. Even in the shade, the light was bright on the newsprint and hurt my eyes. Then the sun went behind clouds and the day was suddenly gray and the breeze came up and ruffled the water and bent the cattails and reeds along the bank. I pinched my eyes with my fingers, and glanced again at the state wrap-up column in the second section. At the bottom of the column was a five-line wire service story about the arrest in north eastern Louisiana of a man who was suspected of robbing apartment mailboxes in a welfare project and assaulting elderly people for their social security checks. His name was Jerry Falgout.

I went inside the bait shop and called the sheriff's office there. The sheriff wasn't in, and the deputy I spoke to, who sounded black, wasn't cooperative.

'Is this guy a bartender in New Orleans?' I said.

'I don't know.'

'What did you get on him from Baton Rouge?'

'You gotta ask the sheriff that.'

'Come on, he's in your custody. You must know something about him. Has he been in Angola?'

'I don't know. He don't say.'

'What's his bond?'

'A hundred thousand.'

'Why so high?'

'He pushed an old woman down the stairs at the project. She's got a fractured skull.'

I was about to give up talking to the deputy and call the sheriff at his home. I tried one more question.

'What *does* he tell you?'

'He don't like it here and he ain't no swinging dick.'

Fifteen minutes later I was in the pickup truck on the road to Lafayette, headed towards the northbound four-lane, while the arching limbs of oak trees swept by overhead.

The country began to change as I drove north of the Red River. The sugarcane and rice fields were behind me now. The black earth and flooded cypress and oak trees were replaced by pastureland and piney woods, lumber mills and cotton acreage, sandy red roads that cut through limitless pecan orchards, Negro towns of paintless shacks and clapboard beer joints and old brick warehouses built along railroad spurs. The French and Spanish names were gone from the mailboxes and the fronts of general stores, too. I was back into the Anglo-Saxon South, where the streets were empty on Sunday and the Baptist churches were full and Negroes baptized in the river bottoms. It was peckerwood country, where Klansmen still burned crosses on rural roads at night and rednecks had coon-on-a-log contests in which a raccoon was chained by his foot to a log in a pond while people sicced their hunting dogs on him.

But history had had its joke with some of those northern parishes. Since the 1960s, Louisiana Negroes had become registered voters in large numbers, and in those parishes and towns where whites were a minority, the mayors' offices and the sheriffs' departments and the police juries had become filled with black people. Or at least that was what had happened in the town upriver from Natchez where Jerry Falgout was being held in the old brick jail behind a courthouse that Yankee soldiers had tried to burn during the Civil War.

It was a poor town, with brick streets and wooden colonnades built over the dilapidated storefronts. On the town square were a bail-bond office, a café, a dime store, and a barber college with a Confederate flag, now flaked and peeling, painted above the door. The elevated sidewalks were cracked and sagging, and the iron tethering rings set in the concrete bled rusty streaks into the gutters. The courthouse building and lawn and the Confederate cannon and the World War I monument were covered in deep shadow by the oak trees that towered above the second story. I walked up the courthouse sidewalk past the scrolled-iron benches where groups of elderly Negro men, in overalls or seersucker slacks, sat and stared out of the shade at the shimmering blaze of light on the street.

A black deputy walked me out the back door of the courthouse into the visiting room of the jail. The bars on the windows and the grid of iron strips on the main door were layered with both white and yellow paint. The room wasn't air-conditioned, and it was hot and close inside and smelled of the oil on the wood floors and tobacco juice that someone had been spitting in a box of sawdust in one corner. A white trusty in jail denims brought Jerry Falgout down a spiral metal stairs at the back of a dark hall and walked him into the visiting area.

His bottom lip was purple and swollen, and there was a crust of blood in one of his nostrils. He kept widening his nostril and sniffing as though he were trying to open a blocked nasal passage. At the corner of one eye was a long, red, scraped area, like a smear of dirty rouge. The trusty went back upstairs, and the deputy locked us in. Jerry sat across from me, his hands limp on top of the wooden table, his eyes sullen and pained as they looked into mine. I could smell the sour reek of his dried sweat.

'What's going on up there?' I said.

'It's a nigger jail. What do you think?'

'Were these black people you've been robbing?'

'I didn't rob nobody man. I was up here visiting my relatives.'

'Cut the dogshit, Jerry.'

'Come on, man. You think I'm gonna rob somebody, I'm gonna rob niggers in a welfare project? Some old lady got thrown down a stairs or something. She was already senile, now she's got a fractured skull, and she says I done it. The night screw is her nephew. So guess what he tells all the boons upstairs?'

'Sounds like a bad situation, all right.'

'Yeah, you're all heart.'

I looked at him a moment before I spoke again.

'You haven't hit the shower in a while, Jerry.'

He turned his face away from me, and a small circle of color formed in one cheek.

'They got you made for stuff, partner?' I said.

'Look, man, I tried to get along. It didn't matter to me if they were colored or not. I tried to make a stinger, you know, a hot plate for these guys so we could warm up the macaroni in the evening. Then this big black bastard walks dripping wet out of the shower and picks up the pot, with his bare feet on the concrete floor. It popped him so hard he looked like somebody shoved a cattle prod up his butt. So he blames me for it. First, he starts throwing shit at me – macaroni and plates and tin cups. Then he starts grinning and tells me his cock is all charged up now. He says he's gonna take a white boy's cherry the next time I come into the shower. And then the other boons are gonna get seconds.'

His face was flushed now, his eyes narrow and glistening.

I walked over to a rust-streaked sink against one wall and filled a paper cup from the tap. I set the water in front of him and sat back down.

'Is your mother going to go bond?' I said.

'She's gotta put up ten grand for the bondsman. She ain't got that kind of gelt, man.'

'How about a property bond?'

'She ain't got it. I told you.' His eyes avoided mine.

'I see.'

'Look, man, I did five years in Angola. I did it with guys that'd cut your face up with a razor for twenty dollars. I seen a snitch burned up in his cell with a Molotov cocktail. I seen a kid drowned in a toilet because he wouldn't suck some guy off. I'm not gonna get broke by a nigger jail in some backwater shithole.'

'You want out of here?'

'Yeah. You got connections with Jesse Jackson?'

'Save the hard-guy routine for another day, Jerry. Do you want out of here?'

'What do you think?'

'You robbed the mails, which is a federal offense. They'll file against you eventually, but I know somebody who can probably hurry it up. We'll get you into federal custody, and you can forget this place.'

'When?'

'Maybe this week. In the meantime I'll call the FBI in Shreveport and tell them there's a serious civil rights violation going on here. That ought to get you into isolation until you're transferred to federal custody.'

'What do you want?'

'Victor Romero.'

'I told you everything I know about the guy. You got a fucking obsession, man.'

'I need a name, Jerry. Somebody who can turn him.'

'I ain't got any. I'm telling you the truth. I got no reason to cover for this cat.'

'I believe that. But you're plugged into a lot of people. You're a knowledgeable man. You sell information. If you remember, you sold me and Robin for a hundred dollars.'

His eyes looked out the barred window at the shade trees on the lawn. He brushed at the dried blood in his nostril with one knuckle.

'I'm floating round on an ice cube that's melting in a toilet,' he said. 'What can I tell you? I got nothing to deal with. You wasted your drive up here. Why don't you get those vice cops to help you? They think they know everything.'

'They have the same problem I do. A guy with no family and no girlfriend is hard to find.'

'Wait a minute. What do you mean no family?'

'That's the information at the First District.'

I saw a confident mean light come back into his eyes.

'That's why they don't never catch anybody. He's got a first cousin. I don't know the cat's name, but Romero brought him into the bar six or seven years ago. The guy pulled a scam that everybody in the Quarter was laughing about. Some guys robbed Maison Blanche of about ten thousand dollars in Bottany 500 suits. Of course, there's a big write-up about it in the Picayune. So Romero's cousin gets ahold of a bunch of these Hong Kong specials, you know, these twenty-buck suits that turn into lint and threads the first time you dry-clean them. He stops business guys up and down Canal and says, "I got a nice suit for you. A hundred bucks. No labels. Know what I mean?" I heard he made two or three grand off these stupid shits. After they found out they got burned, they couldn't do anything about it, either.'

'Where is he now?'

'I don't know. I only saw him once or twice. He's the kind of guy that only makes a move once in a while. I think he ran a laundry or something.'

'A laundry? Where?'

'In New Orleans.'

'Come on, where in New Orleans?'

'I don't know, man. What the fuck I care about a laundry?'

'And you're sure you don't know this guy's name?'

'Hell, no. I told you, it was a long time ago. I been straight with you. You gonna deliver or not?'

'Okay, Jerry. I'll make some phone calls. In the meantime, you try to remember this laundry man's name.'

'Yeah, yeah. Y'all always got to go one inch deeper in a guy's hole, don't you?'

I walked to the iron door and rattled it against the jamb for the deputy to let me out.

'Hey, Robicheaux, I don't have any cigarettes. How about a deck of Luckies?' Jerry said.

'All right.'

'Put a piece of paper with how many packs are in the carton, too. That trusty helps himself.'

'You got it, partner.'

The deputy let me out, and I walked back into the breezy area between the jail and the courthouse. I could smell the pines on the lawn, the hydrangeas blooming against a sunny patch of wall, hot dogs that a Negro kid was selling out of a cart on the streetcorner. I looked back through the jail window at Jerry, who sat alone at the wooden table, waiting for the trusty to take him back upstairs, his face now empty and dull and as lifeless as tallow.

10

I waited until Monday, when business would be open, and drove to New Orleans in the pink light of dawn and began looking up and down the St Charles Avenue streetcar line for laundries and dry cleaners. At one time New Orleans was covered with streetcar tracks, but now only the St Charles streetcar remains in service. It runs a short distance down Canal, the full length of St Charles through the Garden District, past Loyola and Tulane and Audubon Park, then goes up South Carrollton and turns around on Claiborne. This particular line has been left in service because it travels along what is probably one of the most beautiful streets in the world. St Charles and the esplanade in its center are covered by a canopy of enormous oak trees and lined on each side by old, iron-scrolled brick homes and antebellum mansions with columned porches and pike-fenced yards filled with hibiscus, blooming myrtle and oleander, bamboo, and giant philodendron. So most of the area along the streetcar line is residential, and I had to look only in a few commercially zoned neighborhoods for a laundry or dry cleaner's that might be operated by Victor Romero's cousin.

I found only four. One was run by black people, another by Vietnamese. The third one was run by a white couple on Carrollton, but I believed it was set too far back from the street for me to have heard the streetcar bell over the telephone. However, the fourth one, a few blocks southwest of Lee Circle, was only a short distance from the tracks, and its front doors were open to let out the heat from inside, and through the big glass window I could see a telephone on the service counter and behind it a white man thumping down a clothes press in a hiss of steam.

The laundry was on the corner, with an alley behind it, and by the garbage cans a wooden stairway led up to a living area on the second floor. I parked my pickup across the street under an oak tree in the parking lot of a small take-out café that sold fried shrimp and dirty rice. It was a hot, languid day, and the grass on the esplanade was still wet with dew in the shade, the bark on the palm trees was stained darkly with the water that had leaked from the palm fronds during the night, and the streetcar tracks looked burnished and hot in the sunlight. I went inside the café, called the city clerk's office, and found out the laundry was operated by a man named Martinez. So there was no help by way of connection with family names, except for the fact that the laundry operator was obviously Latin. It was going to be a long wait.

I opened both doors of the truck to let in the breeze and spent the morning watching the front door and back entrance and stairway of the laundry. At noon I bought a paper-plate lunch of shrimp and rice from the café and ate it in the truck while a sudden shower beat down on the street and the oak tree above my head.

I was never good at surveillance, in part because I didn't have the patience for it. But more important was the fact that my own mind always became my worst enemy during any period of passivity or in-activity in life, no matter how short the duration. Old grievances, fears, and unrelieved feelings of guilt and black depression would surface from the unconscious without cause and nibble on the soul's edges like iron teeth. If I didn't do something, if I didn't take my focus outside myself, those emotions would control me as quickly and completely as whiskey did when it raced through my blood and into my heart like a dark electrical current.

I watched the rain drip out of the oak branches and hit on the windshield and hood of my truck. The sky was still dark, and low black clouds floated out of the south like cannon smoke. Annie's death haunted me. No matter who had fired the shotguns in our bedroom, no matter who had ordered and paid for it, the inalterable fact remained that her life had been made forfeit because of my pride.

Now I had to wonder what it was I really planned if I caught Victor Romero and learned that he had killed Annie. In my mind I saw myself spread-eagling him against a wall, kicking his feet apart, ripping a pistol loose from under his shirt, cuffing him so tightly that the skin around his wrists bunched like putty, and forcing him down into the backseat of a New Orleans police car.

I saw those images because they were what I knew I should see. But they did not represent what I felt. They did not represent what I felt at all.

It stopped raining around three, and then, with the sun still shining, it showered again around five and the trees along the avenue were dark green in the soft yellow light. I went inside the café and ate supper, then went back out to the truck and watched the traffic thin, the laundry close, the shadows lengthen on the street, the washed-out sky become pink and lavender and then streaked with bands of crimson in the west. The neon signs came on along the avenue and reflected off the pools of water in the gutters and on the esplanade. A Negro who ran a shoeshine stand in front of a package store had turned on a radio in a window, and I could hear a ball game being broadcast from Fenway Park. The heat had gone out of the day, lifting gradually out of the baked brick and concrete streets, and now a breeze was blowing through the open doors of my truck. The big olive-green streetcar, its windows now lighted, rattled down the tracks under the trees. Then, just as the twilight faded, an electric light went on in the apartment above the laundry.

Five minutes later, Victor Romero came down the wooden back stairs. He wore a pair of Marine Corps utilities, an oversized Hawaiian print shirt with purple flowers on it, a beret on his black curls. He stepped quickly over the puddles in the brick alley and entered the side door of a small grocery store. I took my .45 from the glove box, stuck it inside my belt, pulled my shirt over the butt, and got out of the truck.

I had three ways I could go, I thought. I could take him inside the store, but if he was armed (and he probably was, because his shirt was pulled outside his utilities) an innocent person could be hurt or be taken hostage. I could wait for him at the side entrance to the store and nail him in the alley, but that way I would lose sight of the front door, and if he didn't go directly back to the apartment and instead left by the front, I could lose him altogether. The third alternative was to wait in the shadows by my truck, the angular lines of the .45 hard against my stomach, my pulse racing in my neck.

I opened and closed my hands, wiped them on my trousers, breathed deeply and slowly through my mouth. Then the screen door opened into the alley, and Romero stepped out into the neon light with a sack of groceries in his arm and looked blankly toward the street. His black curls hung down from under his beret, and his skin looked purple in the neon reflection off the bricks. He hitched his belt up with his thumb, looked down toward the other end of the alley, and jumped across a puddle. When he did, he pressed his hand against the small of his back. I watched him climb the stairs, go inside the apartment, close the screen, and walk in broken silhouette past a window fan.

I crossed the street, paused at the bottom of the stairs, pulled back the receiver on the .45, and slid a hollow-point round into the chamber. The pistol felt heavy and warm in my hand. Upstairs I could hear Romero pulling groceries out of his sack, pouring tap water in a pan, clattering pans on a stove. I held on to the bannister for balance and eased up the stairs two at a time while the streetcar rattled down the tracks out on St Charles. I ducked under the window at the top of the stairs and then flattened myself against the wall between the screen door and the window. Romero's shadow moved back and forth against the screen. Swallows glided above the trees across the street in the sun's last red light.

I heard him set something heavy and metal on a tabletop, then walk past the screen again and into another room. I took a deep breath, tore open the door, and went in after him. In the hard electric light, he and I both seemed caught as though in the sudden flash of a photographer's camera. I saw the stiff spaghetti noodles protruding from a pot of steaming water on the stove, a loaf of French bread and a block of cheese and a dark bottle of Chianti on the drainboard, an army .45 like mine, except chrome-plated, where he had placed it on a breakfast table. I saw the animal fear and anger in his face as he stood motionless in the bedroom doorway, the tight mouth, the white quiver around his pinched nostrils, his hot black eyes that stared both at me and at the pistol that he had left beyond his grasp.

'You're busted, sonofabitch! Down on your face!' I yelled.

But I should have known (and perhaps I already did) that a man who had lived on snakes and insects and crawled alone through elephant grass with an .03 Springfield to the edge of a Vietcong village would not allow himself to be taken by a small-town cop who was foolish enough to extend the game after one side had just lost badly.

One of his hands rested on the edge of the bedroom door. His eyes stared into mine, his face twisted with some brief thought, then his arm shot forward and slammed the door in my face. I grabbed the knob, turned it, pushed and threw my weight against the wood, but the spring lock was set solidly in the jamb.

Then I heard him jerk a drawer out on the floor and a second later I heard the clack of metal sliding back on metal. I leaped aside and tumbled over a chair just as the shotgun exploded a hole the size of a pie plate through the door. The buckshot blew splinters of wood all over the kitchen, raked the breakfast table clean of groceries, whanged off the stove and the pot heating on the burner. I was off balance, on my knees, pressed against the wall by the jamb, when he let off two more rounds at a different angle. I suspected the barrel was sawed off, because the pattern spread out like cannister, ripped through the wood as though it had been touched with a chain saw, and blew dishes into the air, water out of the pot, a half-gallon bottle of ketchup all over the far wall.

But when he ejected the spent casing and fired again, I gave him something to think about, too. I remained flat against the wall, bent my wrist backwards around the doorjamb, and let off two rounds flush against the wood. The recoil almost knocked the pistol from my hand, but a .45 hollow-point fired through one surface at a target farther beyond makes an awe-inspiring impression on the person who happens to be the target.

'You've had it, Romero. Throw it down. Cops'll be all over the street in three minutes,' I said.

The room was hot and still. The air smelled heavily of cordite and an empty pot burning on the stove. I heard him snick two shells into the shotgun's magazine and then heard his feet thundering up a wooden stairway. I stood quickly in front of the door, the .45 extended in both arms, and fired the whole clip at an upward angle into the bedroom. I chopped holes out of the wood that looked like a jack-o'-lantern's mouth, and even among the explosions of smoke and flame and splintered lead and flying pieces of door I could hear and even glimpse the damage taking place inside the room: a mirror crashing to the floor, a wall lamp whipped into the air against its cord, a water pipe bursting inside a wall, a window erupting into the street.

The breech locked open, and I ripped the empty clip out of the handle, shoved in another one, slid the top round into the chamber, and kicked the shattered door loose from the jamb. By the side wall, safe from my angle of fire, was a stairway that pulled out of the ceiling by a rope. I pointed my .45 at the attic's dark opening, my blood roaring in my ears.

The room was quiet. There was no movement upstairs. Particles of dust and threads of fiberboard floated in the light from the broken ceramic lamp that swung back and forth on its cord against the wall. Down the street I heard sirens.

I had every reason to believe that he was trapped – even though Victor Romero had survived Vietnam, thrived as a street dealer and pimp, gotten out from under federal custody after he probably killed the four people in the plane at Southwest Pass, escaped unhurt in the Toyota when I punched it full of holes with the .45, and managed in all probability to blow away Eddie Keats. It wasn't a record to ignore.

For the first time I glanced through the side window and saw a flat, tarpapered roof outside. There were air vents on it from the laundry, a lighted neon sign, two peaked enclosures with small doors that probably housed ventilator fans, the rusted top of an iron ladder that dropped down to ground level.

Then I saw the boards at the edge of the attic entrance bend with his weight as he moved quietly toward the wall and a probable window that overlooked the roof. I raised the .45 and waited until one board eased back into place and the edges of the next one moved slightly out of the flat, geometric pattern that formed the ceiling, then I aimed just ahead of the spread between his two feet and began firing. I pulled the trigger five times, deliberately and with calculation, saving three shells in the clip, and let the recoil bring each round farther back from the point of his leading foot and the attic entrance.

I think he screamed at one point. But I can't be sure. I didn't really care, either. I've heard that scream before; it represents the failure of everything, particularly of hope and humanity. You hear it in your dreams; it replays itself even when they die silently.

He fell back through the attic opening and crashed on the floor by the foot of the ladder. He lay on his back, one leg bent under him, his eyes filled with black light, his mouth working for air. A round had cut off three fingers of his right hand. The hand trembled with shock on the floor, the knuckles rattling on the wood. There was a deep sucking wound in his chest, and the wet cloth of his shirt fluttered in the wound each time he tried to breathe. Outside, the street was filled with sirens and the revolving blue and red lights of emergency vehicles.

He was trying to speak. His mouth opened, his voice clicked in the back of his throat, and blood and saliva ran down his cheek into his black curls. I knelt by him, as a priest might, and turned my ear toward his face. I could smell his dried sweat, the oil in his hair.

'. . . did her,' he rasped.

'I can't understand.'

He tried again, but he choked on the saliva in his throat. I turned his face to the side with my fingers so his mouth would drain.

His lips were bright red, and they formed a wet smile like a clown's. Then the voice came out in a long whisper, smelling of bile and nicotine: 'I did your wife, motherfucker.'

He was dead two minutes later when three uniformed cops came through the apartment door. A flattened round had caught him in the lower back, tunneled upward through his trunk, and torn a hole in his lung. The coroner told me that the spine had probably been severed and that he was paralyzed when he crashed down the ladder. After the paramedics had lifted him on a stretcher and taken him away, his blood left a pattern like horsetails on the wooden floor.

I spent the next half hour in the apartment answering questions asked by a young homicide lieutenant named Magelli. He was tired and his clothes were wilted with perspiration, but he was thorough and he didn't cut corners. His brown eyes seemed sleepy and expressionless, but when he asked a question, they remained engaged with mine until the last word of my answer was out of my mouth, and only then did he write on his clipboard.

Finally he put a Lucky Strike in his mouth and looked around again at the litter in the kitchen and the buckshot holes in the walls. A drop of perspiration fell out of his hair and spotted the cigarette paper.

'You say this guy worked for Bubba Rocque?' he said.

'He did at one time.'

'I wish he'd made enough to buy an air conditioner.'

'Bubba has a way of dumping people after their function is over.'

'Well, you might have a little trouble about jurisdiction and not calling us when you made the guy, but I don't think it'll be serious. Nobody's going to mourn his passing. Come down to the district and make a formal statement, then you're free to go. Does any of his stuff help you out?'

In the other room the bed was covered with bagged articles of evidence and clothing and personal items taken by the scene investigator from the attic, kitchen, bedroom floor, dressers, and closets: Romero's polyester suits, loud shirts, and colored silk handkerchiefs; the chrome-plated .45 that he had probably used to kill Eddie Keats; a twelve-gauge Remington sawed off at the pump, with a walnut stock that had been cut down, tapered, and sanded until it was almost the size of a pistol grip; the spent shell casings; a whole brick of high-grade reefer; a glass straw with traces of cocaine in it; an Italian stiletto that could cut paper as easily as a razor blade; a cigar box full of pornographic photographs; a bolt-action, scoped .30–06 rifle; a snapshot of him in uniform and two other marines with three Vietnamese bar girls in a nightclub; and finally a plastic bag of human ears, now withered and black, laced together on a GI dogtag chain.

His life had been used to till a garden of dark and poisonous flowers. But in all his memorabilia of cruelty and death, there wasn't one piece of paper or article of evidence that would connect him with anyone outside his apartment.

'It looks like a dead end,' I said. 'I should have called you all.'

'It might have come out the same way, Robicheaux. Except maybe with some of our people hurt. Look, if he'd gotten out on that roof, he'd be in Mississippi by now. You did the right thing.'

'When are you going to pick up his cousin?'

'Probably in the morning.'

'Are you going to charge him with harboring?'

'I'll tell him that, but I don't think we can make it stick. Take it easy. You did enough for one night. All this shit eventually gets ironed out one way or another. How do you feel?'

'All right.'

'I don't believe you, but that's all right,' he said, and put his unlit, sweat-spotted cigarette back in his shirt pocket. 'Can I buy you a drink later?'

'No, thanks.'

'Well, all right, then. We'll seal this place, and you can follow us on down to the district.' His sleepy brown eyes smiled at me. 'What are you looking at?'

The breakfast table was an old round one with a hard rubber top. Among the streaks of canned food that had been blown off the table by Romero's shotgun blast was a pattern of dried rings that looked as if they had been left there by the wet impressions of glasses or cups. Except one set of rings was larger than the other, and they were both on the same side of the table. The rings were gray and felt crusty under my fingertips.

'What's the deal?' he said.

I wet my fingertip, wiped up part of the residue, and touched it to my tongue.

'What's it taste like to you?' I said.

'Are you kidding? A guy who collected human ears. I wouldn't drink out of his water tap.'

'Come on, it's important.'

I wet my finger and did it again. He raised his eyebrows, touched a finger to one of the gray rings, then licked it. He made a face.

'Lemon or lime juice or something,' he said. 'Is this how you guys do it out in the parishes? We use the lab for this sort of stuff. Remind me to buy some Listerine on the way home.'

He waited. When I didn't speak, the attention sharpened in his face.

'What's it mean?' he said.

'Probably nothing.'

'On no, we don't play it that way here, my friend. The game is show-and-tell.'

'It doesn't mean anything. I messed up tonight.'

He took the cigarette back out of his pocket and lit it. He blew the smoke out and tapped his finger in the air at me.

'You're giving me a bad feeling, Robicheaux. Who'd you say he confessed to killing before he died?'

'A girl in New Iberia.'

'You knew her?'

'It's a small town.'

'You knew her personally?'

'Yes.'

He chewed on the corner of his lips and looked at me with veiled eyes.

'Don't make me revise my estimation of you,' he said. 'I think you need to go back to New Iberia tonight. And maybe stay there, unless we call you. New Orleans is a lousy place in the summer, anyway. We're clear about this, aren't we?'

'Sure.'

'That's good. I aim for simplicity in my work. Clarity of line, you might call it.'

He was quiet, his eyes studying me in the kitchen light. His face softened.

'Forget what I said. You look a hundred years old,' he said. 'Stay over in a motel tonight and give us your statement in the morning.'

'That's all right. I'd better be on my way. Thank you for your courtesy,' I said, and walked out into the darkness and the wind that blew over the tops of the oak trees. The night sky was full of heat lightning, like the flicker of artillery beyond a distant horizon.

Three hours later I was halfway across the Atchafalaya basin. My eyes burned with fatigue, and the center line on the highway seemed to drift back and forth under my left front tire. When I thumped across the metal bridge spanning the Atchafalaya River, the truck felt airborne under me.

My system craved for a drink: four inches of Jim Beam straight up, with a sweating Jax draft on the side, an ambergold rush that could light my soul for hours and even let me pretend that the serpentarium was closed forever. On both sides of the road were canals and bayous and wind-dimpled bays and islands of willows and gray cypresses that were almost luminous in the moonlight. In the wind and the hum of the truck's engine and tires, I thought I could hear John Fogerty singing:

Don't come 'round tonight,
It's bound to take your life,
A bad moon's on the rise.
I hear hurricanes a-blowing,
I know the end is coming soon.
I feel the river overflowing,
I can hear the voice of rage and ruin.

I pulled into a truck stop and bought two hamburgers and a pint of coffee to go. But as I continued down the road, the bread and meat were as dry and tasteless in my mouth as confetti, and I folded the hamburgers in the grease-stained sack and drank the coffee with the nervous energy of a man swallowing whiskey out of a cup with the morning's first light.

Romero was evil. I had no doubt about that. But I had killed people before, in war and as a member of the New Orleans police department, and I know what it does to you. Like the hunter, you feel an adrenaline surge of pleasure at having usurped the province of God. The person who says otherwise is lying. But the emotional attitude you form later varies greatly among individuals. Some will keep their remorse alive and feed it as they would a living gargoyle, to assure themselves of their own humanity; others will justify it in the name of a hundred causes, and they'll reach back in moments of their own inadequacy and failure and touch again those flaming shapes that somehow made their impoverished lives historically significant.

But I always feared a worse consequence for myself. One day a curious light dies in the eyes. The unblemished place where God once grasped our souls becomes permanently stained. A bird lifts its span of wings and flies forever out of the heart.

Then I did a self-serving thing that impersonated a charitable act. I pulled off the causeway into a rest area to use the men's room, and saw an elderly Negro man under one of the picnic shelters. Even though it was a summer night, he wore an old suitcoat and a felt hat. By his foot was a desiccated cardboard suitcase tied shut with rope, the words *The Great Speckled Bird* painted on one side. For some reason he had lighted a fire of twigs under the empty barbecue grill and was staring out at the light rain that had begun to fall on the bay.

'Did you eat tonight, partner?' I asked.

'No, suh,' he said. His face was covered with thin brown lines, like a tobacco leaf.

'I think I've got just the thing for us, then,' I said, and took my half-eaten hamburger and the untouched one from the truck and heated them on the edge of the grill. I also found two cans of warm Dr Pepper in my toolbox.

The rain slanted in the firelight. The old man ate without speaking. Occasionally his eyes looked at me.

'Where are you going?' I said.

'Lafayette. Or Lake Charles. I might go to Beaumont, too.' His few teeth were long and purple with rot.

'I can take you to the Salvation Army in Lafayette.'

'I don't like it there.'

'It might storm tonight. You don't want to be out here in an electrical storm, do you?'

'What chu doing this for?' His eyes were red, the lines in his face as intricate as cobwebs.

'I can't leave you out here at night. It's not good for you. Sometimes bad people are out at night.'

He made a sound as though a great philosophical weariness were escaping from his lungs.

'I don't want no truck with them kind. No, suh,' he said, and allowed me to pick up his suitcase and walk him to the pickup.

It started raining hard outside of Lafayette. The sugarcane fields were green and thrashing in the wind, and the oak trees along the road trembled whitely in the explosions of lightning on the horizon. The old man fell asleep against the far door, and I was left alone in the drumming of the rain against the cab, in the sulfurous smell of the air through the wind vane, in the sulfurous smell that was as acrid as cordite.

When I awoke in the morning, the house was cool from the window fans, and the sunlight looked like smoke in the pecan trees outside the window. I walked barefoot in my undershorts to the bath room, then started toward the kitchen to make coffee. Robin opened her door in her pajamas and motioned me inside with her fingers. I still slept on the couch and she in the back room, in part because of Alafair and in part, perhaps, because of a basic dishonesty in myself about the nature of our relationship. She bit down quietly on her lip with a conspiratorial smile.

I sat on the edge of the bed with her and looked out the window into the backyard. It was covered in blue shadow and dripping with dew. She put her hands on my neck and face, rubbed them down my back and chest.

'You came in late,' she said.

'I had to take an old man to the Sally in Lafayette.'

She kissed my shoulder and traced her hand down my chest. Her body was still warm from sleep.

'It sounds like somebody didn't sleep too well,' she said.

'I guess not.'

'I know a good way to wake up in the morning,' she said, and touched me with her hand.

She felt me jerk involuntarily.

'You got your chastity belt on this morning?' she said. 'Scruples about mommy again?'

'I blew away Victor Romero last night.'

I felt her go quiet and stiff next to me. Then she said in a hushed voice, 'You killed Victor Romero?'

'He dealt it.'

Then she was quiet again. She might have been a tough girl raised in a welfare project, but she was no different from anyone else in her reaction to being in proximity to someone who has recently killed another human being.

'It comes with the fucking territory, Robin.'

'I know that. I wasn't judging you.' She placed her hand on my back.

I stared out the window at the yard, my hands on my knees. The red-wood picnic table was dark with moisture.

'You want me to fix breakfast for you?' she said finally.

'Not now.'

'I'll make toast in a pan, the way you like it.'

'I don't want anything to eat right now.'

She put her arms around me and squeezed me. I could feel her cheek and her hair on my shoulder.

'Do you love me, Dave?' she said.

I didn't answer.

'Come on, Streak. Fair and square. Do you love me?'

'Yes.'

'No, you don't. You love things about me. There's a difference. It's a big one.'

'I'm not up to this today, Robin.'

'What I'm telling you is I understand and I got no complaint. You were decent to me when nobody else was. You know what it meant to me when you took me to midnight Mass at the Cathedral? I never had a man treat me with that kind of respect before. Mommy thought she had Cinder-ella's glass slippers on.'

She picked up my hand in hers and kissed it on the back. Then, almost in a whisper, she said, 'I'll always be your friend. Anytime, anywhere, for anything.'

I slipped my hand up her back, under her pajama top, and kissed the corner of her eye. Then I drew her against me felt her breath on my chest, felt her fingers on my thighs and stomach, and I lay down next to her and looked at her eyes, the tanned smoothness of her skin, the way her lips parted when I touched her; then she pressed hard against me for a brief moment, got up from the bed and slid the bolt on the door, and took off her pajamas. She sat beside me, leaned over my face and kissed me, her mouth smiling as though she were looking at a little boy. I pulled off my undershorts, and she sat on top of me, her eyes closing, her mouth opening silently, as she took me inside her. She put her hands in my hair, kissed my ear, then stretched herself out against my body and tucked her feet inside my calves.

A moment later she felt me tense and try to hold back before I gave in to that old male desire that simply wants to complete that bursting moment of fulfillment, whether the other person gets to participate or not. But she raised herself on her arms and knees and smiled at me and never stopped her motion, and when I went weak inside and felt sweat break out on my forehead and felt my loins heat like a flame burning in a circle through paper, she leaned down on my chest again and kissed my mouth and neck and forced her hands under my back as though some part of me might elude her in that final, heart-twisting moment.

Later we lay on top of the sheets under the fan while the sunlight grew brighter in the tree limbs outside. She turned on her side, looking at my profile, and took my fingers in hers.

'Dave, I don't think you should be troubled like this,' she said. 'You tried to arrest him, and he tried to kill you for it.'

I looked at the shadows of the wood-bladed fan turning on the ceiling.

'Look, I know New Orleans cops who would have just killed the guy and never given him a chance. Then they'd plant a gun on him. They've got a name for it. What do they call it?'

'A "drop" or a "throwaway".'

'You're not that kind of cop. You're a good man. Why do you want to carry this guilt around?'

'You don't understand, Robin. I think maybe I'm going to do it again.'

Later I called the office and told them I wouldn't be in that day, then I put on my running shorts and shoes, lifted weights under the mimosa tree in the backyard, and ran three miles along the bayou road. Wisps of fog still hung around the flooded roots of the cypress trees. I went inside the paintless wood-frame general store at the four-corners, drank a carton of orange juice and talked French with the elderly owner of the store, then jogged back along the road while the sun climbed higher into the sky and dragonflies dipped and hovered over the cattails.

When I came through the front screen, hot and running with sweat, I saw the door of Annie's and my bedroom wide open, the lock and hasp pried loose from the jamb, the torn wood like a ragged dental incision. Sunlight streamed through the windows into the room, and Robin was on her hands and knees, in a white sun halter and a pair of cutoff blue jean shorts, dipping a scrub brush into a bucket of soapy water and scouring the grain in the cypress floor. The buckshot-pocked walls and the headboard of the bed were wet and gleaming, and by a bottle of Clorox on the floor was another bucket filled with soaking rags, and the rags and the water were the color of rust.

'What are you doing?' I said.

She glanced at me, then continued to scrub the grain without replying. The stiff bristles of the brush sounded like sandpaper against the wood. The muscles of her tan back rippled with her motion.

'Damn you, Robin. Who gave you the fucking right to go into my bedroom?'

'I couldn't find your keys, so I pried the lock off with a screwdriver. I'm sorry about the damage.'

'You get the fuck out of this room.'

She paused and sat back on her heels. There were white indentations on her knees. She brushed the perspiration out of her hairline with the back of her wrist.

'Is this your church where you go every day to suffer?' she said.

'It's none of your business what it is. It's not a part of your life.'

'Then tell me to get out of your life. Say it and I'll do it.'

'I'm asking you to leave this room.'

'I have a hard time buying your attitude, Streak. You wear guilt like a big net over your head. You ever know guys who are always getting the clap? They're not happy unless some broad has dosed them from their toenails to their eyes. Is that the kind of gig you want for yourself?'

The sweat was dripping off my hands onto the floor. I breathed slowly and pushed my wet hair back over my head.

'I'm sorry for being profane at you. I truly am. But come outside now,' I said.

She dipped the brush in the bucket again and began to enlarge the scrubbed circle on the floor.

'Robin?' I said.

She concentrated her eyes on the strokes of the brush across the wood.

'This is my house, Robin.'

I stepped toward her.

'I'm talking to you, kiddo. No more free pass,' I said.

She sat back on her heels again and dropped the brush in the water.

'I'm finished,' she said. 'You want to stand here and mourn or help me carry these buckets outside?'

'You didn't have the right to do this. You mean well, but you didn't have the right.'

'Why don't you show some respect for your wife and stop using her? If you want to get drunk, go do it. If you want to kill somebody, do that. But at least have the courage to do it on your own, without all this remorse bullshit. It's a drag, Dave.'

She picked up one of the buckets with both hands to avoid spilling it, and walked out the door past me. Her bare feet left damp imprints on the cypress floor. I continued to stand alone in the room, the dust spinning in the shafts of light through the windows, then I saw her cross the backyard with the bucket and walk toward the duck pond.

'Wait!' I called through the window.

I gathered up the soiled rags from the floor, put them in the other bucket, and followed her outside. I stopped by the aluminum shed where I kept my lawn mower and tools, took out a shovel, and walked down to the small flower garden that Batist's wife had planted next to a shallow coulee that ran through my property. The soil in the garden was loamy and damp from the overflow of the coulee and partly shaded by banana trees so the geraniums and impatiens didn't burn up in the summer; but the outer edge was in full sun and it ran riot with daisies and periwinkles.

They weren't the cornflowers and bluebonnets that a Kansas girl should have, but I knew that she would understand. I pushed the shovel into the damp earth and scooped out a deep hole among the daisy roots, poured the two buckets of soap and water and chemicals into the dirt, put the brush and rags into the hole, then put the buckets on top and crushed them flat with my foot, and covered the hole back up with a wet mound of dirt and a tangle of severed daisy and periwinkle roots. I uncoiled the garden hose from the side of the house and watered the mound until it was as slick and smooth as the ground around it and the chemicals had washed far below the root system of the flower bed.

It was the kind of behavior that you don't care to think about or to explain to yourself later. I cleaned the shovel under the hose, replaced it in the shed, and walked back into the kitchen without speaking to Robin. Then I took a shower and put on a fresh pair of khakis and a denim shirt and read the newspaper at the redwood table under the mimosa tree. I could hear Robin making lunch in the kitchen and Alafair talking to her in a mixture of Spanish and English. Then Robin brought a ham and onion sandwich and a glass of iced tea to me on a tray. I didn't look up from the table when she set it on the table. She remained standing next to me, her bare thigh only an inch from my arm, then I felt her hand touch me lightly on the shoulder and finger my damp collar and tease the hair along my neck.

'I'll always be your biggest fan, Robicheaux,' she said.

I put my arm around her soft bottom and squeezed her against me, my eyes shut.

*

Late that afternoon Minos Dautrieve was at my front door, dressed in blue jeans, tennis shoes without socks, and a paintflecked gold shirt. A fishing rod stuck out the passenger's window of his parked Toyota jeep.

'I hear you know where all the big bass are,' he said.

'Sometimes.'

'I've got some fried chicken and Dixie beer and soda in the cooler. Let's get it on down the road.'

'We were thinking of going to the track tonight.'

'I'll have you back early. Get your butt moving, boy.'

'You've really got the touch, Minos.'

We hitched my trailer and one of my boats to his jeep and drove twenty-five miles to the levee that fronts the southwestern edge of the Atchafalaya swamp. The wind was down, the water quiet, the insects just beginning to rise from the reeds and lily pads in the shadows of the willow islands. I took us across a long bay dotted with dead cypresses and oil platforms, then up a bayou, deep into the swamp, before I cut the engine and let the boat drift quietly up to the entrance of a small bay with a narrow channel at the far end. I still didn't know what Minos was up to.

'On a hot day like this, they get deep in the holes on the shady side of the islands,' I said. 'Then just before dusk they move up to the edge of the channel and feed where the water curves around the bank.'

'No kidding?' he said.

'You have a Rapula?'

'I might have one of those.'

He popped open his tackle box, which had three layers of compartments in it, all of them filled with rubber worms, spinners, doll flies, surface plugs, and popping bugs.

'What's it look like?' he said.

'Guess what, Minos? I gave up being a straight man for government agents when I resigned from the New Orleans department.'

He clipped a Devil Horse on his swivel and flipped it neatly across the channel into open water with a quick spring of his wrist. Then he retrieved it through the channel back into the bay and cast again. On the third cast I saw the quiet surface of the water balloon under the lily pads, then the dorsal fin of a bigmouth bass roll like a serpent right in front of the lure, the scales hammered with green and gold light, and then the water exploded when he locked down on the lure and Minos socked the treble hook hard into his jaw. The bass went deep and pulled for a hole among the reeds, clouding the water with mud, but Minos kept the tip of the rod up, the drag tight, and turned him back into the middle of the bay. Then the bass broke through the surface into the air, rattling the lure and swivel against his head, and splashed sideways like a wood plank whipped against the surface, before he went deep again and tried for the channel and open water.

'Get him up again,' I said.

'He'll tear it out of his mouth.'

I started to speak again, but I saw the line stop and quiver against the current, tiny beads of water glistening on the stretched monofilament. When Minos tried to turn the handle of the spinning reel, the rod dipped over the side. I put the hand net, which I had been holding, back under the seat of the boat. Suddenly the rod flipped up straight and lifeless in Minos's palm, the broken line floating in a curlicue on top of the water.

'Sonofabitch,' he said.

'I forgot to tell you there are a bunch of cypress stumps under this bay. Don't feel bad, though. That same bass has a whole collection of my lures.'

He didn't speak for almost five minutes. He drank a bottle of Dixie beer, put the empty back in the cooler, then opened another one and lit a cigar.

'You want some chicken?' he said.

'Sure. But it's getting late, Minos. I still want to go to the track tonight.'

'I'm keeping you?'

I joined the sections of my Fenwick fly rod and tied a black popping bug with a yellow feather and red eyes to the tapered leader. I stuck the hook into the cork handle and handed him the rod.

'This is a surefire killer for goggle-eye,' I said. 'We'll go out into open water and throw back into the bank, then I've got to hit the road, partner.'

I pulled the foot-long piece of train rail that I used as an anchor, left the outboard engine tilted up on the stern, and paddled us through the channel into the larger bay. The air was purple, swallows covered the sky, and a wind had come up and was blowing the insects back into the flooded trees so that the bream and sunfish and goggle-eye perch were feeding deep in the shadows. The western sky was a burnt orange, and cranes and blue herons stood in the shallows on the tips of the sandbars and islands of cattails. Minos dropped his cigar hissing into the water, false-cast in a figure eight over his head, and lay the popping bug right on the edge of the lily pads.

'How do you feel about wasting Romero?' he asked.

'I don't feel anything.'

'I don't believe you.'

'So what?'

'I don't believe you, that's all.'

'Is that why we're out here?'

'I had a phone conversation with that homicide lieutenant, Magelli, this morning. You didn't tell him it was your wife Romero killed.'

'He didn't ask.'

'Oh yeah, he did.'

'I don't feel like talking about this, Minos.'

'Maybe you ought to learn who your friends are.'

'Listen, if you're saying I was out to pop Romero, you're wrong. That's just the way it worked out. He thought he might have another season to run. He lost. It's that simple. And I think day-after analysis is for douchebags.'

'I don't give a damn about Romero. He should have been a bar of soap a long time ago.' He missed a strike among the lily pads and ripped the popping bug angrily back through a leaf.

'Then what's all this stuff about?'

'Magelli said you figured out something in Romero's apartment. Something you weren't telling him about.'

I drew the paddle through the water and didn't answer.

'It had to do with lime juice or something,' he said.

'The only thing that counts is the score at the end of the game. I made a big mistake in not using the New Orleans cops to bust Romero. I don't know how to correct it. Let it go at that, Minos.'

He sat down in the boat and stuck the hook of the popping bug into the cork handle of the rod.

'Let me tell you a quick story,' he said. 'In Vietnam I worked for a major who was both a nasty and stupid man. In free-fire zones he liked to go dink-pinking in his helicopter – farmers in a field, women, water buffalo, whatever was around. Then his stupidity and incompetence compromised a couple of our agents and got them killed. I won't go into detail, but the VC could be imaginative when they created object lessons. One of those agents was a Eurasian schoolteacher I had something of a relationship with.

'I thought a lot about our major. I spent many nights thinking long and hard about him. Then one day an opportunity presented itself. Out in Indian country where you could paint the trees with a fat, incompetent fellow and then smoke a little dope and just let a bad day float away in the wind. But I didn't do it. I wasn't willing to trade the rest of my life – my conscience, if you will – for one asshole. So he's probably still out there, fucking people up, getting them killed, telling stories about all the dinks he left floating in the rice fields. But I'm not crazy today, Robicheaux. I don't have to live with a shitpile of guilt. I don't have to worry about the wrong people showing up at my house one day.'

'Save your concern. I've got nothing of any value to go on. I blew it.'

'I'd like to believe you're that humble and resigned.'

'Maybe I am.'

'No, I know guys like you. You're out of sync with the rest of the world, and you don't trust other people. That's why you're always thinking.'

'Is that right?'

'You just haven't figured out how to pull it off yet,' he said. His face was covered with the sun's last red light. 'Eventually, you'll try to hang them up in a meat market.'

11

He was wrong. I had already quit trying to figure out how to pull it off. Instead, I had spent the entire day brooding on an essential mistake I had made in the investigation, a failure to act upon a foregone conclusion about how Bubba and his wife operated – namely, that they used people. They used them in a cynical and ruthless fashion and then threw them away like soiled Kleenex. Johnny Dartez muled for Bubba and drowned in the plane at Southwest Pass; Eddie Keats kept Bubba's whores in line and Toot trimmed ears for him, and now one had been dumped in a swamp and the other had been cooked in his own bathtub; and finally in my pride and single-mindedness I had stumbled into the role of Victor Romero's executioner.

The board was swept clean. I had always thought of myself as a fairly smart cop, an outsider within the department, a one-eyed existentialist in the country of the blind, but I could not help comparing my situation with the way cops everywhere treat major crimes. We unconsciously target the most available and inept in that myriad army of metropolitan lowlifes: addicts, street dealers, petty thieves, hookers and a few of their johns, storefront fences, and the obviously deranged and violent. With the exception of the hookers, most of these people are stupid and ugly and easy to convict. Check out the residents in any city or county jail. In the meantime the people who would market the Grand Canyon as a gravel pit or sell the Constitution at an Arab rug bazaar remain as socially sound as a silver dollar dropped into a church basket.

But you don't surrender the ballpark to the other team, even when your best pitch is a letter-high floater that they drill into your breastbone. Also, there are certain advantages in situations in which you have nothing to lose: you become justified in throwing a bucketful of monkey shit through the ventilator fan. It might not alter the outcome of things, but it certainly gives the other side pause.

I found Bubba the next morning at his fish-packing house south of Avery Island, a marsh and salt-dome area that eventually bleeds into Vermilion Bay and the Gulf. The packing house was made of tin and built up on pilings over the bayou, and the docks were painted silver so that the whole structure looked as bright and glittering as tinfoil in a sea of sawgrass, dead cypress, and meandering canals. His oyster and shrimp boats were out, but a waxed yellow cigarette boat floated in the gasoline-stained water by the dock.

I parked my truck in the oyster-shell lot and walked up a ramp onto the dock. The sun was hot, reflecting off the water and the air smelled of dead shrimp, oil, tar, and the salt breeze off the Gulf. Bubba was filling an ice chest with bottles of Dixie beer. He was bare-chested and sweating, and his denims hung low on his narrow hips so that the elastic of his undershorts showed. There wasn't a half-inch of fat on his hips or flat stomach. His shoulders were covered with fine brown hair, and across his deeply tanned back were chains of tiny scars.

Behind him, two pale men with oiled dark hair, who wore print shirts, slacks, tassel loafers, and sunglasses, were leaning over the dock rail and shooting pigeons and egrets with a pellet rifle. The dead egrets looked like melting snow below the water's surface. I thought I recognized one of the men as an ex-driver for a notorious, now-deceased New Orleans gangster by the name of Didoni Giacano.

Bubba smiled up at me from where he squatted by the ice chest. There were drops of sweat in his eyebrows and his spiked hair.

'Take a ride with us,' he said. 'That baby there can eat a trench all the way across the lake.'

'What are you doing with the spaghetti and meatball crowd?'

One of the pale-skinned, dark-haired men looked over his shoulder at me. The sun clicked on his dark glasses.

'Friends from New Orleans,' Bubba said. 'You want a beer?'

'They're shooting protected birds.'

'I'm tired of pigeons shitting on my shrimp. But I don't argue. Tell them.' He smiled at me again.

The other man at the rail looked at me now, too. Then he leaned the pellet rifle against the rail, unwrapped a candy bar, and dropped the paper into the water.

'How big is the mob into you, Bubba?'

'Come on, man. That's movie stuff.'

'You pay big dues with that crowd.'

'No, you got it wrong. People pay me dues. I win, they lose. That's why I got these businesses. That's why I'm offering you a beer. That's why I'm inviting you out on my boat. I don't bear grudges. I don't have to.'

'You remember Jimmy Hoffa? There was none tougher. Then he thought he could make deals with the Mob. I bet they licked their teeth when they saw him coming.'

'Listen to this guy,' he said, and laughed. He opened a bottle on the side of the ice chest, and the foam boiled over the top and dripped flatly on the dock.

'Here,' he said, and offered me the bottle, the beer glistening on the back of his brown hand.

'No, thanks,' I said.

'Suit yourself,' he said, and raised the bottle to his mouth and drank. Then he blew air out through his nose and looked at his cigarette boat. The scars on his back were like broken necklaces spread across his skin. He shifted his weight on his feet.

'Well, it's a beautiful day, and I'm about to go,' he said. 'You got something you want to tell me, 'cause I want to get out before it rains.'

'I just had a couple of speculations. About who's making decisions for you these days.'

'Oh yeah?' he said. He drank from the beer with one hand on his hip and looked away at the marsh, where some blue herons were lifting into the sky.

'Maybe I'm all wet.'

'Maybe you got a brain disease, too.'

'Don't misunderstand me. I'm not taking away from your accomplishment. I just have a feeling that Claudette has turned out to be an ambitious girl. She's been hard to keep in the kitchen, hasn't she?'

'You're starting to piss me off, Dave. I don't like that. I got guests here, I got a morning planned. You want to come along, that's cool. Don't be messing with me no more, podna.'

'That is the way I figure it. Tell me if I'm wrong. Johnny Dartez wasn't a stand-up guy, was he? He was a dumb lowlife, a street dip not to be trusted. You knew that one day he'd trade your butt to the feds, so either you or Claudette told Victor Romero to take him out. Except he killed everybody in the plane, including a priest.

'Then I stumble into the middle of things and complicated matters even more. You should have left me alone, Bubba. I wasn't any threat to you. I'd already disengaged when your monkeys started coming around my house.'

'What's all this about?' one of the Italians said.

'Stay out of it,' Bubba said. Then he looked back at me. His thick hand was tight around the beer bottle. 'I'll tell you something, and I'll tell you only once, and you can accept it or stick it sideways up your ass. I'm *one* guy. I'm not a crime wave. You're supposed to be a smart college guy, but you always talk like you don't understand anything. When you mess with the action out of New Orleans, you fuck with hundreds of people. You wouldn't leave it alone, they slammed the door on your nose. Stop laying your shit off on me.'

'Claudette was in Romero's apartment.'

'What are you talking about?'

'You heard me.'

'She don't go anyplace I don't know about.'

'She had her thermos of gin rickeys with her. She left wet prints all over his kitchen table.'

His gray-blue eyes stared at me as though they had no lids. His face was frozen, his jaw hooked sideways like a barracuda's.

'You really didn't know, did you?' I said.

'Say all that again.'

'No, it's your problem. You work it out, Bubba. I'd watch my ass, though. If she doesn't eat up your operation, these guys will. I don't think you're in control of things anymore.'

'You want to find out how much I'm in control? You want that nose busted all over your face right here? Come on, is that what you want?'

'Grow up.'

'No, you grow up. You come out to my home, you come out to my business, you talk trash about my family in front of my friends, but you don't do nothing about it. It's like you're always leaking gas under people's noses.'

'You should have seen a psychiatrist a long time ago. You're fucking pathetic, Bubba.'

He swirled the beer in his bottle.

'That's your best shot?' he said.

'You couldn't understand. You don't have the tools to.'

'All right, you had your say. How about getting out of here now?'

'You don't have your father around anymore to slap your face in front of other people or beat you with a dog chain, so you married a woman like Claudette. You're pussywhipped by a dyke. She's pulling apart your whole operation, and you don't even know it.'

The skin around his eyes stretched tight. His eyes looked like marbles.

'I'll see you around,' I said. 'Rat-hole some money in Grand Cayman, I think you'll need it when Claudette and these guys get finished with you.'

I started down the wooden ramp toward the parking lot and my truck. His beer bottle clattered to the dock and rolled across the boards, twisting a spiral of foam out of the neck.

'Hey! You don't walk off! You hear me? You don't walk off!' he said, jabbing his finger at my face.

I continued toward the truck. The oyster-shell parking lot was white and hot in the sunlight. He was walking along beside me now, his face as tight as the skin of an overinflated balloon. He pushed at my arm with his stiffened hand.

'Hey, you got wax?' he said. 'You don't talk to me like this! You don't get in my face in front of my friends and walk away!'

I opened my truck door. He grabbed my shoulder and turned me back toward him. His sweating chest was crisscrossed with veins.

'Swing on me and you're busted. No more high school builshit,' I said.

I slammed the truck door and drove slowly out of the lot over the oyster shells. His dilated face, slipping past the window, wore the expression of a man whose furious energies had suddenly been transformed into a set of knives turning inside him.

That afternoon I left work early and enrolled Alafair in kindergarten at the Catholic school in New Iberia for the fall semester, then I took her with Batist and me to seine for shrimp in the jug boat out on the salt. But I had another reason to be out on the Gulf that day: it was the twenty-first anniversary of my father's death. He had been a derrick man on a drilling rig, working high up on the monkey board, when the crew hit an oil sand earlier than they had expected. There was no blowout preventer on the wellhead, and as soon as the drill bit tapped into that gas dome far below the Gulf's floor, the rig began to tremble and suddenly salt water, sand, and oil exploded from the hole under thousands of pounds of pressure, and then the casing jettisoned, too. Metal spars, tongs, coils of chain, huge sections of pipe clattered and rang through the rigging, a spark jumped off a steel surface, and the wellhead ignited. The survivors said the roar of flame looked like someone had kicked open hell's front door.

My father clipped his safety belt onto the wire that ran from the monkey board to the roof of the quarter-boat and jumped. But the rig caved with him, crashed across the top of the quarter-boat, and took my father and nineteen other roughnecks down to the bottom of the Gulf with it.

His body was never found, and sometimes in my dreams I would see him far below the waves, still wearing his hardhat and overalls and steel-toed boots, grinning at me, his big hand raised to tell me that everything was all right.

That was my old man. Sheriff's deputies could jail him, saloon bouncers could bust chairs across his back, a *bourée* dealer could steal his wife, but the next morning he would pretend to be full of fun and brush yesterday's bad fortune aside as something not even worth mentioning.

I let Alafair sit behind the wheel in the pilot's cab, an Astros baseball cap sideways on her head, while Batist and I took in the nets and filled the ice bins with shrimp. Then I made a half-mile circle, cut the engine, and let the boat drift back over the spot where my father's rig had gone down in a torrent of cascading iron and geysers of steam twenty-one years ago.

It was twilight now, and the water was black-green and covered with froth that slipped down in the troughs between the waves. The sun was already down, and the red and black clouds on the western horizon looked as though they had risen from a planet burning under the water's surface. I opened the scuba gear box, took out a bunch of yellow and purple roses I had snipped earlier, and threw them out on the flat side of a wave. The petals and clustered stems broke apart in the next wave and floated away from each other, then dimmed and sank below the surface.

'He like that, him,' Batist said. 'Your old man like flowers. Flowers and women. Whiskey, too. Hey, Dave, you don't be sad. Your old man wasn't never sad.'

'Let's boil some shrimp and head for home,' I said.

But I was troubled all the way in. The twilight died in the west and left only a green glow on the horizon, and as the moon rose, the water turned the color of lead. Was it the memory of my father's death that bothered me, or my constant propensity for depression?

No, something else had been stirring in my unconscious all day, like a rat working its whiskers through a black hole. A good cop puts people away; he doesn't kill them. So far I had made a mess of things and hadn't turned the key on anyone. To compensate, I had wrapped barbed wire around the head of a mental cripple like Bubba Rocque. I didn't feel good about it.

Minos called me at the office the next morning.

'Did you hear from the Lafayette sheriff's department about Bubba?' he said.

'No.'

'I thought they kept you informed.'

'What is it, Minos?'

'He beat the shit out of his wife last night. Thoroughly. In a bar out on Pinhook Road. You want to hear it?'

'Go ahead.'

'Yesterday afternoon they started fighting with each other in their car outside the Winn Dixie, then three hours later she's slopping down the juice in the bar on Pinhook with a couple of New Orleans grease-balls when Mad Man Muntz skids his Caddy to a stop in the parking lot, crashes through the front door, and slaps her with the flat of his hand into next week. He knocked her down on the floor, kicked her in the ass, then picked her up and threw her through the men's room door. One of the greasers tried to stop it, and Bubba splattered his mouth all over a wall. That's no shit. The bartender said Bubba hit the guy so hard his head almost twisted off his neck.'

'You're enjoying this, Minos.'

'It beats watching these fuckers park their twenty-grand cars at the racetrack.'

'Where is he now?'

'Back home, I guess. She had to go to Lourdes for stitches, but she and the greaseball aren't filing charges. They don't seem to like participating in the legal process, for some reason. Do you have any idea what triggered Bubba's toggle switch?'

'I went out to his fish business by Avery Island yesterday.'

'So?'

'I poured some iodine on a couple of severed nerve endings.'

'Ah.'

'Let's get it all out here, Minos. I think Claudette Rocque was behind my wife's death. Bubba's a sonofabitch, but I'm convinced he would have come after me head-on. He's prideful, and he's wanted to put out my light since we were kids. He'd never admit to himself that he had to hire somebody to do it. I think Claudette sent Romero and the Haitian to kill me, and when they murdered Annie instead and then Romero missed me again, she came around the house with a poontang act and a hundred-thou-a-year job. When that didn't work, she got Bubba jealous and turned him loose on me. Anyway, I'm sure she was in Romero's apartment. She left stains on the table from that thermos of gin rickeys she always carries around.'

'So that's what the lime-juice business was about?'

'Yes.'

'And of course it's worthless as evidence.'

'Yes.'

'So you decided to stick a fork in Bubba's nuts about his old lady?'

'That's about it.'

'You want absolution now?'

'All right on that stuff, Minos.'

'Quit worrying about it. They're both human toilets. My advice to you now is to stay away from them.'

'Why?'

'Let things run their course.'

I was silent.

'He's psychotic. She collects *cojones*,' he said. 'You spit in the soup. Now let them drink it. It might prove interesting. Just stay the fuck away from it, though.'

'No one will ever accuse you of euphemism.'

'You know what your problem is? You're two people in the same envelope. You want to be a moral man in an amoral business. At the same time you want to blow up their shit just like the rest of us. Each time I talk to you, I never know who's coming out of the jack-in-the-box.'

'I'll see you. Stay in touch.'

'Yeah. Don't bother thanking me for the call. We do this for all rural flatfeet.'

He hung up. I tried to call him back, but his line was busy. I drove home and ate lunch with Batist out on the dock under the canvas awning. It was hot and still and the sun was white in the sky.

I couldn't sleep that night. The air was breathless and dry, and the window and ceiling fans seemed unable to remove the heat that had built up in the wood of the house all day long. The stars looked hot in the sky, and out in the moonlight I could see my neighbour's horses lying down in a muddy slough. I went into the kitchen in my underwear and ate a bowl of ice cream and strawberries, and a moment later Robin stood in the doorway in her lingerie top and panties, her eyes adjusting sleepily to the light.

'It's just the heat. Go back to sleep, kiddo,' I said.

She smiled and felt her way back down the hall without answering.

But it wasn't just the heat. I turned off the light and sat outside on the steps in the dark. I wanted to put Claudette and Bubba Rocque away more than anything else in the world; no, I wanted worse for them. They epitomized greed and selfishness; they injected misery and death into the lives of others so they could live in wealth and comfort. And while they had dined on blackened redfish in New Orleans or slept in a restored antebellum home that overlooked carriage house and flower garden and river and trees, their emissaries had torn my front door open and watched my wife wake terrified and alone in front of their shotgun barrels.

But I couldn't take them down by provoking a sociopath into assaulting his wife. This may sound noble; it's not. The alcoholic recovery program I practiced did not allow me to lie, manipulate, or impose design control over other people, particularly when its intention was obviously a destructive one. If I did, I would regress, I would start to screw up my own life and the lives of those closest to me, and eventually I would become the same drunk I had been years ago.

I fixed coffee and drank it out on the front porch and watched the first pale band of light touch the eastern sky. It was still hot, and the sun broke red over the earth's rim and turned the low strips of cloud on the horizon to flame; it was a sailor's warning, all right, but this morning was going to be one of the endings and beginnings for me. I would no longer flay myself daily because I couldn't extract the vengeance my anger demanded; I wouldn't try to control everything that swam into my ken, and I would humbly try to accept my Higher Power's plan for my life.

And finally I would refuse to be a factor in the squalor and violence of Bubba and Claudette Rocque's lives.

As always when I surrendered a problem or a self-serving mechanism inside myself to my Higher Power, I felt as though an albatross had been cut from my neck. I watched the sun's red glow rise higher into the pewter sky, saw the black border of trees on the far side of the bayou become gray and gradually green and distinct, heard my neighbour turn on his sprinkler hose in a hiss of water. There was no wind, and because it hadn't rained in two days there was dust from the road on the leaves of my pecan trees, and the shafts of spinning light between the branches looked like spun glass.

But I had learned long ago that resolution by itself is not enough; we are what we do, not what we think and feel. In my case that meant I didn't want any more damage to Claudette Rocque on my conscience, it meant no more rat-fucking, no more insertion of fishhooks in Bubba's head, the game was simply going into extra innings. It meant telling both of them all that.

I shaved and showered, put on my loafers and seersucker slacks, clipped on my badge and belt holster, drank another cup of coffee in the kitchen, then drove down the dirt road toward New Iberia and the old highway to Lafayette. The weather had started to change abruptly. A long, heavy bank of gray clouds that stretched from horizon to horizon was moving out of the south, and as the first shadows passed across the sun, a breeze lifted above the marsh, stirred the moss on the cypresses, and flickered the dusty leaves of the oaks along the road.

I could feel the barometric pressure dropping. The bream and goggle-eye had already started hitting along the edge of the lily pads, as they always did before a change in the weather, and the sparrow hawks and cranes that had been gliding on the hot updrafts from the marsh were now circling lower and lower out of the darkening sky. Main Street in New Iberia was full of dust, the green bamboo along the banks of Bayou Teche bending in the wind. At the city limits the Negro owner of a fruit stand, which had been there since I was a boy, was carrying his lugs of strawberries from the shade tree by the highway back inside the stand.

Twenty minutes later I was approaching the Vermilion River and the antebellum home of Bubba and Claudette Rocque. The air was cool now, the clouds overhead blueblack, the sugarcane green and rippling in the fields. I could smell rain in the south, smell the wet earth on the wind. Up ahead I could see the pea-gravel entrance to Bubba's home, the white fences entwined with yellow roses, the water sprinklers twirling among the oak, mimosa, lime, and orange trees on his lawn. Then I saw his maroon Cadillac convertible, the immaculate white top buttoned down on the tinted windows, turn out of the drive in a scorch of gravel and roar down the highway toward me. Its weight and speed actually buffeted my truck as it sucked past me like an arrow off an archer's bow. I watched it grow smaller in the rearview mirror, then saw its brake lights come on by a filling station and restaurant. I turned into his drive.

Even though it was cool, the curtains were drawn on the windows and the fans for the central air-conditioning hummed on the side of the house and a couple of window units upstairs were turned on full blast and dripping with moisture. I walked up on the wide marble porch and twisted the brass bell handle, waited and twisted again, then knocked loudly with my fist. I could hear no sound inside the house. I walked around the side, past a flower bed of wilted geraniums that was sopping from a soak hose, and tapped on the glass of the kitchen door. There was still no answer, but the MG and the Oldsmobile were parked in the carriage house and I thought I could smell fried bacon. The light in the sky had changed, and the air was moist and looked green through the trees, and dead oak leaves clicked and tumbled across the grass like bits of dried parchment.

I put my hands on my hips and looked in a circle at Bubba's clay tennis court and gazebos and myrtle hedges on the river and stone wells hung with ornamental chains and brass buckets and was about to give it up and mark it off when I saw the wind blow smoke and powdered ash and red embers from behind an aluminum lawn shed in back.

I walked across the grass and around the shed and looked down upon an old ash and garbage heap, on top of which were the collapsed and blackened remains of a mattress. The cover had almost all burned away, and the stuffing was smoldering and rising in the wind in black threads. But one side of the mattress had not burned entirely, and on it was a dirty red stain that was steaming from the heat. I opened my Puma knife, knelt, and cut the stained material away. It felt stiff and warm between my fingers as I folded it and placed it in my pocket. Then I found a garden hose in the shed, connected it to a spigot by a flower bed, and sprinkled the mattress until all the embers were dead. A rancid odor rose in the steam.

I walked back across the lawn, pried a brick up from the border of the geranium bed, and knocked out a pane in the back door. I turned the inside handle and stepped into a Colonial-style kitchen of brass pots and pans hung on hooks above a brick hearth. The smell of bacon came from a skillet on the stove and from a single grease-streaked plate on the breakfast table. The air-conditioning was turned so high that my skin felt instantly cold and dead, as though the house had been refrigerated with dry ice. I walked through a pine-paneled television den with empty bookshelves and two black bearskins nailed at angles on the wall, into a chandeliered dining room whose walnut cabinets were filled with shining crystal ware, and finally into the marble-floored entrance area by the spiral staircase.

I walked slowly upstairs with my hand on the bannister. The furnishings and colors and woodwork of the second story had the same peculiar, mismatched quality as the downstairs, like an impaired camera lens that wouldn't focus properly. The bathroom door gaped open at the top of the stairs, exposing a pink shag rug, gold fixtures on the washbasin and bathtub, and pink wallpaper with a silver erotic design on it. The plastic rings on the shower bar hung empty, except for one of them that still held a torn eyelet and a small piece of vinyl from the curtain.

I found the master bedroom farther down the hall. Through the French doors that gave onto the gallery I could see the tops of the oak trees beating in the wind. I turned on the light and looked at the canopied bed that was centered against one wall. The sheets, bedspread, pillows, and mattress were gone. Only the box spring remained in the wooden frame. I walked in a circle around the bed and felt the rug. It was still damp in two places and smelled of dry-cleaning fluid or spot remover.

I knew it was time to call the Lafayette Parish sheriff's office. I was overextended legally, in the home on questionable grounds, and perhaps even in danger of tainting evidence in a homicide. But legality is often a matter that is decided after the fact, and I believed sincerely that someone owed me ten more minutes.

I went out a side door onto the flagstone patio, past the screened-in pool and the breezeway where Bubba kept his dumbbells, universal gym, and punching bags, and found a garden rake leaned against the carriage house. The wind was blowing stronger now, the first raindrops clicking against the upstairs windows.

Even though the flower bed by the side of the house was flooded from the soak hose, the leaves of the geraniums still looked like wilted green paper. I began to rake the dirt and the plants out of the bed. The soil was rich and black and had been built up with compost, and as I scooped it out on the gravel, milky puddles formed in the hollows. A foot down the rake's head struck something solid. I worked the dirt and torn-plants and root systems back over the brick border and created a long, shallow depression through the center of the garden, the rake's teeth again touching something thick and resistant. Then I saw the edge of a vinyl shower curtain rise on one of the teeth and a pajama-clad knee protrude through the soil. I scraped around the edges of the body, watched the feet and shoulders and brow take shape, as though I were its creator and sculpting it from the earth.

I set the rake on the gravel and cut the soak hose in half with my knife to release a strong jet of water. Then I washed the soft dirt, which looked like black coffee grounds, from Bubba's face. He rested on top of the shower curtain, his gray-blue eyes open, his face and hands and feet absolutely bloodless. The handle and the metal back of the cane knife she had used stuck out of the dirt by his head. The cut across the side of his neck went all the way to the bone.

I turned off the soak hose and went back through the kitchen door and called the Lafayette Parish sheriff's office and Minos Dautrieve, then I started toward my truck. Dead leaves swirled all over the yard in the wind, the sky was black, and the few raindrops that struck my face were as hard as BBs.

Behind me I heard the phone ring. I went back inside and picked up the receiver.

'Hello,' I said.

'Bubba? This is Kelly. What's the deal on this dago linen service?' a man's voice said over the hum of long-distance wires. 'Claudette says I'm supposed to hire these guys. What the fuck's going on over there?'

'Bubba's dead, partner.'

'What? Who is this?'

'I'm a police officer. What's your name?'

He hung up the phone.

I drove back down the gravel lane toward the highway while the thick limbs of the oak trees beat against one another overhead. The black thunder-heads on the southern horizon were veined with lightning. The air was almost cold now, and the young sugarcane was bent to the ground in the wind. I rolled up my windows, turned on the windshield wipers, and felt the steering wheel shake in my hand. Pieces of newspaper and cardboard were flying in the air across the highway, and the telephone wires flopped and bounced like rubber bands between the poles.

I passed a cement plant and a sidetracked Southern Pacific freight, and then I saw the maroon convertible parked in front of a truck stop that had a small lounge attached to it. It began raining hard just as I walked inside.

Because the Negro janitor was mopping the floor and wiping down the tables, the curtains were open and the overhead lights were turned on. In the light you could see the cigarette burns on the floor, the mending tape on the booths, and the stacked beer cases in a back corner. An overweight barmaid was drinking coffee and talking with two oilfield roughnecks at the bar. The roughnecks wore tin hats and steel-toed boots and had drilling mud splattered on their clothes. One of them rolled a matchstick in his mouth and said something to me about the weather. When I didn't answer, he and his friend and the woman continued to look at me and the pistol and badge on my belt.

Claudette Rocque was at a table by the back door. The door was open and mist was blowing through the screen. Out on the railway tracks I could see the rust-colored SP freight cars shining in the rain. She sipped her gin rickey and looked at me across the top of the glass. Her face was bruised and fatigued, and her brown eyes, which had that strange red cast to them, were glazed and sleepy with alcohol. There was an outline of adhesive tape around the stitches on her chin, and the skin was puckered on the tip of the bone. But her yellow sundress and the orange bandana in her hair were fresh and clean and even looked attractive on her, and I guessed that she had showered and changed after she had dragged Bubba downstairs on the shower curtain, dug up the garden, buried him, re-planted the geraniums, and burned the mattress and pillows and sheets. She inhaled from her filter-tipped cigarette and blew smoke out toward me.

'You had a hard night,' I said.

'I've had worse.'

'You should have taken him somewhere else. You might have gotten away with it.'

'What *are* you talking about?'

'I dug him up. The cane knife, too.'

She drank from her glass and puffed on the cigarette again. Her eyes looked vaguely amused.

'Drink it up, Claudette. You're going on a big dry.'

'Oh, I wouldn't count on that, pumpkin. You ought to watch more television. Battered wives are in fashion these days.'

I slipped the handcuffs off the back of my belt, took the cigarette out of her mouth and dropped it on the floor, and cuffed her wrists through the back of the chair.

'Oh, our law officer is so uncorruptible, so noble in his AA sobriety. I bet you might like a slightly bruised fuck, though. It's your last chance, sugarplum, because I'll be out on bond tomorrow morning. You should give it some thought.'

I turned a chair around backwards and sat across from her.

'You did three years and you think you're conwise, but you're still a fish,' I said. 'Let me give you the script. You won't do time because you cut Bubba's throat. Nobody cares when somebody like Bubba gets killed, except maybe the people he owes money to. Instead, a jury of unemployed roughnecks, fundamentalist morons, and welfare blacks who don't like rich people will send you up the road because you're an ex-con and a lesbian.

'Of course, you'll think that's unfair. And you'll be right, it is. But the greatest irony is that the people who'll send you back to St Gabriel will never hear the name of the innocent girl you had murdered. Some people might call it comedy. It'll make a good story in the zoo.'

Her reddish-brown eyes were narrow and mean. The bruise over the lid of one eye looked like a small blue mouse. I walked to the pay phone on the wall by the bar and called the sheriff's office. Just as I was about to hang up, I heard Claudette scrape the chair across the floor and smash it with her weight against the wall. She snapped the back loose from the seat, and then with the broken wood supports hanging from her manacled wrists, she went out the screen door into the rain.

I followed her across a field toward the railroad tracks. The bottom of her yellow dress was flecked with mud, and her bandanna fell off her head and her hair stuck wetly to her face. The rain was driving harder now, and the drops were big and flat and cold as hell. I grabbed her by the arm and tried to turn her back toward the truck stop, but she sat down in a puddle of gray water. Her arms, twisted behind her by the handcuffs, were rigid with muscle.

I leaned over and tried to lift her to her feet. She sat in the water with her legs apart, her shoulders stooped, her head down. I pulled her by the arms, her dead weight and wet skin slipping out of my hands. She fell sideways in the water, then she got to her knees and I thought she was going to stand up. I bent down beside her and lifted under one arm. She looked up at me in the rain, as though she were seeing me for the first time, and spit in my face.

I stepped back from her, used my handkerchief, and threw it away. She stared fixedly across the fields at the green line of trees on the horizon. Water ran in rivulets out of her soaked hair and down over her face. I walked to an empty freight car on the siding and pulled an old piece of canvas off the floor. It was stiff and crusted with dirt but it was dry. I spread it over her so that she looked like she was staring out of a small, peaked house.

'It's the Mennonite way of doing things,' I said.

But she wasn't interested in vague nuances. She was looking at the sheriff's deputies and Minos Dautrieve stepping out of their cars in the truck-stop parking lot. I stood beside her and watched them make their way across the drenched field toward us. Through the open doors of the freight car I could see chaff spinning in the wind, and in the distance the gray buildings of the cement plant looked like grain elevators in the rain. Minos was calling to me in the echo of thunder across the land, and I thought of drowned voices out on the salt and wheat fields in the rain. I thought of white-capping troughs out on the Gulf and sunflowers and wheat fields in the rain.

Epilogue

I worked two more weeks with the sheriff's department and then hung it up. In August the sun came up white every morning and the air was hazy with humidity and even your lightest clothes stuck to your body like wet paper. I rented a clapboard bungalow by the Texas coast, and Robin and Alafair and I spent two weeks fishing for gafftop and white and speckled trout. At dawn, when the tide was drawn out over the flats, the gulls squeaked and circled in the sky and dipped their beaks into the pools of trapped shellfish, then the long, flat expanses of wet sand became rose-tinted and purple, and the palm tree in our side yard would stand like a black metal etching against the sun.

It was always cool when we took the boat out in the morning, and the wind would come up out of the southeast and we could smell the schools of trout feeding under the slicks they made on the water. We took the boat across a half-moon bay that was bordered on each side by sand pits, sawgrass, and dead cypress, and just as we crossed over the last sandbar into deep water and entered the Gulf, we would see those large floating slicks, like oil that had escaped from a sunken freighter, and we'd bait our hooks with live shrimp, cast on the edge of the slick, and pop our wood floats loudly against the surface. Occasionally we'd hook gafftop, and we always knew it was a catfish by the way he'd pull straight down for the bottom and not break the surface until we had socked the treble hook all the way through his head and forced him to the top. But a speckled trout would run and strip line off the drag, turn across your bow or stern and go under your boat if he could, and even when you got the net under him he'd still try to break your rod across the gunnel. We'd put cold drinks and sausage, cheese, and onion sandwiches in the ice chest, and by noon, when we had eaten our lunch and the sun was straight up in the sky and the salt was crusty on the hot bow of the boat, the ice would be covered with rows of silver trout, their gills open and red, their teeth hooked wide, their eyes like black glass.

It was late August when we went back to New Iberia, and then one morning Robin was gone. I read the letter at the breakfast table in my underwear while the backyard turned from blue to gray in the early light. She had left coffee for me on the stove and a bowl of Grape-Nuts and strawberries on the table.

I had the cab stop up on the road so I wouldnt wake you. Goodbyes and apologys are for the Rotary and the dipshits, right? I love you, babe. Its important you understand and believe that. You turned me around and cared about me when nobody else did. And I mean nobody. Your not like any guy I new before. You hurt for other people and for some reason you feel guilty about them. But thats not love, Dave. Its something else and I dont understand it really. I think maybe you still love Annie. I guess thats the way its suppose to be. But I think youve got to find out for yourself and you dont need me in the way.

Hey, this is no big deal. Im going to work as a cashier at your brothers resterant on Dauphine, so if you ever want to hit on a hot broad you know where to go. Im off the juice and pills too thanks to a good hearted roach I know. Thats not a bad thing to put on your score card.

My love to Alafair
Take it easy,
Streak Robin

I did strange things during that last week in August. On a twilight evening I walked across the deserted campus of USL in Lafayette, where I attended college in the 1950s. The quadrangle was filled with shadows, the warm breeze blew through the brick walkways, and the dark green oaks were filled with the sounds of birds in the gathering dusk. I sat in a late-hour café by the SP yard and listened over and over to a 1957 Jimmy Clanton record on the jukebox while redbone gandy walkers, glistening with sweat, tore up the track outside in the glare of burning flares, and long strips of freights clattered by in the darkness. I played dominoes with the old men in the back of Tee Neg's pool hall, chipped minié balls out of the coulee's dirt wall by the ruined sugar planter's house on the bayou, and drove my truck down the levee deep into the marsh, where an abandoned community of shacks on stilts still stood, rotting and gray, against the willows and cypress. Forty years ago my father and I had come here for a *fais dodo* on July Fourth, and the people had cooked a pig in the ground and drunk wine out of Mason jars and danced to an accordion band on a houseboat until the sun was a red flare on the horizon and the mosquitoes were black on our skin.

As I stared out the truck window at the gray tops of the trees, the shacks hanging in pieces on the stilts, the water black and still in the dying light, I heard a solitary bullfrog croak, then the flooded woods ached with sound. Three blue herons sailed low against the late sun, and with a sinking of the heart I knew that the world in which I had grown up was almost gone and it would not come aborning again.

And maybe Bubba Rocque and I had been more alike than I cared to admit. Maybe we both belonged to the past, back there in those green summers of bush-league baseball and crab boils and the smoke of neighborhood fish fries drifting in the trees. Every morning came to you like a strawberry bursting on the tongue. We ran crab traps and trotlines in the bay with our fathers, baited crawfish nets with bloody chunks of nutria meat, cleaned boxes of mudcat with knife and pliers, and never thought of it as work. In the heat of the afternoon we sat on the tailgate of the ice wagon at the depot, watching the troop trains roll through town, then fought imaginary wars with stalks of sugarcane, unaware that our little piece of Cajun geography was being consumed on the edges like an old photograph held to a flame. The fiery rifts in evening skies marked only the end of a day, not the season or an era.

But perhaps age has taught me that the earth is still new, molten at the core and still forming, that black leaves in a winter forest will crawl with life in the spring, that our story is ongoing and it is indeed a crime to allow the heart's energies to dissipate with the fading of light on the horizon. I can't be sure. I brood upon it and sleep little. I wait like a denied lover for the blue glow of dawn.

Black Cherry Blues

For John and Flavia McBride

I would like to thank the John Simon Guggenheim Foundation for its generous assistance, and I also would like to thank the National Endowment for the Arts for its past support.

1

Her hair is curly and gold on the pillow, her skin white in the heat lightning that trembles beyond the pecan trees outside the bedroom window. The night is hot and breathless, the clouds painted like horsetails against the sky; a peal of thunder rumbles out on the Gulf like an apple rolling around in the bottom of a wood barrel, and the first raindrops ping against the window fan. She sleeps on her side, and the sheet molds her thigh, the curve of her hip, her breast. In the flicker of the heat lightning the sun freckles on her bare shoulder look like brown flaws in sculpted marble.

Then a prizing bar splinters the front door out of the jamb, and two men burst inside the house in heavy shoes, their pump shotguns at port arms. One is a tall Haitian, the other a Latin whose hair hangs off his head in oiled ringlets. They stand at the foot of the double bed in which she sleeps alone, and do not speak. She awakes with her mouth open, her eyes wide and empty of meaning. Her face is still warm from a dream, and she cannot separate sleep from the two men who stare at her without speaking. Then she sees them looking at each other and aim their shotguns point-blank at her chest. Her eyes film and she calls out my name like a wet bubble bursting in her throat. The sheet is twisted in her hands; she holds it against her breasts as though it could protect her from twelve-gauge deer slugs and double-aught buckshot.

They begin shooting, and the room seems to explode with smoke and flame from their shotgun barrels, with shell wadding, mattress stuffing, splinters gouged out of the bedstead, torn lampshades, flying glass. The two killers are methodical. They have taken out the sportsman's plug in their shotguns so they can load five rounds in the magazine, and they keep firing and ejecting the smoking hulls on the floor until their firing pins snap empty. Then they reload with the calmness of men who might have just stood up in a blind and fired at a formation of ducks overhead.

The sheet is torn, drenched with her blood, embedded in her wounds. The men have gone now, and I sink to my knees by my wife and kiss her sightless eyes, run my hand over her hair and wan face, put her fingers in my mouth. A solitary drop of her blood runs down the shattered headboard and pools on

404

my skin. A bolt of lightning explodes in an empty field behind the house. The inside of my head is filled with a wet, sulphurous smell, and again I hear my name rise like muffled, trapped air released from the sandy bottom of a pond.

It was four in the morning on a Saturday and raining hard when I awoke from the dream in a West Baton Rouge motel. I sat on the side of the bed in my underwear and tried to rub the dream out of my face, then I used the bathroom and came back and sat on the side of the bed again in the dark.

First light was still two hours away, but I knew I would not sleep again. I put on my raincoat and hat and drove in my pickup truck to an all-night café that occupied one side of a clapboard roadhouse. The rain clattered on my truck cab, and the wind was blowing strong out of the southwest, across the Atchafalaya swamp, whipping the palm and oak trees by the highway. West Baton Rouge, which begins at the Mississippi River, has always been a seedy area of truck stops, marginal gambling joints, Negro and blue-collar bars. To the east you can see the lighted girders of the Earl K. Long Bridge, plumes of smoke rising from the oil refineries, the state capital building silhouetted in the rain. Baton Rouge is a green town full of oak trees, parks, and lakes, and the thousands of lights on the refineries and chemical plants are regarded as a testimony to financial security rather than a sign of industrial blight. But once you drive west across the metal grid of the bridge and thump down on the old cracked four-lane, you're in a world that caters to the people of the Atchafalaya basin – Cajuns, redbones, roustabouts, pipeliners, rednecks whose shrinking piece of American geography is identified only by a battered pickup, a tape deck playing Waylon, and a twelve-pack of Jax.

The rain spun in the yellow arc lights over the café parking lot. It was empty inside, except for a fat Negro woman whom I could see through the service window in the kitchen, and a pretty, redheaded waitress in her early twenties, dressed in a pink uniform with her hair tied up on her freckled neck. She was obviously tired, but she was polite and smiled at me when she took my order, and I felt a sense of guilt, almost shame, at my susceptibility and easy fondness for a young woman's smile. Because if you're forty-nine and unmarried or a widower or if you've simply chosen to live alone, you're easily flattered by a young woman's seeming attention to you, and you forget that it is often simply a deference to your age.

I ordered a chicken-fried steak and a cup of coffee and listened to Jimmy Clanton's recording of 'Just a Dream' that came from the jukebox next door. Through the open doorway that gave on to the empty dance floor, I could see a half-dozen people at the bar against the far wall. I watched a man my age, with waved blond hair, drink his whiskey down to the ice, point to the glass for the bartender to refill it, then rise from his stool and walk across the dance floor into the café.

He wore gray slacks, a green sport shirt with blue flowers on it, shined loafers, white socks, a gold watch, and gold clip-on ballpoint pens in his shirt pocket. He wore his shirt outside his slacks to hide his paunch and love handles.

'Hey, hon, let me have a cheeseburger and bring it up to the bar, will you?' he said.

Then his eyes adjusted to the light and he looked at me more carefully.

'Great God Almighty,' he said. 'Dave Robicheaux. You son of a buck.'

A voice and a face out of the past, not simply mine but from an era. Dixie Lee Pugh, my freshman roommate at Southwestern Louisiana Institute in 1956: a peckerwood kid from a river town north of Baton Rouge, with an accent more Mississippi than Louisiana, who flunked out his first semester, then went to Memphis and cut two records at the same studio where Carl Perkins, Johnny Cash, and Elvis began their careers. The second record put him on New York television, and we watched in awe while he played his sunburst rhythm-and-blues guitar or hammered his fingers on the piano keyboard while an audience of thousands went insane and danced in the aisles.

He was one of the biggest in the early rock 'n' roll era. But he had something more going for him than many of the others did. He was the real article, an honest-to-God white blues singer. He learned his music in the Baptist church, but somebody in that little cotton and pecan-orchard town rubbed a lot of pain into him, too, because it was in everything he sang and it wasn't manufactured for the moment, either.

Then we read and heard other stories about him: the four or five failed marriages, the death of one of his children in a fire, a hit-and-run accident and DWI in Texas that put him in Huntsville pen.

'Dave, I don't believe it,' he said, grinning. 'I saw you ten or twelve years ago in New Orleans. You were a cop.'

I remembered it. It had been in a low-rent bar off Canal, the kind of place that featured yesterday's celebrities, where the clientele made noise during the performances and insulted the entertainers.

He sat down next to me and shook hands, almost as an afterthought.

'We got to drink some mash and talk some trash,' he said, then told the waitress to bring me a beer or a highball.

'No, thanks, Dixie,' I said.

'You mean like it's too late or too early in the day or like you're off the jug?' he said.

'I go to meetings now. You know what I mean?'

'Heck yeah. That takes guts, man. I admire it.' His eyes were green and filled with an alcohol shine. He looked at me directly a moment, then his eyes blinked and he looked momentarily embarrassed.

'I read in the newspaper about your wife, man. I'm sorry.'

'Thank you.'

'They caught the guys that did it?'

'More or less.'

'Huh,' he said, and studied me for a moment. I could see that he was becoming uncomfortable with the knowledge that a chance meeting with an old friend is no guarantee that you can reclaim pleasant moments out of the past. Then he smiled again.

'You still a cop?' he asked.

'I own a bait and boat-rental business south of New Iberia. I came up here last night to pick up some refrigeration equipment and got stuck in the storm.'

He nodded. We were both silent.

'Are you playing here, Dixie?' I said.

Mistake.

'No, I don't do that anymore. I never really got back to it after that trouble in Texas.'

He cleared his throat and took a cigarette out of the pack in his shirt pocket.

'Say, hon, how about getting me my drink out of the bar?'

The waitress smiled, put down the rag she had been using to clean the counter, and went into the nightclub next door.

'You know about that stuff in Texas?' he asked.

'Yes, I think so.'

'I was DWI, all right, and I ran away from the accident. But the guy run that stop sign. There wasn't no way I could have avoided it. But it killed his little boy, man. That's some hard shit to live with. I got out in eighteen months with good time.' He made lines on a napkin with his thumbnail. 'A lot of people just don't want to forget, though.'

I didn't know what to say. I felt sorry for him. He seemed little different from the kid I used to know, except he was probably ninety-proof most of the time now. I remembered a quote in a *Newsweek* story about Dixie Lee that seemed to define him better than anything else I had ever seen written about him. The reporter had asked him if any of his band members could read music. He replied, 'Yeah, some of them can, but it don't hurt their playing any.'

So I asked him what he was doing now, because I had to say something.

'Leaseman,' he said, 'Like Hank Snow used to say, "From old Montana down to Alabam." I cover it all. Anyplace there's oil and coal. The money's right, too podna.'

The waitress put his bourbon and water down in front of him. He drank from it and winked at her over his glass.

'I'm glad you're doing okay, Dixie,' I said.

'Yeah, it's a good life. A Caddy convertible, a new address every week, it beats collard greens and grits.' He hit me on the arm. 'Heck, it's all rock 'n' roll, anyway, man.'

I nodded good-naturedly and looked through the service window at the Negro woman who was scraping my hash browns and chicken-fried steak on to a plate. I was about to tell the waitress that I had meant the order to go.

'Well, I got some people waiting on me,' Dixie Lee said. 'Like, some of the sweet young things still come around, you know what I mean? Take it easy, buddy. You look good.'

I shook hands with him, ate my steak, bought a second cup of coffee for the road, and walked out into the rain.

The wind buffeted my truck all the way across the Atchafalaya basin. When the sun came up the light was gray and wet, and ducks and herons were flying low over the dead cypress in the marsh. The water in the bays was the color of lead and capping in the wind. A gas flare burned on a drilling rig set back in a flooded stand of willow trees. Each morning I began the day with a prayer, thanking my Higher Power for my sobriety of yesterday and asking Him to help me keep it today. This morning I included Dixie Lee in my prayer.

I drove back to New Iberia through St Martinville. The sun was above the oaks on Bayou Teche now, but in the deep, early morning shadows the mist still hung like clouds of smoke among the cattails and damp tree trunks. It was only March, but spring was roaring into southern Louisiana, as it always does after the long gray rains of February. Along East Main in New Iberia the yards were filled with blooming azalea, roses, and yellow and red hibiscus, and the trellises and gazebos were covered with trumpet vine and clumps of purple wisteria. I rumbled over the drawbridge and followed the dirt road along the bayou south of town, where I operated a fish dock and lived with a six-year-old El Salvadorean refugee girl named Alafair in the old home my father had built out of cypress and oak during the Depression.

The wood had never been painted, was dark and hard as iron, and the beams had been notched and joined with pegs. The pecan trees in my front yard were thick with leaf and still dripping with rainwater, which tinked on the tin roof of the gallery. The yard always stayed in shadow and was covered with layers of blackened leaves. The elderly mulatto woman who baby-sat Alafair for me was in the side yard, pulling the vinyl storm covers off my rabbit hutches. She was the color of a copper penny and had turquoise eyes, like many South Louisiana Negroes who are part French. Her body looked put together out of sticks, and her skin was covered with serpentine lines. She dipped snuff and smoked hand-rolled cigarettes constantly, and bossed me around in my own home, but she could work harder than anyone I had ever known, and she had been fiercely loyal to my family since I was a child.

My boat dock was in full sunlight now, and I could see Batist, the other black person who worked for me, loading an ice chest for two white men in their outboard. He was shirtless and bald, and the weight of the ice chest made his wide back and shoulders ridge with muscle. He broke up kindling for my barbecue pit with his bare hands, and once I saw him jerk a six-foot alligator out of the water by its tail and throw it up on a sandbar.

I stepped around the puddles in the yard to the gallery.

'What you gonna do this coon?' Clarise, the mulatto woman, said.

She had put my three-legged raccoon, Tripod, on his chain, which was attached to a wire clothesline so he could run up and down in the side yard. She pulled him up in the air by the chain. His body danced and curled as though he were being garroted.

'Clarise, don't do that.'

'Ax him what he done, him,' she said. 'Go look my wash basket. Go look your shirts. They blue yesterday. They brown now. Go smell you.'

'I'll take him down to the dock.'

'Tell Batist not to bring him back, no.' She dropped Tripod, half strangled, to the ground. 'He come in my house again, you gonna see him cooking with the sweet potato.'

I unsnapped his chain from the clothesline and walked him down to the bait shop and café on the dock. I was always amazed at the illusion of white supremacy in southern society, since more often than not our homes were dominated and run by people of color.

Batist and I bailed the rainwater from the previous night's storm out of my rental boats, filled the cigarette and candy machines, seined dead shiners out of the live-bait tanks, drained the water out of the ice bins and put fresh ice on top of the soda pop and beer, and started the barbecue fire for the lunch that we prepared for midday fishermen. Then I opened up the beach umbrellas that were set in the holes of the huge wooden telephone spools that I used as tables, and went back up to the house.

It had turned out to be a beautiful morning. The sky was blue, the grass in the fields a deeper green from the rain; the wind was cool on the gallery, the backyard still deep in shadow under the mimosa tree, and my redwood flower boxes were streaked with water and thick with petunias and Indian paintbrush. Alafair was at the kitchen table in her pajama bottoms, coloring in the Mickey Mouse book I had bought her the day before. Her black hair was cut in bangs; her eyes were big and brown, her face as round as a pie plate, and her skin had already started to grow darker with tan. If there was any physical imperfection in her, it was her wide-set front teeth, which only made her smile look larger than it actually was. It was hard to believe that less than a year ago I had pulled her from a downed plane out at Southwest Pass just off the Gulf, a drowning little girl whose bones had felt hollow as a bird's, whose gasping mouth had looked like a guppy's in my wife's lap.

I brushed her fine black hair under my palm.

'How you doing, little guy?' I said.

'Where you went, Dave?'

'I got caught in the storm and had to stay in Baton Rouge.'

'Oh.'

Her hand went back to coloring. Then she stopped and grinned at me, full of glee.

'Tripod went ca-ca in Clarise basket,' she said.

'I heard about it. Look, don't say "ca-ca". Say "He went to the bathroom."'

'No ca-ca?'

'That's right. "He went to the bathroom."'

She repeated it after me, both of our heads nodding up and down.

She was in the first grade at the Catholic school in New Iberia, but she seemed to learn more English from Clarise and Batist and his wife than she did from me and the nuns. (A few lines you might hear from those three on any particular day: 'What time it is?' 'For how come you burn them leafs under my window, you?' 'While I was driving your truck, me, somebody pass a nail under the wheel and give it a big flat.')

I hugged Alafair, kissed her on top of the head, and went into the bedroom to undress and take a shower. The breeze through the window smelled of wet earth and trees and the gentle hint of four o'clocks that were still open in the shade. I should have been bursting with the spring morning, but I felt listless and spent, traveling on the outer edge of my envelope, and it wasn't simply because of bad dreams and insomnia the previous night. These moments would descend upon me at peculiar times, as though my heart's blood were fouled, and suddenly my mind would light with images and ring with sounds I wasn't ready to deal with.

It could happen anywhere. But right now it was happening in my bedroom. I had replaced several boards in the wall, or filled the twelve-gauge buckshot and deer-slug holes with liquid wood, and sanded them smooth. The gouged and splintered headboard, stained brown with my wife's blood as though it had been flung there by a paintbrush, lay in a corner of the old collapsed bar at the foot of my property. But when I closed my eyes I saw the streaks of shotgun fire in the darkness, heard the explosions that were as loud as the lightning outside, heard her screams as she cowered under a sheet and tried to shield herself with her hands while I ran frantically toward the house in the rain, my own screams lost in the thunder rolling across the land.

As always when these moments of dark reverie occurred in my waking day, there was no way I could think my way out of them. Instead, I put on my gym trunks and running shoes and pumped iron in the backyard. I did dread lifts, curls, and military presses with a ninety-pound bar in sets of ten and repeated the sets six times. Then I ran four miles along the dirt road by the bayou, the sunlight spinning like smoke through the canopy of oak and cypress trees overhead. Bream were still feeding on insects among the cattails and lily pads, and sometimes in a shady cut between two cypress trees I would see the back of a largemouth bass roll just under the surface.

I turned around at the drawbridge, waved to the bridgetender, and hit it hard all the way home. My wind was good, the blood sang in my chest, my stomach felt flat and hard, yet I wondered how long I would keep mortality and memory at bay.

Always the racetrack gambler, trying to intuit and control the future with only the morning line to operate on.

Three days later I was using a broomstick to push the rainwater out of the folds of the canvas awning over my dock when the telephone rang inside the bait shop. It was Dixie Lee Pugh.

'I'll take you to lunch,' he said.

'Thanks but I'm working.'

'I want to talk to you.'

'Go ahead.'

'I want to talk to you alone.'

'Where are you?'

'Lafayette.'

'Drive on over. Go out East Main, then take the bayou road south of town. You'll run right into my place.'

'Give me an hour.'

'You sound a little gray, podna.'

'Yeah, I probably need to get married again or something. Dangle loose.'

Every morning Batist and I grilled chickens and links on the barbecue pit that I had made by splitting an oil drum horizontally with an acetylene torch and welding hinges and metal legs on it. I sold paper-plate lunches of barbecue and dirty rice for three-fifty apiece, and I usually cleared thirty dollars or so from the fishermen who were either coming in for the day or about to go out. Then after we had cleaned the cable-spool tables, Batist and I would fix ourselves plates and open bottles of Dr Pepper and eat under one of the umbrellas by the water's edge.

It was a warm, bright afternoon, and the wind was lifting the moss on the dead cypress tress in the marsh. The sky was as blue and perfect as the inside of a teacup.

'That man drive like he don't know the road got holes in it,' Batist said. His sun-faded denim shirt was open on his chest. He wore a dime on a string around his neck to keep away the *gris-gris*, an evil spell, and his black chest looked like it was made of boiler-plate.

The pink Cadillac convertible, with its top down, was streaked with mud and rippled and dented along the fenders. I watched the front end dip into a chuckhole and shower yellow water all over the windshield.

'Dixie Lee never did things in moderation,' I said.

'You ain't renting him our boat?'

'He's just coming out to talk about something. He used to be a famous country and rock 'n' roll star.'

Batist kept chewing and looked at me flatly, obviously unimpressed.

'I'm serious. He used to be big stuff up in Nashville,' I said.

His eyes narrowed, as they always did when he heard words that he didn't recognize.

'It's in Tennessee. That's where they make a lot of country records.'

No help.

'I'll get us another Dr Pepper. Did you feed Tripod?' I said.

'You t'ink that coon don't know where the food at?'

I didn't understand.

'He ain't lost his nose, no.'

'What are you saying, Batist?'

'He ate all your fried pies. Go look your fried pies.'

Dixie Lee cut his engine, slammed the car door behind him, and lumbered down the dock into the bait shop, flipping one hand at us in recognition. His face was bloodless, the skin stretched tight on the bone, beaded with perspiration like drops of water on a pumpkin. His charcoal shirt, which was covered with roses, was damp along the buttons and under the armpits.

I followed him inside the bait shop. He dropped a five-dollar bill on the counter, opened a long-necked Jax on the side of the beer box, and upended it into his mouth. He kept swallowing until it was almost empty, then he took a breath of air and opened and closed his eyes.

'Boy, do I got one,' he said. 'I mean wicked, son, like somebody screwed a brace and bit through both temples.'

He tilted the bottle up again, one hand on his hip, and emptied it.

'A mellow start, but it don't keep the snakes in their basket very long, do it?'

'Nope.'

'What we're talking about here is the need for more serious fluids. You got any JD or Beam lying around?'

'I'm afraid not, Dixie,' I rang up his sale and put his change on the counter.

'These babies will have to do, then.' He opened another Jax, took a long pull, and blew out his breath. 'A preacher once asked me, "Son, can you take two drinks and walk away from it?" I said, "I can't tell you the answer to that sir, 'cause I never tried." That ought to be funny, but I guess it's downright pathetic, ain't it?'

'What's up, partner?'

He looked around the empty bait shop.

'How about taking me for a boat ride?' he said.

'I'm kind of tied up right now.'

'I'll pay you for your time. It's important, man.'

His green eyes looked directly into mine. I walked to the baitshop door.

'I'll be back in a half hour,' I called to Batist, who was still eating his lunch under the umbrella.

'I appreciate it, Dave. You're righteous people,' Dixie Lee popped open a paper bag and put four bottles of Jax inside.

I took him in an outboard down the bayou, past the four-corners, where the old flaking general store with its wide gallery sat in the shade of an enormous oak tree. Some old men and several Negroes from a road-maintenance crew were drinking soda pop on the gallery.

The wake from the outboard swelled up through the lily pads and cattails and slapped against the cypress roots along the bank. Dixie Lee lay back against the bow, the beer bottle in his hand filled with amber sunlight, his eyes narrowing wistfully in the sun's refraction off the brown water. I cut the engine and let us float on our own wake into an overhang of willow trees. In the sudden quiet we could hear a car radio playing an old Hank Williams song in the shell parking lot of the general store.

'Good God Almighty, is that inside my head or outside it?' he asked.

'It's from the four-corners,' I said, and smiled at him. I took out my Puma pocketknife and shaved the bark off a wet willow stick.

'Boy, it takes me back, though. When I started out, they said if you don't play it like Hank or Lefty, it ain't worth diddly-squat on a rock. They were right, too. Hey, you know the biggest moment I ever had in my career? It wasn't them two gold records, and it sure wasn't marrying some movie actress with douche water for brains. It was when I got to cut a live album with the Fat Man down in New Orleans. I was the only white artist he ever recorded with. Man, he was beautiful. He looked like a little fat baby pig up on that piano bench, with a silver shirt on and rhinestone coat and rings all over his fingers. He was grinning and rocking and pounding the keys with those little sausage fingers, sweat flying off his face, and the whole auditorium going apeshit. I mean with white broads trying to climb on the stage and people doing the dirty boogie in front of the cops. I mean it was his show, he owned them, man, but each time he finished a ride he'd point at me so the spotlight would swing over on my guitar and I'd get half of all that yelling out there. That cat had a generous heart, man.'

Dixie Lee shook his head and opened another Jax with his pocketknife.
I looked at my watch.

'Yeah, I'm sorry,' he said. 'It's a problem I got, getting wrapped up in
yesterday's scrapbook. Look, I got something bad on my mind. In fact,
it's crazy. I don't even know how to explain it. Maybe there's nothing to
it. Hell, I don't know.'

'How about just telling me?'

'Star Drilling sent me and a couple of other leasemen up to Montana.
On the eastern slope of the Rockies, what they call the East Front up
there. Big gas domes, son. Virgin country. We're talking hundreds of
millions of dollars. Except there's a problem with some wilderness area
and the Blackfeet Indian Reservation.

'But that don't concern me. I'm just a leaseman, right? Fooling
around with the Forest Service or Indians or these crazy bastards spiking
trees—'

'Doing what?'

'A bunch of cult people or something don't want anybody cutting
down trees, so they hammer nails and railroad spikes way down in the
trunk. Then some lumberjack comes along with a McCullough and
almost rips his face off. But I don't have any beef with these people.
Everybody's got their own scene, right? Let Star Drilling take care of the
PR and the politics, and Dixie Lee will get through the day with a little JD
and God's good grace.

'But we came back for six weeks of deals and meetings at the Oil Center
in Lafayette. So I'm staying at the motel with these two other lease guys.
The company picks up all the bills, the bar's always open, and a black guy
serves us Bloody Marys and chilled shrimp by the pool every morning. It
should have been a nice vacation before I go back to wheeling and dealing
among the Indians and the crazies.

'Except two nights ago one of the other lease guys has a party in his
rooms. Actually it's more like a geek show. Broads ripping off their bras,
people spitting ice and tonic on each other. Then I guess I got romantic
and went into the bedroom with this big blond gal that looked like she
could throw a hog over a fence.'

His eyes shifted away from me, and his cheeks colored slightly. He
drank again from the Jax without looking back at me.

'But I was deep into the jug that night, definitely not up to her level of
bumping uglies,' he said. 'I must have passed out and rolled off the side
of the bed between the bed and the wall, because that's where I woke up
about five in the morning. The snakes were starting to clatter around in
their basket then I heard the two other lease guys talking by themselves in
the other room.

'One guy – I ain't using his name – says, "Don't worry about it. We did
what we had to do." Then the other guy says, "Yeah, but we should have

taken more time. We should have put rocks on top of them or something. Animals are always digging up stuff in the woods, then a hunter comes along."

'Then the first guy says, "Nobody's going to find them. Nobody cares about them. They were both troublemakers. Right or wrong?"

'Then the second guy says, "I guess you're right."

'And the first guy says, "It's like a war. You make up the rules when it's over."

'I stayed quiet in the bedroom till I heard them call room service for breakfast and a couple of bottles of Champale, then I walked into the living room in my skivvies, looking like I'd just popped out of my momma's womb. I thought both of them was going to brown their britches right there.'

'You think they killed some people?'

He touched his fingers nervously to his forehead.

'Good God, man, I don't know,' he said. 'What's it sound like to you?'

'It sounds bad.'

'What d'you think I ought to do?'

I rubbed my palm on the knee of my khaki work trousers, then clicked my nails on the metal housing of the outboard engine. The dappled sunlight fell through the willows on Dixie's flushed face.

'I can introduce you to the Iberia sheriff or a pretty good DEA agent over in Lafayette,' I said.

'Are you kidding, man? I need a drug agent in my life like a henhouse needs an egg-sucking dog.'

'Well, there's still the sheriff.'

He drank the foam out of the Jax bottle and looked at me with one eye squinted shut against the light.

'I'm getting the impression you think I'd just be playing with my swizzle stick,' he said.

I raised my eyebrows and didn't answer.

'Come on, Dave. I need some help. I can't handle worry. It eats my lunch.'

'Where do you think this happened?'

'Up in Montana, I guess. That's where we been the last three months.'

'We can talk to the FBI, but I don't think it's going anywhere. You just don't have enough information, Dixie.' I paused for a moment. 'There's another bump in the road, too.'

He looked at me as a child might if he was about to be brought to task.

'When I was on the grog, I had a hard time convincing people about some things I heard and saw,' I said. 'It's unfair, but it goes with the territory.'

He stared at the water and pinched his eyes with his fingers.

'My advice is to get away from these guys,' I said.

'I work with them.'

'There're other companies.'

'Be serious. I was in Huntsville. The Texas parole office don't give you the best letter of recommendation.'

'I don't know what to tell you, then.'

'It's a mess of grief, huh?'

I began pulling in the anchor rope.

'You're gonna turn to stone on me?' he said.

'I wish I could help. I don't think I can. That's the way it is.'

'Before you crank that engine, let me ask you a question. Your father was killed on a rig out in the Gulf, wasn't he?'

'That's right.'

'It was a Star rig, wasn't it?'

'Yep.'

'They didn't have a blowout preventer on. It killed a couple of dozen guys when it blew.'

'You've got a good memory, Dixie.' I twisted the throttle to open the gas feed and yanked the starter rope. It didn't catch.

'It don't matter to you that I'm talking about Star Drilling Company?' he said.

I kept yanking the rope while oil and gas bled away from the engine into the water. Then I put one knee on the plank seat, held the engine housing firm with ray palm, and ripped the starter handle past my ear. The engine roared, the propeller churned a cloud of yellow mud and dead hyacinth vines out of the bottom, and I turned us back into the full sunlight, the slap of water under the bow, the wind that smelled of jasmine and wisteria. On the way back Dixie sat on the bow with his forearms lying loosely between his legs, his face listless and empty now, his rose-emblazoned shirt puffing with warm air.

Late that afternoon the wind shifted out of the south and you could smell the wetlands and just a hint of salt in the air. Then a bank of thunderheads slid across the sky from the Gulf, tumbling across the sun like cannon smoke, and the light gathered in the oaks and cypress and willow trees and took on a strange green cast as though you were looking at the world through water. It rained hard, dancing on the bayou and the lily pads in the shallows, clattering on my gallery and rabbit hutches, lighting the freshly plowed fields with a black sheen.

Then suddenly it was over, and the sky cleared and the western horizon was streaked with fire. Usually on a spring evening like this, when the breeze was cool and flecked with rain, Batist and I headed for Evangeline Downs in Lafayette. But the bottom had dropped out of the oil business in Louisiana, the state had the highest rate of unemployment in the country and the worst credit rating, and the racetrack had closed.

I boiled crawfish for supper, and Alafair and I shelled and ate them on the redwood picnic table under the mimosa tree in the backyard. That night I dreamed of a bubble of fire burning under the Gulf's green surface. The water boiled and hissed, geysers of steam and dirty smoke rose into air, and an enormous blue-green oil slick floated all the way to the western horizon. Somewhere far down below among the twisted spars and drill pipe and cables and the flooded wreckage of the quarter boat were the bodies of my father and nineteen other men who went down with the rig when the drill bit punched into a pay sand and the wellhead blew.

The company's public relations men said that they didn't have a blowout preventer on because they had never hit an oil sand at that depth in that part of the Gulf before. I wondered what my father thought in those last moments of his life. I never saw fear in him. No matter how badly he was hurt by circumstances or my mother's unfaithfulness, and eventually by drunken brawls in bars and the time she was locked up in the parish jail, he could always grin and wink at me and my brother and convincingly pretend to us that misfortune was not even worthy of mention.

But what did he feel in those last moments, high up on the monkeyboard in the dark, when the rig started to shake and groan and he saw the roughnecks on the platform floor dropping tongs and chain and running from the eruption of sand, salt water, gas oil, and cascading drill pipe that in seconds would explode into an orange and yellow flame that melted steel spars like licorice? Did he think of me and my brother, Jimmie?

I bet he did. Even when he clipped his safety belt on to the Geronimo wire and jumped into the black, even as the rig caved with him on top of the quarter boat, I bet his thoughts were of us.

They never found his body, but even now, almost twenty-two years later, he visited me in my sleep and sometimes I thought he spoke to me during my waking day. In my dream I saw him walking out of the surf, the green waves and foam sliding around the knees of his overalls, his powerful body strung with rust-coloured seaweed. His wind-burned skin was as dark as a mulatto's, his teeth white, his thick, curly hair black as an Indian's. His tin hat was cocked at an angle on his head, and when he popped a wet kitchen match on his thumbnail and lit a cigar stub in the corner of his mouth and then crinkled his eyes at me, a shaft of morning sunlight struck his hat and flashed as bright as a heliograph. I could feel the salt water surge over my legs as I walked toward him.

But it's the stuff of dreams. My father was dead. My wife was, too. The false dawn, with its illusions and mist-wrapped softness, can be an inadequate and fleeting as Morpheus' gifts.

2

The days became warmer the first week in April, and on some mornings I went out on the salt at dawn and seined for shrimp in the red sunrise. In the afternoon I helped Batist in the bait shop, then worked in my flower beds, pruning the trellises of purple and yellow roses that I grew on the south side of the house. I pumped iron and did three miles along the dirt road by the bayou. At four o'clock I would hear the school bus stop, and five minutes later I would hear Alafair's lunch box clatter on the kitchen table, the icebox open; then she would come looking for me in the backyard.

I sometimes wondered if perhaps she were simply fascinated with me as she would be by a strange and interesting animal that had come unexpectedly into her life. Her mother had drowned while holding her up in a wobbling bubble of air inside a crashed and sunken plane flown out of El Salvador by a Sanctuary priest. Her father had either been killed by the army in the mountains or he had been 'disappeared' inside a military prison. Now through chance and accident she lived with me in my rural Cajun world on the edge of the Louisiana wetlands.

One afternoon I had moved the picnic table out in the sunlight and had gone to sleep on top of it in my running shorts. I heard her bang the screen door, then when I didn't open my eyes she found a duck feather by the pond and began to touch peculiar places on my body with it: the white patch in my hair, my mustache, the curled pungi-stick scar on my stomach. Then I felt her tickle the thick, raised welts on my thigh, which looked like small arrowheads embedded under the skin, where I still carried shrapnel from a mine and sometimes set off airport metal detectors.

When I still refused to respond I heard her walk across the grass to the clothesline, unsnap Tripod from his chain, and suddenly he was sitting on my chest, his whiskers and wet nose and masked beady eyes pointed into my face. Alafair's giggles soared into the mimosa tree.

That evening while I was closing the bait shop and folding up the umbrellas over the tables on the dock, a man parked a new Plymouth that looked like a rental or a company car by my shale boat ramp and walked down the dock toward me. Because of his erect, almost fierce posture, he looked taller than he actually was. In reality he probably wasn't over five and a half feet tall, but his neck was thick and corded with vein, his shoulders wide and sloping like a weight lifter's, his eyebrows one dark, uninterrupted line. His muscles seemed so tightly strung together that one muscular motion seemed to activate a half-dozen others, like pulling on the center of a cobweb with your finger. If anything, he reminded me of a pile of bricks.

He wore his slacks high up on his hips, and the collar of his short-sleeved white shirt was unbuttoned and his tie pulled loose. He didn't smile. Instead, his eyes flicked over the bait shop and the empty tables, then he opened a badge on me.

'I'm Special Agent Dan Nygurski, Mr Robicheaux,' he said. 'Drug Enforcement Administration. Do you mind if I talk with you a little bit?'

The accent didn't go with the name of the man. It was hillbilly, nasal, southern mountains, a bobby pin twanging in your ear.

'I'm closing up for the day and we're about to go to a crawfish boil in the park,' I said.

'This won't take long. I talked with the sheriff in New Iberia and he said you could probably help me out. You used to be a deputy in his department, didn't you?'

'For a little while.'

His face was seamed and coarse, the eyes slightly red around the rims. He flexed his mouth in a peculiar way when he talked, and it caused the muscles to jump in his neck, as though they were attached to a string.

'Before that you were on the force in New Orleans a long time? A lieutenant in homicide?'

'That's right.'

'I'll be,' he said, and looked at the red sun through the cypress trees and the empty boats tied to the dock.

My experience with federal agents of any kind has always been the same. They take a long time to get to it.

'Could I rent a boat from you? Or maybe could you go with me and show me some of these canals that lead into Vermilion Bay?' he asked. His thinning dark hair was cut GI, and he brushed his fingers back through it and widened his eyes and looked around again.

'I'll rent you a boat in the morning. But you'll have to go out by yourself. What is it exactly I can help you with, Mr Nygurski?'

'I'm just messing around, really.' He flexed his mouth again. 'I heard some guys were off-loading some bales down around Vermilion Bay. I just like to check out the geography sometimes.'

'Are you out of New Orleans?'

'No, no, this is my first trip down here. It's nice country. I've got to try some of this crawfish while I'm here.'

'Wait a minute. I'm not following you. You're interested in some dope smugglers operating around Vermilion Bay but you're from somewhere else?'

'It's just an idle interest. I think they might be the same guys I was after a few years ago in Florida. They were unloading a cigarette boat at night outside of Fort Myers, and some neckers out in the dunes stumbled right into the middle of the operation. These guys killed all four of them. The girls were both nineteen. It's not my case anymore, though.'

The twang, the high-pitched voice, just would not go with the subject matter nor the short, thick-bodied dark man who I now noticed was slew-footed and walked a bit sideways like a crab.

'So you're out of Florida?' I said.

'No, no, you got me all wrong. I'm out of Great Falls, Montana, now, and I wanted to talk with you about—'

I shook my head.

'Dixie Lee Pugh,' I said.

We walked up the dock, across the dirt road and through the shadows of the pecan trees in my front yard. When I asked him how he had connected me with Dixie Lee, he said that one of his people had written down my tag number the morning I had met Dixie in the café outside Baton Rouge. I went in side the house, brought out two cold cans of Dr Pepper, and we sat on the porch steps. Through the trunks of the pecan trees I could see the shadows lengthening on the bayou.

'I don't mean any disrespect toward your investigation, Mr Nygurski, but I don't think he's a major drug dealer. I think y'all are firing in the well.'

'Why?'

'I believe he has a conscience. He might be a user, but that doesn't mean he's dealing.'

'You want to tell me why he came out to see you?'

'He's in some trouble. But it doesn't have anything to do with drugs, and he'll have to be the one to tell you about it.'

'Did he tell you he celled with Sal the Duck in Huntsville?'

'With who?'

'Sal the Duck. Also known as Sally Dio or Sally Dee. You think that's funny?'

'I'm sorry,' I said. I wiped my mouth with my hand. 'But am I supposed to be impressed?'

'A lot of people would be. His family used to run Galveston. Slots, whores, every floating crap game, dope, you name it. Then they moved out to Vegas and Tahoe and about two years ago they showed up in

Montana. Sal came back to visit his cousins in Galveston and got nailed with some hot credit cards. I hear he didn't like Huntsville at all.'

'I bet he didn't. It's worse than Angola.'

'But he still managed to turn a dollar or two. He was the connection for the whole joint, and I think he was piecing off part of his action to Pugh.'

'Well, you have your opinion. But I think Dixie's basically an alcoholic and a sick man.'

Nygurski took a newspaper clipping out of his shirt pocket and handed it to me.

'Read this,' he said. 'I guess the reporters thought this was funny.'

The headline read 'CURIOSITY KILLED THE BEAR.' The dateline was Polson, Montana, and the lead paragraph described how a duffel bag containing forty packages of cocaine had been dropped by parachute into a heavily wooded area east of Flathead Lake and was then found by a black bear who strung powder and wrappers all over a hillside before he OD'd.

'That parachute came down on national forestland. But guess who has a hunting lease right next door?'

'I don't know.'

'Sally Dio and his old man. Guess who acted as their leasing agent?'

'Dixie Lee.'

'But maybe he's just a sick guy.'

I looked away at the softness of the light on the bayou. Out of the corner of my eye I could see the knuckles on his hand as he clenched the soda can.

'Come on, what do you think?' he said.

'I think you're in overdrive.'

'You're right. I don't like these cocksuckers—'

'Nobody does. But I'm out of the business. You're tilting with the wrong windmill.'

'I don't think killing bears is funny, either. I don't like to see these guys bring their dirt and greed into a beautiful country. Your friend Pugh is standing up to his bottom lip in a lake of shit and the motorboat is just about to pass.'

'Then tell him that,' I said, and looked at my watch. The breeze dented the leaves in the pecan trees.

'Believe me, I will. But right now I'm fiigmo here.'

'What?'

'It means "Fuck it, I got my orders." In three days I go back to Great Falls.' He drained his soda can, crushed it in his palm, and set it gently on the porch step. He stood up and handed me his card.

'My motel number in Lafayette is on the back. Or later you can call me collect in Montana if you ever want to share any of your thoughts.'

'I've got nothing worth sharing.'

'It sounds depressing.' His mouth made that peculiar jerking motion again. 'Tell me, do you find something strange about my face?'

'No, I wouldn't say that.'

'Come on, I'm not sensitive.'

'I meant you no offense.' I said.

'Boy, you're a careful one. A woman once told me my face looked like soil erosion. I think it was my wife. Watch out for Dixie Pugh, Robicheaux. He'll sell you a bowl of rat turds and call it chocolate chip.'

'I changed my mind. I'll share one thought with you, Mr Nygurski. You didn't come all the way down here to follow a guy like Dixie Lee around. No matter how you cut it, he's not a long-ball hitter.'

'Maybe he is, maybe he isn't.'

'What's really going on up there?'

'Everything that's going on in the rest of the country, except accelerated. It's a real zoo story. All the big players are there, nosing up to the trough. Keep fooling around with that rock 'n' roller and you'll meet some of them.'

He walked off through the trees, his feet loud on the dead leaves and dried pecan husks.

The moon was down that night, the sky black, and trees of lightning trembled on the southern horizon. At four in the morning I was awakened by the rumble of dry thunder and the flickering patterns of light on the wall. A tuning fork was vibrating in my chest, but I couldn't explain why, and my skin was hot and dry to the touch even though the breeze was cool though the window. I heard sounds that were not there: a car engine dying on the road, the footsteps of two men coming through the trees, a board squeaking on the porch, the scrape of a prizing bar being inserted between the front door and the jamb. They were the sounds of ghosts, because one man had been electrocuted in his bathtub with his radio in his lap and the other had died in an attic off St Charles when five hollow-point rounds from my .45 had exploded up through the floor into the middle of his life.

But fear is an irrational emotion that floats from object to object like a helium balloon that you touch with your fingertips. I opened my dresser drawer, took my .45 from under my work shirts, slipped the heavy clip into the magazine, and lay back down in the dark. The flat of the barrel felt hot against my thigh. I put my arm across my eyes and tried to fall asleep again. It was no use.

I put on my sandals and khakis and walked through the dark trunks of the pecan trees in the front yard, across the road and down to the dock and the bait shop. Then the moon rose from behind a cloud and turned the willow trees to silver and illuminated the black shape of a nutria swimming across the bayou toward the cattails. What was I doing here? I told myself that I would get a head start on the day. Yes, yes, certainly that was it.

I opened the cooler in which I kept the soda pop and the long-necked bottles of Jax, Dixie, and Pearl beer. Yesterday's ice had melted, and some of the beer labels floated in the water. I propped my arms on the lip of the cooler and shut my eyes. In the marsh I heard a nutria cry out to its mate, which always sounds like the hysterical scream of a woman. I plunged my hands into the water, dipped it into my face, and breathed deeply with the shock of the cold. Then I wiped my face on a towel and flung it across the counter on to the duckboards.

I went back up to the house, sat at the kitchen table in the dark, and put my head on my forearms.

Annie, Annie.

I heard bare feet shuffle on the linoleum behind me. I raised my head and looked up at Alafair, who was standing in a square of moonlight, dressed in her pajamas that were covered with smiling clocks. Her face was filled with sleep and puzzlement. She kept blinking at me as though she were waking from a dream, then she walked to me, put her arms around my neck, and pressed her head against my chest. I could smell baby shampoo in her hair. Her hand touched my eyes.

'Why your face wet, Dave?' she said.

'I just washed it, little guy.'

'Oh.' Then, 'Something ain't wrong?'

'Not "ain't." Don't say "ain't." '

She didn't answer. She just held me more tightly. I stroked her hair and kissed her, then picked her up and carried her back into her bedroom. I laid her down on the bed and pulled the sheet over her feet. Her stuffed animals were scattered on the floor. The yard and the trees were turning gray, and I could hear Tripod running up and down on his clothesline.

She looked up at me from the pillow. Her face was round, and I could see the spaces between her teeth.

'Dave, is bad people coming back?'

'No. They'll never be back. I promise.'

And I had to look away from her lest she see my eyes.

One week later I took Alafair for breakfast in New Iberia, and when I unfolded a discarded copy of the *Daily Iberian* I saw Dixie Lee's picture on the front page. It was a file photo, many years old, and it showed him onstage in boatlike suede shoes, pegged and pleated slacks, a sequined white sport coat, a sunburst guitar hanging from his neck.

He had been burned in a fire in a fish camp out in Henderson swamp. A twenty-two-year-old waitress, his 'female companion', as the story called her, had died in the flames. Dixie Lee had been pulled from the water when the cabin, built on stilts, had exploded in a fireball and crashed into the bayou. He was listed in serious condition at Our Lady of Lourdes in Lafayette.

He was also under arrest. The St Martin Parish sheriff's department had found a dental floss container of cocaine under the front seat of his Cadillac convertible.

I am not going to get involved with his troubles, I told myself. When you use, you lose. A mean lesson, but when you become involved with an addict or a drunk, you simply become an actor in a script that they've written for you as well as themselves.

That afternoon Alafair and I made two bird feeders out of coffee cans and hung them in the mimosa tree in the backyard, then we restrung Tripod's clothesline out in the pecan trees so he wouldn't have access to Clarise's wash. We moved his doghouse to the base of a tree, put bricks under it to keep it dry and free of mud, and set his food bowl and water pans in front of the door. Alafair always beamed with fascination while Tripod washed his food before eating, then washed his muzzle and paws afterward.

I fixed *étoufée* for our supper, and we had just started to eat on the picnic table in the backyard when the phone rang in the kitchen. It was a nun who worked on Dixie Lee's floor at Lourdes. She said he wanted to see me.

'I can't come, Sister. I'm sorry,' I said.

She paused.

'Is that all you want me to tell him?' she asked.

'He needs a lawyer. I can give you a couple of names in Lafayette or St Martinville.'

She paused again. They must teach it in the convent, I thought. It's an electric silence that makes you feel you're sliding down the sides of the universe.

'I don't think he has many friends, Mr Robicheaux,' she said. 'No one has been to see him. And he asked for you, not an attorney.'

'I'm sorry.'

'To be frank, so am I,' she said, and hung up.

When Alafair and I were washing the dishes, and the plowed and empty sugarcane fields darkened in the twilight outside the window, the telephone rang again.

His voice was thick, coated with phlegm, a whisper into the receiver.

'Son, I really need to see you. They got me gauzed up, doped up, you name it, an enema tube stuck up my ringus.' He stopped and let out his breath into the phone. 'I need you to listen to me.'

'You need legal help, Dixie. I won't be much help to you.'

'I got a lawyer. I can hire a bagful of his kind. It won't do no good. They're going to send me back to the joint, boy.'

I watched my hand open and close on top of the counter.

'I don't like to tell you this, podna, but you were holding,' I said. 'That fact's not going away. You're going to have to deal with it.'

'It's a lie, Dave.' I heard the saliva click in his throat. 'I don't do flake, anymore. It already messed up my life way back there. Maybe sometimes a little reefer. But that's all.'

I pinched my fingers on my brow.

'Dixie, I just don't know what I can do for you.'

'Come over. Listen to me for five minutes. I ain't got anybody else.'

I stared out the screen at the shadows on the lawn, the sweep of night birds against the red sky.

It was windy the next morning and the sky was light blue and filled with tumbling white clouds that caused pools of shadow to move across the cane fields and cow pastures as I drove along the old highway through Broussard into Lafayette. Dixie Lee's room was on the second floor at Lourdes, and a uniformed sheriff's deputy was playing checkers with him on the edge of the bed. Dixie Lee lay on his side, his head, chest, right shoulder, and right thigh wrapped in bandages. His face looked as though it were crimped inside a white helmet. There was mucus in his eyes, and a clear salve oozed from the edges of his bandages. An IV was hooked into his arm.

He looked at me and said something to the deputy, who set the checkerboard on the nightstand and walked past me, working his cigarette pack out of his shirt pocket.

'I'll be right in the hall. The door stays open, too,' he said.

I sat down next to the bed. There were oaks hung with moss outside the window. The pressure of Dixie's head against the pillow made him squint one eye at me.

'I knew you'd come. There's some guys that can't be any other way,' he said.

'You sound better,' I said.

'I'm on the edge of my high and about ready to slide down the other side of it. When the centipedes start crawling under these bandages, they'll be back with the morphine. Dave, I got to get some help. The cops don't believe me. My own lawyer don't believe me. They're going to send my butt to Angola. I can't do no more time, man. I ain't good at it. They tore me up over there in Texas. You get in thin cotton, you don't pick your quota, the boss stands you up on an oil barrel with three other guys. Hot and dirty and hungry, and you stand there all night.'

'They don't believe what?'

'This—' He tried to touch his fingers behind his head. 'Reach around back and feel on them bandages.'

'Dixie, what are—'

'Do it.'

I reached across him and touched my fingertips across the tape.

'It feels like a roll of pennies under there, don't it?' he said. 'That's because I woke up just before some guy with a tire iron or a jack handle came down on my head. He was going to bust me right across the lamps, but I twisted away from him just before he swung. The next thing I knew I was in the water. You ever wake up drowning and on fire at the same time? That's what it was like. There was a gas tank for the outboards under the cabin, and it must have blown and dumped the whole thing in the bayou. Burning boards was hanging off the stilts, the water was full of hot ash, steam hissing all over the fucking place. I thought I'd gone to hell, man.'

He stopped talking and his lips made a tight line. I saw water well up in his green eyes.

'Then I seen something awful. It was the girl, you remember, that redheaded waitress from the café in West Baton Rouge. She was on fire, like a big candle burning all over, hung in all them boards and burning against the sky.

'I can't clean it out of my head, not even when they hit me with the joy juice. Maybe they hit her in the head like they done me. Maybe she was already dead. God, I hope so. I can't stand thinking about it, man. She didn't do nothing to anybody.'

I wiped my palms on my slacks and blew out my breath. I wanted to walk back out into the sunshine, into the windy morning, into the oak trees that were hung with moss.

'Who was the guy with the tire iron?' I said.

'One of those fuckers I work with.'

'You saw his face?'

'I didn't have to. They knew I was going to drop the dime on them. For all the damn good it would do.'

'You told them that?'

'Sure. I got fed up with both of them. No, wait a minute. I got fed up being afraid. I was a little swacked when I stuck it in their face, but I done it just the same. Dalton Vidrine and Harry Mapes. One's a coonass and the other's a stump-jumper from East Texas.'

'I'm having one problem with all this. There's some people who think you're mixed up in dope. Up in Montana.'

His green eyes closed and opened like a bird's.

'They're wrong,' he said.

'—that maybe you're mixed up with a trafficker named Dio.'

His mouth smiled slightly.

'You been talking to the DEA,' he said. 'But they're sniffing up the wrong guy's leg.'

'You didn't lease land for him in Montana?'

'I leased and bought a bunch of land for him. But it don't have anything to do with dope. Sally Dee was my cell partner. Some guys were going to cut me up in the shower. Till Sally Dee told them they treat me just like they treat him. Which means they light my cigarettes, they pick in my sack when we get in thin cotton. The cat's half crazy, man, but he saved my butt.'

'What was the land deal about, Dixie?'

'I didn't ask. He's not the kind of guy you ask those things to. He's got a lot of holdings. He hires people to act as his agents. He likes me for some reason. He paid me a lot of bread. What's the big deal?'

'As an old friend, Dixie, I'm going to ask you to save the Little Orphan Annie routine for the DEA.'

'You believe what you want.'

'What's your bond?'

'Fifteen thou.'

'That's not too bad.'

'They know I ain't going anywhere. Except maybe to Angola. Dave, I ain't giving you a shuck. I can't take another fall, and I don't see no way out of it.'

I looked out the window at the treetops, the way their leaves ruffled in the breeze, the whiteness of the clouds against the dome of blue sky.

'I'll come back and visit you later,' I said. 'I think maybe you have too much faith in one guy.'

'I'll tell you a story I heard Minnie Pearl tell about Hank. This was right after he brought the whole auditorium down singing "I Saw the Light" at the Opry. Backstage he turned to her and said, "But, Minnie, they ain't no light. They just ain't no light." That's when your soul is hanging on a spider's web right over the fire, son. That's right where I'm at now.'

That afternoon I stood on the levee and looked down at the collapsed and blackened remains of the fish camp that, according to Dixie Lee, had belonged to Star Drilling Company. Mattress springs, charred boards, a metal table, a scorched toilet seat, half the shingle roof lay in the shallows at the bottom of the stilt supports. A paste of gray ash floated among the cattails and lily pads.

I walked down to the water's edge. I found what was left of a Coleman stove and a pump twelve-gauge shotgun whose shells had exploded in the magazine. The gasoline drum that had been used to fuel outboard engines was ripped outward and twisted like a beer can.

The fire had made a large black circle from the water to halfway up the levee. Extending out from the circle were trails of ash though the butter-cups and new grass like the legs of a spider. One of them led up to the road at the top of the levee.

I dug the soil loose from around the trail with my pocketknife and smelled it. It smelled like burnt grass and dirt.

I knew little about arson investigation, but I saw nothing on the levee that would help Dixie Lee's case.

I drove to St Martinville and parked across from the old church where Evangeline and her lover are buried under an enormous spreading oak. The wind blew the moss in the trees along Bayou Teche, and the four-o'clocks were opening in the shade along the banks. I was told by the dispatcher in the sheriff's department that the sheriff was out for a few minutes but that a detective would talk to me.

The detective was penciling in a form of some kind and smoking a cigarette when I walked into his office. He affected politeness but his eyes kept going to the clock on the wall while I talked. A side door opened on to the sheriff's office, and I could see his desk and empty chair inside. I told the detective the story that Dixie had told me. I told him about the leasemen, Dalton Vidrine and Harry Mapes.

'We know all about that,' he said. 'That's why the sheriff been talking to them. But I tell you right now, podna, he don't believe that fella.'

'What do you mean he's been talking with them?'

He smiled at me.

'They in his office right now. He went down to the bat'room,' he said. Then he got up and closed the door to the sheriff's office.

I looked at him, stunned.

'They're sitting in there now?' My voice was incredulous.

'He called them up and ax them to come in and make a statement.'

I stood up, took a piece of paper off his desk, and wrote my name and telephone number on it.

'Ask the sheriff to call me,' I said. 'What's your name again?'

'Benoit.'

'Get into another line of work.'

I walked back outside to my pickup truck. The shadows were purple on the bayou and the church lawn. An elderly Negro was taking down the flag from the pole in front of the courthouse and a white man was closing and locking the side doors. Then two men came out the front entrance and walked hurriedly across the grass toward me, one slightly ahead of the other.

The first was a tall, angular man, dressed in brown slacks, shined loafers, a yellow sport shirt with a purple fleur-de-lis on the pocket, a thin western belt with a silver buckle and tongue. I could hear the change in his pocket when he walked. On his bottom lip was a triangular scar that looked like wet plastic.

The man behind him was shorter, dark, thick across the middle, the kind of man who wore his slacks below the navel to affect size and strength and disguise his advancing years. His eyebrows dipped down and met over his nose. Even though it was warm, he wore a long-sleeved white shirt, the pocket filled with a notebook and clip-on ballpoint pens.

Both men had the agitated look of people who might have seen their bus pass them by at their stop.

'Just a minute there, buddy,' the tall man said.

I turned and looked at him with my hand on the open truck door.

'You were using our names in there. Where the hell do you get off making those remarks?' he said. His eyes narrowed and he ran his tongue over the triangular scar on his lip.

'I was just passing on some information. It didn't originate with me, partner.'

'I don't give a goddamn where it came from. I won't put up with it. Particularly from some guy I never saw before,' he said.

'Then don't listen to it.'

'It's called libel.'

'It's called filing a police report,' I said.

'Who the fuck are you?' the other man said.

'My name's Dave Robicheaux.'

'You're an ex-cop or some kind of local bird dog?' he said.

'I'm going to ask you guys to disengage,' I said.

'You're asking us! You're unbelievable, man,' the tall man said.

I started to get in my truck. He put his hand around the window jamb and held it.

'You're not running out of this,' he said. The accent was East Texas, all right, piney woods, red hills, and sawmills. 'Pugh's a pathetic man. He melted his brains a long time ago. The company gave him a break when nobody else would. Obviously it didn't work out. He gets souped up with whiskey and dope and has delusions.' He took his hand from the window jamb and pointed his finger an inch from my chest. 'Now, if you want to spend your time talking to somebody like that, that's your damn business. But if you spread rumors about me and I hear about it, I'm going to look you up.'

I got in my truck and closed the door. I breathed through my nose, looked out at the shadows on the church, the stone statue of Evangeline under the spreading oak. Then I clicked my key ring on the steering wheel. The faces of the two men were framed through my truck window.

Then I yielded to the temptations of anger and pride, two serpentine heads of the Hydra of character defects that made up my alcoholism.

'It was the Coleman fuel for the stove, wasn't it?' I said. 'You spread it around the inside of the cabin, then strung it down the steps and up the levee. As an added feature maybe you opened the drain on the gas drum, too. You didn't expect the explosion to blow Dixie Lee out into the water, though, did you?'

It was a guess, but the mouth of the short man parted in disbelief. I started the engine, turned out into the traffic, and drove past the old storefronts and wood colonnades toward the edge of town and the back road to New Iberia.

In my dreams is a watery place where my wife and some of my friends live. I think it's below the Mekong River or perhaps deep under the Gulf. The people who live there undulate in the tidal currents and are covered with a green-gold light. I can't visit them there, but sometimes they call me up. In my mind's eye I can see them clearly. The men from my platoon still wear their pots and their rent and salt-caked fatigues. Smoke rises in bubbles from their wounds.

Annie hasn't changed much. Her eyes are electric blue, her hair gold and curly. Her shoulders are still covered with sun freckles. She wears red flowers on the front of her nightgown where they shot her with deer slugs. On the top of her left breast is a strawberry birthmark that always turned crimson with blood when we made love.

How you doing, baby love? she asks.

Hello, sweetheart.

Your father's here.

How is he?

He says to tell you not to get sucked in. What's he mean? You're not in trouble again, are you, baby love? We talked a long time about that before.

It's just the way I am, I guess.

It's still rah-rah for the penis, huh? I've got to go, Dave. There's a big line. Are you coming to see me?

Sure.

You promise?

You bet. I won't let you down, kiddo.

'You really want me to tell you what it means?' the psychologist in Lafayette said.

'Dreams are your province.'

'You're an intelligent man. You tell me.'

'I don't know.'

'Yes, you do.'

'Sometimes alcoholics go on dry drunks. Sometimes we have drunk dreams.'

'It's a death wish. I'd get a lot of distance between myself and those kinds of thoughts.'

I stared silently at the whorls of purple and red in his carpet.

The day after I visited the St Martin Parish courthouse I talked with the sheriff there on the phone. I had met him several times when I was a detective with the Iberia Paris sheriff's office, and I had always gotten along well with him. He said there was nothing in the coroner's report that would indicate the girl had been struck with a tire iron or a jack handle before the fish camp burned.

'So they did an autopsy?' I said.

'Dave, there wasn't hardly anything left of that poor girl to autopsy. From what Pugh says and what we found, she was right over the gas drum.'

'What are you going to do with those two clowns you had in your office yesterday?'

'Nothing. What can I do?'

'Pugh says they killed some people up in Montana.'

'I made some calls up there,' the sheriff said. 'Nobody has anything on these guys. Not even a traffic citation. Their office in Lafayette says they're good men. Look, it's Pugh that's got the record, that's been in trouble since they ran him out of that shithole he comes from.'

'I had an encounter with those two guys after I left your department yesterday. I think Pugh's telling the truth. I think they did it.'

'Then you ought to get a badge again, Dave. Is it about lunch-time over there?'

'What?'

'Because that's what time it is here. Come on by and have coffee sometime. We'll see you, podna.'

I drove into New Iberia to buy some chickens and sausage links from my wholesaler. It was raining when I got back home. I put 'La Jolie Blonde' by Iry LeJeune on the record player, changed into my gym shorts, and pumped iron in the kitchen for a half hour. The wind was cool through the window and smelled of rain and damp earth and flowers and trees. My chest and arms were swollen with blood and exertion, and when the rain slacked off and the sun cracked through the mauve-colored sky, I ran three miles along the bayou, jumping across puddles, boxing with raindrops that dripped from the oak limbs overhead.

Back at the house I showered, changed into a fresh denim shirt and khakis, and called Dan Nygurski collect in Great Falls, Montana. He couldn't accept the collect call, but he took the number and called me back on his line.

'You know about Dixie Lee?' I said.

'Yep.'

'Do you know about the waitress who died in the fire?'

'Yes.'

'Did y'all have a tail on him that night?'

'Yeah, we did but he got off it. It's too bad. Our people might have saved the girl's life.'

'He lost them?'

'I don't think it was deliberate. He took the girl to a colored place in

Breaux Bridge, I guess it was, a zydeco place or something like that. What is that, anyway?'

'It's Negro-Cajun music. It means "vegetables" all mixed up.'

'Anyway, our people had some trouble with a big buck who thought it was all right for Pugh to come in the club but not other white folks. In the meantime Pugh, who was thoroughly juiced, wandered out the side door with the girl and took off.'

'Have you heard his story?'

'Yeah.'

'Do you believe it?'

'What difference does it make? It's between him and the locals now. I'll be square with you, Robicheaux. I don't give a damn about Pugh. I want that lunatic Sally Dio in a cage. I don't care how I get him there, either. You can tell Dixie Lee for me I'll always listen when he's on the subject of Sally Dee. Otherwise, he's not in a seller's market.'

'Why would he be buying leasing land for this character Dio? Is it related to the oil business?'

'Hey, that's good, Robicheaux. The mob hooking up with the oil business.' He was laughing out loud now. 'That's like Frankenstein making it with the wife of Dracula. I'm not kidding you, that's great. The guys in the office'll love this. You got any other theories?'

Then he started laughing again.

I quietly replaced the telephone receiver in the cradle, then walked down to the dock in the wet afternoon sunlight to help Batist close up the bait shop.

That evening Alafair and I drove down to Cypremort Point for boiled crabs at the pavilion. We sat at one of the checker-cloth tables on the screened porch by the bay, a big bib with a red crawfish on it tied around Alafair's neck, and looked out at the sun setting across the miles of dead cypress, saw grass, the sandy inlets, the wetlands that stretched all the way to Texas. The tide was out, and the jetties were black and stark against the flat gray expanse of the bay and the strips of purple and crimson cloud that had flattened on the western horizon. Seagulls dipped and wheeled over the water's edge, and a solitary blue heron stood among the saw grass in an inlet pool, his long body and slender legs like a painting on the air.

Alafair always set about eating bluepoint crabs with a devastating clumsiness. She smashed them in the center with the wood mallet, snapped off the claws, and cracked back the shell hinge with slippery hands and an earnest innocence that sent juice and pulp flying all over the table. When we finished eating I had to take her into the washroom and wipe off her hair, face, and arms with wet paper towels.

On the way back home I stopped in New Iberia and rented a Walt

Disney movie, then I called up Batist and asked him and his wife to watch it with us. Batist was always fascinated by the VCR and never could quite understand how it worked.

'Them people that make the movie, they put it in that box, huh, Dave?' he said.

'That's right.'

'It just like at the show, huh?'

'That's right.'

'Then how it get up to the antenna and in the set?'

'It doesn't go up to—'

'And how come it don't go in nobody else's set?' he said.

'It don't go out the house,' Alafair said.

'Not "It don't." Say "It doesn't," ' I said.

'Why you telling her that? She talk English good as us,' Batist said.

I decided to heat up some *boudin* and make some Kool-Aid.

I rented a lot of Disney and other films for children because I didn't like Alafair to watch ordinary television in the evening or at least when I was not there. Maybe I was overly protective and cautious. But the celluloid facsimile of violence and the news footage of wars in the Middle East and Central America would sometimes cause the light to go out of her face and leave her mouth parted and her eyes wide, as though she had been slapped.

Disney films, Kool-Aid, *boudin*, bluepoint crabs on a breezy porch by the side of the bay were probably poor compensation for the losses she had known. But you offer what you have, perhaps even bless it with a prayer, and maybe somewhere down the line affection grows into faith and replaces memory. I can't say. I'm not good at the mysteries, and I have few solutions even for my own problems. But I was determined that Alafair would never again be hurt unnecessarily, not while she was in my care, not while she was in this country.

'This is our turf, right, Batist?' I said as I gave him a paper plate with slices of *boudin* on it.

'What?' His and Alafair's attention was focused on the image of Donald Duck on the television screen. Outside, the fireflies were lighting in the pecan trees.

'This is our Cajun land, right, podna?' I said. 'We make the rules, we've got our own flag.'

He gave me a quizzical look, then turned back to the television screen. Alafair, who was sitting on the floor, slapped her thighs and squealed uproariously while Donald Duck raged at his nephews.

The next day I visited Dixie Lee again at Lourdes and took him a couple of magazines. The sunlight was bright in his room, and someone had placed a green vase of roses in the window. The deputy left us alone, and

Dixie lay on his side and looked at me from his pillow. His eyes were clear, and his cheeks were shaved and pink.

'You're looking better,' I said.

'For the first time in years I'm not full of whiskey. It feels weird, I'm here to tell you. In fact, it feels so good I'd like to cut out the needle, too. But the centipedes start waking up for a snack.'

I nodded at the roses in the window and smiled.

'You have an admirer,' I said.

He didn't answer. He traced a design on the bed with his index finger, as though he were pushing a penny around on the sheet.

'You grew up Catholic, didn't you?' he said.

'Yes.'

'You still go to church?'

'Sure.'

'You think God punishes us right here, that it ain't just in the next world?'

'I think those are bad ideas.'

'My little boy died in a fire. A bare electric cord under a rug started it. If I hadn't been careless, it wouldn't have happened. Then I killed that man's little boy over in Fort Worth, and now I been in a fire myself and a young girl's dead.'

I looked at the confusion and pain in his face.

'I had preachers back home tell me where all that drinking and doping was going to lead me. I wouldn't pay them no mind,' he said.

'Come on, don't try to see God's hand in what's bad. Look outside. It's a beautiful day, you're alive, you're feeling better, maybe you've got alternatives now that you didn't have before. Think about what's right with your life, Dixie.'

'They're going to try and pop me.'

'Who?'

'Vidrine and Mapes. Or some other butthole the company hires.'

'These kinds of guys don't come up the middle.'

He looked back at me silently, as if I were someone on the other side of a wire fence.

'There're too many people looking at them now,' I said.

'You don't know how much money's involved. You couldn't guess. You don't have any idea what these bastards will do for money.'

'You're in custody.'

'Save the dog shit, Dave. Last night Willie out there said he was going for some smokes. It was eleven o'clock. He handcuffed my wrist to the bed rail and came back at one in the morning, chewing on a toothpick and smelling like hamburger and onions.'

'I'll talk to the sheriff.'

'The same guy that thinks I've got fried grits for brains? You think like

435

a cop, Dave. You've probably locked a lot of guys up, but you don't know what it's like inside all that clanging iron. A couple of winging dicks want a kid brought to their cell, that's where he gets delivered. A guy wants you whacked out because you owe for a couple of decks of cigarettes, you get a shank in your spleen somewhere between the mess hall and lockup. Guys like Willie out there are a joke.'

'What do you want me to do?'

'Nothing. You tried. Don't worry about it.'

'I'm not going to leave you on your own. Give me a little credit.'

'I ain't on my own. I called Sally Dee.'

I looked again at the roses in the green vase.

'Floral telegram. He's a thoughtful guy, man,' Dixie Lee said.

'It's your butt.'

'Don't ever do time. You won't hack it inside.'

'What you're doing is not only stupid, you're starting to piss me off, Dixie.'

'I'm sorry.'

'You want to be on these guys' leash the rest of your life? What's the matter with you?'

'Everything. My whole fucking life. You want to pour yourself some iced tea? I got to use the bedpan.'

'I think I've been jerked around here, partner.'

'Maybe you been jerking yourself around.'

'What?'

'Ask yourself how much you're interested in me and how much you're interested in the drilling company that killed your old man.'

I watched him work the stainless steel bedpan out from the rack under the mattress.

'I guess you have dimensions I haven't quite probed.' I said.

'I flunked out my freshman year, remember? You're talking way above my league.'

'No, I don't think so. We'll see you around, Dixie.'

'I don't blame you for walking out mad. But you don't understand. You can't, man. It was big back then. The Paramount Theatre in Brooklyn with Allan Freed, on stage with guys like Berry and Eddie Cochran. I wasn't no drunk, either. I had a wife and a kid, people thought I was decent. Look at me today. I'm a fucking ex-convict, the stink on shit. I killed a child, for God's sake. You come in here talking an AA shuck about the beautiful weather outside when maybe I'm looking at a five-spot on Angola farm. Get real, son. It's the dirty boogie out there, and all the cats are humping to it in three-four time.'

I stood up from my chair.

'I'll speak with the sheriff about the deputy. He won't leave you alone again. I'll see you, Dixie,' I said.

I left him and walked outside into the sunlight. The breeze was cool and scented with flowers, and across the street in a grove of oak trees a Negro was selling rattlesnake watermelons off the back of a truck. He had lopped open one melon on the tailgate as an advertisement, and the meat was dark red in the shade. I looked back up at Dixie Lee's room on the corner of the second floor and saw a nun close the venetian blinds on the sunlight.

3

I had never liked the Lafayette Oil Center. My attitude was probably romantic and unreasonable. As chambers of commerce everywhere are fond of saying, it provided jobs and an expanded economy, it meant progress. It was also ugly. It was low and squat and sprawling, treeless, utilitarian, built with glazed brick and flat roofs, tinted and mirrored windows that gave on to parking lots that in summer radiated the heat like a stove.

And to accommodate the Oil Center traffic the city had widened Pinhook Road, which ran down to the Vermilion River and became the highway to New Iberia. The oak and pecan trees along the road had been cut down, the rural acreage subdivided and filled with businesses and fast-food restaurants, the banks around the Vermilion Bridge paved with asphalt parking lots and dotted with more oil-related businesses whose cinder-block architecture had all the aesthetic design of a sewage-treatment works.

But there was still one café on Pinhook left over from my college days at Southwestern in the 1950s. The parking lot was oystershell, the now-defunct speakers from the jukebox were still ensconced in the forks of the spreading oak trees, the pink and blue and green neon tubing around the windows still looked like a wet kiss in the rain.

The owner served fried chicken and dirty rice that could break your heart. I finished eating lunch and drinking coffee and looked out at the rain blowing through the oaks, at the sheen it made on the bamboo that grew by the edge of the parking lot. The owner propped open the front door with a board, and the mist and cool air and the smell of the trees blew inside. Then a Honda stopped in a rain puddle out front, the windshield wipers slapping, and an Indian girl with olive skin and thick black hair jumped out and ran inside. She wore designer jeans, which people had stopped wearing, a yellow shirt tied across her middle, and yellow tennis shoes. She touched the raindrops out of her eyes with her fingers and glanced around the restaurant until she saw the sign over the women's room. She walked right past my table, her damp wrist almost

438

brushing my shoulder, and I tried not to look at her back, her thighs, the way her hips creased and her posterior moved when she walked; but that kind of resolution and dignity seemed to be more and more wanting in my life.

I paid my check, put on my rain hat, draped my seersucker coat over my arm, and ran past the idling Honda to my truck. Just as I started the engine the girl ran from the restaurant and got into the Honda with a package of cigarettes in her hand. The driver backed around so that he was only ten feet from my cab and rolled his window down.

I felt my mouth drop open. I stared dumbfounded at the boiled pigskin face, the stitched scar that ran from the bridge of his nose up through one eyebrow, the sandy hair and intelligent green eyes, the big shoulders that made his shirt look as though it were about to rip.

Cletus Purcel.

He grinned and winked at me.

'What's happening, Streak?' he said into the rain, then rolled up the window, and splashed out on to Pinhook Road.

My old homicide partner from the First District in the French Quarter. Bust 'em or smoke 'em, he used to say. Bury your fist in their stomachs, leave them puking on their knees, click off their light switch with a slapjack if they still want to play.

He had hated the pimps, the Nicaraguan and Colombian dealers, the outlaw bikers, the dirty-movie operators, the contract killers the mob brought in from Miami, and if left alone with him, they would gladly cut any deal they could get from the prosecutor's office.

But with time he became everything that he despised. He took freebies from whores, borrowed money from shylocks, fought the shakes every morning with cigarettes, aspirin, and speed, and finally took ten thousand dollars to blow away a potential government witness in a hog lot.

Then he had cleaned out his and his wife's bank account, roared the wrong way down a one-way street into the New Orleans airport, bounced over a concrete island, and abandoned his car with both doors open in front of the main entrance. He just made the flight to Guatemala.

A month later I received a card from him that had been postmarked in Honduras.

Dear Streak,

Greetings from Bongo-Bongo Land. I'd like to tell you I'm off the sauce and working for the Maryknolls. I'm not. Guess what skill is in big demand down here? A guy that can run through the manual of arms is an automatic captain. They're all kids. Somebody with a case of Clearasil could take the whole country.

See you in the next incarnation,

C.

PS If you run into Lois, tell her I'm sorry for ripping her off. I left my toothbrush in the bathroom. I want her to have it.

I watched his taillights glimmer and fade in the rain. As far as I knew, there was still a warrant on him. What was Cletus doing back in the States? And in Lafayette?

But he was somebody else's charge now, not mine. So good luck, partner, I thought. Whatever you're operating on, I hope it's as pure and clean as white gas and bears you aloft over the places where the carrion birds clatter.

I drove across the street and parked in front of the Star Drilling Company's regional office. Confronting them probably seems a foolish thing to do, particularly in the capacity of a citizen rather than that of a law officer. But my experience as a policeman investigating white-collar criminals always led me to the same conclusion about them: they might envision a time when they'll have to deal with the law, but in their minds the problem will be handled by attorneys, in a court proceeding that becomes almost a gentlemen's abstraction. They tremble with both outrage and fear when a plainclothes cop, perhaps with an IQ of ninety-five, a .357 showing under his coat, a braided blackjack in his pocket, steps into the middle of their lives as unexpectedly as an iron door slamming shut and indicates that he thinks habeas corpus is a Latin term for a disease.

I put on my coat and ran through the rain and into the building. The outer offices of Star Drilling, which was separated by half-glass partitions, were occupied by draftsmen and men who looked like geologists or lease people. The indirect lighting glowed on the pine paneling, and the air-conditioning was turned so high that I felt my skin constrict inside my damp seersucker. The geologists, or whatever they were, walked from desk to desk, rattling topography maps between their outstretched hands, their faces totally absorbed in their own frame of reference or a finger moving back and forth on the numbers of a township and range.

The only person who looked at me was the receptionist. I told her I wanted to see the supervisor about a mineral lease in Montana.

His desk was big, made of oak, his chair covered with maroon leather, the pine walls hung with deer's heads, a marlin, two flintlock rifles. On a side table was a stuffed lynx, mounted on a platform, the teeth bared, the yellow glass eyes filled with anger.

His name was Hollister. He was a big man, his thick, graying hair cut military, his pale blue eyes unblinking. Like those of most managerial people in the Oil Center, his accent was Texas or Oklahoma and his dress eccentric. His gray Oshman coat hung on a rack, his cufflinks were the size of quarters and embossed with oil derricks. His bolo tie was fastened with a brown and silver brooch.

He listened to me talk a moment, his square hands motionless on the desk, his face like that of a man staring into an ice storm.

'Wait a minute. You came to my office to question me about my employees? About a murder?'

I could see tiny stretched white lines in the skin around the corners of his eyes.

'It's more than one, Mr Hollister. The girl in the fire and maybe some people in Montana.'

'Tell me, who do you think you are?'

'I already did.'

'No, you didn't. You lied to my receptionist to get in here.'

'You've got a problem with your leasemen. It won't go away because I walk out the door.'

His pale eyes looked steadily at me. He lifted one finger off his desk and aimed it at me.

'You're not here about Dixie Pugh,' he said. 'You've got something else bugging you. I don't know what it is, but you're not a truthful man.'

I touched the ball of my thumb to the corner of my mouth, looked away from him a moment, and tapped my fingers on the leather arm of my chair.

'You evidently thought well enough of Dixie Lee to give him a job,' I said. 'Do you think he made all this up and then set himself on fire?'

'I think you're on your way out of here.'

'Let me tell you a couple of things about the law. Foreknowledge of a crime can make you a co-conspirator. Knowledge after the fact can put you into an area known as aiding and abetting. These guys aren't worth it, Mr Hollister.'

'This discussion is over. There's the door.'

'It looks like your company has made stonewalling an art form.'

'What?'

'Does the name Aldous Robicheaux mean anything to you?'

'No. Who is he?'

'He was my father. He was killed on one of your rigs.'

'When?'

'Twenty-two years ago. They didn't have a blowout preventer on. Your company tried to deny it, since almost everybody on the rig went down with it. A shrimper pulled a floorman out of the water two days later. He cost you guys a lot of money.'

'So you got a grudge that's twenty-two years old? I don't know what to tell you, Robicheaux, except I wasn't with the company then and I probably feel sorry for you.'

I took my rain hat off my knee and stood up.

'Tell Mapes and Vidrine to stay away from Dixie Lee,' I said.

'You come in here again, I'll have you arrested.'

I walked back outside into the rain, got in my truck, and drove out of the maze of flat, uniform brick buildings that composed the Oil Center. On Pinhook Road I passed the restaurant where I had seen Cletus an hour before. The spreading oak trees were dark green, the pink and blue neon like smoke in the blowing mist. The wind blew hard when I crossed the Vermilion River, ruffling the yellow current below and shuddering the sides of my truck.

'I don't buy that stuff about a death wish. I believe some guys in Vienna had too much time to think,' I said to the therapist.

'You don't have to be defensive about your feelings. Facile attitudes have their place in therapy, too. For example, I don't think there's anything complex about depression. It's often a matter of anger turned inward. What do you have to say about that, Dave?'

'I don't know.'

'Yes, you do. How did you feel in Vietnam when the man next to you was hit?'

'What do you think I felt?'

'At some point you were glad it was him and not you. And then you felt guilty. And that was very dangerous, wasn't it?'

'All alcoholics feel guilt. Go to an open meeting sometime. Learn something about it.'

'Cut loose from the past. She wouldn't want you to carry a burden like this.'

'I can't. I don't want to.'

'Say it again.'

'I don't want to.'

He was bald and his rimless glasses were full of light. He turned his palms up toward me and was silent.

I visited Dixie Lee one more time and found him distant, taciturn, perhaps even casually indifferent to my presence in the room. I wasn't pleased with his attitude. I didn't know whether to ascribe it to the morphine-laced IV hooked into his arm, or possibly his own morose awareness of what it meant to throw in his lot with his hold cell partner.

'You want me to bring you anything else before I leave?' I asked.

'I'm all right.'

'I probably won't be back, Dixie. I'm pretty tied up at the dock these days.'

'Sure, I understand.'

'Do you think maybe you used me a little bit?' I grinned at him and held up my thumb and forefinger slightly apart in the air. 'Maybe just a little?'

His voice was languid, as though he were resting on the comfortable edge of sleep.

'Me use somebody else? Are you kidding?' he said. 'You're looking at the dildo of the planet.'

'See you around, Dixie.'

'Hell, yes. They're kicking me out of here soon, anyway. It's only second-degree stuff. I've had worse hangovers. We're in tall cotton, son.'

And so I left him to his own menagerie of snapping dogs and hungry snakes.

That Saturday I woke Alafair early, told her nothing about the purpose of our trip, and drove in the cool, rose-stippled dawn to the Texas side of Sabine Pass, where the Sabine River empties into the Gulf. A friend of mine from the army owned a small, sandy, salt-flecked farm not far from the hard-packed gray strip of sandbar that tried to be a beach. It was a strange, isolated place, filled with the mismatched flora of two states: stagnant lakes dotted with dead cypress, solitary oaks in the middle of flat pasture, tangles of black-jack along the edges of coulees, an alluvial fan of sand dunes that were crested with salt grass and from which protruded tall palm trees silhouetted blackly against the sun. Glinting through the pines on the back of my friend's farm were the long roll and pitch of the Gulf itself, and a cascade of waves that broke against the beach in an iridescent spray of foam.

It was a place of salt-poisoned grass, alligators, insects, magpies, turkey buzzards, drowned cows whose odor reached a half mile into the sky, tropical storms that could sand the paint off a water tower, and people like my friend who had decided to slip through a hole in the dimension and live on their own terms. He had a bad-conduct discharge from the army, had been locked up in a mental asylum in Galveston, had failed totally at AA, and as a farmer couldn't grow thorns in a briar patch.

But he bred and raised some of the most beautiful Appaloosa horses I had ever seen. He and I had coffee in his kitchen while Alafair drank a Coke, then I picked up several sugar cubes in my palm and we walked out to his back lot.

'What we doing, Dave?' Alafair said. She looked up at me in the sunlight that shone through the pine trees. She wore a yellow T-shirt, baggy blue jeans, and pink tennis shoes. The wind off the water ruffled her bangs.

My friend winked and went inside the barn.

'You can't ride Tripod, can you, little guy?' I said.

'What? Ride Tripod?' she said, her face confused, then suddenly lighting, breaking into an enormous grin as she looked past me and saw my friend leading a three-year-old gelding out of the barn.

The Appaloosa was steel gray, with white stockings and a spray of black and white spots across his rump. He snorted and pitched his head against the bridle, and Alafair's brown eyes went back and forth between the horse and me, her face filled with delight.

'You think you can take care of him and Tripod and your rabbits, too?' I said.

'Me? He's for me, Dave?'

'You bet he is. He called me up yesterday and said he wanted to come live with us.'

'What? Horse call up?'

I picked her up and set her on top of the fence rail, then let the Appaloosa take the sugar cubes out of my palm.

'He's like you, he's got a sweet tooth,' I said. 'But when you feed him something, let him take it out of your palm so he doesn't bite your fingers by mistake.'

Then I climbed over the fence, slipped bareback on to the horse, and lifted Alafair up in front of me. My friend had trimmed the horse's mane, and Alafair ran her hand up and down it as though it were a giant shoe brush. I touched my right heel against the horse's flank, and we turned in a slow circle around the lot.

'What his name?' Alafair said.

'How about Tex?'

'How come that?'

'Because he's from Texas.'

'What?'

'This is Texas.'

'This where?'

'Never mind.'

I nodded for my friend to open the gate, and we rode out through the sandy stretch of pines on to the beach. The waves were slate green and full of kelp, and they made a loud smack against the sand and slid in a wet line up to a higher, dry area where the salt grass and the pine needles began. It was windy and cool and warm at the same time, and we rode a mile or so along the edge of the surf to a place where a sandbar and jetty had created a shallow lagoon, in the middle of which a wrecked shrimp boat lay gray and paintless on its side, a cacophony of seagulls thick in the air above it. Behind us the horse's solitary tracks were scalloped deep in the wet sand.

I gave my friend four hundred for the Appaloosa, and for another three hundred he threw in the tack and a homemade trailer. Almost all the way home Alafair stayed propped on her knees on the front seat, either looking backward through the cab glass or out the window at the horse trailer tracking behind us, her fine hair flattening in white lines against her scalp.

*

On Monday I walked up to the house for lunch, then stopped at the mailbox on the road before I went back to the dock. The sun was warm, the oak trees along the road were full of mockingbirds and blue jays, and the mist from my neighbor's water sprinkler drifted in a wet sheen over his hydrangea beds and rows of blooming azalea and myrtle bushes. In the back of the mailbox was a narrow package no more than ten inches long. It had been postmarked in New Orleans. I put my other mail in my back pocket, slipped the twine off the corners of the package, and cracked away the brown wrapping paper with my thumb.

I lifted off the cardboard top. Inside on a strip of cotton was a hypodermic needle with a photograph and a sheet of lined paper wrapped around it. The inside of the syringe was clouded with a dried brown-red residue. The photograph was cracked across the surface, yellowed around the edges, but the obscene nature of the details had the violent clarity of a sliver of glass in the eye. A pajama-clad Vietcong woman lay in a clearing by the tread of a tank, her severed head resting on her stomach. Someone had stuffed a C-ration box in her mouth.

The lined paper looked like the kind that comes in a Big Chief notebook. The words were printed large, in black ink.

Dear Sir,

The guy that took this picture is one fucked up dude. He liked it over there and didn't want to come back. He says he used this needle in a snuff flick out in Oakland. I don't know if I'd believe him or not. But your little pinto bean gets on the bus at 7:45. She arrives at school at 8:30. She's on the playground at 10 and back out there at noon. She waits on the south corner for the bus home at 3:05. Sometimes she gets off before her stop and walks down the road with a colored kid. It's hardball. Don't fuck with it. It's going to really mess up your day. Check the zipper-head in the pic. Now there's somebody who really had a hard time getting her C's down.

'For what your face like that? What it is, Dave?'

Batist was standing behind me, dressed in a pair of navy bell-bottoms and an unbuttoned sleeveless khaki shirt. There were drops of sweat on his bald head, and the backs of his hands and wrists were spotted with blood from cleaning fish.

I put the photograph, letter, and torn package back in the mailbox and walked hurriedly down to the dock. I called the elementary school, asked the principal to make sure that Alafair was in her classroom, then told her not to let Alafair board the school bus that afternoon, that I would be there to pick her up. When I walked back toward the house Batist was still at the mailbox. He was illiterate and so the letter inside meant nothing to him, but he had the photograph cupped in his big palm, an unlit cigar in the corner of his mouth, and there was an ugly glaze in his eyes.

'*Que ça veut dire*, Dave? What that needle mean, too?' he said.

'Somebody's threatening Alafair.'

'They say they gonna hurt that little girl?'

'Yes.' The word created a hollow feeling in my chest.

'Who they are? Where they at, them people that do something like this?'

'I believe it's a couple of guys in Lafayette. They're oil people. Have you seen any guys around here who look like they don't belong here?'

'I ain't paid it no mind, Dave. I didn't have no reason, me.'

'It's all right.'

'What we gonna do?'

'I'm going to pick up Alafair, then I'll talk to the sheriff.' I picked the photograph out of his palm by the edges and set it back inside the mailbox. 'I'm going to leave this stuff in there, then take it in later and see if we can find fingerprints on it. So we shouldn't handle it anymore.'

'No, I mean what we gonna *do*?' he said. His brown eyes looked intently into mine. There was no question about his meaning.

'I'm going to pick up Alafair now. Watch the store and I'll be back soon.'

Batist's mouth closed on his dry cigar. His eyes went away from me, stared into the shade of the pecan trees and moved back and forth in his head with a private thought. His voice was quiet when he spoke.

'Dave, in that picture, that's where you was at in the war?'

'Yes.'

'They done them kind of things?'

'Some did. Not many.'

'In that letter, it say that about Alafair?'

I swallowed and couldn't answer him. The hollow feeling in my chest would not go away. It was like fear but not of a kind that I had ever experienced before. It was an obscene feeling, as though a man's hand had slipped lewdly inside my shirt and now rested sweatily on my breastbone. The sunlight shimmered on the bayou, and the trees and blooming hyacinths on the far side seemed to go in and out of focus. I saw a cotton-mouth coiled fatly on a barkless, sun-bleached log, its triangular head the color of tarnished copper in the hard yellow light. Sweat ran out of my hair, and I felt my heart beating against my rib cage. I snicked the mailbox door shut, got into my truck, and headed down the dirt road toward New Iberia. When I bounced across the drawbridge over Bayou Teche, my knuckles were white and as round as quarters on the steering wheel.

On the way back from the school the spotted patterns of light and shadow fell though the canopy of oaks overhead and raced over Alafair's tan face as she sat next to me in the truck. Her knees and white socks and patent leather shoes were dusty from play on the school ground. She kept looking curiously at the side of my face.

'Something wrong, Dave?' she said.

'No, not at all.'

'Something bad happen, ain't it?'

'Don't say "ain't." '

'Why you mad?'

'Listen, little guy, I'm going to run some errands this afternoon and I want you to stay down at the dock with Batist. You stay in the store and help him run things, okay?'

'What's going on, Dave?'

'There's nothing to worry about. But I want you to stay away from people you don't know. Keep close around Batist and Clarise and me, okay? You see, there're a couple of men I've had some trouble with. If they come around here, Batist and I will chase them off. But I don't want them bothering you or Clarise or Tripod or any of our friends, see.' I winked at her.

'These bad men?' Her face looked up at me. Her eyes were round and unblinking.

'Yes, they are.'

'What they do?'

I took a breath and let it out.

'I don't know for sure. But we just need to be a little careful. That's all, little guy. We don't worry about stuff like that. We're kind of like Tripod. What's he do when the dog chases him?'

She looked into space, then I saw her eyes smile.

'He gets up on the rabbit hutch,' she said.

'Then what's he do?'

'He stick his claw in the dog's nose.'

'That's right. Because he's smart. And because he's smart and careful, he doesn't have to worry about that dog. And we're the same way and we don't worry about things, do we?'

She smiled up at me, and I pulled her against my side and kissed the top of her head. I could smell the sun's heat in her hair.

I parked the truck in the shade of the pecan trees, and she took her lunch kit into the kitchen, washed out her thermos, and changed into her playclothes. We walked down to the dock, and I put her in charge of soda pop and worm sales. In the corner behind the beer cases I saw Batist's old automatic Winchester twelve-gauge propped against the wall.

'I put some number sixes in it for that cotton-mouth been eating fish off my stringer,' he said. 'Come see tonight. You gonna have to clean that snake off the tree.'

'I'll be back before dark. Take her up to the house for her supper,' I said. 'I'll close up when I get back.'

'You don't be worry, you,' he said, dragged a kitchen match on a wood post, lit his cigar, and let the smoke drift out through his teeth.

Alafair rang up a sale on the cash register and beamed when the drawer clanged open.

I put everything from the mailbox in a large paper bag and drove to the Iberia Parish sheriff's office. I had worked a short while for the sheriff as a plainclothes detective the previous year, and I knew him to be a decent and trustworthy man. But when he ran for the office his only qualification was the fact that he had been president of the Lions Club and owned a successful dry cleaning business. He was slightly overweight, his face soft around the edges, and in his green uniform he looked like the manager of a garden-supply store. We talked in his office while a deputy processed the wrapping paper, box, note, and hypodermic needle for fingerprints in another room.

Finally the deputy rapped on the sheriff's door glass with one knuckle and opened the door.

'Two identifiable sets,' he said. 'One's Dave's, one's from that colored man, what's his name?'

'Batist,' I said.

'Yeah, we have his set on file from the other time—' His eyes flicked away from me and his face colored. 'We had his prints from when we were out to Dave's place before. Then there's some smeared stuff on the outside of the wrapping paper.'

'The mailman?' the sheriff said.

'That's what I figure,' the deputy said. 'I wish I could tell you something else, Dave.'

'It's all right.'

The deputy nodded and closed the door.

'You want to take it to the FBI in Lafayette?' the sheriff said.

'Maybe.'

'A threat in the mails is in a federal area. Why not make use of them?'

I looked back at him without answering.

'Why is it that I always feel you're not a man of great faith in our system?' he said.

'Probably because I worked for it too long.'

'We can question these two guys, what's their names again?'

'Vidrine and Mapes.'

'Vidrine and Mapes, we can let them know somebody's looking over their shoulder.'

'They're too far into it.'

'What do you want to do?'

'I don't know.'

'Dave, back off of this one. Let other people handle it.'

'Are you going to keep a deputy out at my house? Will one watch Alafair on the playground or while she waits for the bus?'

He let out his breath, then looked out the window at a clump of oak trees in a bright, empty pasture.

'Something else bothers me here,' he said. 'Wasn't your daddy killed on a Star rig?'

'Yes.'

'You think there's a chance you want to twist these guys, no matter what happens?'

'I don't know what I think. That box didn't mail itself to me, though, did it?'

I saw the injury in his eyes, but I was past the point of caring about his feelings. Maybe you've been there. You go into a police or sheriff's station after a gang of black kids forced you to stop your car while they smashed out your windows with garbage cans; a strung-out addict made you kneel at gunpoint on the floor of a grocery store, and before you knew it the begging words rose uncontrollably in your throat; some bikers pulled you from the back of a bar and sat on your arms while one of them unzipped his blue jeans. Your body is still hot with shame, your voice full of thumbtacks and strange to your own ears, your eyes full of guilt and self-loathing while uniformed people walk casually by you with Styrofoam cups of coffee in their hands. Then somebody types your words on a report and you realize that this is all you will get. Investigators will not be out at your house, you will probably not be called to pull somebody out of a lineup, a sympathetic female attorney from the prosecutor's office will not take a large interest in your life.

Then you will look around at the walls and cabinets and lockers in that police or sheriff's station, the gun belts worn by the officers with the Styrofoam coffee cups, perhaps the interior of the squad cars in the parking lot, and you will make an ironic realization. The racks of M-16 rifles, scoped Mausers, twelve-gauge pumps loaded with double-aught buckshot, .38 specials and .357 Magnums, stun guns, slapjacks, batons, tear gas canisters, the drawers that contain cattle prods, handcuffs, Mace, wrist and leg chins, hundreds of rounds of ammunition, all have nothing to do with your safety or the outrage against your person. You're an increase in somebody's work load.

'You've been on this side of the desk, Dave. We do what we can,' the sheriff said.

'But it's not enough most of the time. Is it?'

He stirred a paper clip on the desk blotter with his finger.

'Have you got an alternative?' he said.

'Thanks for your time, Sheriff. I'll think about the FBI.'

'I wish you'd do that.'

The sky had turned purple and red in the west and rain clouds were building on the southern horizon when I drove home. I bought some ice cream in town, then stopped at a fruit stand under an oak tree by the bayou and bought a lug of strawberries. The thunder-heads off the gulf slid across the sun, and the cicadas were loud in the trees and the fireflies were lighting in the shadows along the road. A solitary raindrop splashed on my windshield as I turned into my dirt yard.

It rained hard that night. It clattered on the shingles and the tin roof of the gallery, sluiced out of the gutters and ran in streams down to the coulee. The pecan trees in the yard beat in the wind and trembled whitely when lightning leapt across the black sky. I had the attic fan on, and the house was cool, and I dreamed all night. Annie came to me about four AM, as she often did, when the night was about to give way to the softness of the false dawn. In my dream I could look through my bedroom window into the rain, past the shining trunks of the pecan trees, deep into the marsh and the clouds of steam that eventually bleed into the saw grass and the Gulf of Mexico, and see her and her companions inside a wobbling green bubble of air. She smiled at me.

Hi, sailor, she said.

How you doing, sweetheart?

You know I don't like it when it rains. Bad memories and all that. So we found a dry place for a while. Your buddies from your platoon don't like the rain, either. They say it used to give them jungle sores. Can you hear me with all that thunder? It sounds like cannon.

Sure.

It's lightning up on top of the water. That night I couldn't tell the lightning from the gun flashes. I wish you hadn't left me alone. I tried to hide under the bed sheet. It was a silly thing to do.

Don't talk about it.

It was like electricity dancing off the walls. You're not drinking, are you?

No, not really.

Not really?

Only in my dreams.

But I bet you still get high on those dry drunks, don't you? You know, fantasies about kicking butt, 'fronting the lowlifes, all that stuff swinging dicks like to do.

A guy has to do something for kicks. Annie?

What is it, baby love?

I want—

Tell me.

I want to—

It's not your time. There's Alafair to take care of, too.

It wasn't your time, either.

She made a kiss against the air. Her mouth was red.

450

So long, sailor. Don't sleep on your stomach. It'll make you hard in the morning. I miss you.

Annie—

She winked at me through the rain, and in my dream I was sure I felt her fingers touch my lips.

It continued to rain most of the next day. At three o'clock I picked up Alafair at the school and kept her with me in the bait shop. The sky and the marsh were gray; my rental boats were half full of water, the dock shiny and empty in the weak light. Alafair was restless and hard to keep occupied in the shop, and I let Batist take her with him on an errand in town. At five-thirty they were back, the rain slacked off, and the sun broke through the clouds in the west. It was the time of day when the bream and bass should have been feeding around the lily pads, but the bayou was high and the water remained smooth and brown and un-dented along the banks and in the coves. A couple of fishermen came in and drank beer for a while, and I leaned on the window jamb and stared out at the mauve- and red-streaked sky, the trees dripping rain into the water, the wet moss trying to lift in the evening breeze.

'Them men ain't gonna do nothing. They just blowing they horn,' Batist said beside me. Alafair was watching a cartoon on the old black-and-white television set that I kept on the snack shelf. She held Tripod on her lap while she stared raptly up at the set.

'Maybe so. But they'll let us wonder where they are and when they're coming,' I said. 'That's the way it works.'

'You call them FBI in Lafayette?'

'No.'

'How come?'

'It's a waste of time.'

'Sometime you gotta try, yeah.'

'There weren't any identifiable prints on the package except yours and mine.'

I could see in his face that he didn't understand.

'There's nothing to tell the FBI,' I said. 'I would only create paperwork for them and irritate them. It wouldn't accomplish anything. There's nothing I can do.'

'So you want get mad at me?'

'I'm not mad at you. Listen—'

'What?'

'I want her to stay with you tonight. I'll pick her up in the morning and take her to school.'

'What you gonna do, you?'

'I don't know.'

'I been knowing you a long time, Dave. Don't tell me that.'

'I'll tell Clarise to pack her school clothes and her pajamas and toothbrush. There's still one boat out. Lock up as soon as it comes in.'

'Dave—'

But I was already walking up toward the house in the light, sun-spangled rain, in the purple shadows, in the breeze that smelled of wet moss and blooming four-o'clocks.

It was cool and still light when I stopped on the outskirts of Lafayette and called Dixie Lee at the hospital from a pay phone. I asked him where Vidrine and Mapes were staying.

'What for?' he said.

'It doesn't matter what for. Where are they?'

'It matters to me.'

'Listen, Dixie, you brought me into this. It's gotten real serious in the last two days. Don't start being clever with me.'

'All right, the Magnolia. It's off Pinhook, down toward the river. Look, Dave, don't mess with them. I'm about to go bond and get out of here. It's time to ease off.'

'You sound like you've found a new confidence.'

'So I got friends. So I got alternatives. Fuck Vidrine and Mapes.'

The sun was red and swollen on the western horizon. Far to the south I could see rain falling.

'How far out are these guys willing to go?' I said.

He was quiet a moment.

'What are you talking about?' he said.

'You heard me.'

'Yeah, I did. They burn a girl to death and you ask me a question like that? These guys got no bottom, if that's what you mean. They'll go down where it's so dark the lizards don't have eyes.'

I drove down Pinhook Road towards the Vermilion River and parked under a spreading oak tree by the motel, a rambling white stucco building with a blue tile roof. Rainwater dripped from the tree on to my truck cab, and the bamboo and palm trees planted along the walks bent in the wind off the river and the flagstones in the courtyard were wet and red in the sun's last light. A white and blue neon sign in the shape of a flower glowed against the sky over the entrance of the motel, an electrical short in it buzzing as loud as the cicadas in the trees. I stared at the front of the motel a moment, clicking my keys on the steering wheel, then I opened the truck door and started inside.

Just as I did the glass door of a motel room slid open and two men and women in bathing suits with drinks in their hands walked out on the flagstones and sat at a table by the pool. Vidrine and Mapes were both laughing at something one of the women had said. I stepped back in the shadows and watched Mapes signal a Negro waiter. A moment later the waiter brought them big silver shrimp-cocktail bowls and a platter of fried crawfish. Mapes wore sandals and a bikini swimming suit, and his body was as lean and tan as a long-distance runner's. But Vidrine wasn't as confident of his physique; he wore a Hawaiian shirt with his trunks, the top button undone to show his chest hair, but he kept crossing and recrossing his legs as though he could reshape the protruding contour of his stomach. The two women looked like hookers. One had a braying laugh; the other wore her hair pulled back on her head like copper wire, and she squeezed Mapes's thigh under the table whenever she leaned forward to say something.

I got back in the truck, took my World War II Japanese field glasses out of the glove box, and watched them out of the shadows for an hour. The underwater lights in the swimming pool were smoky green, and a thin slick of suntan oil floated on the surface. The waiter took away their dishes, brought them more rounds of tropical drinks, and their gaiety seemed unrelenting. They left the table periodically and went back through the sliding glass door into the motel room, and at first I thought they were simply using the bathroom, but then one of the women came back out touching one nostril with her knuckle, sniffing as though a grain of sand were caught in her breathing passage. At ten o'clock the waiter began dipping leaves out of the pool with a long-handled screen, and I saw Mapes signal for more drinks and the waiter look at his watch and shake his head negatively. They sat outside for another half hour, smoking cigarettes, laughing more quietly now, sucking on pieces of ice from the bottoms of their glasses, the women's faces pleasant with a nocturnal lassitude.

Then a sudden rain shower rattled across the motel's tile roof, clattered on the bamboo and palm fronds, and danced in the swimming pool's underwater lights. Vidrine, Mapes, and the women ran laughing for the sliding door of the room. I waited until midnight, and they still had not come back out.

I put on my rain hat and went into the motel bar. It was almost deserted, and raindrops ran down the windows. Outside, I could see the white and blue neon flower against the dark sky. The bartender smiled at me. He wore black trousers, a white shirt that glowed almost purple in the bar light, and a black string tie sprinkled with sequins. He was a strange-looking man. His eyes were close-set and small as dimes, and he smoked a Pall Mall with three fingers along the barrel of the cigarette. I sat at the corner of the bar, where I could see the front door of Vidrine and Mapes's rooms, and ordered a 7-Up.

'It's pretty empty tonight,' I said.

'It sure is. You by yourself tonight?' he said.

'Right now I am. I was sort of looking for some company.' I smiled at him.

He nodded good-naturedly and began rinsing glasses in a tin sink. Finally he said, 'You staying at the motel?'

'Yeah, for a couple of days. Boy, I tell you I got one.' I blew out my breath and touched my forehead with my fingertips. 'I met this lady last night, a schoolteacher, would you believe it, and she came up to my room and we started hitting the JD pretty hard. But I'm not kidding you, before we got serious about anything she drank me under the table and I woke up at noon like a ball of fire.' I laughed. 'And with another problem, too. You know what I mean?'

He ducked his head and grinned.

'Yeah, that can be a tough problem,' he said. 'You want another 7-Up?'

'Sure.'

He went back to his work in the sink, his small eyes masked, and a moment later he dried his hands absently on a towel, turned on a radio that was set among the liquor bottles on the counter, and walked into a back hallway, where he picked up a house phone. He spoke into the receiver with his back turned toward me so that I could not hear him above the music on the radio. Outside the window, the trees were black against the sky and the blue tile of the motel roof glistened in the rain.

The girl came through the side door ten minutes later and sat one stool down from me. She wore spiked heels, Levi's, a backless brown sweater, and hoop earrings. She shook her wet hair loose, lit a cigarette, ordered a drink, then had another, and didn't pay for either of them. She talked as though she and I and the bartender were somehow old friends. In the neon glow she was pretty in a rough way. I wondered where she came from, what kind of trade-off was worth her present situation.

I wasn't making it easy for her, either. I hadn't offered to pay for either of her drinks, and I had made no overture toward her. I saw her look at her watch, then glance directly into the bartender's eyes. He lit a cigarette and stepped out the door as though he were getting a breath of fresh air.

'I hate lounges, don't you? They're all dull,' she said.

'It's a pretty slow place, all right.'

'I'd rather have drinks with a friend in my room.'

'What if I buy a bottle?'

'I think that would be just wonderful,' she said, and smiled as much to herself as to me. Then she bit down on her lip, leaned toward me, and touched my thigh. 'I've got a little trouble with Don, though. Like a seventy-five dollar bar tab. Could you lend it to me so they don't eighty-six me out of this place?'

'It's time to take off, kiddo.'

'What?'

I took my sheriff's deputy badge out of my back pocket and opened it in front of her. It was just an honorary one, and I kept it only because it

454

got me free parking at Evangeline Downs and the Fairgrounds in New Orleans, but she didn't know that.

'Don's in deep shit. Go home and watch television,' I said.

'You bastard.'

'I told you you're not busted. You want to hang around and have some of his problems?'

Her eyes went from my face to the bartender, who was coming back through the side door. Her decision didn't take long. She took her car keys out of her purse, threw her cigarettes inside, snapped it shut, and walked quickly on her spiked heels out the opposite door into the rain. I held up the badge in front of the bartender's small, close-set eyes.

'It's Iberia Parish, but what do you care?' I said. 'You're going to do something for me, right? Because you don't want Lafayette vice down here, do you? You're a reasonable guy, Don.'

He bit down on the corner of his lip and looked away from my face.

'I got a number I can call,' he said.

'Not tonight you don't.'

I could see his lip discolor where his tooth continued to chew on it. He blew air out of his nose as though he had a cold.

'I don't want trouble.'

'You shouldn't pimp.'

'How about lightening up a bit?' He looked at the two remaining customers in the bar. They were young and they sat at a table in the far corner. Behind them, through the opened blinds, headlights passed on the wet street.

'Two of your girls are in room six. You need to get them out,' I said.

'Wait a minute . . .'

'Let's get it done, Don. No more messing around.'

'That's Mr Mapes. I can't do that.'

'Time's running out, partner.'

'Look, you got a beef here or something, that's your business. I can't get mixed up in this. Those broads don't listen to me, anyway.'

'Well, I guess you're a stand-up guy. Your boss won't mind you getting busted, will he? Or having heat all over the place? You think one of those girls might have some flake up her nose? Maybe it's just sinus trouble.'

'All right,' he said, and held his palms upward. 'I got to tell these people I'm closing. Then I'll call the room. Then I'm gone, out of it, right?'

I didn't answer.

'Hey, I'm out of it, right?' he said.

'I'm already having trouble remembering your face.'

Five minutes after the bartender phoned Mapes's room the two prostitutes came out the front door, a man's angry voice resounding out of the room behind them, and got into a convertible and drove away. I opened the wooden toolbox in the bed of my pickup truck and took out a five-foot length of chain that I sometimes used to pull stumps. I folded it in half and wrapped the two loose ends around my hand. The links were rusted and made an orange smear across my palm. I walked across the gravel under the dripping trees toward the door of room six. The chain clinked against my leg; the heat lightning jumped in white spiderwebs all over the black sky.

Vidrine must have thought the women had come back because he was smiling when he opened the door in his boxer undershorts. Behind him Mapes was eating a sandwich in his robe at a wet bar. The linen and covers on the king-sized bed were in disarray, and the hallway that led into another bedroom was littered with towels, wet bathing suits, and beer cups.

Vidrine's smile collapsed, and his face suddenly looked rigid and glazed. Mapes set his sandwich in his plate, wet the scar on his lower lip as though he were contemplating an abstract equation, and moved toward a suitcase that was opened on a folding luggage holder.

I heard the chain clink and sing through the air, felt it come back over my head again and again, felt their hands rake against the side of my face; my ears roared with sound – a rumble deep under the Gulf, the drilling-rig floor trembling and clattering violently, the drill pipe exploding out of the wellhead in a red-black fireball. My hand was bitten and streaked with rust; it was the color of dried blood inside a hypodermic needle used to threaten a six-year-old child; it was like the patterns that I streaked across the walls, the bedclothes, the sliding glass doors that gave on to the courtyard where azalea petals floated on the surface of a lighted turquoise pool.

4

Alafair woke up with an upset stomach the next morning, and I kept her home from school. I fixed her soft-boiled eggs and weak tea, then took her down to work with me in the bait shop. The sun had come up in a clear sky that morning, and the trees along the dirt road were bright green from the rain. The myrtle bushes were filled with purple bloom in the sunlight.

'Why you keep looking down the road, Dave?' Alafair asked. She sat on one of the phone-cable spools on the dock, watching me unscrew a fouled spark plug from an outboard engine. The canvas umbrella in the center of the spool was folded, and her Indian-black hair was shiny in the bright light.

'I'm just admiring the day,' I said.

I felt her looking at the side of my face.

'You don't feel good?' she said.

'I'm fine, little guy. I tell you what, let's take a ride down to the store and see if they have any kites. You think you can put a kite up today?'

'There ain't no wind.'

'Don't say "ain't."'

'Okay.'

'Let's go get some apples for Tex. You want to feed him some apples?'

'Sure.' She looked at me curiously.

We walked up to the truck, which was parked under the pecan trees, got in, and drove down the road toward the old store at the four-corners. Alafair looked at the floor.

'What's that, Dave?'

'Don't mess with that.'

Her eyes blinked at my tone.

'It's just a chain. Kick it under the seat,' I said.

She leaned down toward the floor.

'Don't touch it,' I said. 'It's dirty.'

'What's wrong, Dave?'

'Nothing. I just don't want your hands dirty.'

I took a breath, stopped the truck, and went around to Alafair's side. I opened her door and lifted the loops of chain off the floor. They felt as though they were coated with paint that had not quite dried.

'I'll be right back,' I said.

I walked down on the bank of the bayou and sailed the chain out into the middle of the current. Then I stooped by the cattails in the shallows and scrubbed my palms with water and sand. Dragon-flies hovered over the cattails, and I saw a cotton-mouth slide off a log and swim into the lily pads. I pushed my hands into the sand, and water clouded around my wrists. I walked back up on to the bank with my hands dripping at my sides and wiped them on the grass, then I took a cloth out of the toolbox and wiped them again.

The ramshackle general store at the four corners was dark and cool inside, the wood-bladed ceiling fan turning over the counter. I bought a sack of apples for Alafair's horse, some sliced ham, cheese, and French bread for our lunch, and two soda pops to drink out on the gallery. The sun was brilliant on the white shale parking lot, and through the trees across the road I could see a Negro man cane fishing in a pirogue close into the cypress roots.

We went back to the house, and Alafair helped me weed my hydrangea and rose beds. Our knees were wet and dirty, our arms covered with fine grains of black dirt. My flower beds were thick with night crawlers, all of them close to the surface after the rain, and when we ripped weeds from the soil, they writhed pale and fat in the hard light. I knew almost nothing of Alafair's life before she came to Annie and me, but work must have been a natural part of it, because she treated almost any task that I gave her as a game and did it enthusiastically in a happy and innocent way. She worked her way through the rosebushes on all fours, pinging the weeds and Johnsongrass loudly in the bucket, a smear of dirt above one eyebrow. The smell of the hydrangeas and the wet earth was so strong and fecund it was almost like a drug. Then the breeze came up and blew through the pecan trees in the front yard; out on the edge of the trees' shade my neighbor's water sprinkler spun in the sunlight and floated across my fence in a rainbow mist.

They came just before noon. The two Lafayette plainclothes detectives were in an unmarked car, followed by the Iberia Parish sheriff, who drove a patrol car. They parked next to my truck and walked across the dead pecan leaves toward me. Both of the plainclothes were big men who left their coats in the car and wore their badges on their belts. Each carried a chrome-plated revolver in a clip-on holster. I rose to my feet, brushing the dirt off my knees. Alafair had stopped weeding and was staring at the men with her mouth parted.

'You've got a warrant?' I said.

One of the plainclothes had a matchstick in his mouth. He nodded without speaking.

'Okay, no problem. I'll need a few minutes, all right?'

'You got somebody to take care of the little girl?' his partner said. A Marine Corps emblem was tattooed on one of his forearms and a dagger with a bleeding heart impaled upon it on the other.

'Yes. That's why I need a minute or so,' I said. I took Alafair by the hand and turned toward the house. 'You want to come in with me?'

'Lean up against the porch rail,' the man with the matchstick said.

'Can't you guys show some discretion here?' I said. I looked at my friend the sheriff, who stood in the background, saying nothing.

'What the fuck are you talking about?' the tattooed man said.

'Watch your language,' I said.

I felt Alafair's hand close tightly in mine. The other detective took the matchstick out of his mouth.

'Put your hands on the porch rail, spread your feet,' he said, and took Alafair by her other hand and began to pull her away from me.

I pointed my finger at him.

'You're mishandling this. Back off,' I said.

Then I felt the other man shove me hard in the back, pushing me off-balance through the hydrangeas into the steps. I heard his pistol come out of his leather holster, felt his hand clamp down on my neck as he stuck the barrel of the revolver behind my ear.

'You're under arrest for murder. You think being an ex-cop lets you write the rules?' he said.

Out of the corner of my eye I saw Alafair staring at us with the stunned, empty expression of a person wakened from a nightmare.

They booked me into the parish jail on top of the old courthouse in the middle of Lafayette's original town square. The jail was an ancient one, the iron doors and bars and walls painted battleship gray. The words 'Negro Male' were still faintly visible on the door of one of the tanks. During the ride from New Iberia I had sat handcuffed in the back of the car, asking the detectives who it was I had killed. They responded with the silence and indifference with which almost all cops treat a suspect after he's in custody. Finally I gave up and sat back against the seat cushion, the cuffs biting into my wrists, and stared at the oak trees flicking past the window.

Now I had been fingerprinted and photographed, had turned over my wallet, pocket change, keys, belt, even my scapular chain, to a deputy who put them in a large manila envelope, realizing even then that something important was missing, something that would have a terrible bearing on my situation, yes, my Puma knife; and now the jailer and the detective who chewed on matchsticks were about to lock me in a six-cell area that was reserved for the violent and the insane. The jailer turned the key on the large, flat iron door that contained one narrow viewing slit, pulled it open wide, and pushed lightly on my back with his fingers.

'Who the hell was it?' I said to the detective.

'You must be a special kind of a guy, Robicheaux,' he said. 'You cut a guy from his scrot to sternum and don't bother to get his name. Dalton Vidrine.'

The jailer clanged the door behind me, turned the key, shot the steel lock bar, and I walked into my new home.

It was little different from any other jail that I had seen or even been locked in during my drinking years. The toilets stank, the air smelled of stale sweat and cigarette smoke and mattresses that had turned black with body grease. The walls were scratched with names, peace signs, and drawings of male and female genitalia. More enterprising people had climbed on top of the cells and burned their names across the ceiling with cigarette lighters. On the floor area around the main door was a 'deadline', a white line painted in a rectangle, inside of which no one had better be standing when the door swung open or while the trusties were serving out of the food cart.

But the people in that six-cell area were not the ordinary residents of a city or parish prison. One was an enormous demented Negro by the name of Jerome who had smothered his infant child. He told me later that a cop had worked him over with a baton; although he had been in jail two weeks, there was still purple gashes on his lips and lumps the size of birds' eggs on his nappy head. I would come to know the others, too: a biker from New Orleans who had nailed a girl's hands to a tree; a serial rapist and sodomist who was wanted in Alabama; a Vietnamese thug who, with another man, had garroted his business partner with jump cables for a car battery; and a four-time loser, a fat, grinning, absolutely vacant-eyed man who had murdered a whole family after escaping from Sugarland Farm in Texas.

I was given one phone call and I telephoned the best firm in Lafayette. Like all people who get into serious trouble with the law, I became immediately aware of the incredible financial burden that had been dropped upon me. The lawyer's retainer was $2,000, his ongoing fee $125 an hour. I felt as though my head were full of spiders as it tried to think in terms of raising that kind of money, particularly in view of the fact that my bail hadn't been set and I had no idea how high it would be.

I found out at my arraignment the next morning: $150,000. I felt the blood drain out of my face. The lawyer asked for bail reduction and argued that I was a local businessman, an ex-police officer, a property owner, a war veteran, and the judge propped his chin on one knuckle and looked back at him as impassively as a man waiting for an old filmstrip to run itself out.

We all rose, the judge left the bench, and I sat dazed and light-headed in a chair next to the lawyer while a deputy prepared to cuff me for the trip back to jail. The lawyer motioned to the deputy with two fingers.

'Give us a minute, please,' he said. He was an older, heavyset man, with thinning cropped red hair, who wore seersucker suits and clip-on bow ties.

The deputy nodded and stepped back by the side door to the courtroom.

'It's the pictures,' he said. 'Vidrine's entrails are hanging out in the bathtub. It's mean stuff to look at, Mr Robicheaux. And they've got your knife with your prints on it.'

'It must have fallen out of my pocket. Both of those guys were all over me.'

'That's not what Mapes says. The bartender has some pretty bad things to say, too. What'd you do to him?'

'Told him he was going to be busted for procuring.'

'Well, I can discredit him on the stand. But Mapes—' He clicked his tongue against the roof of his mouth. 'There's the fellow we have to break down. A man with chain burns all over his face and back can make a hell of a witness. Tell me, what in God's name did you have in mind when you went through that door?'

My palms were damp. I swallowed and wiped them on my trousers.

'Mapes knew Vidrine was a weak sister,' I said. 'After I was gone, he picked up my knife and took him out. That's what happened, Mr Gautreaux.'

He drummed his fingers on the arm of the chair, made a pocket of air in his jaw, cleared his throat and started to speak, then was silent. Finally, he stood up, patted me on the shoulder, and walked out the side door of the courtroom into the sunlight, into the wind ruffling the leaves of the oak trees, the noise of black kids roaring by on skateboards. The deputy lifted my arm and crimped one cuff around my wrist.

Batist and his wife kept Alafair with them the day I was arrested, but the next day I arranged for her to stay with my cousin, a retired schoolteacher in New Iberia. She was taken care of temporarily, Batist was running the dock, and my main worry had become money. Besides needing a huge unknown sum for the lawyer, I had to raise $15,000 for the bondsman's fee in order to make bail. I had $8,000 in savings.

My half brother, Jimmie, who owned all or part of several restaurants in New Orleans, would have written a check for the whole amount, but he had gone to Europe for three months, and the last his partners heard from him he was traveling through France with a group of Basque jai alai players. I then discovered the bankers whom I had known for years were not anxious to lend money to a man who was charged with first-degree murder and whose current address was the parish jail. I had been locked up nine days, and Batist was still visiting banks and delivering loan papers to me.

Our cells were unlocked at seven AM when a trusty and the night screw wheeled in the food cart, which every morning was stacked with aluminum containers of grits, coffee, and fried pork butts. Until lockup at five in the afternoon, we were free to move around in an area called the bull run, take showers, play cards with a deck whose missing members had been replaced with cards fashioned out of penciled cardboard, or stare listlessly out the window at the tops of the trees on the courthouse lawn. But most of the time I stayed in my cell, filling out loan applications or reading a stiffened, water-stained issue of *Reader's Digest*.

I was sitting on the side of my iron bunk, which hung from the wall on chains, printing across the top of an application, when a shadow moved across the page. Silhouetted in the open door of my cell was the biker who had nailed his girl's hands to a tree. He was thick-bodied and shirtless, his breasts covered with tattooed birds, and his uncut hair and wild beard made his head look as though it were surrounded by a mane. I could feel his eyes move across the side of my face, peel away tissue, probe for the soft organ, the character weakness, the severed nerve.

'You think you can cut it up there?' he said.

I wet my pencil tip and kept on writing without looking up.

'What place is that?' I said.

'Angola. You think you can hack it?'

'I'm not planning on being there.'

'That's what I said my first jolt. Next stop, three years up in the Block with the big stripes. They got some badass dudes there, man.'

I turned to the next page and tried to concentrate on the printed words.

'The night screw says you're an ex-cop,' he said.

I sat my pencil down and looked at the opposite wall.

'Does that make a problem for you?' I said.

'Not me, man. But there's some mean fuckers up on that farm. There's guys that'll run by your cell and throw a gasoline bomb in on you. Melt you into grease.'

'I don't want to be rude, but you're standing in my light.'

He grinned, and there was a malevolent light in his face. Then he stretched, yawned, laughed outright as though he were witnessing an absurdity of some kind, and walked away to the window that gave on to the courthouse lawn.

I did push-ups, I did curls by lifting the bunk with my fingertips, I took showers, and I slept as much as I could. At night I could hear the others breaking wind, talking to themselves, masturbating, snoring. The enormous Negro sometimes sang a song that began, 'My soul is in a paper bag at the bottom of your garbage can.' Then one night he went crazy in his cell, gripping the bars with both hands and bashing his head against them until blood and sweat were flying out into the bull run and we heard the screw shoot the steel lock bar on the door.

On the thirteenth day I received two visitors I wasn't prepared for. A deputy escorted me down the spiral metal stairs to a windowless room that was used as a visiting area for those of us who were charged with violent crimes. Sitting at a wood table scarred with cigarette burns were Dixie Lee Pugh, one arm in a sling, his yellow hair crisscrossed with bandages, and my old homicide partner, Cletus Purcel. As always, Clete looked too big for his shirt, his sport coat, the tie that was pulled loose from his throat, the trousers that climbed above his socks. His cigarette looked tiny in his hand, the stitched scar through his eyebrow a cosmetic distraction from the physical confidence and humor in his face.

Clete, old friend, why did you throw it in?

They were both smiling so broadly they might have been at a party. I smelled beer on Dixie's breath. I sat down at the table, and the deputy locked a barred door behind me and sat on a chair outside.

'You made your bail all right, huh, Dixie?' I said.

He wore a maroon shirt hanging outside his gray slacks, and one foot was bandaged and covered with two athletic socks. His stomach made a thick roll against the bottom of his shirt.

'Better than that, Dave. They cut me loose.'

'They did what?'

'I'm out of it. Free and clear. They dropped the possessions charge.' He was looking at the expression on my face.

'They lost interest,' Clete said.

'Oh? How's that?'

'Come on, Dave. Lighten up. You know how it works,' Clete said.

'No, I think my education is ongoing here.'

'We already have a firm on retainer in New Orleans, and I hired the best in Lafayette. You know these local guys aren't going to get tied up in court for months over a chickenshit holding bust.'

'Who's this "we" you're talking about? What the hell are you doing with Dixie Lee?' I said.

'He's got a friend. I work for the friend. The friend doesn't like to see Dixie Lee suffering a lot of bullshit he doesn't deserve. You don't deserve it, either, Dave.'

'You work for this character Dio?'

'He's not such a bad guy. Look, there's not a lot of jobs around for a cop who had to blow the country, uh, with a few loose ends lying around.'

'How'd you get out of it? I thought there was still a warrant on you.'

'You've never learned, partner. First, they didn't have dog-doo to go on. Second, and this is what you don't understand, nobody cares about a guy like that. The best part of that guy ran down his daddy's leg. He met a bad fate. He should have met it earlier. The world goes on.'

'Do you know what he's talking about?' I said to Dixie Lee.

'It's his business,' he said quietly, and took a cigarette out of his pocket so that his eyes avoided mine.

'Forget the past, Dave. It's a decaying memory. That's what you used to tell me, right? Great fucking line. Let's look at the problem we got now, namely, getting your butt out of here. I hear they've got you in a special place with the lovelies.'

I didn't answer. Both of them looked at my face, then Dixie's eyes wandered around the room.

'Come on, Streak, be my mellow man for a few minutes,' Clete said.

When Dixie Lee's eyes lighted on mine again, I said. 'To tell you the truth, Dixie, I feel like killing you.'

'So he feels bad. What the fuck's he supposed to do? Go to prison?' Clete said. 'Look, I was coming here on my own, anyway, but as soon as I got him kicked loose he told me we got to get your ass out, too. That's a fact.'

'You got the right to be mad,' Dixie Lee said to me. 'I got a way of pissing in the soup, and then everybody's got to drink out of it. I just didn't know you were going to—'

'What?' I said.

'Hell, I don't know. Whatever it was you did in that motel room. Lord, Dave, I heard a cop say they stuck Vidrine's guts back in his stomach with a trowel.'

'That was Mapes's work, not mine.'

I could see the amusement in Clete's face.

'Sorry,' he said. Then he laughed. 'But let's face it. I remember a couple of occasions when you really decorated the walls.'

'This wasn't one of them.'

'Whatever you say. Who cares anyway? The guy was a bucket of shit,' Clete said. 'Let's talk about getting you out of the zoo.'

'Wait a minute. You knew Vidrine?'

'Montana's a small community in a lot of ways. You'd like it there. I rent a place from Sally Dee right on Flathead Lake.'

'You used to hate those guys, Clete.'

'Yeah . . . well,' he said, and sucked his teeth. 'The CIA deals dope, guys in the White House run guns. You used to say it yourself – we keep the lowlifes around so we can have a dartboard we can hit.'

'Where'd you hook up with this guy?'

'Sal?' He scraped a piece of paint on the table with his fingernail. 'I've got a brother-in-law who's connected in Galveston. He got me a job dealing blackjack in one of Sal's places in Vegas. After a month they moved me up into house security. Most of the rent-a-cops in Vegas have chewing gum for brains. It's like running for president against Harpo Marx. In six months I was in charge of security for the whole casino. Now I do whatever needs doing – Vegas, Tahoe, Flathead.' He looked up at me. 'It beats cleaning up puke in a john, which is what I was doing in a dump over in Algiers. Look, you want out of here?'

'Hell, no. Clete. The ambience really grows on you.'

'I can do it in twenty minutes.'

'You're going to put up fifteen thousand?'

'I don't have to. There's a couple of bondsmen here who'd love to do a favor for Sally Dee. Why not? It doesn't cost them anything. Unless you jump the bond.'

'Let him do it for you, Dave,' Dixie Lee said.

'I think I'm going to have to sweat this one out.'

'Why? You got to prove you're an honest man?' Clete said.

'Thanks just the same, Cletus.'

'You're pissing me off. You think I'm trying to sign you up for the Mafia or something?'

'I don't know what you're trying to do. In fact, I don't understand anything you've done.'

'Maybe it's because you're not listening too well.'

'Maybe so.'

He lit a cigarette and flipped the burnt match against the wall. He blew smoke out his nose.

'There's no strings,' he said.

'Come on.'

'You got my word.'

'They'll boil you down to glue, Clete. Bartend in Algiers, sell debit insurance. Just get away from them.'

'I thought maybe I could make up for some bad things I did to you, partner.'

'I don't hold a grudge.'

'You never forget anything, Dave. You store it up in you and feed it and stoke it until it's a furnace.'

'I'm changing.'

'Yeah, that's why they got you locked up with the shitbags.'

'What can I say?'

'Nothing,' Clete said. 'Here's my cigarettes. Trade them to the geeks for their food.'

'Dave, I'd go your bond if I had the money,' Dixie Lee said. 'But if I stepped on a dime right now, I could tell you if it was heads or tails.'

'But the man's not hearing us,' Clete said. 'Right, Dave? You're up on the high road, and the rest of us sweaty bastards have to toil our way through the flies.'

He went to the door and banged the side of his fist against one of the bars.

'Open up,' he said.

'I'm sorry,' I said.

'Yeah, yeah, yeah. Write me a postcard. Polson, Montana, in fact, if you get out of this dog shit, come see me. The beer's cold, you got to knock the trout back in the lake with an oar. A reasonable person might even say it's better than taking showers with queers and child molesters. But what do I know?'

He mashed his cigarette out on the concrete floor while the deputy unlocked the door. The deputy took him and Dixie Lee downstairs in the elevator, and I sat alone in the room, waiting for the deputy to return, my back bent over, my forearms propped loosely on my thighs, my eyes staring at the tiny webbed cracks in the floor.

The next day two deputies brought Jerome back from the jail ward at the charity hospital. The stitches on his forehead looked like small black butterflies laced in his skin. He stared out the windows, talked to himself, urinated on the floor of his cell. The biker and the rapist from Alabama told him the jailer had left the key to the main door in the toilet. He knelt by the bowl, staring into the water, while the other two encouraged him.

'You can't see it. It's way down in the pipe,' the biker said, and grabbed himself and grinned at the other man.

Jerome's arm went into the bowl, and he worked his hand down deep in the drain, splashing water up on his shirt and face.

I put my hands on his shoulders. He looked up at me with his mouth open, his tongue pink and thick on his bottom teeth.

'Don't do that, Jerome. There's no key in there,' I said.

'What?' he said. He talked like a man who was drugged.

'Take off your shirt and wash yourself in the shower,' I said. 'Come on, walk over here with me.'

'We're just giving the cat a little hope,' the biker said.

'Your comedy act is over,' I said.

The biker wore black sunglasses. He looked at me silently and worked his tongue around his gums. The hair on his face and head looked like brown springs.

'Wrong place to be telling people shit,' he said.

I released Jerome's arm and turned back toward the biker.

'Go ahead,' I said.

'Go ahead, what?'

'Say something else clever.'

'What are you talking about, man?'

'I want you to get in my face one more time.'

I couldn't see his eyes behind the sunglasses, but his mouth was as still as though it had been painted on his skin.

Then he said, because the others were watching him, 'We're a family here, man. That's how you hack it inside. You don't know that, you ain't gonna make it.'

I turned on the shower for Jerome, helped him pull off his shirt, and gave him a bar of soap from my cell. Then I picked up my tin plate and banged it loudly on the main door. It didn't take long for the jailer to open up. I was standing inside the deadline when he did.

His lean face was electric with outrage.

'What the hell do you think you're doing, Robicheaux?' he said.

'You've got a retarded man here who's being abused by other inmates. Either put him in isolation or send him to Mandeville.'

'Get your ass back across that line.'

'Fuck you.'

'That's it. You're going into lockdown,' he said, and slammed the iron door.

I turned around and stared into the grinning face of the four-time loser who had murdered a family after breaking out of Sugarland. He was completely naked, and the huge rolls of fat on his thighs and stomach hung off his frame almost like curtains. His eyes were pale, empty of all emotion, but his mouth was as red as a clown's. He took a puff of his cigarette and said, 'Sounds like you're getting pretty ripe, buddy.'

Then he laughed so hard, his eyes squinted shut with glee, that tears ran down his round cheeks.

Fifteen minutes later they moved me into a small room that contained a two-bunk cage, perforated with small squares and covered with thick layers of white paint that had been chipped and scratched with graffiti and prisoners' names. Years ago the cage had been used to hold men awaiting execution in the days when the electric chair, with two huge generators, traveled from parish to parish under tarpaulins on the back of a semi truck. Now it was used to house troublemakers and the uncontrollable. I was told that I would spend the next five days there, would have no visitors other than my lawyer, would take no showers, and would receive one meal a day at a time of my choosing.

That afternoon Batist tried to visit me and was turned away, but a Negro trusty brought me an envelope that contained a half-dozen crayon-filled pages from Alafair's coloring book, along with a note that she had printed out on lined paper. The colored-in pages showed palm trees and blue water, a lake full of fish, a brown horse by whose head she had written the word 'Tex.' Her note read: *I can spell. I can spell ant in the can. I can spell cat in the hat. I love Dave. I don't say ain't no more. Love. Alafair.*

I hung the coloring-book pages on the inside of the cage by pressing their edges under the iron seams at the tops of the walls. It started to rain, and mist blew through the window and glistened on the bars. I unrolled the thin striped mattress on the bottom bunk and tried to sleep. I was unbelievably tired, but I couldn't tell you from what. Maybe it was because you never really sleep in a jail. Iron doors slam all day and night; drunks shake doors against the jambs, and irritated street cops retaliate by raking their batons across the bars; people are gang-banged and sodomized in the shower, their cries lost in the clouds of steam dancing off the tiles; the crazies howl their apocalyptic insight from the windows like dogs baying under a yellow moon.

But it was an even deeper fatigue, one that went deep into the bone, that left the muscles as flaccid as if they had been traversed by worms. It was a mood that I knew well, and it always descended upon me immediately before I began a two-day bender. I felt a sense of failure, moral lassitude, defeat, and fear that craved only one release. In my troubled dream I tried to will myself into one of the pages from Alafair's coloring book – onto a stretch of beach dotted with palm trees, the sun hot on my bare shoulders while flecks of rain struck coldly on my skin. The water was blue and green, and red clouds of kelp were floating in the ground swell. Alafair rode her horse bareback along the edge of the surf, her mouth wide with a smile, her hair back and shiny in the sunlight.

But the pure lines of the dream wouldn't hold, and suddenly I was pouring rum into a cracked coconut shell and drinking from it with both hands. Like the sun and the rain, it was cool and warm at the same time, and it lighted my desires the way you touch a match to old newspaper stored in a dry box. I traveled to low-life New Orleans and Saigon bars, felt a woman's breath on my neck, her mouth on my ear, her hand brush my sex. Topless girls in G-strings danced barefooted on a purple-lit runway, the cigarette smoke drifting across their breasts and braceleted arms. I knocked back double shots of Beam with draft chasers, held on to the edge of the bar like a man in a gale, and looked at their brown bodies, the watery undulations of their stomachs, their eyes that were as inviting as the sweet odor of burning opium.

Then I was back on the beach, alone, trembling with a hangover. The back of Alafair's horse was empty, and he was shaking the loose reins against his neck and snorting with his nose down by the edge of the surf.

Don't lose it all, I heard Annie say.

Where is she?

She'll be back. But you've got to get your shit together, sailor.

I'm afraid.

Of what?

They're serious. They're talking about life in Angola. That's ten and a half years with good time. They've got the knife and the witnesses to pull it off, too. I don't think I'm going to get out of this one.

Sure you will.

I'd be drunk now if I was out of jail.

Maybe. But you don't know that. Easy does it and one day at a time. Right? But no more boozing and whoring in your dreams.

Annie, I didn't do it, did I?

It's not your style, baby love. The rain's starting to slack and I have to go. Be good, darlin'.

I woke sweating in a bright shaft of sunlight through the window. I sat on the side of my bunk, my palms clenched on the iron edges, my mind a tangle of snakes. It was hot, the room was dripping with humidity, but I trembled all over as though a cold wind were blowing across my body. The water faucet in my rust-streaked sink ticked as loudly as a clock.

Two days later my loan was approved at a New Iberia bank, and fifteen minutes after I paid the bondsman's fee I was sprung. It was raining hard when I ran from the courthouse to the pickup truck with my paper sack of soiled clothes and toilet articles under my arm. Alafair hugged me in the snug, dry enclosure of the truck, and Batist lit a cigar and blew the smoke out his teeth as though we all had a lock on the future.

I should have been happy. But I remembered a scene I had witnessed years ago when I was a young patrolman in New Orleans. A bunch of Black Panthers had just been brought back to a holding cell on a wrist chain from morning arraignment, and their public defender was trying to assure them that they would be treated fairly.

'Believe it or not, our system works,' he said to them through the bars.

An unshaved black man in shades, beret, and black leather jacket rolled a matchstick across his tongue and said, 'You got it, motherfucker. And it *work* for somebody else.'

5

Once out of jail I felt like the soldier who returns to the war and discovers that the battlefield is empty, that everyone else has tired of the war except him and gone home.

Dixie Lee had left a note at the house the day before:

Dave,
What I done to you grieves me. That's the honest to God truth, son. I got no excuse except everything I touch turns to shit. I'm leaving a box of milky ways for the little girl that lives with you. Big deal. Me and Clete and his lady friend are headed for the big sky today. Maybe later I might get a gig at one of Sals casinos. Like my daddy used to say, it don't matter if we're colored or not, we all got to pick the white mans cotton. You might as well pick it in the shade next to the water barrel.
   Dave, dont do time.

Dixie Lee

And what about Harry Mapes, the man whose testimony could send me to Angola? (I could still smell his odor from the motel room – a mixture of rut, perfume from the whores, chlorine, bourbon and tobacco and breath mints.) I called Star Drilling Company in Lafayette.

'Mr Mapes is in Montana,' the receptionist said.

'Where in Montana?'

'Who is this, please?'

'An acquaintance who would like to talk with him.'

'You'll have to speak to Mr Hollister. Just a moment, please.'

Before I could stop her he was on the line.

'I need to know where Mapes is. Deposition time and all that,' I said.

'What?'

'You heard me.'

There was a pause.

'Is this Robicheaux?' he asked.

'If we don't get it from you, we'll get it from the prosecutor's office.'

'The only thing I'll tell you is that I think you're a sick and dangerous man. I don't know how they let you out of jail, but you stay away from my people.'

'You have Academy Award potential, Hollister,' I said. But he hung up.

I worked in the bait shop, shoed Alafair's horse, weeded the vegetable garden, cleaned the leaves out of the rain gutters and the coulee, tore down the old windmill and hauled it to the scrapyard. I tried to concentrate on getting through the day in an orderly fashion and not think about the sick feeling that hung like a vapor around my heart. But my trial was six weeks away and the clock was ticking.

Then one bright morning I was stacking cartons of red wrigglers on a shelf in the bait shop and one spilled out of my hand and burst open on the countertop. The worms were thin and bright red in the dark mixture of loam and coffee grounds, and I was picking them up individually with my fingertips and dropping them back in the carton when I felt that sickness around my heart again and heard the words in my head: *They're going to do it. In five and a half weeks.*

I had no defense except my own word, that of an alcoholic ex-cop with a history of violence who was currently undergoing psychotherapy. My trial wouldn't last more than three days, then I would be locked on a wrist chain in the back of a prison van and on my way to Angola.

'What's wrong your face, Dave?' Batist said.

I swallowed and looked at my palms. They were bright with a thin sheen of sweat.

I went up to the house, packed two suitcases, took my .45 automatic out of the dresser drawer, folded a towel around it, snapped it inside a suitcase pouch with two loaded clips and a box of hollow-points, and called the bondsman in Lafayette. I had known him for twenty-five years. His name was Butter Bean Verret; he wasn't much taller than a fire hydrant, wore tropical suits, neckties with palm trees painted on them, rings all over his fingers, and ate butter beans and ham hocks with a spoon in the same café every day of his life.

'What's happening, Butter Bean? I need to get off the leash,' I said.

'Where you going?'

'Montana.'

'What they got up there we ain't got here?'

'How about it, partner?'

He was quiet a moment.

'You're not going to let me get lonely down here, are you? You're gonna call me, right? Every four, five days you gone, maybe.'

'You got it.'

'Dave?'

'What?'

'You done got yourself in a mess here in Lou'sana. Don't make no mo' mess up there, no.'

I told Batist that I was leaving him and Clarise in charge of the dock, my house and animals, that I would call him every few days.

'What you gonna do Alafair?' he said.

'My cousin will keep her in New Iberia.'

He made a pretense of wiping off the counter with a rag. His blue cotton work shirt was unbuttoned, and his stomach muscles ridged above his belt buckle. He put a gumdrop in the side of his mouth and looked out the window at the bayou as though I were not there.

'All right, what's wrong?' I said.

'You got to ask me that?'

'I have to do it, Batist. They're going to send me to prison. I'm looking at ten and a half years. That's with good time.'

'That don't make it right.'

'What am I supposed to do?'

'Her whole life people been leaving her, Dave. Her mama, Miz Annie, you in the jail. She don't need no mo' of it, no.'

I filled up the truck at the dock and waited on the gallery for the school bus. At four o'clock it stopped in the leafy shade by the mailbox, and Alafair walked through the pecan trees toward me, her tin lunch box clanging against her thigh. Her tan skin was dark in the shadows. As always, she could read a disturbed thought in my face no matter how well I concealed it.

I explained to her that I had to leave, that it wouldn't be for long, that sometimes we simply had to do things that we didn't like.

'Cousin Tutta is always nice to you, isn't she?' I said.

'Yes.'

'She takes you to the show and out to the park, just like I do, doesn't she?'

'Yes.'

'Batist will come get you to ride Tex, too. That'll be all right, won't it?'

This time she didn't answer. Instead she sat quietly beside me on the stop and looked woodenly at the rabbit hutches and Tripod eating out of his bowl under the pecan tree. Then pale spots formed in her cheeks, and the skin around her bottom lip and chin began to pucker. I put my arm around her shoulders and looked away from her face.

'Little guy, we just have to be brave about some things,' I said. 'I've got some big problems to take care of. That's just the way it is.'

Then I felt incredibly presumptuous, vain, and stupid in talking to her about bravery and acceptance. She had experienced a degree of loss and violence in her short life that most people can only appreciate in their nightmares.

I stared across the road at a blue heron rising from the bayou into the sunlight.

'Have you ever seen snow?' I said.

'No.'

'I bet there's still snow on the ground in Montana. In the ponderosa and the spruce, high up on the mountain. I went out there once with a friend from the army. I think you and I had better go check that out, little guy.'

'See snow?'

'You better believe it.'

Her teeth were white and her eyes were squinted almost shut with her smile.

By that evening we were highballing through the red-clay piney woods of East Texas, the warm wind blowing through the open truck windows, the engine humming under the hood, the inside of the cab aglow with the purple twilight.

We rode into the black, rain-swept night until the sky began to clear out in the Panhandle and the moon broke through the clouds in a spoked wheel of silver over the high plains. The next day, outside of Raton, New Mexico, I bought a bucket of fried chicken and we ate in a grove of cottonwoods by a stream and slept four hours on a blanket in the grass. Then we climbed out of the mesa country into Trinidad, Colorado, and the tumbling blue-green roll of the Rocky Mountains, through Pueblo, Denver, and finally southern Wyoming, where the evening air turned cold and smelled of sage, and the arroyo-cut land and buttes were etched with fire in the sunset. That night we stayed in a motel run by Indians; in the morning it rained and you could smell bacon curing in a smoke-house.

We crossed into Mountain south of Billings, and the land began to change. It was green and rolling, the rivers slow-moving and lined with cottonwood and willow trees, with sharp-toothed mountains in the distance. Then as we headed toward the Continental Divide the rivers became wider with the spring runoff, roiling in the center, flooding the trees along the banks, and the mountains in the distance tumbled higher and higher against the sky, their crests still packed with snow, the slopes covered with ponderosa pine and Douglas fir and blue spruce. Alafair slept on the seat beside me, her head on a comic book, while I topped the Divide outside of Butte and began the long grade down the western slope toward Missoula. White-tailed deer grazed near the road in the evening shadows, their heads flickering at me as I roared past them. Log ranch houses were set back against the base of the hills, their windows lighted, smoke flattening off their stone chimneys.

I followed the Clark Fork River through a cut in the mountains called

Hellgate Canyon, and suddenly under a bowl of dark sky the city spilled out in a shower of light all the way across the valley floor. Missoula was a sawmill and university town, filled with trees and flowers, old brick homes, wooded parks, intersecting rivers glazed with neon light, the tinge of processed wood pulp, rows of bars where bikers hung in the doorways and the rock music thundered out into the street. My palms were thick and ringing with the pressure of the steering wheel, my ears almost deaf from the long hours of road wind. When I climbed the motel stairs with Alafair asleep on my shoulder, I looked out over the night sheen of the river, at the circle of mountains around the town and the way the timber climbed to the crests, and I wondered if I had any chance at all of having a normal life again, of being an ordinary person who lived in an ordered town like this and who did not wake up each morning with his fears sitting collectively on his chest like a grinning gargoyle.

All of my present troubles had begun with Dixie Lee Pugh, and I felt that their solution would have to begin with him, too. But first I had to make living arrangements for Alafair and me. One of the advantages of being Catholic is that you belong to the western world's largest private club. Not all of its members are the best or most likable people, but many of them are. I rented a small yellow-brick house, with maple and birch trees in the yard, in a working-class neighborhood by the river, only two blocks away from a Catholic church and elementary school. The pastor called the principal at Alafair's school in New Iberia, asked to have her records sent to the rectory, then admitted her to the first-grade class. Then he recommended his housekeeper's widowed sister, who lived next door to the rectory, as a baby-sitter. She was a red-complected, bovine, and good-natured Finnish woman, and she said she could take care of Alafair almost any afternoon or evening, and in case I had to go out of town overnight Alafair could stay at her house.

I bought Alafair a new lunch box, crayons, pencils, and a notebook, and on our third morning in town, I walked her down the tree-lined street to the schoolyard and watched her form in ranks with the other children while a lay teacher waited to lead them in the Pledge of Allegiance. Drinking a cup of coffee on the front steps of my home, I watched the high, brown current of the river froth around the concrete pilings of a railway bridge and the sun break above Hellgate Canyon and fall across the valley, lighting the maples as though their leaves were waxed. Then I chewed on a matchstick and studied the backs of my hands. Finally, when I could delay it no longer, in the way you finally accept major surgery or embark on a long journey that requires much more energy than you possess, I got in my truck and headed for the town of Polson and Flathead Lake and the home of Sally Dio.

The Jocko Valley was ranch and feed-grower country, covered with large areas of sun and shadow; the river ran along the side of the highway and was tea-colored with a pebbled bottom and bordered with willows and cottonwoods. In the distance the Mission Mountains rose up blue and snowcapped and thunderous against the sky. The rural towns were full of Indians in work denims, curled-brim straw hats, heel-worn cowboy boots, and pickup trucks, and when I stopped for gas they looked through me as though I were made of smoky glass. There were lakes surrounded by cattails set back against the mountain range, and high up on the cliffs long stretches of waterfall were frozen solid in the sunlight like enormous white teeth.

I passed a Job Corps camp and an old Jesuit mission, and followed the highway over a pine-covered hill. Suddenly I saw Flathead Lake open up before me, so blue and immense and dancing with sunlight that it looked like the Pacific Ocean. Young pines grew on the slopes of the hills above the beaches, and the eastern shore was covered with cherry orchards. Out in the lake were islands with gray cliffs and trees rooted among the rocks, and a red sailboat was tacking between two islands, clouds of spray bursting of its bow.

I stopped in Polson, which was at the south end of the lake, and asked a filling station operator for directions to Sal Dio's house. He took a cigar out of his mouth, looked at me, looked at my license plate, and nodded up the road.

'It's about two miles,' he said.

'Which side of the road?'

'Somebody up there can tell you.'

I drove up the road between the cherry orchards and the lake, then passed a blue inlet, a restaurant built out over the water, a strip of white beach enclosed by pine trees, until I saw a mailbox with the name Dio on it and a sign that said Private Road. I turned into the dirt lane and started up an incline toward a split-level redwood home that was built on a triangular piece of land jutting out above the lake. But up ahead was an electronically operated iron gate that was locked shut, and between the gate and the lake was a small redwood house whose veranda was extended on pilings over the edge of the cliff. It was obvious that the small and the large houses had been designed by the same architect.

I stopped the truck at the gate, turned off the engine, and got out. I saw a dark-skinned girl with black hair looking at me from the veranda of the small house; then she went inside through sliding glass doors and Clete walked out in a pair of Bermuda shorts, a T-shirt that exposed his bulging stomach, a crushed porkpie fishing hat, and a powder-blue windbreaker that didn't conceal his revolver and nylon shoulder holster.

He walked across the lawn and down the hill to the road.

'Man, I don't believe it. Did they cut you loose?' he said.

'I'm out on bond.'

'Out on bond and out of the state? That doesn't sound right, Streak.'
He was grinning at me in the sunlight.

'I know the bondsman.'

'You want to go fishing?'

'I need to talk to Dixie Lee.'

'You came to the right place. He's up there with Sally.'

'I need to talk to you, too.'

'Sounds like our First District days.'

'It becomes that way when you're about to do a jolt in Angola.'

'Come on, it's not going to happen. You had provocation to go after
those guys. Then it was two against one, and finally it's your word against
Mapes's about the shank. Besides, check out Mapes's record. He's a sick
motherfucker if you ask me. Wait till your lawyer cross-examines him on
the stand. The guy's as likeable as shit on melba toast.'

'That's another thing that bothers me, Cletus – how you know about
these guys.'

'It's no mystery, partner,' he said, and took a package of Lucky Strikes
out of his windbreaker pocket. The outline of his revolver was blue and
hard against the nylon holster. 'Dixie Lee brought them around a couple
times. They liked to cop a few free lines off Sal and hang around some of
those rock people he's always flying in. Sal collects rock people. Vidrine
was a fat dimwit, but Mapes should have been eased off the planet a long
time ago.'

The skin of Clete's face was tight as he lit his cigarette and looked off at
the lake.

'It sounds personal,' I said.

'He got coked to the eyes one night and started talking about blowing
up a VC nurse in a spider hole. Then he tried to take Darlene into
the bedroom. Right there in the living room, like she was anybody's
punch.'

'Who?'

'She's the girl who lives with me. Anyway, Sal told me to walk him
down the road until he was sober. When I got him outside he tried to
swing on me. I got him right on the mouth. With a roll of quarters in my
hand. Dixie had to take him to the hospital in Polson.'

'I think you ought to have an early change of life.'

'Yeah, you were always big on advice, Dave. You see this .38 I have on?
I have a permit to carry it in three states. That's because I work for Sally
Dee. But I can't work as a cop anywhere. So the same people who won't
let me work as a crossing guard license me to carry a piece for Sal. Does
that tell you something? Anyway, I'm using the shortened version of your
AA serenity prayer these days – "Fuck it." '

'Do I get through the gate?'

He blew cigarette smoke out into the wind. His green eyes were squinted, as though the sun hurt them, as though a rusted piece of wire were buried deeply in the soft tissue of his brain.

'Yeah, come on up to the house. I have to call up to Sal's,' he said. 'Meet Darlene. Eat lunch with us if you like. Believe it or not, I'm glad to see you.'

I didn't want to have lunch with them, and I surely didn't want to meet Sally Dio. I only wanted for Dixie Lee to walk down to Clete's and talk with me, and then I would be on my way. But it wasn't going to work out that way.

'They're just getting up. Sal said to bring you up in about an hour,' Clete said, hanging up the phone in his living room. 'They had a big gig last night. Have you ever met the Tahoe crowd? For some reason they make me think of people cornholing each other.'

His girlfriend, whose full name was Darlene American Horse, was making sandwiches for us in the kitchen. Clete sat in a sway-backed canvas chair with a vodka Collins in his hand, one sandaled foot crossed on his knee, the other on a blond bearskin rug. Outside the sliding glass doors the lake was a deep blue, and the pines on an island of gray boulders were bending in the wind.

'The thing you won't forget,' he said, 'the guy who got whacked out back there in Louisiana – all right, the guy I whacked out – that psychotic sonofabitch Starkweather, I *had* to kill him. They said they'd give me ten grand, and I said that's cool, but I was going to run him out of town, take their bread, and tell them to fuck off if they complained about it later. Except he was feeding his pigs out of a bucket with his back to me, telling me how he didn't rattle, how he wouldn't piss on a cop on the pad if he was on fire, then he put his hand down in his jeans and I saw something bright in the sun and heard a click, and when he turned around with it I put a big one in his forehead. It was his Zippo lighter, man. Can you dig that?'

Maybe the story was true, maybe not. I just wasn't interested in his explanation or his obvious obsession, one that left his eyes searching for that next sentence, hanging unformed out there in the air, which would finally set the whole matter straight.

'Why do they call him "the Duck"?' I said.

'What?'

'Why do they call Sally Dio "the Duck"?'

'He wears ducktails.' He took a long drink out of his Collins. His mouth looked red and hard. He shrugged as though dismissing a private, troubling thought. 'There's another story. About a card game and drawing a deuce or something. The deuce is the duck, right? But it's all guinea stuff. They like titles. Those stories are usually bullshit.'

'I tell you, Clete, I'd really appreciate it if you could just bring Dixie Lee down here. I really don't need to meet the whole crowd.'

'You're still the same guy, your meter always on overtime.' Then he smiled. 'Do you think I'm going to call up the man I work for and say, "Sorry, Sal, my old partner here doesn't want to be caught dead in the home of a greaseball"?' He laughed, chewing ice and candied cherries in his jaws. 'But it's a thought, though, isn't it? Dave, you're something else.' He kept smiling at me, the ice cracking between his molars. 'You remember when we cooled out Julio Segura and his bodyguard? We really made the avocado salad fly.'

'Last season's box score.'

'Yeah, it is.' He looked idly out the sliding doors at the lake a moment, then slapped his knee and said, 'Man, let's eat.'

He walked up behind his girlfriend in the kitchen, picked her up around the ribs, and buried his face in her hair. He half walked and carried her back into the living room with his arms still locked around her waist. She turned her face back toward him to hide her embarrassment.

'This is my mainline mama, her reg'lar daddy's sweet little papoose,' he said, and bit the back of her neck.

That's really cool, Cletus, I thought.

She wore a denim skirt with black stockings and a sleeveless tan sweater. There were three moles by the edge of her mouth, and her eyes were turquoise green, like a Creole's. Her hands were big, the backs nicked with gray scars, the nails cut back to the quick. The gold watch she wore on one wrist and the bracelet of tiny gold chains on the other looked like misplaced accidents above her work-worn hands.

'She's the best thing in my life, that's what she is,' he said, still pushing his mouth into her hair. 'I owe Dixie Lee for this one. She got his drunk butt off of a beer joint floor on the reservation and drove him all the way back to Flathead. If she hadn't, a few bucks there would have scrubbed out the toilet with his head. Dixie's got a special way about him. He can say good morning and sling the shit through the fan.'

She eased Clete's arms from around her waist.

'Do you want to eat out on the porch?' she said.

'No, it's still cool. Spring has a hard time catching on here,' he said. 'What's it in New Orleans now, ninety or so?'

'Yeah, I guess.'

'Hotter than hell. I don't miss it,' he said.

His girlfriend set the table for us by the sliding doors, then went back into the kitchen for the food. A wind was blowing across the lake, and each time it gusted, the dark blue surface rippled with light.

'I don't know why she hooked up with me, but why question the fates?' he said.

'She looks like a nice girl.'

'You better believe she is. Her husband got killed felling trees over by

Lincoln. A Caterpillar backed over him, ground him all over a rock. She spent five years opening oysters in a restaurant in Portland. Did you see her hands?'

I nodded.

'Then she was waiting tables in that Indian beer joint. You ought to check out a reservation bar. Those guys would make great pilots in the Japanese air force.'

'They're going to send me up the road unless I nail Mapes.'

He pushed at the thick scar on his eyebrow with his finger.

'You're really sweating this, aren't you?' he said.

'What do you think?'

'I can't blame you. An ex-cop doing time. Bad scene, mon. But I got off the hook, zipped right out of it, and if anybody should have gone up the road, it was me. Tell your lawyer to get a couple of continuances. Witnesses go off somewhere, people forget what they saw, the prosecutor loses interest. There's always a way out, Streak.'

His girl brought out a tray filled with ham sandwiches, glasses of iced tea, a beet and onion salad, and a fresh apple pie. She sat down with us and ate without talking. The three moles by the corner of her mouth were the size of BBs.

'You actually think Dixie can help you?' Clete said.

'He has to.'

'Good luck. He told me once his life's goal is to live to a hundred and get lynched for rape. He's an all-right guy, but I think he has a wet cork for a brain.'

'He said Mapes and Vidrine killed a couple of guys and buried them back in a woods. Can you connect that to anything?'

His big face looked vague. 'No, not really,' he said.

I saw his girl, Darlene, look directly into the plate, her head turned down, as though she wanted to hide her expression. But I noticed the color of her eyes darken in the corners.

'I'm sorry for the way I talk,' I said. 'I think Clete and I were cops too long. Sometimes we don't think about what we say in front of other people.' I tried to smile at her.

'I don't mind,' she said.

'I appreciate you having me for lunch, it's very good.'

'Thank you.'

'I came out here fishing with a friend of mine years ago,' I said. 'Montana's a beautiful place to live, isn't it?'

'Some of it is. When you have a job. It's a hard place to find work in,' she said.

'Everything's down here,' Clete said. 'Oil, farming, cattle, mining. Even lumber. It's cheaper to grow trees down south. These dumb bastards voted for Reagan, then got their butts reamed.'

'Then why is your buddy up here? And these lease people?'

His green eyes moved over my face, then he grinned.

'You never could resist mashing on a guy's oysters,' he said. 'He's not my buddy. I work for him. I get along with him. It's a professional relationship.'

'All right, what's he doing here?'

'It's a free country. Maybe he likes the trout.'

'I met a DEA man who had some other theories.'

'When it comes to Sal's business dealings, I turn into a potted plant. I'm also good at taking a smoke in the yard.'

'Tell it to somebody else. You were the best investigative cop I ever knew.'

'At one time,' he said, and winked. Then he looked out at the lake and the inland sea gulls that were wheeling over the shoreline. He pushed a piece of food out from behind his teeth with his tongue. 'You've read a lot more books than I have. You remember that guy Rhett Butler in *Gone With the Wind*? He's a blockade runner for the Confederates or something. He tells Scarlett that fortunes are made during a county's beginning and during its collapse. Pretty good line. I think Sal read that book in the Huntsville library. He wheels and deals, mon.'

I didn't say anything. I finished the rest of my sandwich and glanced casually at my watch.

'All right, for God's sake,' Clete said. 'I'll take you up there. But do me a favor. That's my meal ticket up there. Don't look at these people like they're zoo creatures. Particularly Sal's father. He's a bloated old degenerate, but he's also a vicious sonofabitch who never liked me to begin with. I mean it, Dave. Your face doesn't hide your feelings too well. It gets that glaze on it like an elephant broke wind in the room. Okay? We got a deal, right, partner?'

'Sure,' I said.

'Oh boy.'

Sally Dio had brought Galveston, Texas, with him. His glassed-in sun porch, which gave on to the lake, was filled with potted banana, umbrella, orange, and Hong Kong orchid tees, and in the center of the house was a heavily chlorinated, lime-green swimming pool with steam rising off the water. A half-dozen tanned people sat on the edge of the tiles or drifted about lazily on inflated rubber rafts. The living room was paneled with white pine, the carpet was a deep red, and the waxed black piano, with the top propped open, gleamed in the indirect lighting. Dixie Lee, dressed only in a pair of Hawaiian beach shorts and an open bathrobe, sat at the piano bench and ran his fingers back and forth over the keys, his shoulders hunched, then suddenly his arms outspread, his florid face confident with his own sound. He sang,

'I was standing on the corner
Corner of Beale and Main,
When a big policeman said,
"Big boy, you'll have to tell me your name."
I said, "You'll find my name
On the tail of my shirt.
I'm a Tennessee hustler
And I don't have to work." '

Sally Dio sat behind a set of drums and cymbals in a pair of pleated gray slacks, bare-chested, his red suspenders hooked over his shoulders. He was a lean, hard-bodied man, his face filled with flat and sharp surfaces like a person whose bone is too close to the skin so that the eyes look overly large for the face. Under his right eye was a looped scar that made his stare even more pronounced, and when he turned his head toward Dixie Lee and fluttered the wire brushes across the snare drum, the ridge of his ducktails glistened against the refracted sunlight off the lake.

Out on the redwood veranda I could see the back of a wheelchair and a man sitting in it. Sally Dio and Dixie finished their song. No one asked me to sit down.

'Dixie says you used to be a police officer. In New Orleans,' Sally Dio said. His voice was flat, his eyes casually interested in my face.

'That's right.'

'What do you do now?'

'I'm a small-business man.'

'Probably pays better, doesn't it?'

'Sometimes.'

He made a circular pattern on the drumhead with the wire brushes.

'You like Louisiana?' he asked.

'Yes.'

'Why are you up here, then?'

Clete walked to the wet bar by the pool's edge and started fixing a drink.

'I have some things to take care of. I wanted a few words with Dixie,' I said.

'He says you're in a lot of trouble down there. What's he got to do with your trouble?'

'A lot.'

He looked me evenly in the eyes. Then he fluttered and ticked the brushes lightly on the drum skin.

'Dixie never hurt anybody. Not intentionally, anyway,' he said.

'I mean him no harm, Mr Dio.'

'I'm glad of that.'

A dripping blond girl in a silver swimsuit that was as tight as tin on her body, with a terry cloth robe over her shoulder, walked toward us, drying her hair with a towel.

'You want me to take Papa Frank in, Sal?' she said.

'Ask Papa Frank.'

'He gets cold if he stays out there too long.'

'Then go ask him, hon.'

She walked to the glass doors, then stopped and hooked up the strap on her sandal, pausing motionlessly against the light as though she were caught in a photographer's lens. Sally Dio winked at her.

I looked at Dixie Lee. I had to talk to him alone, outside. He refused to see any meaning in my face. A moment later the blond girl pushed the man in the wheelchair into the living room.

He wore a checkered golf cap, a knitted sweater over his protruding stomach, a muffler that almost hid the purple goiter that was the size of an egg in his neck. His skin was gray, his eyes black and fierce, his face unevenly shaved. Even from several feet away his clothes smelled of cigar smoke and Vick's VapoRub. With his wasted legs and swollen stomach, he reminded me of a distended frog strapped to a chair.

But there was nothing comical about him. His name had been an infamous one back in the forties and fifties. He had run all the gambling on Galveston Island and all the prostitution and white slavery on Post Office and Church streets. And I remembered another story, too, about a snitch on Sugarland Farm who tried to cut a deal by dropping the dime on Frank Dio. Somebody caught him alone in the shower and poured a can of liquid Drāno down his mouth.

He fixed one watery black eye on me.

'Who's he?' he said to his son.

'Somebody Clete used to know,' Sally Dio said.

'What's he want?'

'He thinks Dixie Lee can get him out of some trouble,' Sally Dio said.

'Yeah? What kind of trouble you in?' the father said to me.

'He's up on a murder charge, Pop. Mr Robicheaux used to be a police officer,' Sally Dio said. He smiled.

'Yeah?' His voice raised a level. 'Why you bring this to our house?'

'I didn't bring anything to your house,' I said. 'I was invited here. By Clete over there. Because the man I wanted to talk with couldn't simply walk down the hill and spend five minutes with me.'

'I invite. Sal invites. You don't get invited by somebody that works for me,' the father said. 'Where you used to be a cop?'

'New Orleans.'

'You know—?' He used the name of an old-time Mafia don in Jefferson parish.

'Yes, I helped give him a six-year jolt in Angola. I heard he complained a lot about the room service.'

'You a wiseguy, huh?'

'You want me to fix you a drink, Mr Frank?' Clete said.

The old man flipped his hand at Clete, his eyes still fixed on me, as though he were brushing away bad air.

'That's my cousin you're talking about,' he said.

I didn't reply. I looked again at Dixie Lee, who sat hunched forward on the piano bench, his hands in his lap, his gaze averted from us.

'Tell him to get the fuck out of here,' the father said. 'Tell that other one he don't bring smartass guys up to our house, either.' Again, he didn't bother to look in Clete's direction.

Then he motioned with his hand again, and the girl in the silver bathing suit wheeled him through a far door into a bedroom. The bed was piled with pink pillows that had purple ruffles around them. I watched the girl close the door.

'Got to do what Pop says. See you around, Mr Robicheaux,' Sally Dio said. He tapped one wire brush across the drumhead.

'Dixie, I want you to walk down to my car with me,' I said.

'Conversation time's over, Mr Robicheaux.'

'The man can speak for himself, can't he?' I said.

But before all my words were out, Sally Dio did a rat-a-tat-tat on the drum with the brushes.

'Are you coming, Dixie?'

Again he slapped the brushes rapidly on the drum, looking me steadily in the eyes with a grin at the corner of his mouth.

'A footnote about your relative in Angola,' I said. 'I not only helped put him away, I maced him in the face after he spit on a bailiff.'

'Clete, help our man find his car,' he said.

Clete took his drink away from his mouth. His face reddened. Behind him, the people in the pool were in various attitudes of embrace among the rubber cushions and wisps of steam.

'Sal, he's a good guy. We got off to a bad start this morning,' he said.

'Mr Robicheaux's late for somewhere else, Clete.'

Clete looked as though he had swallowed a thumbtack.

'No problem. I'm on my way. Take it easy, Clete,' I said.

'Sal, no kidding, he's a solid guy. Sometimes things just go wrong. It's nobody's fault,' Clete said.

'Hey, Robicheaux – something to take with you,' Sally Dio said. 'You came in here on somebody's shirttail. Then you talked rude to an old man. But you're in my house and you get to leave on a free pass. You been treated generous. Don't have any confusion about that.'

I walked outside into the sunlight, the wind riffling the lake, the hazy blue-green roll of the hills in the distance. The flagstone steps that led down the hill to Clete's place and my truck were lined with rosebushes and purple clematis.

'Wait a minute, Dave,' I heard Clete say behind me.

He had on his crushed porkpie hat, and as he descended the flagstone steps in his Bermuda shorts his legs looked awkward, the scars on his knees stretched and whitened across the bone.

'Hey, I'm sorry,' he said.

'Forget it.'

'No, that was bad in there. I'm sorry about it.'

'You weren't a part of it. Don't worry about it.'

'Everybody was saying the wrong things, that's all.'

'Maybe so.'

'I didn't want it to go like that. You know that.'

'I believe you, Cletus.'

'But why do you have to scratch a match on their scrots, man?'

'I thought I was pretty well behaved.'

'Oh fuck yeah, Absolutely. Dave, a half dozen like you could have this whole state in flames.'

'What's Dio's gig here?'

He snuffed inside this nose.

'I take his money. I don't care what he does. End of subject,' he said.

'See you around. Thanks again for the lunch. Say good-bye to Darlene for me.'

'Yeah, anytime. It's always a kick. Like having a car drive through your house.'

I smiled and started toward my pickup.

'Stay in your truck a few minutes. Dixie'll be down,' he said, walking up a gravel path toward his house.

'How do you know?'

'Because even though he acts like a drunk butthole, he wants to help. Also because I told him I'd beat the shit out of him if he didn't.'

I sat in my pickup for ten minutes and was about to give it up when I saw Dixie Lee walk down from Sally Dio's. He had put on a yellow windbreaker and a pair of brown slacks, and the wind blew strands of his blond hair on his forehead. He opened the door on the passenger's side and got in.

'How about we go down to the restaurant on the water for a brew?' he said. 'I'm so dry right now I'm a fire hazard.'

'All right, but I want you to understand something first, Dixie. I don't want you to talk to me because of something Clete said to you.'

'Clete didn't say anything.'

'He didn't?'

'Well, he's a little emotional sometimes. I don't pay him any mind. He don't like to see you in trouble.'

'But this is what's going to happen if I don't hear what I need from you. I'm going to take down Mapes one way or another. If that means getting you locked up as a material witness, that's what's going to happen. I can't promise I'll pull it off, but I'll use all the juice I can to turn the key on you, Dixie.'

'Oh man, don't tell me stuff like that. Not this morning, anyway. My nerve endings are fried as it is.'

'That's another item. I don't want to hear any more about your drinking problems, your theological concerns, or any of the other bullshit you spoon out to people when you're in a corner. Are we clear on this?'

'You come down with both feet son.'

'You dealt me into this mess. You'd better be aware of that, partner.'

'All right. Are we going for a brew or are you going to sit here and saw me apart?'

I started the truck and drove up the dirt lane through the spines to the main road, which was bordered on the far side by a short span of cherry orchards and then the steep rock face of the mountain. We drove along the lake toward the restaurant that was built on pilings out over the water. Dixie Lee had his face turned into the breeze and was looking wistfully at the sandy beaches, the dense stands of pine, the sailboats that tacked against the deep blue brilliance of the lake.

'Why don't you let me get you some real estate here?' he said.

'To tell you the truth, Dixie, I mortgaged my house and business to make bail.'

'Oh.'

'Why is the Dio family buying up land around here?'

'The state is recessed. Property values are way down. The Dios are going to make a lot of money later on.'

I pulled into the parking lot of the restaurant. A narrow dock protruded out from behind the building, and skiffs and sailboats were moored to it. There was a glaze of gasoline and oil on the water, and see gulls dipped and turned over an open bait well in one of the boats. I turned off the ignition.

'I don't think you've been hearing me very well, Dixie,' I said.

'What?'

'I'm really tired of you trying to pull strings on me. We're operating on the outer edges of my patience here.'

'What'd I say?'

'The mob doesn't make money out of real estate speculation. You stop lying to me.'

'You hurt me, man. Maybe I'm a lush, but that don't mean I'm a liar.'

'Then tell me why they're buying up property.'

'Dave, if you go to prison, and, Lord, I hope you don't, you'll learn two things in there. You stay out of the boss man's eye, and you *never* try to find out the other side of a cat like Sal. You go along and you get along. When you were a cop, did you want to know everything that was going on in your department? How many guys were on a pad? How many of them copped some skag or flake at a bust and sold it off later? Look, in another three or four weeks I'm going to start playing a gig at one of Sal's places in Tahoe. It's not a big deal – a piano bar, a stand-up bass, maybe a guitar. But it's Tahoe, man. It's rhythm and blues and back in the lights. I just got to ease up on the fluids, get it under control.'

'Why not get it the hell out of your life?'

'Everybody don't chop cotton the same way. I'm going inside for a brew. You want to come?'

I watched him walk across a board ramp into the bar side of the restaurant. I had wasted most of the morning, part of the afternoon, had accomplished nothing, and I felt a great weariness both with Dixie Lee and my situation. I followed him inside. He sat at the far end of the bar, by the windows, silhouetted against the sunlight on the lake. The walls of the bar were decorated with life preservers and nautical ropes and fishnets. Dixie was drinking from a bottle of Great Falls with a shot of whiskey on the side.

The bartender walked toward me, but I motioned him away.

'You don't want anything?' Dixie said.

'Who would Mapes and Vidrine have reason to kill?' I said.

'Not Vidrine. Mapes.'

'All right.'

He looked out the window.

'I don't know,' he said.

'It was somebody who was in his way, somebody who would cost him money.'

'Yeah, I guess so.'

'So who would cause Mapes trouble?'

'Maybe the crazoids. The tree spikers. Star Drilling wants to get into a wilderness area on the eastern slope. The tree spikers want everybody out.'

'But they don't represent anybody. You said they were cultists or something.'

'I don't know what they are. They're fucking wild men.'

'What could they do to keep Star out of a wilderness area?'

'Nothing, really. People up here don't like them. Them gyppo loggers will rip their ass if they get the chance.'

'Who's that leave?'

He sipped off his whiskey, chased it with beer, and looked out at the lake. His face was composed and his green eyes were distant with either thought or perhaps no thought at all.

'Come on, partner, who could really mess up Mapes's plans?'

'The Indians,' he said finally. 'Star wants to drill on the Blackfeet Reservation. It shouldn't be a problem, because in 1896 the Indians sold all their mineral rights to the government. But there're some young guys, AIM guys, that are smart, that are talking about a suit.'

'The American Indian Movement?'

'Yeah, that's them. They can tie everything up in court, say the treaty was a rip-off or the reservation is a religious area or some other bullshit. It can cost everybody a lot of money.'

'You know some of these guys?'

'No, I always stayed away from them. Some of them been in federal pens. You ever know a con with a political message up his butt? I celled with a black guy like that. Sonofabitch couldn't read and was always talking about Karl Marx.'

'Give me one name, Dixie.'

'I don't know any. I'm telling you the truth. They don't like white people, at least white oil people. Who needs the grief?'

I left him at the bar and drove back toward Missoula. In the Jocko Valley I watched a rain shower move out from between two tall white peaks in the Mission Mountains, then spread across the sky, darken the sun, and march across the meadows, the clumped herds of Angus, the red barns and log ranch houses and clapboard cottages, the poplar windbreaks, the willow-lined river itself, and finally the smooth green hills that rose into another mountain range on the opposite side of the valley. Splinters of lightning danced on the ridges, and the sky above the timberline roiled with torn black clouds. Then I drove over the tip of the valley and out of the rain and into the sunshine on the Clark Fork as though I had slipped from one piece of geographical climate into another.

I picked up Alafair at the baby-sitter's, next door to the rectory, then took her to an ice cream parlor by the river for a cone. There was a big white *M* on the mountain behind the university, and we could see figures climbing up to it on a zigzag trail. The side of the mountain was green with new grass, and above the *M* ponderosa pine grew through the saddle on the mountain and over the crest into the next valley. Alafair looked small at the marble-topped table, licking her cone, her feet not touching the floor. Her red tennis shoes and the knees of her jeans were spotted with grass stains.

'Were they nice to you at school?' I said.

'Sure.' Then she thought for a moment. 'Dave?'

'Yes.'

'The teacher says I talk like a Cajun. How come she say that?'

'I can't imagine,' I said.

We drove back to the house, and I used my new phone to call Dan Nygurski at the DEA in Great Falls. At first he didn't know where I was calling from, then I heard his interest sharpen when I told him I was in Montana.

'What do you think you're doing here?' he said.

'I'm in some trouble.'

'I know about your trouble. I don't think you're going to make it any better by messing around up here in Montana.'

'What do you mean, you know about it?'

'I got feedback from our office in Lafayette. Vidrine and Mapes worked with Dixie Pugh, and Pugh lives with Sally Dio. It's like keeping track of a daisy chain of moral imbeciles. You shouldn't have gotten involved, Robicheaux.'

I couldn't resist it.

'I was at Sally Dio's today,' I said.

'I think that's dumb, if you're asking my opinion.'

'You know who Cletus Purcel is?'

'Yeah, he was your old homicide partner. I heard he blew away a witness. It looks like he found his own level.'

'He told me Dio is called the Duck because he wears ducktails, but I think he left something out of the story.'

'I bet he did. Dio was playing poker with one of the Mexico City crowd on a yacht out in the Gulf. They were playing deuces wild, and the greaseball had taken six or seven grand off our friend. Except Dio caught him with a deuce hidden under his thigh. Sal's old man used to be known as Frankie "Pliers". I won't tell you why. But I guess Sal wanted to keep up the tradition. He had another guy hold the greaseball down on the deck and he cut off most of his ear with a pair of tin snips. Then he told him, "Tell everybody a duck ate your ear." That's the guy you were visiting today. That's the guy who takes care of your buddy Dixie Lee.'

'Why does he care about Dixie Lee?'

'He gets something out of it. Sal doesn't do anything unless there's a blow job in it for him somewhere.'

'Leasing or buying land for him?'

'Maybe. But don't concern yourself. Go back to Louisiana.'

'You know anything about some AIM members who might have disappeared from the Blackfeet Reservation?'

'I'm really wondering about the soundness of your mind at this point.'

'It's a simple question.'

'If you really want to step into a pile of shit, you've found a good way to do it.'

'Look, Mr Nygurski, I'm all on my own. Maybe I'm going to Angola pen. That's not hyperbole, I'm just about wiped out financially, my own testimony is my only defense, and my personal history is one that'll probably make a jury shudder. Tell me what you'd do in my circumstances. I'd really appreciate that.'

He paused, and I heard him take a breath.

'I never heard anything about any AIM guys disappearing,' he said.

'You'll have to talk with the tribal council or the sheriff's department. Maybe the FBI, although they don't have any love lost for those guys. Look, the reservation is a world unto itself. It's like a big rural slum. Kids cook their heads huffing glue, women cut each other up in bars. The Browning jail is a horror show on Saturday night. They're a deeply fucked-up people.'

'I may be over to see you in Great Falls.'

'Why?'

'Because I think Dio is mixed up in this. Harry Mapes has been around his place, and I don't think it's simply because he knows Dixie Lee.'

'Dio is mixed up with narcotics, whores, and gambling. Let me set you straight about this guy. He's not Bugsy Siegel. Comparatively speaking, he's a small-time player in Vegas and Tahoe. Any thing he owns, he's *allowed* to own. But he's an ambitious guy who wants to be a winging dick. So he's come up here to Lum 'n' Abner land to make the big score. Now, that's all you get, Robicheaux. Stay away from him. You won't help your case, and in the meantime you might get hurt. If I hear anything about missing Indians, I'll let you know.'

'Is it possible you feel you have the franchise on Sally Dio?'

'That could be, my friend. I grew up in West Virginia. I don't like what shitheads can do to good country. But I'm also a federal agent. I get paid for doing certain things, which doesn't include acting as an information center. I think I'm already overextended in this conversation. So long, Mr Robicheaux.'

That evening I walked Alafair downtown in the twilight, and we ate fried chicken in a restaurant by the river. Then we walked over the Higgins Street Bridge, where old men fished off the railing in the dark swirls of current far below. The mountains in the west were purple and softly outlined against the red sun, and the wind was cold blowing across the bridge. I could smell chimney smoke and wood pulp in the air, diesel and oil from a passing Burlington Northern. We walked all the way to the park, where a group of boys was trying to hurry summer with a night baseball game. But in the hard glare of the lights the wind grew colder and the dust swirled in the air and finally drops of rain clicked across the tin roof of the dugout. The sky over the valley was absolutely black when we made it home.

Firewood was stacked on the back porch of our hose, and I broke up kindling from an orange crate in the fireplace, placed it and balls of newspaper under three pine logs on the andirons, and watched the bright red cone of flame rise up into the brick chimney. It was raining hard outside now, clattering against the roof and windows, and I could see a sawmill lighted across the river in the rain.

During the night lightning flickered whitely on the far wall of my bedroom. It created a window in the soft green plaster, and through it I

saw Annie sitting on a rock by a stream's edge. Cylindrical stone forma-
tions rose against the cobalt sky behind her. Her hair and denim shirt
were wet, and I could see her breasts through the cloth.

I'm worried, Dave, she said.

Why's that?

*You haven't been going to AA meetings. You think maybe you're setting
yourself up for a slip?*

I haven't had time.

She pulled her wet shirtfront loose from her skin with her fingers.

Will you promise me to look in the yellow pages today and find a meeting?
she said.

I promise.

*Because I think you're flying on the outer edges now. Maybe looking at
something worse than a slip.*

I wouldn't do that.

What?

I'm Catholic.

*I'm talking about something else, baby love. You blow out your doors and
they put you in a place like Mandeville.*

I've still got it between the ditches. I'm sober.

*But you keep calling on me. I'm tired, sweetheart. I have to come a long
way so we can talk.*

I'm sorry.

She put a finger to her lips.

I'll come again. For a while. But you have to keep your promise.

Annie.

When I woke I was sleepwalking, and my palms were pressed against
the cold green plaster of the bedroom wall.

6

It was still raining and cold in the morning. The logs in the fireplace had crumbled into dead ash, and the sky outside was gray. The trees in the yard looked wet and black in the weak light. I turned on the furnace, put fresh logs in the fireplace, lit the kindling and balls of wadded newspaper, and tried to fix French toast for me and Alafair while she dressed for school. I thought I could hear the drone of mosquitoes in my brain, I had on a long-sleeved flannel shirt, and I kept wiping the perspiration out of my eyes on my forearm.

'Why you shaking, Dave?' Alafair said.

'I have malaria. It comes back sometimes. It's not bad, though.'

'What?'

'I got it in the army. In the Philippines. It comes from mosquito bites. It goes away soon.'

'You ain't suppose to be up when you sick. I can fix my own breakfast. I can cook yours, too.'

'Don't say "ain't." '

She took the spatula and the handle of the frying pan out of my hands and began turning the toast. She wore fresh denims with an elastic waistband, and a purple sweater over her white shirt. Her black hair was shiny under the kitchen light.

I felt weak all over. I sat down at the kitchen table and wiped my face with a dry dish towel. I had to swallow before I could speak.

'Can you put on your raincoat and walk yourself to school this morning?' I said.

'Sure.'

'Then if I don't pick you up this afternoon you go to the babysitter's. Okay?'

'Okay.'

I watched her pack her lunch box and put on her yellow raincoat and hood.

'Wait a minute. I'll drive you,' I said.

'I can take myself. You sick, you.'

'Alafair, try not to talk like Batist. He's a good man, but he never went to school.'

'You still sick, Dave.'

I rubbed the top of her head and hugged her briefly around the shoulders, then put on my raincoat and hat. The wind outside was cold and smelled of the pulp mill down the river. In the wet air the smell was almost like sewage. I drove Alafair to the school and let her off by the entrance to the playground. When I got back home I was trembling all over, and the heat from the fireplace and the furnace vents wouldn't penetrate my skin. Instead, the house seemed filled with a dry cold that made static electricity jump off my hand when I touched a metal door-knob. I boiled a big pot of water on the kitchen stove to humidify the air, then sat in front of the fireplace with a blanket around my shoulders, my teeth clicking, and watched the resin boil and snap in the pine logs and the flames twist up the chimney.

As the logs softened and sank on the andirons, I felt as though I had been sent to a dark and airless space on the earth where memory became selective and flayed the skin an inch at a time. I can't tell you why. I could never explain these moments, and neither could a psychologist. It hap-pened first when I was ten years old, after my father had been locked up a second time in the parish jail for fighting in Provost's Pool Room. I was at home by myself, looking at a religious book that contained a plate depicting the souls in hell. Suddenly I felt myself drawn into the illustra-tion, caught forever in their lake of remorse and despair. I was filled with terror and guilt, and no amount of assurance from the parish priest could relieve me of it.

When these moments occurred in my adult life, I drank. I did it full tilt, too, the way you stand back from a smoldering fire of wet leaves and fling a glass full of gasoline on to the flames. I did it with Beam and Jack Daniel's straight up, with a frosted Jax on the side; vodka in the morning to sweep the spiders into their nest; four inches of Wild Turkey at noon to lock Frankenstein in his closet until the afternoon world of sunlight on oak and palm trees and the salt wind blowing across Lake Pontchartrain reestablished itself in a predictable fashion.

But this morning was worse than any of those other moments that I could remember. Maybe it *was* malaria, or maybe my childlike psycho-logical metabolism still screamed for a drink and was writing a script that would make the old alternative viable once again. But in truth I think it was something else. Perhaps, as Annie had said, I had found the edge.

The place where you unstrap all your fastenings to the earth, to what you are and what you have been, where you flame out on the edge of the spheres, and the sun and moon become eclipsed and the world below is as dead and remote and without interest as if it were glazed with ice.

Is this the way it comes? I thought. With nothing dramatic, no three-day bender, no delirium tremens in a drunk tank, no cloth straps and Thorazine or a concerned psychiatrist to look anxiously into your face. You simply stare at the yellow handkerchief of flame in a fireplace and fear your own thoughts, as a disturbed child would. I shut my eyes and folded the blanket across my face. I could feel my whiskers against the wool, the seat running down inside my shirt; I could smell my own odor. The wind blew against the house, and a wet maple branch raked against the window.

Later, I heard a car stop outside in the rain and someone run up the walk on to the porch. I heard the knock on the door and saw a woman's face through the steamed glass, but I didn't get up from my chair. She wore a flat-brim black cowboy hat with a domed crown, and her hair and face were spotted with rain. She knocked more loudly, straining to see me through the glass, then she opened the door and put her head inside.

'Is something wrong?' she asked.

'Everything's copacetic. Excuse me for not getting up.'

'Something's burning.'

'I've got a fire. I built one this morning. Is Clete out there?'

'No. Something's burning in your house.'

'That's what I was saying. Somebody left some firewood on the back porch. The furnace doesn't work right or something.'

Her turquoise eyes looked at me strangely. She walked past me into the kitchen, and I heard metal rattle on the stove and then ring in the sink. She turned on the faucet, and steam hissed off something hot. She walked back into the living room, her eyes still fixed on me in a strange way. She wore rubber boots, a man's wide belt through the loops of her Levi's, and an army field jacket with a First Cav patch over her red flannel shirt.

'The pot was burned through the center,' she said. 'I put it in the sink so it wouldn't smell up the place.'

'Thank you.'

She took off her hat and sat down across from me. The three moles at the corner of her mouth looked dark in the firelight.

'Are you all right?' she said.

'Yes. I have malaria. It comes and goes. They just buzz around in the bloodstream for a little while. It's not so bad. Not anymore, anyway.'

'I think you shouldn't be here alone.'

'I'm not. A little girl lives with me. Where'd you get the First Cav jacket?'

'It was my brother's.' She leaned out of her chair and put her hand on my forehead. Then she picked up one of my hands and held it momentarily. 'I can't tell. You're sitting too close to the fire. But you should be in bed. Get up.'

'I appreciate what you're doing, but this is going to pass.'

'Yeah, I can tell you're really on top of it. Do you know a pot holder was burning on your stove, too?'

She helped me up by one arm and walked me into the bedroom. I sat on the edge of the bed and looked numbly out the window at the wet trees and the rain on the river. When I closed my eyes my head spun and I could see gray worms swimming behind my lids. She took the blanket off my shoulders and pulled off my shirt, pushed my head down on the pillow and covered me with the sheet and bedspread. I heard her run water in the bathroom and open my dresser drawers, then she sat on the side of the mattress and wiped my face and chest and shoulders with a warm, damp towel and pulled a clean T-shirt over my head.

She felt my forehead again and looked down in my face.

'I don't think you take very good care of yourself,' she said. 'I don't think you're a wise man, either.'

'Why have you come here?'

'Leave Sally Dee and his father alone. It's bad for you, it's bad for Clete.'

'Clete got in bed with that bunch on his own.' I blew out my breath and opened my eyes. I could feel the room spinning, the same way it used to spin when I would try to go to sleep drunk and I'd have to hang my head off the side of the mattress or couch to put the blood back in my brain.

'He's done some bad things, but he's not a bad man,' she said.

'He looks up to you. He still wants you to be his friend.'

'He betrayed me when I needed him.'

'Maybe he's paid for it, too. You sleep. I'll stay here and fix lunch for you when you wake up.'

She spread the blanket on top of me and pulled it up to my chin. Her hand touched mine, and involuntarily I cupped her palm in my fingers. Her hand was wide across the back and callused on the edges, and her knuckles were as hard as dimes under the skin. I could not remember when I had last touched a woman's hand. I closed her fingers in my palm, felt the grainy coarseness of her skin with my thumb, let both our hands rest on my chest as though the moment had given me a right that was in reality not mine. But she didn't take her hand away. Her face was kind, and she wiped the wetness out of my hair with the towel and remained on the edge of the bed while the rain swept across the yard and the roof and I felt myself slipping down to the bottom of my own vertigo, down inside a cool, clean, and safe place where no fires burned, where the gray morning was as harmless as the touch of my forehead against her thigh.

It was early afternoon when I woke again, and the sun was out, the sky blue, the yard a deeper green. I felt weak all over, but whatever had invaded my metabolism had gone away like a bored visitor. I opened the front door in my bare feet, and the air was cool and full of sunlight, and in the south the ragged peaks of the Bitterroot Mountains were white and with new snow. Out on the river the rooted end of an enormous tree bounced wet and shining through the current. I heard her in the kitchen behind me, then remembered my earlier behaviour the way a shard of memory comes back from a drunken dream.

She saw it in my face, too.

'I called Clete. He knows where I am. He doesn't mind,' she said.

'I want to thank you for your kindness.'

Her eyes softened and moved over my face. I felt uncomfortable.

'I have strange moments in my life. I can't explain them,' I said. 'So I tell people it's malaria. Maybe it's true, but I don't know that. Maybe it's something else, too. Sometimes people at AA call it a dry drunk. It's nothing to wear on your chest.'

I took a bottle of milk out of the icebox and sat down at the kitchen table. Through the back screen I could see an elderly woman hoeing in her vegetable garden. Next door somebody was cutting his grass with a hand mower. Darlene's eyes had never left my face.

'Clete said you lost your wife,' she said.

'Yes.'

'He said two men murdered her.'

'That's right.'

'How did it happen?' Her hand turned off the burner under a soup pot.

'I messed with some people I should have let alone.'

'I see.' She took two soup bowls out of the cabinet and set them on the table with spoons. 'It bothers you a lot?'

'Sometimes.'

'I blamed myself when my husband got killed. I'd locked him out of the house the night before. I'd found out he was cheating with a white girl who worked in the truck stop. He had to stay all night in the car in zero weather. He went to work like that in the morning and a bulldozer backed over him. He was like a little boy. Always in the wrong place. He always got caught. He spent a year in Deer Lodge for stealing game meat out of some rental lockers at a grocery. He used to lie about it and tell people he went to jail for armed robbery.'

'Why do you tell me this?'

'You shouldn't hurt yourself because of what happened to your wife. You don't realize what you did yesterday. Sally Dee's crazy.'

'No, he's not. He just likes people to think he is. His kind come by the boxcarload.'

She filled our bowls and sat down across from me.

'You don't know Sal. Clete said you made Sal look bad in front of his friends. He came down to the house after you left and they went out on the veranda. I could hear Sal yelling through the glass. I didn't think Clete would let anyone talk to him like that.'

'It's expensive to work for a guy like Sally Dio.'

'He degraded him.'

'Listen, there's an expression in the oil field – "I was looking for a job when I found this one." You tell Clete that.'

'Sal said something else, too. About you.'

'What?'

' "Don't bring him around here again, don't let him be talking to Dixie Lee, either. He does, I'm gonna cut off his dick." '

I looked to the door again at the woman hoeing in her garden across the alley. Her face was pink, her hair white, and her arms were as thick as a man's.

'That's what our man had to say?'

'Clete and Dixie Lee pretend he's all right because they have to. But he's cruel. He frightens me.'

'You should get away from him.'

She put her spoon in her soup and lowered her eyes.

'You're an intelligent woman,' I said. 'You're a good person, too. You don't belong among those people.'

'I'm with Clete.'

'Clete's going to take a big fall with that guy. Or he'll take a fall *for* him, one or the other. Down inside, he knows it, too. Until he started screwing up his life, he was the best partner I ever had. He carried me down a fire escape once while a kid put two .22 rounds in his back. He used to put the fear of God in the wiseguys. They'd cross the street when they saw him on the sidewalk.'

'He's been good to me. Inside he's a good man. One day, he'll see that.'

Her attitude toward him struck me as strange. It seemed more protective than affectionate. But maybe she was that kind of woman. Or maybe it was what I wanted to believe.

'I wonder if you can help me with something,' I said.

'What?'

'Did Clete tell you about some trouble I've had in Louisiana?'

'Yes.'

'Harry Mapes is my way out of it. I think he killed two people up here. Maybe they were Indians, members of AIM.'

She looked down at her food again, but I saw her eyes narrow, the light in them sharpen.

'Why do you think that? About the Indians?' she said.

'Mapes killed these people because they were in the way of his oil deals. Dixie Lee said these AIM guys can tie the oil companies up in court over a nineteenth-century treaty.'

'It's a big fight over on the Rocky Mountain Front.'

'The what?'

'It's the eastern face of the Continental Divide. The Blackfeet called it the backbone of the world. The oil companies want into the roadless areas by Glacier Park. That was Blackfeet land. The government took it or got it for nothing,'

'Did you ever hear about any AIM people disappearing?'

'Why don't you ask up at the reservation?'

'I plan to. Why are you angry?'

'It has nothing to do with you.'

'It seems to.'

'You don't understand the reservation.'

She stopped, and it was obvious that she regretted her abruptness. She wet her lips and began again, but her voice had the quiet, tense quality of someone who had bought seriously into a private piece of discontent.

'Whites have always taken from the Blackfeet. They massacred them on the Marias River, then they starved them and gave them a rural slum to live in. Now they've given us their missile sites. The government admits that in a war everybody on the eastern slope will be killed. But what whites don't understand is that Indians believe spirits live in the earth. That all the treaties and deeds that took our land don't mean anything. Sometimes people hear the crying of children and women in the wind on the Marias. An Indian woman in a white doeskin dress appears at missile silos. Air Force people have seen her. You can talk to them.'

'You believe in these spirits?'

'I've been on the Marias at night. I've heard them. The sound comes right off the edge of the water, where the camp was. It happened in the winter of 1870. An army officer named Baker attacked an innocent band of Blackfeet under Heavy Runner. They killed a hundred and thirty people, then burned their robes and wickiups and left the survivors to freeze in the snow. You can hear people weeping.'

'I guess I don't know about those things. Or the history of your people.'

She ate without answering.

'I think maybe it's not a good idea to keep things like that alive in yourself, though,' I said.

She remained silent, her face pointed downward, and I gave it up.

'Look, will you give Clete a message for me?' I said.

'What is it?'

'That he doesn't owe me, that he doesn't need to feel bad about anything, that I don't sweat a character like Sally Dio. You also tell him to take himself and a nice girl to New Orleans. That's the place where good people go when they die.'

She smiled. I looked at her eyes and her mouth, then caught myself and glanced away.

'I have to go now,' she said. 'I hope you're feeling better.'

'I am. You were a real friend, Darlene. Clete's a lucky guy.'

'Thank you, but he's not a lucky guy. Not at all.'

I didn't want to talk about Clete's problems anymore or carry any more of his load. I walked outside with her to her Toyota jeep and opened the door for her. The sidewalks were still drying in the sunlight, and the pines on the mountains were sharp and green against the sky.

'Maybe you all would like to come into town and have dinner one evening, or walk up one of those canyons in the Bitterroots and try for some cutthroat,' I said.

'Maybe. I'll ask him,' she said, and smiled again.

I watched her drive past the school yard and turn toward the interstate. It was one of those moments when I did not care to reflect upon my own honesty or to know in reality what I was thinking about.

I washed the dishes, put on my running shoes, shorts, and a sweatshirt, and did two miles along the river, then circled back through a turn-of-the-century neighborhood of yellow- and orange-brick homes whose yards were dotted with blue spruce, fir, maple, birch, and willow trees. I was sweating heavily in the cool air, and I had to push hard to increase my speed across an intersection; but my wind was good, the muscles tight in my thighs and back, my mind clear, the rest of the day a bright expectation rather than an envelope of grayness and gloom and disembodied voices.

Ah, voices, I thought. She believes in them. Which any student of psychology will tell you is a mainline symptom of a schizophrenic personality. But I had never bought very heavily into the psychiatric definitions of singularity and eccentricity in people. In fact, as I reviewed the friendships I had had over the years, I had to conclude that the most interesting ones involved the seriously impaired – the Moe Howard account, the drunken, the mind-smoked, those who began each day with a nervous breakdown, people who hung on to the sides of the plant with suction cups.

When I rounded the corner on my block by the river, I heard the bell ring at the elementary school and saw the children burst out of the doors on to the sidewalks. Alafair walked with her lunch box among three other children. I ran backward when I passed her.

'Meet you at the house, little guy,' I said.

I shaved and showered and took Alafair with me to an AA meeting three blocks from our house. She drank a can of pop and did her homework in the coffee room while I sat in the nonsmokers' section of the meeting and listened. The members of the group were mostly mill workers, gyppo loggers, Indians, waitresses, tough blue-collar kids who talked as much about dope as they did about alcohol, and skid-row old-timers who had etched the lines in their face a shot glass at a time. When it was my turn to talk, I gave my name and passed. I should have talked about my nightmares, the irrational depression that could leave me staring eviscerated and numb at a dying fire; but for most of them their most immediate problem was not psychological or in the nature of their addiction – they were unemployed and on food stamps – and my own basket of snakes seemed an unworthy subject for discussion.

Alafair and I ate an early supper, then we walked up on a switchback trail to the big white concrete *M* on the mountain overlooking the university. We could see out over the whole valley: the Clark Fort winding high and yellow through town, the white froth over the breakers, the tree-filled neighborhoods, the shafts of sunlight in the canyons west of town, the plume from the pulp mill flattening out on the river's surface, the bicyclists and joggers like miniature figures on the campus far below. Then as the sun dimmed behind a peak and the air became more chill and the valley filled with a purple haze, house and street and neon lights came on all over town, and in the south we could see the sun's afterglow on the dark strands of ponderosa high up in the Bitterroots.

Alafair sat beside me on the concrete *M*. She brushed dirt off her knees; I saw her frown.

'Dave, whose hat that is?' she said.

'What?'

'In the chair. By the fireplace. That black hat.'

'Oh,' I said. 'I think a lady must have left that there.'

'I sat on it. I forgot to tell you.'

'Don't worry about it.'

'She won't be mad?'

'No, of course not. Don't worry about things like that, little guy.'

The next day I made arrangements for Alafair to stay with the babysitter if I had to remain out of town that night, and I headed for the Blackfeet Reservation, on the other side of the Divide, east of Glacier Park. In the early morning light I drove up the Blackfoot River through the trees from the cabins set back in the meadows. The runoff from the snowpack up in the mountains was still high, and the current boiled over the boulders in the center of the river. Then the country opened up into wider valleys and ranch-land with low green hills and more mountains in the distance. I started to climb into more heavily wooded country, with sheer rock cliffs and steep-sided mountains that ran right down to the edge of the road; the canyons and trees were dark with shadow, and by the time I hit the logging town of Lincoln the air had turned cold and my windows were wet with mist. I drove into clouds on the Divide at Rogers Pass, my ears popping now, and rivulets of melted snow ran out of the pines on the mountainside, bled across the highway, and washed off the dirt shoulder into a white stream far below. The pine trees looked almost black and glistened with a wet sheen.

Then I was out into sunlight again, out on the eastern slope, into rolling wheat and cattle country with no horizon except the Rocky Mountain Front in my rearview mirror. I made good time into Choteau and Dupuyer, and a short while later I was on the Blackfeet Indian Reservation.

I had been on or through several Indian reservations, and none of them was a good place. This one was not an exception. Ernest Hemingway once wrote that there was no worse fate for a people than to lose a war. If any of his readers wanted to disagree with him, they would only have to visit one of the places in which the United States government placed its original inhabitants. We took everything they had and in turn gave them smallpox, whiskey, welfare, federal boarding schools, and penitentiaries.

At a run-down filling station I got directions to the tribal chairman's office, then drove through several small settlements of clapboard shacks, the dirt yards littered with the rusted parts of junker cars, old washing machines on the porches, chicken yards, privies, and vegetable patches in back, with seed packages stuck up on sticks in the rows.

The tribal chairman was a nice man who wore braids, jewelry, a western vest, green-striped trousers, and yellow cowboy boots. On his office wall was an associate of arts degree from a community college. He was polite and listened well, his eyes staying focused attentively on my face while I spoke; but it was also obvious that he did not want to talk about AIM or the oil business with a white man whom he didn't know.

'Do you know Harry Mapes?' I said.

This time his gaze broke. He looked out the window on to the street, where three Indian men were talking in front of a poolroom. The neon sign above the door said only Pool.

'He's a leaseman. He's around here sometimes,' he said. 'Most of the time he works on the edge of the reservation.'

'What else do you know about him?'

He unwrapped the cellophane from an inexpensive cherry-blend cigar. 'I don't have any dealings with him. You'll have to ask somebody else.'

'You think he's bad news?'

'I don't know what he is.' He smiled to be pleasant and lit his cigar.

'He killed his partner, Dalton Vidrine, down in Louisiana.'

'I don't know about that Mr Robicheaux.'

'I think he killed two of your people, too.'

'I don't know what to tell you, sir.'

'Do you know of two guys from AIM who disappeared?'

'Not on the reservation. And that's what I'm elected to take care of – the reservation.'

'What do you mean, "not on the reservation"?'

'I'm not in AIM. I don't mix in their business.'

'But you've heard about somebody disappearing?'

He gazed out the window against the men in front of the poolroom and breathed cigar smoke out his nose and mouth.

'Just south of here, down in Teton County. Clayton Desmarteau and his cousin,' he said. 'I don't remember the cousin's name.'

'What happened?'

'I heard they didn't come home one night. But maybe they just went off somewhere. It happens. Talk to the sheriff's office in Teton. Talk to Clayton's mother. She lives just off the reservation. Here, I'll draw you directions.'

A half hour later I was back off the reservation and driving down a narrow gray dirt road by the edge of a stream. Cottonwoods grew along the banks, then the ground sloped upward into thick stands of lodgepole pine. Ahead I could see the plains literally dead-end into the mountains. They rose abruptly, like an enormous fault, sheer-faced and jagged against the sky. The cliff walls were pink and streaked with shadow, and the ponderosa was so thick through the saddles that I doubted a bear could work his way through the trunks.

I found the home the tribal chairman had directed me to. It was built of logs and odd-sized pieces of lumber, up on a knoll, with a shingled roof and sagging gallery. Plastic sheets were nailed over the windows for insulation, and coffee cans filled with petunias were set along the gallery railing and the edges of the steps. The woman who lived there looked very old. Her hair was white, with dark streaks in it, and her leathery skin was deeply lined and webbed around the eyes and mouth.

I sat with her in her living room and tried to explain who I was, that I wanted to find out what happened to her son, Clayton Desmarteau, and his cousin. But her face was remote, uncertain, her eyes averted whenever I looked directly at them. On a table by the tiny fireplace was a framed photograph of a young Indian soldier. In front of the picture were two open felt boxes containing a Purple Heart and a Silver Star.

'The tribal chairman said maybe your son simply left the area for a while,' I said. 'Maybe he went looking for other work.'

This time she looked at me.

'Clayton didn't go off nowhere,' she said. 'He had a job in the filling station in town. He came home every night. They found his car in the ditch, two miles from here. He wouldn't go off and leave his car in the ditch. They did something to him.'

'Who?'

'People that want to hurt his organization.'

'AIM?'

'He was beat up one time. They were always trying to hurt him.'

'Who beat him up?'

'People that's no good.'

'Mrs Desmarteau, I want to help you find out what happened to Clayton. Did he ever mention someone's name, somebody who gave him trouble?'

'The FBI. They came around the filling station and called up people on the phone about him.'

'How about Harry Mapes or Dalton Vidrine? Do you remember his using those names?'

She didn't answer. She simply looked out into space, took a pinch of snuff out of a Copenhagen can, and put it between her lip and gum. Motes of dust spun in the light through the windows. I thanked her for her time and drove back down the road toward the county seat, the shadows of the cottonwoods clicking across my windshield.

The sheriff was out of town, and the deputy I spoke to at the court-house soon made me feel that I was a well-meaning, obtuse outsider who had as much understanding of rural Montana and reservation life as a seasonal tourist.

'We investigated that case about four months ago,' he said. He was a big, lean man in his khaki uniform, and he seemed to concentrate more on the smoking of his cigarette than on his conversation with me. His desk was littered with papers and manila folders. 'His mother and sister filed a missing-persons report. We found his car with a broken axle in the ditch. The keys were gone, the spare tire was gone, the radio was gone, somebody even tore the clock out of the dashboard. What's that tell you?'

'Somebody stripped it.'

'Yeah, Clayton Desmarteau did. It was going to be repossessed. Him and his cousin were in the bar three miles up the road, they got juiced, they ran off the road. That's the way we see it.'

'And he just didn't bother to come home after that?'

'Where are you from again?'

'New Iberia, Louisiana.'

He blew smoke out into a shaft of sunlight shinning through the window. His hair was thin across his pate.

'Believe it or not, that's not uncommon here,' he said. Then his voice changed and assumed a resigned and tired note. 'We're talking about two guys in AIM. One of them, Clayton's cousin, was in the pen in South Dakota. There's also a warrant out on him for nonsupport. Clayton's had his share of trouble, too.'

'What kind?'

'Fights, carrying a concealed weapon, bullshit like that.'

'Has he ever just disappeared from his home and job before?'

'Look, here's the situation. There's one bar on that road. They were in there till midnight. It's five miles from that bar up to Clayton's house.

Three miles up the road they wrecked the car. Maybe they walked up to Clayton's house without waking the old lady and took off before she got up. Maybe she doesn't remember what they did. Maybe they hitched a ride with somebody after they stripped the car. I don't know what they did. You think a bear ate them?'

'No, I think you're telling me Desmarteau was an irresponsible man. His mother says otherwise. The guy had the Silver Star. What do you make of that?'

'I don't guess I'm communicating with you very well. What you don't understand is the way some people live around here. Come back on a Saturday night and take your own tour. Look, when a white person hires Indians to work for him, he hires six so maybe three will show up in the morning. They cut up their own relatives at wedding parties, they hang themselves in jail cells, they get souped up and drive into the sides of trains. Last winter three kids climbed in a boxcar with a gallon of dago red and a tube of airplane glue. The train went on up into Canada and stopped on a siding in a blizzard. I went up with the families to bring their bodies back. The RCMP said they were frozen so hard you could break their parts off with a hammer.'

I asked him to show me where Clayton Desmarteau's car had gone off the road. He was irritated, but he consented and drove me down the same dirt road I had been on earlier. We passed the bar where Desmarteau and his cousin had been last seen, a wide, flat log building with neon Grain Belt and Great Falls beer signs in the windows; then we curved up the road through bare, hardpan fields and finally picked up the creek, the cottonwoods, and the sloping stands of lodgepole pine that began on the far bank. The deputy stopped his car on the shoulder and pointed.

'Right over there in the ditch,' he said. 'He hooked one wheel over the side and went in. Snapped the axle like a stick. No mystery, my friend. It's a way of life.'

I got back to Missoula late but in time to pick up Alafair at the babysitter's before she went to sleep. The babysitter had run an errand, and a friend of hers, a third-grade teacher and assistant principal at the school named Miss Regan, had come over to stay with Alafair. The two of them were watching television and eating from a bowl of popcorn in the enclosed side porch. Miss Regan was a pretty girl in her late twenties, with auburn hair and green eyes, and although her skin was still pale from the winter months, I could see sun freckles on her shoulders and the bottom of her neck.

'Come see, Dave,' Alafair said. 'Miss Regan drew a picture of Tex and she ain't ever seen him.'

'Don't say "ain't", little guy,' I said.

'Look,' Alafair said, and held up a piece of art paper with a pastel drawing of an Appaloosa on it.

'That's very nice of Miss Regan,' I said.

'My name's Tess,' she said, and smiled.

'Well, thank you for watching Alafair. It was good meeting you.'

'She's a sweet little girl. We had a lot of fun together,' she said.

'Do you live in the neighborhood?'

'Yes, only two blocks from the school.'

'Well, I hope to see you again. Thanks for your help. Good night.'

'Good night,' she said.

We walked home in the dark. The air was warm, and the maple trees looked black and full under the moon. The lights of the bridge reflected off the swirling brown surface of the river.

'Everybody says she's the best teacher in the school,' Alafair said.

'I bet she is.'

'I told her to come down to New Iberia and visit us.'

'That's good.'

'Because she don't have a husband.'

'Say "doesn't." '

'She doesn't have a husband. How come that, Dave?'

'I don't know. Some people just don't like to get married.'

'How come?'

'You got me.'

We ate a piece of pie before we turned out the lights and went to bed. Our bedrooms adjoined, and the door was opened between them. Across the river I could hear the whistle of a Burlington Northern Freight.

'Dave?'

'What?'

'Why don't you marry Miss Regan?'

'I'll give it some thought. See you tomorrow, little guy.'

'Okay, big guy.'

'Good night, little guy.'

'Good night, big guy.'

The next morning I made long-distance calls to Batist, the bondsman, and my lawyer. Batist was managing fine at the bait shop and the bondsman was tranquil about my returning to Louisiana by trial date, but the lawyer had not been able to get a continuance and he was worried.

'What have you come up with in Montana?' he said.

'Nothing definite. But I think Dixie Lee was telling the truth about Mapes, that he killed a couple of people here, maybe Indians.'

'I tell you, Dave, that might be our only out. If you can get him locked up in Montana, he won't be a witness against us in Louisiana.'

'It's not the ninth race yet.'

'Maybe not, but so far we don't have a defense. It's that simple. I hired a PI to do a background on Mapes. He beat the shit out of another kid with a golf club in Marshall, Texas, when he was seventeen, but that's the only trouble he's been in. He graduated from the University of Texas and flew an army helicopter in Vietnam. The rest of the guy's life is a blank. It's hard to make him out as Jack the Ripper.'

'We'll see,' I said. I didn't want to concede the truth in his words, but I could feel my heart tripping.

'The prosecutor's talking a deal,' he said.

I remained silent and listened to the wire of long-distance sound in the earpiece. Through the window I could see the maple tree in my front yard ruffling with the breeze.

'Dave, we're reaching the point where we might have to listen to him.'

'What deal?'

'Second-degree homicide. We'll show provocation, he won't contend with us, you'll get five years. With good time, you can be out in three or less.'

'No deal.'

'It may turn out to be the only crap game in town.'

'It's bullshit.'

'Maybe so, but there's something else I'm honor-bound to tell you. We're going up against Judge Mouton. He's sent six men I know of to the electric chair. I don't think he'd do that in this case. But he's a cranky, old sonofabitch, and you never know.'

After I hung up the phone I tried to read the paper on the front porch with a cup of coffee, but my eyes couldn't concentrate on the words.

I washed the dishes, cleaned the kitchen, and started to change the oil in my truck. I didn't want to think about my conversation with my lawyer. One day at a time, easy does it, I told myself. Don't live in tomorrow's problems. Tomorrow has no more existence than yesterday, but you can always control *now*. We live in a series of nows. Think about now.

But that sick feeling around the heart would not go away. I worked my way under my truck, fitted a crescent wrench around the nut on the oil pan, and applied pressure with both hands while flakes of dried mud fell in my eyes. Then the wrench slipped and I raked my knuckles across the pan. I heard the telephone ring inside.

I crawled out from under the truck, went in the house, and picked up the receiver. The skin was gone on the tops of two of my knuckles.

'What's happening, Dave?'

'Dixie?'

'Yeah. What's happening?'

'Nothing important. What is it?'

'Are you always this happy in the morning?'

505

'What do you want, Dixie?'

'Nothing. I'm in the lounge over in that shopping center on Brooks. Come on over.'

'What for?'

'Talk. Relax. Listen to a few sounds. They got a piano in here.'

'You sound like your boat already left the dock.'

'So?'

'It's nine o'clock in the morning.'

'Big deal. It's twelve o'clock somewhere else. Come on over.'

'No thanks.'

'Darlene dumped me in here while she went running around town. I don't want to sit in here by myself. It's a drag, man. Get your butt over here.'

'I've got a few other things on my mind.'

'That's what I want to talk with you about. Dave, you think you're the only guy who understands your problem. Look, man, I pick cotton everyday in the same patch.'

'What are you talking about?'

'Some people are born different. That's just the way we are. You go against what you are, you're gonna have a mess of grief. Like Hank Junior says, some people are born to boogie, son. They just got to be willing to pay the price.'

'I appreciate all this, but I'm going to sign off now.'

'Oh no you don't. You listen to me, 'cause I been there in spades, right where you're at now. When I got to Huntsville from the county jail, I hadn't had a drink in six weeks. I felt like I had fire ants crawling on my brain. Except I learned you can get almost anything in the joint you can get outside. There was a Mexican cat who sold short-dogs of black cherry wine for five bucks a bottle. We'd mix it with syrup, water, and rubbing alcohol, and it'd fix you up just about like you stuck your head in a blast furnace.

'So one time we had a whole crock of this beautiful black cherry brew stashed in a tool shack, and one time while the boss man was working some guys farther on down the road, we set one guy out as a jigger and the rest of us crapped out in the shack and decided to coolerate our minds a little bit. Except about an hour later, when we're juiced to the eyes, the guy outside comes running through the door, yelling, "Jigger, jigger."

'The boss man was a big redneck character from Lufkin named Buster Higgins. He could pick up a bale of hay and fling it from behind the truck all the way to the cab. When he took a leak he made sure everybody saw the size of his dick. That's no shit, man. The next thing I know, he's standing there in the door of the toolshed, sweat running out of his hat, his face big as a pumpkin. Except this guy was not funny. He thought rock 'n' roll was for niggers and Satan worshipers. He looks down at me and says, "Pugh, didn't your parents have enough money?"

'I said, "What d'you mean, Mr Higgins?"

'He says, "For a better quality rubbers," then he took his hat off and whipped the shit out of me with it. Next stop – one month in isolation, son. I'm talking about down there with the crazoids, the screamers, the guys who stink so bad the hacks have to wash them down with hoses. And I had delirium tremens for two fucking days. Weird sounds snapping in my head, rockets going off when I closed my eyes, a big hard-on and all kinds of real sick sexual thoughts. You know what I'm talking about, man. It must have been ninety degrees in the hole, and I was shaking so bad I couldn't get a cup of water to my mouth.

'I got through two days and thought I was home free. But after a week I started to have all kinds of guilt feelings again. About the little boy in the accident in Forth Worth, about my own little boy dying in the fire. I couldn't stand it, man. Just that small isolation cell and the light through the food slit and all them memories. I would have drunk gasoline if somebody would have given it to me. So you know what I done? I didn't try to get the guilt out of my mind. I got high on it. I made myself so fucking miserable that I was drunk again. When I closed my eyes and swallowed, I could even taste that black cherry wine. I knew then it wasn't never gonna be any different. I was always gonna be drunk, whether I was dry or out there juicing.

'So in my head I wrote a song about it. I could hear all the notes, the riffs, a stand-up bass backing me up. I worked out the lyrics for it, too—

You can toke, you can drop,
Drink or use.
It don't matter, daddy,
'Cause you never gonna lose
Them mean old jailhouse
Black cherry blues.'

I rubbed my forehead with my hand. I didn't know what to say to him.

'You still there?' he said.

'Yes.'

'You gonna come over?'

'Maybe I'll see you another time. Thanks for the invitation.'

'Fuck, yeah, I'm always around. Sorry I wasted your time.'

'You didn't. We were good friends in college. Remember?'

'Everybody was good friends in college. It all died with Cochran and Holly. I got to motivate on over to another bar. This place bugs me. Dangle easy, Dave.'

He hung up. I stared listlessly out into the sunlight a moment, then walked outside and finished changing the oil in my truck.

She drove up in her red Toyota jeep a half hour later. I guess I knew that she was coming, and I knew that she would come when Alafair was at school. It was like the feeling you have when you look into the eyes of another and see a secret and shared knowledge there that makes you ashamed of your own thoughts. She wore a yellow sundress, and she had put on lipstick and eye shadow and hoop earrings. The sacks of groceries in the back of the jeep looked as though they were there only by accident.

Her lipstick was dark, and when she smiled her teeth were white.

'Your hat,' I said.

'Yes. You found it?'

'It's in the living room. Come in. I have some South Louisiana coffee on the stove.'

She walked ahead of me, and I looked at the way her black hair sat thickly on her neck, the way the hem of her dress swung across her calves. When I opened the screen for her I could smell the perfume behind her ears and on her shoulders.

I went into the kitchen while she found her hat in the living room. I fooled with cups and saucers, spoons, a bowl of sugar, milk from the icebox, but my thoughts were as organized as a puzzle box that someone had shaken violently between his hands.

'I try to shop in Missoula. It's cheaper than Polson,' she said.

'Yeah, food's real cheap here.'

'Dixie Lee came along with me. He's in a bar right now.'

'He called me. You might have to drag him out of the place on a chain.'

'He'll be all right. He's only bad when Sal lets him take cocaine.' She paused a moment. 'I thought maybe you wouldn't be home.'

'I got a late start today. A bunch of phone calls, stuff like that.'

She reached for the cups and saucers on the drainboard and her arm brushed against mine. She looked at my eyes and raised her mouth, and I slipped my arms around her shoulders and kissed her. She stepped close against me, so that her stomach touched lightly against my loins, and moved her palms over my back. She opened and closed her mouth while she held and kissed me, and then she put her tongue in my mouth and felt her body flatten against me. I ran my hands over her bottom and her thighs and gently bit her shoulder as she wrapped one calf inside my leg and rubbed her hair on the side of my face.

We pulled the shades in the bedroom and undressed without speaking, as if words would lead both of us to an awareness about morality and betrayal that we did not care to examine in the heated touch of our skin, the dry swallow in the throat, the silent parting of our mouths.

There had been one woman in my life since my wife's death, and I had lived celibate almost a year. She reached down and took me inside her and stretched out her legs along me and ran her hands along the small of my back and down my thighs. The breeze clattered the shades on the windows, the room was dark and cool, but my body was rigid and hot and my neck filmed with perspiration, and I felt like an inept and simian creature laboring above her. She stopped her motion, kissed me on the cheek and smiled, and I stared down at her, out of breath and with the surprise of a man whose education with women always proved inadequate.

'There's no hurry,' she said quietly, almost in a whisper. 'There's nothing to worry about.'

Then she said, 'Here,' and pressed on my arm for me to move off her. She brushed her hair out of her eyes, sat on top of me, kissed me on the mouth, then raised herself on her knees and put me inside her again. Her eyes closed and opened, she tightened her thighs against me, and propped herself up on her hands and looked quietly and lovingly into my face.

She came before I did, her face growing intense and small, her mouth suddenly opening like a flower. Then I felt all my nocturnal erotic dreams, my fear, my aching celibacy, rise and swell in my loins, and burst away outside of me like a wave receding without sound in a cave by the sea.

She lay close to me under the sheet, her fingers in the back of my hair. A willow tree in the backyard made shadows on the shade.

'You feel bad, don't you?' she said.

'No.'

'You think what you've done is wrong, don't you?'

I didn't answer.

'Clete's impotent, Dave,' she said.

'What?'

'He goes to a doctor, but it doesn't do any good.'

'When did he become impotent?'

'I don't know. Before I met him. He says a fever did it to him in Guatemala. He says he'll be all right eventually. He pretends it's not a problem.'

I raised up on my elbow and looked into her face.

'I don't understand,' I said. 'You moved in with an impotent man?'

'He can't help what he is. He's good to me in other ways. He's generous, and he respects me. He takes me places where Indians don't go. Why do you have that look on your face?'

'I'm sorry. I don't mean to,' I said.

'What are you thinking?'

'Nothing. I just don't quite understand.'

'Understand what?'

'Your relationship. It doesn't make sense.'

'Maybe it isn't your business.'

'He was my partner, I'm in bed with his girl. You don't think I have some involvement here?'

'I don't like the way you're talking to me.'

I knew that anything else that I said would be wrong. I sat on the edge of the bed with my back toward her. The wind fluttered the shade in the window, casting a brilliant crack of sunlight across the room. Finally I looked over my shoulder at her. She had pulled the sheet up over her breasts. ·

'I try not to be judgmental about other people. I apologize,' I said. 'But he and I used to be good friends. You said he was impotent. You were suggesting I didn't have anything to feel bad about. There's something wrong in the equation here. Don't pretend there isn't.'

'Look the other way, please,' she said, gathered the sheet around her, picked up her clothes from the chair, and walked into the bathroom. A few minutes later she came back out in her yellow dress, pushing the top back on her lipstick, pressing her lips together.

'I like you just the same,' I said.

'You don't know anything,' she said.

And she left me there, with a wet spot in the center of my bed and a big question mark as to whether I had acquired any degrees of caution or wisdom in the fiftieth year of my life.

7

I needed to go back of the Divide and talk to more people about the disappearance of Clayton Desmarteau and his cousin. But I had gotten too late a start that day, and instead I drove up to Flathead Lake and spent two hours searching through property records in the county clerk's office. I was still convinced that there was some tie between Sally Dio, Dixie Lee, Harry Mapes, and Star Drilling Company. I didn't buy the story that Sally Dio kept Dixie Lee around to effect innocuous real estate deals or because he simply liked over-the-hill rockabilly musicians. I had known too many like him in New Orleans. They liked women but didn't consider them important; they liked power but would share it out of necessity; they were cruel or violent upon occasion but usually in a pragmatic way. However, they loved money. It was the ultimate measure of success in their lives, the only subject of interest in their conversations. They paid with cash in restaurants, not with credit cards, and their elaborate tipping was as much a part of their predictable grandiosity as their lavender Cadillacs and eight-hundred-dollar tropical suits.

But all I found in the courthouse with Dixie Lee's or Dio's name on them were deeds or leases to house lots, corner business property, and a couple of marinas, nothing that surprised me, nothing that suggested anything more than investments in local real estate.

I drove up the east shore of the lake, through the orchards of cherry trees, past the restaurant built put over the water and the blue lagoon with the rim of white beach and the pines growing thickly up the incline back toward the road, and finally to the entrance of Sally Dio's split-level redwood home built up on a cliff that overlooked the dazzling silklike sheen of the lake. I drove around the next curve, parked my truck off the shoulder, and walked back through a stand of pine trees that ended abruptly at the lip of a cliff that fell away to the lake's edge. Green, moss-covered rocks showed dully in the sunlight just below the water's surface.

Across the lagoon I could see Dio's house and the cottage below where Clete and Darlene lived. I knelt on one knee among the pine needles and steadied my World War II Japanese field glasses against a tree trunk. An

American flag popped in the breeze on Dio's veranda, his flower boxes were brilliant with pink and blue and crimson petunias, and a cream-colored Mercury and black Porsche with Nevada plates were parked in the gravel at the edge of his lawn. I wrote the tag numbers down in a notebook, buttoned it in my shirt pocket, then watched a big van with bubble side windows, followed by a Toyota jeep, drive out on the beach. The side door, which was painted with a tropical sunset, slid open and a group of swimmers jumped out on the sand and began inflating a huge yellow raft with a foot-operated air pump.

I refocused the glasses on their faces. It was Dio and what Clete called the Tahoe crowd. Dio wore an open shirt, flop sandals, and a luminescent purple bikini that fitted tightly against his loins and outlined his phallus. He was in a good mood, directing the outing of his entourage, pointed at a milk-white two-engine amphibian plane that came in low over the hills of the far side of the lake, unlocking his father's wheelchair from the mechanical platform that extended from the van's open door and lowered to the sand. Clete walked from the Toyota, wheeled Dio's father by a barbecue pit, lighted a bag of charcoal, and began forking a box of steaks on to the grill. He wore his crushed porkpie fishing hat, and I could see his nylon shoulder holster and revolver under his sweater.

The amphibian made one pass over the beach, gunned its engines and banked into the cloudless sky over my head, then made a wide turn and came in over the top of a cherry orchard and a sailboat dock, flattening out and touching its belly and wing pontoons down on the water in a spray of white foam and mist from the back draft of the propellers.

While Clete cooked and attended to the elder Dio, who sat sullen and wrapped in a shawl with a glass of red wine in his hand, the others took rides on the plane. I was amazed at the carelessness of the pilot and the faith of those who flew with him. They lifted off the water and into the wind and cleared the pines by no more than thirty feet, then climbed high into the sun, banked at a sharp angle, and came back between a cut in the hills, dipping down over beachfront houses in a roar of noise that made fishermen in outboards pull their anchors and turn in to shore.

I watched them for two hours. They smoked dope in the lee of the van, drank wine and canned beer out of a washtub filled with crushed ice, ate bleeding steaks and tossed salads off paper plates, swam out breathlessly into the lake and climbed laughing into their yellow raft, their bodies hard and pickled with cold. The girls were pretty and tan and good to look at. Everyone was happy, except maybe Clete and the elder Dio. The Tahoe crowd were the kind of people who knew that they would never die.

The sun had moved into the western sky, which was absolutely blue above the green hills, and the light must have glinted on my field glasses because I saw Sally Dio look up suddenly and squint at the pine trees in which I knelt. I stepped back into the shadows and refocused through the branches. Dio stood by Clete and his father and was pointing in my direction. Clete stopped cleaning up paper plates from a picnic table, glanced up briefly at the cliff, then resumed his work. But Sally Dio and his father looked as if they were staring at an angry dog that was running against its chain. The elder Dio's mouth was wide when he spoke to Clete again, and Clete flung a handful of picnic trash into a garbage can, walked down to the water's edge where the swimmers had left the raft, dragged it up on the sand, and began pulling out the air plugs. Then he loaded the hampers, the washtub of beer and wine coolers, and the elder Dio back into the van.

I could have gotten out of there, I suppose, without being seen. But sometimes self-respect requires that you float one down the middle, letter high, big as a balloon, and let the batter have his way. I walked through the trees back to the road. The air was cool in the shade and heavy with the smell of pine needles on the ground. Bluebirds with yellow wings flew in and out of the smoky light at the tops of the trees. I walked up the shoulder of the road, got in my truck, put my field glasses inside their case, put the case inside the glove box, and started the engine just as Dio's van and Clete's jeep turned out of the entrance to the public beach and headed toward me.

I saw Sally Dio's face through the wide front window of the van, saw the recognition and anger grow in it as he looked back at me and took his foot off the accelerator. Clete was slowing behind him at the same time.

Dio stopped opposite my cab and stared at me.

'What the fuck you think you're doing, man?' he said.

Through the bubble side window of the van I could see people sitting in leather swivel chairs. Their faces gathered at the window as though they were looking out of a fishbowl.

'Wonderful day,' I said.

'What the fuck you doing up in that woods?'

'What do you care? You're not shy. Come on, Dio. That air show was first-rate.'

I saw his nostrils whiten around the edges.

'We told you the other day you don't come around,' he said. 'You're not a cop. You seem to have confusion about that.'

I turned off my engine and clicked my nails on the window jamb. He turned off his engine, too. It was silent on the road, except for the wind blowing through the pines. The western sun over the lake made his waxed black van almost glow with an aura.

'I heard you like to take off parts of people,' I said.

'You heard what?'

'The Sal the Duck story. It's the kind of stuff they enjoy at the DEA. It brightens up a guy's file.'

He opened the door and started to step out on the road. I saw his father lean forward from the back and try to hold his shoulder. The father's lips looked purple against his gray skin; his goiter worked in this throat and his eyes were intense and black when he spoke. But Sally Dio was not listening to his father's caution, and he slid off the seat and stepped out on the road.

I set my sunglasses on the dashboard and got out of the truck. Out of the corner of my eye I could see Clete standing by his jeep. Dio had put on a pair of Levi's over his bathing suit. His denim shirt was open, and his stomach was flat and ridged with muscle. I heard the van door slide open on the far side, and a sun-bleached boy and girl walked around the back and stared at me, but it was obvious they intended to remain spectators. Through the trees I could see the sun click on the deep-blue rippling sheen of the lake.

'You've got a serious problem,' Sally Dio said.

'How's that?' I said, and I smiled.

'You hear an Italian name, you think you can piss on it. A guy's been up the road, you think he's anybody's fuck.'

'You're not a convincing victim, Dio.'

'So you keep coming around, provoking a guy, bothering his family, bothering his friends.' He touched me lightly on the chest with three stiff fingers. There were small saliva bubbles in the corner of his mouth. His ducktailed hair was the color of burnt copper in the slanting light.

'It's time to back off, partner,' I said, and smiled again.

'And it don't matter you been warned. You get in people's faces, you got no respect for an old man, you got no respect for people's privacy. You're a jitterbird, man.' His three stiffened fingers tapped against my chest again, this time harder. 'You get off hanging around swinging dicks, 'cause you got nothing going on your own.'

His face came closer to mine and he poked me in the chest again. The looped scar under his right eye looked like a flattened piece of string on his skin. I slipped my hands into the back pockets of my khakis, as a third-base coach might, and looked off at the sunlight winking through the pine trees.

'Let me run something by you, Sal,' I said. 'Did you ever ask yourself why you have a certain kind of people hanging around you? Hired help, rummy musicians, beachboys with rut for brains. Do you think it's just an accident that everybody around you is a gumball? When's the last time somebody told you you were full of shit?'

I could hear his breathing.

'You got a death wish, man. You got something wrong with you,' he said.

'Let's face it, Sal. I'm not the guy with the electronic gate on my driveway. You think the Fuller Brush man is going to whack you out?'

He wet his lips to speak again, the suddenly one side of his face tightened and he swung at my head. I ducked sideways and felt a ring graze across my ear and scalp. Then I hooked him, hard, between the mouth and the nose. His head snapped back, and his long hair collapsed over his ears. Then he came at me, swinging wildly with both fists, the way an enraged child would. Before I could hit him squarely again, he locked both arms around me, grunting, wheezing in my ear, I could smell his hair tonic and deodorant and the reefer smoke in his clothes. Then he released one of his arms, bent his knees, and swung at my phallus.

But his aim was not as good as his design. He hit me inside the thigh, and I brought my elbow into his nose, felt it break like a chicken bone, saw the shock and pain in his eyes just before I hit him again, this time in the mouth. He bounced off the van's side panel, and I hit him hard in the face again. He was trying to raise his hands in front of him, but it did him no good. I heard the back of his head bounce off the metal again, saw the genuine terror in his eyes, saw his blood whipped across the glass bubble in the panel, felt my fists hit him so hard that his face went out of round.

Then Clete was between us, his revolver drawn, one arm held out stiffly toward me, his eyes big and glaring.

'Back away, Dave! I'll shoot you in the foot! I swear to God I will!' he said.

On the edge of my vision I could see cars stopped on the road in each direction. Clete was breathing through his mouth, his eyes riveted on mine. Sally Dio had both hands pressed to his face. His fingers were red in the sunlight through the trees. In the distance I heard a police siren. I felt the heat go out of my chest the way a hot-eyed, hook-beaked raven would fly out of a cage.

'Sure,' I said.

'I mean it, all the way across the road,' he said.

I held up my palms.

'No problem,' I said. 'Don't you want me to move my truck, though? We're blocking a lot of traffic.'

I saw the sun-bleached boy and the girl walk Sally Dio around to the other side of the van. A sheriff's car was driving around the traffic jam on the edge of the road. Cletus put his revolver back in his nylon shoulder holster.

'You crazy sonofabitch,' he said.

The holding cell in the county jail was white and small, and the barred door gave on to a small office area where two khaki-uniformed deputies did their paperwork. The cell contained nothing to sit or sleep on but a narrow wood bench that was bolted into the back wall, and no plumbing except a yellow-streaked drain in the center of the cement floor. I had already used the phone to call the babysitter in Missoula to tell her that I would probably not be home that night.

One of the deputies was a big Indian with a plug of chewing tobacco buttoned down tightly in his shirt pocket. He bent over a cuspidor by the side of his desk and spit in it. He had come into the office only a few minutes earlier.

'They already told you Dio's not pressing charges?' he asked.

'Yes.'

'So it's just a disorderly conduct charge. Your bond's a hundred bucks.'

'I don't have it.'

'Write a check.'

'I don't have one.'

'You want to use the phone again?'

'I don't know anyone I can call.'

'Look, guilty court's not for two days.'

'There's nothing I can do about it, podna.'

'The judge's already gone home or the sheriff could ask him to let you out on your own recognizance. We'll see what we can do tomorrow.'

'I appreciate it.'

'You came all the way up here from Louisiana to stomp Sally Dio's ass?'

'It sort of worked out that way.'

'You sure picked on one bad motherfucker. I think you'd be better off if you'd blown out his light altogether.'

For supper I ate a plate of watery lima beans and a cold Spam sandwich and drank a can of Coca-Cola. It was dark outside the window now, and the other deputy went home. I sat in the gloom on the wood bench and opened and closed my hands. They felt thick and stiff and sore on the knuckles. Finally the Indian looked at his watch.

'I left a message for the judge at his house. He didn't call back,' he said. 'I got to take you upstairs.'

'It's all right.'

As he took the keys to the cell out of his desk drawer his phone rang. He nodded while he listened, then hung up.

'You got the right kind of lady friend,' he said.

'What?'

'You're cut loose. Your bail's your fine, too. You ain't got to come back unless you want to plead not guilty.'

He turned the key in the iron lock, and I walked down the wood-floored corridor toward the lighted entrance that gave on to the parking lot. She stood under the light outside, dressed in blue jeans and a maroon shirt with silver flowers stitched on it. Her black hair was shiny in the light, and she wore a deerskin bag on a string over her shoulder.

'I'll drive you back to your truck,' she said.

'Where's Clete?'

'Up at Sal's.'

'Does he know where you are?'

'I guess he does. I don't hide anything from him.'

'Nothing?' I said.

She looked at me and didn't answer. We walked toward her jeep in the parking lot. The sheen on her hair was like the purple and black colors in a crow's wing. We got in and she started the engine.

'What's China pearl?' she asked.

'High-grade Oriental skag. Why?'

'You knocked out one of Sal's teeth. They gave him a shot of China pearl for the pain. You must have been trying to kill him.'

'No.'

'Oh? I saw his face. There're bloody towels all over his living room rug.'

'He dealt it, Darlene. He's a violent man and one day somebody's going to take him out.'

'*He's* a violent man? That's too much.'

'Listen, you're into some kind of strange balancing act with these people. I don't know what it is, but I think it's crazy. Clete said he met you when you drove Dixie Lee all the way back to Flathead from a reservation beer joint. Why would you do that for Dixie Lee?'

'He's a human being, isn't he?'

'He's also barroom furniture that usually doesn't get hauled across the mountains by pretty Indian girls.'

She drove up the east short of the lake without answering. The trunks of the aspens and birch trees were silver in the moonlight, the rim of the mountains around the lake black against the sky. I tried one more time.

'What does it take to make you understand you don't belong there?' I said.

'Where do I belong?'

'I don't know. Maybe with another guy.' I swallowed when I said it.

The scars on the backs of her hands were thin and white in the glow of moon- and starlight though the window.

'Do you want to take a chance on living with me and my little girl?' I said.

She was silent a moment. Her mouth looked purple and soft when she turned her face toward me.

'I won't always be in this trouble. I've had worse times. They always passed,' I said.

'How long will you want me to stay?'

'Until you want to leave.'

Her hands opened and then tightened on the steering wheel.

'You're lonely now,' she said. 'After we were together, maybe you'd feel different.'

'You don't know that.'

'I know the way people are when they're lonely. It's like the way you feel at night about somebody. Then in the daylight it's not the same.'

'What would you lose by trying?'

She slowed the jeep on the gravel shoulder a few feet behind my parked pickup truck and cut the engine. It was dark in the heavy shadow of the pines. Out over the lake the sky was bursting with constellations.

'You're a nice man. One day you'll find the right woman,' she said.

'That's not the way you felt this morning. Don't put me off, Darlene.'

I put my arm around her shoulders and turned her face with my hand. Her eyes looked up quietly at me in the dark. I kissed her on the mouth. Her eyes were still open when I took my mouth away from hers. Then I kissed her again, and this time her mouth parted and I felt her lips become wet against mine and her fingers go into my hair. I kissed her eyes and the moles at the corner of her mouth, then I placed my hand on her breast and kissed her throat and tried to pull aside her shirt with my clumsy hand and kiss the tops of her breasts.

Then I felt her catch her breath, tear it out of the air, stiffen, push against me and turn her face out into the dark.

'No more,' she said.

'What—'

'It was a mistake. It ends here, Dave.'

'People's feelings don't work like that.'

'We're from different worlds. You knew that this morning. I led you into it. It's my fault. But it's over.'

'Are you going to tell me Clete's from your world?'

'It doesn't matter. It's not going anywhere. Maybe at another time—'

'I'm just not going to listen to that stuff, Darlene.'

'You have to accept what I tell you. I'm sorry about all of it. I'm sorry I'm hurting you. I'm sorry about Clete. But you go back home or you're going to be killed.'

'Not by the likes of Sally Dee, I'm not.'

I put my arm around her shoulders again and tried to brush back her hair with my hand.

'I'm sorry,' she said, but this time calmly, with her eyes straight ahead. Then she got out of the jeep and stood in the dark with her arms folded and her face turned toward the lake. The water's surface was black and flecked with foam in the wind. I walked up next to her and put my fingers lightly on her neck.

'It's not good,' she said softly.

I could not see her face in the shadows. I walked away from her toward my truck. The gravel crunched loudly under my feet, and the wind was cold through the pines.

*

The next morning was Friday. I was headed back to the other side of the Divide when my water pump went out at Bonner, on the Blackfoot River, ten miles east of Missoula. I had my truck towed to a garage in town and was told by the mechanic that he would not have the repairs done until Monday at noon. So I had to mark off two days that I could sorely afford to lose.

The air was cool and smelled of woodsmoke when I woke Monday morning, and the sun was bright on the lip of Hellgate Canyon and the valley was filled with blue shadows. I made *cush-cush* for Alafair and me, walked her to school in the spreading sunlight, then sat on the front porch in a long-sleeved flannel shirt and drank another cup of coffee and read the paper. A few minutes later a Landrover with a fly rod case in the gun rack pulled to a stop in front. Dan Nygurski got out, dressed in a pair of beltless jeans, an army sweater, and a floppy hat covered with trout flies.

'I've got a day off. Take a drive with me up the Blackfoot,' he said.

'I have to pick up my truck in the shop later.'

'I'll take you there. Come on. You got a fishing rod?'

His seamed, coarse face smiled at me. He looked like he could bench three hundred pounds or break a baseball bat across his knee. I invited him in and gave him a cup of coffee in the kitchen while I got my Fenwick rod out of the closet and tied on my tennis shoes.

'What have you got in the way of flies?' he asked.

'Nothing really, popping bugs.'

'I've got what you need, brother. A number-fourteen renegade. It drives them crazy.'

'What's this about?'

His mouth twitched, and the muscles in the side of his face and throat jumped.

'I thought I'd pick up some tips from you on how to handle Sally Dee,' he said. 'I think you've got a first there. I don't believe anybody's ever cleaned Sal's clock before.'

'How'd you hear about it?'

'The sheriff's office reports to us whenever Sal comes to their attention. A deputy told me you tried to use Sal's face to repaint the side of his van. I always knew he had some worthwhile potential.'

'He's got skag and coke in that house.'

'How do you know?'

'A friend told me.'

'Purcel?'

'No.'

'Ah, the Indian girl.'

'What do you know about her?'

'Nothing. She's just some gal Purcel picked up. They come and go at Sally Dee's. What's your point about the coke and the skag?'

'Get a warrant and bust the place.'

'When I put Sal away, it's going to be for the rest of his worthless life, not on a chickenshit possessions charge. He'd have one of those lame-brain beachboys doing his time, anyway.'

'I spent some time up at the Flathead courthouse. Why's he buying and leasing up property around the lake?'

Nygurski set his cup in the saucer and looked out the window at the backyard. The grass was wet and green in the shade, and the sunlight was bright on the tops of the trees across the alley.

'He thinks casino gambling's going through the legislature,' he said. 'The time's right for it. People are out of work, they've used up all their compo, agriculture's in the toilet. Casino gambling could turn Flathead Lake into another Tahoe. Sal would be in on the ground floor.'

'It's that simple?'

'Yeah, more or less. I don't think it's going to happen, though. People here don't like outsiders, anyway. Particularly greasers and Californians.'

'What did you come over here to tell me?'

'Don't worry about it. Come on, I've got an appointment with an eighteen-inch rainbow.'

We drove up through the Blackfoot River canyon, which was still dark and cool with shadows and smelled of woodsmoke blowing up from the mill at Bonner. Then we broke out into meadowland and ranch country and sunshine again, turned off the highway and crossed the river on a planked log bridge, and began climbing on a dirt road through hills and lodgepole pine and scrub brush, where white-tailed deer sprang in a flick of the eye back into the dense cover of the woods. Then we came back into the canyon again, into the most beautiful stretch of river that I had ever seen. The rock cliffs were red and sheer and rose straight up three hundred feet. The crests were thick with ponderosa, and the water, blue and green, turned in deep pools where the current had eaten under the cliffs. The rocks along the shore were bone white and etched with dried insects, and out beyond the canyon's shadows, the great boulders in the middle of the river were steaming in the sun and flies were hatching out in a gray mist above the riffle.

I tied a renegade fly on the tippet of my nylon leader and followed Nygurski into the shallows. The water was so cold inside my tennis shoes and khakis that my bones felt as though they had been beaten with an ice mallet. I false-cast in a figure eight above my head, laid out the line upstream on the riffle, and watched the fly swirl through the eddies and around the boulders toward me. I picked it up, false-cast again, drying it in the air with whistling sound inches from my ear, and dropped it just beyond a barkless, sun-bleached cottonwood that beavers had toppled into the stream. The riffle made a lip of dirty foam around the end of the log, and just as my leader swung around it and coursed across the top of a deep pool, I saw a rainbow rise from the bottom like an iridescent bubble released from the pebble-and-silt bed and snap my renegade down in a spray of silvery light.

I raised my rod high and stripped off-line with my left hand and let him run. He headed out into the current, into deep water, and my Fenwick arched and vibrated in my palm, drops of water glistening and trembling on the line. Then he broke the surface, and the sun struck the red and pink and green band on his side. I had to go deeper into the current with him, up to my chest now, and strip off my line to keep from breaking the tippet. I kept walking with him downstream while he pumped against the rod and tried to wrap the line around a submerged boulder, until I was back in the deep shade of the canyon, with the wind cold on my neck and the air heavy with the smell of ferns and wet stone.

Then I was around a bend, up into shallow water again, the gravel firm under my tennis shoes. It was all over for him. I worked him up into a small lagoon, watched him gin impotently over the clouded bottom with his dorsal fin out of the water; then I wet my hand and knelt in the shallows and picked him up under the stomach. He felt cold and thick in my hand, and his mouth and gills pumped hard for oxygen. I slipped the fly loose from the corner of his mouth and placed him back in the water. He hovered momentarily over the gravel, his tail moving for balance in the light current, before he dropped away over a ledge and was gone in the current.

While Nygurski fished farther upstream, I kicked together a pile of driftwood out in the sunlight, started a fire on the stones, and fixed a pot of cowboy coffee from his rucksack. It was warm in the sun. I sat on a dead cottonwood and drank the coffee black from one of his tin cups and watched him fish. There was a ranch farther upstream, and curious Angus wandered out of the unfenced pasture, through the willows and clattered across the stones on the beach into the shallows. I saw Nygurski break his leader on a snag, then look back at me in frustration. I pointed to my watch.

He walked up the beach with his fly rod over his shoulder. His jeans were wet up to his thighs. He slipped his straw creel off his shoulder, slit open the stomachs of three rainbow, scooped out the guts and threw them back into the willows. Then he stooped by the edge of the stream and dug the blood and membrane out of the vertebrae with his thumbnail.

'I saw you turn that big one loose,' he said.

'I don't keep them much anymore. I don't have a Montana license, anyway.'

'You hunt?'

'I used to. I don't much anymore.'

'You give it up in the army?'

'Something like that.'

He poured himself a cup of coffee, took two wax-paper-wrapped pork chop sandwiches out of his rucksack and gave me one, then sat down on the log next to me. The veins in his thick neck stuck out like webs of cord when he chewed.

'What kind of gun do you have?' he said.

'An army .45 automatic.'

'You have a permit for it?'

'In Louisiana I do. Not here.'

'They're not real big on gun permits in Montana, but let's get you one, anyway.'

'What are we talking about?'

'We have a tap on Sally Dio's telephone. He knows it.'

'So?'

'He doesn't know that we have a tap on a pay phone down the shore from his house. The one that he uses for some of his long-distance calls.'

I picked up a small, flat, gray stone and skipped it out on the water.

'He called a bar in Vegas,' Nygurski said. 'He said to the guy who answered, "Tell Charlie I've got a yard job for him up here." You know what that is?'

'No, that's a new one.'

'I've heard a couple of Quentin graduates use it. It's when they do somebody out on the yard. The last time we heard Sal say something like that on a tap, a witness against him got a .22 Magnum round behind the ear. But we don't know who Charlie is.'

I tossed another small stone in a gentle arc out on the water. It made a circle like a trout rising, then the circle floated on down the riffle into white water.

'Maybe it doesn't have anything to do with you,' he said. 'The Dios have lots of enemies.'

I brushed the gravel off my palms and I didn't say anything for a while. The sun was hot now, and flies were hatching out of the cattails and rainbows popping at them in a shaded pool under the cliff.

'What do you think I ought to do?' I said finally.

'Maybe it's time to go back to New Iberia.'

'You think he'd bring in a mechanic, risk his whole operation, because of pride?'

'Look, he's got a little clout in the mob because he's Frank Dio's son. But basically Sal's a loser. He's a lousy musician, he did time for stolen credit cards, his wife dumped him after he broke her nose, his friends are bought-and-paid-for rummies and cokeheads. Then you come along and remodel his face while everybody gets to watch. What do you think a guy like that is feeling for you right now?'

'It won't matter, then, if I go back to Louisiana or not.'

'Maybe not.'

I looked at my watch. Across the stream I saw a hawk drop suddenly into a meadow and hook a field mouse in its talons.

'Thanks for the fishing trip. I need to pick up my truck now,' I said.

'I'm sorry to be the one to drop this on you.'

'Don't worry about it.'

'Why in God's name did you do it, Robicheaux?'

I didn't sleep that night. As we say in AA, the executive committee held a session in my head. I thought about sending Alafair back to Louisiana, to stay with my cousin or Batist and his wife, but then I would lose all control over her situation. I doubted that Harry Mapes would make a move against either of us as long as my trial was pending and it looked like I was going to take the fall for Dalton Vidrine's murder; but then again you can't second-guess a psychopath, and I believed that's what he was.

I still wasn't convinced by Dan Nygurski about Sally Dio's calling Vegas to bring in a contract killer. The mob, or at least its members I had known in New Orleans, did not operate like that. They whacked out witnesses, Colombian competitors, and each other, but they didn't hit ordinary people because of a personal grudge. Their own leadership didn't allow it; it brought down too much heat on their operation and compromised their hard-bought relationships with politicians, police officials, and judges. Sally Dee was a vicious punk, but his father was smart and cautious, a survivor of gang wars and Mafia power struggles. I just didn't believe they would be willing to blow it all over a broken tooth.

So the executive committee stayed in session until the false dawn and then adjourned with little resolved. As always when I was weak and drained and absolutely burnt-out with my own failed attempts at reasoning through a problem, I turned it over to my Higher Power; then I cooked sausage and eggs for our breakfast, walked Alafair to school, made arrangements for her to stay with the babysitter, put my .45 and an extra clip under the truck seat, and headed over the Divide for the Blackfeet Reservation.

My fan belt broke ten miles south of the reservation, and I hitched a ride with an Indian feed grower to a filling station at a four-corners four miles up the road. I bought a new fan belt, then started walking on the shoulder of the road back toward my truck. It was a mistake. Rain clouds drifted down over the low green hills to the east, shadowing the fields and sloughs and clumps of willows and cottonwoods; suddenly the sky burst open and a hard, driving rain stung my skin and drenched my clothes in minutes. I took cover against the rock face of a small hill that the road cut through, and watched the storm shower work its way across the land.

Then a paintless and battered school bus, with adhesive tape plastered on its cracked windows, with bicycles, collapsed tents, shovels, and two canoes roped to its sides and roof, came highballing around the corner like a highway-borne ghost of the 1960s.

When the driver stopped for me I could hear screws scouring into brake shoes, the twisted exhaust pie hammering against the frame, the engine firing as if all the spark plug leads had been deliberately crossed. The driver threw open the folding door with a long lever, and I stepped inside of what could have been a time capsule. The seats had all been torn out and replaced with hammocks, bunks, sleeping bags, a butane stove, a bathtub, cardboard boxes bursting with clothes. A woman nursed a child at her breast; a white man with Indian braids sat on the floor, carving an animal out of a soap bar; another woman was changing an infant's diapers on the backseat; a bearded man in a ponytail slept facedown in a hammock, so that his body looked like a netted fish's suspended from the ceiling. I could smell sour milk, reefer, and burnt food.

The driver had dilated blue eyes and a wild red beard, and he wore leather wristbands and a fatigue jacket open on his bare chest, which was deeply tanned and scrolled with dark blue jailhouse tattoos. He told me to sit down in a wood chair that was located next to him at the head of the aisle. Then he slammed the door shut with the lever, crunched the transmission into gear, and we careened down the road in the blowing rain. I told him where I was going, and held on to a metal rail to keep from bouncing out of the chair.

'That's a bad place to stand, man,' he said. 'There's fuckers come around that curve seventy miles an hour, crazy sonsobitches in log trucks think they own the fucking road. What one of them needs is somebody to wind up a brick on a string and put it through his window. You live around here?'

'No. I'm just a visitor.'

'That's a weird accent. I thought maybe you was a Canuck.'

'No, I'm from Louisiana.'

His eyes were curious, and they moved over my face. The bus drifted toward the shoulder.

'Say, there's a café up on the right. I think I'll get off and get something to eat,' I said.

'I said we'd take you to your truck. You'll get there, man. Don't worry about it.'

The woman who was breast-feeding the child wiped his chin with her shirt, then put his mouth on the nipple again and looked impassively out the window. Her face was without makeup, her hair dull brown, long, and stuck together on the tips.

'You keep looking in the back of the bus. Something bothering you?' the driver said.

'Not at all.'

'You think we're spikers or something?'

'What?'

'Spikers. You think we go around driving railroad spikes in trees?'

'No, I don't think that.'

''Cause we don't, man. A tree is a living thing, and we don't wound living things. Does that make sense to you?'

'Sure.'

'We live up on the reservation. We're a family. We lead a natural way of life. We don't get in nobody's face. All we ask is nobody fuck with us. That ain't a lot to ask, is it?'

I looked out the streaked windowpanes of the folding door. The countryside was green and wet and covered with a gray mist.

'Is it?' he said.

'No, it's not.'

''Cause a lot of people won't let you alone. They're at war with the earth, man. That's their fucking problem. You don't do it their way, they try to kick a two-by-four up your ass.'

The ride was becoming increasingly more uncomfortable. I figured it was three more miles to my truck.

'Do you know a girl named Darlene American Horse on the reservation?' I said.

'I don't know her.'

'She's from there.'

'That might be man, but I don't know her. Check with my old lady.' He nodded backward toward the woman with the child at her breast.

I asked her about Darlene. She wore large wire-rimmed glasses, and she looked at me quietly with no expression in her face.

'I don't know her,' she said.

'You've lived there long?'

'A year.'

'I see.'

'It's a Blackfeet reservation,' she said. Her speech had that flat quality of quasi-omniscience that you hear in women who have reached a certain gray plateau in their lives from which they know they'll never escape.

'Yes?' I said.

'They're all Blackfeet. The Sioux live over in South Dakota.'

'I don't understand what you mean.'

'American Horse is a Sioux name,' she said. 'He fought with Sitting Bull and Crazy Horse against the whites.'

It's her married name, I thought.

'You know how they bought it, too?' the driver said. 'Dealing with the Man under a flag of truce. They went into the fort and got their asses shot. That's what happens when you trust those fuckers.'

My God, why didn't I see it, I thought.

'Hey, you're looking a little gray,' the driver said.

'What?'

'You want some food? We got extra,' he said.

'No. Thank you. D y'all know a guy by the name of Clayton Desmarteau?'

'You better believe it. Same outfit as me. First Cav.'

'Did he have a sister?'

'What d'you mean "did"?'

'You haven't seen him around in a while, have you?'

He thought for a moment.

'I guess not,' he said.

'Do you know if he had a sister?'

'I don't know nothing about his family. He don't live on the reservation. He used to come on it to organize for AIM against them oil and gas companies. They're gonna mess up the East Front, try to build pipelines and refineries and all kinds of shit.'

'What color were his eyes?'

'His eyes?' He turned and grinned at me through his red beard. His teeth were missing in back. 'I look like I go around looking at guys' eyes?'

'Come on, were they turquoise?'

'What the fuck I know about a guy's eyes? What kind of stuff are you into, man?'

'He's a policeman,' the woman with the child said.

'Is that for real?' the driver said.

'No.'

'Then why you asking all these questions? You trying to give some shit to Clayton's people?' The hair on his forearms grew like red metal wires on the edges of his leather wristbands.

'No.'

'Cause the Indians don't need no more hassle. These are native people, man, I mean it was their *place*, and whites been taking a dump on them for two hundred years.'

'I'll get off here,' I said.

'You bothered by something I said?'

'Not in the least, partner. The rain's stopping now, and I need to walk. My truck's just over the rise.'

'Cause we got no beef with nobody. We thought we were helping you out. You gotta watch out for a lot of people in this state. I ain't blowing gas, Jack. It's the times,' he said.

I stood on the side of the road in the damp, sunlit air, a green pasture behind me, and watched the bus disappear over the rise. My truck was still a mile down the road.

*

The old woman was hoeing in a rocky vegetable patch behind her house. She wore laced boots, a man's oversized wool trousers, and a khaki shirt, and a shawl was wrapped around her head. In the distance the wet land sloped toward the Divide, where the mountains thrust up violently against the sky, their sheer cliffs now purple with shadow. Up high it had snowed, and the ponderosa was white on the crests and through the saddles. The old woman glanced sideways at me when I opened her wood gate and walked into the yard, then continued chopping weeds in the rows as though I were not there.

'Darlene American Horse is your daughter, isn't she?' I asked.

She didn't answer. Her white hair bunched out under her shawl, and the corners of her eyes were creased with concentration on her work.

'Mrs Desmarteau, believe me, I'm a friend,' I said. 'I want to find out what happened to your son. I want to help Darlene, if I can.'

She thudded and raked the hoe in the dirt and stones and notched out weeds between the cabbages without ever touching a leaf.

'I think Darlene lives among some bad people. I want to get her away from them,' I said.

She pulled back the door of an abandoned, dilapidated privy, put away the hoe and took out a shovel. In the back of the privy a calico cat was nursing her litter on top of a pile of gunnysacks. Mrs Desmarteau laid the shovel across a wheel-barrow leaded with manure and began pushing it toward the edge of the vegetable patch. I took the handles out of her hands and wheeled it across the dirt yard, then began spreading the manure at the end of each row. The clouds were purple on top of the mountains, and snow was blowing off the edges of the canyons. Behind me I heard the plastic sheets of insulation rattling on her windows.

'She's your daughter, isn't she?' I said again.

'Are you one of the FBI?' she said.

'No, I'm not. But I used to be a policeman. I'm not any longer. I'm just a man who's in some trouble.'

For the first time her eyes looked directly at mine.

'If you know Darlene, why are you asking me if she's my daughter?' she said. 'Why are you here and asking that question? You don't make sense.'

Then I realized that perhaps I had under-estimated this elderly lady. And like most people who consider themselves educated, I had perhaps presumed that an elderly person – like someone who is foreign-speaking or unschooled – could not understand the complexities of my life and intellect.

'I didn't relate the name to yours,' I said. 'But I should have. She wears her brother's First Cav army jacket, doesn't she? She also has turquoise eyes. Your family name is French-Canadian, not Indian. Darlene and Clayton's father was part white, wasn't he?'

'Why do you say she lives among bad people?'

'The man she stays with isn't bad, but the people he works for are. I believe she should come back home and not stay with these people on the lake.'

'You've been there?'

'Yes.'

'Are they criminals?'

'Some of them are.'

Her hand slipped down over mine and took the shovel. Her palm was rough and edged with callus. She was motionless, the shovel propped against her wool trousers, her eyes fixed on the jagged outline of the mountains against the sky. The clouds on the high peaks looked full of snow.

'Are they the ones that killed my boy?' she said.

'Maybe they were involved in some way. I don't know.'

'Why is she with them?'

'She thinks she can find out what happened to Clayton and his cousin. She worked in a bar. Where is it?'

'Five miles down the road. You passed it when you came here.'

'Do you know a man named Dixie Lee Pugh?'

'No.'

'Do you see Darlene?'

'She comes one day a week and brings groceries.'

'Talk to her, Mrs Desmarteau. She's a good girl. Between the two of us we'll get her back home.'

I saw her breathe through the mouth. Her lips moved without sound.

'What?' I said.

'Clayton never did no harm to anybody. They said he carried a gun. If he did, they made him. They wouldn't let him alone. They were afraid of him because he was brave.'

It was turning cold, I helped her finish spreading manure in her vegetable patch, then said good-bye and latched the wooden gate behind me. The sky was overcast and gray now. She looked small and alone with her hoe, in her dirt yard, in the ward that blew down off the backbone of the world.

I drove back down the dirt road and stopped at the place where Clayton Desmarteau and his cousin had put their car in the ditch. Did Mapes and Vidrine kidnap and drive them someplace, or did it all happen here? I asked myself. I jumped across the stream that bordered the far side of the road and walked up the slope into the lodgepole pine. The ground was thick with pine needles. Chipmunks played in the rocks, and red squirrels chased each other around the tree trunks. I walked about a quarter of a mile through the pines, then intersected a trace of a road that somebody had used at one time to dump garbage. The road dead-ended in a pile of rusted box springs, tin cans, mattresses, beer and wine bottles, and plastic soap containers. I went on another four hundred yards or so through the pines, then the trunks thinned and I came out on a tea-colored stream coursing over gray rocks. The stream cut along the edge of a low, rock-faced hill that rose abruptly into box elder, wild rosebushes, and thick scrub brush. I walked up and down the stream bank, crossed the sculpted tracks of deer, the delicate impressions of turkey and grouse in the wet sand, found the rotted, soft logs of an old cabin, tripped over the half-buried remains of a wood stove, and flushed a white-tailed buck that must have had ten points on his rack; but I saw nothing that was out of the ordinary or that could be helpful in discovering the fate of Clayton Desmarteau and his cousin.

Finally I came to a spring that flowed out of the hillside on the far bank of the stream. The spring dripped over rocks, and had eroded away the dirt and exposed the gnarled roots of small pines on the hillside. The water drained over a wide area of wet pine needles and black leaves, and the ground there was spongy and bursting with mushrooms and dark fern. I could smell the water, the coolness of the stone, the dank humus, the exposed tree roots that trailed like brown cobweb in the current. It smelled like the coulee on my property back in Louisiana. I wondered when I would be going back there, or if in fact I would be able to. Because I had decided that if I did not develop a better defense than the one I presently had, I was not going to deliver myself up for trial and a sure jolt in Angola pen.

I was tired. After hiking back to my truck, I drove up the road in the gray light between the wet fields, then I glanced in the side mirror at a black Willys Jeepster, a remake of the classic model manufactured right after World War II. Because the road was wet and there was no dust, I could see the driver's tall outline behind the steering wheel. Then he accelerated and closed on my rear bumper, as though he wanted to see my reflection in the side mirror or some detail of my pickup – the dealer's name, a bumper sticker that read Mulate's, Breaux Bridge, Louisiana.

Up ahead was the wide, squat log tavern where Clayton Desmarteau and his cousin had probably spent the last night of their lives, where Darlene had waited tables, and where she had probably met Dixie Lee Pugh while he was in a drunken stupor, saved him from getting his head kicked in, and driven him over the mountains to Sally Dio's on Flathead Lake. It was starting to mist, and a purple and orange neon war bonnet was lighted on the roof against the gray sky.

I pulled on to the gravel parking lot and waited to see what the driver in the Jeepster would do. He slowed abreast of me, his long hands on the top of the steering wheel, and stared intently out the passenger's window. His face, forehead, and neck were streaked with thin scabs, as though he had walked through a nest of rust-colored spiderweb.

I wanted him to stop, to open his door, to confront me with his injury and his anger. I wanted to see a weapon in his hand and feel that adrenaline surge, that violent sanction, that lights and clarifies the mind and resolves all the complexities.

But Harry Mapes was holding all the good cards. Harry Mapes had been a helicopter pilot in Vietnam, and he knew that you don't change the terms of your situation when your Gatling guns are locked in on a solitary pajama-clad target in the middle of a glassy rice field.

He turned into the parking lot and parked by the front door, where three Indians in work clothes were drinking canned beer next to a truck. He lit a cigarette with a gold lighter before he got out of his Jeepster, then went inside without looking back at me.

By the time I got back to Missoula that night Alafair had already had her supper at the babysitter's, but I took her for a late snack at a pizza place called Red Pies Over Montana. She wore her soft denim jeans with the elastic waistband, patent leather shoes with white socks that were now gray and with dust from the playground, and her yellow T-shirt printed with a smiling purple whale and the words 'Baby Orca' on it. Her cheeks were spotted with red pizza sauce. Through the restaurant window I could see the stars over the mountains.

'Dave?' she said.

'What is it, little guy?'

'When we going back home?'

'Don't you like it here?'

'I want to see Tex. Maybe Batist needs us at the shop. He can't read.'

'You don't have to read to sell worms and shiners.'

'Nothing here is like it is at home.'

'It has a lot of good things, though, doesn't it?'

'I miss Tripod. I miss Clarise. It's cold at night.'

I brushed her shiny black hair with my hand.

'It won't be long. You'll see,' I said.

But my assurance was an emotional lie. I didn't know when we could go back. I wasn't sure if I ever could. That night in the dark, with the door open between our bedrooms, I heard her saying her prayers by the side of the bed, then climbing in under the covers.

'Dave?'

'What?'

'Are people trying to hurt us? Is that why we had to move?'

I got up and walked barefoot into her room and sat on the edge of the bed. Her face looked round and tan in the moonlight through the window. Her blanket was pulled up to her chin.

'Don't think like that, Alf. Nobody wants to hurt guys like us. We're good guys,' I said. 'Think of all the people who love you. Batist and

Clarise and your friends and teachers at school. They all love you, Alfie. And I love you most of all.'

I could see her wide-spaced teeth and the brightness of her eyes when she smiled up from the pillow.

But her thoughts were not far from my own. That night I dreamed of South Louisiana, of blue herons standing among flooded cypress trees, fields of surgarcane beaten with purple and gold light in the fall, the smell of smoldering hickory and pork dripping into the ash in our smokehouse, the way billows of fig rolled out of the swamp in the morning, so thick and white that sound – a bass flopping, a bullfrog falling off a log into the water – came to you inside a wet bubble, pelicans sailing out of the sun over the breaks out on the Gulf, the palm trees ragged and green and clacking in the salt breeze, and the crab and crawfish boils and fish fries that went on year-round, as though there were no end to a season and death had no sway in our lives, and finally the song that always broke my heart, 'La Jolie Blonde', which in a moment made the year 1945. Our yard was abloom with hibiscus and blue and pink hydrangeas and the neighbours came on horseback to the *fais-dodo* under our oaks.

The next morning I got a call from Tess Regan, the third-grade teacher and assistant principal at Alafair's school. She said she had a one-hour break at eleven o'clock, and she asked if she would walk down to the house and talk with me.

'Is there something wrong?' I said.

'Maybe it's nothing. I'd rather talk to you about it at your house.'

'Sure. Come on down.'

A few minutes later she knocked on the screen door. She wore a pale green cotton dress, and her auburn hair was tied back with a green kerchief. I could see baby powder on her freckled shoulders.

'I hope I'm not bothering you,' she said.

'No, not at all. I have some iced tea made. It's a beautiful day. Let's have some on the porch.'

'All right,' she said. The corners of her eyes wrinkled good-naturedly at the deference to her situation as a layperson in a Catholic elementary school.

I brought the tea out on the porch, and we sat on two old metal chairs. The light was bright on the lawn and the trees, and bumblebees hummed over the clover in the grass.

'A man called earlier,' she said. 'He said he was a friend of yours from Louisiana. He wanted to know where you and Alafair lived.'

'What was his name?'

'He wouldn't give it.'

'Did you tell him?'

'No, of course not. We don't give out people's addresses. I told him to call information. He said he tried, but your number was unlisted.'

'It isn't, but my address isn't in the phone book, and information usually won't give out addresses. Why did the call bother you?' I leaned slightly forward.

'He was rude. No, it was more than that. His voice was ugly.'

'What else did he say?'

'He kept saying he was an old friend, that it was important he talk with you, that I should understand that.'

'I see.'

'Alafair said you used to be a police officer. Does this have something to do with that?'

'Maybe. Could you tell if it was long-distance?'

'It didn't sound like it.'

I tried to think. Who knew that Alafair went to a parochial school in Missoula? Darlene, perhaps. Or maybe I said something to Clete. Or maybe the person called New Iberia and got something out of Batist or Clarise. Then he could have phoned every Catholic elementary school in town until he hit the right combination.

'What was the first thing this guy said?' I asked.

Her mouth was wet and red when it came away from her glass. Her green eyes looked thoughtfully out into the sunlight.

'He said, "I'm calling for Dave Robicheaux," ' she said. 'I told him I didn't understand. Then he said it again, "I'm calling for Dave." So I said, "You mean you're delivering a message for him?" '

'Then he knew he'd found the right school.'

'What?'

'He's a slick guy.'

'I'm sorry if I handled it wrong,' she said.

'Don't worry about it. He's probably a bill collector. They follow me around the country.' I smiled at her, but she didn't buy it.

She set her iced tea on the porch railing and sat with her knees close together and her hands folded in her lap. She dropped her eyes, then looked up at me again.

'I'm probably being intrusive, but you're in some trouble, aren't you?'

'Yes.'

'Who is this man?'

'I'm not sure. If he called again, though, I'd appreciate your letting me know.'

'Is he a criminal?'

I looked at her face and eyes. I wondered how much of the truth she was able to take. I decided not to find out.

'Maybe,' I said.

She pinched her fingers together in her lap.

'Mr Robicheaux, if he's a threat to Alafair, we need to know that,' she said. 'You have an obligation to tell us that, I think.'

'This guy didn't have a Texas accent, did he?'

'No. He didn't have an accent.'

'A couple of guys have a beef with me. Maybe he works for one of them. But their beef is with me. It's not going to affect anything at your school.'

'I see,' she said, and her eyes went away into the sunlight on the yard.

'I'm sorry. I didn't mean to sound sharp,' I said.

'You weren't. I'm sorry you're having this trouble.' She stood up to go. 'I think you should consider calling the police. Your daughter is a beautiful little girl.'

'There's no law against a guy asking for somebody's address.'

'You probably understand these things better than I, then. Thank you for the tea.'

'Wait a minute. I appreciate your help. I really do. And Alafair thinks the world of you. But I could start explaining my situation to you now and we'd still be talking tomorrow morning. It's a mess, and it involves a bunch of bad people. I don't have any answers for it, either. Sometimes cops can't do any good. That's why as I get older I believe more and more in prayer. At least I feel like I'm dealing with somebody who's got some real authority.' I smiled again, and this time it took.

'I'll bet you handle it all right,' she said, and her eyes crinkled. She squeezed my hand and walked down the steps on to the sidewalk, out of the porch's shadow, into the sunshine, her calves clicking with light in the bright air.

I went into the kitchen and fixed a bowl of Grape-Nuts for lunch. While I ate I stared out the window at the neighbor's orange cat climbing up the roof of the garage out by the alley. Overhead, two doves sat on the telephone wires. Who had been the man on the telephone? I thought. Sally Dio's mechanic out of Vegas? Or maybe somebody who worked with Harry Mapes. Why not? It would be a safe way for Mapes to keep me agitated and off-balance. He was a mailer of hypodermic needles and threats against a child. A telephone call to the school would be consistent with his past behavior. At least that's what a police department psychologist would say.

Except for the fact that I was the defendant in an upcoming murder trial and Mapes was the prosecution witness. The apparatus of the law was on his side; he was the friend of the court, the chain-whipped victim of an alcoholic, burnt-out cop. Mapes didn't need to shave the dice.

Which brought me back to my original speculation and Dan Nygurski's warning, one I truly did not want to confront. A faceless button man whose only name was Charlie.

Call the police, she had said. Suffering God, I thought, why is it that in problematic situations almost everyone resorts to axioms and societal remedies that in actuality nobody believes in? Tess Regan was a good girl, and obviously I was being too hard on her in my frustration, but ask yourself, have you ever known anyone whose marriage was saved by a marriage counselor, whose drinking was cured by a psychiatrist, whose son was kept out of reform school by a social worker? In a badass, beer-glass brawl, would you rather have an academic liberal covering your back or a hobnailed redneck?

I drove to Bob Ward's Sporting Goods, a mountaineering and tackle-and-gun store I had heard about even in Louisiana, and used my MasterCard to buy a .38 revolver, a box of rounds and a cutaway holster for it, a secondhand twelve-gauge shotgun, and a box of double-aught buckshot. Back home I carried the tool chest from my truck into the kitchen, slipped the top shelf out of the cupboard, and tacked the .38 holster to its bottom. I replaced the shelf, loaded five rounds into the revolver, set the hammer on the empty chamber, slipped the revolver into the holster, and snapped the leather strap across the base of the hammer.

Then I took a hacksaw from the tool chest, lay the shotgun on the back-porch step, placed my knee hard against the stock, and sawed through the ventilated rib sight and both barrels ten inches above the chambers. I broke open the breech, looked through the barrels at the clean, oily whorls of light, plopped two double-aughts in the chambers, snapped the breech shut, set the safety, and put the shotgun on the top shelf of the closet in the front hallway.

With the .45 in the bedroom, there would now be no place in the house where I would not have almost immediate access to a weapon. It wasn't a panacea, but it was all I had. I could have spent time regretting that I had bounced Sally Dio's head off his van in front of his friends, but if he was involved with Harry Mapes or Star Drilling Company, and I believed he was, it would have been only a matter of time before I had trouble with the Dio family, anyway.

I was still tired from yesterday's drive over the Divide. No, it went deeper than that. I was tired of pursuing a course that seemed to have no resolution, of walking about in what seemed to be a waking nightmare, of feeling that I deserved all this, that somehow I had asked for it, that it was inevitable that I ride in a wood cart like a condemned seventeenth-century criminal, creaking over the cobbled street through the mob toward the elevated platform where a hooded man waited with wheel and iron bar.

I put on my gym shorts, running shoes, and a cutoff sweatshirt, and ran four miles along the river. It was a cloudless day, the sky hard and blue, and the pines high up on the mountains seemed to tremble with light. In the south the Bitterroots were as sharp and etched against the sky as if they had been cut out with a razor blade. The spring runoff of melted snow was starting to abate in the river, and great round boulders that had been covered by the current only two days ago were now exposed and hot-looking in the sun, the skeletal remains of hellgrammites welded to their sides. I ran all the way to the university district, thumped across the river on an abandoned railroad bridge, and looked down below at a fisherman horsing a rainbow out of the current on to the gravel. The riverbank was lined with cottonwoods and willows, and the wind blew out of Hellgate Canyon and flattened the new leaves so that the trees looked like they had changed, in a flick of the eye, to a pale green against the brown rush of water.

When I turned into my block my body was running with sweat, and I could feel the sun's heat deep in my skin. I did fifty push-ups off the back steps, fifty stomach crunches, one hundred leg lefts, and twenty-five chin-ups on the iron stanchion that supported the clothesline, while my neighbor's orange cat watched me from the garage roof. Then I sat quietly in the grass, my forearms on my knees, breathing the sweet smell of the clover, my heartbeat as regular and strong and temporarily as confident as it had been twenty years before.

The moon was down that night, somewhere beyond the black outline of the Bitterroots, and dry lightning leapt whitely between the clouds over the mountains. I could smell electricity and impending rain through the screen door, and the trees along the street were dark and shaking in the wind. At nine o'clock the phone rang.

'Hello,' I said.

'Can you come up here, Dave?' The line was heavy with static.

'Clete?'

'I need you up here, man. Real bad.'

'What is it?'

'Darlene . . . Fuck, man. She's dead.'

8

The regular babysitter wasn't home. I found Tess Regan's number in the telephone book, called her, then took Alafair over to her house.

An hour and a half later I drove up the dirt lane to Clete's small redwood house on Flathead Lake. All the lights were on. It was raining, and the lake was black in the background, and I could see the rain blowing in the light from the windows. Farther up the dirt lane, past the electronic gate, the Dio house was dark. I knocked on Clete's front door; when no one answered, I went inside.

I heard a toilet flush somewhere in back, then he walked out of the bedroom with a wet towel held to his mouth. His face looked bloodless, the skin as tight as a lampshade. His tie was pulled loose, and his white shirt was wet down the front. He sat down at the table by the sliding glass doors and drank noisily out of a coffee cup, his whole hand wrapped around the cup to keep it from shaking. On the table were a carton of milk and a fifth of Cutty Sark. He drew in deeply on a Camel and held the smoke down as though he were taking a hit off a reefer. His breath jerked in his chest when he let the smoke out. Out on the lake a lighted, anchored sailboat pitched in the troughs.

He rubbed the towel on his mouth again, then on the back of his thick neck.

'I can't keep anything down. I think I got a peptic ulcer,' he said.

'Where is she?'

'In the main bathroom.' He looked up at me with his poached face and swallowed.

'Get yourself together.'

'I came back from Missoula, she was like that. I can't take this shit.'

But I wasn't listening to him. I walked down the hall to the bathroom. When I looked inside I had to clasp one hand on the doorjamb. The safety razor lay on the tile floor, glued thickly to the surface with her blood. She was nude and had slipped down in the tub on her side so that only half her face floated above the soapy red water. There was a deep incision across the inside of both forearms.

Oh, Lord God, I thought, and had to take a deep breath and look away.

She had bled until she was almost white. I sat on the edge of the tub and touched her soft, wet hair with my fingertips. It felt like wet feathers.

Written in lipstick on the bathroom mirror were the words:

> C,
>
> > *Checking out,*
> > *Bye-bye, love,*
> >
> > > D

I ran my hand through my hair and stared numbly at her. Then I saw the tiny scratches and the red discolorations, like pale strawberry bruises, like love bites, on her neck and shoulder. I took a sheet out of the bedroom and draped it over her, then went back into the living room.

Clete was pouring another scotch and milk at the table. The smoke from his Camel curled up over the nicotine stains on his fingers. The skin around his eyes flexed abruptly when he saw my expression.

'Hey, you get that look out of your face, man,' he said.

'What were you doing in Missoula?' I said.

'I pick up cigars for Sal's old man. There's only one store in Missoula that carries his brand.'

'Why tonight?'

'He told me to.'

'Why haven't you called the locals?'

'They're going to bust me for it.'

'For a suicide?' I watched his face carefully.

'It's no suicide. You know it's not.'

'Clete, if you did this—'

'Are you crazy? I was going to ask her to marry me. I'm seeing a therapist now because I'm fucked up, but when I'm straightened out I was going to see about taking us back to New Orleans, living a regular life, opening up a bar maybe, getting away from the greaseballs.'

I looked steadily into his eyes. They stared back at me, hard as green marbles, as though they had no lids. The stitched scar that ran from the bridge of his nose through one eyebrow looked as red as a bicycle patch. Then his eyes broke, and he took a hit of the scotch and milk.

'I don't care what you believe,' he said. 'If you think I got jealous over you and her, you're right. But I didn't blame her for it. I got a condition I can't do anything about right now. The therapist says it's because of all that stuff back in New Orleans and because I'm working for greaseballs and pretending I like it when actually I wouldn't spit on these guys. But I didn't blame her. You got that?'

'She told you?'

'What's to tell? There's ways a guy knows. Butt out of my personal affairs, Streak.'

'I put a sheet over her. Don't go back in there till the cops get here.' I picked up the telephone. The moon had broken through a crack in the clouds over the mountains on the far side of the lake, and I could see the froth on the waves blowing in the wind.

'You saw the bruises?' Clete said.

'Yes.'

'Most of the locals aren't real bright. But when the coroner does the autopsy, they're going to pick them up.'

'Maybe. What's the point.'

He drank out of the cup again, then drew in on the cigarette. His breath was ragged coming out.

'You're not big on sympathy tonight, are you?' he said.

'To be honest, I don't know what I feel toward you, Clete.'

'It's Sal. It's gotta be. I'm going to be on ice, he's going to be playing rock 'n' roll with Dixie Lee and the Tahoe cornholers. I'm going to nail that fucker, man. I'm going to blow up his shit. I'm going to do it in pieces, too.'

'What's his motive?' I set the receiver back down.

'He doesn't need one. He's psychotic.'

'I don't buy that.'

'She was on to something. It's got to do with oil, with Dixie Lee, maybe with dope. I don't know. She believed in spirits. She thought they told her things. Then yesterday she saw Sal chopping up lines for Dixie Lee and a couple of the Tahoe broads, and she told him he was a fucking cancer, that one day his kind were going to be driven into holes in the earth. Can you dig that? Holes in the earth.'

'Where are the Dios now?'

'They said they were going to play up in Bigfork.'

'Have you heard Sally Dio say anything about a guy named Charlie?'

'Charlie? No. Who is he?'

'A hit man out of Vegas.'

'Wait a minute, they picked up a guy at the airport in Missoula last night. I thought he was just another one of Sal's buttwipes. I offered to drive in and get him, but Sal said I needed a night off.'

'What did he look like?'

'I don't know, I didn't see him.'

The clouds over the lake were silver where the moon had broken through, and the water below was black and glazed with light.

'I'm going to call the cops now, then I'm taking off,' I said. 'I don't want my name in it, all right?'

'Whatever you say.' Then he said, 'You're pretty cool. A cool operator.

You always were. Nobody shakes ole Streak's cookie bag. They could strike matches on your soul and not make you flinch.'

I didn't answer him. I walked out into the misting rain and the broken moonlight and drove my pickup truck back down the lakefront road toward Polson. The cherry trees in the orchards were dripping with rainwater in my headlights. The wooded hills were dark, and down on the beach I could see a white line of foam sliding up on the sand. With the windows up I was sweating inside the cab. I passed a neon-lit bar, a boat dock strung with light bulbs, a wind-sheltered cove where the pines grew right down to the water's edge, a clapboard cottage where people were having a party and somebody was still barbecuing in the darkness of the porch. Then I turned east of Polson, at the foot of the lake, and headed for the Jocko Valley, and I knew that I would be all right. But suddenly the clouds closed over the moon again, the sky became as black as scorched metal, and a hard wind blew out of the ice-capped Missions. A curtain of driving rain swept across meadow, irrigation canal, slough, poplar windbreak, and willow-lined stream. Lightning leapt from the crest of the Missions to the black vault of sky overhead, thunder rolled out of the canyons, and hailstones the size of dimes clattered on my truck like tack hammers.

I pulled to the side of the road, sweat boiling off my face, my windows thick with steam. The truck shook violently in the wind. My knuckles were round and white on the steering wheel. I felt my teeth grinding, felt the truck's metal joints creak and strain, the tailgate tremble and reverberate against the hooked chain; then a shudder went though me that made my mouth drop open, as though someone had clapped me on both ears with the flats of his hands. When I closed my eyes I thought I saw a copper-colored stream beaten with raindrops, and in it a brown trout with a torn mouth and blood roaring in clouds from its gills.

The next morning I walked down to the old brick church next to Alafair's school. The sun was brilliant in the bowl of blue sky above the valley. High up on one of the mountains above Hellgate Canyon, I could see horses grazing in the new grass and lupine below the timber, and the trees along the river were dark green from the rain. The current looked deep and cold between the sunbaked boulders that protruded from the water's surface. Someone had planted a garden by the side door of the church, and yellow roses and spearmint bloomed against the red-brick wall. I went inside, crossed myself at the holy water fount, and knelt in a pew close to the altar. Like almost all Catholic churches, this one smelled like stone and water, incense, and burning wax. I think that fact is no accident inside a Catholic church. I think perhaps the catacombs, where the early Christians celebrated mass, smelled the same way.

I prayed for Darlene, for Alafair, my father and brother, and finally for myself. A muscular, blond-headed priest in black trousers, scuffed cowboy boots, and a T-shirt came out of the sacristy and began removing the flower vases from the altar. I walked to the communion rail, introduced myself, and asked if he would hear my confession.

'Let's go out into the garden,' he said.

Between the church and the rectory was a sunny enclosure of lawn and flower beds, stone benches, bird feeders, and a small greenhouse. The priest and I sat next to one another on a bench, and I told him about my relationship with Darlene and finally about her death. While I talked he flipped small pieces of dirt at the leaves of a potted caladium. When I finished he was silent a moment; then he said. 'I'm not quite sure what you're confessing to. Do you feel that you used this woman?'

'I don't know.'

'Do you think you contributed to her death?'

'I don't think so. But I'm not sure.'

'I think that something else is troubling you, something that we're not quite talking about.'

I told him about Annie, the shotgun blasts that leapt in the darkness of our bedroom, the sheet drenched with her blood, the coldness of her fingers when I put them in my mouth. I could hear him breathing next to me. When I looked up at him I saw him swallow.

'I'm sorry,' he said.

'It won't go away, Father. I don't believe it ever will.'

He picked up another piece of hard dirt off the grass and started to flip it at the plant, then dropped it from his hand.

'I feel inadequate in trying to advise you,' he said. 'But I think you're a good man and you're doing yourself an unnecessary injury. You were lonely when you met the Indian lady. You obviously cared for her. Sometimes maybe it's a vanity to judge ourselves. Did you ever think of it that way? You make your statement in front of God, then you let Him be the measure of right and wrong in your life. And I don't believe you caused your wife's death. Sometimes when that kind of evil comes into our lives, we can't explain it, so we blame it on God or ourselves. In both cases we're wrong. Maybe it's time you let yourself out of prison.'

I didn't answer him.

'Do you want absolution?'

'Yes.'

'What for?'

'I don't know. For my inadequacies. My failures. For any grief or injury I've brought an innocent person. That's the best I can say. I can't describe it.'

His forearms were folded on his thighs. He looked down at his boots, but I could see a sad light in his eyes. He took a deep breath.

'I wish I could be of more help to you,' he said. 'We're not always up to the situation. Our experience is limited.'

'You've been more than kind.'

'Give it time, Mr Robicheaux.' Then he smiled and said, 'Not everybody gets to see a blinding light on the way to Damascus.'

When I left that sunny, green enclosure between the buildings, he was kneeling down in a flower bed, troweling out a hole for the pink-and-gray-striped caladium, his eyes already intent with his work, his day obviously ordered and serene and predictable in a way that I could not remember mine being since I walked off the plane into a diesel-laced layer of heat at Tan Son Nhut air base in 1964.

I wanted to go into yesterday. And I don't think that's always bad. Sometimes you simply have to walk through a door in your mind and lose thirty or forty years in order to remember who you are. Maybe it's a self-deception, a mental opiate that I use to escape my problems, but I don't care. We are the sum total of what we have done and where we have been, and I sincerely believe that in many ways the world in which I grew up was better than the one in which we live today. I stuck a paperback copy of Ernest Gaines's *Of Love and Dust* in my pocket, and walked down to Bonner Park and sat on a bench under a maple tree and read. The fountain and concrete wading pool looked dry and white in the sun, and in the distance the mountains were a sharp blue against the clouds. The wind was cool blowing out of the shade, but I was already inside the novel, back on a hot sugarcane and sweet potato plantation in South Louisiana in the 1940s. No, that's not really true. I was back in New Iberia the summer after my second year in college, when my brother, Jimmie, and I worked on an offshore seismograph rig and bought a 'forty-six Ford convertible that we put dual Hollywood mufflers on, lowering blocks and fender skirts, painted canary yellow and lacquered and waxed until the metal seemed to have the soft, deep gleam of butter. It was the best summer of my life. I fell in love seriously for the first time, with a girl who lived on Spanish Lake, outside of town, and as is always the case with your first love, I remembered every detail of the season, as though I had never experienced summer before, sometimes with a poignancy that would almost break my heart. She was a Cajun like myself, and her hair was brown and bleached in streaks by the sun so that it looked like dark honey when the wind blew it. We danced at Voorhies Roof Garden in Lafayette and Slick's in St Martinville, drank twenty-cent long-necked Jax beer under the oaks at Deer's Drive-In in New Iberia; we fished for white trout out on the salt, went to crab boils and fish fries at Cypermort Point and drove home in the lilac evening, down that long two-lane black-top parish road between the cypress and the oaks, with the wind warm off the gulf, the new cane green in the fields, the western sky streaked with fire, the cicadas deafening in the trees.

She was one of those girls who love everything about the man they choose to be theirs. She never argued or contended, she was happy in any place or situation where we were together, and I only had to touch her cheek with my fingers to make her come close to me, to press herself against me, to kiss my throat and put her hand inside my shirt. It rained every afternoon, and sometimes after it cleared and clouds were pink and maroon on the horizon, we'd drive down the levee to the dock where my father kept his boat, the cypress dripping into the dead water, and in the soft light her face would have the color and loveliness of a newly opened flower.

Jimmy Clanton's 'Just a Dream' was on every jukebox in southern Louisiana that summer, and car radios at the drive-in were always tuned to 'Randy's Record Shop' in Memphis at midnight, when Randy kicked it off with 'Sewannee River Boogie'. Each morning was one of expectation, of smoky light in the pecan trees outside my bedroom window, of innocent desire and the confidence that within a few hours I would be with her again, and that absolutely nothing would ever come between us. But it ended over an unreasonable and youthful concern. I hurt her without meaning to, in a way that I could not explain to myself, much less to her, and my silence caused her an even greater injury that these many years later still troubles me on occasion.

I'll never forget that summer, though. It's the cathedral I sometimes visit when everything else fails, when the heart seems poisoned, the earth stricken, and dead leaves blow across the soul's windows like bit of dried parchment.

My experience has been that grief and loss do not necessarily become more acceptable with time, and commitment to them is of no value to either the living or the dead. The next morning I was back in the Lake County courthouse.

The sheriff looked as hard and round as a wooden barrel. His dark blue suit was spotted with cigarette ash that he had tried to clean off with a wet paper towel; he wore his gray hair in a crew cut, his white shirt lapels ironed flat so that his chest hair stuck out like a tangle of wire. He was one of those elected law officers who have probably been diesel mechanics or log-truck drivers before someone had talked them into running for office. He sat at the corner of his desk when he talked, rather than behind it, and smoked a cigarette and looked out the window at the lake with such private concentration that I had the feeling that he already knew the outcome of our conversation, and that he was talking to me now only because of a public relations obligation that the office imposed upon him.

'You were a homicide detective in New Orleans?' he said.

'That's right.'

'Then a detective in the sheriff's department in . . . what's the name of that place?'

'New Iberia. Where they make Tabasco sauce.' I smiled at him, but his eyes were looking through his cigarette smoke at the blue wink off the lake.

'You know a DEA agent named Dan Nygurski?'

'Yep.'

'He was here yesterday. He said I could count on you coming to see me.'

'I see.'

'He said I should tell you to go back to Louisiana. What do you think about that?'

'Advice is cheap.'

'You wondering about the coroner's report?'

I let out my breath. 'Yes, sir, I am,' I said.

'Because you think she was murdered?'

'That's right.'

'What for? Who had reason to kill her?'

'Check out Sally Dee's record. Check on a guy name Harry Mapes, too.' I felt the heat start to rise in my voice, and I paused. 'I'd give some thought to Purcel, too.'

'From what I've been told, these are all people you've had trouble with at one time or another. You think you're being entirely objective here?'

'The Dios are animals. So is Mapes. Purcel killed a guy for some para-military crazies in New Orleans. I wouldn't underestimate the potential of any of them.'

'Why would Purcel kill her?'

He looked at me with interest for the first time. I dropped my eyes to my shoes. Then I looked back at him.

'I was involved with Darlene,' I said. 'He knew about it.'

The sheriff nodded and didn't reply. He opened his desk drawer and took out a clipboard on which were attached Xeroxed copies of the kinds of forms that county medical examiners use in autopsies.

'You were right about the bruises,' he said. 'She had them on her neck and her shoulders.'

I waited for him to continue.

'She also had a bump on the back of her head,' he said.

'Yes?'

'But it's going down as a suicide.'

'What?'

'You got it the first time.'

'What's the matter with you? You're discounting your own autopsy report?'

'Listen, Robicheaux, I don't have any evidence that she didn't kill herself. On the other hand, I have every indication that she did. She could have hit her head on the tub. She could have gotten the bruises anywhere. Maybe you don't like to hear this, but Indians around here get into trouble. They get drunk, they fight in bars, families beat the shit out of each other. I'm not knocking them. I've got nothing against them. I think they get a lousy break. But that's the way it is. Look, if I suspected anybody, it'd have to be Purcel. But I don't believe he did it. The guy's really strung out on this.'

'What about Sally Dee?'

'You give me the motive, you put him in the house, I'll cut the warrant.'

'You're making a big mistake, Sheriff.'

'Tell me how. Fill me in on that, please.'

'You're taking the easy choice, you're letting them slide. The Dios sense weakness in you, they'll eat you alive.'

He opened a deep drawer in the bottom of his desk and took out a baton. The layers of black paint were chipped, and the grip had been grooved in a leather and drilled to hold a leather wrist loop. He dropped it loudly on the desktop.

'The guy I replaced gave me this the day I took office,' he said. 'He told me, "Everybody doesn't have to go to jail." And there's days when maybe I got that kind of temptation. I see Dio in the supermarket and I shudder. This is good country. He doesn't belong here. But I don't bust heads, I don't let my deputies do it, either. If that don't sit right with somebody, that's their problem.' He mashed out his cigarette without looking at me.

'I guess I'll be on my way,' I said, and stood up. Then, as an afterthought, I said, 'Did the autopsy show anything else unusual?'

'Not to me or the medical examiner.'

'What else?'

'I think we've ended this discussion.'

'Come on, Sheriff, I'm almost out of your day.'

He glanced again at his clipboard.

'What she had for supper, traces of semen in the vagina.'

I took a breath and looked out the window at the electric blueness of the lake in the sunlight and the low green hills and pine trees in the distance. Then I pinched my eyes and the bridge of my nose with my fingers and put on my sunglasses.

'You were on the money about Cletus,' I said.

'What are you talking about?'

'He didn't do it. He's impotent. She was raped before she was murdered.'

He sucked his teeth, smiled to himself, shook his head slightly, and opened his newspaper to the sports page.

'You'll have to excuse me,' he said. 'It's the only chance I get to read it.'

I found out from the medical examiner's office that Darlene's family had picked up the body that morning and that the funeral was the next afternoon on the Blackfeet Reservation. The next day was Saturday, so Alafair drove across the mountains with me to Dupuyer, on the south end of the reservation. I found out from the local newspaper that the service was to be held at a Baptist church up on the Marias River at two o'clock. We had lunch in a clapboard café that was built on to the side of a grease-stained, cinder-block filling station. I had little appetite and couldn't finish my plate, and I stared out the window at the dusty street while Alafair ate her hamburger. The bars were doing a good business. Rusted pickup trucks and oversized jalopy gas burners were parked at an angle to the curb, and sometimes whole families sat listlessly in them while the old man was inside the juke joint. People who looked both devastated and broke from the night before sat on the curb, their attention fixed on nothing, their mouths open like those of silent, newly hatched birds.

Then I saw Alafair watching them, her eyes squinting, as though a camera lens were opening momentarily in her mind.

'What do you see, little guy?' I said.

'Are those Indians?'

'Sure.'

'They're like me?'

'Well, not exactly, but maybe you're part Indian. An Indian Cajun from Bayou Teche,' I said.

'What language they talk, Dave?'

'English, just like you and me.'

'They don't know no Spanish words?'

'No, I'm afraid not.'

I saw a question mark, then a troubled look slip into her face.

'What's on your mind, little guy?' I asked.

'The people in my village. They sat in front of the clinic. Like those people there.' Her eyes were looking at an elderly man and woman on the curb. The woman was fat and wore army shoes and dirty athletic socks, and her knees were splayed open so that you could see up her dress. 'Dave, they ain't got soldiers here, have they?'

'You get those thoughts out of your head,' I said. 'This is a good country, a safe place. You have to believe what I tell you, Alf. What happened in your village doesn't happen here.'

She put her hamburger on her plate and lowered her eyes. The corners of her mouth were turned downward. Her bangs hung in a straight line across her tan forehead.

'It did to Annie,' she said.

I looked away from her face and felt myself swallow. The sky had clouded, the wind had come up and was blowing the dust in the street, and the sun looked like a thin yellow wafer in the south.

The funeral was in a wood-frame church whose white paint had blistered and peeled into scales. All the people inside the church were Indians, people with braided hair, work-seamed faces, hands that handled lumber without gloves in zero weather, except for Clete and Dixie Lee, who sat in a front pew to the side of the casket. It was made of black metal, lined and cushioned with white silk, fitted with gleaming brass handles. Her hair was black against the silk, her face rouged, her mouth red as though she had just had a drink of cold water. She had been dressed in a doeskin shirt, and a beaded necklace with a purple glass bird on it, wings outstretched in flight, rested on her breast. Only the top portion of the casket was opened, so that her forearms were not visible.

The skin of Clete's face was shiny and stretched tight on the bone. He looked like a boiled ham inside his blue suit. I could see his cigarettes tight against his shirt pocket; his big wrists stuck out of his coat sleeves; his collar had popped loose under the knot of his tie; the strap of his nylon shoulder holster made a hard line across his back. His eyes had the glare of a man staring at a match flame.

I didn't hear, or rather listen to, much of what the preacher said. He was a gaunt and nervous man who read from the Old Testament and made consoling remarks in the best fashion he was probably capable of, but the rain that began clicking against the roof and windows, sweeping in a lighted sheet across the hardpan fields and river basin, was a more accurate statement of the feelings that were inside me.

I made a peculiar prayer. It's a prayer that sometimes I say, one that is perhaps self-serving, but because I believe that God is not limited by time and space as we are, I believe perhaps that He can influence the past even though it has already happened. So sometimes when I'm alone, especially at night, in the dark, and I begin to dwell on the unbearable suffering that people probably experienced before their deaths, I ask God to retroactively relieve their pain, to be with them in mind and body, to numb their senses, to cool whatever flame licked at their eyes in their final moments. I said that prayer now for Darlene. Then I said it again for my wife, Annie.

The cemetery, a windswept and weed-grown square of land enclosed by wire strung between concrete posts, was located a short distance from the edge of the river bottoms. The Marias basin was string country; the bluffs and the gradated channelings of the river looked as if they had been formed with a putty knife, the clay and slit layered and smoothed in ascending plateaus. Even the colors were strange. The eroded bluffs on the far side of the basin were gray and yellow and streaked with a burnt orange that looked like rust. The water in the main channel was high and brown, and leafless cottonwood limbs floated in it. The sky was sealed with gray clouds from horizon to horizon; in the thin rain the country-side looked as if it were poisoned by the infusion of toxic waste. This was the place Darlene had told me about, the site of what was called the Baker massacre of 1870. On this afternoon, except for a solitary purple dogwood blooming by the cemetery fence, it looked as though the spring had never touched the land here, as thought this place had been predestined as moonscape, a geographical monument to what was worst in us.

I watched the pallbearers lower Darlene's casket into the freshly dug hole in the cemetery. The piled orange-and-gray dirt next to the grave was slick with rainwater. The graves around hers were littered with jelly glasses and dime-store vases filled with dead wild-flowers. A small American flag lay sideways on a soldier's grave, spotted with mud. A picture of a little girl, not more than five or six, was wrapped in plastic and tied to a small stone marker with baling wire. On the incline to one side of the cemetery a long length of black plastic pipe ran from a house trailer down to the lip of the river basin. The pipe had cracked at a joint, and a stream of yellow-black effluent had leaked its way in rivulets into one side of the cemetery.

I walked over to the pickup truck, where Alafair slept on the seat with the door open; I stared out over the wet land. In the distance I could see rain falling heavily on some low gray-green hills dotted with a few pine trees. After a while I heard cars and pickups driving away over the dirt road, rocks knocking up under their fenders; then it became quiet again, except for the sound of the two gravediggers spading the mound of dirt on Darlene's casket. Then a strange thing happened: the wind began to blow across the fields, flattening the grass, wrinkling the pools of rain-water in the road. It blew stronger and stronger, so unexpectedly hard, in fact, that I opened my mouth to clear my ears and looked at the sky for the presence of new storm clouds or even a funnel. A cloud shifted temporarily away from the sun and a curtain of light moved suddenly across the bluffs and the gradated layers of the river basin. As it did, the wind stripped away the purple flowers of the dogwood blooming by the cemetery fence and blew them in a pocket of air out over the river's surface like a fragmented bird.

Then it was all over. The sky was gray again, the wind dropped, the weeds stood up stiffly in the fields.

I heard someone standing behind me.

'It looks like the end of the earth, don't it?' Dixie Lee said. He wore a gray western suit and a maroon shirt that had pearl snap buttons on it. 'Or what the earth'll look like the day Jesus ends it.'

I saw Clete behind the wheel of Dixie's pink Cadillac convertible, waiting for him.

'Who paid for the casket?' I said.

'Clete.'

'Who did it, Dixie?'

'I don't know.'

'Sally Dio?'

'I can't believe something like that.'

'Don't tell me that.'

'Fuck, I don't know.' He looked at Alafair, who was sleeping with her rump in the air. 'I'm sorry . . . but I don't know. I ain't sure about anything anymore.'

I continued to look out over the river flats, the swirl of dark current in the middle of the river, and the orange-streaked bluffs beyond.

'It ain't any good to stand out here studying on things,' he said. 'Convoy on back with us and we'll stop in Lincoln for something to eat.'

'I'll be along after a while.'

I heard him light a cigarette, click his lighter shut and put it in his pocket. I could smell his cigarette smoke drifting from behind me.

'Walk over here with me. I don't want to wake up that little girl,' he said.

'What is it, Dixie?' I said irritably.

'Some people say life's a bitch and you die. I don't know if that's right or not. But it's what you're starting to think right now, and it ain't your way. You get yourself a lot of distance between you and them kind of thoughts, son. Look, you got involved with her. Everything ain't lost on me. I know what you're feeling.'

'You're sober.'

'So I eased up a couple of days. I got my own program. You guys stay sober a day at a time. I get drunk a day at a time. Convoy on back with us. Give me a break from Clete. Sonofabitch is driving me crazy. It's like being next to a balloon that's fixing to float down on a hot cigarette. I tell you, he catches the guy that did this, it ain't ever getting to the jailhouse.'

I followed them back toward the Divide, across the greening plains and into the mountains, up the glistening black highway into thick stands of ponderosa pine, blue shadow in the canyons, white water breaking over the boulders in the streambeds far below, long strips of cloud hanging wetly in the trees. It was misting heavily in the town of Lincoln; the air was cool and purple in the twilight and smelled of cut logs and woodsmoke and food cooking and the diesel exhaust from the eighteen-wheel log trucks idling in café parking lots. I saw Clete and Dixie pull off the road next to a café and look back at me. I shifted into second, accelerated through the traffic light, and kept going through town. Alafair looked at me in the light from the dashboard. Her window was half down, and there were drops of water in her hair and on her face.

'We ain't going to stop?' she said.

'How about I buy you a buffalo burger on the other side of the mountain?'

'They wanted you to stop with them, didn't they?'

'Those guys want lots of things. But like somebody once told me, I just don't want to be there when they find it.'

'Sometimes you don't make no sense, Dave.'

'I've got to have a talk with your teacher,' I said.

On Monday morning I started to call my lawyer, then decided I didn't need higher phone bills or more depressing news. If he had gotten a continuance, he would have called me, and anything else he might have to say would be largely irrelevant. I walked Alafair to school, then ate a bowl of Grape-Nuts at the kitchen table and tried to think, as I had all day Sunday, of a reasonable plan to push Harry Mapes and Sally Dio to the wall. But I was quickly running out of options. I would never be able to find the bodies of the dead Indians, much less prove that they were killed by Harry Mapes and Dalton Vidrine. I wondered how I had ever thought I could solve my legal problems by myself, anyway. I wasn't a cop; I had no authority, access to police information, power of warrant, arrest, or interrogation. Most motion pictures portray private investigators as chivalric outsiders who solve crimes that mystify the bumbling flatfeet of officialdom. The reality is that most PIs are former jocks, barroom bouncers, and fired or resigned cops who would cut off their fingers to still have their civil service ratings. Their licenses gave them about as much legal authority as a postman.

I could go back on the eastern slope of the Divide and start checking oil leases in county courthouses. Maybe somehow I would tie Dio into Harry Mapes and Star Drilling Company and the Indians, but even if the connection existed, how would they help my defense on the murder charge in Louisiana? And who had killed Darlene and why? My thoughts became like dogs snapping at each other.

I was distracted by the sound of somebody walking between my house and the neighbor's. I got up from the table and looked through the bedroom door and out the screen window. In the leafy shade I saw a thick-bodied blond man in a yellow hard hat and denim shirt with cut-off sleeves disappear through some bushes into the backyard. A tool belt clinked on his side. I walked quickly to the back door and saw him standing in the sunlight, in the middle of the lawn, staring up at the telephone pole with his hands on his hips. His biceps were big and red with sunburn.

'Could I help you?' I said.

'Telephone company. There's trouble on the line.'

I nodded and didn't reply. He continued to stare up the pole, then he glanced back at me again.

'Did you use your phone this morning?' he asked.

'No.'

'Did it ring and just stop?'

'No.'

'Well, it's no big thing. I got to get up on your pole, and then maybe I'll have to use your phone in a little bit. We'll get it fixed, though.' He grinned at me, then walked out into the alley and behind the garage where I couldn't see him.

I went into the hallway, picked up the telephone, and listened to the dial tone. Then I dialed the operator. When she answered, I hung up. I looked out the back door again and couldn't see the repairman. I sat back down at the kitchen table and continued eating from my cereal bowl.

Something bothered me about the man, but I couldn't think what it was. Maybe I'm just wired, I thought. Or maybe I wanted the dragons to come finally into my own yard. No, that wasn't it. There was something wrong in the picture, something that was missing or that didn't fit. I went to the front of the house and stepped out on the porch. There was no telephone truck parked on the street. Four houses down a short man in a cloth cap with two canvas sacks cross-strung on his chest was putting handbills with rubber bands on people's doors. The bags were full and heavy, and there were sweat marks on his T-shirt.

I returned to the kitchen and thought I heard somebody between the houses again. I looked out the screen door, but the backyard was empty and the repairman was nowhere in sight. Then two doves settled on the telephone wire, and I glanced at the pole for the first time. The lowest iron climbing spikes were set in the wood some fifteen feet above the ground so children could not get up on the pole.

That's it, I thought. He didn't have climbing spurs strapped on to his boots and ankles, and he didn't wear a safety belt. I went back into the hallway and picked up the telephone receiver. It was dead.

I took the .45 out of the drawer of the nightstand next to my bed. It felt cold and heavy in my hand. I pulled back the receiver, eased a hollow-point round into the chamber, and reset the hammer. It was quiet outside, and the bushes next to the bedroom windows made deep shadows on the screens. I went to the front door just as the handbill carrier was stepping up on the porch. I stuck the .45 inside the back of my trousers and went outside.

'Listen, go to the little grocery on the corner, dial the operator, ask for the police,' I said. 'All you have to say is "Assault in progress at 778 Front Street." Can you do that for me, podna?'

'What?' He was middle-aged, but his stiff, straw-colored hair sticking out from under his cap and his clear blue eyes gave him a childlike appearance.

'I've got some trouble here. I need some help. I'll give you five dollars after the cops get here. Look, just tell the operator you need the cops out here and give them this number—' I pointed to the tin numerals on the screen door. Then I took out my pocketknife, pried the set of attached numbers loose from the wood, and handed it to him. 'Just read the numbers into the phone. Seven-seventy-eight Front Street. Then say "Emergency." Okay, podna?'

'What's going on?' His face looked confused and frightened.

'I'll fill you in later.'

'Just dial?' A drop of sweat ran out of his cloth cap.

'You got it.'

He started off the porch, the heavy canvas sacks swinging from his sides.

'Leave your sacks here. Okay?' I said.

'Yeah, sure. I'll be right back with the cops.'

He headed down the street, the metal house numbers in his hand. I watched him go inside the little yellow-brick grocery store on the corner, then I headed around the side of the house, through the shrubs and shadows toward the backyard. I could see my telephone box, partly obscured by hedge under the bathroom window, and I was sure that the wires on it had been cut; but before I could look I saw the repairman walk across the sunny lawn toward my back door.

I moved quickly up to the edge of the house, the .45 in my right hand. I could feel the moisture in my palm against the thin slick of oil on the metal. The wind was cool between the houses and smelled of damp earth and old brick. The repairman pushed his yellow hard hat up on his forehead, rested his hand on the leather pouch of his tool bag, and started to knock on the screen door. Surprise time, motherfucker, I thought, cocked the .45, stepped out into the yard, and pointed it at him with both hands.

'Right there! Hands behind your head, down on your knees!' I shouted.

'What?' His face went white with shock. He stared incredulously at the automatic.

'Do it! Now!'

I saw his right hand flutter on his tool pouch.

'You're an inch from the next world, bubba,' I said.

'All right, man! What the hell is this? All right! All right! I'm not arguing.' He knelt on the wood steps and laced his fingers behind his neck. His hard hat slipped down over his eyes. His arms looked thick and red in the sunlight, and I could see the taut whiteness of his chest where the sleeves of his denim shirt were cut off. He was breathing loudly.

'You got me mixed up with somebody else,' he said.

'Where's your truck?'

'Down the street. In the fucking alley.'

'Because you're shy about parking it on the street. With your left hand

551

unstrap your tool belt, let it drop, then put your hand behind your head again.'

'Look, call my company. You got the wrong guy.'

'Take off the belt.'

His hand worked the buckle loose, and the heavy pouch clattered to the step. I rattled the tools loose out on the concrete pad – pliers, blade and Phillips screwdrivers, wire cutters, an ice pick with a small cork on the tip. I held the ice pick up to the corner of his vision.

'You want to explain this?' I asked.

'Wasps build nests inside the boxes sometimes. I use it to clean out the corners.'

'Drop your wallet behind you.'

His fingers went into his back pocket, jerked the wallet loose, and let it fall. I squatted down, the .45 pointed at the center of his back, picked up the wallet, moved back on the grass, and shook everything out. The back of his neck was red and hot-looking in the bright air, and his shirt was peppered with sweat marks. I fingered through the dollar bills, ID cards, photographs, and scraps of paper at my feet, and gradually became more and more uncomfortable. He had a Montana driver's license with his picture on it, a social security card with the same name on it, a local Elks membership card, and two tickets to a US West Communications employees dance.

I let out my breath.

'Where did you say your truck was?' I asked.

'Down the alley.'

'Let's take a look,' I said, getting to my feet. 'No, you walk ahead of me.'

He stayed in front of me, as I had told him, but by this time I had eased down the hammer on the .45 and had let it hang loose at my side. We walked past the garage into the alley. Parked at the end of the alley, hard against somebody's toolshed in the shade of a maple tree, was his company truck. I stuck the pistol in my back pocket. His face was livid with anger, and he closed and unclosed his fists at his sides.

'I'm sorry,' I said.

'You're sorry? You sonofabitch, I ought to knock your fucking teeth down your throat.'

'You got a right to. You probably won't understand this, but somebody is trying to do me and maybe a little girl a lot of harm. I thought you were that guy.'

'Yeah? Well, you ought to call the cops, then. I tell you, buddy, I feel like ripping your ass.'

'I don't blame you.'

'That's all you got to say? You don't blame me?'

'You want a free shot?'

There was an intense, measured look in his eye. Then the moment passed. He pointed his finger at me.

'You can tell the cops about it. They'll be out to see you. I guarantee it,' he said. Then he walked to the back steps, put his tools back in his leather pouch, and replaced all the articles in his wallet. He didn't bother to look at me as he recrossed the lawn toward the alley and his parked truck. My face felt round and tight in the wind.

Two uniformed cops were there ten minutes later. I didn't try to explain my troubles with Sal Dio; instead, I simply told them that I was an ex-police officer, that the DEA had warned me that an attempt might be made on my life, that they could call Dan Nygurski in Great Falls to confirm my story, and that I had made a serious mistake for which I wanted to apologize. They were irritated and even vaguely contemptuous, but the telephone man had not filed charges against me, he had only phoned in a report, and I knew that it wasn't going anywhere and that all I had to do was avoid provoking them.

'I just didn't act very smart, I'm sorry,' I said.

'Where is the gun?' the older of the two cops said. He was big and bareheaded and wore pilot's sunglasses.

'In the house.'

'I suggest you leave it there. I also suggest you call us the next time you think somebody's trying to hurt you.'

'Yes, sir, I'll do that. Actually I tried. Didn't the handbill man call you all?'

'The what?'

'A guy who puts handbills on front doors. I sent him to the grocery to call you when I thought my line was cut.' I realized that I was getting back into the story again when I should let it drop.

'I don't know anything about it. Believe me, I hope I don't hear any more reports from this address. Are we fairly straight on that?'

'Yes, sir, you're quite clear.'

They left, and I tried to reorder my morning. When the squad car had pulled up out front, some of the neighbors had come out on the porches. I determined that I was not going to be a curiosity who would hide in his house, so I put on my running shorts and an old pair of boat shoes and began pulling weeds in the front flower bed. The sun was warm on my back, and the clover among the rye grass in the yard was full of small bees. The willow trees out on the river were bent in the breeze. After a few minutes a man's shadow fell across my face and shoulders.

'The phone was broke. I had to go up on Broadway,' the man said. His clear blue eyes looked down at me from under his cap.

'Oh, yeah, how you doing?' I said. 'Look, I'm sorry to send you running off like that. It was sort of a misfire.'

'I saw the cops leave from the corner. So I had me a soda. Everything worked out all right, huh?'

'Yeah, and I owe you five bucks. Right?'

'Well, that's what you said. But you don't have to, though. It was three blocks before I found a phone.'

'A deal's a deal, partner. Come inside. I'll get my wallet.'

I opened the screen and walked ahead of him. He caught the screen with his elbow rather than his hand when he came in.

'Could I have a glass of water?' he asked.

'Sure.'

We went into the kitchen, and as I took a jelly glass out of the cabinet I saw him slip both hands into his back pockets and smile. I filled the glass from the tap and thought how his smile reminded me of lips painted on an Easter egg. He was still smiling when I turned around and he raised the slapjack and came across my forehead with it. It was black and flat and weighted at the end with lead, and I felt it knock into bone and rake across my eye and nose, then I was falling free into a red-black place deep under the basement floor, with a jelly glass that tumbled in slow motion beside me.

I woke as though I were rising from a dark, wet bubble into light, except my arms were locked behind my head, I couldn't breathe or cry out, and I was drowning. Water cascaded over my face and ran down my nostrils and over the adhesive tape clamped across my mouth. I gagged and choked down in my throat and fought to get air into my lungs and felt the handcuffs bite into my wrists and the chain clank against the drainpipe under the sink. Then I saw the handbill man squatting on his haunches next to me, an empty iced tea pitcher in his hand, a curious expression on his face as though he were watching an animal at the zoo. His eyes were sky blue and laced with tiny threads of white light. He wadded up a ball of paper towels in his hand and blotted my face dry, then widened my eyes with his fingers as an ophthalmologist might. By his foot was one of his handbill sacks.

'You're doing all right. Rest easy and I'll explain the gig to you,' he said. He took an Instamatic camera from his bag, focused on my face and the upper half of my body, his mouth askew with concentration, and flashed it twice in my eyes. My head throbbed. He dropped the camera back in his bag.

'I got to take a piss. I'll be right back,' he said.

I heard him urinate loudly in the toilet. He flushed it, then walked back into the kitchen and knelt beside me.

'The guy wants before-after shots,' he said. 'So I give him before-after shots. He's paying for it, right? But that don't mean I have to do everything else he wants. It's still my gig. Hell, it's both our gig. I don't think you're a bad dude, you just got in the wrong guy's face. So I'm going to cut you all the slack I can.'

He looked steadily into my face. His eyes were vacuous, as clear and devoid of meaning as light itself.

'You don't understand, do you?' he asked. 'Look, you piss a guy off bad, you make him look like shit in front of people, you keep turning dials on him, you show him up a punk in front of his gash so they ain't interested in his Dream-sicle anymore, he's going to stay up nights thinking about you.'

His eyes were serene, almost kind, as though it had all been explained in a way that should be acceptable to even the most obtuse.

'You're a little thick, aren't you?' he said. 'Look, you're supposed to go in pieces, left lung, then cock in the mouth. But I say fuck that. At least not while the guy knows it. Nobody tells me how to do my work, man. Hey, this maybe isn't much comfort to you, but it could be a lot worse. Believe me.'

He put his left palm flat on my chest, almost as if he were reassuring or comforting me or feeling for my heartbeat as a lover might, and reached behind him into the canvas sack with his right hand. The knife was a foreign imitation of the Marine Corps K-Bar, with a stainless steel blade, sawteeth on the top, a black aluminum handle with a bubble compass inserted in the butt. I remembered seeing them advertised for six dollars in the *Times-Picayune* Sunday magazine.

The back door was shut, the yellow linoleum floor glistened with sunlight from the window, water ran from my hair and drenched shirt like ants on my skin, my own breathing sounded like air being forced through sand. His hand moved down my sternum over my stomach, toward my loins, and he shifted his weight on his knees, cupped the knife palm up in his right hand, and moved his eyes slowly over my face. I clanged the handcuff chain against the drainpipe, tried to twist away from him, then jerked my knees up in front of my stomach as a child might, my voice strangling in my throat.

He took his hand away from my body and looked at me patiently.

'Come on, man. Trust me on this one,' he said.

A shadow went across the glass window in the back door, then the handle turned and Clete came through the door as though he were bursting through barrel slats, flinging the door back against the wall, knocking a chair across the linoleum, his .38 revolver aimed straight out at the handbill man's face. He looked ridiculous in his old red and white Budweiser shorts, T-shirt, blue wind-breaker, crushed porkpie hat, loafers without socks, and nylon shoulder holster twisted across one nipple.

'What's happening, Charlie?' he said, his face electric with anticipation. 'Throw away the shank or I blow your shit all over Streak's wallpaper.'

The handbill man's vacuous blue eyes never changed expression. The white threads of light in them were as bright as if some wonderful promise were at hand. He set the knife on the floor and grinned at nothing, resting comfortably on one knee, his right forearm draped across his thigh.

'Charlie almost got away from me,' Clete said. 'Sal told me he took his rental back to Missoula and caught a flight last night. Except Charlie's been getting some nook up on the lake and his punch told me she's supposed to meet him at the airport tonight. I thought you were a pro, Charlie. You ought to keep your hammer in your pants when you're working. Roll over on your stomach and put your hands behind your neck.'

Clete knelt behind him and shook him down, patting his pockets, feeling inside his thighs.

'Where's the key to the cuffs?' Clete said.

The handbill man's face was flat against the floor, pointed at me. His eyes were bright with light.

'Hey, you got problems with your hearing?' Clete said, and kicked him with the point of his loafer in the rib cage.

Still, the handbill man didn't say anything. His breath went out of his lungs, and he breathed with his mouth open like a fish out of water. Clete started to kick him again, then his eyes went to the top of the kitchen table. He slid the knife across the linoleum with his foot and picked up the handcuff key from the table. He knelt beside me and unlocked one of my wrists. I started to raise up, but before I could he snapped the loose cuff around the drainpipe.

'Sorry, Streak, not just yet,' he said. 'Get the tape off your mouth and dangle loose a minute while we talk to Charlie here.' He picked up the canvas sack by the bottom and shook it out on the floor. The Instamatic, a roll of pipe tape, and a .22 revolver clattered on the linoleum among the scatter of handbills. 'Sal wanted some pictures for his scrapbook, huh? And it looks like we got a Ruger with a magnum cylinder. Streak, we're looking at your genuine, all-American psychopath here. I got a friend at Vegas PD to pull Charlie's sheet for me.'

I had the tape worked loose from my mouth now. I sat up as best I could under the lip of the sink and pinched the skin around my mouth. It was stiff and dead to the touch. I could feel a swollen ridge through my hairline and down my forehead.

'What are you doing, Clete?' I said. My words sounded strange and outside of myself.

'Meet Charlie Dodds. Vegas says he's been tied to five syndicate hits they know about, and maybe he iced a guy on the yard at Quentin. His finest hour was whacking out a federal witness, though. The guy's fourteen-year-old daughter walked in on it, so Charlie took her out, too.'

'Give me the key,' I said.

'Be mellow, Dave.' He had put the .22 in one of the big pockets of his Budweiser shorts. He started to lean over the man on the floor.

'Call the locals, Clete.'

He straightened up and looked at me as he would at a lunatic.

'You think you or I can keep this guy in jail? What's the matter with you?' he said. 'He'd be out on bond in three hours, even if these hicks would file charges. No matter how you cut it, he'd be back doing lines with the cornholers before the five o'clock news. I'll tell you something else, too, Dave. The mortician told me a tear was sealed inside Darlene's eye, he couldn't clean it out. You know what she must have gone through before she died?'

His jaw flexed, the skin of his face tightened, the scar that ran through his eyebrow and across his nose reddened, and he kicked the man on the floor hard in the rectum. He kicked him in the same place again, then leaned over him and whipped the barrel of the .38 across the back of his head. Then he said 'Fuck' as though an insatiable rage had released itself in him, put his revolver in his other deep pocket, hoisted the man to his feet by his belt, as if he were made of rags and sticks, threw him against the wall and drove his huge fist into his face.

Then Clete held him erect by the throat, hit him again and again, until his knuckles were shiny and red and the man's eyes were crossed and a bloody string of saliva hung from his mouth.

'For God's sakes, cut it out, Clete!' I said. 'The guy's all we've got. Use your head, man.'

'Bullshit. Charlie's no sissy. Our man here is a stand-up con.' And with that, he wrapped his hand around the back of the man's neck, ran him across the room, and smashed his head down on the side of the stove. I saw the skin split above the eye; then Clete threw him to the floor. The man's eyes had rolled, and his straw-colored hair was matted with sweat.

Clete stuck his wrist down at my face.

'Feel my pulse,' he said. 'I'm calm, I'm copacetic, I'm fucking in control of my emotions. I don't have a hard-on. I'm extremely tranquil. I saved your fucking ass this morning. How about a little gratitude for a change?'

'You unlock me, Clete, or I'm going to square this. I swear it.'

'You'll never change, Streak. You're unteachable.'

Clete picked up the roll of pipe tape and the survival knife from the floor and knelt next to the unconscious man. He ripped off a ten-inch length of tape, sliced through it with the knife, and wrapped the man's mouth. Then he pulled his arms behind him, wrapped each wrist individually, made a thick figure eight between both wrists, and sliced the tape again. The knife was honed as sharp as a barber's razor. He wrapped the man's ankles just as he had done the wrists.

'I don't know what your plan is, but I think it's a bad one,' I said.

'I'm not the one up on a murder charge in Louisiana. I'm not the guy cuffed to a drainpipe. I don't have a knot on my head. Maybe I do something right once in a while. Try some humility along with the gratitude.'

He went into the front of the house, and I heard him pushing furniture around, tumbling a chair or a table to the floor. A moment later he came back into the kitchen, dragging my living room rug behind him. His face was flushed, and sweat ran out of the band of his porkpie hat. He ripped off his windbreaker and used it to wipe the sweat out of his eyes. The powder-blue sleeves were flecked with blood.

'Sorry to fuck up your house. See if you can write it off on the IRS as part of Neighborhood Watch,' he said.

He kicked the rug out flat on the floor and began rolling the man up in it.

'Clete, we can bring Dio down with this guy.'

But he wasn't listening. He breathed hard while he worked, and there was a mean bead in his eye.

'You got out of that murder beef in New Orleans. You want them to stick you with another one?' I said.

Again he didn't answer. He went out the back door, then I heard his jeep grinding in reverse across the lawn to the steps. Clete came back into the kitchen, unhooked the spring from the screen door, lifted up the man inside the rolled rug, and dragged him outside to the jeep. When he came back inside his face was dusty from the rug and running with sweat and his big chest heaved up and down for air. He put a cigarette in his mouth, lit it from a book of matches, and flipped the burnt match out through the open screen into the sunlight.

'You got a hacksaw?' he said.

'In my toolbox. Behind the driver's seat.'

He went back outside, and I heard him clattering around in my truck. Then he walked back up the wood steps with the saw hanging from his hand.

'You can cut through the chain in about fifteen minutes,' he said. 'If you want to call the locals then, ask yourself how much of this they'll believe. Also ask yourself how much trouble you want over a shitbag like that guy out there.'

'What are you going to do with him?'

'It's up to him. Are you really worried about a guy who'd kill a fourteen-year-old girl? The guy's a genetic accident.' He pulled up a chair, sat down, and leaned toward me while he puffed on his cigarette and tried to get his breath back at the same time. 'Did you ever think about it this way, Streak? You know how the real world works, just like I do. But half the time you act like you don't. But it lets you feel good around guys like me. What do your AA pals call it – "drinking down"?'

'That's not the way it is, Cletus.'

'Why'd you keep partnering with me at the First District after you saw me bend a couple of guys out of shape?' He grinned at me. 'Maybe because I'd do the things you really wanted to. Just maybe. Think about it.'

'Don't kill this guy.'

'Hey, I got to be on the road. You want anything before I split? A glass of water or something?' He put the hacksaw in my hand.

'It's never to late to turn it around.'

'That's solid gold, Dave. I wonder if ole Charlie out there thinks of something like that while he's doing a job on somebody. Man, that's fucking noble. I got to remember that.'

He hooked the spring on the screen door again, worked it back and forth a couple of times, then looked at me and said, 'After you cut through the chain, the cuff key's there on the table. You want to take down Sal and that other fart that framed you in Louisiana, get real or buy yourself some Mouseketeer ears. In an hour I'll have Charlie's life story. You want in on it, call me at the Eastgate Lounge at six o'clock.'

Then he was gone.

9

I filled a clean dish towel with ice cubes and cracked them into a fine, wet paste with a rolling pin on the edge of the sink, then lay down on the living room couch and held the towel to my head. What a sharp ex-cop I proved myself this morning, I thought. I had managed to roust, terrify, and infuriate an innocent telephone man, then invite a contract killer into my house, right after the cops had left, turn my back on him unarmed, when I had access to a .45, a double-barreled twelve-gauge, and a .38 revolver nailed in a holster under a cabinet shelf, and get sapped and manacled to a drainpipe. I didn't want to think about the rest of it: the moist touch of his hand sliding across the quivering muscles of my stomach, the total absence of moral light in his eyes, the transfixed, almost opiated shine in his face while he let the knife hover over my heart cavity.

I had seen the work of his kind before, in New Orleans. They created object lessons that no one in the criminal community ever forgot: a grand jury witness garroted with wire, a hooker drenched with gasoline and turned into a cone of flame, a mob member who had cuckolded a friend emasculated and his phallus stuffed in his mouth. The men who did the work made you shudder. I've heard all kinds of explanations for their behavior and their perverse nature. My personal feeling is that they're simply evil. The hooker, the street dips, the check writers, the fences and hot-money passers at the track, that bumbling urban army of brain-fried misfits, are often people with families and other jobs who eventually disappear into the normalcy of American life without ever leaving more than a forgettable scratch on it. Charlie Dodds's kind are a special bunch, however. I don't think there are many of them around, but enough perhaps to remind us that not every human being can be fixed or explained and that the jailer who keeps them in maximum-security lock-down, chained ankle, waist, and wrist when they're moved only a short distance in the prison, knows and appreciates something about them that the rest of us do not.

I had decided not to call the heat about Charlie Dodds's visit. As Clete had said, how much of it would they be willing to believe, particularly after I had rousted the telephone man? Also, I was tired of having to prove myself to cops. Sometimes it's not good to interfere with the fates. Maybe Clete and Dodds had found each other.

The ice melted in the towel. I got up from the couch, my forehead numb and tight from the cold and swelling, and cleaned up the kitchen. I wiped Dodd's blood off the wall, stove, and linoleum with wet paper towels, cleaned the same areas again with detergent and rubbing alcohol, then put the towels, his survival knife, his cloth cap, and the sawed handcuffs into his canvas handbill bag, wadded it up, and threw the whole mess down the basement stairs.

Then I showered and took a nap in the bedroom. The breeze ruffled the bushes outside the window and blew coolly across the sheets. In my dream I saw Annie sitting on the rail of my father's houseboat in the misty early morning light down in the Atchafalaya marsh. The houseboat was weathered and paintless, streaked with moisture, and clouds of vapor billowed out of the islands of willow and cypress trees and hung low on the motionless water. Her hair was gold, her skin tan, her mouth red in the mist, but she wouldn't speak to me. She smiled and looked toward my father, who waited for me in the outboard, and I realized that I was only fifteen and that I had to help him run the crab line, dripping with catfish heads, that we had strung across the bay the night before. As the sun burned the mist off the water and back into the trees, we filled the bait well with bluepoint crabs, then began picking up the conical fishnets that we had weighted with bricks, marked with sealed, plastic Clorox containers, and dropped into deep current yesterday morning. We worked through lunch, shaking huge mud cat and *gaspagoo*, what Texans called buffalofish and Negroes goo-fish, into the bottom of the boat, our backs hot and striped with sweat under the white sun. My father's hair was curly and wild, like black wire, his hands big as skillets, his teeth strong and white, his laugh genuine and full of fun, his shoulders and arms so powerful and corded with muscle that he could fight three men at one time in the middle of a dance floor and take blows from every direction without going down. On the pipeline and in the oil field they called him Big Al Robicheaux with the kind of respect and affection that working people have for a man who possesses their best qualities. I leaned over the gunnel, grabbed a floating Clorox container, and got the lip of the net almost to the surface. But it was as heavy as concrete, the wooden hoops fouled, the netting torn, and no matter how I strained I couldn't life the first hoop clear of the water.

My father cut the engine, climbed to the bow so he wouldn't capsize the boat, and jerked net up with his massive arms, until he could see the outline of the trapped gar just below the yellow surface.

'*Fils p'tain*,' he said. He hadn't shaved in three days, and his hair and beard were dripping with sweat.

The gar must have been five feet long. Its fins and tail and armorlike scales and long, teeth-filled snout were mired in the netting, and there was no way to get it back out through the series of hoops. My father pulled up the bricks that we used to anchor the net, cut them loose, and dropped them into the bottom of the boat; then we towed the net slowly behind us back to the willow island where the houseboat was moored in the shade.

We shook the gar out the ruined net on the bank and watched it flop and gasp for air and coat its gills with sand. Its teeth could cut a bass in half like a razor slicing through it. My father got behind it, hit it once on the head with a brick, then drove his skinning knife through a soft place between the head and the armored shell, pushing down with both hands until the knife point went through the throat into the sand and blood roared from the gar's mouth and gills. But the gar continued to flop, to twist against the knife and flip sand into the air, until my father crushed its head and its eyes became as suddenly lifeless and cold as black glass. Then he brought the knife straight back along the dorsal fin, and the black-green armor cracked away from the rows of pink meat as cleanly as pecan shell breaking.

It wasn't a good day. The gar wasn't a commercial fish, and we couldn't afford the loss of a net, but my father always put the best light on a situation.

'We can't sell him, no,' he said. 'But he gonna be some good garfish balls. You mess with Aldous and Dave, you gonna get fry, you gonna get eat, you better believe, podna.'

We cleaned the filleted fish in pans of bloody water until evening, when the mosquitoes started to boil out of the shadows and purple rain clouds gathered on the horizon and lightning flashed far out on the Gulf. We packed the fish in the ice bin, so tomorrow we could take them downriver to sell in Morgan City. I went to sleep in my bunk bed with the wind blowing cool through the window from across the bay, then I woke to a smell that shouldn't have been there. It was thick and gray, as fetid as excrement and sweet at the same time. But we had thrown all the fish guts and heads and piles of stripped mud-cat skins into the current and had washed the deck and all the pans clean. I kept the pillow over my head and tried to push myself deeper into sleep, but I could feel the stench against my face like a rat's breath.

In the first blue light of dawn I went out on the deck, and Annie was leaning against the rail in the mist, dressed like a Cajun fisher girl in sun-faded jeans, tennis shoes without socks, a khaki shirt with the arms cut off. The smell was everywhere. She pointed toward my father, who waited for me on the sandbar, a shovel over his shoulder.

Don't be afraid, she said. *Go with Al.*

I don't want to this time.

You mustn't worry about those things. We both love you.

You're about to go away from me, aren't you?

Her face was kind, and her eyes moved over my face as though she were an older sister looking at her younger brother.

I followed my father into the marsh, our tennis shoes splashing through the sloughs, the wet willow branches winging back into our faces. The early sun was big and hot on the edge of the flooded woods, and the cypress trees looked black against the red light. The water was dead and covered with green algae; cottonmouth moccasins were coiled on the low branches of the trees. The smell became stronger, so that I had to hold my hand to my face and breathe through my mouth. We came up out of a slough on to a hard-packed sandbar, and lying stretched on the sand, huge divots cut out of its back by a boat propeller, was the rotting carcass of the biggest bull alligator I had ever seen. His tail drag and the sharp imprints of his feet trailed off the sandbar back through the trees. I could see the open water where he had probably been hit by a commercial boat of some kind, or the screw on a seismograph drill barge, and had beached himself and begun his crawl to this spot, where he had died on high ground and turkey buzzards and snakes had begun feeding on his wounds.

'*Mais,* that stink,' my father said, and waved at the air in front of his face. 'You start dig a hole.' He handed me the shovel, then he grinned as he sometimes did when he was about to play a joke on me. 'Where you gonna dig a hole, you?'

I didn't understand him. I started to scrape in the dry sand with the shovel's tip.

'*Que t'as près faire, cher? Tu veux travailler comme un neg?*' he said, and laughed. ('What are you doing, dear one? You want to work like a Negro?')

I pressed down again into the hard sand, felt it grate and slide over the blade. He took the shovel out of my hand, walked to a dip in the sandbar where the water from two sloughs had washed a small channel, and dug deeply and easily into the wet sand and flung it out into the sunlight, his face grinning at me.

'You do it where it soft,' he said. 'Ain't you learned nothing from your old man?'

I woke to a clatter of birds in the trees outside the window, my head thick with afternoon sleep. I rinsed my face in the bathroom sink and looked at the tight purple lump that ran down through my hairline. The dream made no sense to me, other than the facts that I missed my father and Annie, that I feared death, and that I conducted a foolish quarrel with the irrevocable nature of time.

Al, what are you trying to tell me? I thought, as the water streamed off my face in the mirror's silent reflection.

Shortly before three o'clock I walked down to the school and waited for Alafair by the side of the playground. A few minutes later the doors of the building were flung open, and she came running across the small softball diamond with a group of other children, her Donald Duck lunch box clanging against her thigh. Her elastic-waisted jeans were grimed at the knees, and there were dirt and sweat rings around her neck.

'What did you guys do today at recess? Mud wrestling?' I said.

'Miss Regan let us play dodgeball. It's fun. I got hit in the seat. You ever play it, Dave?'

'Sure.'

'What happened to your head?'

'I hit it when I was working on the truck. Not too smart, huh?'

Her eyes looked at me curiously, then she put her hand in mine and swung her weight on my arm.

'I forgot,' she said. 'Miss Regan said to give you this note. She said she'd call you anyway.'

'About what?'

'About the man.'

'What man?'

'The one at the school yard.'

I unfolded the piece of paper she had taken from her lunch box. It read: *Mr Robicheaux, I want to have a serious talk with you. Call me at my home this afternoon – Tess Regan.* Under her name she had written her phone number.

'Who's this man you're talking about, Alafair?' I said.

A bunch of children ran past us on the sidewalk. The sunlight through the maple trees made patterns on their bodies.

'The other kids said he was in a car on the corner. I didn't see him. They said he was looking through, what you call those things, Dave? You got some in the truck.'

'Field glasses?'

'They called them something else.'

'Binoculars?'

'Yeah.' She grinned up at me when she recognized the word.

'Who was he looking at, Alafair?'

'I don't know.'

'Why does Miss Regan want to talk to me about it?'

'I don't know.'

'What time was this guy out there?'

'At recess.'

'What time is recess?'

'First- through third-graders go at ten-thirty.'

'Is that when he was out there?'

'I don't know, Dave. Why you look so worried?'

I took a breath, released her hand, and brushed my palm on the top of her head.

'Sometimes strange men, men who are not good people, try to bother little children around schools or at playgrounds. There're not many people like this, but you have to be careful about them. Don't talk with them, don't let them give you anything, don't let them buy you anything. And no matter what they say, never go anywhere with them, never get in a car with them. Do you understand that, little guy?'

'Sure, Dave.'

'That kind of man will tell you that he's a friend of your father's. That your father sent him to pick you up, maybe. But if he was a friend, you'd recognize him, right?'

'They hurt children?'

'Some of them do. Some of them are very bad people.'

I saw doubt and fear working into her face like a shadow. Her throat swallowed. I picked up her hand in mine again.

'Don't be scared, little guy,' I said. 'It's the same thing I've told you before. We just have to be cautious sometimes. Miss Regan tells all the children that, doesn't she? It's no big deal.'

But it wasn't working. Her eyes were locked on images in her memory that I could not touch or eradicate.

'Look, when I tell you not to stick your hand in the window fan, that doesn't mean you should be afraid of the fan, does it?' I said.

'No.'

'If I tell you not to put your finger in Tripod's mouth, that doesn't mean you should be afraid of Tripod, does it?'

'No.' Her eyes crinkled slightly at the corners.

'If Clarise won't let Tex eat at the breakfast table, that doesn't mean she's afraid of horses, does it?'

She grinned up at me, her face squinting in the sunlight. I swung her on my arm under the maple trees, but there was a feeling in my chest like a chunk of angle iron.

At the house she poured a glass of milk and cut a piece of pie at the kitchen table for her afternoon snack, then washed out her lunch box and thermos and began straightening her room. I took the telephone into the bathroom so she could not hear me talking to Tess Regan.

'What's the deal with this guy at the school ground?' I said.

'I beg your pardon?'

'You sent a note home. Then Alafair told me about the guy with binoculars.'

'I was referring to your tone. Are you always this cross with people over the telephone?'

'It's been an unusual day. Look, Miss Regan – Tess – what's the deal?'

'At recess we use some of the eighth-graders as monitors for the lower grades. Jason, one of the monitors, said a man was parked in his car under the trees across the street. He said the man walked over to the fence and asked where Alafair Robicheaux was. He said he was a friend of her father's, and he had a message for her. We teach all the children not to talk to people off the street, to direct all visitors to the principal's office. Jason told him he should see Sister Louise inside the building. Then the man pointed to where the little ones were playing dodgeball and said, "Oh, there she is." Jason said, "Yeah, but you have to see Sister Louise." The man said he didn't have time but he'd be back later. When he got back in the car, the children said, he looked at the school ground through a pair of binoculars.'

'What time was he there?'

'It must have been about eleven o'clock.'

Then it wasn't Charlie Dodds, I thought. He was already inside my house by then.

'What kind of car?'

'The kids said it was yellow.'

'What did the guy look like? Did he have an accent?'

'Jason just said he was tall. I didn't ask about an accent.'

'That's all right. Was there anything unusual about him? A scar on his lip?'

'Children usually don't remember those kinds of details about adults. In their world adults are simply "big people" whom they either trust or dislike.'

'I'd like to talk to Jason.'

'Then you'll need to make an appointment with Sister Louise, and maybe she'll ask the parents to bring Jason in. But I doubt it. Not unless you want to tell us what this is about and also call the police. Because that's what we're going to do.'

'That's good. But you need to listen to me now and not be afraid of what I'm going to tell you. This guy is not a child molester. He wanted to get at me through Alafair. He may work for the mob out of Vegas or Reno. I had one like that in my house this morning. That's why it's been an unusual day. Or he may be somebody connected with an oil company, a guy named Mapes or somebody who works for him. Either way, the local cops don't have much experience with this kind of guy.'

'The mob?' she said.

'That's right.'

'You mean like in *The Godfather*? The honest-to-God Mafia?'

'The real article.'

'And you didn't tell me this before?'

'It wouldn't have changed anything. Except maybe to alarm you.'

'I think I'm very angry right now.'

'Look, I don't want to be the guy to mess up your day. You asked for the truth, I gave it to you. There's no big revelation what I told you, either. There's some Reno transplants right up there at Flathead Lake. The mob's any place there's money to be made in gambling or dope or any kind of vice.'

She didn't answer.

'Listen,' I said, 'if that guy comes back, you try to get his license number, then you call the heat, then you call me. Okay?'

'What do you plan to do?' she said. Her voice was dry, the way heat is when it lifts off a metal surface.

'I'm going to seriously impair this interest in children on school yards.'

'I'll give your words some thought. In the meantime you might reflect a bit on the need for a little more candor in your relationships with other people. Maybe they don't like to feel that they're not be trusted with this great body of private information that you have.'

The line went dead in my hand.

I couldn't blame her. How would any ordinary person deal with the knowledge that an emissary of the mob could stroll into a world as innocent and predictable as a children's playground? But was the man indeed one of Dio's people, a partner of or a backup for Charlie Dodds? Why would Dodds need a backup? It was a simple hit, probably a five-thou whack that a guy like Dodds considered a cakewalk. Unless Dio's outraged pride was so great that he wanted a child's death as well as my own.

It didn't compute, though. If Dodds had been paid to hurt Alafair also, he would have waited until after three o'clock, when we were both home, or he would have come on the weekend.

So that left Harry Mapes. He had been driving a black Jeepster when I had seen him just south of the Blackfeet Reservation, but maybe the man in the yellow car with the binoculars worked with Mapes or had been hired by him. Why would he want to turn the screws on me now? Did he think I was close to finding something or turning it around on him? If he did, he had a lot more confidence in me than I did in myself.

I called Sister Louise, the principal, at the school and caught her just before she left the office. She had already talked with Tess Regan, and she was no more happy with me than Tess Regan had been. She sounded like some of the nuns I had known as a child, the ones who wore black habits that were probably like portable stoves and who whacked your knuckles with tricorner rules and who could hit you on the run with their fifteen-decade rosaries. She told me that she had just made a police report, that I should do the same, and that a patrol car would be parked by the school tomorrow morning.

'I'd still like to talk with the little boy, what's his name, Jason,' I said.

'He's told me everything he knows. He's a shy boy. He's not one to study detail in adults.'

'Does he remember if the man had an accent?'

'He's fourteen years old, he's not a linguist.'

'Sister, it's good that you'll have a patrol car out there tomorrow. But our man won't be back while the cops are around.'

'That's the point, isn't it?'

'But he may well be when they're gone. That's when we can nail him.'

'There's no "we" involved in this, Mr Robicheaux.'

'I see.'

'I'm glad you do. Good-bye.'

For the second time in ten minutes someone had hung up on me.

I took Alafair to the park to play, then we went back home and fixed supper. Clete had told me I could call him at the Eastgate Lounge at six o'clock. I wasn't sure that I should. Whatever he had done with Charlie Dodds, it wasn't good. But at that point my legal problems as well as the threat to Alafair's and my safety were so involved and seemingly without solution that I wondered why I should be troubled over some marginal involvement with the fate of a depraved and psychotic character like Dodds, whom nobody cared about except perhaps Sally Dio because he had probably paid him half the hit money up front. It was five-thirty, and we were five minutes into our meal when I heard a car park in front and somebody walk up on the porch.

Even before I could make out his silhouette against the screen door, I saw Dixie Lee's battered pink Cadillac convertible parked with two wheels on the edge of my grass. The top was up, but I could see that the backseat was loaded with suitcases, boxes of clothing and cowboy boots, hangered western suits racked on a wire.

His sudden change of fortune, his plans for himself, his rehearsed entreaty, were altogether too obvious and predictable. I didn't open the door. I was even a bit ashamed at my lack of sympathy. But it had been a bad day, and I really didn't need Dixie Lee in it. He was eloquent in his desperation, though. He had marshaled all the raw energies of a drunk who knew that he was operating on the last fuel in his tank.

'Things are coming apart up there at the lake,' he said. 'You were right,

Sal's a shit. No, that ain't right. He's a crazy person. He wants your ass cooked in a pot. I couldn't abide it. I had to get out.'

'Watch your language. My daughter's here.'

'I'm sorry. But you don't know what Sal's like when lights start going off in his head. He's got this twisted-up look on his face. Nobody can say anything around him unless you want your head snapped off. One of the broads is eating her dessert at the dinner table, and Sal keeps smoking his cigarette and looking at her like she crawled up out of a drain hole. Her eyes are blinking and she's trying to smile and be pretty and cute and get off the hook, then he says, "You eat too much," and puts out his cigarette in her food.

'He hates you, Dave. You really got to him. You bend up the wheels inside a guy like Sally Dee, and smoke starts to come out of the box. I don't want to be around it. That's where it stands. You tell me to get out of your life, I can relate to it. But I picked myself into some thin cotton, son, and I got nowhere to turn. I'll be straight with you on something else, too. I'm in to Sal for fifteen thou. That's how much flake I put up my nose on the tab. So I got that old Caddy out there, thirty-seven dollars in my pocket, and a quarter tank of gas. I'm trying to keep it all in E major, but I blew out my amps on this one.'

'Save the rock 'n' roll corn pone for somebody else,' I said. 'I had Charlie Dodds in my house this morning.'

'Dodds? I thought he went back to Vegas last night. What was he doing here?'

'You don't know?'

'You mean he's a mechanic? I didn't know. I swear in front of God I didn't. I thought he was one of Sal's mules. Is that how you got that purple knot on your head?'

'Something like that.'

'Man, I'm sorry. I didn't have any idea. The guy didn't say three words when he was around me. I thought he was retarded. All those mules got that meltdown look in their eyes. They swallow balloons full of skag, fly in and out of canyons, land on dirt roads at night. We're talking about the dumbest white people you ever met.'

'I think he might have a backup man still after me. Is there some other new guy hanging around Sal's place?'

'No.'

'You're sure?'

'Yeah.'

'Anyway, I can't help you, Dixie.'

He looked at me blankly through the screen. He swallowed, glanced up the street as though something of significance were waiting for him there, then started to speak again.

'I've got too many problems of my own. That's about it, partner,' I said.

'No way, huh?'

'I'm afraid not.'

He blew his breath up into his face.

'I can't blame you,' he said. 'I just ain't got many selections right now.'

'Start over.'

'Yeah, why not. It ain't my first time washing dishes or living in a hallelujah mission. Hey, I want you to remember one thing, though, Dave. I ain't all bad. I never set out to harm anybody. It just worked out that way.'

'Whatever you do, good luck with it, Dixie,' I said, and closed the inside door on him and went back to the kitchen table, where Alafair had already started in on her dessert.

I looked at my watch – it was a quarter to six now – and tried to finish supper. The food seemed tasteless, and I couldn't concentrate on something Alafair was telling me about the neighbor's cat chasing grasshoppers in the flower bed.

'What's wrong?' she said.

'Nothing. It's just a little headache. It'll pass.'

'That man made you mad or something?'

'No, he's just one of those guys who'll always have his elevator stuck between floors.'

'What?'

'Nothing, little guy. Don't worry about it.'

I chewed my food and looked silently out the window at the shadows and the cool gold light on the backyard. I heard Alafair wash her dishes in the sink, then walk toward the front of the house. A moment later she was back in the kitchen.

'That man's still out there. Just sitting in his car. What's he doing, Dave?' she said.

'Probably figuring out ways to sell the Rocky Mountains to Arab strip miners.'

'What?'

'Just ignore him.'

But I couldn't. Or at least I couldn't ignore the twelfth-step AA principle that requires us to help those who are afflicted in the same way we are. Or maybe I knew that I had asked for all my own troubles, and it wasn't right any longer to blame it on Dixie Lee. I set my knife and fork down on my plate and walked outside to his car. He was deep in thought, a cigarette burned almost down to his fingers, which rested on top of the steering wheel. His face jerked around with surprise when he heard me behind him.

'Lord gold, you liked to give me a heart attack,' he said.

'You can't drink while you stay with us,' I said. 'If you do or if you come home with it on your breath, you're eighty-sixed. No discussion, no second chance. I don't want any profanity in front of my daughter, and you go outside if you want to smoke. You share the cooking and the cleaning, you go to bed when we do. The AA group down the street has a job service. If they find you some work, you take it, whatever it is, and you pay one third of the groceries and the rent. That's the deal, Dixie. If there are any rules here you can't live with, now's the time to tell me.'

'Son, you say "Frog" and I'll say "How high?"'

He began unloading the backseat of his car. His face wore the expression of a man who might have been plucked unexpectedly from the roof of a burning building. As he piled his boxes and suitcases and clothes on the sidewalk, he talked without stop about the 1950s, Tommy Sands, Ruth Brown, the Big Bopper, the mob, cons in Huntsville, the actress wife who paid goons to beat him up behind Cook's Hoe Down in Houston. I looked at my watch. It was five minutes to six.

He was still talking while I looked up the number of the Eastgate Lounge.

'—called him "the hippy-dippy from Mississippi, yes indeed, Mister Jimmy Reed,"' he said. 'When that cat went into "Big Boss Man", you knew he'd been on Parchman Farm, son. You don't fake them kind of feelings. You don't grow it in New York City, either. You don't put no mojo in your sounds unless you picked cotton four cents a pounds and ate a mess of them good ole butter beans. My daddy said he give up on me, that somebody snuck me into the crib, that I must have been a nigra turned inside out.'

Alafair sat delighted and amazed as she listened to Dixie Lee's marathon storytelling. I dialed the Eastgate Lounge, then listened to the hum and clatter of noise in the background while a woman called Clete to the phone. I heard him scrape the receiver off a hard surface and place it to his ear.

'Streak?'

'Yep.'

'Did I surprise you? Did you think maybe your old partner had headed for Taco Greaso Land again?'

'I wasn't sure.'

'I don't rattle, mon. At least not over the shitbags.'

'Maybe you should be careful what you tell me.'

'Do I sound like I'm sweating it? When are you going to stop pretending you still got your cherry?'

'You're starting to get to me, Clete.'

'What else is new? All I did was save your life today.'

'Is there something you want me to say?'

571

'Yeah. Get your butt over here. You know where the Eastgate is?'

'Yeah, but I'm bringing Alafair with me. I'll meet you in the park across the river from the shopping center. You walk across an old railway trestle that's been made into a footbridge.'

'And you'll be eating ice cream cones at a picnic table. Man, how do I get in on the good life?' he said, and hung up.

I told Dixie Lee there was a cold roast, bread, and mayonnaise in the icebox, and he could fix himself sandwiches if he hadn't eaten yet. Then Alafair and I drove across town to the ice cream place on the north bank of the Clark Fork, bought cones, and walked across the river on the footbridge to the park on the opposite side. In the past, there had been a bad fire up the sides of Hellgate Canyon, and the pines that grew down from the crest had been scorched black and then the ash and the burnt needles had been washed away by rain and the spring snowmelt so that the steep gray-pink cliffs of the canyon were exposed high above the river. The wind was up, and the leaves of the cottonwoods along the river's edge clicked and flickered in the soft light; because the spring runoff had ended and the water was dropping each day, more and more white, moss-scaled stones were exposed in the riverbed and the main channel was turning from copper-colored to a dark green. The white water had formed into long, narrow trout riffles that fanned out behind big rocks into deep pools.

The park was full of blue spruce and Russian olive trees, and kids from the university, which was only a block away, sailed Frisbees overhead and played rag football. We sat on the mowed grass, high up on the riverbank, so we could look out over the tops of the willows and watch two men who were fishing with worms and spinning rods, throwing lead weights far out into the channel. I saw Clete walk across the bridge with a paper sack hefted in one arm. I got Alafair started on one of the swing sets and then sat back down on the bank. His knees cracked, his stomach hung over his Budweiser shorts, and he grunted hard in his chest when he sat down beside me.

'You look undressed,' I said.

'Oh.' He touched his chest and smiled. 'I don't work for Sal any-more. I don't have to walk around with a piece all the time. Feels good, mon.'

He twisted the cap off a bottle of Great Falls.

'Dixie Lee says he didn't know Dodds was a hit man.'

'He probably didn't. Where'd you see Dixie Lee?'

'He's living at my house.'

'I'll be damned. He cut the umbilical cord? I didn't think he had the guts. Sal doesn't handle rejection well.'

'Dodds may have had a partner, a backup guy. Does Dio have another guy in town?'

'If he does, I don't know about it. I know a lot of them, too. At least the ones Sal hangs with. They're New York transplants who think the essence of big time is playing bridge by the pool with a lot of gash lying around. Hey, dig this. Sal had a bunch of them staying at his motel, and the motel manager is this little Jewish guy who used to run a book for the mob out of a pizza joint in Fort Lauderdale. Of course, the Jew can't do enough for the dagos because they scare the shit out of him. But he's got this kid who's a wiseass college student at Berkeley, and the kid works for his old man as the poolside waiter during the summer. So four of the dagos are playing cards at one of the umbrella tables. And these are big, mean-looking cocksuckers, shades, wet black hair all over their stomachs, big floppers tucked in their bikinis, and they're giving the kid a terrible time – sending food back to the kitchen, complaining the drinks taste like there's bathroom antiseptic in them, running the kid back and forth for cigarettes and candied cherries and sun cream for the gash and anything else they think of.

'Then one guy spills ice and vodka all over the table and tells the kid to mop it up and bring him another deck of cards. The kid says, "Hey, I've been studying Italian at school this year. What does *Eatta my shitta* mean?"

'The old man hears it and slaps his kid's face in front of everybody. Then he starts swallowing and sweating and apologizing to the dagos while they stare at him from behind those black shades. Finally one of them stands up, hooks his finger in the old man's mouth, and throws him down in an iron chair. He said, "He don't have manners 'cause you didn't teach him none. So you shut up your face and don't be talking to impress nobody. You clean this up, and bring everybody what they want, you sit over there and you don't go nowhere till we say."

'They made him sit out there in the sun like an organ-grinder's monkey for four hours. Till the kid finally begged them to let the old man go back inside.

'It's good to say *Ciao, ciao, bambino* to the grease-balls. The next time the United States drops an A-bomb on anyone, I think it should be Palermo.'

'Where's Dodds?'

'You really want to know?'

'I want to know if he's going to be back after me.'

'First you tell me why you didn't drop the dime on me.' There was a half grin on his face as he raised the beer bottle to his mouth.

'No games, Clete.'

'Because a guy out on bond for murder doesn't like to introduce cops to his blood-splattered kitchen. Because maybe he knows they might just take the easy route and haul his butt down to the bag. Sounds like your faith might be waning, Streak.'

'Is that guy going to be back?'

'That's one you don't have to worry about.'

'Where is he?' I asked.

'Get serious. You don't need to know any more, Streak. Except the fact that our man didn't like heights.'

'What?'

'Did you ever meet a psychopath yet that wasn't scared of something? It's what makes them cruel. Charlie didn't like high places. At least not the one I showed him.'

I looked out silent at the river. A Frisbee sailed by overhead.

'Too grim for you?' Clete said.

'Did he kill Darlene?'

'No, I'm convinced that's one he didn't do.'

'Dio, then?'

'He didn't know. Put it in the bank, too.'

I stood up and began brushing the grass off my pants.

'You're going to turn to stone on me, huh?' he said.

'It's a school night. Alafair has to get home.'

'Why is it you always make me feel like anthrax, Streak?'

'You're right about one thing today. I didn't call the heat because I didn't want to be part of another criminal investigation. Particularly when I was left with the problem of explaining how somebody's blood got smeared all over my walls and stove and floor. Right now I'm going to believe that Charlie Dodds is on a flight to new opportunities in Mexico City. Beyond that, I wouldn't count on anything, Clete.'

'I'm going to get the guy that did her. You want to sit around and bite your nails, that's cool with me.'

I walked off toward a group of children with whom Alafair was playing tag. Then Clete called after me, in a voice that made people turn and stare. 'I love you anyway, motherfucker.'

I needed some help. I had accomplished virtually nothing on my own; I had been locked up for punching out Sally Dio, had persuaded nobody of my theories, and instead had managed to convince a couple of local cops that I was a gun-wielding paranoid. That night I called Dan Nygurski at his home in Great Falls. A babysitter answered and said that he was at a movie with his wife, that she would take down my name and number. He returned my call just after ten, when I was drifting off to sleep with a damp towel folded across the lump on my forehead. I took the phone into the kitchen and closed the hallway door so as not to wake Alafair or Dixie Lee, who was sleeping on the living room couch.

I told him about Charlie Dodds in my house. About the slapjack across the head, the handcuffs, the Instamatic camera, the survival knife that he had started to shove into my heart. Then I told him about Clete, the working over that Dodds had taken, the rolled rug, and the trip in the jeep probably up a log road in either the Bitterroot Valley or the Blackfoot Canyon.

'You realize what you're telling me?' Nygurski said.

'I don't give a damn about Dodds. That's not why I called.'

'You didn't tell the cops any of this?'

'I'm telling you. Do with it what you want. I'll bet nobody ever finds Dodds, though. Clete's done this kind of thing before and gotten away with it.'

'You should have called the cops.'

'Bullshit. I'd be trying to arrange bond right now.'

'I'll have to report this to them.'

'Go ahead. I think their interest level on a scale of one to ten will be minus eight. Look, Nygurski, there's somebody else after me or my daughter. He was hanging around her school this morning. Maybe it's Mapes, maybe it's another one of Dio's people. I need some help.'

'I think it takes a hell of a lot of nerve to ask a federal agent for help after you run around two states with a baseball bat.'

'We both want the same thing – Sally Dee doing some serious time.'

'No, you've got it wrong. I want to do my job. You want to write your own rules on a day-to-day basis.'

'Then you give me a solution. You pledge the safety of my daughter, you assure me that I won't be headed for Angola Farm in about three weeks, and I won't be a problem to you.'

'What kind of help do you want?'

'Can you find out if Dio might have another hit man in town?'

'If he does, we don't know about it. Maybe he put out the contract and let Dodds hire a backup guy. I tell you, though, if this new guy is working with Dodds, he's not going to try for any "before and after" stuff, not after Dodds blew it. He'll go for a clean hit, one that you'll never see coming. I don't want to be graphic, but you know how they usually do it – one behind the head, one in the ear, and three under the chin.'

'Run Mapes for me.'

'What do you expect to find?'

'I don't know. My lawyer says he was in trouble only once, for beating up a kid with a golf club when he was seventeen. But I've seen this guy in action, and I can't believe he hasn't bumped into the furniture more than once.'

'Where's he from?'

'He beat up the kid in Marshall, Texas.'

'I'll see what I can do.'

'There's one other thing. Dixie Lee moved out of Dio's place. He says he's through with him. You might talk to him.'

'About what?'

'That's your province. How about grand jury testimony? It took guts to walk out on Dio, particularly when he owes him fifteen thou.'

'When did you decide to start sharing Pugh's secrets?'

'He's probably going to need federal protection sometime. He might be a drunk, but his head sops up information and people's conversations like a blotter.'

'Where is he?'

'He's staying with me.'

'What did you do for kicks as a kid? Swallow thumbtacks?'

'The guy's up against the wall,' I said.

'No, I take that crack back. You're a slick operator. Robicheaux. Pugh becomes a federal witness, Pugh lives at your house, your house and the people in it go under our umbrella. Right?'

'Not really.'

'I hope not. Because we choose the accommodations.'

'Clever people don't end up in the mess I'm in, Nygurski.'

'I think maybe there's solid truth in that statement. I'll get back to you. In the meantime you watch your butt.'

'When can I hear from you about Mapes?'

'I'm going the extra mile for you. Ease up on the batter, okay? Have a little trust. If you ever get out of this, get your badge back. I think everybody would rather have you inside the tent pissing out the flap rather than the other way around. I'm sure of it.'

Dixie Lee was up early the next morning and had breakfast with me and Alafair at the kitchen table. He was one of those drunks whose eyes clear and whose skin becomes pink and unlined with only a twenty-four-hour respite from alcohol. This morning his face was shaved and bright, and he wore a pair of pleated, white summer shorts and a white sport shirt with green parrots on it. I walked Alafair to school, then made him go to an AA meeting with me down the street and put his name in with the job-placement service. His mood was not as cheerful on the way home as it had been earlier.

'Them people make me nervous, son,' he said. 'I feel like a turd floating around in somebody's soup bowl.'

'It's the one place where maybe people can understand guys like us, Dixie.'

'Yeah, well, I've been to them meets before, and it didn't take. I think that's just the way it is with some guys. Jesus pointed his finger at the people he wanted. I ain't seen nobody point his finger at me. Hey, you remember those jokes we used to tell in the fifties? Like, what'd the bathtub say to the toilet? "I get the same amount of ass you do, but I don't have to take all that shit." '

'Come on, partner, what's really bothering you?'

'I don't relate to that fourth- and fifth-step stuff. Where you got to go over all you done wrong and confess everything to somebody. I really don't dig that at all. I got enough damn guilt without poking at it all with a stick.'

'Take it a step at a time. You don't have to do that now. Besides, haven't you owned up to a lot of things already? You told me some pretty honest stuff when you were in the hospital in Lafayette.'

'I got all kinds of things that make me ashamed. Hell, I knew Sal was no good when I met him in the pen. He was a geek. But he had bread, a lot of dope, and he liked me. So I didn't have to sweat the wolves and the swinging dicks and the guys who'd blow out your candle if they ever thought you snitched for the boss man. So I pretended not to see what went on in our cell. I wrote it off. A lot of guys turn homosexual inside the joint. I didn't go for it myself, but I didn't knock the guys who did. So Sal had a punk. Big deal, I thought. The fucking system does it to guys. That's what I said to myself. So I'd take a walk when this Mexican kid would come to our cell. It wasn't my business, right? Except something very weird started happening.'

We sat down on the front steps of my porch. Birds flew in and out of the shade. There was no wind, and the maple trees looked green and bright and stiff against the sky.

'You see, in that kind of relationship, in the pen, I mean, the punk is disposable,' Dixie Lee said. 'A pair of pork chops. All right, it's sickening stuff, but that's the way it is. But this kid was a real lover for Sal. He'd bring lipstick and women's underwear to the cell, and he'd wash and comb Sal's hair and then they'd hang a blanket down off the top bunk and really go at it. Except the kid turned out to be a lot more than Sal's punk. Sal really fell for him. The kid always had cigarettes, candy bars, ludes, magazines, an easy job in the infirmary, safe-conduct pass with the badasses. Then the kid started acting like a celebrity, walking around with a little pout on his face, making cow eyes at some very dangerous guys in the shower. A couple of guys told Sal he'd better straighten out his punk, but it wasn't too long before everybody knew that his kid could jerk Sal around any way he wanted to.

'The problem was some black guys wanted to take over Sal's drug action. But he had too many mean guys working for him, and they knew he was connected on the outside, too, so they always walked around him. Then the kid started making him look like a douche bag, and they decided it was time for them to get into some serious pharmaceutical sales. Sal had been bringing in about four or five hundred bucks a week, which is a lot of money in the joint, and in three weeks' time the blacks cut that in half. His mules came around the cell like scared mice and asked him what he was going to do about it, since the blacks were telling them they were out of the business for good, and Sal tried to blow it off and tell them everything was cool and that he was bringing in a load of Afghan skunk that would cook brains all over the joint.

'But everybody was laughing at him behind his back. The kid treated Sal like he was the punk instead of the other way around, and in the meantime he was hanging with a couple of other yard bitches who were anybody's punchy, and the three of them would go swishing around the place while the kid talked in a loud voice about Sal like he was some Dagwood Bumstead the kid put up with.

'But somebody called up Sal's old man in Galveston, and the shit hit the fan. The old man came up to Huntsville, and I don't know what he said to Sal in the visiting room, but whatever it was it put the fear of God in him. His face was white when he came back to our cell. He sat up all night smoking cigarettes on the side of his bunk, and in the morning he puked his breakfast out on the work detail. I asked him what was wrong, and he said, "I got to do something." I said, "What?" He said, "Something I don't want to do."

'So I said, "Don't do it." Then he said, "I'm a made guy. When you're a made guy, you do what they tell you."

'See, that's that dago stuff. They got some kind of ritual with knives and blood and magical bullshit, and they get to be made guys, which means they can smoke cigars at front tables in Vegas and pretend they're not a bunch of ignorant fish peddlers anymore.

'Two days later, right before lockup, Sal went to the kid's cell, where the kid was reading a comic book on his bunk with another fairy. He told the other kid to take off, then he took a piece of pipe out of his pants and beat that Mexican boy almost to death. He broke his nose, busted out his teeth, cauliflowered his ears, hurt that boy so bad his mother wouldn't know him.

'When he come back to the cell he had his shirt wadded up in his hand to hide the blood. After lights-out he tore it up in strips and flushed it down the toilet. In the morning he was all smiles, like he'd just made his first jump in the airborne or something. That kid was in the hospital three weeks. They shaved his head bald and put a hundred stitches in it. He looked like a lumpy white basketball with barbed wire wrapped all over it.

'Then Sal put out the word the kid was anybody's bar of soap. You know what that means in the joint for a kid like that? They're some cruel, sick sonsobitches in there, son. That kid had an awful time of it. I don't like remembering it.'

'Why are you telling me this, Dixie?'

'Because most of them people at the meet are just drunks. Liquor's only part of my problem. I lived off a guy like Sal. The reason I done it was because it was easy. You can't beat lobster and steak every day, plus the sweet young things were always ready to kick off their panties. If I didn't cut it with the oil business, life was still a pure pleasure around Sal's swimming pool. It didn't have nothing to do with liquor or dope. It has to do with a lack of character.'

'It's part of the illness. You'll learn that if you keep going to meetings,' I said.

He pulled a long-bladed weed from the edge of the step and bounced it up and down between his feet.

'You'll see,' I said.

'You want me to talk to the DEA, don't you?'

'Why do you think that?'

'I heard you on the phone last night.'

'You want to?'

'No.'

He bounced the weed on the toe of his loafer, then picked up a small red bug with the weed's tip and watched it climb toward his hand.

'You wouldn't use me, would you, Dave?' he said.

'No, I wouldn't do that.'

'Because I'd be sorely hurt. I mean it, son. I don't need it. I surely don't.'

I stood up and brushed off the seat of my pants.

'I don't know how you do it,' I said.

'What's that?' He squinted up at me in the sunlight. His hair was gold and wavy and shiny with oil.

'No matter what I talk to you about, somehow I always lose.'

'It's your imagination. They don't come much more simple than me.'

I remember one of the last times I saw my mother. It was 1945, just before the war ended, and she came to our house on the bayou with the gambler she had run away with. I was out front the dirt road, trying to catch my dog, who was chasing chickens in the ditch, when he stopped his coupe, one with a rumble seat and hand-cranked front window with gas-ration stamps on it, thirty yards down the house. She walked fast up the lane into the shade of our oaks and around to the side yard, where my father was nailing together a chicken coop. She worked in a drive-in and beer garden in Morgan City. Her pink waitress uniform had white trim on the collar and sleeves, and because her body was thick and muscular it looked too small on her when she walked. Her back was turned to me while she talked to my father, but his face was dark as he listened and his eyes went up the road to where the coupe was parked.

The gambler had his car door open to let in the breeze. He was thin and wore sideburns and brown zoot pants with suspenders and a striped shirt and a green necktie with purple dots on it. A brown fedora sat in the back window.

He asked me in French if the dog was mine. When I didn't answer, he said, 'You don't talk French, boy?'

'Yes, sir.'

'That your dog?'

'Yes, sir.'

'You know how to make him stop running them chicken? Break a stick on him. You ain't got to do it but once.'

I walked away in the dust toward the house and the trees, and I didn't look at my dog. I heard my father say to my mother, 'In five minutes I'm coming there. That little gun won't do him no good, neither.'

She took me by the hand and walked me quickly to the front steps and sat me in her lap. She brushed my face and hair with her hands and kissed me and patted my thighs. There were drops of perspiration behind her neck, and I could smell her perfume, like four-o'clocks, and the powder on her breasts.

'You been good at school, huh?' she said. 'You been going to mass, too, you? You been making confess and go to communion? Aldous been taking you? You got to do good in school. The brothers gonna teach you lots of t'ings.'

'Why you stay with him?'

She pressed my face against her breasts. I could feel the hard shape of her stomach and her thighs.

'He shot somebody. In a card game,' I said.

'He ain't bad. He's good to me. We brung you a present. You gonna see.'

She picked me up and carried me to the road. I could see my father watching from the side yard, the hammer in his hand. She sent me down by the open door of the coupe. The air was humid and hot in the sun, and the cattails in the ditch were coated with dust.

'Come see,' she said. 'Show it him, Mack. Behind the seat.'

His face had no expression. He reached behind the seat, his eyes looking out the yellow road, and pulled out a paper bag. It was folded across the top and tied with string.

'Here,' she said, and unwrapped it for me. Her dress was tight across her thighs and there were dimples in her knees. The man got out of the car and walked out on the road and lit a cigarette. He didn't look in my father's direction, but they could see each other well.

'You like a top, huh?' my mother said. 'See, it got a crank. You push it up and down and it spin around and whistle.'

There was perspiration in her black hair. She put the top in my hands. The metal felt hot against my palms.

'Is he coming out?' the man said.

'No. He promised.'

'The last time was for free. You told him that?'

'He don't want no more trouble, Mack. He ain't gonna bother us.'

'I give a damn, me.'

'Don't be talking that way. We gotta go. Don't be looking over there. You hear me, Mack?'

'They gonna keep him in jail next time.'

'We going right now. Get in the car. I gotta be at work. Dave don't need be standing out in the hot road. Ain't that right, Davy? Mack, you promised.'

He flipped his cigarette away in the ditch and got behind the steering wheel. He wore two-tone brown and white shoes, and he wiped the dust off the shine with a rag from under the seat. I saw my father toss his hammer up on the workbench, then pick up the chicken coop and look at the angles of its side.

My mother leaned over me and pressed me against her body. Her voice was low, as though the two of us were under a glass bell.

'I ain't bad, Davy,' she said. 'If somebody tell you that, it ain't true. I'll come see you again. We'll go somewheres together, just us two. Eat fried chicken, maybe. You gonna see, you.'

But a long time would pass before I would see her again. The Victory gardens, the picket-fenced donation centers of worn tires and bundled coat hangers, the small tasseled silk flags with blue and gold service stars that hung in house windows to signify the number of family members who were in uniform or killed in action, would all disappear within the year, an era would end, and the oil companies would arrive from Texas. I would hear that my mother worked in the back of a laundry with colored women in Baton Rouge, that Mack died of tuberculosis, that she married a man who operated carnival rides. Then when I was sixteen years old and I went for the first time to the Boundary Club on the Breaux Bridge highway, a rough, ramshackle roadhouse where they fought with knives and bottles in the shale parking lot, I saw her drawing draft beer behind the bar. Her body was thicker now, her hair blacker than it would have been, and she wore a black skirt that showed a thick scar above one knee. She brought a beer tray to a table full of oil-field workers, then sat down with them. They all knew her and lit her cigarettes, and when she danced with one of them she pressed her stomach against his loins. I stood by the jukebox and waved at her, and she smiled back at me over the man's shoulder, but there was no recognition in her face.

I waited out in the car for my friends to come out of the club. I saw a drunk man pushed out the side door on to the shale. I saw some teenagers throw a Coke bottle at a car full of Negroes. I saw a man in a yellow cowboy shirt and tight blue jeans without a belt slap a woman against the side of a car. He hit her hard and made her cry and shoved her in the backseat and made her stay there by herself while he went back inside. It was hot and still in the parking lot, except for the sounds of the woman. The willow trees were motionless on the banks of the Vermilion River, and the moonlight looked like oil on the water's surface. Dust drifted through the car window, and I could smell the stench of dead garfish out on the mudbank and hear the woman weeping quietly in the dark.

The option of certain people has always been important to me. Most of those people have been nuns, priests, Catholic brothers, and teachers. When I was a child the good ones among them told me I was all right. Some in that group were inept and unhappy with themselves and were cruel and enjoyed inculcating guilt in children. But the good ones told me that I was all right. As an adult, I still believe that we become the reflection we see in the eyes of others, so it's important that someone tell us we're all right. That may seem childish, but only to those who have paid no dues and hence have no question mark about who they are, because their own experience or lack of it has never required them to define themselves. You can meet some of these at university cocktail parties; or sometimes they are journalists who fear and envy power and celebrity but who love to live in its ambience. There is always a sneer buried inside their laugher. They have never heard a shot fired in anger, done time, walked through a mortared ville, seen a nineteen-year-old door gunner go apeshit in a free-fire zone. They sleep without dreaming. They yawn at the disquietude of those whom they can't understand. No one will ever need to tell them that they are all right.

I think for some the soul has the same protean shape as fire, or a collection of burning sticks that melts and hisses through the snow until only an ill-defined and soot-streaked hollow remains to indicate the nature of flame and its passage through ice.

Then somebody tells you that you are all right.

I had to go back on the other side of the Divide. It was a good time to take Alafair out of Missoula, too. I walked down to the school and found Tess Regan in her office. A vase of mock orange sat on her desk, and her corkboard was a litter of thumbtacked crayon drawings. Through a sunny window I could see the children on the playground, a solitary basketball hoop, and the brick wall of the church next door. She wore a cotton knit yellow dress, a gold neck chain, and gold earrings that were almost hidden by her auburn hair. Her nails were cut short and painted with clear polish, and her fingers were spread on her desk blotter while she listened to me talk. I liked her and respected her feelings, and I didn't want her to be angry with me any longer or to be uncomfortable because of our conversation yesterday.

'People hang up on me all the time. I expect it,' I said. 'A Treasury agent once told me I had the telephone charm of Quasimodo.'

'That purple lump on your head, that happened at your house yester-day?'

'I was careless. It'll be gone soon.'

'You want to take Alafair out of school today and tomorrow?'

'That's right. She'll be back Thursday.'

'Where are you going, if you don't mind my asking?'

'I have to take care of some business across the mountains.'

'I'm very concerned about all this. You give me bad feelings. These men you talk about are evil, aren't they? But you seem almost cavalier.'

'You're wrong about that, kiddo.'

'I wish you wouldn't call me that.'

'All right.'

'Alafair is a wonderful little girl. I worry about her. I worry about your attitudes.'

'She thinks the world of you, too. I don't want to be unpleasant or to upset you in any way, but I want you to understand something. Somebody sent me a used hypodermic needle and a letter and a photo-graph. I won't tell you what was in the photograph, but the person who wrote the letter said the needle had been used in a snuff film. His threat was not aimed at me. It was directed at Alafair. I believe he was serious, too.

'Now, in the movies potential murder or assault victims are given twenty-four-hour protection by the cops. But it doesn't happen that way. You're on your own. If you don't believe me, ask anybody who has been hunted down by a guy who they had locked up and who made bail by the next morning. They tell a great story. A lot of them tend to become NRA members.'

Her green eyes were steady and intelligent. She was a good soldier and obviously was trying to look beyond the abrasive quality of my words; but I had gone over a line, almost like an emotional bully, and she wasn't up to handling it.

'I'll get Alafair for you,' she said.

'Miss Regan . . . Tess, I'm at a real bad place in my life. I apologize for the way that I talk, but I'm really up against it. Don't make me walk out of here feeling like a shit.'

But it was no use. She brushed past me, her hips creasing inside her knit dress, her eyes welling with tears.

Later that day Alafair and I drove into the clouds on the Divide. It rained hard and the trees looked thick and black in the wet light, and water sluiced off the road into the canyons far below. It was too late to get anything done at the Teton County courthouse, so we stayed the night at a motel in Choteau, the county seat.

The next day I found the connection between Sally Dee and the oil business. I found it all over the East Front, in Teton, Pondera, and Glacier counties. And I found out the service that Dixie Lee had been performing for him.

10

That evening I called Dan Nygurski at his house in Great Falls.

'Where've you been? I called you three times today,' he said.

'Over here, east of the Divide.'

'Now? Where?'

'Right outside of Great Falls.'

'What are you doing right now?'

'Nothing. Going to a motel. I don't feel like driving back tonight.'

'We're fixing to cook out in the backyard in a few minutes. You want to come over?'

'My little girl's with me.'

'Bring her. We've got three kids she can play with. I've got some heavy stuff on Mapes that you ought to know about.'

'The DEA had a file on him?'

'FBI. He was part of a kidnap investigation. You better come over.'

He gave me his address and directions, and Alafair and I drove in the twilight to a 1950s suburb of split-level ranch homes, maple-lined streets, sprinklers twirling on the lawns, flower beds full of blue clematis, yellow and red roses, with tree bark packed on the dirt to prevent the growth of weeds. We sat on the redwood deck built out back, behind sliding glass doors, while Alafair played on a small seesaw with two of his little girls. The coals in his hibachi had already turned gray and hot before we arrived, and his wife brought out a tossed salad and a pitcher of iced tea on a tray, then laid a row of venison and elk steaks on the grill. The grease hissed and steamed off the coals and the smell was wonderful.

His wife was attractive and polite and had the same accent as he.

She wore makeup and a dress, and her eyes were shy when you looked too closely at them. She went back into the kitchen and began slicing a loaf of French bread on a cutting board.

'You're wondering why a woman who looks like that married a guy who looks like me,' he said.

'Not at all.'

'Come on, Robicheaux.'

'Women have kind hearts.'

'Yeah, they do,' he said, and got up from his chair and closed the sliding glass door. 'So let's walk around the side of the house so nobody else has to hear what I have to tell you. In fact, maybe we ought to wait until after you've eaten.'

'Let's do it.'

We walked into his side yard, which was planted with apple trees and climbing red roses on trellises set in small circular beds. There were small, hard green apples in the leaves of the trees. A picket fence separated his yard from his neighbor's swimming pool. It was dusk now, and the reflection of the neighbor's porch light looked like a yellow balloon under the pool's surface. He picked up two metal chairs that were leaned against the side of his house and shook them open. His mouth twitched when he started to speak, and I saw the web of vein and sinew flex and pulse in his throat.

'Where'd your lawyer get his information on Mapes?'

'He hired a PI.'

'Tell him to get your money back. The PI blew it. I suspect he checked the sheriff's and city police's office in Mapes's hometown, came up with the assault arrest, the golf club deal, when Mapes was seventeen, then sent your lawyer a bill for two days' services, which is usually about six hundred dollars. In the meantime he didn't check anything else.'

'What's the story?'

'Look, you were a cop a long time. You know that once in a while you run across a guy, a guy who everybody thinks is normal, maybe a guy with an education, a good job, service record, a guy who doesn't focus much attention on himself. At least he doesn't give cops reason to think about him. But there's something wrong with him. The conscience isn't there, or maybe the feelings aren't. But he's out there, in suburbs just like this, and he's the one who commits the murders that we never solve. I think that's your man Harry Mapes.

'In 1965 an eighteen-year-old soldier on leave from Fort Polk picked up his girlfriend in Tyler, Texas, and took her to a drive-in movie. Then it looks like they went on a back road and parked behind an old greenhouse where somebody used to grow roses. At least that's where the sheriff department found that girl's dress and underwear. They found the car five miles away in a creek bed. Somebody had torn the gas line loose and set it on fire. Both those kids were in the trunk. The pathologist said they were alive when it burned.'

I leaned forward on the folding metal chair and picked a leaf from a rosebush. My throat felt tight. I could hear the children playing on the seesaw in the backyard.

'Mapes was involved?' I said.

'That's the big question. The fingerprints of another kid from Marshall were on the victims' car, but not Mapes's. But that would figure, if Mapes drove one car and the other kid drove the victims' car to the place where they burned it. Both of them were seen together earlier that night, and it took two people to pull it off, unless the kid they had dead-bang was on foot, which is improbable, since he owned a car and was driving around in it with Mapes earlier.'

'The other kid didn't implicate Mapes?'

'He denied everything. Evidently he had a reputation around Marshall as a lunatic. Acid, speed, all that bullshit. In his cell he wrapped himself in toilet paper, soaked it in lighter fluid, and set himself on fire. It looked like good theater. But later on he showed everybody he was sincere. He unwrapped some wire from a broom and hanged himself.

'In the meantime, Mapes's old man, who owned a sawmill there, hired a law firm, and they got a Mexican prostitute to swear Mapes and another friend of his were trying out their magic twangers that night. The other kid backed her up. But later on it looks like he might have had problems with his conscience.'

'And he was the one Mapes worked over with the golf club.'

'You got it, brother. Case closed. On top of it, that other kid got zapped in Vietnam two years later.'

I rubbed my hands up and down on my trousers.

'I've got to nail him, Dan. I'm all out of leads, and I keep coming up with a handful of air.'

'Let's eat some dinner.'

'I don't think I'm up to it. I'm sorry. I've got less than one and a half weeks to trial. I'm being straight with you. I'm just not going to do time.'

'You're a good man, and you're going to be all right,' he said, and put his big hand on the corner of my shoulder. It felt hard and cupped, like a starfish that had dried on hot sand.

It was time to turn things around on Sally Dee, to plant some dark thoughts in his head about his own vulnerability, so I could concentrate on Harry Mapes. I knew that Charlie Dodds had probably become bear food at the bottom of a canyon, but Sally Dee didn't. However, he was well aware of Charlie Dodds's potential, and I doubted if he would enjoy being in an adversarial relationship with him. Snapping dogs don't like having their collars chained together.

After Alafair and I got back to Missoula, I rented an hour's typewriter time at the University of Montana library and composed the following letter. I worked hard on it. Chaucer and Dickens created wonderful rogues. I wondered what they would have thought of my attempt. But the more I read over my final draft, the more I was certain that they just might have winked at me with approval.

Dear Sal,

The flowers that go with this you can stick up your butt. When you called Vegas, you said it was a simple yard job. You didn't say anything about pictures and this before and after bullshit. That little stunt almost got me killed. In fact, maybe I think you set me up. You go around telling everybody you're a made guy but made guys don't get their nose bent out of joint by some ex-cop that nobody cares about. I think you're not only a dago shitbag and a welsher but a yellow cunt, too. I heard about you from some guys that were in Huntsville. They say your punk had the whole joint laughing at you behind your back. The only reason you got straight is because you were more afraid of your old man than you were of your punk. But you're not getting out of this one. You owe me the rest of the money, and you know where to deliver it, I don't get it, and I mean right away, I'm coming after you. Nobody back in Vegas is going to make a beef about it, either. They all think you're a prick that should have been clipped a long time ago.

    C.D.

I drove up to Polson, found a florist's, then called them from a pay phone across the street and got the price of a small floral delivery to Sally Dio's house. Then I found the state employment office, parked by the curb, and watched the men who went in and out of the entrance or who sat against the wall in the shade and smoked cigarettes and passed a bottle back and forth in a paper sack. Finally a middle-aged man in work clothes with uncut dull blond hair came out the door and sat down on the curb with his friends.

I got out of my truck and walked up to him.

'Say, I'll pay you five bucks to go into a florist's and put in an order for me,' I said. 'I'm playing a joke on a guy, and I don't want him to know where the flowers came from. How about it?'

He took a hand-rolled cigarette out of his mouth and looked at me quizzically. He shrugged his shoulders.

'I don't give a shit,' he said.

I drove him back over to the street where the florist's was located, parked three stores down, and gave him the money for the order and a sealed envelope with the letter inside. I didn't know Dio's address, but I had printed his name on the envelope and drawn the approximate location of his house on Flathead Lake.

'Don't tell them you're doing this for anybody else,' I said. 'Just give them the money and the order and the envelope. Okay?'

'Can you make it ten? If I don't buy them other guys a can of beer or something, they might cut me out of a job they get.'

He went into the store and was back out in five minutes. I drove him back to the state employment office.

'You didn't tell them anything, did you?' I asked.

'What's to talk about in a flower place? I give them the money, I give them the envelope. You got any more jobs like this one you want done?'

That night Dixie Lee and I took Alafair to a movie. Before I went to bed I got Dixie to give me Sally Dee's unlisted telephone number.

'What for? You don't want no more truck with that man,' he said. He sat in his undershirt, candy-striped undershorts, and black shoes at the kitchen table, eating a piece of pie.

'Don't worry about it.'

'Are you kidding? He's got mental diseases they haven't named yet. I ain't putting you on, son. He's got a hard-on for you you couldn't knock down with a hammer.'

'Don't use that language in the house.'

'Sorry, it's a speech defect or something. His head reminds me of a flowerpot somebody dropped on the concrete. It's full of cracks and the dirt's starting to leak out, but he don't know it yet. Dig this. Sal built an elevator platform for the piano at his club, one of these deals that rises up into the spotlight while the guy's playing. Except after the club closed this two-hundred-and-eighty-pound bouncer got on top of the piano with this topless dancer for some serious rumba boogie, and somehow the machinery got cranked up and the elevator went right up to the ceiling and mashed them both against a beam. It broke the guy's neck, and the broad was trapped up there with him all night. So Sal says it's a real big tragedy, and he holds the funeral on a Sunday afternoon at the club, with the casket covered with flowers out in the middle of the dance floor. But the undertaker messed up the job, and the guy's neck was bent and his head was out of round, like a car tire had run over it, and the dagos were slobbering and wailing all over the place while Sal's singing on the mike in a white suit like he's Tony Bennett. It was so disgusting the waiters went back to the union and threatened to quit. Later Sal says to me, "It was a class send-off, don't you think? Jo-Jo would have liked it." Except I found out he only rented the casket, and he had Jo-Jo planted in a cloth-covered box in a desert cemetery outside of town that lizards wouldn't crawl across.'

'Good night, Dixie.'

He shook his head and forked another piece of pie in his mouth.

'You worry about my bad language, and you're fixing to squeeze Sal in the peaches. You're a wonder to behold, son.'

I set the alarm on my Seiko watch for two AM and went to sleep. It was raining lightly when I was awakened by the tiny dinging sound on my wrist. I dialed Sal's number, then hung up when a man with sleep in his voice answered. I waited fifteen minutes, then hung up again as soon as the same man said 'Hello' irritably into the receiver. I drank a glass of milk and watched the rain fall in the yard and run down the window, then at two-thirty I called again. I put a pencil crossways in my teeth and covered the mouthpiece with my handkerchief.

'Who the fuck is this?' the same man said.

'Where's Sal?' I kept my voice in the back of my throat and let it come out in a measured rasp.

'Asleep. Who is this?'

'Go wake him up.'

'Are you crazy? It's two-thirty in the morning. What's with you, man?'

'Listen, you get that dago welsher out of bed.'

'I think you're loaded, man, and you'd better stop playing on the phone and forget you ever called here.'

'You don't recognize my voice, huh? Maybe it's because a guy put a wrench across my windpipe, a guy that gutless kooze sent me to see. I didn't catch a plane back to Vegas, either. I'm one hour away. I better not find out you're hitting on my broad, either.'

He was quiet a moment, then he said, 'Charlie?'

I didn't answer.

'Charlie?' he said. 'Hey, man . . .'

'What?'

'I didn't know. Hey, man, I'm sorry. You should have told me. It's late, and I been asleep, and I didn't know it was you.'

'Get him on the phone.'

'Man, he's out. I mean, like him and Sandy must have smoked a whole shoe box of shit before they crashed. How about he calls you in the morning?'

'You got some kind of skin growth over your ears?'

'Look, man, I go in there, he'll tear my dick off. He's been crawling the walls all day, anyway. Look, I don't know what's going on between you guys, but I don't want to get caught in it. Okay? I'm not putting you on, man, he can't talk to you. He really smoked his brains tonight.'

I waited five seconds and listened to him breathe.

'Tell him I'm coming,' I said, and hung up.

I overslept the next morning and was awakened by the sound of Alafair fixing breakfast in the kitchen. She was too short to function well around the stove, and she clattered the pan loudly on the burners.

'I can walk myself today, Dave,' she said.

'No, that's out. We do everything together, little guy. We're a team, right?'

She stood in front of the stove, her face quiet, her head even with the top of the stove, looking at the skillet full of French toast.

'It makes me feel funny in front of the other kids,' she said.

'I'll drive you, then. It'll be like I'm dropping you off on the way to work. That'll be okay, won't it?'

'Clarise don't know how to take care of Tripod. She's always mad at him.'

I turned off the stove, picked up the skillet with a dish towel, and set it in the sink to cool. The French toast was burned around the edges.

'We're just going to have to accept some things now. That's the way it is, Alf,' I said.

She packed her lunch box silently, then ate only half of her French toast, and went outside and waited for me on the front step. The wind was blowing off the river, and the sunlight through the maple tree made shifting patterns of leaves on her face.

Later, Dixie and I went to an early AA meeting. Afterward, one of the members who worked in the job-placement service told Dixie that he had found him a part-time job operating a forklift at the pulp mill out on the river. We walked home, and it was obvious that Dixie was not happy at the news. He sulked around the house, then took his sunburst guitar out on the back steps and began playing with a thumb pick and singing a song that I had heard only once before, many years ago. The words went to the tune of 'Just a Closer Walk with Thee.'

'Now, bread and gravy is all right,
And a turnip sandwich is a delight,
But my kids always scream
For more of them ole butter beans.

Well, just a little piece of country ham,
Just pass the butter and the jam,
Just pass the biscuits if you please,
And some more of them good ole butter beans.

Just see that woman over there,
The one with both her hands in the air.
She's not pregnant as she seems
She's just full of good ole butter beans.'

I opened the screen and sat down on the steps beside him. It was warm, and the clover in the grass was alive with bees.

'You're supposed to report to the plant at noon, aren't you?' I said.

'That's what he said.'

'You going out there in slacks and a Hawaiian shirt?'

'Look, that job ain't exactly what I had in mind.'

'Oh?'

'Ain't that place a toilet paper factory or something? Besides, I don't have experience running heavy equipment.'

'A forklift isn't heavy equipment. And I thought you told me you operated one in Huntsville.'

'For about two days, till I dropped the prongs on a guy's foot.'

'We had a deal, podna. We don't renegotiate the terms.'

He made a sliding blues chord high up on the guitar's neck, then ran it all the way down to the nut.

'I learned that from Sam Hopkins,' he said. 'I went out to his house in the Fifth Ward in Houston. People said them nigras'll leave you bleeding in the street for the garbageman to find. They treated me like royalty, man.'

'I spent some time Wednesday in some court-houses east of the Divide.'

His face went blank.

'I found some of the deals you made over there.'

He continued to look out at the lawn and the bees lifting off the clover.

'I'm not an expert on the oil business, but I saw some peculiar stuff in those lease files,' I said.

'They're public records. A person can look all they want to.' He began fishing in his shirt pocket for a cigarette.

'Every time you leased up a big block of land for Star Drilling, there was a hole or two left in it.'

He lit his cigarette and smoked it with his elbow propped on the belly of his guitar.

'Those holes were leased or bought up by one of Sal's businesses in Vegas,' I said. 'The same company name is on some of the deals you made for him around Flathead Lake.'

'I'm not proud of it.'

'So he does want into the oil and gas business.'

'He wants to cover his action every way he can. He's shooting for the big score in gambling and lake property development, he wants in on the gas domes on the East Front. In the drilling business, it don't matter if they tap in on top of your property or not. As long as you're in the pool, part of the dome, you're going to get royalties. That ain't all he's got on his mind, either. They make a big strike over there, it could be like that pipeline deal up in Alaska. All them sonsobitches are horny, and they got plenty of money for dope, too. Them conservation people are hollering because the gas is full of hydrogen sulfide, it stinks like rotten eggs, but they ought to hear what Sal's got planned for the place.'

'So you took Star over the hurdles?'

'That's about it.'

'And you helped Sal start out in a brand-new enterprise.'

'You want me on the cross? I told you I done it. I ain't lied about it.'

'But that's not all of it.'

'What?'

'Dalton Vidrine and Harry Mapes had to know what you were doing.'

'At first they didn't but Vidrine heard about it from another guy who was working the same township and range as me. He told Mapes, and they stuck it to me at the motel one night. I thought they were going to drop the dime on me with the home office, but they just wanted me to piece off the action. Sal said no problem. It cost him a little coke. Everybody was happy.'

'You've got to give me something I can use against Mapes.'

'I got nothing to offer. I told you all of it. They're like piranha in a goldfish bowl. You stick your finger in it, you take back a polished bone.'

I left him thumbing the bass string on his guitar and staring out at the lawn, as though the blue and green shades in the grass held a secret for him. A few minutes later he came into the house and changed into an old shirt and a pair of ripped and faded pink slacks and drove off toward the smoking stacks of the pulp mill west of town.

After he was gone, I sat alone in the silence of the house with the realization that there was nothing I could do today to help my case. I knew of nothing I could do tomorrow or the next day either. I had run out of options. The time has come, I thought, to think not in terms of what to do but instead of where to go. Any jail or prison is a bad place. The person who thinks otherwise has never been in one. Angola is worse than most. The man who would willingly submit to do time unjustly in a place like that would take pleasure in his own crucifixion, I thought. It was a big country, and there were lots of places to get lost in it.

But the idea of being a permanent fugitive from the law was so strange and removed from any concept I had ever had about my fate in this world that thinking about it left me numb and staring at phantasms in the air.

Annie, I thought.

But she came to me only in the darkness, and her visits had become less frequent and her voice had grown weaker across the water and in the din of the rain. I had only myself to depend on now, and my Higher Power and the AA program that I followed. Maybe, as I had told Dixie Lee in the hospital, it was time to look at the things that I had rather than at the problems that seemed to beset me without a solution. I was sober, even though I had set myself up for a fall by not attending meetings. When I had wanted to join Annie in that watery place more than anything in the world, I had gone into therapy rather than let that morning arrive when I would awaken in the blue-gray light, sit quietly on the side of my bed in my underwear, and fit the iron sight of my .45 against the roof of my mouth. And, last, I had Alafair, who was given to me inside a green bubble of air from below the Gulf's surface.

Maybe it's like the seventh-inning stretch, I thought, when they've shelled your fastball past your ears and blown your hanging curve through the boards. Afternoon shadows are growing on the field, your arm aches, the movement and sound of the fans are like an indistinct hum in the stands. Then a breeze springs up and dries the sweat on your face and neck, you wipe your eyes clear on your sleeve, scrub the ball against your thigh, fork your fingers tightly into the stitches, and realize that the score is irrelevant now, that your failure is complete, that it wasn't so bad after all because now you're free and alone in a peculiar way that has put you beyond the obligations of victory and defeat. The batter expects you to float another balloon past his letters, and instead you take a full windup, your face dry and cool in the breeze, your arm now weightless, and you swing your leg and whole butt into the delivery, your arm snaps like a snake, and the ball whizzes past him in a white blur. And that's the way you pitch the rest of the game, in the lengthening shadows, in the dust blowing off the base paths, in the sound of a flag popping on a metal pole against the blue sky; you do it without numbers in your head, right into the third out in the bottom of the ninth.

And I wasn't going to let Tess Regan have the final statement, either. You don't walk out of a room on someone, with tears in your eyes, as though he's an ogre, unless you want to inflict a certain amount of damage. I ate lunch, then told her that over the phone. Then I asked her to have dinner with me and Alafair at a restaurant that evening.

'I don't know what to say. I don't want to be unkind to you. I just don't understand you,' she said.

'Stop hiding behind that elementary-school-teacher stuff.'

'You stop talking to me like that.'

'Don't treat me like I fell through a hole in the dimension, either.'

'You're an incredible person. You can't say everything that's on your mind to somebody, then ask them out to dinner.'

'I've been straight with you, Tess. I'm indebted to you for the care you've given Alafair. I respect and like you. I don't want you to be unaware of that fact. That's all I had to say. We'll leave it at that.'

She paused a moment, then away from the receiver, cleared her throat.

'I have a PTA buffet at five-thirty,' she said. 'We could go out for dessert later, if you'd like to.'

That evening I shined my loafers, put on a pair of seersucker slacks, a long-sleeved blue shirt with a red-and-black-striped tie, and Alafair and I picked her up in the truck at seven-thirty. She lived on the bottom floor of an old orange-brick apartment building, with a wood porch and thick wood columns and an enormous white-trunked birch tree in the front yard. She wore beige sandals and a print dress covered with small blue and pink flowers. We went to an outdoor café by the river and had ice cream and Black Forest chocolate cake, and I paid for it with my MasterCard, hoping that it hadn't been canceled yet. It rained briefly;

now the sky looked like an ink wash above the mountains and I could see lightning striking hard on a distant ridge.

Alafair was overjoyed at the thought of Tess Regan and me being together. But it wasn't a romantic overture on my part. Or at least that was what I told myself, although she was surely good to look at. I think she reminded me of one of those girls whom Catholic boys were always told, when I was growing up, that they should marry. I doubt that a girl of that kind ever existed, but we believed she did, anyway. Before I met Darlene, I was involved seriously with only three women in my adult life. My first wife was from Martinique, a descendant of French Huguenots, or probably iconoclasts who liked to smash statues in cathedrals. She tired quickly of living with a drunk, for which I couldn't blame her, but she also tired of living on a policeman's salary and became fond of wealth and clubhouse society. She married a Houston geologist, and the last I heard they lived in River Oaks and raced quarter horses at Rio Dosa.

Annie was not only the best woman I ever knew; she was also the best human being. I called her my Mennonite girl, sewn together from cornflowers and bluebonnets. He faults were those of excess – in love, forgiveness, worry over others, faith that goodness would always prevail over evil. She was seldom if ever critical of others, and when their views didn't coincide with her eccentric Kansas vision of the world, she saw them as victims of what she called weirdness, a condition that she saw virtually everywhere.

I became involved with Robin Gaddis after Annie's death. She was a stripper and sometime-hooker on Bourbon Street, but she was brave in her way and kind and gave much more than she received. What some will not understand is that it takes courage to grow up in a place like the welfare project by the old St Louis Cemetery in New Orleans. Ask a tourist who has visited that cemetery in anything less than a large group, even in broad daylight. Or if one is suicidal and would like to have a truly existential experience, he might try walking though Louis Armstrong Park, right next to the welfare project, at night. Robin's body was outraged in many ways long before she began taking off her clothes for men simply for money. I don't know where she is today. I wish I did. I have two Purple Hearts. I believe they belong much more to Annie, Robin, and Darlene than they do to me.

The wind began to blow, and in the fading twilight I could see the smoke from the pulp mill flatten in the valley west of town and smell its odor like a tinge of sewage in the wet air. We drove Tess Regan back to her apartment house, and I walked her to her door. The porch light was on, and there was a sheen in her auburn hair, and her shoulders looked pale against her pink-and-blue-flowered dress.

'Thank you for this evening,' she said, and she touched me lightly on the arm with her fingers and let them rest there for perhaps three seconds.

Her green eyes were warm and genuine, and I wondered if she had been rehearsing for a long time to be that Catholic girl the nuns and the brothers had told us about.

We drove under the dark shadows of the trees toward our house, and the glow from the street lamps looked like long slicks of yellow light ironed into the street's wet surface. I turned the corner on to our block while Alafair kept looking out the passenger window at a pair of headlights behind us.

'That same car stopped down from Miss Regan's,' she said.

'What?'

'That car stopped behind us while you were talking to Miss Regan on the porch.'

I parked in front of our house. The street was dark, and the strings of lights on the sawmill across the river shone on the water's surface.

'Don't get out of the truck,' I said, and I reached under the seat for my .45. The vehicle behind me pulled to the curb, and the driver cut the headlights just as I stepped out of the cab with the automatic held behind my leg.

Clete stuck his head out of the window of his Toyota jeep, his mouth grinning, a white billed cap cocked over his eye.

'Hey, can you tell me where I can catch the St Charles streetcar?' he said. 'What have you got hidden behind you, noble mon? Are we into heavy shit here?'

'What are you doing following me?'

'I was on my way over and just happened to see you on the other street. Slow your pulse down, Streak.' He got out of the Toyota and stretched and yawned. He wore a purple and gold LSU football jersey with big tiger's head on the front. His love handles stuck out from the sides of his blue jeans. He reached back through the car window and took out a pint of whiskey in a paper bag, unscrewed the cap, and took a neat drink.

'Who was the broad?' he said.

I didn't answer him. I walked Alafair into the house, turned on all the lights, looked in each of the rooms, and came back outside. He sat on the steps, smoking a cigarette, the pink bottle by his knee.

'Who's the new broad?' he said.

'Wrong word.'

'All right, who's the *lady*?'

'Just a friend, one of the teachers at the school. She looks after Alafair sometimes.'

'I wonder why she isn't homely. Probably just a coincidence.'

'What are you up to, Clete?'

'Nothing. Maybe I just want to talk a minute. You got a minute don't you?'

I sat down next to him on the steps. Against the lights on the sawmill, I could see the outline of suitcases and a couple of rolled sleeping bags in the back of his jeep. He took his billfold out of his back pocket and began counting through a thick sheaf of twenties in the bill holder.

'How you doing on money?' he said.

'Not bad.'

'I bet.'

'I've still got my credit cards.'

'You remember that time I dropped a deuce at Jefferson Downs? You lent it to me so Lois wouldn't find out.'

'You paid it back. When we took that charter fishing trip out of Gulfport.'

'Not quite. I didn't pay the guy.'

I looked at him.

'He was a lousy guy. He ran us up on the sandbar, he didn't bring enough bait, his mate was a smartass. You think I'm going to give a guy like that four hundred dollars?' he said.

'Thanks, Clete. I don't need it right now.'

He folded a stack of bills between his fingers and shoved them into my shirt pocket.

'Take it and stop irritating me.'

'It looks like you're packed up.'

'You can't ever tell.'

'What are you doing, partner?'

'I think my greatest potential lies in population control and travel. Who'd you tell about Charlie Dodds?'

'The DEA.'

'I knew it.'

'The agent said he was going to the locals with it, too.'

'Big deal. But I knew you'd do it, Streak. You'll always be a straight cop.'

'There's worse things.'

'What's that mean?'

'Nothing. I'm just talking about myself. I've got to go inside now. You want to come in?'

'No, thanks. I think I'll just take a drive somewhere, maybe eat a steak.'

'You've been lucky so far, Clete. Walk away from it.'

'You ought to come up to the Nine Mile House at Alberton with me. They've got steaks you can cut with a spoon. Watch out for that school-teacher. Those kind will marry you.'

I watched him drive away in the darkness. I went into the kitchen and put the folded sheaf of bills from my pocket on the table. Then I looked at the bills again and counted them. Some of the bills were fifties, not twenties. He had given me over six hundred dollars.

Later that night, Dixie came home with a black-and-white television set that he had bought for ten dollars, and was watching the late show on the couch in his underwear when the phone rang. I sat up sleepily on the edge of the bed and looked out at him in the lighted hallway as he answered the phone. His hairy stomach protruded over the elastic of his candy-striped shorts. He put his hand over the mouthpiece of the receiver.

'It's that DEA Polack in Great Falls,' he said. 'You want me to tell him you're bombed out?'

'That's all right,' I said, took the phone from him, went into the bathroom, and closed the door.

'What's up, Dan?' I said.

'I'm just glad to find you home.'

'I'm glad to be home, too. My watch says it's one in the morning.'

'An hour ago, somebody took a shot at Sally Dee. They damn near got him, too. The sheriff over there is going to have you high up on his list.'

'Give him a call in the morning, will you, and tell him what time you got ahold of me. I don't want any more dealings with that guy.'

'Sure. Hey, the deputy who called me said Sal's real shook up. The shooter got up on the knoll above the house and parked a big one right through the kitchen window while Sal was drinking a glass of milk and eating cookies at the table. It blew glass and parts of a flowerpot all over him. Guess who wants police protection now?'

'What do they have so far?'

'Not much. They know about where the shot came from. That's about it.'

'No witnesses?'

'Not so far. You got some ideas?'

'Put is this way. How many people *wouldn't* like to see him cooled out?'

'No, no, let's be a little more candid here.'

'My speculations aren't of much value these days.'

'We're talking about Purcel.'

'He was here earlier tonight.'

'How much earlier?'

'Three hours.'

'That'd give him time to get up there, wouldn't it?'

'Yeah, it would.'

'You think he did it, don't you?'

'Maybe.'

'Well, ole Sal's on the other end of the stick now. I wonder how he's going to handle it.'

'He'll bring in some more of his hired shitheads. I'm real tired, Dan. Is there anything else?'

'Stay clear of Purcel.'

'You better tell that to the Dio family. I wouldn't want Clete hunting me.'

'I don't think these guys want advice from the DEA. It's not a federal situation, anyway. Sometimes you get to sit back and watch the show.'

I went back to bed and slept until the sun came up bright in my eyes and I heard the Saturday morning sound of children rollerskating out on the sidewalk.

For one morning I didn't want to think about my troubles, so when the lady next door gave me a venison roast, Alafair and I packed my rucksack for a picnic, took Dixie Lee with us, and drove down into the Bitterroot Valley to Kootenai Creek Canyon. The sky was cloudless, a hard ceramic blue from the Sapphire Mountains all the way across the valley to the jagged, snow-tipped ridges of the Bitterroots. We walked two miles up a US Forest Service trail by the streambed, the water white and boiling over the rocks, the floor of the canyon thick with cottonwoods and ponderosa pine, the layered rock walls rising straight up into saddles of more pine and peaks that were as sharp as ragged tin. The air was cool and so heavy with the smell of mist from the rocks, wet fern, pine needles, layers of dead cottonwood leaves, logs that had rotted into humus, that it was almost like breathing opium.

We climbed down the incline of the streambed and started a fire in a circle of rocks. The stream flattened out here, and the current flowed smoothly over some large boulders and spread into a quiet pool by the bank, where we set out cans of pop in the gravel to cool. I had brought along an old refrigerator grill, and I set it on the rocks over the fire, cut the venison into strips, put them on the grill with potatoes wrapped in tinfoil, then sliced up a loaf of French bread. The grease from the venison dripped into the fire, hissed and smoked in the wind, and because the meat was so lean it curled and browned quickly in the heat and I had to push it to the edge of the grill.

After we ate, Dixie Lee and Alafair found a pile of rocks that was full of chipmunks, and while they threw bread crumbs down into the crevices I walked farther down the stream and sat by a pool whose surface was covered by a white, swirling eddy of froth and leaves and spangled sunlight. Through the cottonwoods on the other side of the stream I could see the steep, moss-streaked cliff walls rise up straight into the sky.

Then a strange thing happened, because she had never appeared to me during the waking day. But I saw her face in the water, saw the sunlight spinning in her hair.

Don't give up, sailor, she said.

What?

You've had it worse. You always got out of it before.

599

When?

How about Vietnam?

I had the US Army on my side.

Listen to the voices in the water and you'll be all right. I promise. Bye-bye, baby love.

Can you stay a little longer?

But the wind blew the cottonwoods and the light went out of the water, and the pool turned to shadow and an empty pebble-and-sand bottom.

'Don't be down here talking to yourself, son,' Dixie Lee said behind me. 'You'll give me cause to worry.'

I didn't have to wait long to learn how Sally Dio would try to handle his new situation. He called me that evening at the house.

'I want a meet,' he said.

'What for?'

'We talk some stuff out.'

'I don't have anything to say to you.'

'Look, man, this is going to get straightened out. One way or another. Right now.'

'What have I got that you're interested in?'

'I ain't interested in anything you got. What's the matter with you? You got impacted shit in your head or something?'

'I'm busy tonight. Plus, I don't think I want to see you again, Sal.'

I could almost hear his exasperation and anger in the silence.

'Look, I'm making an effort,' he said. 'I'm going the extra mile. I don't have to do that. I can handle it other ways. But I'm treating you like a reasonable man.'

I deliberately waited a good five seconds.

'Where?' I said.

'There's a bar and restaurant in Missoula, the Pink Zebra, right off Higgins by the river. It's in an alley, but it's a class place. Nine o'clock.'

'I'll think it over.'

'Listen, man—'

I hung up on him.

Later, I put the .45 back under the seat of the truck, dropped Alafair off at the babysitter's, then drove to the Pink Zebra downtown. It was located in a brick-paved alley that had been refurbished into a pedestrian walkway of small cafés and shops and bars that offered philodendron and brass elegance more than alcohol.

I went inside and walked past the espresso machines and a row of booths that had copper champagne buckets affixed to the outside. The brick walls and the ceiling were hung with gleaming kettles and pots of ivy and fern, and in the back was a small private dining room, where I saw Sally Dio at a table with two men whom I hadn't seen before. But they came out of the same cookie cutter as some I had known in New Orleans. They were both around thirty, heavier than they should have been for their age, their tropical shirts worn outside their gray slacks, their necks hung with gold chains and religious medals, their pointed black shoes shined to the gloss of patent leather, their eyes as dead and level and devoid of emotion as someone staring into an empty closet.

I stopped at the door, and one of them stood up and approached me.

'If you'll step inside, Mr Robicheaux, I need to make sure you're not carrying nothing that nobody wants here,' he said.

'I don't think we'll do that,' I said.

'It's a courtesy we ask of people. It's not meant to insult nobody,' he said.

'Not tonight, podna.'

'Because everybody's supposed to feel comfortable,' he said. 'That way you have your drink, you talk, you're a guest, there ain't any tensions.'

'What's it going to be, Sal?' I said.

He shook his head negatively at the man next to me, and the man stepped back as though his body were attached to a string.

Sal wore a cream-colored suit, black suspenders, and an open-necked purple sport shirt with white polka dots. His ducktails were combed back on the nape of his neck, and he smoked a cigarette without taking his hand from his mouth. He looked at me steadily out of his blade-face, his stare so intense that the bottom rim of his right eye twitched.

'Get the waiter,' he said to the man who was standing.

'What are you having, Mr Robicheaux?' the man said.

'Nothing.'

He motioned the waiter to the door anyway.

'Bring a bottle of something nice for Mr Dio's guest,' he said.

'Bring Mr Dio another Manhattan, too. You want anything else, Sal?'

Sal shook his head again, then motioned the two men out of the room. I sat down across the table from him. A half-dozen cigarette butts were in the ashtray, and ashes were smeared on the linen tablecloth. I could smell the heavy odor of nicotine on his breath. The looped scar under his right eye was tight against his skin.

'What the fuck's going on?' he said.

'What do you mean?'

'With Charlie Dodds.'

'I don't know anything about him.'

'Cut the shit. He tried to clip me last night.'

'What has that got to do with me?'

He breathed through his nose and wet his lips.

'I want to know what's going on,' he said.

'You got me, Sal. I don't know what you're talking about.'

'You and Dodds cut some kind of deal.'

'I think maybe you've burned out some cells in your brain.'

'Listen, you stop trying to fuck with my head. You and him got something going. You paid him or something, you turned him around. I don't know what kind of deal you're working, but believe me, man, it ain't worth it.'

'This is why you wanted to meet? Big waste of time.'

'What do you want?'

'Nothing.'

'I mean it, you quit jerking me around. We're talking business. We straighten all this out right now. We don't, my old man will. You understand that? You and Charlie Dodds aren't going to fuck up millions of dollars in deals people got around here.'

'You're hitting on the wrong guy, Sal.'

The waiter brought in a Manhattan and a green bottle of wine in a silver ice bucket. He uncorked the wine and stared to pour it into a glass for me to taste.

'Get out of here,' Sal said.

After the waiter was gone, Sal lit a fresh cigarette and drew the smoke deep into his lungs.

'Listen,' he said, 'there's nothing between us.'

'Then you shouldn't send bad guys around my house.'

'It was a personal beef. It's over. Nobody got hurt. It ends now. There's a lot of money going to be made here. You can have in on it.'

I looked at my watch.

'I have to be somewhere else,' I said.

'What the fuck is with you? I'm talking a score you couldn't dream about. I'm talking three, four large a week. Broads, a condo in Tahoe, any fucking thing you want. You going to turn that down because you got a personal beef to square?'

'I'll see you, Sal. Don't send anybody else around my house. It won't help your troubles with Charlie Dodds.'

I started to get up. He put his hand on my forearm.

'I know something you want, you need, man. And I'm the cat can give it to you,' he said.

'What's that?'

'That guy Mapes. Dixie said he can send you up the road. How'd you like it if Mapes wasn't around to worry you anymore?' He took a drink from his Manhattan. His eyes were level and intent over the glass.

'I don't even know where he is,' I said.

'You say the word, you end this bullshit between you and me, you deliver up that cocksucker Charlie Dodds, Mapes is dead meat. You'll get Polaroids, then you burn them. You don't have any connection with it. Nobody'll ever see the guy again. It'll be like he never existed.'

'I'll think about it.'

'You'll think about it?'

'That's what I said, Sal. Call me tomorrow afternoon.'

I walked out of the restaurant into the coolness of the night. The streets were full of college kids, and I could smell pine woodsmoke from people's chimneys and the heavy, cold smell of the river in the air.

When I got home Dixie showed me the business card a Missoula city detective had left in the mailbox. The detective had penciled a note on the back to the effect that he wanted me to call him, since he had missed me twice at the house. I suspected this had to do with Dan Nygurski's calling the local police about Charlie Dodds's visit to my house. I dropped the card on top of the icebox, put Alafair to bed, and watched the late show with Dixie Lee.

I slept through until morning without dreaming or once getting up in the night. When I woke and stepped out on the porch with a cup of coffee, the river was green and running fast in the shadows of the bridge, riffling over the boulders in the deepest part of the current, and the sunlight through the maples in the yard looked like spun glass.

11

It was Sunday morning. I took Alafair to nine o'clock mass, then we fixed *cush-cush* and ate breakfast with Dixie Lee. He had shaved, pressed his slacks, and put on a white shirt.

'Where are you going?' I said.

'Some Holy Rollers asked me to play piano at their church. I hope the plaster don't fall out of the ceiling when I walk in.'

'That's good.'

He looked down at his coffee cup, then played with the big synthetic diamond ring on his finger.

'I got something bothering me,' he said.

'What is it?'

He looked at Alafair.

'Alafair, why don't you start on the dishes while Dixie helps me with something outside?' I said.

We went out to the truck, and I took the small whisk broom from behind the seat and began sweeping out the floor.

'I'm afraid I'm going to drink. I woke up scared about it this morning,' he said.

'Just do it a day at a time. Do it five minutes at a time if you have to.'

'Why the fuck am I scared, man?'

'Because it's fear that makes us drink.'

'I don't understand. It don't make sense. I felt real good yesterday. Today I'm shaking inside. Look at my hands. I feel like I just got off a jag.'

'Dixie, I'm not a psychologist, but you're going into a church today that's like the one you grew up in. Maybe you're dealing with some memories that bring back some bad moments. Who knows? Just let it go, partner. You're sober this morning. That's all that counts.'

'Maybe some people ain't supposed to make it.'

'You're not one of them.'

'You'd really throw me out if I went back on the juice?'

'Yep.'

'Somehow that just made a cold wind blow through my soul.'

'You work the steps, and I promise all that fear, all those weird mechanisms in your head, will go away.'

'What mechanisms?'

'Strange thoughts and images, things that don't make any sense, stuff that you won't talk about with anybody. If you work the program, all those things will gradually disappear.'

The morning was cool, and there was a breeze off the river, but there were drops of perspiration on his forehead and in his eyebrows.

'Dave, I just feel downright sick inside. I can't explain it.'

'It's going to pass,' I said. 'Just don't drink today.'

But his eyes were forlorn, and I well understood the peculiar chemical misery he was experiencing at the moment; I also knew that my words would mean more to him later than they did now.

'While we're out here, let me tell you about something else,' I said 'I'm going to receive a phone call this afternoon. I don't want you to answer it.'

'All right.'

'It'll be from Sally Dee. I don't want him to know you're living here.'

'You're putting me on?'

I continued sweeping the floor mat with the whisk broom.

'Dave, that ain't true?'

'It's complicated.'

'So is shit. This is some kind of nightmare. What are you doing, man?'

'Just don't answer the phone.'

'I wouldn't touch the sonofabitch at gunpoint.'

An hour later the phone rang. But it was Tess Regan, not Sally Dio.

'Jason, the eighth-grader I told you about, the one who talked with the man in the yellow car, he just came over on his bicycle,' she said. 'Last night he went to the Heidelhaus for dinner with some of his relatives. He saw the yellow car behind the restaurant. He's sure it's the same one. He remembered that the back window was cracked and there was a University of Wyoming sticker on it.'

'What kind of car?'

'A Mercury.'

'Did he get the license number?'

'No, I asked him. He said he didn't have a piece of paper or a pencil. Kids don't quite pull it all off sometimes, Dave.'

'He did just fine,' I said. 'It was at dinnertime, you say?'

'Yes. He said the Mercury was there when he went into the restaurant, and it was still there when he left. He tried to tell his uncle about it, but it was a birthday party and adults tend not to hear children sometimes.'

'Thanks very much, Tess. Tell Jason I appreciate what he's done.'

Alafair and I drove over to the Heidelhaus, a large Bavarian-style restaurant on the south side of town. The lunch crowd had started to come in, and the parking lot was half filled with cars, but none of them was a yellow Mercury. I drove behind the building and around the sides but had no luck there, either. I took Alafair for an ice cream cone, returned in a half hour, and still came up empty.

When we got home Dixie Lee was reading the newspaper on the front steps.

'It ain't rung. At least not while I was here,' he said.

'How was church?'

'It went okay. They asked me to play again Wednesday night. They ain't a bad bunch for people that probably left their toast in the oven too long.'

Alafair went inside just as the phone rang.

'Damn, there it is,' Dixie Lee said. 'Go easy, boy. Let's stay on the sunny side for a while.'

Alafair had picked up the receiver, but I eased it out of her hand before she could speak. I stepped into the bathroom and closed the door on the cord.

'You had time to think, Robicheaux?' Sally Dee said.

'I still believe you have things mixed up.'

'I'm not interested in opinions. You want to do some business, or you want to keep fucking around?'

'You've got it backwards, Sal. You hired Charlie Dodds to take me out.'

'That's past history. You come up to the lake uninvited, you provoked my father, you started that beef out on the road. I mark it off even. That's the way I see it.'

'What's the offer?'

'What d'you mean, what's the offer? I spelled it out to you yesterday.'

'No, you didn't. You said three or four grand a week. Are you going to pay that kind of money for house security?'

'We'll set you up with your own action. You manage a club in Vegas. All you got to do is count the receipts. You know what the skim is on a half-dozen lobby slots?'

'I'm about to go on trial.'

'You're breaking my knob off.'

'No, I think you're trying to do a number on me, Sal. You'll talk a lot of shit about the big score out in Vegas, let me think I got no worries about Harry Mapes, then a little time passes and I'm back in Louisiana in handcuffs.'

'You think I'm playing games while that crazy fucker is shooting at me?'

'That's your problem. My big worry is prison. That and your shitheads coming around my house.'

'I told you, there ain't anybody after you now. What is it I can't get through to you? This is a simple deal. You make money, I make money,

Mapes gets whacked. You're home free. I guarantee it. People don't get out from under us. You were a cop. You know that.'

'I don't think I want to do business with you, Sal.'

'What?'

'I think you're about to take another fall.'

'What is this? What the fuck are you up to, man?'

'Don't call here again. I'm out of your life. Don't even have thoughts about me.'

'You shit-eating motherfucker, you're setting me up . . . It won't work, cocksucker . . . it's entrapment . . . you tell that to Nygurski . . . I've got lawyers that'll shove it up his ass.'

I placed the receiver quietly in the cradle and went outside and sat down on the steps beside Dixie Lee, who was reading the comics in the newspaper. He turned the page and popped the paper straight between his hands.

'Don't start telling me about it. My system's puny as it is. I just as soon drink razor blades,' he said.

I called Nygurski at his house a few minutes later. He wasn't home, so I put Alafair in the truck and we drove back to the Heidelhaus. This time the yellow Mercury with the cracked back window and the University of Wyoming sticker was parked in the shade of the building behind the dumpster.

I parked in the main lot, away from the Mercury, took Alafair inside and bought her a Coke by a stone fireplace that was now filled with a huge tropical aquarium.

I went up to the male cashier at the bar.

'I backed into a yellow Mercury by the side of the building,' I said. 'I think it might belong to somebody who works here. I think I just scatched it, but I'd like to make it right.'

'Next to the building? Right out there?' he asked, gesturing toward the side of the restaurant where the dumpster was located.

'Yeah, that's it.'

'It sounds like Betty's. That's her down the bar.'

She was around thirty, blond, thick across the stomach, overly rouged, too old for the Bavarian waitress costume that she wore.

'Is that your Mercury by the side of the building, the one with the Wyoming sticker?' I said.

'Sure.' She stopped washing glasses and smiled at me. There were tiny lines in the corners of her eyes.

'I'm afraid I backed into it. I don't think I really hurt it, but you might take a look at it to be sure.'

'You couldn't hurt that thing. It's twelve years old and has eighty-five thousand miles on it.'

'Well, I just didn't want to drive off and not say anything.'

'Just a minute.' She took several glass steins out of the tin sink, set them top down on a folded dish towel, then said something to the cashier. 'I have to hurry. We're real busy right now.'

I told Alafair I would be right back, and the waitress and I went outside to her car. I ran my hand over some scratches by the Mercury's taillight.

'That's about where I hit it,' I said. 'I couldn't tell if that was old stuff or not. Maybe I just hit the bumper.'

'Forget it. It's not worth worrying about. I'm getting rid of it, anyway.'

'Aren't you a friend of Harry's?' I said.

'Which Harry?'

'Mapes.'

'Sure. How'd you know that?'

'I guess I saw y'all together.'

'How do you know Harry?'

'Through the oil business. I thought he was doing lease work east of the Divide.'

'He is. He's just visiting right now.'

'Well, I'm sorry to have taken you away from your work.'

'It's all right. It's nice of you to be concerned. Not many people would bother.'

She was a nice lady, and I didn't like to deceive her. I wondered how she had gotten involved with Harry Mapes. Maybe because it's a blue-collar, male-oriented town, I thought, where a woman's opportunities are limited. Regardless, I felt sorry for her.

I took Alafair back to the house, called the baby-sitter, then Tess Regan, but neither of them was at home.

'There's a dollar double feature at the Roxy. How about I take her to that?' Dixie Lee said.

Before I could hide it he saw the hesitation in my face.

'You think I'm gonna get drunk, I'm gonna run off and leave her alone?' he said.

'No.'

'Or maybe I ain't worked up to the step where you can trust me as good as that old woman down at the church.'

'I just didn't know what you had planned for today.'

'You want me to look after her or not?'

'I'd appreciate your doing that, Dixie.'

'Yeah, I can see that. But that's all right. I ain't sensitive. It all bounces off me.'

'I probably won't be home until late this evening,' I said. 'Can you fix her supper?'

'Show me a little trust, son. I'd be grateful for it.'

I drove back across town and parked on a side street behind the

Heidelhaus so I could see the yellow Mercury. It was a long wait, but at eight o'clock she came out of the restaurant, walked to her car with her purse on her arm, started the engine, and drove south into the Bitterroot Valley.

I followed her twenty-five miles along the river. The light was still good in the valley, and I could see her car well from several hundred yards away, even though other cars were between us; but then she turned on to a dirt road and headed across pastureland toward the foot of the mountains. I pulled to the shoulder of the highway, got out with my field glasses, and watched the plume of white dust grow smaller in the distance, then disappear altogether.

I drove down the dirt road into the purple shadows that were spreading from the mountains' rim, crossed a wide creek that was lined with cottonwoods, passed a rotted and roofless log house with deer grazing nearby, then started to climb up on a plateau that fronted a deep canyon in the mountains. The dust from her Mercury still hung over the rock fence that bordered the property where she had turned in. The house was new, made of peeled and lacquered logs that had a yellow glaze to them, with a railed porch, a peaked shingle roof, and boxes of petunias and geraniums in the windows. But her car was the only one there.

I drove on past the house to the canyon, where there was Forest Service parking area, and watched the house for a half hour through my field glasses. She fed a black Labrador on the back steps, she took some wash off the line, she carried a carton of mason jars out of the shed back into the house, but there was no sign of Harry Mapes.

I went back home and found Alafair asleep and Dixie Lee putting a new set of strings on his sunburst Martin.

I didn't have to call Dan Nygurski again. He called me at five minutes after eight the next morning.

'You beat me to it,' I said. 'I tried to catch you at home yesterday.'

'About Sally Dio.'

'That's right.'

'About your phone conversation with him.'

'That's right. So he did use the pay phone down the road from his house?'

'Yeah, he sure did. In fact, he was using it several times a day. Calls to Vegas, Tahoe, LA, Galveston. Notice I'm using the past tense here.'

I squinted my eyes closed and pressed my forefinger and thumb against my temples.

'I've sympathized with you, I've tried to help you,' he said. 'I took you into my confidence. I just had a conference call with a couple of federal agents who are very angry right now. My explanations to them didn't seem to make them feel any better.'

'Dan—'

'No, you got to talk yesterday. It's my turn now. You blew a federal wiretap. You know how long it took us to set that up?'

'Listen to what you've got on that tape. Solicitation to commit murder. He stepped in his own shit.'

'You remember when I told you that Sal is not Bugsy Siegel? I meant it. He did time for stolen credit cards. He's a midlevel guy. But he's connected with some big people in Nevada. They're smart, he's not. He makes mistakes they don't. When he falls, we want a whole busload to go up the road with him. Are you starting to get the big picture now?'

'All right, I screwed it up.'

'That doesn't bother me as much as the fact that I think you knew better.'

'He walked into it. I let it happen. I'm sorry it's causing you problems.'

'No, you wanted to make sure he thought he was tapped. That way he wasn't about to try to whack you again.'

'What would you do?'

'I would have stayed away from him to begin with.'

'That's a dishonest answer. What would you do if a guy like Dio was trying to whack you out, maybe you and your daughter both?'

I could hear the long-distance hum of the wires in the receiver.

'Did that Missoula detective get a hold of you?' he asked.

'He came out and left his card.'

'I hope he'll be of some help to you if you have more trouble there.'

'Look, Dan—'

'I have another call. We'll see you,' he said.

I went into the kitchen to fix a bowl of Grape-Nuts and spilled the box all over the floor. I cleaned up the cereal with a wet paper towel and threw it in the trash.

'I'm heading out for work,' Dixie Lee said.

'All right.'

'Who was that?'

'Nobody.'

'Yeah . . . well, what do you want to do after Wednesday?'

'What?'

'About Alafair. That job ain't but four hours a day. I can put them in any time I want.'

'What are you talking about?'

'School's out for the summer, ain't it? I can help look after her. What's the best time for me to be home?'

'I don't know, Dixie. I can't think about it right now.'

I felt him looking quietly at the side of my face, then he turned and walked outside of his automobile. I looked at my watch. It was eight-thirty. I locked the house, put the .45 under the truck seat, and drove south once again into the Bitterroot Valley.

This time the black Jeepster was parked right next to the Mercury, and when I pulled into the yard and got out of the truck woodsmoke was blowing off the stone chimney. Through the front window I could see the woman named Betty drinking coffee with a man at a table in the living room.

The porch rails and the lacquered yellow logs of the house were wet with dew. I stepped up on the porch, knocked on the door, and when the woman opened it I saw Harry Mapes stare at me with his mouth parted over his coffee cup. Then he got up and walked out of my line of sight into a side room.

'Hi,' she said, and smiled with recognition. 'You're—'

'I didn't tell you my name yesterday. It's Dave Robicheaux. I'd like to talk to Harry.'

'Sure. He's here. But how'd you know where I lived?'

'I'm sorry for disturbing you, but I'd appreciate it if you'd ask him to step out here.'

'I don't understand this,' she said, then turned and saw Mapes standing behind her. 'Harry, this is the guy I told you about.'

'I figured it was you,' he said to me.

He wore jeans and a flannel shirt, and a black automatic hung from his left hand. The chain scars on his face were almost totally gone now.

'Harry, what are you doing?' she said.

'This is the guy who attacked me in Louisiana,' he said.

'Oh!' she said. Then she said it again, 'Oh!'

'Come outside, Mapes,' I said.

'You don't know when to leave it alone, do you?' he said. 'My lawyer told me you might try something like this. He also told me what to do about it.'

'What's that?'

'You try to intimidate a witness, you just create more trouble for yourself. Figure it out.'

'So you're holding all the cards. Look, I don't have a weapon. Why don't you step outside? Nobody's going to eat you.'

His fingers were long on the sides of the automatic. I had seen only one or two like it since I had left Vietnam. It was a 7.62-millimeter Russian Tokarev, a side arm often carried by NVA officers.

I saw Mapes wet the triangular scar on his lip, his mouth tight, his eyes narrowed as though he were biting down softly on a piece of string. He wasn't a bad-looking man. He still had the build of a basketball player or a man who could do an easy five-mile morning run. You wouldn't pay particular attention to him in a supermarket line. Except for his eyes.

He was the kind who was always taking your inventory, provided you represented or possessed something he was interested in; and sometimes when you studied the eyes in his kind you saw a hidden thought there that made you look away hurriedly.

'You're right,' he said, and set the pistol on the arm of a couch by the door. 'Because you're all smoke. A guy who's always firing in the well. A big nuisance who couldn't mind his own business.'

He opened the screen door and stepped out on the porch.

'You think it's going to come out different somehow at your trial?' he said. 'You think following me around Montana is going to make all that evidence go away?'

'You've got it wrong, Harry. I gave up on trying to nail you. You're too slick a guy. You've fooled people all your life. You burned two people to death when you were seventeen, you murdered the Indians, the waitress in Louisiana, your partner, and I think you raped and murdered Darlene. You got away with all of it.'

I saw the blood drain out of the face of the woman behind the screen. Mapes's chest rose and fell with his breathing.

'Listen, you asshole—' he said.

'But that's not why I'm here. You were at the school ground, in that Mercury there, looking at my daughter through field glasses, asking questions about her. Now, my message here is simple. If you come around her again, I'm going to kill you. Believe it. I've got nothing to lose at this point. I'm going to walk up to you, wherever you are, and blow your fucking head off.'

I walked off the porch into the yard.

'Oh, no, you don't,' he said. 'You, too, Betty. You stay out here and listen to this. My lawyer did some checking on this guy. He's a drunk, he's a mental case, he's got an obsession because he got his wife killed by some drug dealers. Then somebody threatened his daughter, and he accused me and my partner. The fact that he's an ex-cop with dozens of people who'd like to even a score with him doesn't seem to enter his head. Let me tell you something, Robicheaux. Betty's son goes to a Catholic school in Missoula. She and her ex-husband have shared custody. Sometimes I pick him up or drop him off for her. If that's the same school your daughter goes to, it's coincidence, and that's all it is.'

'You heard what I said. No warning light next time,' I said.

I got inside my truck and closed the door.

'No, Harry, bring him back,' the woman said. 'Who's Darlene? What's he talking about a rape? Harry?'

'He's leaving. Close the door,' he said to her.

'Harry, I'll call the sheriff. He can't get away with saying that.'

'He's leaving. He's not coming back.'

Then he walked toward the truck window just as I started the engine.

'You're going to prison,' he said. 'Nothing's going to change that. You can mess me up with my girl, you can say stuff about blowing me away if it makes you feel good, but in a few weeks you're going to be hoeing sweet potatoes in Angola.'

I put the transmission in reverse and began backing around in a half circle. The wind blew his hair, and his skin looked grained and healthy in the sunlight. His eyes never left my face. My knuckles were ridged on top of the gearshift knob, and my thighs were shaking as I depressed the floor pedals.

It had all been for nothing.

But there was still time, the moment was still there. To pull the .45 from under the seat, to aim it suddenly at his face, knock him to his knees, screw the barrel hard into his neck and cock the hammer, let him experience the terror of his victims who clawed the inside of an automobile trunk while the metal heated and the flames spread to the gasoline tank. I could feel the .45 leap into my hand as though it had a life of its own.

I shut off the engine and stepped out of the truck. My face felt cool in the bright air. The yellow log house and the ponderosa and blue spruce on the hillsides seemed dazzling in the sun. His eyes dropped to my hands. I held my palms up.

'Did you ever go to the stake in Saigon?' I said.

'What?'

'Some ARVN and white mice would march them out to the stake, tie them to it, and put a round behind the ear. At least that was what I was told. I never saw it.'

'I think you had some head damage over there. You've got thirty seconds to be past Betty's property line, then we call the sheriff.'

'You'd better concentrate on my words, Harry. The executioner was probably a special kind of guy. He could kill people and go home and have lunch. He's somebody you can understand. You'd recognize each other in a group. But you know I'm not like you, and that's why you're not afraid of me. I can come out here and talk about cooling you out, but you know I won't do it. But how about Sally Dio?'

'Dio? You must truly be out of your mind. Get out of here, man.'

'He was talking about whacking you out. That's not a shuck. He's got some new guys up at the lake. They're the real article, genuine syndicate hit men. You can call Dan Nygurski at the DEA in Great Falls and ask him. Or, better yet, ask him to deny it. If that's not enough for you, I can give you Sal's unlisted number and you can talk with him about it. If I'm just jerking you around, you can clear the whole matter up in a few minutes.'

'What's Dio care about me? I only met the guy twice.'

'Ask him. Maybe you shouldn't have gotten mixed up in his and Dixie

Lee's lease deals. He's probably a borderline psychotic. I doubt if he thinks too straight.'

His eyes looked like they were focused on a thought ten inches in front of his face. Then they came back on me.

'Where'd you hear this?' he asked.

'Stay away from my daughter. Don't come near that school. I don't care if your lady friend's son goes there or not,' I said, and I got back into the truck and drove out on the dirt toad.

In the rearview mirror I saw him standing alone in the yard, staring after me, the woman holding the screen door wide behind him.

I went back home, walked down the street to a noon AA meeting, brought groceries for our supper that evening, then sat on the back steps in the shade and tried to put myself inside the mind of Harry Mapes. He was a smart man. He had killed a number of people over the years – his first when he was seventeen and God only knew how many in Vietnam – and he had never spent a day in jail for it. He wasn't compulsive; he was calculating, and he used fear and violence to achieve an immediate, practical end. Like any sociopath's, his emotions were simple ones and concerned entirely with desires, survival, and the destruction of his enemies. He remained passive, functional, and innocuous in appearance until he felt threatened. Then he rose to the occasion.

When he saw me east of the Divide, on the dirt road between the Indian beer joint and the home of Clayton Desmarteau's mother, I scared him in some way. He went to the school ground to keep my mind on other things or, perhaps, to provoke me into attacking him again. Somehow he had also concluded that Darlene had sent me east of the Divide, had put me on that dirt road south of the Blackfeet Reservation, and he feared that somewhere in that hardpan country I would discover what had happened to Clayton Desmarteau and his cousin.

In the last two days I had managed to turn it around on both Dio and Mapes, to use some smoke and their own frame of reference against them, so that in all probability they wouldn't come around me and Alafair again. But my legal situation remained the same as it had been when I left Louisiana. My victory had become the restoration of the status quo. I lay down on the living room couch in a funk, with my arm across my eyes, and fell asleep.

The image in my dream was brief, like needles of light in the afternoon haze. *Darlene kneeling by water, white-tailed deer thudding across the wet ground between the cottonwoods.*

I felt feathers brushing across my forearm and cheek. I opened one eye and looked at Alafair's grinning face. The other day she had found an old feather duster in the house.

'How you doing, you cute little guy?' I said.

'How you doing, you cute little Dave?' she said. She wore jeans and her Baby Orca T-shirt.

I sat up on the couch.

'How'd you get home?' I said.

'Dixie Lee walked down and got me. You was asleep. Dave?'

'What?' I rubbed my face and tried to make the afternoon come into focus.

'We only got two more days of school. We going home then?'

'Maybe so, little guy.'

'We better call Batist and tell him.'

'Alafair, when we go back home, it might be for just a few days. I might have to sell a few things and raise some money so we can take another trip.'

'Trip?'

'To a different place for a while. Down by the ocean, maybe.'

'We're not going to live at the house no more?'

'I don't know, Alf.'

I looked at the confusion in her face.

'Let's take things as they come,' I said. 'I just don't want you to be disappointed later if we move somewhere else for a while.'

I heard the phone ring in the hallway. Alafair picked up her lunch box from the coffee table and started toward the kitchen.

'Miss Regan asked if we eat redfish,' she said. 'Why she ask that? What's she care about redfish? I got pushed down on the school ground. I threw a dirt clod at the boy that did it.'

I let her go and didn't say anything more.

'Dave, you better take this,' Dixie Lee said in the doorway, the telephone receiver in his hand.

'What is it?'

'St Pat's Hospital. They got Clete in there.'

We drove to the hospital on Broadway, left Alafair in the second-floor waiting room with a comic book, and walked down the corridor to Clete's room. A plaincothes cop, with his badge on his belt, was just coming out the door. He had a blond mustache and wore a white shirt and knit tie. He was putting a small notebook in his shirt pocket.

'What happened?' I said.

'Who are you?' he said.

'A friend of Cletus Purcel.'

'What's your name?'

'Dave Robicheaux.'

He nodded slowly, and I saw the name meant nothing to him.

'Your friend got worked over,' he said. 'He says he didn't know the two guys who did it. But the bartender who phoned us said the two guys called him by name. Tell your friend it's dumb to protect people who'll slam a man's hand in a car door.'

He brushed past me and walked to the elevator. Dixie Lee and I went inside the room, which Clete shared with an elderly man who had an IV connected to his wasted arm. Clete's bed was on the far side of the partition, one end elevated so he could look up at the television set that was turned on without sound. One eye was swollen into a purple egg, and his head was shaved in three places where the scalp had been stitched. His right hand was in plaster; the ends of his fingers were discolored as though they were gangrenous.

'I heard you with the detective,' he said.

'He doesn't seem to believe your story,' I said.

'He's probably got marital trouble. It makes a cynic out of you. What's happening, Dixie?'

'Oh man, who did this to you?' Dixie Lee said.

'A couple of Sal's meatballs.'

'Who?' Dixie Lee said.

'Carl and Foo-Foo. I got Foo-Foo one shot in the rocks, though. He's not going to be unlimbering his equipment for a while.'

'What happened?' I said.

'I stopped at this bar off Ninety. They must have seen the jeep in the parking lot. They caught me with a baton when I came out the side door. When I thought they were through, they dragged me to a car and slammed my hand in the door. If the bartender hadn't come out, they'd have done my other hand.'

'Tell the cops,' Dixie Lee said. 'Why do you want to protect Carl and Foo-Foo?'

'What goes round, comes round,' Clete said. 'I ain't sweating it, mon.'

'You used to say "Bust 'em or smoke 'em." Let the cops bust them,' I said.

'Maybe they've got a surprise coming out of the jack-in-the-box,' Clete said. He looked at my face. 'All your radio tubes are lit up, Streak. What are you thinking about?'

'Why'd they do it?'

'Sal's running scared. He's got nobody but his old man and his hired dagos. Even the cornholers cut out on him.'

'That's not it,' I said.

'How do I know what goes on in his head?'

'Come on, Clete,' I said.

'When I left, he owed me fifteen hundred in back salary. Plus I'd already paid my rent to him in advance. So I went in his house and took a couple of gold ashtrays.'

'You crazy bastard,' Dixie Lee said.

'He didn't kill Darlene, then, did he?'

'I don't know,' Clete said.

'Yes, you do. Somebody shot at him. He thinks it was Charlie Dodds. If he had killed Darlene, you'd be the first person he would fear. Those two guys wouldn't have just broken your hand, either. They would have passed you on the road and taken you out with a shotgun.'

'Maybe,' he said.

'No maybe about it, Cletus,' I said. 'It was Mapes. He thought she sent me over by the reservation where he killed the two Indians. He found her alone, and he raped and killed her. You've got a beef with the wrong guy, and you know it.'

'I got a beef with Sal for all kinds of reasons,' he said. 'But that's all right. Our man's going to have a sandy fuck.'

'What?' I said.

'A fifties joke. Sand in the Vaseline,' he said. 'Forget it. Hey, do me a favor. My jeep's still out at that bar. It's a log place, right where Broadway runs into Ninety. Take it to your house, will you? The keys are on the table. I don't want some local punks to clean it out.'

'All right.'

'Where's Mapes?' he said.

'You'll have to find him on your own, partner.'

'You know where he is, then.'

'Do you want us to bring you anything?'

'Come on, you think I'm going to get out of bed and scramble Mapes's eggs? You give me too much credit.'

'You'd find a way, Clete.'

He wet his mouth and smiled.

'Dixie, can you give me and Streak a minute?' he said.

'Sure.'

'It's just something from our First District days,' Clete said.

'I don't mind,' Dixie Lee said.

'Then come on back later,' Clete said.

'Don't be talking down to me. It hurts my feelings,' Dixie Lee said. 'I'll come see you tomorrow.'

He walked out of the room.

'He's not full of booze,' Clete said.

'What do you need, Cletus?'

'I screwed up a lot of things back there in New Orleans. Blew my marriage, took juice, knocked a girl up, got into the shylocks. Then I cooled out that shitbag in the hog lot. But I paid for it. In spades. I'd like to change it but I can't. I guess that's what remorse is about. But the big one that's been eating my lunch all this time is that I could have brought that guy in and gotten you off the hook. For ten grand I helped them turn you into toilet paper.'

'The lowlifes all took a fall one way or another.'

'Yeah, your fourteen years with the department went down the hole, too.'

'It was my choice, Clete.'

'You want to act like a stand-up guy about it, that's copacetic. But I don't buy it. I fucked you over. It's the worst thing I did in my life. I'm telling you I'm sorry. I'm not asking you to say anything. I'm telling you how I feel. I'm not bringing it up again. You were my best friend. I stuck it to you.'

'It's all right. Maybe you were doing the best you could at the time.'

His one open eye stared up at me. It looked like a piece of green glass in his battered face.

'It's time to write it off, partner,' I said.

'That's straight?'

'Who cares about last year's box score?'

He swallowed. His eye was watery along the bottom rim.

'Fuck, man,' he said.

'I have to go. Alafair is in the waiting room.'

'I've got to tell you something,' he said.

'What?'

'I've got to whisper it. Come here.'

'What is it, Clete?'

'No, closer.'

I leaned over him, then his good hand came up, clamped around the back of my neck like a vise, and pulled my face down on his. He kissed me hard on the mouth, and I could smell the cigarettes on his breath, the salve and Mercurochrome painted on his stitches and shaved scalp.

We drove out west of town to the bar where Clete had been beaten up by Sally Dee's goons and found his Toyota jeep in the parking lot. Dixie Lee drove it back to the house, parked it in back, and locked it. A few minutes later Tess Regan called.

'Can you come over?' she said.

'When?'

'Tonight. For redfish. Didn't Alafair say anything?'

'It came out a little confused.'

'I called you earlier, but nobody was home. It's nothing special, really. We could make it another night.'

'Tonight's fine,' I said.

And it was. The evening was cool and smelled of flowers and sprinkled yards, and she blackened the redfish on a grill in the backyard and served it in her small dining room, which glowed with the sun's reflection through the tall turn-of-the-century windows. She wore tight blue jeans and low heels, a short-sleeved blouse with tiny pink roses on it, and gold hoop earrings, but her apartment gave her away. The wood floors and mahogany trim on the doors gleamed; the kitchen was spotless; the hung pictures and those on the marble mantel were all of relatives. The wallpaper was new, but the design and color did nothing to remove the apartment from an earlier era. A Catholic religious calendar, with an ad for a mortuary on it, was affixed to the icebox door with small magnets. She had crossed two palm strangs in an *X* behind the crucifix on the dining room wall.

After supper we did the dishes together while Alafair watched television. When her leg bumped against me, she smiled awkwardly as though we had been jostled against one another on a bus, then her eyes looked at my face with both expectation and perhaps a moment's fear. I suspected she was one of those whose heart could be easily hurt, one to whom a casual expression of affection would probably be interpreted as a large personal commitment. The moon was up now. The window was open and I could smell the wet mint against the brick wall and the thick, cool odor of lawn grass that had been flooded by a soak hose. It was the kind of soft moment that you could slip into as easily as you could believe you were indeed able to regain the innocence of your youth.

So I squeezed her hand and said good night, and I saw the flick of disappointment in her eyes before she smiled again and walked with me back into the living room. But she was one with whom you dealt in the morning's light, unless you were willing to trust the nocturnal whirrings of your own heart.

She came to me in a dream that night, a dream as clear in its detail as though you had suddenly focused all the broken purple and tan glass in a kaleidoscope into one perfect image. Darlene's hair was braided on her shoulders, and she wore the doeskin dress she had been buried in, the purple glass bird on her breast. I saw her look first at me from the overhang of the cliff, then squat on her moccasins by a spring that leaked out of rocks into a tea-colored stream. She put her hands into the trailing moss, into the silt and wet humus and mud, and began to smear it on her face. She looked at me again, quietly, her mouth cold and red, her cheeks streaked with mud; then she was gone, and I saw a huge golden deer crash through the underbrush and cottonwoods.

I sat straight up in bed, my breath coming hard, my hands shaking. I looked at my watch. It was two in the morning. I shook Dixie Lee awake on the couch.

'I've got to go east of the Divide. You have to take care of Alafair until I get back,' I said.

'What?'

'You heard me. Can you do that? Fix breakfast for her, walk her to school, pick her up in the afternoon?'

'What's going on?' His face was puffy and full of sleep.

'I have to depend on you, Dixie. I'll be back by tomorrow evening. But you've got to take good care of her. Call in sick at work if you have to.'

'All right,' he said irritably. 'But what are you doing?'

'I think I'm going to nail Mapes. I think I'm going to do it.'

He sat up on the edge of the couch in his underwear, his arms draped between his thighs. He widened his eyes and rubbed his face.

'I hate to tell you, son, you still act like a drunk man,' he said.

Fifteen minutes later I stopped at an all-night diner on the edge of town, bought a thermos of black coffee, then I was roaring up the highway along the Blackfoot River, the tree-covered crests of the mountains silhouetted blackly against the starlight, the river and the cottonwoods and willows along the banks aglow with the rising moon.

It was dawn when I drove down the dirt road where Clayton Desmarteau had gone in the ditch. The hardpan fields were wet with dew, and the long rays of the sun struck against the thick green timber high up in the saddles of the mountains that formed the Divide. I took an army entrenching tool out of the back of my truck, jumped across the stream on the north side of the road, and walked up the incline into the lodgepole pine. It was cool and the wind was blowing, but I was sweating inside my shirt and my hand was tight on the wood shaft of the E-tool. Low pools of mist hung around the trees, and I saw a doe and her fawn eating the bear grass. Then I intersected the thin trace of a road that had been used as an access to a garbage dump, and walked on farther across the pine needles until I hit the stream that flowed under a heavy canopy of trees at the foot of a rock-faced hill, and followed it across the soft moldy remains of a log cabin, a rusted-out wood stove half buried in the wet soil, and carpets of mushrooms whose stems cracked under my shoes. Finally I saw the spring that flowed out of the hillside, glistened on the dark rocks and moss, and spread into a fan of blackened leaves and rivulets of silt at the end of the stream

Annie and my father had tried to tell me in the dream, but I hadn't understood. It was winter when Vidrine and Mapes had murdered Clayton Desmarteau and his cousin. It was winter, and the ground must have been frozen so hard that a posthole digger could only chip it. My heart was beating as I unscrewed the metal ring under the blade of the E-tool, folded the blade into a hoe, and tightened the ring. I scraped away the layers of leaves and raked back long divots of silt and fine gravel, creating half a wagon wheel that spread out from the stream's edge back to the spring's source. My pants were wet up to my knees, my shoes sloshing with water. Then I reset the blade and began digging out a level pit in five-inch scoops and setting the mud carefully in a pile on the bank. I worked a half hour, until my shirt was sweated through and my arms and face were streaked with mud. I had begun to think that maybe Dixie Lee was right; I was simply behaving as though I were on a dry drunk.

Then my shovel hit the toe of a work boot, and I worked the sand and mud off the edges, the congealed laces, back along the gray shank of shinbone that protruded from the rotted sock. I uncovered the other leg, then the folded knees and the collapsed, flattened thigh that was much too small now for the cloth that lay in strips around it. The second man was buried right next to the first, curled in an embryonic position, the small, sightless, tight gray ball of his face twisted up through the soil.

I stepped back from the pit into the middle of the stream, cleaned the shovel blade in the gravel, then knelt on the opposite bank and washed my arms and face in the water. But I was trembling all over and I couldn't stop sweating. I sat on the bank, with my knees pulled up in front of me, and tried to stop hyperventilating, to think in an orderly fashion about the rest of the morning. I hadn't hit the perfecta in the ninth race, but it was close, if I just didn't do anything wrong. Then, as I wiped the sweat out of my eyes with my thumb and looked across the stream at the glistening mound of mud and silt that I had dug from the bodies, at the nests of white worms that I had lifted into the light, I saw a corroded green cartridge that had been ejected from an automatic. It had the same bottleneck shape as the 7.62-millimeter round fired by a Russian Tokarev.

I had to drive three miles down the dirt road before I found a pay phone outside of a closed filling station. It had started to rain over the mountains but the sky in the east was still pink and blue, and the air smelled of pine and sage. When I got Dan Nygurski on the phone at his office, I told him all of it, or I thought all of it, but my words came out in a rush, and my heart was still beating fast, and I felt as if I were standing at the finish line at the track, my fingers pinched tight on that perfecta ticket, trying in the last thunderous seconds of the race to will the right combination under the wire.

'Let your motor idle a little bit,' he said. 'How'd you find them?'

'They were run off the road between the beer joint and Clayton Desmarteau's house. I think Mapes and Vidrine took them out of the truck at gunpoint and drove them into the woods. An old road leads off the main one and runs back to a garbage dump. They got out there and walked back to the stream. But the ground was probably covered with snow and frozen solid. I bet you could bust a pick on it in wintertime. Then they walked across a warm-water spring, where the ground stayed soft and wet year-round, and that's where they shot Desmarteau and his cousin.'

'Tell me about the shell again.'

'It came up in a shovelful of mud. I didn't even see it until I had stopped digging. It's bottlenecked, like a 7.62 round. Mapes has got a Tokarev. He had it in his hand at his girl's house down in the Bitterroot. I think he had it in Lafayette, too. He was trying to get to his open suitcase when I hit him with the chain. Look, it's enough for a search warrant. But it's got to be done right. You can bring the FBI in on it, let them coordinate it.'

'Oh?'

'They can use kidnapping and interstate flight, or depriving a minority of his civil rights by taking his life. The locals might blow it. If Mapes gets a sniff of what's going on before they serve the warrant, he'll lose the Tokarev.'

'I had to take a lot of heat because of that phone tap.'

'I'm sorry.'

'It hasn't quieted down yet.'

'I was up against the wall. I don't know what else to tell you. You want me to hang up and call the sheriff's office?'

He waited a moment.

'No, don't do that,' he said finally. 'I guess we've got a vested interest. This whole Indian thing started with Pugh, and Pugh's had a longtime involvement with Sally Dee. Give me the directions again.'

I told him in detail once more. The shower had moved eastward across the fields, and rain was now clicking on the roof of the phone booth. An Indian boy on an old bicycle with fat tires rattled past me on the road, his face bent down against the rain.

'I'll call the FBI and the Teton sheriff's office,' Nygurski said. 'Then I'll be out myself. I want a promise from you, though.'

'What is it?'

'Other people take it from here on in. You're out of it. Absolutely.'

'All right.'

'I want your word. You don't go near Mapes.'

'You have it, but you've got to get him with the Tokarev.'

'I think you've made your point. But are you sure that's what you saw in his hand? I wonder why he didn't get rid of it.'

'They were prize souvenirs in Vietnam. Besides, he always sailed out of everything he ever did.'

'Where are you going to be?'

'On the road where their truck went into the ditch. We can walk in from there, or find the access road that leads back to the garbage dump.'

'Did you hear anything more from Dio?'

'Nope. Except two of his goons broke Purcel's hand. He says he took a couple of gold ashtrays out of Dio's house.'

'Bad guy to steal from. Purcel must not have pressed charges, because we didn't hear anything about it.'

'He said something strange when I went to see him in the hospital yesterday. He said, "Our man's going to have a sandy fuck." Or maybe I misunderstood him. I think Dio has a girlfriend named Sandy. Anyway, it didn't make any sense to me.'

'Where is he?'

'St Pat's in Missoula.'

'Maybe it's time we have a talk with him. I'll see you a little later this morning. In the meantime, congratulations. You're a good cop, Robicheaux. Get your badge back.'

'You've been a good friend, too, Dan.'

'And, lastly, keep your name out of my paperwork for a while.'

I drove back up the road in the rain and parked by the stream where I had entered the woods at dawn. Then the clouds moved eastward and the rain drifted away over the land behind me, and in the distance the sheer red cliffs of the mountains rose into the tumbling plateaus of ponderosa. When I closed my eyes and laid my head back against the seat I heard robins singing in a lone cottonwood by the stream.

The next morning I drank almost two pots of coffee and waited for the phone to ring. I had spent nearly all of the previous day at the murder site, the Teton's sheriff's department, and the coroner's office. I watched three deputies finish the exhumation and put the bodies gingerly in black bags, I gave a statement to the FBI and one to the sheriff's office, I talked to the pathologist after we had opened up the brainpans of both Indians with an electric saw and had picked out the 7.62 slugs that had been fired at close range into the back of their skull. I had them contact the St Martin Parish sheriff's office about Dixie Lee's deposition in which he claimed to have overheard Vidrine and Mapes talking about the murder of the Indians. I told them where to find Mapes in the Bitterroot Valley, where his girlfriend worked in Missoula, the kind of cars he drove; I talked incessantly, until people started to walk away from me and Nygurski winked at me and said he would buy me a hamburger so I could be on my way back to Missoula.

So I drank coffee on the back steps and waited for someone to call. Dixie Lee went to work and came back in the early afternoon, and still no one had phoned.

'Ease up, boy. Let them people handle it,' he said.

We were in the kitchen, and I was shining my shoes over some newspapers that I had spread on the floor.

'That's what I'm doing,' I said.

'You put me in mind of a man who spent his last cent on Ex-Lax and forgot the pay toilet cost a dime.'

'Give me a break on the scatology.'

'The what?'

'It's not a time for humor, Dixie.'

'Go to a meet. Get your mind off it. They got his butt dead-bang. You're out of it, boy.'

'You have them dead-bang when you weld the door on them.'

Finally I called Nygurski's office. He wasn't in, he had left no message for me, and when I called the Teton sheriff's office a deputy there refused to talk with me. I had become a spectator.

I sat down at the kitchen table and started buffing my loafers again.

'While you were gone yesterday I put all Clete's stuff in the basement,' Dixie Lee said. 'Was that all right?'

'Sure.'

'He'll probably get out in a couple more days. He's got one rib that's broke bad, though. The doc says he's got ulcers, too.'

'Maybe he'll go back to New Orleans and get started over again.'

'There was something funny in his jeep.'

'What's that?' But I really wasn't listening.

'A pillowcase. With sand in it.'

'Huh.'

'Why would he put sand in a pillowcase?'

'I don't know.'

'He must have had a reason. Clete never does anything without a reason.'

'Like I say, I don't know.'

'But it's funny to do something like that. What d'you think?'

'I don't care, for God's sakes. Dixie, cut me some slack, will you?'

'Sorry.'

'It's all right.'

'I just thought I'd get your mind off of things.'

'Okay.'

'I want to see you loosen up, smile a little bit, start thinking about Louisiana, let them people handle it.'

'I'll do all those things. I promise,' I said, and I went into the bathroom, washed my face, then waited out on the front porch until it was time for Alafair to get out of school.

But he was right. I was wired, and I was thinking and acting foolishly. In finding the bodies of the Indians I had been far more successful than I had ever thought I would be. Even if the FBI or the locals didn't find the Tokarev, Mapes would still remain the prime suspect in the murder because of motive and Dixie Lee's testimony, and he could be discredited as a prosecution witness against me in Louisiana. No matter how it came out, it was time to pack our bags for New Iberia.

And that's what I started doing. Just as the phone rang.

'Mr Robicheaux?' a woman said.

'Yes.'

'This is the secretary at the DEA in Great Falls. Special Agent Nygurski called a message in from his car and asked me to relay it to you.'

'Yes?'

'He said, "They found the weapon. Mapes is in custody. Call in a couple of days if you want ballistic results. But he's not going to fly on this one. Enjoy your trip back to Louisiana." Did you get that, sir?'

'Yes.'

'Did you want to leave a message?'

'Tell him *Playgirl* magazine wants him on a centerfold.'

She laughed out loud.

'I beg your pardon?' she said.

'Tell him I said thank you.'

Five minutes later Alafair came through the front door with her lunch box.

'How'd you like to head home day after tomorrow?' I said.

Her grin was enormous.

We cooked out in the backyard that evening and had Tess Regan over, then Alafair and I climbed the switchback trail to the concrete *M* on the mountain behind the university. The whole valley was covered with a soft red glow. The wind was cold at that altitude, even though we were sweating inside our clothes, and rain and dust were blowing up through the Bitterroot Valley. Then the wind began to blow harder through the Hellgate, flattening the lupine and whipping grains of dirt against our skin. Overhead a US Forest Service fire-retardant bomber came in low over the mountains and turned toward the smoke jumpers' school west of town, its four propellers spinning with silver light in the sun's afterglow.

The thought that had kept bothering me all afternoon, that I had tried to push into a closed compartment in the back of my mind, came back like a grinning jester who was determined to extend the ball game into extra innings.

When we got home I unlocked Clete's jeep and picked up the soiled pillowcase that was on the floorboard. I turned it inside out and felt the residue of dry sand along the seams. Then I called Sally Dio's number at the lake. It was disconnected. I had reserved the next day for packing, shutting off the utilities, greasing the truck, making sandwiches for our trip home, and having a talk with Tess Regan about geographic alternatives. But Sally Dee was to have one more turn in my life.

'What time are you going in to work?' I said to Dixie Lee at breakfast the next morning.

'I ain't. The boss man said he don't need me today. That's something I want to talk with you about, Dave. With you cutting out, I don't know what kind of future I got here. Part-time forklifting ain't what you'd call a big career move.'

'Will you watch Alafair while I go up to the lake?'

'Why you going up there?'

'I need to talk with Dio. If he's not there, I'll leave him a note. Then I'll be back.'

'You're going to do what?' He set his coffee cup down on the table and stared at me.

I drove to Polson, then headed up the east side of the lake through the cherry orchards. I could have called Dan Nygurski or the sheriff's office, but that would have forced me to turn in Cletus, and I thought that a man with ulcers, a broken rib, a crushed hand, and stitches in his head had paid enough dues.

It was cold and bright on the lake. The wind was puckering the electric-blue surface, and the waves were hitting hard against he rocks along the shore. I parked in front of the Dios' redwood house on the cliff, took off my windbreaker and left it in the truck so they could see I wasn't carrying a weapon, and used the brass knocker on the door. There was no answer. I walked around the side of the house, past the glassed-in porch that was filled with tropical plants, and saw the elder Dio in his wheelchair on the veranda, his body and head wrapped in a hooded, striped robe. In his hand was a splayed cigar, and inside the hood I could see the goiter in his throat, his purple lips, the liquid and venomous expression in his eyes. He said something to me, but it was lost in the wind, because I was looking down the tiers of redwood steps that led to the rocks below and the short dock where Sally Dee and his two hoods had just carried armloads of suitcases and cardboard boxes. Even Sal's set of drums was stacked on the dock.

The three of them watched me silently as I walked down the steps toward them. Then Sal knelt by a big cardboard box and began reinforcing a corner of it with adhesive tape as though I were not there. He wore a yellow jumpsuit, with the collar flipped up on his neck, and the wind had blown his long copper-colored hair in his face.

'What d'you want us to do, Sal?' one of his men said.

Sally Dee stood erect, picked up a glass of iced coffee from the dock railing, drank out of it, and looked at me with an almost amused expression.

'Nothing,' he said. 'He's just one of those guys who get on the bottom of your shoe like chewing gum.'

'I'll just take a minute of your time, Sal,' I said. 'I think somebody fucked your airplane.'

'Yeah?'

'Yeah.'

'My airplane?'

'That's right.'

'How'd they fuck my airplane?'

'I think maybe somebody put sand in your gas tank.'

'Who's this somebody you're telling me about?'

'That's all you get. You can make use of it or forget I was here.'

'Yeah? No shit? Fuck with my airplane.'

'If I were you, I'd check it out.'

'You see my airplane around here?'

'Well, I told you what I had to say, Sal. I'll be going now.'

'Why you doing me these favors?' he said, and grinned at the two men, who were leaning against the dock rail.

'Because I don't want a guy like you on my conscience.'

He winked at the two men, both of whom wore shades.

'Keep looking at that spot between those two islands,' he said to me, and pointed. 'That's it, right over there. Keep watching. You hear that sound? It's an airplane. You know whose plane that is? You see it now, coming past those pine trees? It sounds like there's sand in the gas tank? It looks like it's going to crash?'

The milk-white amphibian came in low between the islands and touched down into the dark-blue surface of the water, the backwash of the propellers blowing clouds of spray in the air.

'Number one, I got locks on those gas tanks,' Sal said. 'Number two, I got a pilot who's also a mechanic, and he checks out everything before we go anywhere.' Then he looked at the other two men again and laughed. 'Hey, man, let me ask you an honest question. I look like I just got off the boat with a bone in my nose and a spear in my hand? Come on, I ain't mad. Nothing's going to happen to you. Give me an honest answer.'

I turned to go.

'Hey, hey, man, don't run off yet. You're too fucking much.' His mouth was grinning widely. 'Tell me for real. You think we're all that dumb? That we weren't going to catch on to all these games? I mean, I look that dumb to you?'

'What are you trying to say?'

'It was a good scam. But you ought to quit when you're ahead. Foo-Foo promised the florist a hundred bucks if he should see the guy who sent flowers and the note. So he came out yesterday and told us he seen the guy. So we found the guy, and the guy told us all about it. Charlie Dodds hasn't been anywhere around here.'

'It looks like you're on top of everything. I'm sorry I wasted your time.'

He tried to hold his grin, but I saw it fading, and I also saw the hard brown glint in his eyes, like a click of light you see in broken beer glass.

'I'll tell you what's going to happen a little ways down the road,' he said. 'I'm going to be playing card with some guys in Nevada. Not Carl or Foo-Foo here. Guys you never heard of or saw before. I'll just mention your name and the name of that shithole you come from. I'll mention Purcel's name, too. And I might throw Dixie's in as a Lucky Strike extra. That's all. I won't say nothing else. Then one day a guy'll come to your door. Or he'll be standing by your truck when you come out of a barbershop. Or maybe he'll want to rent a boat from you. It's going to be a big day in your life. When it happens, I want you to remember me.'

His two men grinned from behind their shades. The sunlight was brilliant and cold on the lake, the wind as unrelenting as a headache.

12

The story was on the front page of the *Missoulian* the next morning. The amphibian went down on the Salish Indian Reservation, just south of the lake. Two Indians who saw it crash said they heard the engines coughing and misfiring as the plane went by overhead, then the engines seemed to stall altogether and the plane veered sideways between two hills, plowing a trench through a stand of pines, and exploded. A rancher found a smashed wheelchair hanging in a tree two hundred yards away.

I wondered what Sal thought about in those last moments while the pilot jerked impotently against the yoke and Sal's hired men wrenched about in their seats, their faces stretched with disbelief, expecting him to do *something*, and the horizon tilting at a violent angle and the trees and cliffs rushing up at him like a fist. I wondered if he thought of his father or his lover in Huntsville pen or the Mexican gambler whose ear he mutilated on a yacht. I wondered if perhaps he thought that he had stepped into history with Ritchie Valens, the Big Bopper, and Buddy Holly.

But I doubted that he thought any of these things. I suspected that in his last moments Sal thought about Sal.

I folded the paper and dropped it into the trash sack in the kitchen. Alafair was putting our Styro-foam cooler, with our sandwiches and soft drinks, on the front seat of the truck.

'How would Clete get into Sally Dee's house to steal those ashtrays?' I asked Dixie Lee.

'He probably just let himself in. Sal didn't know it, but Clete copied all his keys. He could get into everything Sal owned – house, boat, cars, airplane, meat locker in town. Clete ain't nobody's fool, son. Like the Wolfman used to say, "You got the curves, baby, I got the angles." I saw them in one of his boxes when I put his junk in the basement.'

'Would you mind getting them for me?' I said.

Dixie went down the basement stairs and came back with a fistful of keys that were tied together with a length of baling wire.

I walked out on the front porch into the morning, across the lawn and the street and down the embankment to the river's edge. The sun was not up over the mountains yet, trout were feeding in the current around the stanchions of the steel railway bridge, and the sawmill across the river was empty and quiet. I unfastened the looped baling wire and flung the keys out into the water like a shower of gold and silver coins.

Dixie Lee was standing on the curb, watching me, when I walked back up the embankment.

'Ain't that called destroying evidence or something?' he said.

'It's all just rock 'n' roll,' I said.

'How come Dixie always says "ain't"?' Alafair asked.

'Try not to say "how come", little guy.'

'Great God in heaven, leave that little girl's grammar alone,' Dixie said.

'I think maybe you're right,' I said.

'You better believe it, boy,' he said, then took a deep breath down in his chest and looked out at the ring of blue mountains around the valley as though he held title to them.

'Ain't this world a pure pleasure?' he said.

Epilogue

Harry Mapes was sentenced to two life terms in the Montana state penitentiary at Deer Lodge, and the charges against me in Louisiana were dropped. I'm up to my eyes in debt, but it's late fall now, the heat has gone out of the days, and the sky has turned a hard, perfect blue, the way it does in South Louisiana after the summer exhausts itself in one final series of red dawns and burning afternoons. The water is now cool and still in the bays and coves, and the fishermen who go out of my dock bring back their ice chests loaded with *sac-a-lait* that are as thick as my hand across the back.

I invited Tess Regan to visit us, made arrangements for her to stay with my cousin in town, but when the time drew near for her to catch the plane, I knew she wouldn't be here. She said it was a sick grandparent in Bozeman. But we both knew better, and that's all right. I believe every middle-aged man remembers the girl he thinks he should have married. She reappears to him in his lonely moments or he sees her in the face of a young girl in the park, buying a snowball under an oak tree by the baseball diamond. But she belongs back *there*, to somebody else, and that thought sometimes rends your heart in a way that you never share with anyone else.

Clete moved back to New Orleans and opened a bar right down from Joe Burda's Golden Star on Decatur. I don't know where he got the capital. Maybe he came away from Sally Dee's house with more than two gold ashtrays. Dixie Lee worked with me in the bait shop for a month, played weekends at a Negro nightclub in St Martinville, then moved to New Orleans and organized a trio. They play regularly at Clete's place and one of my brother's clubs. One night I was down on Decatur, and I passed Clete's place when the door was open. I saw Dixie at the piano, way in back by the dance floor, his white rhinestone sport coat and pink shirt lighted by the floor lamps. I heard him singing:

'When they lay me down to rest,
Put a rose upon my breast.

I don't want no evergreens,
All I want is a bowl of butter beans.'

Three weeks ago I was deep in the marsh at first light. At that time of day you hear and see many strange things in the marsh: a bull gator calling for his mate, a frog dropping off a cypress knee into the water, the cry of a nutria that sounds like the scream of a hysterical woman. The fog hangs so thick on the dead water and between the tree trunks that you can lose your hand in it. But I know what I saw that morning, and I know what happened, too, and I feel no need to tell a psychologist about it. I was picking up the trotline that I had strung through the trees the night before, and just as it started to rain through the canopy overhead Annie and my father walked through the mist and stood on a sandspit right by the bow of my pirogue.

She was barefoot and wore a white evening gown, and she had strung together a necklace of purple four-o'clocks around her throat.

'It's good-bye for real this time, Dave. It's been special,' she said, then waded into the water, her dress billowing around her. She kissed me on the eyes and mouth, as perhaps my mother would have.

My father's tin hat was at an angle on his head, and he grinned with a matchstick in the corner of his mouth and held up one of his thumbs and winked. Then they walked deeper into the marsh, and the fog became so white and thick and cold that I had to reach out with the paddle and knock against the hard wood of a cypress to know where I was.

Neither sleep nor late-night thunderstorms bring them back now, and I rise each day into the sunlight that breaks through the pecan trees in my front yard. But sometimes at dusk, when the farmers burn the sugarcane stubble off their fields and the cinders and smoke lift in the wind and settle on the bayou, when red leaves float in piles past my dock and the air is cold and bittersweet with the smell of burnt sugar, I think of Indians and water people, of voices that can speak through the rain and tease us into yesterday, and in that moment I scoop Alafair up on my shoulders and we gallop down the road through the oaks like horse and rider toward my house, where Batist is barbecuing *gaspagoo* on the gallery and paper jack-o-lanterns are taped to the lighted windows, and the dragons become as stuffed toys, abandoned and ignored, like the shadows of the heart that one fine morning have gone with the season.